THE
JOURNEY TO
THE WEST

THE JOURNEY TO THE WEST

VOLUME ONE

Translated and Edited by Anthony C. Yu

The University of Chicago Press CHICAGO AND LONDON

The University of Chicago Press, Chicago 60637
The University of Chicago Press, Ltd., London
© 1977 by The University of Chicago
All rights reserved. Published 1977
Paperback edition 1980
Printed in the United States of America

01 00   7 8 9

Library of Congress Cataloging in Publication Data

Wu, Ch'eng-en, ca. 1500–ca. 1582.
  The journey to the west.

  Translation of Hsi yu chi.
  1. Yu, Anthony C., 1938–   II. Title.
PL2697.H75E596   1976   895.1'3'4   75-27896
ISBN: Vol.   I: 0-226-97150-3 (paper)
ISBN: Vol. II: 0-226-97151-1 (paper)
ISBN: Vol. III: 0-226-97153-8 (paper)
ISBN: Vol. IV: 0-226-97154-6 (paper)

For Priscilla and Christopher

Contents

Preface

Though *The Journey to the West* is one of the most popular works of fiction in China since its first publication in the late sixteenth century, and though it has been studied extensively in recent years by both Oriental and Western scholars (notably Hu Shih, Lu Hsün, Chêng Chên-to, Ogawa Tamaki, Ōta Tatsuo, C. T. Hsia, Liu Ts'un-yan, Sawada Mizuho, and Glen Dudbridge), a fully translated text has never been available to Western readers, notwithstanding the appearance in 1959 of what is reputed to be a complete Russian edition.[1] Two early versions in English (Timothy Richard, *A Mission to Heaven*, 1913, and Helen M. Hayes, *The Buddhist Pilgrim's Progress*, 1930) were no more than brief paraphrases and adaptations. The French brought out in 1957 a two-volume edition which presented a fairly comprehensive account of the prose passages, but it left much of the poetry virtually untouched.[2] It was, moreover, riddled with errors and mistranslations. In 1964, George Theiner translated into English a Czech edition which was also greatly abridged.[3] This leaves us finally with the justly famous and widely read version of Arthur Waley, published in 1943 under the misleading title *Monkey, Folk Novel of China*.[4] Waley's work is vastly superior to the others in style

1. A. Rogačev and V. Kolokolov, trans., *Wu Ch'êng-ên: Putešestvije na zapad*, 4 vols. (Moscow, 1959). See Z. Novotná's note in *Revue bibliographique de sinologie* 5 (1959): 304, for a brief descriptive review. I have not been able to obtain a copy of this edition for examination.

2. *Si yeou ki, ou le voyage en occident,* trans. Louis Avenol (Paris, 1957).

3. *The Monkey King*, ed. Zdena Novotná and trans. George Theiner (London, 1964).

4. (London, 1943). The book is currently available in a paper edition by Grove Press.

and diction, if not always in accuracy, but unfortunately it, too, is a severely truncated and highly selective rendition.

Of the one hundred chapters in the narrative, Waley has chosen to translate only chapters 1–15, 18–19, 22, 37–39, 44–49, and 98–100, which means that he has included less than one-third of the original. Even in this attenuated form, however, Waley's version further deviates from the original by having left out large portions of certain chapters (e.g., 10 and 19). What is most regrettable is that Waley, despite his immense gift for, and magnificent achievements in, the translation of Chinese verse, has elected to ignore the many poems —some 750 of them—that are structured in the narrative. Not only is the fundamental literary form of the work thereby distorted, but also much of the narrative vigor and descriptive power of its language which have attracted generations of Chinese readers is lost. The basic reason for my endeavor here, in the first volume of what is hoped to be a four-volume unabridged edition in English, is simply the need for a version which will provide the reader with as faithful an image as possible of this, one of the four or five lasting monuments of traditional Chinese fiction.

My dependence on modern scholarship devoted to this work is apparent everywhere in both the Introduction and the translation itself. I have stressed, however, in my discussion of the work those narrative devices and structural elements which have received comparatively little attention from recent commentators. For, in addition to being a work of comedy and satire masterfully wrought, *The Journey to the West* appears to embody elements of serious allegory derived from Chinese religious syncretism which any critical interpretation of it can ill afford to ignore.

A small portion of the Introduction first appeared as "Heroic Verse and Heroic Mission: Dimensions of the Epic in the *Hsi-yu chi*," *Journal of Asian Studies* 31 (1972): 879–97, while another segment was written as part of an essay, "Religion and Allegory in the *Hsi-yu chi*," for *Persuasion: Critical Essays on Chinese Literature,* edited by Joseph S. M. Lau and Leo Lee (in preparation).

The commitment to so large an undertaking can hardly be kept without the encouragement and support of friends both at the University of Chicago and elsewhere. It has been my good fortune since my arrival at Chicago to have had Nathan Scott as a teacher and a colleague. He is an unfailing and illuminating guide in the area of literary theory and theological criticism, and my gratitude for the sustaining friendship of Professor Scott and his wife for more than a decade cannot be expressed in a few words. From the beginning, Dean Joseph Kitagawa of the University of Chicago's Divinity School has not only urged me to attempt this translation, but has also faithfully provided thoughtful assistance which has enabled me to carry forward, without too great disruption, each phase of research and writing in the face of equally demanding academic and administrative responsibilities. To Herlee Creel, Elder Olson, Mircea Eliade, Frank Reynolds, James Redfield (all of Chicago), C. T. Hsia (Columbia University), Joseph Lau (University of Wisconsin), and Giles Gunn (University of North Carolina at Chapel Hill), I must say that the warmth of their friendship and their enthusiasm for the project have been a constant source of strength and inspiration. David Roy has generously placed his superb library and his vast knowledge of Chinese literature at my disposal; the many discussions with him have saved me from several serious errors. David Grene has taught me, more by example than by precept, a good deal about the art of translation. Portions of this volume have also been read by D. C. Lau (University of London) and Nathan Sivin (M.I.T.); their searching criticisms and suggestions, along with those of an anonymous reader, have decisively improved the manuscript.

I am indebted also to Philip Kuhn and Najita Tetsuo, past and present directors of the Far Eastern Language and Area Center at the University, for making available the needed funds at various stages of research. A grant by the Leopold Schepp Foundation of New York in the summer of 1973 enabled me to visit Japan and Taiwan to study the early editions of the narrative. The gracious hospitality and stimulating conversations provided by Kubo Noritada (Tōyō Bunka Kenkyūjo), Nakamura Kyoko (University of Tokyo), Tanaka Kenji (Jinbun Kagaku Kenkyūjo), and Abe Masao (Nara University) made my stay in Japan unforgettable, though it was all too brief.

My thanks are due, too, to T. H. Tsien and his able staff at the Far Eastern Library of the University of Chicago (Tai Wen-pei, Robert Petersen, Ma Tai-loi, Ho Hoi-lap, and Kenneth Tanaka), who have offered me every assistance in the acquisition of materials and in the investigation of texts, and to Mrs. T. H. Tsien, whose elegant calligraphy has graced the pages of this edition. Araki Michio, doctoral candidate at the Divinity School and my sometime research assistant, has been invaluable in helping me read Japanese scholarship. Edmund Rowan, doctoral candidate at the Department of Far Eastern Languages and Civilizations, has proofread the entire typescript with meticulous care and discerning criticisms. No brief statement is adequate to indicate the selfless and painstaking labor of Mrs. Donna Guido and Miss Susan Hopkins in the preparation of the manuscript.

Finally, I owe the successful completion of this first volume above all else to my wife and my young son. For their affectionate exhortations, for their unswerving devotion to the translation, and for their cheerful forbearance toward long stretches of obsessive work, the dedication betokens only a fraction of my gratitude.

Abbreviations

BSOAS	*Bulletin of the School of Oriental and African Studies.*
Fa-shih chuan	*Ta-T'ang Ta Tz'ŭ-ên-ssŭ San-tsang fa-shih chuan* 大唐大慈恩寺三藏法師傳 . By Hui-li 慧立 and Yen-ts'ung 彥悰. *T.* 50, no. 2053.
HJAS	*Harvard Journal of Asiatic Studies.*
Hu Shih (1923)	Hu Shih 胡適, "*Hsi-yu chi* k'ao-chêng 西游記考證," first published in 1923; reprinted in *Hu Shih wên-ts'un* 胡適文存, 4 vols. (Hong Kong, 1962), ii, 354–99.
HYC	*Hsi-yu chi* 西游記 (Peking, 1954). Abbreviation refers only to this edition.
JA	*Journal asiatique.*
JW	*The Journey to the West*
JAOS	*Journal of the American Oriental Society.*
JAS	*Journal of Asian Studies.*
LSYYCK	*Li-shih yü-yen yen-chiu-so chi-k'an* 歷史語言研究所集刊.
LWC	*"Hsi-yu chi" yen-chiu lun-wên chi* 西游記研究論文集 (Peking, 1957).
SPPY	*Szu-pu pei-yao* 四部備要.
SPTK	*Szu-pu ts'ung-k'an* 四部叢刊.
T.	Taishō Tripiṭaka.
TPKC	*T'ai-p'ing kuang-chi* 太平廣記, 10 vols. (Peking, 1961).
TT	*Tao Tsang* 道藏.

References to all Standard Histories, unless otherwise indicated, are to the *SPTK Po-na* 百衲 edition.

Introduction

HISTORICAL AND LITERARY ANTECEDENTS

The story of the *Hsi-yu Chi* 西游記 (*The Journey to the West*) is loosely based on the famous pilgrimage of Hsüan-tsang (596–664), the monk who went from China to India in quest of Buddhist scriptures. He was not the first to have undertaken such a long and hazardous journey, for according to the tabulations of a modern scholar,[1] at least fifty-four named clerics before him, beginning with Chu Shih-hsing 朱士行 in A.D. 260, had traveled westward both for advanced studies and for the procurement of sacred writings, though not all of them had reached the land of their faith. After Hsüan-tsang, there were another some fifty pilgrims who made the journey, the last of whom was the monk Wu-k'ung 悟空, who stayed in India for forty years and returned in the year 789.[2] Hsüan-tsang's journey, therefore, was not unique, for it was part of the wider movement of seeking the dharma in the West which spanned nearly five centuries, but his extraordinary achievements and his personality did become part of the permanent legacy of Chinese Buddhism. He was, by most accounts, one of the best-known and most revered Buddhist monks.

Born probably in the year 596 into a family of fairly high officials in the province of Honan,[3] Hsüan-tsang, whose secular surname was Ch'ên, is described by his biographers as having been a child of prodigious intelligence.[4] When he was but eight years old, he was taught the Confucian classics by his father, and the influence of an older brother who was a Buddhist monk may have been decisive for his joining the monastic community in the city of Lo-yang at the age of thirteen. Even at this tender age he had developed a deep interest in the study of Buddhist scriptures, and he later journeyed with his brother to Ch'ang-an in the neighboring province of Shensi to continue his studies with the dharma masters of that city.

Hsüan-tsang grew up in a period of tremendous social and intellectual ferment in Chinese history. Yang Chien (r. 581–604), the founding emperor of the Sui dynasty, came to power in 581, and though the dynasty itself lasted less than forty years (581–618), its accomplishments, as Arthur Wright has written, were

> prodigious, and its effects on the later history of China were far-reaching. It represented one of those critical periods in Chinese history—paralleled perhaps only by the Ch'in dynasty (221–207 B.C.)—when decisions made and measures taken wrought a sharp break in institutional development in the fabric of social and political life. The Sui reunified China politically after nearly three hundred years of disunion; it reorganized and unified economic life; it made great strides in the re-establishment of cultural homogeneity throughout an area where subcultures had proliferated for over three centuries. Its legacy of political and economic institutions, of codified law and governmental procedures, of a new concept of empire, laid the foundations for the great age of T'ang which followed.[5]

It was also a time marked by the revival of religious traditions, for Sui Wên-ti (Yang Chien) actively sought the support and sanction of all three religions—Confucianism, Taoism, and Buddhism—to consolidate his empire, thus reversing the persecutive policies of some of his predecessors in the Northern Chou dynasty and providing exemplary actions for the early T'ang emperors in the next dynasty.[6] Though he might lack some of the personal piety of a previous Buddhist emperor such as Liang Wu-ti (r. 502–49), Wên-ti himself was unquestionably a devout believer, whose imperial patronage gave to the Buddhist community the kind of support, security, and stimulus for growth not unlike that received by the Christian church under Constantine. Wên-ti began a comprehensive program of constructing stūpas and enshrining sacred relics in emulation of the Indian monarch Aśoka; he also established various assemblies of priests to propagate the faith and study groups to promote sound doctrines. Even allowing for some exaggerations in the Buddhist sources of the early T'ang period, it was apparent that Buddhism, by the end of the Sui dynasty, had enjoyed remarkable growth, as evidenced by the vast increase of converts, clerics, and temples throughout the land.

That Hsüan-tsang himself at an early age was very much caught up in the intellectual activities spreading through his religious community at this time can perhaps best be seen in the kind of training he received as a young acolyte. His biographers mention specifically that after he first entered the Pure Land Monastery in Lo-yang, he studied with abandonment the *Nieh-p'an ching* 涅槃經 (*Nirvāṇa Sūtra*) and the *Shê-ta-ch'êng lun* 攝大乘論 (*Mahāyāna-saṃparigraha śāstra*) with two tutors.[7] The citation of these two works is significant to the extent that it may reflect a salient part of the doctrinal controversy that went on for some three centuries in Chinese Buddhism. A major Mahāyāna text, the *Nirvāṇa Sūtra* was translated three times: first by Fa-hsien in collaboration with Buddha-bhadra, then by Dharmakshema of Pei-Liang in 421, and again by a group of southern Chinese Buddhists led by Hui-yen (363–443) in the Yüan-chia era (424–453). Its widespread appeal, particularly in the south, and the repeated discussions of it can readily be attributed to its emphasis on a more inclusive concept of enlightenment and salvation. According to Kenneth Ch'en, the Buddhists until this time

> had been taught that there is no self in nirvāṇa. In this sutra, however, they are told that the Buddha possesses an immortal self, that the final state of nirvāṇa is one of bliss and purity enjoyed by the eternal self. *Saṃsāra* is thus a pilgrimage leading to this final goal of union with the Buddha, and this salvation is guaranteed by the fact that all living beings possess the Buddha-nature. All living beings from the beginning of life participated in the Buddha's eternal existence, and this gives dignity to them as children of the Buddha.[8]

On the other hand, the śāstra, though also a Mahāyānist text, belongs to the Yogācāra school of Indian idealism, and it stresses what may be called a more elitist view of salvation.[9] In the biography, Hsüan-tsang is depicted as not only a specially able exponent of this text, but also as deeply vexed by the question of whether all men, or only part of humanity, could attain Buddhahood. It was to resolve this particular question as well as other textual and doctrinal perplexities that he decided to journey to India. Years later, when he was touring the land of the faith, he prayed before a famous image of Kuan-yin (Avalokiteśvara) on his way to Bengal, and his three petitions were: to have a safe and easy journey back to China, to be reborn in Lord Maitreya's palace as a result of the knowledge he gained, and to be personally assured that he would become a Buddha since the holy teachings claimed that not all men had the Buddha-nature.[10]

As he studied with various masters in China during his youth, Hsüan-tsang became convinced that unless the encyclopedic *Yogā-cārya-bhūmi śāstra* (*Yü-chia shih-ti lun* 瑜家師地論), the foundational text of this school of Buddhism, became available, the other idealistic texts could not be properly understood. He resolved to go to India, but his application to the imperial court for permission to travel was refused, probably because the frontier at that time was not yet secured. The second emperor of the T'ang dynasty, T'ai-tsung (r. 627–649), had just assumed his title, but his rule over the empire was hardly complete. Emboldened, however, by an auspicious dream in which he saw himself crossing a vast ocean treading on sprouting lotus leaves and uplifted to the peak of the sacred Sumeru Mountain by a powerful breeze, Hsüan-tsang set out probably, late in 627, by joining in secret a merchant caravan.[11] Sustaining appalling obstacles and hardships, he traversed Turfan, Darashar, Tashkent, Samarkand, Bactria, Kapisa, and Kashmir, until he finally reached the Magadha Kingdom of mid-India (now Bodhgaya) around 631. Here he studied with the aged Silabhadra (Chieh-hsien 戒賢) in the great Nālandā Monastery for five years—in three separate periods. He traveled widely throughout the land of his faith, visited many sacred sites, and, according to his biographers, expounded the Dharma before kings, priests, and laymen. Heretics and brigands alike were converted by his preaching, and scholastics were defeated in debates with him. After sixteen years, in 643, he began his homeward trek, taking the wise precaution while en route in Turfan the following year to send a letter to ask for imperial pardon for leaving China without permission. Readily absolved by T'ai-tsung, who owed his own rise to power in no small way to the decisive support of Buddhists on several occasions, Hsüan-tsang arrived at the capital, Ch'ang-an, in the first month of 645, bearing some 657 items (*pu* 部) of Buddhist scriptures. The emperor, however, was away in the eastern capital, Lo-yang, preparing for his campaign against Koguryŏ.

In the following month, Hsüan-tsang proceeded to Lo-yang where emperor and pilgrim finally met. More interested in "the rulers, the climate, the products, and the customs in the land of India to the west of the Snowy Peaks"[12] than in the fine points of doctrinal development, T'ai-tsung was profoundly impressed by the priest's vast knowledge of foreign cultures and peoples. He offered to make Hsüan-tsang an appointive official, but the priest declined; instead, Hsüan-tsang declared his resolve to devote his life to the translation of sūtras and śāstras. He was first installed in the Hung-fu Monastery and subsequently in the Tz'ŭ-ên Monastery of Ch'ang-an, the latter edifice having been built by the crown prince (later, emperor Kao-tsung) in memory of his mother. Supported by continuous royal favors and a large staff of some of the most able Buddhist clerics of the empire, Hsüan-tsang spent the next nineteen years of his life translating and writing. By the time he died in 664, he had completed translations of seventy-four works in 1,355 volumes (*chüan*), including the lengthy *Yogācārya-bhūmi śāstra* for which T'ai-tsung wrote the famous *Shêng-chiao hsü* 聖教序 (Preface to the Holy Teachings). Among Hsüan-tsang's own writings, his *Ch'êng Wei-shih lun* 成唯識論 (Treatise on the Establishment of the Consciousness-Only System) and the *Ta-T'ang Hsi-yü chi* 大唐西域記 (The Great T'ang Record of the Western Territories) were the best known, the first being an elaborate and subtle exposition of the *Trimsika* by Vasubandhu and a synthesis of its ten commentaries, and the latter a descriptive and anecdotal travelogue dictated to the disciple Pien-chi 辯機 (d. 649).

It should be apparent from this brief sketch of Hsüan-tsang that the account of his life, as told by his biographers, has much of the engaging blend of facts and fantasies, of myth and history, out of which fictions are made. It is not surprising, therefore, that his exploits were soon incorporated into the biographical sections (*lieh-chuan*) of such a standard dynastic history as the *Chiu T'ang Shu*,[13] and subsequently the story of his life was repeatedly celebrated by the literary imagination. Yet, it must be pointed out that that story, as it was finally told in the hundred-chapter narrative published in 1592 and titled *Hsi-yu chi* (literally, the Record of the Westward Journey) of which the present work is a complete translation, and the historical Hsüan-tsang have only the most tenuous relation. In nearly a millennium of evolution, the story of T'ang San-tsang (Tripitaka, the honorific name of Hsüan-tsang) and his acquisition of scriptures in the West has been told by both pen and mouth and through a variety of literary forms which have included the short poetic tale, the drama, and finally the fully developed narrative using both prose and verse. In this long process of development, the theme of the pilgrimage for scriptures is never muted, but added to this basic constituent of the story are numerous features which have more in common with folktales and popular legends than with history. The account of a courageous monk's undertaking, motivated by profound religious zeal and commitment, is thus eventually transformed into a tale of supernatural deeds and fantastic adventures, of mythic beings and animal spirits, of fearsome battles with monsters and miraculous deliverances from dreadful calamities. How all this came about is a study in itself, but since this has already been done systematically and thoroughly by Glen Dudbridge in his authoritative *The Hsi-yu Chi: A Study of Antecedents to the Sixteenth-Century Chinese Novel*,[14] I shall review briefly only the most important literary versions of the westward journey prior to the late Ming narrative.

Between the time of the historical Hsüan-tsang and the first literary version of his journey for which we have solid documentary evidence, there are only a few scattered indications that the story of this pilgrimage was working its way into the popular imagination. In the biography, the monk is represented as having a special fondness for the *Heart Sūtra* (the *Prajñāpāramitāhrdaya*), for it was by reciting it and by calling upon Kuan-yin that he found deliverance from dying of thirst and from hallucinations in the desert.[15] By the time of the *T'ai-p'ing kuang-chi* 太平廣記, the encyclopedic anthology of anecdotes and miscellaneous tales compiled in the late tenth century, the brief account of Hsüan-tsang contained therein already included the motif of the pilgrim's special relation with the sūtra. There we are told that an old monk, his face covered with sores and his body with pus and blood, was the one who had transmitted this sūtra to the pilgrim, for whom, "when he recited it, the mountains and the streams became traversable, and the roads were made plain and passable; tigers and leopards vanished from sight; demons and spirits disappeared. He thus reached the land of Buddha."[16] During the next century, the poet-official Ou-yang Hsiu 歐陽修 (1007–72) recalled drinking one night at the Shou-ling Monastery (壽靈寺) in Yang-chou. He was told by an old monk there that when the place was used as a traveling palace by the Later Chou emperor Shih-tsung (r. 954–59), all the murals were destroyed except that on one wall which depicted the story of Hsüan-tsang's journey in quest of the scriptures.[17]

These two references, while clearly pointing to popular interest in the story, provide us with scant information on how this story has been told. The first representation of a distinctive tale with certain characteristic figures and episodes appears, as Dudbridge puts it, "almost without warning." Two texts preserved in Japanese collections, which contain minor linguistic discrepancies but which recount essentially the same story, have been dated by most scholars as products of the thirteenth century: *Hsin-tiao Ta-T'ang San-tsang Fa-shih ch'ü-ching chi* 新雕大唐三藏法師取經記 (The Newly Printed Record of the Procurement of Scriptures by the Master of the Law, Tripitaka, of the Great T'ang) and the *Ta-T'ang San-tsang ch'ü-ching shih-hua* 大唐三藏取經詩話 (The Poetic Tale of the Procurement of Scriptures by Tripitaka of the Great T'ang). Originally belonging to the monastery Kōzanji 高山寺 northwest of Kyoto, these texts finally gained public attention upon their publication earlier in the present century.[18]

As some of the earliest examples of printed popular fiction in China, the texts have deservedly attracted widespread scholarly interest and scrutiny. For our purpose here, however, they are significant not so much for the history of Chinese popular fiction as for their contribution to the development of the Tripitaka legend. This brief tale of seventeen sections (with section one missing in both texts), narrated by prose interlaced with verse written mostly in the form of the seven-syllabic *chüeh-chü* 絕句, tells of Hsüan-tsang's journey through such mythic and fantastic regions as the palace of Mahābrahmā Devarāja, the Long Pit and the Great Serpent Range, the Nine Dragon Pool, the kingdoms of Kuei-tzu Mu, Women, Po-lo, and Utpala Flowers, and the Pool of Wang-mu (Queen of the West) before his arrival in India. After procuring some 5,048 *chüan* of Buddhist scriptures, Hsüan-tsang returns to the Hsiang-lin Monastery, where he is taught the *Heart Sūtra* by the Dīpaṃkara Buddha. On his way back in the province of Shensi, the pilgrim avenges the crime of a stepmother's murder of her son by splitting open a large fish and restoring the child to life. When he reaches the capital, the priest is met by the emperor and given the title "Master Tripitaka," after which the pilgrim and his companions are conveyed by celestial vehicles to Heaven.

As a primitive version of the *Hsi-yu Chi* story, the poetic tale is hardly to be compared with the scope and complexity of the hundred-chapter narrative. Its importance lies rather in its introduction of a number of themes or motifs which are to receive expansion and development in subsequent literary treatments of the same story. These themes may be summarized as follows:

1. The Monkey Novice-Monk (*hou hsing-chê* 猴行者) as protector and guide of Hsüan-tsang (sec. 2 and passim) who gains the title Great Sage (Ta-shêng 大聖) at the end (sec. 17).
2. The gifts of the Mahābrahmā Devarāja: an invisible hat, a golden-ringed priestly staff, and an alms bowl (sec. 2; cf. *Journey to the West*, chaps. 8 and 12 for the gifts to Hsüan-tsang from Buddha and from the emperor).
3. The snow-white skeleton (sec. 6; cf. *JW*, chaps. 27–31, the Cadaver Monster? or chap. 50).
4. Monkey's defeat of the White Tiger spirit through invasion of its belly (sec. 6; cf. *JW*, chaps. 59, 75, and 82 for similar feats of Monkey).
5. The Deep-Sand God as possible ancestor of Sha Monk of the Ming narrative (sec. 8; *JW*, chap. 22).[19]
6. The Kingdom of Kuei-tzu-mu 鬼子母 (sec. 9; cf. scene 12 of the twenty-four-act drama also titled *Hsi-yu Chi*, and chap. 42 of *JW*).[20]
7. The Kingdom of Women, where Mañjuśrī and Samantabhadra appear as temptresses (sec. 10; cf. *JW*, chaps. 23, 53–54).
8. The reference to Monkey's theft of immortal peaches and his capture by Wang-mu (sec. 11; cf. *JW*, chap. 5).
9. The reference to the ginseng fruit and its childlike features (sec. 11; cf. *JW*, chaps. 24–26).

Among these themes which appeared in the Sung poetic tale, the most significant is surely that which introduces a Monkey Novice-Monk as the companion of the pilgrim. Disguised as a white-robed scholar that Hsüan-tsang met on the way, this simian figure anticipates in some ways the powerful, resourceful, and heroic Sun Wu-k'ung of the hundred-chapter narrative. The place that Monkey claims to be his home is mentioned in exactly the same manner again in the twenty-four-scene *tsa-chü* 雜劇 version of the story (the Purple-Cloud Cave of the Flower-Fruit Mountain), while the hundred-chapter narrative retains only the name of the mountain. Throughout the tale, he is presented as both a past delinquent and a guardian who will deliver Hsüan-tsang from his preordained afflictions during the pilgrimage.

In the biography of the historical monk, we have, of course, no intimations whatever that he was accompanied on his journey by any supernatural beings, let alone animal figures. The tantalizingly cryptic reference to the need for a Monkey Novice-Monk to procure scriptures

(取經煩猴行者) in a line of poetry by the Sung poet, Liu K'o-chuang 劉克莊 (1187–1269), gives an early hint of this figure's association with a scripture pilgrimage, but it has no explanation for the origin of this association.[21] The carved monkey figure located at the K'ai-yüan szŭ 開元寺 of Ch'üan-chou 泉州 (Zayton), completed sometime in 1237, is also, according to the description of G. Ecke and P. Demié-ville,[22] identified by that temple tradition as Sun Wu-k'ung, though the iconographic representation differs significantly from the novelistic figure in terms of clothing and weapon.[23] Neither of these "sources," however, really explains how a popular religious folk hero such as Hsüan-tsang has come to acquire this animal attendant, who gains steadily in popularity in subsequent literary accounts until finally, in the hundred-chapter narrative he almost completely overshadows his master.

It is to the search for the possible origin of this fascinating figure and the reasons for his associations with, and prominence within, the Tripi-taka legend that Dudbridge devotes all of his investigation in the second half of his study. The pertinent documents which he examines in detail range from early prose tales of a white ape figure (The *T'ang Po-yüan chuan* 唐白猿傳 and the vernacular mid-Ming short story *Ch'ên Hsun-chien Mei-ling shih-ch'i chi* 陳巡檢梅嶺失妻記),[24] to Ming *tsa-chü* such as the *Êrh-lang shên so Ch'i-t'ien ta-shêng* 二郎神鎖齊天大聖, *Êrh-lang shên tsui-shê so-mo-ching* 二郎神醉射鎖魔鏡, *Mêng-lieh Ne-cha san pien-hua* 猛烈那吒三變化, *Kuan-k'ou Êrh-lang chan chien-chiao* 灌口二郎斬健蛟, and the *Lung-chi shan yeh-yüan t'ing ching* 龍濟山野猿聽經.[25] None of these works, however, can be shown decisively to be a "source" for the derivation of the later, hundred-chapter narrative. As Dudbridge sees the matter, the essential role of the white ape emerging from the tales under consideration is one of abductor and seducer of women, a characteristic foreign to the Monkey of the *Hsi-yu Chi*. In his opinion, "Tripitaka's disciple com-mits crimes which are mischievous and irreverent, but the white ape is from first to last a monstrous creature which has to be eliminated. The two acquire superficial points of similarity when popular treat-ments of the respective traditions, in each case of Ming date, coincide in certain details of nomenclature."[26] That might well have been the case, or it might have been that there were two related traditions con-cerning the monkey figure: one which emphasizes the monkey as a demon, evil spirit, and recreant in need of suppression by Êrh-lang or Naṭa as in the *Ch'i-t'ien ta-shêng* plays, and one which portrays the monkey as capable of performing religious deeds as in the *t'ing-ching* accounts. Both strands of the tradition might in turn feed into the evolving *Hsi-yu Chi* cycle of stories.[27]

In addition to these literary texts, the figure of Wu-chih-ch'i 無支祈, the water god, has provided many scholars with a prototype of Sun Wu-k'ung, mainly because he, too, was a monster whose delinquent behavior led to his imprisonment beneath a mountain, first by the legendary King Yü, the conqueror of the Flood in China, and again by Kuan-yin.[28] However, Dudbridge points out that such a theory involves the identification of Sun Wu-k'ung as originally a water demon and his early association with the Êrh-lang cult of Szechuan, neither of which assumptions is supported by the Kōzanji text. It may be added that Wu-chih-ch'i, though certainly a figure known to the author of the hundred-chapter narrative (he was referred to in chap. 66 as the Great Sage of the Water Ape [Shui-yüan ta-shêng 水猿大聖]), has been kept quite distinct from the monkey hero. One of Sun Wu-k'ung's specific weaknesses in the hundred-chapter narrative is that he loses much of his power and adroitness once he is in water. Dudbridge's conclusions, therefore, are that the legend about Wu-chih-ch'i "casts no light on the monkey-figure known to us in our basic source" and that "the 'derivation' theory in its strict form should be suspended."[29]

If indigenous materials prove insufficient to establish with any certainty the origin of the monkey hero, does it imply that one must follow Hu Shih's provocative conjectures and look for a prototype in alien literature?[30] An affirmative answer to this question seems inviting, since the universally popular Hanumat adventures in the *Rāmāyaṇa* story might have found their way into China through centuries of mercantile and religious traffic with India. Furthermore, the composition attributed to Vālmīki is known to have reached the Tun-huang texts in the form of Tibetan and Khotanese manuscripts. But more recent research by both Chinese and European scholars, whom Dudbridge follows, has shown that known sources of our early Chinese popular literature, whether in narrative or dramatic form, contain no more than fragmentary and modified traces of the *Rāmāyaṇa* epic. Wu Hsiao-ling, who has canvassed a large number of probable allusions to various episodes and incidents of the *Rāmāyaṇa* in extant Chinese Buddhist scriptures, has also argued the improbability of the author of the hundred-chapter narrative having seen any of these.[31] The many ostensible similarities between Hanumat and the Monkey of the narrative perhaps point to a "fund of shared motifs," but we still lack well-attested evidence of the intervening stages to establish influence or derivation. Dudbridge's cautious suggestion at the end of his study is that the folk hero Mu-lien, who in the Avalambana celebrations observed in nineteenth-century Amoi was attended by animal "apostles," might provide a distant parallel to Tripitaka and his companions. But the questions why "a popular religious folk hero should acquire bizarre animal-attendants" and why a monkey figure should enjoy such preeminence cannot be settled until further knowledge in Chinese folklore is gained and, as Dudbridge asserts, we know more about "the use of comic elements in religious drama, and the functions of Monkey as a figure in heroic tradition."[32]

If the origins of Sun Wu-k'ung remain obscure, we have at least three other texts of major import between the Kōzanji version and the hundred-chapter narrative of the sixteenth century, texts which undoubtedly made their own contributions to the formation of the *Hsi-yu chi* story as it was finally told in the later narrative. First there is a passage of a little less than 1,100 characters which is preserved in the scant surviving remnants of the *Yung-lo ta-tien* 永樂大典 (the encyclopedic collection compiled in 1403–8 under commission of the Ming emperor Ch'êng-tsu). This passage constitutes a remarkable parallel to portions of chapter 9 (chap. 10 in *HYC*) in the hundred-chapter narrative.[33] Though the episodes concerning Tripitaka's genealogy and public debut receive much fuller treatment in the later work, the essential sequences (i.e., the conversations between a fisherman named Chang Shao and a woodcutter named Li Ting, the transgressions of the Dragon King and his conviction by the fortune-teller Yüan Shou-ch'êng, and the dream execution of the dragon by the prime minister Wei Chêng [580–643] in the midst of a chess game with the emperor T'ai-tsung) and certain sentences and phrases (e.g., the Dragon King's address to the emperor: "Your majesty is the true dragon, whereas I am only a false dragon") are nearly identical in both accounts. What is of greater interest here is that the *Yung-lo ta-tien* extract is listed under an old source named *Hsi-yu chi*, which may well have existed as a kind of *Urtext* for all the dramatic and narrative works that are to follow. This text, unfortunately, is now lost, and the lack of information on authorship, texts, and publisher prohibits any conclusion other than the existence of a document or documents by such a name two centuries before the circulation of the full-length narrative.

Such a conclusion may certainly find further support in the *Pak t'ongsa ŏnhae* (in Chinese, the *P'u t'ung shih yen-chieh* 朴通事諺解), a Korean reader in colloquial Chinese first printed probably some time in the mid-fifteenth century, though the surviving version now preserved in the Kyu-chang-kak collection of the Seoul University library has a preface which dates from 1677. This manual contains an account of Tripitaka's experience in the *Ch'ê-ch'ih Kuo* 車遲國 (the Cart-Slow Kingdom of chaps. 44–46 of the *JW*), and, more significantly, "the picture of ordinary people going out to buy popular stories in a book [which] confirms that a *Hsi-yu chi* was among those available."[34] There are, moreover, a number of references to mythic regions and to various demons and gods (including Chu Pa-chieh receiving the title of Janitor of the Altars 淨壇使者 at the end of the journey) which find echoes in subsequent dramatic and narrative accounts.[35] Though the paucity of additional evidence external to the work in question makes it impossible to reconstruct a lost text of the *Hsi-yu chi*, internal analysis of this document, as Dudbridge aptly observes, at least presents "evidence as a trend . . . that the *Hsi-yu chi* story, now well known in published form, was progressively assuming an accepted and less variable form."[36]

That form was finally established by the dramatic versions of the story, of which fortunately we possess at least one more or less complete sample among the six known stage works supposedly devoted to the *Hsi-yu chi* theme. This is the twenty-four-act *tsa-chü* titled *Hsi-yu chi*, which was discovered in Japan and first reprinted there in 1927–28.[37] The play was first thought to be the lost work of the same title by the Yüan playwright, Wu Ch'ang-ling 吳昌齡. The ascription, however, has been conclusively repudiated by Sun K'ai-ti, though Sun's own thesis that the play was written by Yang Ching-hsien 楊景賢 (alternatively Ching-yen 景言) has been challenged also.[38] Whoever the author was, the play is of crucial importance, not only because of its unique length when compared with other *tsa-chü*, but also because of its content. It represents the fullest embodiment of the major themes and figures of the *Hsi-yu chi* story prior to the hundred-chapter narrative. Acts 1–4 present at length the adventures of Hsuan-tsang's parents as well as the abandonment and rescue, of the young priest and his revenge on his father's murderers. Subsequent acts dramatize the royal commission of Hsüan-tsang to procure scriptures, the provision of a dragon-horse by Kuan-yin for the scripture pilgrim, the dispatch of guardian deities by Kuan-yin, the mischievous adventures of the monkey hero Sun Hsing-chê, and his subsequent submission to Tripitaka as the monk's disciple and protector. The figure Chu Pa-chieh is also given extensive coverage (acts 13–16). In this regard, the play is unique not only because the monkey is seen to be subdued by Nata and not by Êrh-lang as in the case of the other *Ch'i-t'ien ta-shêng* plays, but also because Chu Pa-chieh is portrayed as being someone who has to be captured by Êrh-lang. Chu, in fact, makes the assertion that he fears no one except the small hound of that deity. Readers of the hundred-chapter *Hsi-yu chi* will readily recognize these themes when they reappear in the transformed context of the developed narrative, and in the case of Sun and Chu's relations to the divine figures, they may also perceive how the genius of the late Ming author has adapted his "source" to the logic of his massive masterpiece.

TEXT AND AUTHORSHIP

If the antecedents to the sixteenth-century narrative are numerous and complex, the vast family of texts and the different versions of *The Journey to the West* itself, both abridged and unabridged, present no less formidable an area of investigation to the serious student of this work. We are fortunate once again to have the meticulous scholarship of Glen Dudbridge, who has made the most comprehensive examination of the narrative's textual history,[39] and his careful conclusions seem to me to be on the whole beyond dispute.

Part of the critical controversy surrounding the genesis of *The Journey to the West* as a developed narrative has to do with the relation of the hundred-chapter version to two shorter accounts. One of these is the *San-tsang ch'u-shen ch'üan-chuan* 三藏出身全傳 (The Complete Biography of San-tsang's Career), commonly known as the Yang version because its putative author is Yang Chih-ho 楊志和, probably a contemporary of many Fukien publishers at the end of the sixteenth century but of whom little additional information is available. The work is divided into forty chapters, and together with the

Tung-yu chi (Journey to the East), the *Nan-yu chi* (Journey to the South), the *Pei-yu chi* (Journey to the North), three tales of comparable length which recount the voyages of various figures in myth and legend to a particular point of the compass, it forms a familiar group of stories known as the *Szu-yu chi* 四游記 (The Four Journeys). Though the earliest extant reprint dates from 1730, its printing format points to a date in the late Ming period.

The other brief version of the *Hsi-yu chi* is called the *T'ang San-tsang Hsi-yu shih-ni (=o) chuan* 唐三藏西游釋尼(= 厄)傳 (The Chronicle of Deliverances in Tripitaka T'ang's Journey to the West), commonly known as the Chu version because its compiler is acknowledged to be Chu Ting-ch'en 朱鼎臣 of Canton. A work of similar length to the Yang version, the Chu text has as its distinctive feature a lengthy account of the "Ch'ên Kuang-jui story," which tells of the birth and early adventures of Hsüan-tsang as well as the terrible mishaps befalling his parents. That story, with some modifications, appears also as chapter 9 first in an abridged Ch'ing edition of the *Hsi-yu chi* which bears the name of *Hsi-yu chêng-tao shu* 西游證道書 (The Journey to the West, a Book of the Illumination of *Tao*), compiled by Huang T'ai-hung 黄太鴻 and Wang Hsiang-hsü 汪象旭, and dated by Dudbridge as around 1662.[40] The chapter, however, is missing in the earliest hundred-chapter version published in 1592 and in the several other editions almost immediately following which are based on this text. Since the title of the Chu text is also explicitly named in the seven-syllabic *lü-shih* poem which opens the hundred-chapter narrative (see chap. 1), the critical controversy thus centers on the problem of which version precedes the others. Though scholars in the past have advocated the priority of either the Yang or the Chu version, Dudbridge seems to me to have clearly established the supremacy of the text of the hundred-chapter version, published most probably in 1592 by the Shih-tê-t'ang 世德堂 of Nanking, which, as he says, "promises to stand as close to the original as any that survives."[41] The standard modern edition, on which the present translation is based, was published by the Tso-chia ch'u-pan shê 作家出版社 of Peking in 1954. The text is primarily that of the Shih-tê-t'ang, with minor corrections and alterations based on comparison with six other abridged and unabridged editions of *The Journey to the West* brought out in the Ming-Ch'ing period.[42]

When compared with its numerous literary antecedents, the hundred-chapter narrative may be seen at once as a culmination of a long and many-faceted tradition as well as a creative synthesis and expansion of all the major figures and themes associated with the story of Hsüan-tsang's westward journey. Though the narrative far surpasses any of the previous dramatic or narrative accounts in scope and length, the author also reveals a remarkably firm sense of structure and an extraordinary capacity for organizing disparate materials in the presentation of his massive tale. Certain details related to the development of plot and characters evince thoughtful planning, preparation, and execution. The basic outline of the narrative, as we have it in the modern edition, may be divided into the following five sections:

1 (chapters 1–7): the birth of Sun Wu-k'ung, his acquisition of immortality and magic powers under the tutelage of Patriarch Subhodi, his invasion and disturbance of Heaven, and his final subjugation by Buddha under the Mountain of Five Phases:

2 (chapter 8): the Heavenly Council in which Buddha declares his intention to impart the Buddhist canon to the Chinese, the journey of Kuan-yin to the land of the East to find the appropriate scripture pilgrim, and her preparatory encounters with all of Hsüan-tsang's future disciples;

3 (chapters 9–12): the background and birth of Hsüan-tsang, his vengeance on his father's murderers, Wei Chêng's execution of the Ching River Dragon, the journey of T'ang T'ai-tsung to the underworld, his convening of the Mass for the Dead, and the commission of Hsüan-tsang as the scripture pilgrim after the epiphany of Kuan-yin;

4 (chapters 13–97): the journey itself, developed primarily through a long series of captures and releases of the pilgrims by monsters, demons, animal spirits, and gods in disguise which form the bulk of the eighty-one ordeals (*nan* 難) preordained for Hsüan-tsang;

5 (chapters 98–100): the successful completion of the journey, the audience with Buddha, the return with scriptures to Ch'ang-an, and the final canonization of the five pilgrims in the West.

As the present translation is intended to be a complete reproduction of the modern edition, I have not followed Dudbridge's advice to exclude chapter 9. For reasons stated elsewhere,[43] I am persuaded that the "Ch'ên Kuang-jui story" is essential to the plot of the *Hsi-yu chi* as a whole, even though it lacks the best form of textual support.

Despite the popularity which this narrative has apparently enjoyed since its publication, the identity of its author, as in the case of such other major works of Chinese fiction as the *Chin P'ing Mei* and the *Fêng-shên yen-i*, remains unclear. In his preface to the Shih-tê-t'ang edition, Ch'ên Yuan-chih 陳元之 has emphasized that neither he, nor the Hua-yang-tung-t'ien chu-jên 華陽洞天主人 who checked 校 this edition, nor T'ang Kuang-lu 唐光祿, the publisher who "requested the preface" from Ch'ên, has any knowledge of who the author was. Indeed, all the known individuals who had anything to do with published editions of *The Journey to the West* in the Ming dynasty were silent on this point. Though the suggestion had been made by several writers in the Ch'ing period, it was not until after the essay of 1923 by Hu Shih that this theory of the hundred-chapter narrative as being the creation of Wu Ch'êng-ên 吳承恩 (ca. 1500–1582), a native of the Shan-yang 山陽 district in the prefecture of Huai-an 淮安 (Kiangsu), gained wide acceptance. Wu was never more than a minor official during his lifetime, having been selected as a Tribute Student 歲貢生 in 1544, but he achieved a certain reputation as a poet and humorous writer. Modern studies of Wu include an edition of his collected writings and an exhaustive reconstruction of his life and career.[44]

The ascription of *The Journey to the West* to Wu is based primarily on an entry in the *I-wên-chih* 藝文志 section of the *Gazetteer of Huai-an Fu*, compiled in the Ming T'ien-ch'i 天啟 reign period (1621–27), where after Wu's name are listed the following works:

> *Shê-yang chi* 射陽集, 4 *ts'ê*, —— *chüan*; Preface to *Ch'un-ch'iu lieh-chuan* 春秋列傳序; *Hsi-yu chi* 西游記.[45]

An additional reference may be found in the *Ch'ien-ch'ing-t'ang shu-mu* 千頃堂書目, a catalogue completed at the end of the seventeenth century, in which the title *Hsi-yu chi* is printed after the name of Wu Ch'êng-ên. The entry, however, is included within the section on "Geography" (輿地類), in the division of "Histories" (史).

Further listings noted by Hu Shih include the *Huai-an Gazetteer* and the *Shan-yang District Gazetteer* 山陽縣志, compiled during the K'ang-hsi (1662–1722) and T'ung-chih (1862–74) reigns of the Ch'ing dynasty. Of the several writers in this dynasty who affirmed Wu to be the author of the *Hsi-yu chi*, the two most frequently cited are Wu Yü-chin 吳玉搢 (1698–1773) and Ting Yen 丁晏 (1794–1875), a noted textual scholar of the classics. In the *Shan-yang chih-i* 山陽志遺 (Supplement to the Shan-yang Gazetteer), Wu Yü-chin has the following observation:

> The Old Gazetteer of the T'ien-ch'i [1621–27] period listed the Master [i.e., Wu Ch'êng-ên] as the ranking writer of recent years whose works had been collected. He was said to be "a man of exceptional intelligence and many talents who read most widely; able to compose poetry and prose at a stroke of the brush, he also excelled in witty and satirical writing. The various miscellaneous writings 雜記 he produced brought him resounding fame at the time." I did not know at first what sort of books the miscellaneous writings were until I read the *List of Works by Eminent Writers of the Huai Region* [i.e., *chüan* 19, 3 b], where it was recorded that *Hsi-yu chi* was by the Master. I have discovered that *Hsi-yu chi*, whose old title was *The Book of the Illumination of Tao* 證道書, is so named because its content was thought to be consonant with the Principle of the Golden Elixir. Yü Tao-yüan [i.e. Yü Chi 虞集 1272–1348] of the Yüan dynasty had written a preface, in which he claimed that this book was written by the Ch'ang-ch'un Taoist Adept with the surname of Ch'iu 邱長春真人 [i.e. Ch'iu Ch'u-chi 邱處機 1148–1227] at the beginning of the Yüan period. The regional gazetteer, however, claims that it was by the hand of the Master. Since the T'ien-ch'i period is not far removed from the time of the Master, this statement must have some basis. . . . The fact that the book [i.e., *JW*] contains a great number of expressions peculiar to our local dialects should indicate that it must have been the product of someone from the Huai district 書中多吾鄉方言其出淮人手無疑.[46]

Since the appearance of Hu Shih's essay, Wu Ch'êng-ên's authorship has been widely accepted by scholars in both the East and the West.

This thesis, however, has been challenged recently by Glen Dudbridge, who in turn follows the arguments advanced by Tanaka Iwao. Essentially, the objection of Tanaka includes the following points:

1. that the title *Hsi-yu chi* listed in the *Huai-an Gazetteer* cannot be positively identified with the hundred-chapter narrative;
2. that there is no known precedent in Chinese literary history for equating miscellaneous writings (雜記) with works of fiction;

3. that Wu Ch'êng-ên's reputed excellence in humorous compositions itself cannot be regarded as positive evidence of authorship;
4. that none of the known persons associated with the first publication of the hundred-chapter version had any idea who the author was;
5. that the famous critic Li Chih 李 贄 (tzǔ Cho-wu 卓吾 1527–1602), who had edited such major works of literature as the *Shui-hu chuan*, the *Hsi-hsiang chi*, and the *Hsi-yu chi* with his own commentaries, also made no mention that Wu Ch'êng-ên was the author.[47]

The last of Tanaka's five reasons for doubting the authorship of Wu Ch'êng-ên is ostensibly the most cogent, since Li Cho-wu's literary activities related to his editing of *The Journey to the West* could not have occurred more than twenty years after Wu's death. If Wu's fame was as widespread as the *Huai-an Gazetteer* had claimed, why did Li seem to be completely ignorant of it, especially when his annotations of the narrative in many places clearly reflect his admiration for its anonymous author?[48]

The answer to this question, it must be pointed out, can take more than one form, of which Tanaka's inference—that silence is ignorance, and that Li's ignorance further casts doubt on Wu's putative achievements—is only one among several possibilities. As it stands, it is still an argument ex silentio, for Li at no point made the specific assertion that Wu was not the author. Moreover, if Wu Ch'êng-ên was known to be an associate of some of the Seven Masters of Later Times (後七子)[49]—the group of literary theorists and writers of late Ming who championed the imitation of the classics—one wonders if Li Cho-wu would be inclined to suspect Wu's hand in the *JW*, or, even if he had known Wu to be the author, publicly to credit him with the authorship. For we must remember that Li himself was the declared foe and staunch critic of this literary movement, and his own imprisonment and final suicide were caused in no small way by his stubborn iconoclasm in views both political and literary.[50]

With regard to the reputation of Wu Ch'êng-ên as a humorist, it is certainly true that that characteristic alone cannot establish Wu as the author. Nor, of course, should Wu's humor be easily dismissed as evidence, in view of the wealth of comedy and satire in the narrative. In addition to the element of wit, perhaps the more significant aspect of Wu's character which may link him to *The Journey to the West* is his self-declared predilection for the marvelous, the exotic, and the supramundane in literature. In the *Yü-ting-chih hsü* 禹鼎志序, a preface to a group of stories, now lost, which he wrote on one of the legendary sage kings of Chinese antiquity, Wu said:

> I was very fond of strange stories when I was a child. In my village-school days, I used to buy stealthily popular novels and historical recitals. Fearing that my father and my teacher might punish me for this and rob me of these treasures, I carefully hid them in secret places where I could enjoy them unmolested. As I grew older, my love for strange stories became even stronger, and I learned of things stranger than what I had read in my childhood. When I was in my thirties, my memory was full of these stories accumulated through years of eager seeking. I have always admired such writers of the T'ang Dynasty as Tuan Ch'êng-shih [author of the *Yu-yang tsa-tsu* 酉陽雜俎] and Niu Sheng-ju [author of the *Hsüan-kuai lu* 玄怪錄], who wrote short stories so excellent in portrayal of men and description of things. I often had the ambition to write a book (of stories) which might be compared with theirs. But I was too lazy to write, and as my laziness persisted, I gradually forgot most of the stories which I had learned. Now only these few stories, less than a score, have survived and have so successfully battled against my laziness that they are at last written down. Hence this Book of Monsters. I have sometimes laughingly said to myself that it is not I who have found these ghosts and monsters, but they, the monstrosities themselves, which have found me! . . . Although my book is called a book of monsters, it is not confined to them: it also records the strange things of the human world and sometimes conveys a little bit of moral lesson.[51]

That the author of the hundred-chapter narrative was familiar with the contents of the *Yu-yang tsa-tsu* may be seen from the references to the Three Worms in chapter 15 and Wu Kang 吳剛 in chapter 22. And in the following section of this introduction, we shall see not only that the author of *The Journey to the West* is well read in some of the arcane lore of alchemy, but also that this book of monsters and pilgrimage similarly "records the strange things of the human world and sometimes conveys a little bit of moral lesson."

Finally, though the attempt by Liu Ts'un-yan to turn up prosodic parallels between the narrative and Wu's surviving writings has yielded nothing more than rather vague generalizations,[52] there is one little item overlooked by Liu which deserves some consideration. What is of interest here is the description of Wu in the *Jen-wu-chih* section of the *Huai-an Gazetteer*, part of which was already quoted by Wu Yü-chin cited above. The complete entry in *chüan* 16 of the gazetteer reads as follows: "Wu Ch'êng-ên was a man of exceptional intelligence and many talents who read most widely; his prose and poetry, composed at a stroke of the brush, are refined, flowing and elegant—much like the style of Ch'in Shao-yu (清雅流麗有秦少游之風)."[53] The noteworthy part of this brief description is the reference to Ch'in Kuan 秦觀 (1049–1100), one of the masters of *tz'ŭ* in the Northern Sung period. One may wonder why he, of all the major Sung poets, is singled out for comparison with Wu apart from the fact that he too is a native of Kao-yu, a town close to Huai-an in the neighboring prefecture of Yang-chou. As he appears in the collected writings, Wu Ch'êng-ên may certainly be considered a competent poet, if not a consistently inspired one. The surviving *tz'ŭ* poems, furthermore, do reveal such characteristics as the subtle juxtaposition of imageries, the intimate fusion of emotion and natural objects, the occasionally bold erotic language, and the startling insertion of colloquialism which are frequently associated with Sung poets like Su Tung-p'o (1036–1101), Ch'in Kuan, and, in the Southern Sung, with Hsin Ch'i-chi (1140–1207).[54] But my own careful comparison of the fifty-three *tz'ŭ* poems of Wu with the collected *tz'ŭ* of Ch'in Kuan has turned up nothing more specific than a general stylistic resemblance. However, there is one perceptible example of poetic borrowing in the *Hsi-yu chi* which may cast an interesting light on this reference to Ch'in. In the poetic dialogues between the fisherman and the wood-cutter which open chapter 10 of the narrative, we have these lines from a *tz'ŭ* poem composed to the tune of *Hsi-chiang-yüeh* 西江月:

Dense flowers of red smartweeds glow in the moonlight
紅蓼花繁映月
Tousled leaves of yellow rushes shake in the wind.
黃蘆葉亂搖風
The blue sky, clean and distant—an empty Ch'u River;
碧天清遠楚江空
Drawing in my lines, I stir a deep pool of stars.
牽攬一潭星動

That this poem is unmistakably an adaptation of a poem written to the tune of *Man-t'ing-fang* 滿庭芳 by Ch'in Kuan may be seen from the following quotation:

Dense flowers of red smartweeds
紅蓼花繁
Tousled leaves of yellow rushes,
黃蘆葉亂

.   .   .   .

The blue sky empty and wide,
霽天空闊
Light clouds and a clear Ch'u River
雲淡楚江清

.   .   .   .

With a small golden hook
金鉤細
And a line slowly drawn
絲綸慢捲
I stir a pool of stars.[55]
牽動一潭星

In a literary tradition in which rhetorical adaptations and imitations are, in fact, highly cherished and ardently cultivated practices, this particular example in the narrative should occasion no surprise, and it certainly proves nothing more than the fact that its author has knowledge of the Sung poet. But in view of the statement about Wu Ch'êng-ên's stylistic similarity to Ch'in Kuan made by the compilers of the *Huai-an Gazetteer*, even this minor detail should be taken into account in any future research on this perplexing question of authorship.

It seems to me, in conclusion, that Wu Ch'êng-ên, despite scholarly objections to date, remains the most likely author of this late Ming masterpiece. The lack of indisputable evidence, however, has compelled me to refrain, with reluctance, from so identifying him in the present edition.

THE FUNCTIONS OF VERSE, RELIGIOUS THEMES, AND ALLEGORY

Unlike any typical Western work of prose fiction written since the Renaissance, *The Journey to the West* is made up of prose heavily interlaced with verse of many varieties and lengths. The incorporation of

poetry into prose narration is not, of course, unique to Chinese
vernacular fiction. For distant Western parallels, one may point to
the early satiric fragments of Menippus, the later *Consolation of
Philosophy* by Boethius, a work like the *Aucassin and Nicolette*, and the
writings of Bunyan and Rabelais. In Chinese literature, however, this
form of writing has apparently enjoyed more sophisticated and artful
cultivation, for the use of poetry to serve specific literary functions is
already a characteristic of T'ang fiction and drama.[56] In such narrative works as the *Ying-ying chuan* 鶯鶯傳 and the *Sung-yüeh chia-nü*
嵩岳嫁女, there are poems which are made to advance the action by
revealing the emotional conditions of the characters, or poems which
serve as set pieces of dramatic dialogue, a feature which receives
extensive development in subsequent dramatic literature. The employment of verse for narrative, descriptive, and didactic purposes in
prose fiction is no doubt given further impetus by the growing popularity of Buddhist writings and by the development of the *pien-wên*
變文.

No reader of the *Ta-chih-tu lun* 大智度論 or the *Vimalakīrti-nirdeśa
sūtra*, to pick two examples at random, can fail to perceive that
characteristic which Maurice Winternitz has called "an old form of
Buddhist composition": namely, that of "expressing an idea first in
prose and then garbing it in verse, or [of] commencing the presentation of a doctrine in prose and then continuing it in verse."[57] Nor can
that reader fail to notice, when he turns from the Buddhist canon to
the *pien-wên*, how the utilization of poetry to develop the prose
presentation has become one of the defining features of this popular
form of writing.

Since the discovery of these *pien-wên* texts in the cave of Tun-huang
in 1899, their historical basis is well known. Dating from the eighth
and ninth centuries, many of the texts took as their subject the *Leben
und Treiben* of Buddhist saints and heroes, though many other secular
stories dealt with persons and events from Chinese legend or history
as well. The origin of the religious *pien-wên* has been traced to the
evangelistic efforts of Buddhist monks, who sought to accommodate
their more abstruse doctrines to a popular audience through storytelling, a practice for which the Buddha himself might be said to have
provided the exemplary precedent.[58] Not incomparable to some of the
patristic and medieval epic paraphrases of biblical themes in the West

(e.g., the *Libri Evangeliorum IV* of Juvencus, the *Carmen Paschale* of Sedulius, the anonymous but massive Old Saxon *Heliand*, and the *De Vita et Gestis Christi* of Jacobus Bonus), these *pien-wên* consisted of imaginative elaborations and expansions of individual episodes in a Buddhist sūtra, with events and persons freely altered or added. Alternating between short sections of semiliterary prose and lengthier sections composed mainly of the five or seven-syllabic poetic line, the *pien-wên* may amplify a relatively short unit (about one or two hundred characters) of the *Saddharma-puṇḍarīka sūtra* or the *Vimala-kīrti-nirdeśa sūtra* into a narrative of several thousand characters in length.[59] In all probability, these stories were first sung or chanted during temple festivals, and, to judge from observations made in the *Kao-sêng chuan* 髙僧傳 (Biographies of Illustrious Monks), popular reaction to the presentations, especially those describing the agonies of hell, could be extremely emotional.[60]

The popularity and success of the Buddhist *pien-wên* may be seen in the widespread emulation of its form by subsequent authors of secular topics drawn from both history and folklore. The mixture of poetry and prose in narration as a distinctive mode of composition thus made its mark permanently on Chinese literary history by exerting enormous influence on the development of popular drama and the practice of storytelling in the subsequent Sung and Yüan dynasties. The indebtedness of Chinese colloquial fiction to these art forms in turn has been a familiar theme of modern scholarship; scholars who have studied the formal characteristics of the dramatic and narrative literature in medieval China have noted such poetic functions as commentary, moral judgment, exemplum, and summary.[61] By the time of the Ming-Ch'ing novelists, the combination of verse and prose in narration had evolved into a highly flexible medium. And, in the exploitation of this technique, few writers could rival the author of *The Journey to the West* in creative skill, keen observational power, vivid vocabulary, and sure command of a wide variety of poetic forms.

Unlike the poetry of the *San-kuo-chih yen-i* (Romance of the Three Kingdoms), where selections from actual poets provide mainly choric commentary on characters and incidents, or that of the *Chin P'ing Mei*, where the libretti of popular songs and dramas serve frequently to enhance the setting or mood of a particular episode, or even that of the later *Hung-lou mêng* (Dream of the Red Chamber, or The Story of

the Stone), where the lyrical tradition functions to reveal the sub-
jectivity and development of the protagonists and acts as a futile
though deeply moving critique of a decadent Confucian morality, the
original poetry of *The Journey to the West*[62] both excels in formal
varieties and assumes a large share of the narrative responsibility. At
every opportunity, the author seems almost eager to display his poetic
skills by weaving into the fabric of his tale a poem of the style of the
chüeh-chü (a rhymed quatrain of five- or seven-syllabic lines with
fixed tonal pattern), or of the *lü-shih* (an eight-line rhymed poem of
five- or seven-syllabic lines with fixed tonal pattern), or of the *p'ai-lü*
(a long poem using a single rhyme scheme, with the middle parallel
couplets of the *lü-shih* serially extended), or of the *tz'ŭ* (generally a
short, rhymed lyric of irregular meter), or of the *fu* (the rhyme-prose).
Running the length of the first chapter alone, which tells of Monkey's
birth and his life up to the time when he was given the name Wu-
k'ung, are no less than seventeen poems exemplifying nearly all the
forms just mentioned. Though it is not at all apparent in the widely
read, abridged translation by Arthur Waley (pp. 11–12), there is a
poem depicting the monkey's frolic "under the shade of some pine
trees," and another *lü-shih* sketches the curtainlike waterfall immediately after its discovery by the monkeys.

To make a comprehensive study of the narrative's poetry would
require a separate monograph much lengthier than this Introduction.
Here I can only point out some of the most important functions of the
verse in the narrative: that of describing scenery, battles, seasons, and
living beings both human and nonhuman; that of presenting dialogues; and that of providing commentary on the action and the
characters. Poems in the last category make frequent use of religious
themes and rhetoric as well as allegorical devices, and they will be
studied later on in the section on allegory.

It is not without reason that the author of the *JW* has been ranked
by C. T. Hsia as "one of the most skilled descriptive poets in all
Chinese literature,"[63] for much of the descriptive verse in this
narrative is marked by extraordinary realism, vivid delineation,
and vivacious humor. Though it may be impossible to duplicate the
terse rhythm of the three-syllabic line with end rhymes used in the
poem portraying the frolic of the monkeys (chap. 1), I have attempted
to catch something of its characteristic vigor in my translation.

Swinging from branches to branches

Searching for flowers and fruits;
They played two games or three
With pebbles and with pellets.
. . . [see pp. 68–69].

Another example of this type of poetic sketch may be taken from chapter 89, where we have the following poem on a butterfly.

A pair of gossamer wings,
Twin feelers of silvery shade:
It flies so swiftly in the wind,
And dances slowly in the sun.
With nimble speed passing over walls and streams,
It blithely with the fragrant catkins flirts;
Its airy frame loves most the scent of fresh flowers,
Where its graceful form unfolds with greatest ease.

A third example of the poet's descriptive power may be taken from chapter 20, where Tripitaka is asked to depict a violent gust that the pilgrims encounter on their way. "Look at this wind!" he said.

Augustly it blows in a blusterous key,
An immense force leaving the jade-green sky.
It passes the ridge, just hear the trees roar.
It moves in the wood, just see the poles quake.
. . . [see pp. 404–5].

These three poems are but brief illustrations of the author's superb poetic eye and his uncanny ability to capture in a few lines the essential qualities of his subject. That subject may be a mosquito (chap. 16), a bee (chap. 55), a bat (chap. 65), a moth (chap. 84), an ant (chap. 86), a rabbit (chap. 95), or one of the numerous monsters with whom Tripitaka's disciples must engage in combat, or the battle itself, or the scenery of the different regions through which the pilgrims must pass. But what the reader meets again and again in these poems is an enthralling spectacle of exquisite details. Indeed, if judged by some of the traditional norms of Chinese lyric poetry, most of the poems of The Journey to the West might be considered inferior products because of their graphic and, occasionally, unadorned diction. The language is often too explicit, too direct, too bold, to be evocative or suggestive—that quality of metaphorical elusiveness which most Chinese lyric poets cherish and seek to incorporate into their verse.

What is scorned by tradition, however, may turn out to be a poetic trait of special merit in the Hsi-yu chi. For what the author has sought to express in these poems is hardly the kind of lyricism suffused with symbolic imageries so characteristic of the earlier poetry of reclusion, nor is he attempting to achieve the subtle fusion of human emotion and nature which has been the constant aim of many of the T'ang and Sung poets.[64] Most of all, he is not trying to enlist the service of the lyrical tradition to realize the ancient ideal of "expressing serious intent" (*shih yen chih*), and that is why none of these descriptive poems can be said to be the bearer of profound moral ideas or weighty philosophical substances.[65] Rather, what the author of the *Hsi-yu chi* seeks to convey to us seems to be the overpowering immediacy of nature, with all its fullness and richly contrasting variety, as it is often experienced by the main characters in the narrative. To give us this sense of munificence in the natural order, the verse frequently makes use of what may be called the technique of delayed amplification. In the first chapter, where the Flower-Fruit Mountain (the birth place of Sun Wu-k'ung) is introduced, part of the testimonial *fu* poem reads:

> Its majesty commands the wide ocean;
> Its splendor rules the jasper sea;
> Its majesty commands the wide ocean
> When, like silver mountains, the tide sweeps fishes into caves;
> Its splendor rules the jasper sea
> When snowlike billows send forth serpents from the deep.
> . . . [see pp. 66–67].

When the monkeys, the subjects of Sun Wu-k'ung, later enjoy a feast, the delicacies include

> Golden balls and pearly pellets;
> Red ripeness and yellow plumpness.
> Golden balls and pearly pellets are the cherries,
> Their colors truly luscious.
> Red ripeness and yellow plumpness are the plums,
> Their taste—a fragrant tartness.

Again, the setting we are made to see of the abode of the Bear Monster in chapter 17 is a cave which is surrounded by

> Mist and smoke abundant,
> Cypress and pine umbrageous.
> Mist and smoke abundant, their hues surround the door;
> Cypress and pine umbrageous, their green entwines the gate.

In these lines of poetry, the use of repetition is the apparent means by which the poet partially overcomes the limitations inherent in his medium: the extreme economy of construction and the tendency toward traditional diction in literary Chinese. One does not need to read a great deal of classic Chinese verse before one recognizes that phrases such as "wide ocean" (汪洋), "snowlike billows" (雪浪), "red ripeness" (紅綻), "yellow plumpness" (黃肥), and "cypress and pine umbrageous" (松柏森森) have been used so regularly that they may almost be characterized as "formulaic." In his compositions, the author of the *Hsi-yu chi* has shown little interest in moving beyond traditional vocabularies and metaphors. Even his extensive employment of *wu-hsing* (Five Phases) and alchemical terminologies in many of the poems, though a somewhat exceptional practice, has had antecedents in some of the minor T'ang, Sung, and Ming poets. What he has done in the narrative that merits our attention is the way he breaks up into separate lines the phrases that would be ordinarily joined together. Instead of simply stating "Cypress and pine umbrageous, their green entwines the gate," he first mentions the cypresses and the bamboos before proceeding to a full rehearsal of their particular appearance and condition. The immediate result of this procedure is to retard the movement of the poetic line by giving a more leisurely pace to a metrical rhythm that is normally terse and rapid. The repetitions compel our attention and serve to enhance the amplitude of the poetic utterance. Cumulatively these poems impress us with the encyclopedic range of the poet's interest and the fineness of his vision, for there is hardly anything that is too mundane or too exotic for his scrutiny. Foodstuff of all kinds, household utensils, birds, animals, and insects, plants and flowers of sundry varieties, the beings of heaven and hell—all process unhurriedly before us in their colorful and manifold plenitude, and we are also given a profound sense of "God's plenty." In this manner the language of the poems serves a peculiar function that is not unworthy of comparison with that of Homeric verse, for the traditional Chinese diction, with its strict tonal, metrical, and stylistic consistency, is so utilized that it inevitably, as one modern scholar has said of the Homeric epithets, calls attention to "the special excellence of all things."[66]

If the poems of the narrative excel in presenting the concrete excellence of the natural world, they are equally effective in transcribing for us the sense of time passing, the ever recurring pattern of seasonal change.[67] Though the length of Tripitaka's journey in the narrative has been either purposefully or erroneously changed by its author from sixteen years (as with the historical Hsüan-tsang) to fourteen, there is little indication that he thereby wishes to minimize the duration of Tripitaka's undertaking. On the contrary, many details are present in the narrative to emphasize specifically the temporal magnitude of the journey. Not only do the pilgrims themselves repeatedly talk about distance and time (cf. *HYC*, chap. 24, p. 270; chap. 80, p. 911; chap. 86, pp. 986–87; chap. 88, p. 1000; chap. 91, p. 1029; chap. 92, p. 1039; chap. 93, p. 1055), but the narrator also stresses the vast span of the pilgrimage by means of frequent poetic descriptions of seasonal alterations. Soon after Sun Wu-k'ung's submission to the scripture pilgrim, the narrative in chapter 14 reads:

> Tripitaka rode his horse, with Pilgrim [i.e., Wu-k'ung] leading the way; they journeyed by day and rested by night, taking food and drink according to their needs. Soon it was early winter. You see
> > Frost blighted maples and the wizened trees;
> > Few verdant pine and cypress still on the ridge.
> > . . . [see p. 306].

In chapter 18, however, this is the contrasting scene we have after Sun Wu-k'ung has recovered a lost cassock.

> As Pilgrim led the way forward, it was the happiest time of spring. You see
> > The horse making light tracks on grassy turfs;
> > Gold threads of willow swaying with fresh dew.
> > . . . [see p. 368].

It will be seen in these and similar poetic passages (cf. *HYC*, chap. 20, p. 223; chap. 23, p. 256; chap. 56, pp. 643–44) that the author is not interested merely in conveying to us the sense and beauty of seasonal change. More importantly, what he wishes us to grasp through such poetic accounts of the seasons, in themselves no more than familiar literary exercises in the Chinese lyric tradition, is the effect such changes have on those who must take time to reach a distant goal. Constantly exposed to the whims of nature, the pilgrims are the ones who must, as the Chinese put it, "feed on the wind and rest on the dew" (餐風宿露), who must be "capped by the moon and cloaked by the stars" (戴月披星). Just as the cycles of ordeals and adversities accentuate the suffering which Tripitaka and his disciples must undergo, so even the ostensibly charming and innocuous shifts of the seasons add to the hardships ("The strong, cold wind/Tears at the sleeve!/How does one bear this chilly might of night?") encountered on the way. In this sense, time is both spatialized and physicalized, its effect thus reinforcing our impression of the immensity of the journey to the West.

Their compelling descriptive power notwithstanding, these poems can sometimes, paradoxically, be devoid of local color and impression. This is especially true of those designed to depict a place. Invariably the verse refers to precipitous cliffs and exotic flowers, to carved beam buildings and verdant forests of pines and bamboos, to the cries of cranes and phoenixes, and to the congregation of rare and mythic animals. There are, to be sure, variations in the contents and in the syntax, but without explicit authorial identification it would be difficult solely from the poetic descriptions to distinguish between the birthplace of Sun Wu-k'ung (*Hua-kuo shan*) in chapter 1, the Black Wind Mountain (*Hêh-fêng shan*) in chapter 17, the Spirit Mountain (*Ling shan*), which is Buddha's abode, in chapters 52 and 98, or the counterfeit *Ling shan* in chapter 65, where the pilgrims meet one of their most formidable adversaries.

This paradoxical fusion of the particular and the typical is what enables the entire narrative to be imbued with a kind of "epic" grandeur, energy, and expansiveness. In his thoughtful essay "The Realistic and Lyric Elements in the Chinese Medieval Story," Jaroslav Prûšek has suggested that the prose and poetic portions of the *pien-wên* and the *hua-pen* constitute two levels of representing reality. Recalling how Balzac found it praiseworthy that Sir Walter Scott impregnated the novel "with the spirit of olden times, combined in it drama and dialogue, portrait, landscape and description, introduced into it fantasy and truth—elements typical of the epic—and placed poetry in closest intimacy with the most ordinary speech," Prûšek thinks that the lyrical poetical insertions into the realistic prose segments of the Chinese story "form—possibly quite unintentionally—a kind of second plane to the actual story, raise it—even though it be unconsciously—to the demonstrations of a certain philosophical conception of the world."[68]

While Průšek's observation, to some extent, can be applied to *The Journey to the West*, it does not succeed entirely in isolating the particular virtue of the work. For the poetic insertions are neither "interludes" nor "interruptions"; they are, rather, integral parts of the total narrative. Not unlike some of the great landscape paintings of the Sung and the Yüan periods, in which a thousand details subsist in a delicate union of concreteness and ideality, the poetry here at once heightens and elevates by pointing simultaneously to the peculiar quality of a certain site and to its mysterious and elemental character. Most important of all, the lyric impulse is always placed at the service of the epic; the descriptions do not invite attention to themselves as poetic entities in their own right but, rather, are called upon constantly to strengthen the élan and verve of the story itself. As Erich Auerbach has written so perceptively of *The Divine Comedy*, "the vivid descriptions of landscape in which the great poem abounds are never autonomous or purely lyrical; true, they appeal directly to the reader's emotions, they arouse delight or horror; but the feelings awakened by the landscape are not allowed to seep away like vague romantic dreams, but forcefully recapitulated, for the landscape is nothing other than the appropriate scene or metaphorical symbol of human destiny."[69] Similarly, the mountains, the monasteries, the monsters, the deities, the rivers and plains, and the seasons in *The Journey to the West* acquire a significance not in themselves but only in relation to the fate of the pilgrims. The appearance of any locality can be either menacing or tutelary precisely because it can forebode danger or shelter for Tripitaka and his companions. So too, the accounts of the glorious epiphany of Kuan-yin in chapter 12 and of the fearful visages of the Green-Hair Lion, the Yellow-Tusk Elephant, and the Garuda Monster in chapter 75 achieve their greatest impact only when these are understood as forces which can assist or impede the pilgrims' progress.

To stress the central importance of the pilgrims' experience and its determinative influence on the quality of the poetic insertions is not to overlook the element of verbal humor, another aspect of the narrative that has often been praised. One of the best examples of narrative realism masterfully blended with comic irony may be found in chapter 67, where an elder of a village is seeking Monkey's aid to rid the people of a python monster.

Pilgrim [another nickname of Sun Wu-k'ung] said, "Old man, it's easy to catch the monster. There is difficulty only because the families here are not united in their efforts." The elder asked, "How did you reach this conclusion?" Pilgrim replied, "For three years this monster has been a menace, hurting countless creatures. I should think that if each family would contribute one ounce of silver, five hundred families would fetch five hundred ounces. You could find an exorcist anywhere to get rid of this monster. Why did you permit this outrage to last for three years?" The elder said, "Speaking of spending money would be an utter embarrassment! Which one of our families did not disburse three or five ounces of silver! The year before last we found a monk from the south side of this mountain and invited him to come. But he didn't prevail." Pilgrim asked, "How did that monk go about catching the monster?" The elder said:

"Oh, that *Sêng-gha*,
He wore a Kasāya,
He expounded first the *Peacock*;
He then recited the *Lotus*.
Incense he burned within the urn;
He then took the bell in his hand.
As he thus sang and chanted,
He greatly disturbed the monster.
The wind rose and the clouds gathered,
And he arrived at this village.
The monk engaged the monster;
What a battle to relate:
One stroke delivered a punch,
One stroke delivered a scratch.
The monk tried hard to win,
But he possessed no hair.
In a while the monster triumphed
And went back to mist and smoke.
(It's like sunning a dried scab!)
We moved more closely to look:
The bald head was beaten like a rotten watermelon!"

Pilgrim said, laughing, "Well, he really lost out!" The elder said, "He only paid with his life; we were the true victims. We had to pay for his coffin and his funeral, and we gave some money to his disciple. The disciple still hasn't given up and wants to sue us even now. It's a mess!" Pilgrim said, "Did you ask any

other person to catch him?" The elder answered, "Last year
we also located a Taoist." Pilgrim asked, "How did the Taoist
catch him?" The elder said, "That Taoist:

> Wearing on his head a gold cap,
> He put on an exorcist robe.
> He banged aloud his placard;
> He waved his charms and water.
> He sent for gods and spirits:
> He only brought on the ogre!
> Wild wind was howling and churning;
> Black fog dimmed both sky and sight;
> The monster met the Taoist;
> They fought a lengthy battle.
> When twilight at last set in,
> The monster left for his home.
> The cosmos was bright and fair,
> And we were all assembled.
> Going to hunt for the Taoist,
> We found him drowned in a brook;
> We fished him out for a better look:
> He looked like a chicken poached in soup!"

The language of this passage may certainly bring to mind such works
in the West as the Homeric *Batrachomyomachia* (Battle of the Frogs
and Mice) and Pope's *The Rape of the Lock*. But what prevents even this
section of *The Journey to the West* from being merely an episode of the
mock heroic is its serious context. Despite the scene's relaxed, comic
tone, the ordeal facing Pilgrim and his companion, Pa-chieh, is no
illusion. Shortly thereafter they will again have to battle a real and
dangerous opponent in the figure of the monster, which is another
part of the ordeal preordained for the pilgrims.

This deliberate harnessing of the poetic elements to augment the
narrative force may be detected also in many of the poetic speeches of
the narrative. The technique of advancing the action through poetic
dialogues is no doubt inherited directly from the colloquial short
stories and popular dramas of earlier periods, but it has now become
a highly flexible and effective device. Most of these speeches are spoken
as challenges to battle or descriptions of some weapons, for which the
author of *The Journey to the West* exploits the longer form of the
p'ai-lü with utmost virtuosity. The challenges to battle are usually
delivered immediately before the character engages in actual combat.

They provide occasions for the speaker not only to indulge in polemical humor and verbal provocation of his adversary, but also frequently to reminisce, to recount the prior history of his own person. Thus, when Pa-chieh demands from Sha Wu-ching his name and surname before the battle in chapter 22, this is the reply he receives:

> My spirit was strong since the time of birth.
> I had made a tour of the whole wide world,
> Where my fame as a hero became well known—
> A gallant type emulated by all.
> . . . [see pp. 432–34].

Though this speech of Sha Wu-ching, or any of those by other characters in the narrative (cf. chaps. 19, 52, 70, 85, 86), is not in any length comparable to, say, the tales of Odysseus, it serves a similar function, common to most heroic tales, of filling in the background of a hero's life, just as "Homer makes Nestor boast of his lost youth or Phoenix tell of his lurid past."[70]

The last major function of the verse in *The Journey to the West* has to do with authorial commentary, particularly in the form of allegorical interpretation of characters and incidents in the narrative. Since, however, allegory in this instance is intimately linked to certain religious themes and terminologies structured in the narrative, it is to these that we shall first turn our attention.

In an essay on *The Journey to the West* published recently in a volume titled *Ssŭ-pu ku-tien hsiao-shuo p'ing-lun* 四部古典小說評論 (Criticism of Four Classic Novels), a committee on literature at the Normal University of Shanghai has pinpointed the distinctive feature of this work: "In the first place, what distinguishes the *Hsi-yu chi* from most other fiction of antiquity is that it is a novel of the supramundane."[71] Few readers will dispute such a remark on what is certainly the prima facie character of this epic narrative on Buddhist pilgrimage. It is surprising, however, that the bulk of modern criticism has not made any serious investigation into the significance of the supramundane, the mythic, and, indeed, the religious themes and rhetoric that pervade the entire work. This lack in modern criticism no doubt stems in part from scholarly reaction against the emphases of the editors and compilers of the previous centuries who, from the very first moment of the work's public appearance, regarded it as a work of profound allegory. In his preface to the Shih-tê-t'ang edition, for example, Ch'ên Yüan-chih already sees in Tripitaka—the name of the master pilgrim in the narrative—a meaning which transcends its normal associations with Buddhism. Taking Tripitaka (*San-tsang*, three baskets or collections of the Buddhist canonical writings) to mean, rather, the three constitutive elements of the human self (spirit, *shên*, voice, *shêng*, vital energy, *ch'i*), Ch'ên goes on to give the reader what he perceives as the significance hidden in the narrative:

> For demons are the miasmas caused by the mouth, the ears, the nose, the tongue, the body, the will, the fears and the illusions of the imagination. Therefore, as demons are born of the mind, they will be also subdued by the mind. This is why we must subdue the mind in order to subdue the demons; we must subdue the demons in order to return to truth; we must return to truth in order to reach the primal beginning where there will be nothing more to be subdued by the mind. This is what is meant by the accomplishment of the *Tao*, and this is also the real allegory of the book.[72]

In what may be the most widely read and most often reprinted abridged version of the work, the *Hsi-yu chên-ch'üan* 西游真銓 (The True Explanation of the Westward Journey), its early Ch'ing editor Ch'ên Shih-pin 陳士斌 has also developed the most thoroughgoing allegorical interpretation through the use of alchemical, *yin-yang*, and *I Ching* lore. Following, perhaps, the occasional examples provided by the original author himself (cf. the prefatory poem of chap. 26), Ch'ên even makes use of the highly speculative eccentricities of ideography, as when he interprets the Cave of the Three Stars and Slanting Moon (the abode of the Magic Master Subodhi where Sun Wu-k'ung attained enlightenment) as meaning the mind or the heart (*hsin* 心), a Chinese character composed of a crescentlike long stroke surrounded by three short strokes.[73] Perhaps it was this attempt by Ch'ên and others to interpret the narrative as a detailed treatise of internal alchemy that led another Ch'ing editor, half a century later, to take a different tack. In his unabridged hundred-chapter *Hsin-shuo Hsi-yu chi* 新說西游記 (The Journey to the West, Newly Interpreted), Chang Shu-shên declared in the section entitled "Hsi-yu chi tsung-p'i" (Overall Comments on the Journey to the West) that "the book *Hsi-yu* has been designated by the ancients as a book for the illumination of *Tao*, by which it originally means the *Tao* of the sages, the worthies, and the *Ju*. It would be a mistake to consider it to be the illumination of the Tao of Immortals and Buddhism."[74] From such a point of view, Chang defended the story of the quest for Buddhist scriptures as an allegory of the classic Confucian doctrines on the illustration of virtue (*ming-tê* 明德) and the rectification of the mind (*chêng-hsin* 正心).

It was in opposition to this tendency to treat the narrative as a manual for Buddhist, Taoist, or Confucian self-cultivation that Hu Shih emphatically declared in his essay of 1923 that there was neither subtle language nor profound meaning intended by the author, whose overriding purpose in writing the narrative, according to Hu, was simply to air his satiric view of life and the world.[75] For the modern Chinese philosopher, *The Journey to the West* must be regarded primarily as a marvelous comic work; it is, as Hu says in the foreword to Arthur Waley's version, "a book of . . . profound nonsense."[76] How influential this view of Hu has been may be seen in the echoing remarks of Lu Hsün[77] and countless other writers and commentators since. Perhaps the extreme position along this line is represented by the verdict of Tanaka Kenji and Arai Ken, who have asserted that, unlike other traditional tales of the supernatural in China, this late Ming narrative neither is accompanied by the shadow of religion and superstition, nor emphasizes the karmic principle of reward and retribution. Rather, the world of *Hsi-yu chi* manifests what Miki Katsumi has said of it in his *Saiyuki Oboegaki*: "human liberation from mystery and progress from the medieval world to the spirit of modernity."[78]

Not all modern students of this work, however, subscribe to such an astonishing view of its nature. While fully acknowledging the wealth of comedy and satire in the novel, C. T. Hsia has pointedly challenged Hu's judgment when he observes that "the phrase 'profound nonsense' . . . concedes the necessity for philosophical or allegorical interpretation."[79] Chin Meishin 陳明新 has some perceptive comments on the relation of *The Journey to the West* to the *chih-kuai* 志怪 (Chronicles of the Marvelous) tradition in Chinese fiction by calling our attention to the ostensibly strong didactic intent of Wu Ch'êng-ên as a writer of supernatural tales.[80] Though Chin's thesis involves the recognition of Wu Ch'êng-ên as the author of the narrative—a position, as we have seen, not entirely free of critical controversy—an essay by Andrew Plaks of Princeton University has demonstrated powerfully how the text itself, quite apart from the problem of authorship, invites serious reckoning with its allegorical elements.[81] It is my intention, therefore, to examine more closely how and in what significant manner the narrative occasions "the necessity for philosophical or allegorical interpretation." I would also like to determine whether the vast complex of alchemical, *yin-yang*, *wu-hsing*, and Buddhist terminologies in this text bear some organic relation to the action and characters of the story, or whether they merely present a veneer of certain common figures of speech overlaid upon "ready-made fictional characters" and incidents, as Glen Dudbridge has described the Monkey of the Mind and Horse of the Will metaphor in the novel.[82]

The task of such an investigation, I realize, is not easy, since critical uncertainty about the authorship of *The Journey to the West* complicates the problem of tracing the possible religious and philosophical sources of the work. Furthermore, even provisional acceptance of Wu Ch'êng-ên as the author is of little help here, because what we know of him gives but meager information concerning what he might have read in the vast chronicles of Buddhist and Taoist lore. That he had a lifelong passion for the strange and the exotic in literature is evident from what we have already seen in the *Yü-ting-chih hsü* quoted above in the section "Text and Authorship." Also, a short piece titled *Po-ch'ih-shan ch'üan-yüan chi* 鉢池山勸緣偈 (The Gāthā for the Exposition of Affinity on Po-ch'ih Mountain) reveals that Wu was familiar with some of the most common phrases of Buddhism,[83] and a few alchemical terms also turn up in some of his writings.[84] But neither the prose nor the poetry of his collected writings evince the kind of massive appropriation from Chinese religious traditions that is apparent on almost every page of *The Journey to the West*. The study of sources, therefore, must begin with the text itself, though the scope and length of this narrative, not to mention the *Tao Tsang* and the Buddhist canon, rule out any exhaustive comparison of the work with extant religious texts. In what follows, which must be regarded as only a preliminary investigation, I shall discuss some of the most obvious and prominent religious themes and symbols found in the narrative.

Although the story of *The Journey to the West* is based upon the historical pilgrimage of Hsüan-tsang, it is quite remarkable how extensively the themes and rhetoric of Taoism appear in every part of the work. By Taoism, I mean the concepts, ideas, and practices traceable to the *Tao Tsang* (The Taoist Canon), while fully acknowledging that many such elements codified and preserved for religious or non-religious reasons in this collection are no more than folk beliefs and rituals. As so many students of Chinese culture have come to realize, Taoism as a distinct philosophical movement or religious tradition is notoriously difficult to define. My pragmatic proposal here is made strictly in order to facilitate critical analysis, for the pervasive use of Taoist vocabularies in *The Journey to the West*'s titular couplets, in hundreds of its narrative and descriptive poems, and in various parts of the prose narration to illumine the significance of certain episodes, is quite without parallel in classic Chinese fiction. True, the *Fêng-shên yen-i* (Investiture of the Gods) surpasses even the *Hsi-yu chi* in its dramatization of the enormous celestial pantheon, the many sacred sites, and the weapons of stupendous magic power; the *Chin P'ing Mei* may contain concise transcriptions of a number of Taoist masses and rituals; and in the *Dream of the Red Chamber*, as Plak's study has brilliantly shown, there is some subtle interplay between *yin-yang* and *wu-hsing* theories and the development of characters and action in the novel. None of these works, however, is comparable to *The Journey to the West*, in which Taoist elements serve, not merely as a means of providing choric commentary on incidents and characters in the narrative, but frequently as an aid to reveal to the reader the true nature of the fellow pilgrims, to help define their essential relationships, and to advance the action of the narrative itself. Though the numerous literary antecedents to this novel clearly reveal an extended tradition wherein the story of the Buddhist pilgrim-monk becomes progressively assimilated to popular myths and legends, many of them originating from popular Taoism,[85] it remains for the author of the hundred-chapter version to give shape and coherence on an unprecedented scale to this tradition by endowing the Buddhist Hsüan-tsang with four supernatural disciples, the divine status of three of whom is attained through their efforts in alchemical self-cultivation. Indeed, as one examines the story of the pilgrims developed through spagyric themes and rhetoric in the narrative, one may come to the conclusion that the journey to the West also takes on the appearance of an allegorical pilgrimage in self-cultivation.

The first and most prominent member of the monk's disciples is, of course, Sun Wu-k'ung (Monkey), and significantly the narrative begins not with Hsüan-tsang's departure for the West—as might have been the case in the story's earliest prototype, the Sung poetic tale of the Westward journey—but with Monkey's birth and his attainment of immortality. It is because of Monkey's sudden awareness of his own impermanence (*wu-ch'ang*) one day during his insouciant existence on the Flower-Fruit Mountain, an awareness which one of his subordinates saw to be the sprouting of the mind of *Tao*, that led to his eventual encounter with Patriarch Subodhi. Although the name Wu-k'ung (悟空) that Monkey was given had historical precedent in another T'ang Buddhist pilgrim (see the first section of this introduction), the explanation of its meaning by the patriarch clearly followed Taoist emphasis:

> Laughing, the Patriarch said, "Though your features are not the most attractive, you do resemble a monkey (*Hu-sun*) that feeds on pine seeds. . . . [see p. 82] You will hence be given the religious name Awake-to-Vacuity (*Wu-k'ung*)."

This name Wu-k'ung (Awake-to-Vacuity), which the Patriarch gives Monkey, brings quickly to mind such concepts as *śūnya*, *śūnyatā*, and *māyā* in Buddhism, which point to the emptiness, the vacuity, and the unreality of all things and all physical phenomena. These are, in fact, cardinal doctrines of the Yogācāra school of which the historical Hsüan-tsang himself, as we have seen, is an able exponent. It is not without reason, therefore, that when the fictive Tripitaka first learns of Monkey's name in chapter 14, he is very pleased and exclaims, "It exactly fits the emphasis of our denomination." We should remember, of course, that the concept of emptiness and its complementary doctrine of mind cultivation (*hsiu-hsin* 修心) in idealistic Buddhism have also been adopted by many Taoists in their writings. In this early episode of his narrative, the author of *The Journey to the West* reveals how the emphasis on the unity of the Three Religions (*San-chiao kuei-i* 三教歸一), so prevalent in many late medieval authors in the *Tao Tsang*, is also the underlying religious vision of the novel. For, while Monkey's name strongly evokes Buddhist teachings, his surname, as the Patriarch Subodhi says, illustrates the Doctrine of the Baby, which is the classic term in the lore of internal alchemy to designate the maturation of the holy embryo (*shêng-t'ai* 聖胎) in one's body when immortality is achieved.

This is precisely Monkey's achievement, as we learn in the second chapter. In a highly comical interview with his teacher, Monkey rapidly rejects a series of offers by the Patriarch to teach him the arts of divination, conjuration, meditation, breathing exercises, and the taking of medicinal aids on the ground that none of these practices, so the Patriarch tells him, leads to immortality. Only when Monkey steals into the inner chamber where the Patriarch is sleeping that night does Monkey attain his wish, for he gains the secret oral formula from his master:

> Know well this secret formula wondrous and true:
> Spare and nurse the vital forces, this and nothing else.
> . . . [see p. 88].

The interest of this formula lies not merely in its specific use of classic terminologies of internal alchemy but also in what it may reveal about the author's knowledge of such writings in the Taoist canon. Though neither the text itself nor any of the major commentators of *The Journey to the West* I have seen has suggested that the formula is not original with the author, I am surprised to discover a verbatim quotation of it in *Chung-kuo Tao-chiao shih* 中國道教史 (A History of Taoism in China) by Fu Ch'in-chia 傅勤家. What is of the greatest interest here is that Fu does not use the formula to identify Wu Ch'êng-ên or the author of the *Hsi-yu chi*; he simply declares it to be a secret formula, used by those "in the cultivation of the Way in posterity" to explain certain passages in the *Huang-t'ing nei-ching ching* 黃庭內景經 (The Yellow Court Classic on the Interior Condition) and the *San-hua chü-ting* 三花聚頂 (Three Flowers [Forces] Coming Together at the Top) phrase in the *Ch'ien-ch'üeh lei-shu* 潛確類書 (Reference Books for the Penetration of Reality).[86] Whether this formula in fact exists somewhere in the formidable depths of the *Tao Tsang* is a question which cannot be readily resolved without the assistance of time!

If the source for this formula is yet unclear, there are several other places in *The Journey to the West* which indicate quite unambiguously that the author of the narrative may well have direct knowledge of certain segments of the *Tao Tsang*. The first such instance is the prefatory verse of chapter 8 (see p. 180). With the exception of the last three lines,

> In that hour,
> Once you penetrate to the Origin,
> You'll see the three jewels and the Dragon King,

it is a direct quotation of a tz'ŭ poem with the melodic name of
Su-wu-man 蘇武慢, by one Fêng Tsun-shih 馮尊師 (Honored
Teacher Fêng), in the Ming-ho yü-yin 鳴鶴餘音 (The Crying Crane's
Lingering Sound), chüan 2, 2, a collection of Taoist poems compiled
supposedly by a Yüan Taoist by the name of P'êng Chih-chung 彭致中
(Tao Tsang, 84/744). The last three lines of the original poem read
as follows:

> Avoid, in the clumps of vines and creepers,
> The topsy-turvy dreams
> Of the old wives and wayfaring sons.

It is interesting to observe how, in his use of this poem, the author of
The Journey to the West has converted his source to his own purpose.
Whereas the original poem seems to represent a mildly ironic view
of Buddhism, the author of the narrative has made it into a cryptic
statement for the necessity of enlightenment by the alteration of the
last three lines to:

> In that hour,
> Once you penetrate to the Origin,
> You'll see the Three Treasures and the Dragon King.

The author's familiarity with the Ming-ho yü-yin is evident further in
chapter 12 of the narrative, when Hsüan-tsang, during the beginning
of the Grand Mass of Land and Water convened by the T'ang emperor,
presented the latter with the proclamation for the deliverance of the
orphaned souls. The text of this proclamation again utilizes part of a
Shêng-t'ang Wên 昇堂文 (Proclamation upon the Ascension to the
Main Hall) attributed to the same Fêng Tsun-shih (Ming-ho yü-yin,
chüan 9, 13–14; the text also appears as Shêng-t'ang shih-chung
昇堂示眾 [Ascending the Hall to Reveal to the Assembly] in the Tung-
yüan chi 洞淵集 [Collected Writings on the Cave and the Deep],
chüan 4, 9ab, in Tao Tsang, 83/733). I quote the relevant passage from
The Journey to the West:

> The spirit of the pure and the clean circulates freely and flows
> everywhere in the Three Regions. There are a thousand changes
> and ten thousand transformations, all regulated by the forces
> of yin and yang. Boundless and vast indeed are the substance,
> the function, the true nature, and the permanence of such

phenomena. . . . Flinging wide the gates of salvation and setting
in motion many vessels of mercy, we would deliver you, the
multitudes, from the Sea of Woe and save you from perdition
and from the Sixfold Path. You will be led to return to the way
of truth, and to enjoy the bliss of Heaven. Whether it be by
motion, rest, or nonactivity, you will be fused with pure
essences. Therefore, make use of this noble occasion for you are
invited to the pleasures of the Celestial City.

As this proclamation was used in the narrative during what might be
called a Buddhist "All Souls" Mass, it would be illuminating to determine what was the function of the original text in Taoist ritual.

A third instance of the *Hsi-yu chi* author's adaptation from this
particular Taoist volume occurs in the prefatory verse which opens
chapter 11. The first section of another *Shêng-t'ang Wên*, by one
Ch'in Chên-jên 秦真人 (Adept Ch'in) (*Ming-ho yü-yin, chüan* 9, 15ab),
reads as follows:

The time of a hundred years: swift as a flowing stream.
The work of a lifetime: vain as froth and foam.
On your face yesterday, peach and apricot flowers blossom.
Besides the temples today, snow and frost now shine through. . . .
The termites disband as if in a dream;
The cuckoo's earnest call asks you to turn back.

From this passage comes the seven-syllabic *lü-shih* poem of our
narrative, a gently didactic statement of *sic gloria mundi transit* that
seeks to distill the mood of the chapter, which tells of the emperor
T'ai-tsung's tour of the underworld:

A hundred years pass by like a flowing stream;
The work of a lifetime is only froth and foam.
. . . [see p. 237].

These are the three most notable parts of the early segment of the
narrative for which sources clearly can be found, and further investigation of the *Tao Tsang* may turn up other instances of such identifi-
able borrowings. What is more difficult to trace are the origins of the
vast amount of *yin-yang, wu-hsing,* and alchemical terminologies
structured in the narrative, which reveal unambiguous linguistic
affinity with many of the texts of the *Tao Tsang*, though they do not,
at least at this stage of my research, point to any particular one in the

canon. But even without completely resolving the question of sources, it is still possible to determine more precisely the function of these elements and allusions in the narrative.

It is significant, as I mentioned before, that the three main disciples of the pilgrim Tripitaka all acquire immortality and join the celestial hierarchy through the process of self-cultivation (*hsiu-tao*) imparted to them by a teacher. Their supernatural character and their magical powers, on which the master pilgrim must so heavily depend, thus do not stem from their association with Buddhism. Rather, it is their success in internal alchemy, in making the inward elixir of immortality, as it were, that qualifies Sun Wu-k'ung, Chu Wu-nêng, and Sha Wu-ching to be the proper guardians of the mortal monk. The reason their assistance is needed is that the pilgrimage itself is believed to be so filled with hazards and perils that human help and companionship for the scripture pilgrim will not suffice. Already in chapter 8, when the Boddhisattva Kuan-yin is sent by Śākyamuni to seek a scripture pilgrim in the Land of the East, she is given special treasures by Buddha to present to the candidate for his protection. She is also told to persuade any monster possessing great magical power whom she meets on her way to become the disciple of the scripture pilgrim. Her journey to China, which in essence becomes a proleptic journey to the West with the order of events and geographical direction partially reversed, results in four celestial renegades' being made into disciples and thus prepares the reader for subsequent developments in the narrative. When the fictive Hsüan-tsang later departs from the capital of Ch'ang-an, he is quickly divested of his human assistants. At the mountain significantly named the Two Frontiers, which in the structure of the narrative marks the pilgrim's departure from the mundane territory of T'ang China and his entrance into the mythic realm of the journey infested by wild beasts, monsters, and demons, Hsüan-tsang is told by a human hunter who has come to his aid during his first ordeal that he must proceed alone, for the tigers and wolves beyond that mountain are not submissive to the hunter (chap. 13). It is, in fact, at that critical moment that Hsüan-tsang encounters Monkey, who will prove to be his most resourceful and trustworthy disciple. This meeting also initiates the fulfillment of the poetic prophecy announced by the god the night before when he rescues the monk from a band of animal spirits:

I am the planet Venus from the West,
Who came to save you by special request,
Some pupils divine will come to your aid.
Blame not the scriptures for hardships ahead.

The contrast between the limited strength of the human hunter and the fantastic power of Wu-k'ung is dramatically underscored by the episode immediately following the latter's release from the Wu-hsing Mountain. When master pilgrim and disciple encounter another ferocious tiger on their way, Monkey disposes of the beast with one stroke of his rod, causing

> its brain to burst out like ten thousand red petals of peach blossoms, and the teeth to fly out like so many pieces of white jade. So terrified was our Ch'ên Hsüan-tsang that he fell off his horse. "O God! O God!" he cried, biting his fingers. "When Guardian Liu [the hunter] overcame that striped tiger the other day, he had to do battle with him for almost half a day. But without even fighting today, Sun Wu-k'ung reduces the tiger to pulp with one blow of his rod. How true is the saying, 'For the strong, there's always someone stronger!'" [chap. 14]

This note of Hsüan-tsang's reliance on supernatural assistance is sounded again when, some time later, his white horse—his last link to the ordinary human world—is devoured by the Dragon prince exiled at the Eagle Grief Stream. Kuan-yin, who has been asked by Wu-k'ung to come to subdue the dragon, explains to the frustrated disciple:

> I went personally to plead with the Jade Emperor to have the dragon stationed here so that he could serve as a means of transportation for the scripture pilgrim. Those mortal horses from the Land of the East, do you think that they could walk through ten thousand waters and a thousand hills? How could they possibly hope to reach the Spirit Mountain, the land of Buddha? Only a dragon-horse could make that journey!
> [chap. 15]

To recognize the mighty resources of the disciples is to understand why Tripitaka is portrayed in such a manner in the *Hsi-yu-chi*. For no one familiar with the work has failed to notice to what degree this Hsüan-tsang differs from the heroic figure drawn from history and hagiography. With studied irony, the author seems to delight in demeaning the popular religious hero. Joyless and humorless, the fictive Tripitaka is dull of mind and peevish in spirit, his muddle-headedness matched only by his moral pusillanimity. As someone who is supposedly committed to the life of *pravraj* (*ch'u-chia*, a life of having forsaken the family), he is singularly attached to bodily comforts, complaining more than once about the cold and hunger inflicted by the journey. The slightest foreboding of ill or danger terrifies him; the most groundless kind of slander at once shatters his confidence in his most trustworthy follower, Sun Wu-k'ung, who has never failed to come to his rescue. Though he does win admiration from his disciple on a few occasions by his dogged resistance to sexual temptation, most of his encounters with evil, whether in human or supernatural form, find him impotent and paralyzed by fear, never revealing, even at the journey's end, that he has gained any moral or spiritual insight from his experience. It is this characteristic in Tripitaka that elicits an interesting observation from Hsia, who writes:

> From the viewpoint of popular Buddhism, Tripitaka has on all occasions followed the command not to kill, but because the novel inculcates the kind of Buddhist wisdom which excludes even the finest human sentiments as a guide to salvation, he is seen as a victim of perpetual delusion and can never make the same kind of spiritual progress as the hero of a Christian allegory. The novel, however, ultimately demonstrates the paradoxical character of this wisdom in that its nominal hero is granted Buddhahood at the end precisely because he has done nothing to earn it. To consciously strive for Buddhahood would again have placed him under bondage.[87]

As far as Tripitaka is concerned, Hsia's point is well taken, for Tripitaka's achievement does little to merit his final exaltation. However, the weakness of his character, it may be argued, does not necessarily imply that "the finest human sentiments" are not desirable or that they have little value in the religious vision of the work. On the contrary, Tripitaka's frail and fallible character is deliberately magnified by the author in order to stress his absolute need for his supernatural companions and, most especially, for the protective guidance of Sun Wu-k'ung. For this reason, both the narrator and Sun on several occasions have emphasized the fact that the master pilgrim is of "fleshly eyes and mortal stock" (肉眼凡胎). When, in chapter 22, the pilgrims are stranded on the eastern shore of the Flowing-Sand River, Wu-k'ung and Wu-nêng debate on the means of getting Tripitaka across the river. "You have no idea," says Pilgrim, "about the capacity of my cloud-somersault, which with one leap can cover a hundred and eight thousand miles. . . ." "Elder Brother," says Pa-chieh, "if it's so easy, all you need to do is to carry Master on your back: nod your head, stretch your waist, and jump across. . . ." To which Pilgrim, after some reflection, responds: ". . . But it is required of Master to go through all these strange territories before he finds deliverance from the sea of sorrows; hence even one step turns out to be difficult" (p. 436). These remarks by the two disciples point up the fundamental truth concerning Tripitaka's pilgrimage: for all the supernatural forces coming to aid or harm him, Tripitaka must journey to the West as a human mortal. Just as he is conditioned by his physical limitations, and the thousand hills and ten thousand waters cannot be circumvented, so he is also subject to intellectual errors and moral shortcomings. His dependence on his followers, especially Sun Wu-k'ung, is therefore utterly necessary.

What renders all three disciples of the mortal monk so powerful, however, is the fact that each of them (the Dragon is already supernatural) has had success in his quest for immortality. It is to accentuate their special status as those who have penetrated the secret mysteries of longevity that the author of the *Hsi-yu chi* has skillfully woven the language of alchemy into the fabric of their autobiographical declarations. Witness the lengthy *p'ai-lü* poems spoken by Chu Wu-nêng in chapter 19 and by Sha Wu-ching in chapter 22 (quoted earlier). What these poems describe is nothing other than the process of performing internal alchemy, a process which has been discussed with endless variations in so many texts of the *Tao Tsang*,[88] and at the completion of which the practitioner will ascend to Heaven in broad daylight. That which Chu Wu-nêng has been able to attain, despite his early indolence and sloth, is also the achievement of both Wu-k'ung and Wu-ching, who are, by their own testimonies (cf. *HYC*, chap. 17, pp. 192–93; chap. 52, pp. 600–601; chap. 63, p. 721; chap. 70, pp. 795–96; chap. 71, pp. 811–12; chap. 86, p. 980; chap. 94, pp. 1060–61, for Wu-k'ung; chap. 22, pp. 247–48, and chap. 94, p. 1061, for Wu-ching) and by evidence in the narrative, far more alert spiritually and more earnest in the practice of religion.

The supernal might of the disciples, however, is developed not merely in their personal success in acquiring immortality and the attendant powers of magic transformations, of riding the cloud and mounting the wind and transcending the limits of time and space. Most dramatically it is associated with the special magic weapons that each of them possesses, which, in the course of the narrative, become extensions of their characters. To be sure, the famous warriors of Chinese history and fiction are nearly always identified by some peculiar weapons of their own: Thus Kuan Yü 關羽 (160–219) has his Scimitar of the Green Dragon and Crescent Moon 青龍偃月刀 and Lü Pu 呂布 (d. 198) has his Halberd of Square Sky 方天畫戟 in the *San-kuo chih yen-i*; thus "Black Cyclone" Li K'uei 李逵 has his pair of battle axes in the *Shui-hu chuan* (The Water Margin); and the list of fighters with their particular weapons, magical or otherwise, is almost endless in the *Fêng-shên yen-i*. Few such instruments of war, however, receive the kind of eulogistic and meticulous treatment accorded the rod of Pilgrim, the muckrake of Pa-chieh, and the priestly staff of Sha Monk in *The Journey to the West*. Prior to their battle in chapter 19, when Pa-chieh is asked by Pilgrim whether his rake is used "to plough the fields or plant vegetables for the Kao family," Pa-chieh's reply, again in the form of a long *p'ai-lü* poem, draws heavily on mythological allusions to emphasize the celestial splendor of his weapon. "Just listen to my recital!" he says:

> This is fine steel colored like ice divine,
> Polished so highly that it glows and shines.
> . . . [see pp. 385–86].

A little later, in chapter 22, when Sha Wu-ching is in turn questioned by Pa-chieh about his weapon, this is part of his reply:

> It's called the treasure staff good for crushing fiends,
> Placed forever in Divine Mists to rout the ogres.
> . . . [see pp. 437–38].

Needless to say, the iron rod of Wu-k'ung himself, the most famous weapon in the entire narrative, is also the mightiest of all; its origin is traced supposedly to its first use by the legendary King Yü, the conqueror of the Flood in China. This piece of iron, tipped with gold at both ends, is employed by Yü to fix the depths of the rivers and the oceans (chaps. 3 and 88), after which it is stored in the deepest part of the Eastern Ocean until Monkey acquires it.

There are, to be sure, a few occasions on which Wu-k'ung's rod is referred to as something peculiarly fitting for his apish personality, a humorous reference no doubt deriving from the practice of monkeys playing with sticks or poles in vaudeville shows in China,[89] just as the muckrake humorously and constantly reminds us of Wu-nêng's swinish nature and his farming talents prior to his joining the pilgrimage. But Monkey's rod throughout the narrative serves also a more serious purpose, for it is that indispensable instrument by which he overcomes the demons and ogres crowding the pilgrims' journey. As he says in the panegyric on his weapon in chapter 88:

> It can everywhere the Tiger tame and the Dragon subdue;
> It can everyplace the monster exorcise and the demon smelt.

Since the phrases, "tame the Tiger and subdue the Dragon," "exorcise the monster and smelt the demon," can refer not only to the literal action of Monkey in such activities but to the alchemical action within the body as well,[90] the magic rod is thus made a part of the entire process of alchemical self-cultivation practiced by its master. It is for this reason that when it is the turn of the three disciples of Tripitaka to make disciples themselves in chapter 88, the three princes of the Jade-Flower Kingdom are taught martial art (wu-i 武藝). The three of them, in fact, are instructed to use weapons identical to those of the pilgrims, but only after their mortal frames have been transformed by the immortal breath of Sun Wu-k'ung can they carry a rod, a rake, and a staff of comparable weight. Whether, as Okuno Shintarō suggests,[91] the lengthy p'ai-lü poems spoken by the three pilgrims in chapters 19, 22, and 88 reveal vestigial elements of the cult of blacksmiths, whose divine patron since the Sung period has been Lao Tzu, requires further study. But it is clear in the narrative that the peculiar weapons of the three pilgrims are so intimately related to their masters as divine beings that when they are stolen, at the end of chapter 88, the narrator in the closing poetic comment can say:

> Tao can't be left for a moment;
> What can be left is not the Tao.
> When weapons divine are stolen,
> The seekers have labored in vain.

In this poem—the first two lines of which are a verbatim quotation of the opening sentence of the Doctrine of the Mean—the use of divine weapons (shên-ping 神兵) has become intimately associated with the cultivation of Tao, for both require vigilant practice.

The disciples of Tripitaka, however, do not simply serve as the protective guardians of their mortal master, although to defend the human priest against all sorts of perils and to assist him in all kinds of physical hazards along the journey may seem, on the surface of the narrative, their primary functions. In the lengthy course of their travel, the disciples, notably Sun Wu-k'ung himself, on numerous occasions become their master's instructors as well. C. T. Hsia has already called attention to the fact that Wu-k'ung's superior understanding of the *Heart Sūtra* provides periodic illuminations for the earthly monk.[92] But it should be added that Wu-k'ung seems as adept in helping his master to perceive the mystery of alchemical self-cultivation as he is in the exposition of Buddhist writings. In chapter 36, which has the suggestive titular couplets, "When the mind-monkey is rectified, the nidānas cease;/When the side door [*p'ang-mên*, metaphor for heterodoxy] is punctured, one sees the moon," Wu-k'ung's discourse on the analogical significance of the moon in the process of self-cultivation follows a well-known tradition which may be traced to the theory initiated by Ching Fang 京房 (77–37 B.C.) and Yü Fan 虞翻 (164–233). After hearing Tripitaka recite an extemporaneous poem on how the pure splendor of the full moon fills him with nostalgic longings for his homeland, Wu-k'ung proceeds to point out to his master the deeper significance of the moon and how its movement of growth and attenuation reflects nature's own process of cultivation. The standard interpretation here of how the moon reaches its fullness and decline through the alternating addition or reduction of the yin-yang forces follows the widely adopted correlation of the Eight Trigrams (*kua*) with the cycle of the lunar month developed and elaborated in such Han treatises as the *Ts'an T'ung Ch'i* 參同契 (The Kinship of the Three, or The Accordance of the Book of Changes with the Phenomena of Composite Things) of Wei Po-yang (2d century), the *Hsi Tz'û chuan* 繫辭傳 (Commentary of the Appended Judgments of the *I Ching*), and by such thinkers as Mêng Hsi 孟喜 and Chiao Kan 焦贛.[93] This theory has been appropriated by later theorists writing on internal alchemy (*nei-tan*) to develop their concept of picking the forces of the yin to nourish the forces of the yang (*ts'ai-yin pu-yang*), the process whereby the action of internal cultivation imitates the lunar cycle.[94] Thus it is that the seven-syllabic *chüeh-chü* poem with which Wu-k'ung concludes his brief lecture (chap. 36),

> After the First Quarter and before the Last Quarter [i.e., of the moon]:
> The medicine's taste is common, the condition's complete;
> What you acquire from picking, refine in the brazier—
> The fruit of determination is the Western Heaven.

is again a direct quotation (with the exception of the last line) of a poem which may be found in the *Yüan-ch'ing Tzŭ chih-ming p'ien* 袁清子至命篇 (Chapter on the Ultimate Life of Yüan-ch'ing Tzŭ), *chüan* 1, 3ab, attributed to Wang Ch'ing-shêng 王慶升 of the Sung dynasty.[95] The last line of the original poem in the Taoist text reads, "To forge the warm nourishment is like cooking [something] fresh," which is itself undoubtedly another reference to the process of alchemy, whether this process is understood as the internal one or the external one, or both.

When Wu-k'ung finishes speaking, however, Sha Monk also adds briefly his own observation, saying,

> Though Elder Brother spoke most appropriately concerning how the First Quarter belonged to the yang and the Last Quarter belonged to the yin, and how in the midst of yin and in the middle of yang one could obtain the metal of water, he did not mention
> Water and fire blended, each is to the other drawn;
> But you need the earth mother to make such a match.
> Three members are thus united without war or strife:
> The water is in the Long River and the moon in the sky.

This poem of the third disciple of Tripitaka is worthy of our note since it introduces the personifications of alchemical and *wu-hsing* terms to represent the members of the pilgrimage. To this element of religious and "physiological" allegory we must pay brief attention before terminating our discussion of Taoist themes in the narrative.

Few readers of the *Hsi-yu chi* in Chinese can fail to notice the frequent designation of the three disciples of Tripitaka by *wu-hsing* and alchemical nomenclature. A quick glance at the various titular couplets will make such usages apparent:

Chapter 32
   On the Level-Top Mountain the Sentinel brings a message;
   At the Lotus-Flower Cave the *Wood Mother* meets disaster.

Chapter 40
   The playful forms of the Baby the Mind of Zen disturbs;
   The Ape, the Horse, the *Spatula*,[96] and the *Wood Mother* all [fight]
      in vain.

Chapter 47
   The Sage Monk is blocked by night at the Passing-to-Heaven
      River;
   In compassion *Metal* and *Wood* rescue a little child.

Chapter 53
   Eating a meal the Zen Master becomes demonically conceived;
   The *Yellow Hag* carries water to abort the weird child.
                        (emphasis mine)

Though none of the four traditional orders of the Five Evolutive Phases
—cosmogonic, mutual production, mutual conquest, and "modern"[97]
—may be isolated as one representing a satisfactory correlation with
all five members of the pilgrimage, there is nonetheless consistency in
the narrative as far as the associations of Wu-k'ung, Wu-nêng, and
Wu-ching are concerned. Throughout the work, Monkey is invariably
identified with metal or gold (*chin* 金), and he is frequently referred
to as *chin-kung* 金公 or *chin-wêng* 金翁 (the Lord or Squire of Gold or
Metal). The reason for this, at least according to the notes following
chapter 22 of the 1954 Peking edition, is threefold: first, in the
spagyrical literature, lead, one of the two or three most important
ingredients in alchemy, is given the name of Lord or Squire of Gold
(*chin-kung*), for there is the belief that true lead is born from the
Celestial Stem (*t'ien-kan* 天干) of *Kêng* 庚. Since the corresponding
metal to the stem is metal or gold, the name is thus derived. Moreover, the Branches of the Earth (*ti-chih* 地支), which with the Celestial
Stems combine to form the Chinese sexagenary cycle, are so arranged
that the combination of *shên-yu* 申酉 directly matches the combination of *kêng-hsin* in the celestial system. Because the symbolical animal
of the horary character *shên* is a monkey, the correlation is thus made
complete. By the same process of reasoning, Chu Wu-nêng is given
the name Wood Mother (*mu-mu* 木母), in the narrative, for it is a

term used by alchemists to designate mercury. True mercury is supposed to have been born from the horary character of *hai* 亥 for which the symbolical animal is a boar or a pig. As for Sha Wu-ching, he is almost always linked to the earth, bearing at times the name Earth Mother (*t'u-mu* 土母), at times the name Yellow Hag (*huang-p'o* 黃婆), and at times the name Spatula (*tao-kuei* 刀圭). Since in the literature of internal alchemy the five phases are further correlated with the energies or breaths (*ch'i* 氣) of the five viscera, these three disciples of Tripitaka are thereby made symbols of the interior realities in the human body. According to the *Nei-tan huan-yüan chüeh* 內丹還原訣 (Formula for the Internal Elixir to Return to the Origin), for example, metal or gold is correlated with the secretion of the lungs, earth or Yellow Hag points to the liquid of the spleen, and wood corresponds to the *ch'i* of the liver.[98] Such a schematization thus provides the narrator of the *Hsi-yu chi* with a complex system of correspondences by which he may comment on the experience and the action of the pilgrims. When Wu-k'ung first brings Wu-nêng to submission and leads him back to see Tripitaka, the narrator presents at that point the following testimonial poem:

> Strong is metal's nature to vanquish wood:
> Mind Monkey has the Wood Dragon subdued.
> . . . [see p. 388].

We should observe in this poem that the emphasis is placed upon the harmonious relation that exists—and should exist—between Wu-k'ung and Wu-nêng, just as the ideal state of the body sought by those engaging in the process of self-cultivation is one characterized by the harmonious balance of the several internal breaths or energies. It is not without reason, therefore, that when the pilgrims reach one of the lowest points in their journey—the occasion of Wu-k'ung's first banishment, which was caused by Tripitaka's succumbing to the slanderous suasion of Wu-nêng, the narrator presents this contrasting poetic comment on the action:

> The Horse of the Will and the Ape of the Mind are all dispersed;
> The Metal Squire and the Wood Mother are scattered both;
> Yellow Hag is wounded, from everyone divorced;
> With reason and right so divided, what can be achieved?
> [Chap. 30]

In several parts of the narrative (e.g., chaps 31, 40, 57), similar poetic commentaries may be found as there are also certain brief prose passages cast in unambiguously didactic language. After the River of the Flowing Sand episode, for example, the narrator says in the beginning of chapter 23: "We tell you now about the four of them, master and disciples, who, having perceived the suchness of Bhūta-tatathatā, broke asunder at once the lock of dust. Leaping clear from the Flowing Sand of the Sea of Forms, they were completely rid of any hindrance." And after Tripitaka's interview with several tree spirits on the Ridge of Thorns where they have had a poetic conference together, the narrator again alerts the reader to another level of meaning in the episode by his opening remarks in the following chapter:

> We tell you now about Tripitaka, who was most single-minded in his piety and sincerity. We need not mention how he was protected by the gods above; even such spirits of grass and woods also came to keep him company. After one night of conversation on the arts, he was delivered from the thorns and the thistles, no longer encumbered by vines or wistaria.
>
> [Chap. 65]

Through such narrative devices, therefore, we may catch a clear glimpse of the author's unobtrusive allegorical intent and technique. Unlike some allegories in other literary traditions, where the narrative movement may proceed from abstract to graphic personifications or descriptions, the *Hsi-yu chi* reveals through the narrator the ironic meaning of many of the episodes almost as an afterthought. But the juxtaposition of poetic and prose commentaries with the action in the narrative is what definitely conveys to the readers' imagination a vivid picture not only of *bellum intestinum*, "the root of all allegory" according to C. S. Lewis,[99] but of *concordia* as well.

Turning now to the discussion of Buddhist elements in the *Hsi-yu chi*, we may begin with the rather puzzling phenomenon that the narrative presents surprisingly few details traceable to specific Buddhist sources, despite the fact that its story is built on the historical pilgrimage undertaken by one of the most famous Buddhist personalities in Chinese history. We have, of course, the *Heart Sūtra*, the version translated by the historical Hsüan-tsang himself (cf. *T*. 85:169), which is faithfully transcribed in chapter 19; and appearing in the last chapter is a complete reproduction of the *Shêng-chiao*

Hsü, which historically the emperor T'ai-tsung is said to have composed in gratitude for the pilgrim monk and his translation of the *Yogācārya-bhūmi śāstra*. In chapter 12, when T'ai-tsung proposes to convene a Grand Mass of Land and.Water for the dead which he has pledged to hold during his tour of the underworld, the author heightens the drama of the particular episode by presenting a little debate between the emperor's officials on the merits of Buddhism. Fu I 傅奕 (555–639), well known in this period of Chinese history as a trenchant critic of the faith,[100] is here made the antagonist who presents a memorial against Buddhism, but he is, of course, overruled, and the mass leads to the eventual meeting of the emperor and the fictive Hsüan-tsang. There is, moreover, the whole episode of the River of the Flowing Sand, where Sha Wu-ching joins Tripitaka as his disciple. Though it may have its origin in the biographical account of Hsüan-tsang,[101] the story may just as well have been a modification of the Sung poetic tale's account of the Deep-Sand God 深沙神 (fragment from section 8).[102] The gifts which Tripitaka receives from the Buddha through Kuan-yin at the beginning of his journey (a cassock and a nine-ringed priestly staff) and the alms bowl of purple gold he receives from the emperor T'ai-tsung may again have derived from section 3 of the poetic tale (titled "Entrance into the Palace of the Mahābrahmā Devarājā") and from *chüan* 7 of the biography. Hu Shih has also suggested that the account in the biography (*chüan* 1, 15–20) of how Hsüan-tsang becomes the bond-brother of the King of Turfan 高昌王 (r. 619–640) may form the basis for the emperor T'ai-tsung's becoming the monk's brother in the narrative.[103] Finally, in the episode in chapter 23 where the pilgrims are tempted by Mañjuśrī and Samantabhadra disguised as beautiful girls, the debate between Tripitaka and the lovely widow on the benefits of a life at home and a life outside the home (*tsai-chia* 在家 versus *ch'u-chia* 出家) may echo the same sort of dispute found in the *Wên-shu-shih-li wên ching* 文殊師利問經 (cf. T. 14:505, no. 468). Beyond these several obvious examples, the relation of the hundred-chapter narrative to Buddhism seems not vastly different from what Glen Dudbridge has said of the Sung poetic tale: "Many elements of vaguely Buddhist origin are there, but there is certainly no monopoly of Buddhist themes, of whatever degree of orthodoxy."[104]

   To point out this aspect of the *Hsi-yu chi*, however, is not to deny the countless allusions to Buddhist concepts and legends structured in the narrative, from Buddha's luminescent eyebrow (*ūrnā*) to the Hell of Avīci, from the *Dharmacakra* to *Vajradhātu*, that reveal the author's knowledge of Buddhism to be much more than passing acquaintance. Although there may be no systematic exposition of one particular Buddhist doctrine in the narrative comparable to the kind of explicit presentation of Calvinistic thinking on predestination and atonement found in Book Three of Milton's *Paradise Lost*, certain themes and figures do receive consistent development.

The first such theme is the emphasis on the compassionate power of Buddha himself. Because of the immense appeal of the character of Sun Wu-k'ung, many modern critics, especially those who favor a more political interpretation of the narrative,[105] have found it rather difficult to accept Monkey's subjugation in chapter 7, let alone the use of the golden fillet later as a means of gaining continuous control over him by inflicting unbearable pain once recalcitrant behavior is detected. The "conversion" of Monkey in this view is a basic flaw in the narrative, and what we see of him after his release from the Wu-hsing Mountain in chapter 14, as a faithful guardian of the cowardly and ineffectual Buddhist pilgrim, seems to contradict the magnificent heroic character whose defiance and love of independence we have come to cherish and admire in the first seven chapters.

That such a view fails to do full justice to the complexity of the narrative should also be apparent. For, although Buddha and his divine followers do constitute part of the entire celestial hierarchy (the other part being made up of what may be called Taoist divinities), and in this sense the Buddhist pantheon may seem, in Arthur Wright's words, "a victim of its own adaptability,"[106] there are nonetheless some subtle differentiations in the narrative concerning the two groups of deities. Whereas the bureaucratic pretension and incompetence of both groups become frequent targets of the author's biting satire, the wisdom and mercy of Buddha—characteristics hardly shared by any of the Taoist deities, least of all by the Jade Emperor—are constantly emphasized. Unlike the historical pilgrimage of Hsüan-tsang, which had its origin in the profound religious vision of the human monk, the journey of the narrative really begins with the Buddha's benevolent intention to impart the sacred Tripiṭaka to the inhabitants of the East. During the celestial assembly in chapter 8, this is the declaration of Buddha: "Those who reside in the South Jambūdvīpa, however, are prone to practice lechery and delight in evil-doing, indulging in much slaughter and strife. . . . However, I have

three baskets of true scriptures which can persuade man to do good . . .
[see p. 184]. This will provide a source of blessings great as a
mountain and deep as the sea." To be sure, this motive of Buddha is
severely questioned by Sun Wu-k'ung later; when defeated by the
Lion, the Elephant, and the Garuda Monsters, he wonders why
Buddha, instead of asking someone to go through such ordeals to
fetch the scriptures, does not send them to the East in the first place
(chap. 77). But Wu-k'ung's anguished query represents only a
momentary lapse of faith; his unreserved commitment to the journey
and to what it seeks to accomplish is, in fact, what sustains the
pilgrims through all those overwhelming difficulties. For the meaning
of the journey, as it is developed in the narrative, is not confined to
the benefits of acquiring sacred scriptures for the people of T'ang
China. On a more personal and profound level, the journey signifies
for the pilgrims a new beginning, a freely given opportunity for self-
rectification. It is in this way that the theme of the journey as a pro-
tracted process of merit-making complements and magnifies the
theme of Buddha's mercy.

I pointed out earlier how the distinctive characteristic of three of
Tripitaka's disciples is to be found in their status as immortals, as
beings who have succeeded in the way of alchemical self-cultivation.
One further observation must now be added: they are not just immortals with great magic power, they are also delinquent ones. All
three of them, together with the dragon-horse, have been condemned
for certain misdeeds. The widespread fame of Monkey stems from the
turmoils he caused in Heaven; Pa-chieh, Sha Monk, and the dragon-
horse were punished and exiled to the earth below for getting drunk
and insulting Ch'ang O, the legendary beauty of the Lunar Palace, for
breaking crystals during a solemn banquet, and for setting fire to his
father's palace and thereby destroying some precious pearls. The
modern reader of the *Hsi-yu chi* may be offended by the harshness of
their sentences, but it is no less clear that the author's intention is not
so much to dwell on their misery, deserved or not, as to emphasize
their preservation for a "higher" purpose. Thus it is that the narrator,
after Monkey has been imprisoned by Buddha beneath the Wu-hsing
Mountain, closes the chapter with the poetic commentary:

Prideful of his power once the time was ripe,
He [i.e., Monkey] tamed dragon and tiger, exploiting wily might.
. . . [see p. 179].

As Kuan-yin carries out Tathāgata's instruction to persuade any monster with great magical power she may meet on her way to find a scripture pilgrim in the East (chap. 8) to become one of the pilgrim's guardians, all four disciples-to-be of Tripitaka are told by the Bodhisattva to wait for this special emissary from T'ang China. For their willingness to journey to the West with him and their faithful service will win for Sun Wu-k'ung, Chu Wu-nêng, Sha Wu-ching, and the dragon sufficient merit to atone for their past crimes. This motif is repeatedly heard in the narrative, of which one conspicuous example is when the dragon joins the pilgrimage in chapter 15 after Kuan-yin arrives at the Eagle Grief Stream. "The Bodhisattva went up to the little dragon and plucked off the shining pearls hanging around his neck . . . [see pp. 323–24]. After Pilgrim had heard all these kind words, he thanked the Bodhisattva of Great Mercy and Compassion."

It is important for us to note that in the admonition of the Bodhisattva to both the dragon and Wu-k'ung, the journey promises not merely a restoration of their previous divine status, but in fact a higher plane of attainment. This may be part of the reason, too, why Wu-k'ung is made to say to Wu-nêng during their first meeting in chapter 19, "It's old Monkey who turned from wrong to right, who left the Taoist to follow the Buddhist. I am now accompanying the royal brother of the Great T'ang Emperor in the Land of the East, whose name is Tripitaka, Master of the Law." By her words of encouragement and her additional gift of magic power to Monkey, which will indeed prove to be life-saving in a later crisis (chap. 70), the Bodhisattva Kuan-yin of the narrative thus reveals her character to be consistent with a long established tradition, which venerates Avalokiteśvara as one who enlightens and who delivers her followers from all kinds of perils and pains.[107] In her person and in her action, the compassionate power of Buddha extends not only to the disciples of Tripitaka but also to someone like the Bear Monster of chapter 17, whose life she spares in order that he might become a mountain guardian of Potalaka, thus winning for herself the spontaneous compliment of Monkey: "truly a salvific and merciful goddess, who will not hurt a single sentient being!"

It may be asked at this point what sort of merit the disciples do succeed in making during their lengthy journey. The most obvious answer to this question must be, of course, their success in overcoming the marauding hordes of demons and monsters along the way which seek to harm the pilgrim monk. Thus when Pa-chieh kills the

Tiger Vanguard in chapter 20, he is congratulated by both the narrator (in verse) and by Wu-k'ung for achieving his first merit. But to consider the worth of the disciples to reside solely in their protection of the T'ang Monk, however important and however dangerous such a responsibility may be, is to miss some of the more profound intentions of the author. For it is clear from the later sections of the *Hsi-yu chi* that the narrative does not merely focus on what sort of personal, or even national, rewards the action of the pilgrims will bring once they have successfully completed this long and difficult journey. There are also insistent rehearsals of how the excesses, the heroic energies, and the representative individualism of a Sun Wu-k'ung or a Chu Pa-chieh are being transformed and used for the benefit of countless people along the way. It is remarkable how many episodes of encounter with ogres and demons end, not only in their defeat or in Tripitaka's deliverance, but also in a kingdom restored, a lost child recovered, an estranged family reunited, and a Flame-Throwing Mountain extinguished so that travel and agriculture may resume. The conquest of the monsters is not simply a victory for the heavenly powers; the restoration and reestablishment of human social order is just as crucial because it comes as a result of the defeat of the chthonic, antinomian forces resident in the demonic world. That even the rather shallow and insensitive Tripitaka begins to appreciate the character of Monkey and the frequency with which he has performed eleemosynary service of great magnitude is what we see at the beginning of chapter 88, after that disciple has brought rain to a region suffering from intense drought.

> As he rode, the T'ang monk said to Pilgrim: "Worthy disciple! Your virtuous fruit this time even surpasses your achievement when you rescued those infants at the Bishu Kingdom. It's entirely your merit!" "At the Bishu Kingdom," said Sha Monk, "only one thousand and ten little baby boys were saved. How could that be compared with this torrential rain, whose moisture would sustain the lives of thousands and thousands of people. This disciple has long admired in silence Elder Brother, whose dharma-power reaches to Heaven, and whose merciful kindness covers the Earth."
>
> [*HYC*, p. 998]

The solemnity of this moment, assuredly, is somewhat deflated by Pa-chieh's humorous complaint that Wu-k'ung, despite his benevolent acts to others, never shows any regard for his companion's huge appetite—a comment which immediately draws for Pa-chieh his master's rebuke. But there is no question that what is presented in the narrative as their final merit involves not merely the successful completion of their journey but also their virtuous actions during their travel. The ordeals over which they triumph, the sufferings they have undergone, and the deeds of charity they perform throughout this immense trek bring them absolution and the final exaltation in the presence of Buddha.

In his rather speculative essay on the *Hsi-yu chi,* Okuno Shintarō has suggested that this pattern of banishment, wandering, and return in the experiences of Tripitaka's disciples may be compared with the structure characteristic of those tales which exploit the theme of the nobles in exile (*kishu ryūritan* 貴種流離談).[108] What Okuno fails to perceive, however, is that this pattern is discernible not only in the lives of the disciples, but supremely in that of the master pilgrim himself, since the Hsüan-tsang of the narrative is none other than the second disciple of Buddha, Gold Cicada. Because he is inattentive to the discourse of Buddha and thereby slights the Law, he is fated to face tremendous perils in the human world (see chaps. 9, 81, and 100), eighty-one ordeals in all. Seen from this perspective, the journey for Tripitaka is also one of merit-making, for it is those fated ordeals of his which provide the necessary expiatory experience for him and for his followers. We should remember, of course, that the idea of certain figures of fiction having different preexistent identities is nothing new in Chinese literature. The theme of reincarnation may be found in works ranging from the *San-kuo-chih p'ing-hua* 三國志平話 (fourteenth century) to the *Shuo-yüeh ch'üan-chuan* 説岳全傳 (eighteenth century). In *The Journey to the West,* however, this popular theme is given such sustained treatment that it becomes the central element of the narrative action. The journey to obtain scriptures in the Western Heaven is, for Tripitaka and his disciples, also the piacular journey of return to Buddha, and like the Odysseus of the Homeric poem, the scripture pilgrim must pass through appalling obstacles for past offenses against the gods.

It is only when we perceive the religious significance of the journey that we can understand more adequately the relation among the five pilgrims. That the defenseless and hapless monk of the narrative has need of his four supernatural companions in order to traverse "the thousand hills and ten thousand waters" is very much self-evident.

On the other hand, the person and the sacred mission of Tripitaka is also stressed by the author as the means by which the hubristic tendencies of someone like Sun Wu-k'ung are curbed as his mighty and hardwon abilities are converted to serve a less self-centered and self-serving purpose. Both the human monk and his powerful companion must "work out their salvation" on the basis of mutual reliance, as can perhaps best be seen in the events of chapter 14, titled "The Monkey of the Mind returns to the Right;/All the six robbers vanish from sight." This segment of the tale tells of how Wu-k'ung, after his release by Tripitaka from imprisonment beneath the Mountain of Five Phases as a punishment for his delinquent behavior in Heaven, begins his service as guardian and guide to the scripture pilgrim by killing six robbers they meet on the way. Significantly, the chapter begins with the following poem:

> The Mind is the Buddha, and the Buddha is Mind;
> Both Mind and Buddha are important things.
> . . . [see p. 297].

Moments later, master and disciple face the threat of the six robbers (see pp. 306–08). The six robbers represent, of course, the six *cauras*, the Buddhist metaphor for the six sense organs which impede enlightenment. And Monkey's execution of them is intended to portray in an allegorical fashion his greater detachment from the human senses, a freedom of which his master and his fellow pilgrim Chu Pa-chieh have little knowledge. The action of Monkey thus also confirms the significance of his name, Wu-k'ung (Awake-to-Vacuity), given him by his first teacher, and dramatizes his superior understanding of the truth of the emptiness of all things, a truth epitomized in the *Heart Sūtra* of which the prefatory verse of the chapter just referred to reads like a paraphrase.

It is also true, however, that this action of Monkey leads directly to the bestowal of the golden fillet to Tripitaka by the Bodhisattva Kuan-yin, an instrument which, once Wu-k'ung is deceived into wearing it on his head, becomes the ineluctable means of discipline. When they are seen from within the context of the whole narrative, the events of this particular chapter thus become once more an allegorical expansion of what it means to bridle the Monkey of the Mind and the Horse of the Will, a theme central to the entire narrative and which receives repeated and varied developments. To view the work solely in terms of Tripitaka's relation to his disciple as a graphic illustration of human intelligence (of which the wayward and restless tendencies are so aptly symbolized by the ape's active nature) mastered by Buddhist wisdom is, of course, a facile interpretation. Indeed, the familiarity of the "Monkey-Horse" metaphor from both Buddhist and later Taoist sources[109] has led Dudbridge to the assertion that it "cannot be seen as an urgent or spontaneous force" in the work.[110] Nonetheless, we should also remember that Wu-k'ung's impetuous self-assertiveness has been repeatedly dramatized by the author as a potential cause of trouble, and, at least on one occasion, it almost becomes a dangerous liability.[111] And it should be pointed out further that the supremacy of Buddhist wisdom and its ethical norm like the injunction not to kill is never questioned in the narrative. When Wu-k'ung is banished by Tripitaka for the second time as a result again of his killing several brigands and appeals tearfully to Kuan-yin for adjudication, the Bodhisattva explicitly affirms the rectitude of the human monk who seeks to uphold the commandment of not taking human life (JW, chap. 57), even though such wrong-headed exercise of humanitarian pity has more than once led the pilgrims into dire difficulties.

Taking into account the multiple meanings attached to Wu-k'ung's person and action, we can more fully perceive the kind of Buddhist paradox which the various allegorical elements of the narrative seek to emphasize and elucidate. As C. T. Hsia rightly observes, Wu-k'ung surpasses all the members of the pilgrimage in his understanding of the emptiness of all things and the consequential need for detachment.[112] Yet his very comprehension depends on the exercise of his mind, on the use of his intelligence. That is why the narrative constantly stresses Tripitaka's need to control the Monkey of the Mind, no less than the pilgrim's need for the services of Sun Wu-k'ung. Without the presence of his chief disciple, Tripitaka and his other companions are virtually mindless (cf. chaps. 28–30). When they reach almost the nadir of defeat, it is the Great Sage who "uses the Mind to question the Mind" (i-hsin wên-hsin 以心問心) to rescue them from their plight (chap. 51). Revealed in the person and action of Wu-k'ung, therefore, is the true attitude toward the doctrine of emptiness (śūnyatā), which, according to D. T. Suzuki, "signifies, negatively, the absence of particularity, the non-existence of individuals as such, and positively, the ever-changing state of the phenomenal world, a constant flux of becoming, an eternal series of causes and effects."[113] What Monkey has to teach Tripitaka and, perhaps by extension, his human audience as well, is not simply the illusory nature of experience or the unreality of the monsters and ogres infesting the way to the West. More positively, what he tries to help his master see is that these various phenomena themselves can become vehicles for enlightenment. Thus when Tripitaka asks him early in the narrative (chap. 24) how far it is to the Western Heaven, the abode of Buddha, Wu-k'ung replies,

> You can walk from the time of your youth till the time you
> grow old, and after that, till you become youthful again; and
> even after going through such a cycle a thousand times, you
> may still find it difficult to reach the place where you want to go
> to. But when you perceive, by the resoluteness of your will,
> the Buddha-nature in all things, and when every one of your
> thoughts goes back to its very source in your memory, that will
> be the time you arrive at the Spirit Mountain.

At the same time, what Tripitaka has to offer to his four disciples is the occasion by which their antinomian and anarchic tendencies are checked and reoriented toward the good of the human community, and by which their peculiar strengths and talents (even Chu Pa-chieh can serve as a "super bulldozer" for plowing a way through eight hundred miles of thorns and prickles in chapter 64 and through the Rotted-tree Alley in chapter 67) may be put to serve a noble cause. To elaborate these deeper meanings of the journey, the author has made striking use of the rhetoric of two religious traditions. In accordance with folk Taoism, the emphasis is on integration, for the essence of self-cultivation, as Andrew Plaks has succinctly observed, "lies in the subordination of the individual Self to a larger vision of totality." To all four of his imprisoned followers Tripitaka offers the opportunity of finding renewal and release through the subordination of their selves "to the Selfhood of the pilgrimage." But the vision of the spagyrical arts, to quote Plaks further, "leads directly to the illusion that the self-contained world of the individual mind [and, one might add, the individual body as well] can stand alone, since it can encompass the entire universe with its ken."[114] It is to modify such a vision, I believe, that the narrative also places such strong emphasis on the Buddhist concepts of the maturation of good stock 善根 (kuśalamūla), and the accumulation of merits 功果 (puṇyaṃ-karoti), conditions which are socially beneficent and are to be achieved through mutual dependence and communal effort. That is why in the climactic moment of their journey, when the pilgrims finally arrive at the shores of salvation after having been ferried across the Cloud-Transcending Stream by the Buddha of the Light of Ratnadhvaja in a bottomless boat, and having seen in midstream the "proof" of their liberation through the shedding of their "old bodies" or shells, we are allowed to witness this important conversation between master and disciple.

> When Tripitaka realized what had happened, he turned quickly
> to thank his three disciples. Pilgrim said: "We two parties
> need not thank each other, for we are meant to support each
> other. We are indebted to our master for our liberation, through
> which we have found the gateway to the making of merit, and
> fortunately we have achieved the right fruit. Our master also has
> to rely on our protection so that he may be firm in keeping
> both law and faith to find this happy deliverance from the mortal
> stock" [chap. 98].

This segment of *The Journey to the West*, when read within the context of the entire narrative, should help us see that the submission of the disciples to the master pilgrim, and through him to the claims of Buddhism, is not simply a matter of passive acquiescence to a hateful policy of pacification as some critics have suggested when they compare the disciples to the one hundred and eight heroes of the *Shui-hu chuan* (The Water Margin).[115] In this latter novel, the surrender to the political powers that be indeed marks the disintegration and decline of the gallant brigands, but for Sun Wu-k'ung, Chu Wu-nêng, Sha Wu-ching, and the Dragon Prince, the decision to undertake the journey to the West is also the beginning of their discovery of self-fulfillment and a freedom that does not destroy.

THE
JOURNEY TO
THE WEST

One

The divine root being conceived, the origin emerges;
The moral nature once cultivated, the Great Tao is born.

The poem said:
   Before Chaos divided, Heaven and Earth were confused;
   Formless and void—such matter no man had seen.
   But when P'an Ku the nebula dispersed,[1]
   Creation began, the impure parted from the pure.
   The supreme goodness, benefic to every creature,
   Enlightened all things to attain the good.
   If you would know creation's work through the spans of time,
   You must read *The Chronicle of Deliverance in the Westward Journey.*[2]
We heard that, in the order of Heaven and Earth, a single period consisted of 129,600 years. Dividing this period into twelve epochs were the twelve stems of Tzŭ, Ch'ou, Yin, Mao, Ch'ên, Ssŭ, Wu, Wei, Shên, Yu, Hsü, and Hai, with each epoch having 10,800 years. Considered as the horary circle, the sequence would be thus: the first sign of dawn appears in the hour of Tzŭ, while at Ch'ou the cock crows; daybreak occurs at Yin, and the sun rises at Mao; Ch'ên comes after breakfast, and by Ssŭ everything is planned; at Wu the sun arrives at its meridian and declines westward by Wei; the evening meal comes during the hour of Shên, and the sun sinks completely at Yu; twilight sets in at Hsü, and people rest by the hour of Hai. This sequence may also be understood macrocosmically. At the end of the epoch of Hsü, Heaven and Earth were obscure and all things were indistinct. With the passing of 5,400 years, the beginning of Hai was the epoch of darkness. This moment was named Chaos, because there were neither human beings nor the two spheres. After another 5,400 years the Hai ended, and as the creative force began to work after great perseverance, the epoch of Tzŭ drew near and again brought gradual development. Shao K'ang-chieh[3] said:
   When winter moved to the middle of Tzŭ,
   No change occurred in the mind of Heaven.

The male principle had barely stirred,
And all things were as yet unborn.

At this point, the firmament first acquired its foundation. With another 5,400 years came the Tzŭ epoch; the ethereal and the light rose up to form the four phenomena of the sun, the moon, the stars, and the heavenly bodies. Hence it is said, the Heaven was created at Tzŭ. This epoch came to its end in another 5,400 years, and the sky began to harden as the Ch'ou epoch approached. The *I Ching* said, "Great was the male principle; supreme, the female! They made all things, in obedience to Heaven." At this point, the Earth became solidified. In another 5,400 years after the arrival of the Ch'ou epoch, the heavy and the turbid condensed below and formed the five elements of water, fire, mountain, stone, and earth. Hence it is said, the Earth was created at Ch'ou. With the passing of another 5,400 years, the Ch'ou epoch came to its end and all things began to grow at the beginning of the Yin epoch. *The Book of Calendar* said: "The heavenly aura descended; the earthly aura rose up. Heaven and Earth copulated, and all things were born." At this point, Heaven and Earth were bright and fair; the yin had intercourse with the yang. In another 5,400 years, during the Yin epoch, humans, beasts, and fowls came into being, and thus the so-called three forces of Heaven, Earth, and Man were established. Hence it is said, man was born at Yin.

Following P'an Ku's construction of the universe, the rule of the Three Kings, and the ordering of the relations by the Five Emperors,[4] the world was divided into four great continents. They were: the East Pūrvavideha Continent, the West Aparagodānīya Continent, the South Jambūdvīpa Continent, and the North Uttarakuru Continent. This book is solely concerned with the East Pūrvavideha Continent.

Beyond the ocean there was a country named Ao-lai. It was near a great ocean, in the midst of which was located the famous Flower-Fruit Mountain. This mountain, which constituted the chief range of the Ten Islets and formed the origin of the Three Islands,[5] came into being after the creation of the world. As a testimonial to its magnificence, there is the following *fu* poem:

Its majesty commands the wide ocean;
Its spendor rules the jasper sea;
Its majesty commands the wide ocean
When, like silver mountains, the tide sweeps fishes into caves;

Its splendor rules the jasper sea
When snowlike billows send forth serpents from the deep.
Plateaus are tall on the southwest side;
Soaring peaks arise from the Sea of the East.
There are crimson ridges and portentous rocks,
Precipitous cliffs and prodigious peaks.
Atop the crimson ridges
Phoenixes sing in pairs;
Before precipitous cliffs
The unicorn singly rests.
At the summit is heard the cry of golden pheasants;
In and out of stony caves are seen the strides of dragons;
In the forest are long-lived deer and immortal foxes.
On the trees are divine fowls and black cranes.
Strange grass and flowers never wither;
Green pines and cypresses keep eternal their spring.
Immortal peaches are always fruit-bearing;
Lofty bamboos often detain the clouds.
Within a single gorge the creeping vines are dense;
The grass color of meadows all around is fresh.
This is indeed the pillar of Heaven, where a hundred rivers meet—
The Earth's great axis, in ten thousand kalpas unchanged.

There was on top of that very mountain an immortal stone, which measured thirty-six feet and five inches in height and twenty-four feet in circumference. The height of thirty-six feet and five inches corresponded to the three hundred and sixty-five cyclical degrees, while the circumference of twenty-four feet corresponded to the twenty-four solar terms of the calendar.[6] On the stone were also nine perforations and eight holes, which corresponded to the Palaces of the Nine Constellations and the Eight Trigrams. Though it lacked the shade of trees on all sides, it was set off by epidendrums on the left and right. Since the creation of the world, it had been nourished for a long period by the seeds of Heaven and Earth and by the essences of the sun and the moon, until, quickened by divine inspiration, it became pregnant with a divine embryo. One day, it split open, giving birth to a stone egg about the size of a playing ball. Exposed to the wind, it was transformed into a stone monkey endowed with fully developed features and limbs. Having learned at once to climb and run, this monkey also bowed to the four quarters, while two beams of golden light flashed from his eyes to reach even the Palace of the Polestar. The light disturbed the Great Benevolent Sage of Heaven, the Celestial Jade Emperor of the Most Venerable Deva, who, attended by his divine ministers, was sitting in the Cloud Palace of the Golden Arches, in the Treasure Hall of the Divine Mists. Upon seeing the glimmer of the golden beams, he ordered Thousand-Mile Eye and Fair-Wind Ear to open the South Heavenly Gate and to look out. At this command the two captains went out to the gate, and, having looked intently and listened clearly, they returned presently to report, "Your subjects, obeying your command to locate the beams, discovered that they came from the Flower-Fruit Mountain at the border of the small Ao-lai Country, which lies to the east of the East Pūrvavideha Continent. On this mountain is an immortal stone which has given birth to an egg. Exposed to the wind, it has been transformed into a monkey, who, when bowing to the four quarters, has flashed from his eyes those golden beams that reached the Palace of the Polestar. Now that he is taking some food and drink, the light is about to grow dim." With compassionate mercy the Jade Emperor declared, "These creatures from the world below are born of the essences of Heaven and Earth, and they need not surprise us."

That monkey in the mountain was able to walk, run, and leap about; he fed on grass and shrubs, drank from the brooks and streams, gathered mountain flowers, and searched out fruits from trees. He made his companions the tiger and the lizard, the wolf and the leopard; he befriended the civet and the deer, and he called the gibbon and the baboon his kin. At night he slept beneath stony ridges, and in the morning he sauntered about the caves and the peaks. Truly, "in the mountain there is no passing of time; the cold recedes, but one knows not the year."[7] One very hot morning, he was playing with a group of monkeys under the shade of some pine trees to escape the heat. Look at them, each amusing himself in his own way by

Swinging from branches to branches,
Searching for flowers and fruits;
They played two games or three
With pebbles and with pellets;
They circled sandy pits;
They built rare pagodas;
They chased the dragon flies;

They ran down small lizards;
Bowing low to the sky,
They worshiped Bodhisattvas;
They pulled the creeping vines;
They plaited mats with grass;
They searched to catch the louse
They bit or crushed with their nails;
They dressed their furry coats;
They scraped their finger nails;
Some leaned and leaned;
Some rubbed and rubbed;
Some pushed and pushed;
Some pressed and pressed;
Some pulled and pulled;
Some tugged and tugged.
Beneath the pine forest they played without a care,
Washing themselves in the green-water stream.

So, after the monkeys had frolicked for a while, they went to bathe in the mountain stream and saw that its currents bounced and splashed like tumbling melons. As the old saying goes, "Fowls have their fowl speech, and beasts have their beast language." The monkeys said to each other, "We don't know where this water comes from. Since we have nothing to do today, let us follow the stream up to its source to have some fun." With a shriek of joy, they dragged along males and females, calling out to brothers and sisters, and scrambled up the mountain alongside the stream. Reaching its source, they found a great waterfall. What they saw was

A column of rising white rainbows,
A thousand fathoms of dancing waves—
Which the sea wind buffets but cannot sever,
On which the river moon shines and reposes.
Its cold breath divides the green ranges;
Its tributaries moisten the blue-green hillsides.
This torrential body, its name a cascade,
Appears truly like a hanging curtain.

All the monkeys clapped their hands in acclaim: "Marvelous water! Marvelous water! So this waterfall is distantly connected with the stream at the base of the mountain, and flows directly out, even to the Great Ocean." They said also, "If any of us had the ability to penetrate the curtain and find out where the water comes from without hurting himself, we would honor him as king." They gave the call three times, when suddenly the stone monkey leaped out from the crowd. He answered the challenge with a loud voice, "I'll go in! I'll go in!" What a monkey! For

Today his fame will spread,
His fortune arrives with the time;
Fated to live in this place,
He's sent as king to his palace.

Look at him! He closed his eyes, crouched low, and with one leap he jumped straight through the waterfall. Opening his eyes at once and raising his head to look around, he saw that there was neither water nor waves inside, only a gleaming, shining bridge. He paused to collect himself and looked more carefully again: it was a bridge made of sheet iron. The water beneath it surged through a hole in the rock to reach the outside, filling in all the space under the arch. With bent body he climbed on the bridge, looking about as he walked, and discovered a beautiful place that seemed to be some kind of residence. Then he saw

Fresh mosses piling up indigo,
White clouds like jade afloat,
And luminous sheens of mist and smoke;
Empty windows, quiet rooms,
And carved flowers growing smoothly on benches;
Stalactites suspended in milky caves;
Rare blossoms voluminous over the ground.
Pans and stoves near the wall show traces of fire;
Bottles and cups on the table contain leftovers.
The stone seats and beds were truly lovable;
The stone pots and bowls were more praiseworthy.
There were, furthermore, a stalk or two of tall bamboos,
And three or five sprigs of plum flowers.
With a few green pines always draped in rain,
This whole place indeed resembled a home.

After staring at the place for a long time, he jumped across the middle of the bridge and looked left and right. There in the middle was a stone tablet on which was inscribed in regular, large letters: "The Blessed Land of Flower-Fruit Mountain, the Cave Heaven of Water-Curtain Cave."[8] Beside himself with delight, the stone monkey quickly turned around to go back out and, closing his eyes and crouching again, leaped out of the water. "A great stroke of luck," he exclaimed with two loud guffaws, "a great stroke of luck." The other monkeys surrounded him and asked, "How is it inside? How deep is the water?" The stone monkey replied, "There isn't any water at all. There's a sheet iron bridge, and beyond it is a piece of heaven-sent property." "What do you mean that there's property in there?" asked the monkeys. Laughing, the stone monkey said, "This water splashes through a hole in the rock and fills the space under the bridge. Beside the bridge there is a stone mansion with trees and flowers. Inside are stone ovens and stoves, stone pots and pans, stone beds and benches. A stone tablet in the middle has the inscription, 'The Blessed Land of the Flower-Fruit Mountain, The Cave Heaven of the Water-Curtain Cave.' This is truly the place for us to settle in. It is, moreover, very spacious inside and can hold thousands of the young and old. Let's all go live in there, and spare ourselves from being subject to the whims of Heaven. For we have in there

A retreat from the wind,
A shelter from the rain.
You fear no frost or snow;
You hear no thunderclap.
Mist and smoke are brightened,
Warmed by a holy light—
The pines are ever green;
Rare flowers, daily new."

When the monkeys heard that, they were delighted, saying, "You go in first and lead the way." The stone monkey closed his eyes again, crouched low, and jumped inside. "All of you," he cried, "Follow me in! Follow me in!" The braver of the monkeys leaped in at once, but the more timid ones stuck out their heads and then drew them back, scratched their ears, rubbed their jaws, and chattered noisily. After milling around for some time, they too bounded inside. Jumping across the bridge, they were all soon snatching dishes, clutching bowls, or fighting for stoves and beds—shoving and pushing things hither and thither. Befitting their stubbornly prankish nature, the monkeys could not keep still for a moment and stopped only when they were utterly exhausted. The stone monkey then solemnly took a seat above and spoke to them: "Gentlemen! 'If a man lacks trustworthiness, it is difficult to know what he can accomplish!'[9] You yourselves promised just now that whoever could get in here and leave again without hurting himself would be honored as king. Now that I have come in and gone out, gone out and come in, and have found for all of you this heavenly grotto in which you may reside securely and enjoy the privilege of raising a family, why don't you honor me as your king?" When the monkeys heard this, they all folded their hands on their breasts and obediently prostrated themselves. Each one of them then lined up according to rank and age, and, bowing reverently, they intoned, "Long live our great king!" From that moment, the stone monkey ascended the throne of kingship. He did away with the word "stone" in his name and assumed the title, Handsome Monkey King. There is a testimonial poem which says:

When triple spring mated to produce all things,
A divine stone was quickened by the sun and moon:
The egg became a monkey and reached the Great Way.
A name he had and in elixir success.
His inward shape is concealed for it has no form,
But his outward form is by his action plainly known.
All mankind will be his subject in every age:
He's called a king and a sage who rules over all.

The Handsome Monkey King thus led a flock of gibbons and baboons, some of whom were appointed by him as his officers and ministers. They toured the Flower-Fruit Mountain in the morning, and they lived in the Water-Curtain Cave by night. Living in concord and sympathy, they did not mingle with bird or beast but enjoyed their independence in perfect happiness. For such were their activities:

In the spring they gathered flowers for food and drink.
In the summer they went in quest of fruits for sustenance.
In the autumn they collected taros and chestnuts to ward off time.
In the winter they searched for yellow-sperms[10] to live out the
    year.

The Handsome Monkey King had enjoyed this insouciant existence for three or four hundred years when one day, while feasting with the rest of the monkeys, he suddenly grew sad and shed a few tears. Alarmed, the monkeys surrounded him bowed down and asked, "What is disturbing the Great King?" The Monkey King replied, "Though I am very happy at the moment, I am a little concerned about the future. Hence my vexation." The monkeys all laughed and said, "The Great King indeed does not know contentment! Here we daily have a banquet on an immortal mountain in a blessed land, in an ancient cave on a divine continent. We are not subject to the unicorn or the phoenix, nor are we governed by the rulers of mankind. Such independence and comfort are immeasurable blessings. Why, then, does he worry about the future?" The Monkey King said, "Though we are not subject to the laws of man today, nor need we be threatened by the rule of any bird or beast, old age and physical decay in the future will disclose the secret sovereignty of Yama, King of the Underworld. If we die, shall we not have lived in vain, not being able to rank forever among the heavenly beings?"

When the monkeys heard this, they all covered their faces and wept mournfully, each one troubled by his own impermanence. But look! From among the ranks a bareback monkey suddenly leaped forth and cried aloud, "If the Great King is so farsighted, it may well indicate the sprouting of his religious inclination. There are, among the five major divisions of all living creatures,[11] only three species that are not subject to Yama, King of the Underworld." The Monkey King said, "Do you know who they are?" The monkey said, "They are the Buddhas, the immortals, and the holy sages; these three alone can avoid the Wheel of Transmigration as well as the process of birth and destruction, and live as long as Heaven and Earth, the mountains and the streams." "Where do they live?" asked the Monkey King. The monkey said, "They do not live beyond the world of the Jambūdvīpa, for they dwell within ancient caves on immortal mountains." When the Monkey King heard this, he was filled with delight, saying, "Tomorrow I shall take leave of you all and go down the mountain. Even if I have to wander with the clouds to the corners of the sea or journey to the distant edges of Heaven, I intend to find these three kinds of people. I will learn from them how to be young forever and escape the calamity inflicted by King Yama." Lo, this utterance at once led him to leap clear of the Web of Transmigration, and to turn him into the Great Sage, Equal to Heaven. All the monkeys clapped their hands in acclamation, saying, "Wonderful! Wonderful! Tomorrow we shall scour the mountain ranges to gather plenty of fruits, so that we may send the Great King off with a great banquet."

Next day the monkeys duly went to gather immortal peaches, to pick rare fruits, to dig out mountain herbs, and to chop yellow-sperms. They brought in an orderly manner every variety of orchids and epidendrums, exotic plants and strange flowers. They set out the stone chairs and stone tables, covering the tables with immortal wines and food. Look at the

Golden balls and pearly pellets.
Red ripeness and yellow plumpness.
Golden balls and pearly pellets are the cherries,
Their colors truly luscious.
Red ripeness and yellow plumpness are the plums,
Their taste—a fragrant tartness.
Fresh lungans
Of sweet pulps and thin skins.
Fiery lychees
Of small pits and red sacks.
Green fruits of the *Pyrus* are presented by the branches.
The loquats yellow with buds are held with their leaves.
Pears like rabbit heads and dates like chicken hearts
Dispel your thirst, your sorrow, and the effects of wine.
Fragrant peaches and soft almonds
Are sweet as the elixir of life;
Crisply fresh plums and strawberries
Are sour like cheese and buttermilk.
Red pulps and black seeds compose the ripe watermelons.
Four cloves of yellow rind enfold the big persimmons.
When the pomegranates are split wide,
Cinnabar grains glisten like specks of ruby;
When the chestnuts are cracked open,
Their tough brawns are hard like cornelian.
Walnut and silver almonds fare well with tea.
Coconuts and grapes may be pressed into wine.
Hazelnuts, yews, and crabapples overfill the dishes.
Kumquats, sugarcanes, tangerines, and oranges crowd the tables.
Sweet yams are baked,
Yellow-sperms overboiled,
The tubers minced with seeds of waterlily,
And soup in stone pots simmers on a gentle fire.
Mankind may boast its delicious dainties,
But what can best the pleasure of mountain monkeys?

The monkeys honored the Monkey King with the seat at the head of the table, while they sat below according to their age and rank. They drank for a whole day, each of the monkeys taking turn to go forward and present the Monkey King with wine, flowers, and fruits. Next day the Monkey King rose early and gave the instruction, "Little ones, cut me some pinewood and make me a raft. Then find me a bamboo for the pole, and gather some fruits and the like. I'm about to leave." When all was ready, he got onto the raft by himself. Pushing off with all his might, he drifted out toward the great ocean and, taking advantage of the wind, set sail for the border of South Jambūdvīpa Continent. Here is the consequence of this journey:

The heaven-born monkey, strong in magic might,
He left the mount, he rode the raft and caught the fair wind;
He drifted across the sea in search of immortals' way,
Determined in heart and mind to achieve great things.
It is his cause—and his portion—to quit all earthly zeals;
He'll be enlightened without worries or cares.
He may be expected to meet some approving one
Who will reveal the origin and the dharma of all things.

It was indeed his fortune that, after he had boarded the wooden raft, a strong southeast wind which lasted for days sent him to the north-western coast, the border of the South Jambūdvīpa Continent. He took the pole to test the water, and, finding it shallow one day, he abandoned the raft and jumped ashore. On the beach there were people fishing, hunting wild geese, digging clams, and draining salt. He approached them and, making a weird face and some strange antics, he scared them into dropping their baskets and nets and scattering in all directions. One of them could not run and was caught by the Monkey King, who stripped him of his clothes and put them on himself, aping the way humans wore them. With a swagger he walked through counties and prefectures, imitating human speech and human manners in the marketplaces. He rested by night and dined in the morning, but he was bent on finding the way of the Buddhas, immortals, and holy sages, on discovering the formula for eternal youth. He saw, however, that the people of the world were all seekers after profit and fame; there was not one who showed concern for his appointed end. This is their condition:

The quest for fame and fortune, when will it end?
This tyranny of early rising and retiring late!
Riding on mules they long for noble steeds.
Already prime ministers, they seek to be kings.

For food and raiment they suffer stress and strain,
Never fearful of Yama's call to reckoning.
Searching for wealth and power to give to grandsons and sons,
No one is ever willing to turn back.

The Monkey King searched diligently for the way of immortality, but he had no chance of meeting it. Going through big cities and visiting small towns, he unwittingly spent eight or nine years on the South Jambūdvīpa Continent before he suddenly came upon the Great Western Ocean. He thought that there would certainly be immortals living beyond the ocean; so, having built himself a raft like the previous one, he once again drifted across the Western Ocean until he reached the territory of the West Aparagodānīya Continent. After landing, he searched for a long time, when all at once he came upon a tall and beautiful mountain with thick forests at its base. Since he was afraid neither of wolves and lizards nor of tigers and leopards, he went straight to the top to look around. It was indeed a magnificent mountain:

A thousand peaks stand like rows of spears,
Like ten thousand cubits of screen widespread.
The sun's beams lightly enclose the azure mist;
In darkening rain, the mount's color turns cool and green.
Dry creepers entwine old trees;
Ancient fords edge secluded paths.
Rare flowers and luxuriant grass.
Tall bamboos and lofty pines.
Tall bamboos and lofty pines
For ten thousand years grow green in this blessed land.
Rare flowers and luxuriant grass
In all seasons bloom as in the Isles of the Blest.
The calls of birds hidden are near.
The sounds of streams rushing are clear.
Deep inside deep canyons the orchids interweave.
On every ridge and crag sprout lichens and mosses.
Rising and falling, the ranges show a fine dragon's pulse.[12]
Here in reclusion must an eminent man reside.

As he was looking about, he suddenly heard the sound of a man speaking deep within the woods. Hurriedly he dashed into the forest and cocked his ear to listen. It was someone singing, and the song went thus:

I watch chess games, my ax handle's rotted.[13]
I chop at wood, *chêng-chêng* the sound.
I walked slowly by the cloud's fringe at the valley's entrance.
Selling my firewood to buy some wine,
I am happy and laugh without restraint.
When the path is frosted in autumn's height,
I face the moon, my pillow the pine root.
Sleeping till dawn
I find my familiar woods.
I climb the plateaus and scale the peaks
To cut dry creepers with my ax.

When I gather enough to make a load,
I stroll singing through the marketplace
And trade it for three pints of rice,
With nary the slightest bickering
Over a price so modest.
Plots and schemes I do not know;
Without vainglory or attaint
My life's prolonged in simplicity.
Those I meet,
If not immortals, would be Taoists,
Seated quietly to expound the *Yellow Court*.[14]

When the Handsome Monkey King heard this, he was filled with delight, saying, "So the immortals are hiding in this place." He leaped at once into the forest. Looking again carefully, he found a woodcutter chopping firewood with his ax. The man he saw was very strangely attired.

On his head he wore a wide splint hat
Of seed-leaves freshly cast from new bamboos.
On his body he wore a cloth garment
Of gauze woven from the native cotton.
Around his waist he tied a winding sash
Of silk spun from an old silkworm.
On his feet he had a pair of straw sandals,
With laces rolled from withered sedge.
In his hands he held a fine steel ax;
A sturdy rope coiled round and round his load.
In breaking pines or chopping trees

Where's the man to equal him?

The Monkey King drew near and called out: "Reverend immortal! Your disciple raises his hands." The woodcutter was so flustered that he dropped his ax as he turned to return the salutation. "Blasphemy! Blasphemy!" he said, "I, a foolish fellow with hardly enough clothes or food! How can I bear the title of immortal?" The Monkey King said, "If you are not an immortal, how is it that you speak his language?" The woodcutter said, "What did I say that sounded like the language of an immortal?" The Monkey King said, "When I came just now to the forest's edge, I heard you singing, 'Those I meet, if not immortals, would be Taoists, seated quietly to expound the *Yellow Court*.' The *Yellow Court* contains the secret sayings of Taoism. What can you be but an immortal?" Laughing, the woodcutter said, "I can tell you this much: the tune of that *tz'ŭ* poem is 'A Court Full of Blossoms,' and it was taught to me by an immortal, a neighbor of mine. He saw that I had to struggle to make a living and that my days were full of worries; so he told me to recite the poem whenever I was troubled. This, he said, would both comfort me and rid me of my difficulties. It happened that I was anxious about something just now; so I sang the song. It didn't occur to me that I would be overheard." The Monkey King said, "If you are a neighbor of the immortal, why don't you follow him in the cultivation of Tao? Wouldn't it be nice to learn from him the formula for eternal youth?" The woodcutter said, "My lot has been a hard one all my life. When I was young, I was indebted to my parents' nurture until I was eight or nine. As soon as I began to have some understanding of human affairs, my father unfortunately died, and my mother remained a widow. I had no brothers or sisters; so there was no alternative but for me alone to support and care for my mother. Now that my mother is growing old, all the more I dare not leave her. Moreover, my fields are rather barren and desolate, and we haven't enough food or clothing. I can't do more than chop two bundles of firewood to take to the market in exchange for a few pennies to buy a few pints of rice. I cook that myself, serving it to my mother with the tea that I make. That's why I can't practice austerities."

The Monkey King said, "According to what you have said, you are indeed a gentleman of filial piety, and you will certainly be rewarded in the future. I hope, however, that you will show me the way to the immortal's abode, so that I may reverently call upon him." "It's not far. It's not far," the woodcutter said, "This mountain is called The Mountain of Heart and Mind, and in it is the Cave of Slanting Moon and Three Stars. Inside the cave is an immortal by the name of the Patriarch Subodhi, who has already sent out innumerable disciples. Even now there are thirty or forty persons who are practicing austerities with him. Follow this narrow path and travel south for about seven or eight miles, and you will come to his home." Grabbing at the woodcutter, the Monkey King said, "Honored brother, go with me. If I receive any benefit, I will not forget the favor of your guidance." "What a boneheaded fellow you are!" the woodcutter said. "I have just finished telling you these things, and you still don't understand. If I go with you, won't I be neglecting my livelihood? And who will take care of my mother? I must chop my firewood. You go on by yourself!"

When the Monkey King heard this, he had to take his leave. Going out of the forest, he found the path and went past the slope of a hill. After he had traveled seven or eight miles, a cave dwelling indeed came into sight. He stood up straight to take a better look at this splendid place, and this was what he saw:

Mist and smoke in diffusive brilliance,
Flashing lights from the sun and moon,
A thousand stalks of old cypress,
Ten thousand stems of tall bamboo.
A thousand stalks of old cypress
Draped in rain half fill the air with tender green;
Ten thousand stems of tall bamboo
Held in smoke will paint the glen chartreuse.
Strange flowers spread brocades before the door.
Jadelike grass emits fragrance beside the bridge.
On ridges protruding grow moist green lichens;
On hanging cliffs cling the long blue mosses.
The cries of immortal cranes are often heard.
Once in a while a phoenix soars overhead.
When the cranes cry,
Their sounds reach through the marsh to the distant sky.
When the phoenix soars up,
Its plume with five bright colors embroiders the clouds.
Black apes and white deer may come or hide;
Gold lions and jade elephants may leave or bide.

Look with care at this blessed, holy place:
It has the true semblance of Paradise.

He noticed that the door of the cave was tightly shut; all was quiet, and there was no sign of any human inhabitant. He turned around and suddenly perceived, at the top of the cliff, a stone slab approximately eight feet wide and over thirty feet tall. On it was written in large letters: "The Mountain of Heart and Mind; The Cave of Slanting Moon and Three Stars." Immensely pleased, the Handsome Monkey King said, "People here are truly honest. This mountain and this cave really do exist!" He stared at the place for a long time but dared not knock. Instead, he jumped onto the branch of a pine tree, picked a few pine seeds and ate them, and began to play.

After a moment he heard the door of the cave open with a squeak, and an immortal youth walked out. His bearing was exceedingly graceful; his features were highly refined. This was certainly no ordinary young mortal, for he had

His hair bound with two cords of silk,
A wide robe with two sleeves of wind.
His body and face seemed most distinct,
For visage and mind were both detached.
Long a stranger to all worldly things
He was the mountain's ageless boy.
Untainted even with a speck of dust,
He feared no havoc by the seasons wrought.

After coming through the door, the boy shouted, "Who is causing disturbance here?" With a bound the Monkey King leaped down from the tree, and went up to him bowing. "Immortal boy," he said, "I am a seeker of the way of immortality. I would never dare cause any disturbance." Laughing, the immortal youth asked, "Are you a seeker of Tao?" "I am indeed," answered the Monkey King. "My master at the house," the boy said, "has just left his couch to give a lecture on the platform. Before even announcing his theme, however, he told me to go out and open the door, saying, 'There is someone outside who wants to practice austerities. You may go and receive him.' It must be you, I suppose." The Monkey King said, laughing, "It is I, most assuredly!" "Follow me in then," said the boy. With solemnity the Monkey King set his clothes in order and followed the boy into the depths of the cave. They passed rows and rows of lofty towers and huge alcoves, of pearly chambers and carved arches.

After walking through innumerable quiet chambers and empty studios, they finally reached the base of the green jade platform. Patriarch Subodhi was seen seated solemnly on the platform, with thirty lesser immortals standing below in rows. He was truly

An immortal of great perception and purest mien,
The Master Subodhi, whose wondrous form of the West
Had no end or birth—such, the work of Double Three.[15]
His whole appearance was with mercy suffused.
Vacuous, spontaneous, and freely changing,
His Buddha-nature could perform all things.
His majestic body and Heaven's age were the same.
Fully tried and enlightened was this grand priest.

As soon as the Handsome Monkey King saw him, he prostrated himself and kowtowed times without number, saying, "Master! Master! I, your pupil, pay you my sincere homage." The Patriarch said, "Where do you come from? Let's hear you state clearly your name and country before you kowtow again." The Monkey King said, "Your pupil came from the Water-Curtain Cave of the Flower-Fruit Mountain, in the Ao-lai Country of the East Pūrvavideha Continent." "Chase him out of here!" the Patriarch shouted. "He is nothing but a liar and a fabricator of falsehood. How can he possibly be interested in attaining enlightenment?" The Monkey King hastened to kowtow unceasingly and to say, "Your pupil's word is an honest one, without any deceit." The Patriarch said, "If you are telling the truth, how is it that you mention the East Pūrvavideha Continent? Separating that place and mine are two great oceans and the entire region of the South Jambūdvīpa Continent. How could you possibly get here?" Again kowtowing, the Monkey King said, "Your pupil drifted across the oceans and trudged through many regions for more than ten years before finding this place." The Patriarch said, "If you have come on a long journey in many stages, I'll let that pass. What is your *hsing*?"[16] The Monkey King again replied, "I have no *hsing*. If a man rebukes me, I am not offended; if he hits me, I am not angered. In fact, I simply repay him with a ceremonial greeting and that's all. My whole life's without ill temper." "I'm not speaking of your temper," the Patriarch said, "I'm asking after the name of your parents." "I have no parents either," said the Monkey King. The Patriarch said, "If you have no parents, you must have been born from a tree." "Not from a tree," said the Monkey King, "but from a rock. I recall that there used to be an immortal stone on the Flower-Fruit Mountain. I was born the year the stone split open."

When the Patriarch heard this, he was secretly pleased, and said, "Well, evidently you have been created by Heaven and Earth. Get up and show me how you walk." Snapping erect, the Monkey King scurried around a couple of times. The Patriarch laughed and said, "Though your features are not the most attractive, you do resemble a monkey (*hu-sun*) that feeds on pine seeds. This gives me the idea of deriving your surname from your appearance. I intended to call you by the name 'Hu.' Now, when the accompanying animal radical is dropped from this word, what's left is a compound made up of the two characters, *ku* and *yüeh*. *Ku* means aged and *yüeh* means female, but an aged female cannot reproduce. Therefore, it is better to give you the surname of 'Sun.' When the accompanying animal radical is dropped from this word, we have the compound of *tzŭ* and *hsi*. *Tzŭ* means a boy and *hsi* means a baby, so that the name exactly accords with the Doctrine of the Baby. So your surname will be 'Sun.'" When the Monkey King heard this, he was filled with delight. "Splendid! Splendid!" he cried, kowtowing, "At last I know my surname. May the Master be even more gracious! Since I have received the surname, let me be given also a personal name, so that it may facilitate your calling and commanding me." The Patriarch said, "Within my tradition are twelve characters which have been used to name the pupils according to their divisions. You are one who belongs to the tenth generation." "Which twelve characters are they?" asked the Monkey King. The Patriarch said, "They are: wide (*kuang*), great (*ta*), wise (*chih*), intelligence (*hui*), true (*chên*), conforming (*ju*), nature (*hsing*), sea (*hai*), sharp (*ying*), wake-to (*wu*), complete (*yüan*), and awakening (*chüeh*). Your rank falls precisely on the word 'wake-to' (*wu*). You will hence be given the religious name 'Wake-to-Vacuity' (*wu-k'ung*). All right?" "Splendid! Splendid!" said the Monkey King, laughing; "henceforth I shall be called Sun Wu-k'ung." So it was thus:

When the world was first created, there was no name;

To break the stubborn vacuity one needs to wake to vacuity.

We do not know what sort of Taoist cultivation he succeeded in practicing afterward and must await the explanation in the next chapter.

Two

The true wondrous doctrine of Bodhi thoroughly
  comprehended;
The destruction of Māra[1] and the return to origin
  unify the soul.

Now we were speaking of the Handsome Monkey King, who, having
received his name, jumped about joyfully and went forward to give
Subodhi his grateful salutation. The Patriarch then ordered the congregation to lead Sun Wu-k'ung outdoors and to teach him how to
sprinkle water on the ground and dust, and how to speak and move
with proper courtesy. The company of immortals obediently went
outside with Wu-k'ung, who then bowed to his fellow students. They
prepared thereafter a place in the corridor where he might sleep.
Next morning he began to learn from his schoolmates the arts of
language and etiquette. He discussed with them the scriptures and
the doctrines; he practiced calligraphy and burned incense. Such was
his daily routine. In more leisurely moments he would be sweeping
the grounds or hoeing the garden, planting flowers or pruning trees,
gathering firewood or lighting fires, fetching water or carrying drinks.
He did not lack for whatever he needed, and thus he lived in the cave
without realizing that six or seven years had slipped by. One day the
Patriarch ascended the platform and took his high seat. Calling
together all the immortals, he began to lecture on a great doctrine.
He spoke
  With words so florid and eloquent
  That gold lotus sprang up from the ground.
  The doctrine of three vehicles he subtly rehearsed,[2]
  Including even the laws' minutest tittle.
  The yak's-tail[3] waved slowly and spouted elegance;
  His thunderous voice moved e'en the Ninth Heaven.
  For a while he lectured on Tao.
  For a while he discoursed on Zen.
  To harmonize the three schools[4] was a natural thing.
  One word's elucidation in conformity to truth
  Would lead to a life birthless and knowledge most profound.

Wu-k'ung, who was standing there to listen, was so pleased with the talk that he scratched his ear and rubbed his jaw. Grinning from ear to ear, he could not refrain from dancing on all fours! Suddenly the Patriarch saw this and called out to him, "Why are you madly jumping and dancing in the ranks and not listening to my lecture?" Wu-k'ung said, "Your pupil was devoutly listening to the lecture. But when I heard such wonderful things from my reverend master, I couldn't contain myself for joy and started to leap and prance about quite unconsciously. May the master forgive my sins!" "Let me ask you," said the Patriarch, "if you comprehend these wonderful things, do you know how long you have been in this cave?" Wu-k'ung said, "Your pupil is basically feeble-minded and does not know the number of seasons. I only remember that whenever the fire burned out in the stove, I would go to the back of the mountain to gather firewood. Finding a mountainful of fine peach trees there, I have eaten my fill of peaches seven times." The Patriarch said, "That mountain is named the Ripe Peach Mountain. If you have eaten your fill seven times, I suppose it must have been seven years. What kind of Taoist art would you like to learn from me?" Wu-k'ung said, "I am dependent on the admonition of my honored teacher. Your pupil would gladly learn whatever has a smidgen of Taoist flavor."

The Patriarch said, "Within the tradition of Tao, there are three hundred and sixty heteronomous divisions, all the practices of which may result in Illumination. I don't know which division you would like to follow." "I am dependent on the will of my honored teacher," said Wu-k'ung, "your pupil is wholeheartedly obedient." "How would it be," said the Patriarch, "if I taught you the practice of the Art division?" Wu-k'eng asked, "How would you explain the practice of the Art division?" "The practice of the Art division," said the Patriarch, "consists of summoning immortals and working the planchette, of divination by manipulating yarrow stalks, and of learning the secrets of pursuing good and avoiding evil." "Can this sort of practice lead to immortality?" asked Wu-k'ung. "Impossible! Impossible!" said the Patriarch. "I won't learn it then," Wu-k'ung said.

"How would it be," said the Patriarch again, "if I taught you the practice of the Schools division?" "What is the meaning of the Schools division?" asked Wu-k'ung. "The Schools division," the Patriarch said, "includes the Confucians, the Buddhists, the Taoists, the

Dualists, the Mohists, and the Physicians. They read scriptures or recite prayers; they interview priests or conjure up saints and the like." "Can this sort of practice lead to immortality?" asked Wu-k'ung. The Patriarch said, "If immortality is what you desire, this practice is like setting a pillar inside a wall." Wu-k'ung said, "Master, I'm a simple fellow and I don't know the idioms of the marketplace. What's setting a pillar inside a wall?" The Patriarch said, "When people build houses and want them to be sturdy, they place a pillar as a prop inside the wall. But someday the big mansion will decay, and the pillar too will rot." "What you're saying then," Wu-k'ung said, "is that it is not long-lasting. I'm not going to learn this."

The Patriarch said, "How would it be if I taught you the practice of the Silence division?" "What's the aim of the Silence division?" Wu-k'ung asked. "To cultivate fasting and abstinence," said the Patriarch, "quiescence and inactivity, meditation and the art of cross-legged sitting, restraint of language and a vegetarian diet. There are also the practices of yoga, exercises standing or prostrate, entrance into complete stillness, contemplation in solitary confinement, and the like." "Can these activities," asked Wu-k'ung, "bring about immortality?" "They are no better than the unfired bricks on the kiln," said the Patriarch. Wu-k'ung laughed and said, "Master indeed loves to beat about the bush! Haven't I just told you that I don't know these idioms of the marketplace? What do you mean by the unfired bricks on the kiln?" The Patriarch said, "The tiles and the bricks on the kiln may have been molded into shape, but if they have not been refined by water and fire, a heavy rain will one day make them crumble." "So this too lacks permanence," said Wu-k'ung. "I don't want to learn it."

The Patriarch said, "How would it be if I taught you the practice of the Action division?" "What's it like in the Action division?" Wu-k'ung asked. "Plenty of activities," said the Patriarch, "such as gathering the yin to nourish the yang, bending the bow and treading the arrow,[5] and rubbing the navel to pass breath. There are also experimentation with alchemical formulas, burning rushes and forging cauldrons, taking red lead, making autumn stone,[6] and drinking bride's milk and the like." "Can such bring about long life?" asked Wu-k'ung. "To obtain immortality from such activities," said the Patriarch, "is also like scooping the moon from the water." "There you go again, Master!" cried Wu-k'ung. "What do you mean by scooping the moon from the water?" The Patriarch said, "When the moon is high in the sky, its reflection is in the water. Although it is visible therein, you cannot scoop it out or catch hold of it, for it is but an illusion." "I won't learn that either!" said Wu-k'ung.

When the Patriarch heard this, he uttered a cry and jumped down from the high platform. He pointed the ruler he held in his hands at Wu-k'ung and said to him: "What a mischievous monkey you are! You won't learn this and you won't learn that! Just what it is that you are waiting for?" Moving forward, he hit Wu-k'ung three times on the head. Then he folded his arms behind his back and walked inside, closing the main doors behind him and leaving the congregation stranded outside. Those who were listening to the lecture were so terrified that everyone began to berate Wu-k'ung. "You reckless ape!" they cried, "you're utterly without manners! The master was prepared to teach you magic secrets. Why weren't you willing to learn? Why did you have to argue with him instead? Now you have offended him, and who knows when he'll come out again?" At that moment they all resented him and despised and ridiculed him. But Wu-k'ung was not angered in the least and only replied with a broad grin. For the Monkey King, in fact, had already solved secretly, as it were, the riddle in the pot; he therefore did not quarrel with the other people but patiently held his tongue. He reasoned that the master, by hitting him three times, was telling him to prepare himself for the third watch; and by folding his arms behind his back, walking inside, and closing the main doors, was telling him to enter by the back door so that he might receive instruction in secret.

Wu-k'ung spent the rest of the day happily with the other pupils in front of the Divine Cave of the Three Stars, eagerly waiting for the night. When evening arrived, he immediately retired with all the others, pretending to be asleep by closing his eyes, breathing evenly, and remaining completely still. Since there was no watchman in the mountain to beat the watch or call the hour, he could not tell what time it was. He could only rely on his own calculations by counting the breaths he inhaled and exhaled. Approximately at the hour of Tzŭ,[7] he arose very quietly and put on his clothes. Stealthily opening the front door, he slipped away from the crowd and walked outside. Lifting his head, he saw

The bright moon and the cool, clear dew;
In each corner was not a speck of dust.

Secluded fowls rested deep in the woods;
A brook flowed gently from its source.
The glow of darting fireflies dispersed the gloom.
Wild geese passed in calligraphic columns through the clouds.
Precisely it was the third-watch hour—
Time to seek the Truth, the Perfect Way.

You see him following the familiar path back to the rear entrance, where he discovered that the door was, indeed, ajar. Wu-k'ung said happily, "The reverend master truly intended to give me instruction. That's why the door was left open." He reached the door in a few large strides and entered sideways. Walking up to the Patriarch's bed, he found him asleep with his body curled up, facing the wall. Wu-k'ung dared not distrub him; instead, he knelt before his bed. After a little while, the Patriarch awoke. Stretching his legs, he recited to himself:

Hard! Hard! Hard!
· The Way is most obscure!
Deem not the gold elixir a common thing.[8]
He who imparts dark mysteries not to a perfect man
    Is bound to make words empty, the mouth tired, and the tongue
        dry!

"Master," Wu-k'ung responded at once, "Your pupil has been kneeling here and waiting on you for a long time." When the Patriarch heard Wu-k'ung's voice, he rose and put on his clothes. "You mischievous monkey!" he exclaimed, sitting down cross-legged, "Why aren't you sleeping in front? What are you doing back here at my place?" Wu-k'ung replied, "Before the platform and the congregation yesterday, the master gave the order that your pupil, at the hour of the third watch, should come here through the rear entrance in order that he might be instructed. I was therefore bold enough to come directly to the master's bed." When the Patriarch heard this, he was terribly pleased, thinking to himself, "This fellow is indeed an offspring of Heaven and Earth. If not, how could he solve so readily the riddle in my pot!" "There is no one here save your pupil," Wu-k'ung said. "May the master be exceedingly merciful and impart to me the way of long life. I shall never forget this gracious favor." "Since you have solved the riddle in the pot," said the Patriarch, "it is an indication that you are destined to learn, and I am glad to teach you. Come closer and listen carefully. I will impart to you the wondrous way of long life." Wu-k'ung kowtowed to express his gratitude, washed his ears, and listened most attentatively, kneeling before the bed. The Patriarch said:

Know well this secret formula wondrous and true:
Spare and nurse the vital forces, this and nothing else.
All power resides in the semen, the breath, and the spirit;
Guard these with care, securely, lest there be a leak.[9]
Lest there be a leak!
Keep within the body!
Hearken to my teaching and the Way itself will prosper.
Remember the oral formulas so efficacious
To purge concupiscence and lead to purity;
To purity
Where the light is bright.
You may face the elixir platform and enjoy the moon.[10]
The moon holds the jade rabbit, the sun hides the crow;
See there also the snake and the tortoise tightly entwined.[11]
Tightly entwined,
The vital forces are strong.
You can plant gold lotus e'en in the midst of flames.
The Five Phases use together and in order reverse—[12]
When that's attained, be a Buddha or immortal at will!

At that moment, the very origin was revealed to Wu-k'ung, whose mind became spiritualized as happiness came to him. He carefully committed to memory all the oral formulas. After kowtowing to thank the Patriarch, he left by the rear entrance. As he went out, he saw that the eastern sky was just beginning to pale with light, though golden beams were radiant from the Westward Way. Following the same path, he returned to the front door, pushed it open quietly, and went inside. He sat up in his sleeping place and purposely rustled the bed and the covers, crying "It's light! It's light! Get up!" All the other people were still sleeping and did not know that Wu-k'ung had received a good thing. He played the fool that day after getting up, but he persisted in what he had learned secretly by doing breathing exercises before the hour of Tzŭ and after the hour of Wu.[13]

Three years went by swiftly, and the Patriarch again mounted his throne to lecture to the multitude. He discussed the scholastic deliberations and parables, and he discoursed on the integument of external conduct. Suddenly he asked, "Where's Wu-k'ung?"

Wu-k'ung drew near and knelt down. "Your pupil's here," he said. "What sort of art have you been practicing lately?" the Patriarch asked. "Recently," Wu-k'ung said, "your pupil has begun to apprehend the nature of all things and my foundational knowledge has become firmly established." "If you have penetrated to the dharma nature to apprehend the origin," said the Patriarch, "you have, in fact, entered into the divine substance. You need, however, to guard against the danger of three calamities." When Wu-k'ung heard this, he thought for a long time and said, "The words of the master must be erroneous. I have frequently heard that when one is learned in the Way and excels in virtue, he will enjoy the same age as Heaven; fire and water cannot harm him and every kind of disease will vanish. How can there be this danger of three calamities?" "What you have learned," said the Patriarch, "is no ordinary magic: you have stolen the creative powers of Heaven and Earth and invaded the dark mysteries of the sun and moon. Your success in mixing the elixir is something that the gods and the demons cannot countenance. Though your appearance will be preserved and your age lengthened, after five hundred years Heaven will send down the calamity of thunder to strike you. Hence you must be intelligent and wise enough to avoid it ahead of time. If you can escape it, your age will indeed equal that of Heaven; if not, your life will thus be finished. After another five hundred years Heaven will send down the calamity of fire to burn you. That fire is neither natural nor common fire; its name is the Fire of Yin, and it arises from within the soles of your feet to reach even the cavity of your heart, reducing your entrails to ashes and your limbs to utter ruin. The arduous labor of a millennium will then have been made completely superfluous. After another five hundred years the calamity of wind will be sent to blow at you. It is not the wind from the north, south, east, or west; nor is it one of the winds of four seasons; nor is it the wind of flowers, willows, pines, and bamboos. It is called the Mighty Wind, and it enters from the top of the skull into the body, passes through the midriff and penetrates the nine apertures.[14] The bones and the flesh will be dissolved and the body itself will disintegrate. You must therefore avoid all three calamities." When Wu-k'ung heard this, his hair stood on end, and, kowtowing reverently, he said, "I beg the master to be merciful and impart to me the method to avoid the three calamities. To the very end. I shall never forget your gracious favor." The Patriarch said,

"It is not, in fact, difficult, except that I cannot teach you because you are somewhat different from other people." "I have a round head pointing to Heaven," said Wu-k'ung, "and square feet walking on Earth. Similarly, I have nine apertures and four limbs, entrails and cavities. In what way am I different from other people?" The Patriarch said, "Though you resemble a man, you have much less jowl." The monkey, you see, has an angular face with hollow cheeks and a pointed mouth. Stretching his hand to feel himself, Wu-k'ung laughed and said, "The master does not know how to balance matters! Though I have much less jowl than human beings, I have my pouch, which may certainly be considered a compensation." "Very well, then," said the Patriarch, "what method of escape would you like to learn? There is the Art of the Heavenly Ladle, which numbers thirty-six transformations, and there is the Art of the Earthly Multitude, which numbers seventy-two transformations." Wu-k'ung said, "Your pupil is always eager to catch more fishes, so I'll learn the Art of the Earthly Multitude." "In that case," said the Patriarch, "come up here, and I'll pass on the oral formulas to you." He then whispered something into his ear, though we do not know what sort of wondrous secrets he spoke of. But this Monkey King was someone who, knowing one thing, could understand a hundred! He immediately learned the oral formulas and, after working at them and practicing them himself, he mastered all seventy-two transformations.

One day when the Patriarch and the various pupils were admiring the evening view in front of the Three Stars Cave, the master asked, "Wu-k'ung, has that matter been perfected?" Wu-k'ung said, "Thanks to the profound kindness of the master, your pupil has indeed attained perfection; I now can ascend like mist into the air and fly." The Patriarch said, "Let me see you try to fly." Wishing to display his ability, Wu-k'ung leaped fifty or sixty feet into the air, pulling himself up with a somersault. He trod on the clouds for about the time of a meal and traveled a distance of no more than three miles before dropping down again to stand before the Patriarch. "Master," he said, his hands folded in front of him, "this is flying by cloud-soaring." Laughing, the Patriarch said, "This can't be called cloud-soaring! It's more like cloud-crawling! The old saying goes, 'The immortal tours the North Sea in the morning and reaches Ts'ang-wu by night.' If it takes you half a day to go less than three miles, it can't even be considered cloud-crawling." "What do you mean," asked Wu-k'ung, "by saying, 'The immortal tours the North Sea in the morning and reaches Ts'ang-wu by night'?" The Patriarch said, "Those who are capable of cloud-soaring may start from the North Sea in the morning, journey through the East Sea, the West Sea, the South Sea, and return again to Ts'ang-wu. Ts'ang-wu refers to Ling-ling in the North Sea. It can be called true cloud-soaring only when you can traverse all four seas in one day." "That's truly difficult!" said Wu-k'ung, "truly difficult!" "Nothing in the world is difficult," said the Patriarch; "only the mind makes it so." When Wu-k'ung heard these words, he kowtowed reverently and implored the Patriarch, "Master, if you do perform a service for someone, you must do it thoroughly. May you be most merciful and impart to me also this technique of cloud-soaring. I would never dare forget your gracious favor." The Patriarch said, "When the various immortals want to soar on the clouds, they all rise by stamping their feet. But you're not like them. When I saw you leave just now, you had to pull yourself up by jumping. What I'll do now is to teach you the cloud-somersault in accordance with your form." Wu-k'ung again prostrated himself and pleaded with him, and the Patriarch gave him an oral formula, saying, "Make the magic sign, recite the spell, clench your fist tightly, shake your body, and when you jump up, one somersault will carry you a hundred and eight thousand miles." When the other people heard this, they all giggled and said, "Lucky Wu-k'ung! If he learns this little trick, he can become a dispatcher for someone to deliver documents or carry circulars. He'll be able to make a living anywhere!"

The sky now began to darken, and the master went back to the cave dwelling with his pupils. Throughout the night, however, Wu-k'ung practiced ardently and mastered the technique of cloud-somersault. From then on, he had complete freedom, blissfully enjoying his state of long life.

One day early in the summer, the disciples were gathered under the pine trees for fellowship and discussion. They said to him, "Wu-k'ung, what sort of merit did you accumulate in another incarnation that led the master to whisper in your ear, the other day, the method of avoiding the three calamities? Have you learned everything?" "I won't conceal this from my various elder brothers," Wu-k'ung said, laughing. "Owing to the master's instruction in the first place and my diligence day and night in the second, I have fully mastered the several matters!" "Let's take advantage of the moment," one of the pupils said. "You try to put on a performance and we'll watch." When Wu-k'ung heard this, his spirit was aroused and he was most eager to display his powers. "I invite the various elder brothers to give me a subject," he said. "What do you want me to change into?" "Why not a pine tree?" they said. Wu-k'ung made the magic sign and recited the spell; with one shake of his body he changed himself into a pine tree. Truly it was

Thickly held in smoke through all four seasons;
Its chaste fair form rose straight to the clouds,
With not the least likeness to the impish monkey,
But only frost-tried and snow-tested branches.

When the multitude saw this, they clapped their hands and roared with laughter, everyone crying, "Marvelous monkey! Marvelous monkey!" They did not realize that all this uproar had disturbed the Patriarch, who came running out of the door, dragging his staff. "Who is creating this bedlam here?" he demanded. At his voice the pupils immediately collected themselves, set their clothes in order, and came forward. Wu-k'ung also changed back into his true form, and, slipping into the crowd, he said, "For your information, Reverend Master, we are having fellowship and discussion here. There is no one from outside causing any disturbance." "You were all yelling and screaming," said the Patriarch angrily, "and were behaving in a manner totally unbecoming to those practicing the Great Art. Don't you know that those in the cultivation of Tao are wary of opening their mouths lest they dissipate their vital forces, or of moving their tongues lest they provoke arguments? Why are you all laughing noisily here?" "We dare not conceal this from the master," the crowd said. "Just now we were having fun with Wu-k'ung, who was giving us a performance of transformation. We told him to change into a pine tree, and he did indeed become a pine tree! Your pupils were all applauding him and our voices disturbed the reverend teacher. We beg his forgiveness." "Go away, all of you," the Patriarch said. "You, Wu-k'ung, come over here! I ask you what sort of exhibition were you putting on, changing into a pine tree? Did I give you spiritual ability just for showing off to people? Suppose you saw someone with this ability. Wouldn't you ask him at once how he acquired it? So when others see that you are in possession of it, they'll come begging. If you're afraid to refuse them, you will give away the secret; if you don't, they may hurt you. You are actually placing your life in grave jeopardy." "I beseech the master to forgive me," Wu-k'ung said kowtowing. "I won't condemn you," said the Patriarch, "but you must leave this place." When Wu-k'ung heard this, tears fell from his eyes. "Where am I to go, Teacher?" he asked. "From wherever you came," the Patriarch said, "you should go back there." "I came from the East Pūrvavideha Continent," Wu-k'ung said, his memory jolted by the Patriarch, "from the Water-Curtain Cave of the Flower-Fruit Mountain in the Ao-lai Country." "Go back there quickly and save your life," the Patriarch said. "You cannot possibly remain here!" "Allow me to inform my esteemed teacher," said Wu-k'ung, properly penitent, "I have been away from home for twenty years, and I certainly long to see my subjects and followers of bygone days again. But I keep thinking that my master's profound kindness to me has not yet been repaid; I therefore dare not leave." "There's nothing to be repaid," said the Patriarch. "See that you don't get into trouble and involve me; that's all I ask."

Seeing that there was no other alternative, Wu-k'ung had to bow to the Patriarch and take leave of the congregation. "Once you leave," the Patriarch said, "you're bound to end up evildoing. I don't care what kind of villainy and violence you engage in, but I forbid you ever to mention that you are my disciple. For if you but utter half the word, I'll know about it; you can be assured, wretched monkey, that you'll be skinned alive. I will break all your bones and banish your soul to the Place of Ninefold Darkness, from which you will not be released even after ten thousand afflictions!" "I will never dare mention my master," said Wu-k'ung. "I'll say that I've learned this all by myself." Having thanked the Patriarch, Wu-k'ung turned away, made the magic sign, pulled himself up, and performed the cloud-somersault. He headed straight toward the East Pūrvavideha, and in less than an hour he could already see the Flower-Fruit Mountain and the Water-Curtain Cave. Rejoicing secretly, the Handsome Monkey King said to himself:

Heavy with bones of mortal stock I left this place.
But success in Tao has lighten'd both body and frame.
'Tis this world's pity that none is firmly resolved
To learn the mystery, plain to all who seek.
Hard was the advance in that hour of ocean crossing.

How easy the journey of my homecoming today!

Parting words of counsel still echo in my ears.

Mine's not the hope to see so soon the eastern depths!

Wu-k'ung lowered the direction of his cloud and landed squarely on the Flower-Fruit Mountain. He was trying to find his way when he heard the call of cranes and the cry of monkeys; the call of cranes reverberated in the heavens, and the cry of monkeys moved his spirit with sadness. "Little ones," he called out, "I have returned!" From the crannies of the cliff, from the flowers and bushes, and from the woods and trees, monkeys great and small leaped out by the tens of thousands and surrounded the Handsome Monkey King. They all kowtowed and cried, "Great King! What laxity of mind! Why did you you go away for such a long time and leave us here longing for your return like someone hungering and thirsting? Recently, we have been brutally abused by a monster, who wanted to rob us of our Water-Curtain Cave. Out of sheer desperation, we fought hard with him. And yet all this time, that fellow has plundered many of our possessions, kidnaped a number of our young ones, and given us many restless days and nights watching over our property. How fortunate that our great king has returned! If the great king had stayed away another year or so, we and the entire mountain cave would have belonged to someone else!" When Wu-k'ung heard this, he was filled with anger. "What sort of a monster is this," he cried, "that behaves in such a lawless manner? Tell me about this in detail and I will find him to exact vengeance." "Be informed, Great King," the monkeys said, kowtowing, "that the fellow calls himself the Monstrous King of Havoc, and he lives north of here." Wu-k'ung said, "From here to his place, how great is the distance?" The monkeys said, "He comes like the cloud and leaves like the mist, like the wind and the rain, like lightning and thunder. We don't know how great the distance is." "In that case," said Wu-k'ung, "go and play for a while and don't be afraid. Let me go and find him."

Dear Monkey King! He leaped up with a bound and somersaulted all the way northward until he saw a tall and rugged mountain. What a mountain!

Its penlike peak stands erect.

Its winding streams flow unfathomed and deep.

Its penlike peak, standing erect, cuts through the air;

> Its winding streams, unfathomed and deep, reach divers sites on
>   earth.
> On two ridges flowers rival trees in exotic charm;
> At various spots pines match bamboos in verdure.
> The dragon on the left
> Seems docile and tame;
> The tiger on the right
> Seems gentle and meek.
> Iron oxen[15] on occasion are seen plowing.
> Gold-coin flowers are frequently planted.
> Rare fowls make melodious songs;
> The phoenix stands facing the sun.
> Rocks worn smooth and shiny
> By water placid and bright
> Appear by turns grotesque, bizarre, and fierce.
> In countless numbers are the world's famous mountains
> Where flowers bloom and wither; they flourish and die.
> What place resembles this long-lasting scene
> By the four seasons and eight epochs[16] wholly untouched?
> This is, in the Three Regions,[17] the Mount of Northern Spring,
> The Water-Belly Cave, nourished by the Five Phases.[18]

The Handsome Monkey King was silently viewing the scenery when
he heard someone speaking. He went down the mountain to find
who it was, and he discovered the Water-Belly Cave at the foot of a
steep cliff. Several imps who were dancing in front of the cave saw
Wu-k'ung and began to run away. "Stop!" cried Wu-k'ung. "You
can use the words of your mouth to communicate the thoughts of
my mind. I am the lord of the Water-Curtain Cave in the Flower-
Fruit Mountain south of here. Your Monstrous King of Havoc, or
whatever he's called, has repeatedly bullied my young ones, and I
have found my way here with the specific purpose of settling matters
with him."

Hearing this, the imps darted into the cave and cried out, "Great
King, a disastrous thing has happened!" "What sort of disaster?"
asked the Monstrous King. "Outside the cave," said the imps, "there
is a monkey who calls himself the lord of the Water-Curtain Cave in
the Flower-Fruit Mountain. He says that you have repeatedly bullied
his young ones and that he has come to settle matters with you."

Laughing, the Monstrous King said, "I have often heard those monkeys say that they have a great king who has left the family to practice the Great Art. He must have come back. How is he dressed, and what kind of weapon does he have? "He doesn't have any kind of weapon," the imps said. "He is bare-headed, wears a red robe with a yellow sash, and has a pair of black boots on. He looks like neither a monk nor a layman, neither a Taoist nor an immortal. He is out there making demands with naked hands and empty fists." When the Monstrous King heard this, he ordered, "Get me my armor and my weapon." These were immediately brought out by the imps, and the Monstrous King put on his breastplate and helmet, grasped his scimitar, and walked out of the cave with his followers. "Who is the lord of the Water-Curtain Cave?" he cried with a loud voice. Quickly opening wide his eyes to take a look, Wu-k'ung saw that the Monstrous King

Wore on his head a black gold helmet
Which gleamed in the sun;
And on his body a dark silk robe
Which swayed in the wind;
Lower he had on a black iron vest
Tied tightly with leather straps;
His feet were shod in finely carved boots,
Grand as those of warriors great.
Ten spans—the width of his waist;
Thirty feet—the height of his frame;
He held in his hands a sword;
Its blade was fine and bright.
His name: the Monster of Havoc
Of most fearsome form and look.

"You have such big eyes, reckless monster, but you can't even see old Monkey!" the Monkey King shouted. When the Monstrous King saw him, he laughed and said, "You're not four feet tall, nor are you thirty years old; you don't even have weapons in your hands. How dare you be so insolent, looking for me to settle accounts?" "You reckless monster!" cried Wu-k'ung. "You are blind indeed! You think I'm small, not knowing that it's hardly difficult for me to become taller; you think I'm without weapon, but my two hands can drag the moon down from the edge of heaven. Don't be afraid; just have a taste of old Monkey's fist!" He leaped into the air and aimed a blow smack at the monster's face. Parrying the blow with his hand, the Monstrous King said, "You are such a midget and I'm so tall; you want to use your fist but I have my scimitar. If I were to kill you with it, I would be a laughing stock. Let me put down my scimitar, and we'll see how well you can box." "Well said, fine fellow," replied Wu-k'ung. "Come on!" The Monstrous King shifted his position and struck out. Wu-k'ung closed in on him, hurtling himself into the engagement. The two of them pummeled and kicked, struggling and colliding with each other. Now it's easy to miss on a long reach, but a short punch is firm and reliable. Wu-k'ung jabbed the Monstrous King in the short ribs, hit him on his chest, and gave him such heavy punishment with a few sharp blows that the monster stepped aside, picked up his huge scimitar, aimed it straight at Wu-k'ung's head, and slashed at him. Wu-k'ung dodged, and the blow narrowly missed him. Seeing that his opponent was growing fiercer, Wu-k'ung now used the method called the Body beyond the Body. Plucking a handful of hairs from his own body and throwing them into his mouth, he chewed them to tiny pieces and then spat them into the air. "Change!" he cried, and they changed at once into two or three hundred little monkeys encircling the combatants on all sides. For you see, when someone acquires the body of an immortal, he can project his spirit, change his form, and perform all kinds of wonders. Since the Monkey King had become accomplished in the Great Art, every one of the eighty-four thousand hairs on his body could change into whatever shape or substance he desired. The little monkeys he had just created were so keen of eye and so swift of movement that they could be wounded by neither sword nor spear. Look at them! Skipping and jumping, they rushed at the Monstrous King and surrounded him, some hugging, some pulling, some crawling in between his legs, some tugging at his feet. They kicked and punched; they yanked at his hair and poked at his eyes; they pinched his nose and tried to sweep him completely off his feet, until they tangled themselves into confusion. Meanwhile Wu-k'ung succeeded in snatching the scimitar, pushed through the throng of little monkeys, and brought the scimitar down squarely onto the monster's skull, cleaving it in two. He and the rest of the monkeys then fought their way into the cave and slaughtered all the imps, young and old. With a shake, he collected his hair back onto his body, but there were some monkeys that did not return to him. They were the little monkeys kidnaped by the Monstrous King from the Water-Curtain Cave. "Why are you here?" asked Wu-k'ung. The thirty or fifty of them all said tearfully, "After the Great King went away to seek the way of immortality, the monster menaced us for two whole years and finally carried us off to this place. Don't these utensils belong to our cave? These stone pots and bowls were all taken by the creature." "If these are our belongings," said Wu-k'ung, "move them out of here." He then set fire to the Water-Belly Cave and reduced it to ashes. "All of you," he said to them, "follow me home." "Great King," the monkeys said, "when we came here, all we felt was wind rushing past us, and we seemed to float through the air until we arrived here. We don't know the way. How can we go back to our home?" Wu-k'ung said, "That's a magic trick of his. But there's no difficulty! Now I know not only one thing but a hundred! I'm familiar with that trick too. Close your eyes, all of you, and don't be afraid."

Dear Monkey King. He recited a spell, rode for a while on a fierce wind, and then lowered the direction of the cloud. "Little ones," he cried, "open your eyes!" The monkeys felt solid ground beneath their feet and recognized their home territory. In great delight, every one of them ran back to the cave along the familiar roads and crowded in together with those waiting in the cave. They then lined up according to age and rank and paid tribute to the Monkey King. Wine and fruits were laid out for the welcome banquet. When asked how he had subdued the monster and rescued the young ones, Wu-k'ung presented a detailed rehearsal, and the monkeys broke into unending applause. "Where did you go, Great King?" they cried. "We never expected that you would acquire such skills!" "The year I left you all," Wu-k'ung said, "I drifted with the waves across the Great Eastern Ocean and reached the West Aparagodānīya Continent. I then arrived at the South Jambūdvīpa Continent, where I learned human ways, wearing this garment and these shoes. I swaggered along with the clouds for eight or nine years, but I had yet to learn the Great Art. I then crossed the Great Western Ocean and reached the West Aparagodānīya Continent.[19] After searching for a long time, I had the good fortune to discover an old Patriarch, who imparted to me the formula for enjoying the same age as Heaven, the secret of immortality." "Such luck is hard to meet even after ten thousand afflictions!" the monkeys said, all congratulating him. "Little ones," Wu-k'ung said, laughing again, "Another delight is that our entire family now has a name." "What is the name of the great king?" "My surname is Sun," replied Wu-k'ung, "And my religious name is Wu-k'ung." When the monkeys heard this, they all clapped their hands and shouted happily, "If the great king is Elder Sun, then we are all Junior Suns, Suns the Third, small Suns, tiny Suns—the Sun Family, the Sun Nation, and the Sun Cave!" So they all came and honored Elder Sun with large and small bowls of coconut and grape wine, of divine flowers and fruits. It was indeed one big happy family! Lo,

The surname is one, the self's return'd to its source.

This glory awaits—a name recorded in Heaven!

If you do not know what the result was and how Wu-k'ung fared in this territory, you must listen to the explanation in the next chapter.

Three

The Four Seas and the Thousand Mountains all bow
   in submission;
From the Hell of Ninefold Darkness are deleted
   the names of ten species.[1]

Now we were speaking of the Handsome Monkey King's triumphant return to his home country. After slaying the Monstrous King of Havoc and wresting from him his huge scimitar, he practiced daily with the little monkeys the art of war, teaching them how to sharpen bamboos for making spears, how to file wood for making swords, how to arrange flags and banners, how to go on patrol, how to advance or retreat, and how to pitch camp. For a long time he played thus with them. Suddenly he grew quiet and sat down, thinking out loud to himself, "The game we are playing here may turn out to be something quite serious. Suppose we disturb the rulers of men or of fowls and beasts, and they become offended; suppose they say that these military exercises of ours are subversive, and raise an army to destroy us. How can we meet them with our bamboo spears and wooden swords? We must have sharp swords and fine halberds. But what can be done at this moment?" When the monkeys heard this, they were all alarmed. "The great king's observation is very sound," they said, "but where can we obtain these things?" As they were speaking, four older monkeys came forward, two female monkeys with red buttocks and two bareback gibbons. Coming to the front, they said, "Great King, to be furnished with sharp-edged weapons is a very simple matter." "How is it simple?" asked Wu-k'ung. The four monkeys said, "East of our mountain, across two hundred miles of water, is the boundary of the Ao-lai Country. In that country there is a king who has numberless men and soldiers in his city, and there are bound to be all kinds of metalworks there. If the great king goes there, he can either buy weapons or have them made. Then you can teach us how to use them for the protection of our mountain, and this will be the stratagem for assuring ourselves of perpetuity." When Wu-k'ung heard this, he was filled with delight. "Play here, all of you," he said. "Let me make a trip."

Dear Monkey King! He quickly performed his cloud-somersault and crossed the two hundred miles of water in no time. On the other side he did indeed discover a city with broad streets and huge market-places, countless houses and numerous arches. Under the clear sky and bright sun, people were coming and going constantly. Wu-k'ung thought to himself, "There must be ready-made weapons around here. But going down there to buy a few pieces from them is not as good a bargain as getting them by magic." He therefore made the magic sign and recited a spell. Facing the ground on the southwest, he took a deep breath and then blew it out. At once it became a mighty wind, hurtling pebbles and rocks through the air. It was truly terrifying:

Thick clouds in vast formation moved o'er the world;
Black fog and dusky vapor darkened the Earth;
Waves churned in seas and rivers, affrighting fishes and crabs;
Boughs broke in mountain forests, wolves and tigers taking flight.
Traders and merchants were gone from stores and shops.
No single man was seen at sundry marts and malls.
The king retreated to his chamber from the royal court.
Officials, martial and civil, returned to their homes.
This wind toppled Buddha's throne of a thousand years
And shook to its foundations the Five-Phoenix Tower.

The wind arose and scattered the king and his subjects in the Ao-lai Country. Throughout the various boulevards and marketplaces, every family bolted the doors and windows and no one dared go outside. Wu-k'ung then lowered the direction of his cloud and rushed straight through the imperial gate. He found his way to the armory, knocked open the doors, and saw that there were countless weapons inside. Scimitars, spears, swords, halberds, battle-axes, scythes, whips, rakes, drumsticks, drums, bows, arrows, forks, and lances—every kind was available. Highly pleased, Wu-k'ung said to himself, "How many pieces can I possibly carry by myself? I'd better use the magic of body division to transport them." Dear Monkey King! He plucked a handful of hairs, chewed them to pieces in his mouth, and spat them out. Reciting the spell, he cried, "Change!" They changed into thousands of little monkeys, which snatched and grabbed the weapons. Those that were stronger took six or seven pieces, the weaker ones two or three pieces, and together they emptied out the armory. Wu-k'ung then mounted the cloud and performed the magic of displacement by calling up a great wind, which carried all the little monkeys back to their home.

We tell you now about the various monkeys, both great and small, who were playing outside the cave of the Flower-Fruit Mountain. They suddenly heard the sound of wind and saw in midair a huge horde of monkeys approaching, the sight of which made them all flee in terror and hide. In a moment, Wu-k'ung lowered his cloud and, shaking himself, collected the pieces of hair back onto his body. All the weapons were piled in front of the mountain. "Little ones," he shouted, "come and receive your weapons." The monkeys looked and saw Wu-k'ung standing alone on level ground. They came running to kowtow and ask what had happened. Wu-k'ung then recounted to them how he had made use of the mighty wind to transport the weapons. After expressing their gratitude, the monkeys all went to grab at the scimitars and snatch at the swords, to wield the axes and scramble for spears, to stretch the bows and mount the arrows. Shouting and screaming, they played all day long.

The following day, they marched in formation as usual. Assembling the monkeys, Wu-k'ung found that there were forty-seven thousand of them. This assembly greatly impressed all the wild beasts of the mountain—wolves, insects, tigers, leopards, mouse deer, fallow deer, river deer, foxes, wild cats, badgers, lions, elephants, apes, bears, antelopes, boars, musk-oxen, chamois, green one-horn buffaloes, wild hares, and giant mastiffs. Led by the various demon kings of no less than seventy-two caves, they all came to pay homage to the Monkey King. Henceforth they brought annual tributes and answered the roll call made every season. Some of them joined in the maneuvers; others supplied provisions in accordance with their rank. In an orderly fashion, they made the entire Flower-Fruit Mountain as strong as an iron bucket or a city of metal. The various demon kings also presented metal drums, colored banners, and helmets. The hurly-burly of marching and drilling went on day after day.

While the Handsome Monkey King was enjoying all this, he suddenly said to the multitude, "You all have become adept with the bow and arrow and proficient in the use of weapons. But this scimitar of mine is truly cumbersome, not at all to my liking. What can I do?" The four elder monkeys came forward and memorialized, "The great king is a divine sage, and therefore it is not fit for him to use an earthly weapon. We do not know, however, whether the great king is able to take a journey through water?" "Since I have known the Way," said Wu-k'ung, "I have the ability of seventy-two trans- formations. The cloud-somersault has unlimited power. I am familiar with the magic of body concealment and the magic of displacement. I can find my way to Heaven or I can enter the Earth. I can walk past the sun and the moon without casting a shadow, and I can penetrate stone and metal without hindrance. Water cannot drown me, nor fire burn me. Is there any place I can't go to?" "It's a good thing that the great king possesses such powers," said the four monkeys, "for the water below this sheet iron bridge of ours flows directly into the Dragon Palace of the Eastern Ocean. If you are willing to go down there, Great King, you will find the old Dragon King, from whom you may request some kind of weapon. Won't that be to your liking?" Hearing this, Wu-k'ung said with delight, "Let me make the trip!"

Dear Monkey King! He jumped to the bridgehead and employed the magic of water restriction. Making the magic sign with his fingers, he leaped into the waves, which parted for him, and he followed the waterway straight to the bottom of the Eastern Ocean. As he was walking, he suddenly ran into a yakṣa on patrol, who stopped him with the question, "What divine sage is this who comes pushing through the water? Speak plainly so that I can announce your arrival." Wu-k'ung said, "I am the Heaven-born sage Sun Wu-k'ung of the Flower-Fruit Mountain, a near neighbor of your old Dragon King. How is it that you don't recognize me?" When the yakṣa heard this, he hurried back to the Water-Crystal Palace to report. "Great King," he said, "there is outside a Heaven-born sage of the Flower- Fruit Mountain named Sun Wu-k'ung. He claims that he is a near neighbor of yours, and he is about to arrive at the palace." Ao-kuang, the Dragon King of the Eastern Ocean, arose immediately; accom- panied by dragon sons and grandsons, shrimp soldiers and crab generals, he came out for the reception. "High Immortal," he said, "please come in!" They went into the palace for proper introduction, and after offering Wu-k'ung the honored seat and tea, the king asked, "When did the high immortal become accomplished in the Way, and what kind of divine magic did he receive?" Wu-k'ung said, "Since the time of my birth, I have left the family to practice the Great Art. I have now acquired a birthless and deathless body. Recently I have been teaching my children how to protect our mountain cave, but unfortunately I am without an appropriate weapon. I have heard that my noble neighbor, who has long enjoyed living in this green-jade palace and its shell portals, must have many divine weapons to spare. I came specifically to ask for one of them." When the Dragon King heard this, he could hardly refuse. So he ordered a perch commander to bring out a long-handled scimitar, and presented it to his visitor. "Old Monkey doesn't know how to use a scimitar," said Wu-k'ung. "I beg you to give me something else." The Dragon King then commanded a whiting lieutenant together with an eel porter to carry out a nine-pronged fork. Jumping down from his seat, Wu-k'ung took hold of it and tried a few thrusts. He put it down, saying, "Light! Much too light! And it doesn't suit my hand. I beg you to give me another one." "High Immortal," said the Dragon King, laughing, "won't you even take a closer look? This fork weighs three thousand six hundred pounds." "It doesn't suit my hand," Wu-k'ung said, "it doesn't suit my hand!" The Dragon King was becoming rather fearful; he ordered a bream admiral and a carp brigadier to carry out a giant halberd, weighing seven thousand two hundred pounds. When he saw this, Wu-k'ung ran forward and took hold of it. He tried a few thrusts and parries and then stuck it in the ground, saying, "It's still light! Much too light!" The old Dragon King was completely unnerved. "High Immortal," he said, "there's no weapon in my palace heavier than this halberd." Laughing, Wu-k'ung said, "As the old saying goes, 'Who worries about the Dragon King's lacking treasures!' Go and look some more, and if you find something I like, I'll offer you a good price." "There really aren't any more here," said the Dragon King.

As they were speaking, the dragon mother and her daughter slipped out and said, "Great King, we can see that this is definitely not a sage with meager abilities. Inside our ocean treasury is that piece of rare magic iron by which the depth of the Heavenly River[2] is fixed. These past few days the iron has been glowing with a strange and lovely light. Could this be a sign that it should be taken out to meet this sage?" "That," said the Dragon King, "was the measure with which the Great Yü[3] fixed the depths of rivers and oceans when he conquered the Flood. It's a piece of magic iron, but of what use could it be to him?" "Let's not be concerned with whether he could find any use for it," said the Dragon mother. "Let's give it to him, and he can do whatever he wants with it. The important thing is to get him out of this palace!" The old Dragon King agreed and told

Wu-k'ung the whole story. "Take it out and let me see it," said Wu-k'ung. Waving his hands, the Dragon King said, "We can't move it! We can't even lift it! The high immortal must go there himself to take a look." "Where is it?" asked Wu-k'ung. "Take me there." The Dragon King accordingly led him to the center of the ocean treasury, where all at once they saw a thousand shafts of golden light. Pointing to the spot, the Dragon King said, "That's it—the thing that is glowing." Wu-k'ung girded up his clothes and went forward to touch it; it was an iron rod more than twenty feet long and as thick as a barrel. Using all his might, he lifted it with both hands, saying, "It's a little too long and too thick. It would be more serviceable if it were somewhat shorter and thinner." Hardly had he finished speaking when the treasure shrunk a few feet in length and became a layer thinner. "Smaller still would be even better," said Wu-k'ung, giving it another bounce in his hands. Again the treasure became smaller. Highly pleased, Wu-k'ung took it out of the ocean treasury to examine it. He found a golden hoop at each end, with solid black iron in between. Immediately adjacent to one of the hoops was the inscription, "The Compliant Golden-Hooped Rod. Weight: thirteen thousand five hundred pounds." He thought to himself in secret delight, "This treasure, I suppose, must be most compliant with one's wishes." As he walked, he was deliberating in his mind and murmuring to himself, bouncing the rod in his hands, "Shorter and thinner still would be marvelous!" By the time he took it outside, the rod was no more than twenty feet in length and had the thickness of a rice bowl.

See how he displayed his power now! He wielded the rod to make lunges and passes, engaging in mock combat all the way back to the Water-Crystal Palace. The old Dragon King was so terrified that he shook with fear, and the dragon princes were all panic-stricken. Sea-turtles and tortoises drew in their necks; fishes, shrimps, and crabs all hid themselves. Wu-k'ung held the treasure in his hands and sat in the Water-Crystal Palace. Laughing, he said to the Dragon King, "I am indebted to my good neighbor for his profound kindness." "Please don't mention it," said the Dragon King. "This piece of iron is very useful," said Wu-k'ung, "but I have one further statement to make." "What sort of statement does the high immortal wish to make?" asked the Dragon King. Wu-k'ung said, "Had there been no such iron, I would have let the matter drop. Now that I have it in my hands, I can see that I am wearing the wrong kind of clothes to go with it. What am I to do? If you have any martial apparel, you might as well give me some too. I would thank you most heartily." "This, I confess, is not in my possession," said the Dragon King. Wu-k'ung said, "A solitary guest will not disturb two hosts. Even if you claim that you don't have any, I shall never walk out of this door." "Let the high immortal take the trouble of going to another ocean," said the Dragon King. "He might turn up something there." "To visit three homes is not as convenient as sitting in one," said Wu-k'ung, "I beg you to give me one outfit." "I really don't have one," said the Dragon King, "for if I did, I would have presented it to you." "Is that so?" said Wu-k'ung. "Let me try the iron on you!" "High Immortal," the Dragon King said nervously, "don't ever raise your hand! Don't ever raise your hand! Let me see whether my brothers have any and we'll try to give you one." "Where are your honored brothers?" asked Wu-k'ung. "They are," said the Dragon King, "Ao-ch'in, Dragon King of the Southern Ocean; Ao-shun, Dragon King of the Northern Ocean; and Ao-jun, Dragon King of the Western Ocean." "Old Monkey is not going to their places," said Wu-k'ung. "For as the common saying goes, 'Three in bond can't compete with two in hand.' I'm merely requesting that you find something casual here and give it to me. That's all." "There's no need for the high immortal to go anywhere," said the Dragon King. "I have in my palace an iron drum and a golden bell. Whenever there is any emergency, we beat the drum and strike the bell and my brothers are here shortly." "In that case," said Wu-k'ung, "go beat the drum and strike the bell." The turtle general went at once to strike the bell, while the tortoise marshal came to beat the drum.

Soon after the drum and the bell had sounded, the Dragon Kings of the Three Oceans got the message and arrived promptly, all congregating in the outer courtyard. "Elder Brother," said Ao-ch'in, "what emergency made you beat the drum and strike the bell?" "Good Brother," answered the old Dragon, "it's a long story! We have here a certain Heaven-born sage from the Flower-Fruit Mountain, who came here and claimed to be my near neighbor. He subsequently demanded a weapon; the steel fork I presented he deemed too small, and the halberd I offered too light. Finally he himself took that piece of rare, divine iron by which the depth of the Heavenly River was fixed and used it for mock combat. He is now sitting in the palace and also demanding some sort of battle dress.

We have none of that here. So we sounded the drum and the bell to invite you all to come. If you happen to have some such outfit, please give it to him so that I can send him out of this door!" When Ao-ch'in heard this, he was outraged. "Let us brothers call our army together," he said, "and take him captive. What's wrong with that?" "Don't talk about taking him captive!" the old Dragon said, "don't talk about taking him captive! That piece of iron—a small stroke with it is deadly and a light tap is fatal! The slightest touch will crack the skin and a small rap will injure the muscles!" Ao-jun, the Dragon King of the Western Ocean said, "Second elder brother should not raise his hand against him. Let us rather assemble an outfit for him and get him out of this place. We can then present a formal complaint to Heaven, and Heaven will send its own punishment." "You are right," said Ao-shun, the Dragon King of the Northern Ocean, "I have here a pair of cloud-treading shoes the color of lotus root." Ao-jun, the Dragon King of the Western Ocean said, "I brought along a cuirass of chainmail made of yellow gold." "And I have a cap with erect phoenix plumes, made of red gold," said Ao-ch'in, the Dragon King of the Southern Ocean. The old Dragon King was delighted and brought them into the Water-Crystal Palace to present the gifts. Wu-k'ung duly put on the gold cap, the gold cuirass, and cloud-treading shoes, and, wielding his compliant rod, he fought his way out in mock combat, yelling to the dragons, "Sorry to have bothered you!" The Dragon Kings of the Four Oceans were outraged, and they consulted together about filing a formal complaint, of which we make no mention here.

Look at that Monkey King! He opened up the waterway and went straight back to the head of the sheet iron bridge. The four old monkeys were leading the other monkeys and waiting beside the bridge. They suddenly beheld Wu-k'ung leaping out of the waves: there was not a drop of water on his body as he walked onto the bridge, all radiant and golden. The various monkeys were so astonished that they all knelt down, crying, "Great King, what marvels! What marvels!" Beaming broadly, Wu-k'ung ascended his high throne and set up the iron rod right in the center. Not knowing any better, the monkeys all came and tried to pick the treasure up. It was rather like a dragonfly attempting to shake an iron-wood tree: they could not budge it an inch! Biting their fingers and sticking out their tongues, every one of them said, "O Father, it's so heavy! How did you ever manage to bring it here?" Wu-k'ung walked up to the rod, stretched forth his hands, and picked it up. Laughing, he said to them, "Everything has its owner. This treasure has presided in the ocean treasury for who knows how many thousands of years, and it just happened to glow recently. The Dragon King only recognized it as a piece of black iron, though it is also said to be the divine rarity which fixed the bottom of the Heavenly River. All those fellows together could not lift or move it, and they asked me to take it myself. At first, this treasure was more than twenty feet long and as thick as a barrel. After I struck it once and expressed my feeling that it was too large, it grew smaller. I wanted it smaller still, and again it grew smaller. For a third time I commanded it, and it grew smaller still! When I looked at it in the light, it had on it the inscription, 'The Compliant Golden-Hooped Rod. Weight: thirteen thousand five hundred pounds.' Stand aside, all of you. Let me ask it to go through some more transformations." He held the treasure in his hands and called out, "Smaller, smaller, smaller!" and at once it shrank to the size of a tiny embroidery needle, small enough to be hidden inside the ear. Awe-struck, the monkeys cried, "Great King! Take it out and play with it some more." The Monkey King took it out from his ear and placed it on his palm. "Bigger, bigger, bigger!" he shouted, and again it grew to the thickness of a barrel and more than twenty feet long. He became so delighted playing with it that he jumped onto the bridge and walked out of the cave. Grasping the treasure in his hands, he began to perform the magic of cosmic imitation. He bent over and cried, "Grow!" and at once grew to be ten thousand feet tall, with a head like the T'ai Mountain and a chest like a rugged peak, eyes like lightning and a mouth like a blood bowl, and teeth like swords and halberds. The cudgel in his hands was of such a size that its top reached the thirty-third Heaven and its bottom the eighteenth layer of Hell. Tigers, leopards, wolves, and crawling creatures, all the monsters of the mountain and the demon kings of the seventy-two caves, were so terrified that they kowtowed and paid homage to the Monkey King in fear and trembling. Presently he revoked his magical appearance and changed the treasure back into a tiny embroidery needle stored in his ear. He returned to the cave dwelling, but the demon kings of the various caves were still frightened, and they continued to come to pay their respects.

At this time, the banners were unfurled, the drums sounded, and the brass gongs struck loudly. A great banquet of a hundred delicacies was given, and the cups were filled to overflowing with the fruit of the vines and the juices of the coconut. They drank and feasted for a long time, and they engaged in military exercises as before. The Monkey King made the four old monkeys mighty commanders of his troops by appointing the two female monkeys with red buttocks as marshals Ma and Liu, and the two bareback gibbons as generals Pêng and Pa. The four mighty commanders, moreover, were entrusted with all matters concerning fortification, pitching camps, reward, and punishment. Having settled all this, the Monkey King felt completely at ease to soar on the clouds and ride the mist, to tour the four seas and disport himself in a thousand mountains. Displaying his martial skill, he made extensive visits to various heroes and warriors; performing his magic, he made many good friends. At this time, moreover, he entered into fraternal alliance with six other monarchs: the Bull Monster King, the Dragon Monster King, the Garuda Monster King, the Long-Haired Lion King, the Female Monkey King, and the Giant Ape King. Together with the Handsome Monkey King, they formed a fraternal order of seven. Day after day they discussed civil and military arts, exchanged wine cups and goblets, sang and danced to songs and strings. They gathered in the morning and parted in the evening; there was not a single pleasure that they overlooked, covering a distance of ten thousand miles as if it were but the span of their own courtyard. As the saying has it, one nod of the head goes farther than three thousand miles; one twist of the torso covers more than eight hundred.

One day, the four mighty commanders had been told to prepare a great banquet in their own cave, and the six kings were invited to the feast. They killed cows and slaughtered horses; they sacrificed to Heaven and Earth. The various imps were ordered to dance and sing, and they all drank until they were thoroughly drunk. After sending the six kings off, Wu-k'ung also rewarded the leaders great and small with gifts. Reclining in the shade of pine trees near the sheet iron bridge, he fell asleep in a moment. The four mighty commanders led the crowd to form a protective circle around him, not daring to raise their voices. In his sleep the Handsome Monkey King saw two men approach with a summons with the three words "Sun Wu-k'ung" written on it. They walked up to him and, without a word, tied him up with a rope and dragged him off. The soul of the Handsome Monkey King was reeling from side to side. They reached the edge of a city. The Monkey King was gradually coming to himself, when he lifted up his head and suddenly saw above the city an iron sign bearing in large letters the three words "Region of Darkness." The Handsome Monkey King at once became fully conscious. "The Region of Darkness is the abode of Yama, King of Death," he said. "Why am I here?" "Your age in the World of Life has come to an end," the two men said. "The two of us were given this summons to arrest you." When the Monkey King heard this, he said, "I, old Monkey himself, have transcended the Three Regions and the Five Phases; hence I am no longer under Yama's jurisdiction. Why is he so confused that he wants to arrest me?" The two summoners paid scant attention. Yanking and pulling, they were determined to haul him inside. Growing angry, the Monkey King whipped out his treasure. One wave of it turned it into the thickness of a rice bowl; he raised his hands once, and the two summoners were reduced to hash. He untied the rope, freed his hands, and fought his way into the city, wielding the rod. Bull-headed demons hid in terror, and horse-faced demons fled in every direction. A band of ghost soldiers ran up to the Palace of Darkness, crying, "Great Kings! Disaster! Disaster! Outside there's a hairy-faced thunder god fighting his way in!"

Their report alarmed the Ten Kings of the Underworld so much that they quickly straightened out their attire and went out to see what was happening. Discovering a fierce and angry figure, they lined up according to their ranks and greeted him with loud voices: "High Immortal, tell us your name. High Immortal, tell us your name." "I am the Heaven-born sage Sun Wu-k'ung from the Water-Curtain Cave in the Flower-Fruit Mountain," said the Monkey King, "what kind of officials are you?" "We are the Emperors of Darkness," answered the Ten Kings, bowing, "the Ten Kings of the Underworld." "Tell me each of your names at once," said Wu-k'ung, "or I'll give you a drubbing." The Ten Kings said, "We are: King Ch'in-Kuang, King of the Beginning River, King of the Sung Emperor, King of Avenging Ministers, King Yama, King of Equal Ranks, King of the T'ai Mountain, King of City Markets, King of the Complete Change, and King of the Turning Wheel."[4] "Since you have all ascended the thrones of kingship," said Wu-k'ung, "you should be intelligent beings, responsible in rewards and punishments. Why are you so ignorant of good and evil? Old Monkey has acquired the Tao and attained immortality. I enjoy the same age as Heaven, and I have transcended the Three Regions and leapt clear of the Five Phases. Why, then, did you send men to arrest me?" "High Immortal," said the Ten Kings, "let your anger subside. There are many people in this world with the same name and surname. Couldn't the summoners have made a mistake?" "Nonsense! Nonsense!" said Wu-k'ung. "The proverb says, 'Magistrates err, clerks err, but the man with the warrant never errs!'[5] Quick, get out your register of births and deaths, and let me have a look." When the Ten Kings heard this, they invited him to go into the palace to see for himself.

Holding his compliant rod, Wu-k'ung went straight up to the Palace of Darkness and, facing south, sat down in the middle. The Ten Kings immediately had the judge in charge of the records bring out his books for examination. The judge, who did not dare tarry, hastened into a side room and brought out five or six books of documents and the ledgers on the ten species of living beings. He went through them one by one—short-haired creatures, furry creatures, winged creatures, crawling creatures, and scaly creatures—but he did not find his name. He then proceeded to the file on monkeys. You see, though this monkey resembled a human being, he was not listed under the names of men; though he resembled the short-haired creatures, he did not dwell in their kingdoms; though he resembled other animals, he was not subject to the unicorn; and though he resembled flying creatures, he was not governed by the phoenix. He had, therefore, a separate ledger, which Wu-k'ung examined himself. Under the heading "Soul 1350" he found the name Sun Wu-k'ung recorded, with the description: "Heaven-born Stone Monkey. Age: three hundred and forty-two years. A good end." Wu-k'ung said, "I really don't remember my age. All I want is to erase my name. Bring me a brush." The judge hurriedly fetched the brush and soaked it in heavy ink. Wu-k'ung took the ledger on monkeys and crossed out all the names he could find in it. Throwing down the ledger, he said, "That's the end of the account, the end of the account! Now I'm truly not your subject." Brandishing his rod, he fought his way out of the Region of Darkness. The Ten Kings did not dare approach him.

They went instead to the Green Cloud Palace to consult the Bodhisattva King Kṣitigarbha and made plans to report the incident to Heaven, which does not concern us for the moment.

While our Monkey King was fighting his way out of the city, he was suddenly caught in a clump of grass, and stumbled. Waking up with a start, he realized that it was all a dream. As he was stretching himself, he heard the four mighty commanders and the various monkeys crying with a loud voice, "Great King! How much wine did you imbibe? You've slept all night long. Aren't you awake yet?" "Sleeping is nothing to get excited about," said Wu-k'ung, "but I dreamed that two men came to arrest me, and I didn't perceive their intention until they brought me to the outskirts of the Region of Darkness. Showing my power, I protested right up to the Palace of Darkness and argued with the Ten Kings. I went through our ledger of births and deaths and crossed out all our names. Those fellows have no hold over us now." The various monkeys all kowtowed to express their gratitude. From that time onward there were many mountain monkeys which did not grow old, for their names were not registered in the Underworld. When the Handsome Monkey King finished his account of what had happened, the four mighty commanders reported the story to the demon kings of various caves, who all came to tender their congratulations. Only a few days had passed when the six sworn brothers also came to congratulate him, all of them delighted about the cancelation of the names. We shall not elaborate here on their joyful gathering.

We shall turn instead to the Great Benevolent Sage of Heaven, the Celestial Jade Emperor of the Most Venerable Deva, who was holding court one day in the Treasure Hall of Divine Mists, the Cloud Palace of Golden Arches. The divine ministers, civil and military, were just gathering for the morning session when suddenly the Taoist immortal Ch'iu Hung-chi announced, "Your Majesty. outside the Translucent Palace, Ao-kuang, Dragon King of the Eastern Ocean, is awaiting your command to present a memorial to the Throne." The Jade Emperor gave the order to have him brought forth, and Ao-kuang was led into the Hall of Divine Mists. After he had paid his respects, a divine page boy in charge of documents received the memorial, and the Jade Emperor read it from the beginning. The memorial said:

From the lowly water region of the Eastern Ocean at the East Pūrvavideha Continent, the small dragon subject, Ao-kuang, humbly informs the Wise Lord of Heaven, the Most Eminent High God and Ruler, that a bogus immortal, Sun Wu-k'ung, born of the Flower-Fruit Mountain and resident of the Water-Curtain Cave, has recently abused your small dragon, gaining a seat in his water home by force. He demanded a weapon, employing power and intimidation; he asked for martial attire, unleashing violence and threats. He terrorized my water kinsmen, and scattered turtles and tortoises. The Dragon of the Southern Ocean trembled; the Dragon of the Western Ocean was filled with horror; the Dragon of the Northern Ocean drew back his head to surrender; and your subject Ao-kuang flexed his body to do obeisance. We presented him with the divine treasure of an iron rod and the gold cap with phoenix plumes; giving him also a chain-mail cuirass and cloud-treading shoes, we sent him off courteously. But even then he was bent on displaying his martial prowess and magical powers, and all he could say to us was "Sorry to have bothered you!" We are indeed no match for him, nor are we able to subdue him. Your subject therefore presents this petition and humbly begs for imperial justice. We earnestly beseech you to dispatch the heavenly host and capture this monster, so that tranquility may be restored to the oceans and prosperity to the Lower Region. Thus we present this memorial.

When the Holy Emperor had finished reading, he gave the command: "Let the Dragon God return to the ocean. We shall send our generals to arrest the culprit." The old Dragon King gratefully touched his forehead to the ground and left. From below the Immortal Elder Ko, the Divine Teacher, also brought forth the report. "Your majesty, the Minister of Darkness, King Ch'in-kuang, supported by the Bodhisattva King Kṣitigarbha, Pope of the Underworld, has arrived to present his memorial." The jade girl in charge of communication came from the side to receive this document, which the Jade Emperor also read from the beginning. The memorial said:

The Region of Darkness is the nether region proper to Earth. As Heaven is for gods and Earth for ghosts, so life and death proceed in cyclic succession. Fowls are born and animals die; male and female, they multiply. Births and transformations, the male begotten of the procreative female—such is the order of Nature, and it cannot be changed. But now appears Sun Wu-k'ung, a Heaven-born baneful monkey from the Water-Curtain Cave in the Flower-Fruit Mountain, who practices evil and violence, and resists our proper summons. Exercising magic powers, he utterly defeated the ghostly messengers of Ninefold Darkness; exploiting brute force, he terrorized the Ten Merciful Kings. He caused great confusion in the Palace of Darkness; he abrogated by force the Record of Names, so that the category of monkeys is now beyond control, and inordinately long life is given to the simian family. The wheel of transmigration is stopped, for birth and death are eliminated in each kind of monkey. Your poor monk therefore risks offending your heavenly authority in presenting this memorial. We humbly beg you to send forth your divine army and subdue this monster, to the end that life and death may once more be regulated and the Underworld rendered perpetually secure. Respectfully we present this memorial.

When the Jade Emperor had finished reading, he again gave a command: "Let the Lord of Darkness return to the Underworld. We shall send our generals to arrest this culprit." King Ch'in-kuang also touched his head to the ground gratefully and left.

The Great Heavenly Deva called together his various immortal subjects, both civil and military, and asked, "When was this baneful monkey born, and in which generation did he begin his career? How is it that he has become so powerfully accomplished in the Great Art?" Scarcely had he finished speaking when, from the ranks, Thousand-Mile Eye and Fair-Wind Ear stepped forward. "This monkey," they said, "is the Heaven-born stone monkey of three hundred years ago. At that time he did not seem to amount to much, and we do not know where he acquired the knowledge of self-cultivation these last few years and became an immortal. Now he knows how to subdue dragons and tame tigers,[6] and thus he is able to annul by force the Register of Death." "Which one of you divine generals," asked the Jade Emperor, "wishes to go down there to subdue him?" Scarcely had he finished speaking when the Long-Life Spirit of the Planet Venus came forward from the ranks and prostrated himself. "Highest and Holiest," he said, "within the three regions, all creatures endowed with the nine apertures can, through exercise, become immortals. It is not surprising that this monkey, with a body nurtured by Heaven and Earth, a frame born of the sun and moon, should achieve immortality, seeing that his head points to Heaven and his feet walk on Earth, and that he feeds on the dew and the mist. Now that he has the power to subdue dragons and tame tigers, how is he different from a human being? Your subject therefore makes so bold as to ask your majesty to remember the compassionate grace of Creation and issue a decree of pacification. Let him be summoned to the Upper Region and given some kind of official duties. His name will be recorded in the Register and we can control him here. If he is receptive to the Heavenly decree, he will be rewarded and promoted hereafter; but if he is disobedient to your command, we shall arrest him forthwith. Such an action will spare us a military expedition in the first place, and, in the second, permit us to receive into our midst another immortal in an orderly manner."

The Jade Emperor was highly pleased with this statement, and he said, "We shall follow the counsel of our minister." He then ordered the Star Spirit of Songs and Letters to compose the decree, and delegated the Gold Star of Venus to be the viceroy of peace.

Having received the decree, the Gold Star went out of the South Heavenly Gate, lowered the direction of his hallowed cloud, and headed straight for the Flower-Fruit Mountain and the Water-Curtain Cave. He said to the various little monkeys, "I am the Heavenly messenger sent from above. I have with me an imperial decree to invite your great king to go to the Upper Region. Report this to him quickly!" The monkeys outside the cave passed the word along one by one until it reached the depth of the cave. "Great King," one of the monkeys said, "there's an old man outside bearing a document on his back. He says that he is a messenger sent from Heaven, and he has an imperial decree of invitation for you." Upon hearing this, the Handsome Monkey King was exceedingly pleased. "These last two days," he said, "I was just thinking about taking a little trip to Heaven, and the Heavenly messenger has already come to invite me!" The Monkey King quickly straightened out his attire and went to the door for the reception. The Gold Star came into the center of the cave and stood still with his face toward the south. "I am the Gold Star of Venus from the West," he said. "I came down to Earth, bearing the imperial decree of pacification from the Jade Emperor, and invite you to go to Heaven to receive an immortal appointment." Laughing, Wu-k'ung said, "I am most grateful for the Old Star's visit." He then gave the order: "Little ones, prepare a banquet to entertain our guest." The Gold Star said, "As a bearer of imperial decree, I cannot remain here long. I must ask the Great King to go with me at once. After your glorious promotion, we shall have many occasions to converse at our leisure." "We are honored by your presence," said Wu-k'ung; "I am sorry that you have to leave with empty hands!" He then called the four mighty commanders together for this admonition: "Be diligent in teaching and drilling the young ones. Let me go up to Heaven to take a look and to see whether I can have you all brought up there too to live with me." The four mighty commanders indicated their obedience. This Monkey King mounted the cloud with the Gold Star and rose up into the sky. So,

He ascended to the high rank of immortals from the Sky;

His name's enrolled in the cloud columns and treasure scrolls.

We do not know what sort of rank or appointment he received. You must listen to the explanation in the next chapter.

Four

Appointed to the post of Pi-ma, how can he be
   satisfied?
Though his name is Equal to Heaven, he is still
   discontented.

The Gold Star of Venus left the depths of the cave dwelling with the Handsome Monkey King, and together they rose by mounting the clouds. But the cloud-somersault of Wu-k'ung, you see, is no common magic; its speed is tremendous. Soon he left the Gold Star far behind and arrived first at the South Heavenly Gate. He was about to dismount from the cloud and go in when the Devarāja Virūḍhaka, leading P'ang, Liu, Kou, Pi, Têng, Hsin, Chang, and T'ao, the various divine heroes, barred the way with spears, scimitars, swords, and halberds and refused him entrance. The Monkey King said, "What a deceitful fellow that Gold Star is! If old Monkey has been invited here, why have these people been ordered to use their swords and spears to bar my entrance?" He was protesting loudly when the Gold Star arrived in haste. "Old man," said Wu-k'ung angrily to his face, "why did you deceive me? You told me that I was invited by the Jade Emperor's decree of pacification. Why then did you get these people to block the Heavenly Gate and prevent my entering?" "Let the Great King calm down," the Gold Star said, laughing. "Since you have never been to the Hall of Heaven before, nor have you been given a name, you are quite unknown to the various Heavenly guardians. How can they let you in on their own authority? Once you have seen the Heavenly Deva, received an appointment, and had your name listed in the Immortal Register, you can go in and out as you please. Who would then obstruct your way?" "If that's how it is," said Wu-k'ung, "it's all right. But I'm not going in by myself." "Then go in with me," said the Gold Star, pulling him by the hand.

As they approached the gate, the Gold Star called out loudly, "Guardians of the Heavenly Gate, lieutenants great and small, make way! This person is an immortal from the region below, whom I have summoned by the imperial decree of the Jade Emperor." The Devarāja Virūḍhaka and the various divine heroes immediately lowered their weapons and stepped aside, and the Monkey King finally believed what he had been told. He walked slowly inside with the Gold Star and looked around. For it was truly

His first ascent to the Region Above,
His sudden entrance into the Hall of Heaven,
Where ten thousand shafts of golden light whirled as a coral rainbow,
And a thousand layers of hallowed air diffused mist of purple.
Look at that South Heavenly Gate!
Its deep shades of green
From glazed tiles were made;
Its radiant battlements
Adorned with treasure jade.
On two sides were posted scores of celestial sentinels,
Each of whom, standing tall beside the pillars,
Carried bows and clutched banners.
All around were sundry divine beings in golden armor,
Each of them holding halberds and whips,
Or wielding scimitars and swords.
Impressive may be the outer court;
Overwhelming is the sight within!
In the inner halls stood several huge pillars
Coiled around with red-whiskered dragons whose scales of gold gleamed in the sun.
There were, moreover, a few long bridges;
Above them crimson-headed phoenixes circled with soaring plumes of many hues.
Bright mist shimmered in the light of the sky.
Green fog descending obscured the stars.
Thirty-three heavenly mansions were found up here,
With names like the Scattered Cloud, the Vaiśravaṇa, the Pānca-vidyā, the Suyāma, the Nirmāṇarati . . .[1]
On the roof of every mansion the ridge held a stately golden beast.
There were also the seventy-two treasure halls,
With names like the Morning Assembly, the Transcendent Void, the Precious Light, the Heavenly King, the Divine Minister . . .
In every hall beneath the pillars stood rows of jade unicorn.
On the Platform of Canopus,[2]

There were flowers unfading in a thousand millennia;
Beside the oven for refining herbs,
There were exotic grasses growing green for ten thousand years.
He went before the Tower of Homage to the Sage,
Where he saw robes of royal purple gauze
Brilliant as stars refulgent,
Caps the shape of hibiscus,
Resplendent with gold and precious stones,
And pins of jade and shoes of pearl,
And purple sashes and golden ornaments.
When the golden bells swayed to their striking,
The memorial of the three Judges[3] would cross the vermilion[4]
    courtyard;
When the drums of Heaven were sounded,
Ten thousand sages of the royal audience would honor the Jade
    Emperor.
He went, too, to the Treasure Hall of Divine Mists
Where nails of gold penetrated frames of jade,
And colorful phoenixes danced atop scarlet doors.
Here were covered bridges and winding corridors
Displaying everywhere openwork carvings most elegant;
And eaves crowding together in layers three and four,
On each of which reared up phoenixes and dragons.
There was high above
A round dome big, bright, and brilliant—
Its shape, a huge gourd of purple gold,
Below which guardian goddesses hung out their fans
And jade maidens held up their immortal veils.
Ferocious were the sky marshals overseeing the court;
Dignified, the divine officials protecting the throne.
There at the center, on a crystal platter,
Tablets of the Great Monad Elixir were heaped;
And rising out of the cornelian vases
Were several branches of twisting coral.
So it was that
Rare goods of every order were found in Heaven's Hall,
And nothing like them on Earth could ever be seen—
Those golden arches, silver coaches, and that heavenly house,

Those coralline blooms and jasper plants with their buds of jade.
The jade rabbit passed the platform to adore the king.
The golden crow flew by to worship the sage.[5]
Blessed was the Monkey King to come to this heavenly realm,
He who was not mired in the filthy soil of man.

The Gold Star of Venus led the Handsome Monkey King to the Treasure Hall of Divine Mists, and, without waiting for further announcement, they went into the imperial presence. While the Star prostrated himself, Wu-k'ung stood erect by him. Showing no respect, he cocked his ear only to listen to the report of the Gold Star. "According to your decree," said the Gold Star, "your subject has brought the bogus immortal." "Which one is the bogus immortal?" asked the Jade Emperor graciously. Only then did Wu-k'ung bow and reply, "None other than old Monkey!" Blanching with horror, the various divine officials said, "That wild ape! Already he has failed to prostrate himself before the Throne, and now he dares to come forward with such an insolent reply as 'None other than old Monkey'! He is worthy of death, worthy of death!" "That fellow Sun Wu-k'ung is a bogus immortal from the region below," announced the Jade Emperor, "and he has only recently acquired the form of a human being. We shall pardon him this time for his ignorance of court etiquette." "Thank you, Your Majesty," cried the various divine officials. Only then did the Monkey King bow deeply with folded hands and utter a cry of gratitude. The Jade Emperor then ordered the divine officials, both civil and military, to see what vacant appointment there might be for Sun Wu-k'ung to receive. From the side came the Star Spirit of Wu-ch'ü, who reported, "In every mansion and hall everywhere in the Palace of Heaven, there is no lack of ministers. Only at the imperial stables is a supervisor needed." "Let him be made a pi-ma-wên,"[6] proclaimed the Jade Emperor. The various subjects again shouted their thanks, but Monkey only bowed deeply and gave a loud whoop of gratitude. The Jade Emperor then sent the Star Spirit of Jupiter to accompany him to the stables.

The Monkey King went happily with the Star Spirit of Jupiter to the stables in order to assume his duties. The Star Spirit then returned to his own mansion. At the stables, he gathered together the deputy and assistant supervisors, the accountants and stewards, and other officials both great and small and made thorough investigation of all

the affairs of the stables. There were about a thousand celestial
horses,[7] and they were all
    Hua-lius and Ch'i-chis
    Lu-erhs and Hsien-lis,
    Consorts of Dragons and Purple Swallows,
    Folded Wings and Su-hsiangs,
    Chüeh-t'is and Silver Hooves,
    Yao-niaos and Flying Yellows,
    Chestnuts and Faster-than-Arrows,
    Red Hares and Speedier-than-Lights,
    Leaping Lights and Vaulting Shadows,
    Rising Fogs and Triumphant Yellows,
    Wind Chasers and Distance Breakers,
    Flying Pinions and Surging Airs,
    Rushing Winds and Fiery Lightnings,
    Copper Sparrows and Drifting Clouds,
    Dragonlike piebalds and Tigerlike pintos,
    Dust Quenchers and Purple Scales,
    And Ferghanas[8] from the Four Corners.
    Like the Eight Steeds and Nine Stallions
    They have no rivals within a thousand miles!
    Such are these fine horses,
    Every one of which
    Neighs like the wind and gallops like thunder to show a mighty
      spirit.
    They tread the mist and mount the clouds with unflagging
      strength.
Our Monkey King went through the lists and made a thorough
inspection of the horses. Within the imperial stables, the accountants
were in charge of getting supplies; the stewards groomed and washed
the horses, chopped hay, watered them, and prepared their food;
and the deputies and assistants saw to the overall management.
Never resting, the pi-ma oversaw the care of the horses, fussing with
them by day and watching over them diligently by night. Those
horses that wanted to sleep were stirred up and fed; those that
wanted to gallop were caught and placed in the stalls. When the
celestial horses saw him, they all behaved most properly and they
were so well cared for that their flanks became swollen with fat.

More than half a month soon went by, and on one leisurely morning, the various department ministers gave a banquet to welcome him and congratulate him.

While they were drinking happily, the Monkey King suddenly put down his cup and asked: "What sort of rank is this pi-ma-wên of mine?" "The rank and the title are the same," they said. "But what ministerial grade is it?" "It does not have a grade," they said, "If it does not have a grade," said the Monkey King, "I suppose it must be the very highest." "Not at all," they replied, "it can only be called 'the unclassified'!" The Monkey King said, "What do you mean by 'the unclassified'?" "It is really the meanest level," they said. "This kind of minister is the lowest of the low ranks; hence he can only look after horses. Take the case of Your Honor, who, since your arrival, have been so diligent in discharging your duties. If the horses are fattened, you will only earn yourself a 'Fairly Good!' If they look at all thin, you will be roundly rebuked. And if they are seriously hurt or wounded, you will be prosecuted and fined." When the Monkey King heard this, fire leaped up from his heart. "So that's the kind of contempt they have for old Monkey!" he cried angrily, gnashing his teeth. "At the Flower-Fruit Mountain I was honored as king and patriarch. How dare they trick me into coming to look after horses for them? If horse tending is such a menial service, reserved only for the young and lowly, how did they intend to treat me? I won't do this anymore! I won't do this anymore! I'm leaving right now!" With a crash, he kicked over his official desk and took out the treasure from his ear. One wave of his hand and it had the thickness of a rice bowl. Delivering blows in all directions, he fought his way out of the imperial stables and went straight to the South Heavenly Gate. The various celestial guardians, knowing that he had been officially appointed a pi-ma-wên, did not dare stop him and allowed him to fight his way out of the Heavenly Gate.

In a moment, he lowered the direction of his cloud and returned to the Flower-Fruit Mountain. The four mighty commanders were seen drilling troops with the Monster Kings of various caves. "Little ones," this Monkey King cried in a loud voice, "old Monkey has returned!" The flock of monkeys all came to kowtow and received him into the depths of the cave dwelling. As the Monkey King ascended his throne, they busily prepared a banquet to welcome him. "Receive our congratulations, Great King," they said. "Having gone to the region above for more than ten years, you must be returning in success and glory." "I have been away for only half a month," said the Monkey King. "How can it be more than ten years?" "Great King," said the various monkeys, "you are not aware of time and season when you are in Heaven. One day in Heaven above is equal to a year on Earth. May we ask the Great King what ministerial appointment he received?" "Don't mention that! Don't mention that!" said the Monkey King, waving his hand. "It embarrasses me to death! That Jade Emperor does not know how to use talent. Seeing the features of old Monkey, he appointed me to something called the pi-ma-wên, which actually means taking care of horses for him. It's a job too low even to be classified! I didn't know this when I first assumed my duties, and so I managed to have some fun at the imperial stables. But when I asked my colleagues today, I discovered what a degraded position it was. I was so furious that I knocked over the banquet they were giving me and rejected the title. That's why I came back down." "Welcome back!" said the various monkeys, "welcome back! Our Great King can be the sovereign of this blessed cave dwelling with the greatest honor and happiness. Why should he go away to be someone's stable boy?" "Little ones," they cried, "send up the wine quickly and cheer up our Great King."

As they were drinking wine and conversing happily, someone came to report: "Great King, there are two one-horned demon kings outside who want to see you." "Show them in," said the Monkey King. The demon kings straightened out their attire, ran into the cave, and prostrated themselves. "Why did you want to see me?" asked the Handsome Monkey King. "We have long heard that the Great King is receptive to talents," said the demon kings, "but we had no reason to request your audience. Now we learn that our Great King has received a divine appointment and has returned in success and glory. We have come, therefore, to present the Great King with a red and yellow robe for his celebration. If you are not disdainful of the uncouth and the lowly and are willing to receive us plebeians, we shall serve you as dogs or as horses." Highly pleased, the Monkey King put on the red and yellow robe while the rest of them lined up joyfully and did homage. He then appointed the demon kings to be the Vanguard Commanders, Marshals of the Forward Regiments. After expressing their thanks, the demon kings asked again, "Since our Great King was in Heaven for a long time, may we ask what kind of appointment he received?" "The Jade Emperor belittles the talented," said the Monkey King. "He only made me something called the pi-ma-wên." Hearing this, the demon kings said again, "Great King has such divine powers! Why should you take care of horses for him? What is there to stop you from assuming the rank of the Great Sage, Equal to Heaven?" When the Monkey King heard these words, he could not conceal his delight, shouting repeatedly, "Bravo! Bravo!" "Make me a banner immediately," he ordered the four mighty commanders, "and inscribe on it in large letters, 'The Great Sage, Equal to Heaven.' Erect a pole to hang it on. From now on, address me only as the Great Sage, Equal to Heaven, and the title Great King will no longer be permitted. The Monster Kings of the various caves will also be informed so that it will be known to all." Of this we shall speak no further.

We now refer to the Jade Emperor, who held court the next day. The Heavenly Preceptor Chang[9] was seen leading the deputy and the assistant of the imperial stables to come before the vermilion courtyard. "Your Majesty," they said prostrating themselves, "the newly appointed pi-ma-wên, Sun Wu-k'ung, objected to his rank as being too low and left the Heavenly Palace yesterday in rebellion." As they were saying this, the Devarāja Virūḍhaka, leading the various celestial guardians from the South Heavenly Gate, also made the report, "The pi-ma-wên for reasons unknown to us has walked out of the Heavenly Gate." When the Jade Emperor heard this, he made the proclamation: "Let the two divine commanders and their followers return to their duties. We shall send forth celestial soldiers to capture this monster." From among the ranks, Devarāja Li, who was the Pagoda Bearer,[10] and his Third Prince Naṭa came forward and presented their request, saying, "Your Majesty, though your humble subjects are not gifted, we await your authorization to subdue this monster." Delighted, the Jade Emperor appointed Pagoda Bearer Devarāja Li Ching to be grand marshal for subduing the monster, and promoted Third Prince Naṭa to be the great deity in charge of the Three-Platform Assembly of the Saints. They were to lead an expeditionary force at once for the Region Below.

Deva King Li and Naṭa kowtowed to take leave and went back to their own mansion. After reviewing the troops and their captains and lieutenants, they appointed Mighty-Spirit God to be Vanward Commander, the Fish-Belly General to bring up the rear, and the General of the Yakṣas to urge the troops on. In a moment they left by the South Heavenly Gate and went straight to the Flower-Fruit Mountain. A level piece of land was selected for encampment, and the order was then given to the Mighty-Spirit God to provoke battle. Having received his order and having buckled and knotted his armor properly, the Mighty-Spirit God grasped his spreading-flower ax[11] and came to the Water-Curtain Cave. There in front of the cave he saw a great mob of monsters, all of them wolves, insects, tigers, leopards, and the like; they were all jumping and growling, brandishing their swords and waving their spears. "Damnable beasts!" shouted the Mighty-Spirit God. "Hurry and tell the pi-ma-wên that I, a great general from Heaven, has by the authorization of the Jade Emperor come to subdue him. Tell him to come out quickly and surrender, lest all of you be annihilated!" Running pell-mell into the cave, those monsters shouted the report, "Disaster! Disaster!" "What sort of disaster?" asked the Monkey King. "There's a celestial warrior outside," said the monsters, "who claims the title of an imperial envoy. He says he came by the holy decree of the Jade Emperor to subdue you, and he orders you to go out quickly and surrender, lest we lose our lives." Hearing this, the Monkey King commanded, "Get my battle dress!" He quickly donned his red gold cap, pulled on his yellow gold cuirass, slipped on his cloud-treading shoes, and seized the compliant golden-hooped rod. He led the crowd outside and set them up in battle formation. The Mighty-Spirit God opened wide his eyes and stared at this magnificent Monkey King:

The gold cuirass worn on his body was brilliant and bright;
The gold cap on his head also glistened in the light.
In his hands was a staff, the golden-hooped rod,
That well became the cloud-treading shoes on his feet.
His eyes glowered strangely like burning stars.
Hanging past his shoulders were two ears, forked and hard.
His remarkable body knew many ways of change,
And his voice resounded like bells and chimes.
This pi-ma-wên of pointed mouth and gaping teeth
Set high his aim to be the Sage, Equal to Heaven.

"You lawless ape," cried the Mighty-Spirit God with a powerful roar, "do you recognize me?" When the Great Sage heard these words, he asked quickly, "What sort of dull-witted deity are you? Old Monkey has yet to meet you! State your name at once!" "You fraudulent simian," cried the Mighty-Spirit, "what do you mean, you don't recognize me! I am the Celestial General of Mighty-Spirit, the Vanward Commander and subordinate to Devarāja Li, the Pagoda Bearer, from the divine empyrean. I have come by the imperial decree of the Jade Emperor to receive your submission. Strip yourself of your apparel immediately and yield to the Heavenly grace, so that this mountainful of creatures can avoid execution. If you dare but utter half a 'No,' you will be reduced to powder in seconds!" When the Monkey King heard the saying, he was filled with anger. "Reckless simpleton!" he cried. "Stop bragging and wagging your tongue! I would have killed you with one stroke of my rod, but then I would have no one to communicate my message. So, I'll spare your life for the moment. Get back to Heaven quickly and inform the Jade Emperor that he has no regard for talent. Old Monkey has unlimited abilities. Why did he ask me to mind horses for him? Take a good look at the words on this banner. If I am promoted according to its title, I will lay down my arms, and the cosmos will then be fair and peaceable. But if he does not agree to my demand, I'll fight my way up to the Treasure Hall of Divine Mists, and he won't even be able to sit on his dragon throne!" When the Mighty-Spirit God heard these words, he opened his eyes wide and faced the wind. He did indeed see a tall pole outside the cave; on the pole hung a banner bearing in large letters the words "The Great Sage, Equal to Heaven." The Mighty-Spirit God laughed scornfully three times and jeered, "You lawless ape! How fatuous can you be, and how arrogant! So you want to be the Great Sage, Equal to Heaven! Be good enough to take a bit of my ax first!" Aiming at his head, he hacked at him, but, being a knowledgeable fighter, the Monkey King was not unnerved. He met the blow at once with his golden-hooped rod, and this exciting battle was on.

The rod was named Compliant;
The ax was called Spreading Flower.
The two of them, meeting suddenly,
Did not yet know their weakness or strength;
But ax and rod
Clashed left and right.
One concealed secret powers most wondrous;
The other vaunted openly his vigor and might.
They used magic—

Blowing out cloud and puffing up fog;
They stretched their hands,
Splattering mud and spraying sand.
The might of the celestial battler had its way;
But the Monkey King's power of change knew no bounds.
The cudgel uplifted seemed a dragon playing in water;
The ax arrived as a phoenix slicing through flowers.
Mighty-Spirit, though his name was known throughout the world,
In prowess truly could not match the other one.
The Great Sage whirling lightly his iron staff
Could numb the body with one stroke on the head.

The Mighty-Spirit God could oppose him no longer and allowed the Monkey King to aim a mighty blow at his head, which he hastily sought to parry with his ax. With a crack the ax handle split in two, and Mighty-Spirit turned swiftly to flee for his life. "Imbecile! Imbecile!" laughed the Monkey King, "I've already spared you. Go and report my message at once!"

Back at the camp, the Mighty-Spirit God went straight to see the Pagoda Bearer Devarāja. Huffing and puffing, he knelt down saying, "The pi-ma-wên indeed has great magic powers! Your unworthy warrior cannot prevail against him. Defeated, I have come to beg your pardon." "This fellow has blunted our will to fight," said Devarāja Li angrily. "Take him out and have him executed!" From the side came Prince Naṭa, who said, bowing deeply, "Let your anger subside, Father and King, and pardon for the moment the guilt of Mighty-Spirit. Permit your child to go into battle once, and we shall know the long and short of the matter." The Devarāja heeded the admonition and ordered Mighty-Spirit to go back to his camp and await trial.

This Prince Naṭa, properly armed, leaped from his camp and dashed to the Water-Curtain Cave. Wu-k'ung was just dismissing his troops when he saw Naṭa approaching fiercely. Dear Prince!

Two boyish tufts barely cover his skull.
His flowing hair has yet to reach the shoulders.
A rare mind, alert and intelligent.
A noble frame, pure and elegant.
He is indeed the unicorn son from Heaven above,
Truly immortal as the phoenix of mist and smoke.
This seed of dragon has by nature uncommon features.

His tender age shows no relation to any worldly kin.
He carries on his body six kinds of magic weapons.
He flies, he leaps; he can change without restriction.
Now by the golden-mouth proclamation of the Jade Emperor
He is appointed to the Assembly: its name, the Three Platforms.[12]

Wu-k'ung came near and asked, "Whose little brother are you, and what do you want, barging through my gate?" "Lawless monstrous monkey!" shouted Naṭa. "Don't you recognize me? I am Naṭa, third son of the Pagoda Bearer Devarāja. I am under the imperial commission of the Jade Emperor to come and arrest you." "Little prince," said Wu-k'ung laughing, "your baby teeth haven't even fallen out, and your natal hair is still damp! How dare you talk so big? I'm going to spare your life, and I won't fight you. Just take a look at the words on my banner and report them to the Jade Emperor above. Grant me this title, and you won't need to stir your forces. I will submit on my own. If you don't satisfy my cravings, I will surely fight my way up to the Treasure Hall of Divine Mists." Lifting his head to look, Naṭa saw the words "Great Sage, Equal to Heaven." "What great power does this monstrous monkey possess," said Naṭa, "that he dares claim such a title? Fear not! Swallow my sword." "I'll just stand here quietly," said Wu-k'ung, "and you can take a few hacks at me with your sword." Young Naṭa grew angry. "Change!" he yelled loudly, and he changed at once into a fearsome person having three heads and six arms. In his hands he held six kinds of weapons: a monster-stabbing sword, a monster-cleaving scimitar, a monster-binding rope, a monster-taming club, an embroidered ball, and a fiery wheel. Brandishing these weapons, he mounted a frontal attack. "This little brother does know a few tricks!" said Wu-k'ung, somewhat alarmed by what he saw. "But don't be rash. Watch my magic!" Dear Great Sage! He shouted, "Change!" and he too transformed himself into a creature with three heads and six arms. One wave of the golden-hooped cudgel and it became three staffs, which were held with six hands. The conflict was truly earth-shaking and made the very mountains tremble. What a battle!

The six-armed Prince Naṭa.
The heaven-born Handsome Stone Monkey King.
Meeting, each met his match
And found each to be from the same source.
One was consigned to come down to Earth.

The other in guile disturbed the universe.
The edge of the monster-stabbing sword was quick;
The keen, monster-cleaving scimitar alarmed demons and gods;
The monster-binding rope was like a flying snake;
The monster-taming club was like the head of a wolf;
The lightning-propelled fiery wheel was like darting flames;
Hither and thither the embroidered ball rotated.
The three compliant rods of the Great Sage
Protected the front and guarded the rear with care and skill.
A few rounds of bitter contest revealed no victor,
But the prince's mind would not so easily rest.
He ordered the six kinds of weapon to change
Into hundreds and thousands of millions, aiming for the head.
The Monkey King, undaunted, roared with laughter loud,
And wielded his iron rod with artful ease:
One turned to a thousand, a thousand to ten thousand,
Filling the sky as a swarm of dancing dragons,
And shocked the Monster Kings of sundry caves into shutting their
     doors.
Demons and monsters all over the mountain hid their heads.
The angry breath of divine soldiers was like oppressive clouds.
The golden-hooped iron rod whizzed like the wind.
On this side,
The battle cries of celestial fighters appalled everyone;
On that side,
The banner-waving of monkey monsters startled each person.
Growing fierce, the two parties both willed a test of strength.
We know not who was stronger and who weaker.

Each displaying his divine powers, the Third Prince and Wu-k'ung battled for thirty rounds. The six weapons of that Prince changed into a thousand and ten thousand pieces; the golden-hooped rod of Sun Wu-k'ung into ten thousand and a thousand. They clashed like raindrops and meteors in the air, but victory or defeat was not yet determined. Wu-k'ung, however, proved to be the one swifter of eye and hand. Right in the midst of the confusion, he plucked a piece of hair and shouted, "Change!" It changed into a copy of him, also wielding a rod in its hands and deceiving Naṭa. His real person leaped behind Naṭa and struck his left shoulder with the cudgel. Naṭa, still performing his magic, heard the rod whizzing through the air and

tried desperately to dodge it. Unable to move quickly enough, he took
the blow and fled in pain. Breaking off his magic and gathering up
his six weapons, he returned to his camp in defeat.

Standing in front of his battle line, Devarāja Li saw what was
happening and was about to go to his son's assistance. The prince,
however, came to him first and gasped, "Father and King! The
pi-ma-wên is truly powerful. Even your son of such magical strength
is no match for him! He has wounded me in the shoulder." "If this
fellow is so powerful," said the Devarāja, turning pale with fright,
"how can we beat him?" The prince said, "In front of his cave he
has set up a banner bearing the words 'The Great Sage, Equal to
Heaven.' By his own mouth he boastfully asserted that if the Jade
Emperor appointed him to such a title, all troubles would cease. If
he were not given this name, he would surely fight his way up to
the Treasure Hall of Divine Mists!" "If that's the case," said the
Devarāja, "let's not fight with him for the moment. Let us return to
the region above and report these words. There will be time then for
us to send for more celestial soldiers and take this fellow on all sides."
The prince was in such pain that he could not do battle again; he
therefore went back to Heaven with the Devarāja to report, of which
we speak no further.

Look at that Monkey King returning to his mountain in triumph!
The monster kings of seventy-two caves and the six sworn brothers
all came to congratulate him, and they feasted jubilantly in the
blessed cave dwelling. He then said to the six brothers, "If little
brother is now called the Great Sage, Equal to Heaven, why don't all
of you assume the title of Great Sage also?" "Our worthy brother's
words are right!" shouted the Bull Monster King from their midst,
"I'm going to be called the Great Sage, Parallel with Heaven." "I
shall be called the Great Sage, Covering the Ocean," said the Dragon
Monster King. "I shall be called the Great Sage, United with Heaven,"
said the Garuda Monster King. "I shall be called the Great Sage,
Mover of Mountains," said the Lion Monster King. "I shall be called
the Fair Wind Great Sage," said the Female Monkey King. "And I
shall be called the God-Routing Great Sage," said the Giant Ape
Monster King. At that moment, the seven Great Sages had complete
freedom to do as they pleased and to call themselves with whatever
titles they liked. They had fun for a whole day and then dispersed.

Now we return to the Devarāja Li and the Third Prince, who, leading the other commanders, went straight to the Treasure Hall of Divine Mists to give this report: "By your holy decree your subjects led the expeditionary force down to the region below to subdue the baneful immortal, Sun Wu-k'ung. We had no idea of his enormous power, and we could not prevail against him. We beseech Your Majesty to give us reinforcements to wipe him out." "How powerful can we expect one baneful monkey to be," asked the Jade Emperor, "that reinforcements are needed?" "May Your Majesty pardon us from an offense worthy of death!" said the prince, drawing closer. "That baneful monkey wielded an iron rod; he defeated first the Mighty-Spirit God and then wounded the shoulder of your subject. Outside the door of his cave he had set up a banner bearing the words 'The Great Sage, Equal to Heaven.' He said that if he were given such a rank, he would lay down his arms and come to declare his allegiance. If not, he would fight his way up to the Treasure Hall of Divine Mists." "How dare this baneful monkey be so insolent!" exclaimed the Jade Emperor, astonished by what he had heard. "We must order the generals to have him executed at once!" As he was saying this, the Gold Star of Venus came forward again from the ranks and said, "The baneful monkey knows how to make a speech, but he has no idea what's appropriate and what isn't. Even if reinforcements are sent to fight him, I don't think he can be subdued right away without taxing our forces. It would be better if Your Majesty were greatly to extend your mercy and proclaim yet another decree of pacification. Let him indeed be made the Great Sage, Equal to Heaven; he will be given an empty title, in short, rank without compensation." "What do you mean by rank without compensation?" said the Jade Emperor. The Gold Star said, "His name will be Great Sage, Equal to Heaven, but he will not be given any official duty or salary. We shall keep him here in Heaven so that we may put his perverse mind at rest and make him desist from his madness and arrogance. The universe will then be calm and the oceans tranquil again." Hearing these words, the Jade Emperor said, "We shall follow the counsels of our minister." He ordered the mandate to be made up and the Gold Star to bear it hence.

The Gold Star left through the South Heavenly Gate once again and headed straight for the Flower-Fruit Mountain. Outside the

Water-Curtain Cave things were quite different from the way they
had been the previous time. He found the entire region filled with
the awesome and bellicose presence of every conceivable kind of
monster, each one of them clutching swords and spears, wielding
scimitars and staffs. Growling and leaping about, they began to attack
the Gold Star the moment they saw him. "You, chieftains, hear me,"
said the Gold Star, "let me trouble you to report this to your Great
Sage. I am the Heavenly messenger sent by the Lord above, and I
bear an imperial decree of invitation." The various monsters ran
inside to report, "There is an old man outside who says that he is a
Heavenly messenger from the region above, bearing a decree of
invitation for you." "Welcome! Welcome!" said Wu-k'ung. "He must
be that Gold Star of Venus who came here last time. Although it was
a shabby position they gave me when he invited me up to the region
above, I nevertheless made it to Heaven once and familiarized myself
with the ins and outs of the celestial passages. He has come again
this time undoubtedly with good intentions." He commanded the
various chieftains to wave the banners and beat the drums, and to
draw up the troops in receiving order. Leading the rest of the monkeys,
the Great Sage donned his cap and his cuirass, over which he tossed
the red and yellow robe, and slipped on the cloud shoes. He ran to
the mouth of the cave, bowed courteously, and said in a loud voice,
"Please come in, Old Star! Forgive me for not coming out to meet
you."

The Gold Star strode forward and entered the cave. He stood facing
south and declared, "Now I inform the Great Sage. Because the Great
Sage has objected to the meanness of his previous appointment and
absented himself from the imperial stables, the officials of that department, both great and small, reported the matter to the Jade Emperor.
The proclamation of the Jade Emperor said at first, 'All appointed
officials advance from lowly positions to exalted ones. Why should he
object to that arrangement?' This led to the campaign against you by
Devarāja Li and Naṭa. They were ignorant of the Great Sage's power
and therefore suffered defeat. They reported back to Heaven that you
had set up a banner which made known your desire to be the Great
Sage, Equal to Heaven. The various martial officials still wanted to
deny your request. It was this old man who, risking offense, pleaded
the case of the Great Sage, so that he might be invited to receive a
new appointment, and without the use of force. The Jade Emperor

accepted my suggestion; hence I am here to invite you." "I caused you trouble last time," said Wu-k'ung, laughing, "and now I am again indebted to you for your kindness. Thank you! Thank you! But is there really such a rank as the Great Sage, Equal to Heaven, up there?" "I made certain that this title was approved," said the Gold Star, "before I dared come with the decree. If there is any mishap, let this old man be held responsible."

Wu-k'ung was highly pleased, but the Gold Star refused his earnest invitation to stay for a banquet. He therefore mounted the hallowed cloud with the Gold Star and went to the South Heavenly Gate, where they were welcomed by the celestial generals and guardians with hands folded at their breasts. Going straight into the Treasure Hall of Divine Mists, the Gold Star prostrated himself and memorialized, "Your subject, by your decree, has summoned here Pi-ma-wên Sun Wu-k'ung." "Have that Sun Wu-k'ung come forward," said the Jade Emperor. "I now proclaim you to be the Great Sage, Equal to Heaven, a position of the highest rank. But you must indulge no more in your preposterous behavior." Bowing deeply, the monkey uttered a great whoop of thanks. The Jade Emperor then ordered two building officials, Chang and Lu, to erect the official residence of the Great Sage, Equal to Heaven, to the right of the Garden of Immortal Peaches. Inside the mansion, two departments were established, named "Peace and Quiet" and "Serene Spirit," both of which were full of attending officials. The Jade Emperor also ordered the Star Spirits of Five Poles[13] to accompany Wu-k'ung to assume his post. In addition, two bottles of imperial wine and ten clusters of golden flowers were bestowed on him, with the order that he must keep himself under control and make up his mind to indulge no more in preposterous behavior. The Monkey King obediently accepted the command and went that day with the Star Spirits to assume his post. He opened the bottles of wine and drank them all with his colleagues. After seeing the Star Spirits off to their own palaces, he settled down in complete contentment and delight to enjoy the pleasures of Heaven, without the slightest worry or care. Truly

His name divine, forever recorded in the Long-Life Book
And kept from falling into saṃsāra, will long be known.
We do not know what took place hereafter, and you must listen to the explanation in the next chapter.

Five

The Great Sage, stealing elixir, disrupts the Peach Festival;
Many gods try to catch the monster, a rebel in Heaven.

Now we must tell you that the Great Sage, after all, was a monkey monster; in truth, he had no knowledge of his title or rank, nor did he care for the size of his salary. He did nothing but place his name on the Register. At his official residence he was cared for night and day by the attending officials of the two departments. His sole concern was to eat three meals a day and to sleep soundly at night. Having neither duties nor worries, he was free and content to tour the mansions and meet friends, to make new acquaintances and form new alliances at his leisure. When he met the Three Pure Ones,[1] he addressed them as "Your Reverence"; and when he ran into the Four Emperors,[2] he would say, "Your Majesty." As for the Nine Luminaries,[3] the Generals of the Five Quarters,[4] the Twenty-Eight Constellations,[5] the Four Devarājas,[6] the Twelve Horary Branches,[7] the Five Elders of the Five Regions,[8] the Star Spirits of the entire Heaven, and the numerous gods of the Milky Way, he called them all brother and treated them in a fraternal manner. Today he toured the east, and tomorrow he wandered west. Going and coming on the clouds, he had no definite itinerary.

Early one morning, when the Jade Emperor was holding court, the Taoist immortal Hsü Ching-yang stepped from the ranks and went forward to memorialize, kowtowing, "The Great Sage, Equal to Heaven, has no duties at present and merely dawdles away his time. He has become quite chummy with the various Stars and Constellations of Heaven, calling them his friends regardless of whether they are his superiors or subordinates, and I fear that his idleness may lead to roguery. It would be better to give him some assignment so that he will not grow mischievous." When the Jade Emperor heard these words, he sent for the Monkey King at once, who came amiably. "Your Majesty," he said, "what promotion or reward did you have in mind for old Monkey when you called him?" "We perceive," said the Jade Emperor, "that your life is quite indolent, since you have nothing to do, and we have decided therefore to give you an assignment. You will temporarily take care of the Garden of Immortal Peaches. Be careful and diligent, morning and evening." Delighted, the Great Sage bowed deeply and grunted his gratitude as he withdrew.

He could not restrain himself from rushing immediately into the Garden of Immortal Peaches to inspect the place. A local spirit from the garden stopped him and asked, "Where is the Great Sage going?" "I have been authorized by the Jade Emperor," said the Great Sage, "to look after the Garden of Immortal Peaches. I have come to conduct an inspection." The local spirit hurriedly saluted him and then called together all the stewards in charge of hoeing, watering, tending peaches, and cleaning and sweeping. They all came to kowtow to the Great Sage and led him inside. There he saw

Radiantly young and lovely,
On every trunk and limb—
Radiantly young and lovely blossoms filling the trees,
And fruits on every trunk and limb weighing down the stems.
The fruits, weighing down the stems, hang like balls of gilt;
The blossoms, filling the trees, form tufts of rouge.
Ever they bloom, and ever fruit-bearing, they ripen in a thousand
  years;
Not knowing winter or summer, they lengthen out to ten thousand
  years.
Those that first ripen
Glow like faces reddened with wine,
While those half-grown ones
Are stalk-held and green-skinned.
Encased in smoke their flesh retains their green,
But sunlight reveals their cinnabar grace.
Beneath the trees are rare flowers and exotic grass
Which colors, unfading in four seasons, remain the same.
The towers, the terraces, and the studios left and right
Rise so high into the air that often cloud covers are seen.
Not planted by the vulgar or the worldly of the Dark City,
They are grown and tended by the Queen Mother of the Jade
  Pool.[9]

The Great Sage enjoyed this sight for a long time and then asked the local spirit, "How many trees are there?" "There are three thousand six hundred," said the local spirit. "In the front are one thousand two hundred trees with little flowers and small fruits. These ripen once every three thousand years, and after one taste of them a man will become an immortal enlightened in the way, with healthy limbs and a lightweight body. In the middle are one thousand two hundred trees of layered flowers and sweet fruits. They ripen once every six thousand years. If a man eats them, he will ascend to Heaven with the mist and never grow old. At the back are one thousand two hundred trees with fruits of purple veins and pale yellow pits. These ripen once every nine thousand years and, if eaten, will make a man's age equal to that of Heaven and Earth, the sun and the moon." Highly pleased by these words, the Great Sage that very day made thorough inspection of the trees and a listing of the arbors and pavilions before returning to his residence. From then on, he would go there to enjoy the scenery once every three or four days. He no longer consorted with his friends, nor did he take any more trips.

One day he saw that more than half of the peaches on the branches of the older trees had ripened, and he wanted very much to eat one and sample its novel taste. Closely followed, however, by the local spirit of the garden, the stewards, and the divine attendants of the Equal to Heaven Residence, he found it inconvenient to do so. He therefore devised a plan on the spur of the moment and said to them, "Why don't you all wait for me outside and let me rest a while in this arbor?" The various immortals withdrew accordingly. That Monkey King then took off his cap and robe and climbed up onto a big tree. He selected the large peaches that were thoroughly ripened and, plucking many of them, ate to his heart's content right on the branches. Only after he had his fill did he jump down from the tree. Pinning back his cap and donning his robe, he called for his train of followers to return to the residence. After two or three days, he used the same device to steal peaches to gratify himself once again.

One day the Lady Queen Mother decided to open wide her treasure chamber and to give a banquet for the Grand Festival of Immortal Peaches, which was to be held in the Palace of the Jasper Pool. She ordered the various Immortal Maidens—Red Gown, Blue Gown, White Gown, Black Gown, Purple Gown, Yellow Gown, and Green Gown—to go with their flower baskets to the Garden of Immortal Peaches and pick the fruits for the festival. The seven maidens went to the gate of the garden and found it guarded by the local spirit, the stewards, and the ministers from the two departments of the Equal to Heaven Residence. The girls approached them, saying, "We have been ordered by the Queen Mother to pick some peaches for our banquet." "Divine maidens," said the local spirit, "please wait a moment. This year is not quite the same as last year. The Jade Emperor has put in charge here the Great Sage, Equal to Heaven, and we must report to him before we are allowed to open the gate." "Where is the Great Sage?" asked the maidens. "He is in the garden," said the local spirit. "Because he is tired, he is sleeping alone in the arbor." "If that's the case," said the maidens, "let us go and find him, for we cannot be late." The local spirit went into the garden with them; they found their way to the arbor but saw no one. Only the cap and the robe were left in the arbor, but there was no person to be seen. The Great Sage, you see, had played for a while and eaten a number of peaches. He had then changed himself into a figure only two inches high and, perching on the branch of a large tree, had fallen asleep under the cover of thick leaves. "Since we came by imperial decree," said the Seven-Gown Immortal Maidens, "how can we return empty-handed, even though we cannot locate the Great Sage?" One of the divine officials said from the side, "Since the divine maidens have come by decree, they should wait no longer. Our Great Sage has a habit of wandering off somewhere, and he must have left the garden to meet his friends. Go and pick your peaches now, and we shall report the matter for you." The Immortal Maidens followed his suggestion and went into the grove to pick their peaches.

They gathered two basketfuls from the trees in front and filled three more baskets from the trees in the middle. When they went to the trees at the back of the grove, they found that the flowers were sparse and the fruits scanty. Only a few peaches with hairy stems and green skins were left, for the fact is that the Monkey King had eaten all the ripe ones. Looking this way and that, the Seven Immortal Maidens found on a branch pointing southward one single peach that was half white and half red. The Blue Gown Maiden pulled the branch down with her hand, and the Red Gown Maiden, after plucking the fruit, let the branch snap back up into its position. This was the very branch on which the transformed Great Sage was sleeping. Startled by her, the Great Sage revealed his true form and whipped out from his ear the golden-hooped rod. One wave and it had the thickness of a rice bowl. "From what region have you come, monsters," he cried, "that you have the gall to steal my peaches?" Terrified, the Seven Immortal Maidens knelt down together and pleaded, "Let the Great Sage calm himself! We are not monsters, but the Seven-Gown Immortal Maidens sent by the Lady Queen Mother to pluck the fruits needed for the Grand Festival of Immortal Peaches, when the treasure chamber is opened wide. We just came here and first saw the local spirit of the garden, who could not find the Great Sage. Fearing that we might be delayed in fulfilling the command of the Queen Mother, we did not wait for the Great Sage but proceeded to pluck the peaches. We beg you to forgive us." When the Great Sage heard these words, his anger changed to delight. "Please arise, divine maidens," he said. "Who is invited to the banquet when the Queen Mother opens wide her treasure chamber?" "The last festival had its own set of rules," said the Immortal Maidens, "and those invited were: the Buddha, the Bodhisattvas, the holy monks, and the arhats of the Western Heaven; Kuan-yin from the South Pole; the Holy Emperor of Great Mercy of the East, the Immortals of Ten Continents and Three Islands; the Dark Spirit of the North Pole; the Great Immortal of the Yellow Horn from the Imperial Center. These were the Elders from the Five Quarters. In addition, there were the Star Spirits of the Five Poles, the Three Pure Ones, the Four Deva Kings, the Heavenly Deva of the Great Monad, and the rest from the Upper Eight Caves. From the Middle Eight Caves there were the Jade Emperor, the Nine Heroes, the Immortals of the Seas and Mountains; and from the Lower Eight Caves, there were the Pope of Darkness and the Terrestrial Immortals. The gods and devas, both great and small, of every palace and mansion, will be attending this happy Festival of the Immortal Peaches." "Am I invited?" asked the Great Sage, laughing. "We haven't heard your name mentioned," said the Immortal Maidens. "I am the Great Sage, Equal to Heaven," said the Great Sage. "Why shouldn't I, old Monkey, be made an honored guest at the party?" "Well, we told you the rule for the last festival," said the Immortal Maidens, "but we do not know what will happen this time." "You are right," said the Great Sage, "and I don't blame you. You all just stand here and let old Monkey go and do a little detection to find out whether he's invited or not."

Dear Great Sage! He made a magic sign and recited a spell, saying to the various Immortal Maidens, "Stay! Stay! Stay!" This was the

magic of immobilization, the effect of which was that the Seven-
Gown Immortal Maidens all stood wide-eyed and transfixed beneath
the peach trees. Leaping out of the garden, the Great Sage mounted
his hallowed cloud and headed straight for the Jasper Pool. As he
journeyed, he saw over there

A skyful of holy mist with sparkling light,
And sacred clouds of five colors passing unendingly.
The cries of white cranes resounded in the nine Heavens;
The fine color of red blossoms spread through a thousand leaves.
Right in this midst an immortal now appeared
With a face of natural beauty and features most distinguished.
His spirit glowed like a rainbow dancing in the air.
From his waist hung the list untouched by birth or death.
His name, the Great Joyful Immortal of Naked Feet.[10]
Going to the Peach Festival, he would add to his age.

That Great Immortal of Naked Feet ran right into the Great Sage,
who, his head bowed, was just devising a plan to deceive the real
immortal. Since he wanted to go in secret to the festival, he asked,
"Where is the Venerable Wisdom going?" The Great Immortal said,
"On the kind invitation of the Queen Mother, I am going to the happy
Festival of Immortal Peaches." "The Venerable Wisdom has not yet
learned of what I'm about to say," said the Great Sage. "Because of
the speed of my cloud-somersault, the Jade Emperor has sent old
Monkey out to all five thoroughfares to invite people to go first to the
Hall of Perfect Light for a rehearsal of ceremonies before attending
the banquet." Being a sincere and honest man, the Great Immortal
took the lie for the truth, though he protested, "In years past we
rehearsed right at the Jasper Pool and expressed our gratitude there.
Why do we have to go to the Hall of Perfect Light for rehearsal this
time before attending the banquet?" Nonetheless, he had no choice
but to change the direction of his hallowed cloud and go straight to
the Hall.

Treading the cloud, the Great Sage recited a spell and, with one
shake of his body, changed into the form of the Great Immortal of
Naked Feet. It did not take him very long before he reached the
treasure chamber. He stopped his cloud and walked softly inside.
There he found

Swirling waves of ambrosial fragrance,
Dense layers of holy mist,

A jade terrace decked with ornaments,
A chamber full of the life force,
Ethereal shapes of the phoenix soaring and the argus rising,
And undulant forms of gold blossoms with stems of jade.
Set upon there were the Screen of Nine Phoenixes in Twilight,
The Beacon Mound of Eight Treasures and Purple Mist,
A table inlaid with five-color gold,
And a green jade pot of a thousand flowers.
On the tables were dragon livers and phoenix marrow,
Bear paws and the lips of apes.[11]
Most tempting was every item of the hundred delicacies,
And most succulent the color of every kind of fruit and food.

Everything was laid out in an orderly fashion, but no deity had yet
arrived for the feast. Our Great Sage could not make an end of staring
at the scene when he suddenly felt the overpowering aroma of wine.
Turning his head, he saw, in the long corridor to the right, several
wine-making divine officials and grain-mashing stewards. They were
giving directions to the few Taoists charged with carrying water and
the boys who took care of the fire in washing out the barrels and
scrubbing the jugs. For they had already finished making the wine,
rich and mellow as the juices of jade. The Great Sage could not
prevent the saliva from dripping out of the corner of his mouth, and
he wanted to have a taste at once, except that the people were all
standing there. He therefore resorted to magic. Plucking a few hairs,
he threw them into his mouth and chewed them to pieces before
spitting them out. He recited a spell and cried "Change!" They
changed into many sleep-inducing insects, which landed on the
people's faces. Look at them, how their hands grow weak, their
heads droop, and their eyelids sink down. They dropped their activities,
and all fell sound asleep. The Great Sage then took some of the rare
delicacies and choicest dainties and ran into the corridor. Standing
beside the jars and leaning on the barrels, he abandoned himself to
drinking. After feasting for a long time, he became thoroughly drunk,
but he turned this over in his mind, "Bad! Bad! In a little while,
when the invited guests arrive, won't they be indignant with me?
What will happen to me once I'm caught? I'd better go back home
now and sleep it off!"

Dear Great Sage! Reeling from side to side, he stumbled along
solely on the strength of wine, and in a moment he lost his way. It

was not the Equal to Heaven Residence that he went to, but the Tushita Palace. The moment he saw it, he realized his mistake. "The Tushita Palace is at the uppermost of the thirty-three Heavens," he said, "the Griefless Heaven which is the home of the Most High Lao Tzu. How did I get here? No matter, I've always wanted to see this old man but have never found the opportunity. Now that it's on my way, I might as well pay him a visit." He straightened out his attire and pushed his way in, but Lao Tzu was nowhere to be seen. In fact, there was not a trace of anyone. The fact of the matter is that Lao Tzu, accompanied by the Aged Buddha Dīpaṁkara, was giving a lecture on the tall, three-storied Red Mound Elixir Platform. The various divine youths, commanders, and officials were all attending the lecture, standing on both sides of the platform. Searching around, our Great Sage went all the way to the alchemical room. He found no one but saw fire burning in an oven beside the hearth, and around the oven were five gourds in which finished elixir was stored. "This thing is the greatest treasure of immortals," said the Great Sage happily. "Since old Monkey has understood the Way and compre- hended the mystery of the Internal's identity with the External, I have also wanted to produce some golden elixir on my own to benefit people. While I have been too busy at other times even to think about going home to enjoy myself, good fortune has met me at the door today and presented me with this! As long as Lao Tzu is not around, I'll take a few tablets and try the taste of something new." He poured out the contents of all the gourds and ate them like fried beans.

In a moment, the effect of the elixir had dispelled that of the wine, and he again thought to himself, "Bad! Bad! I have brought on myself calamity greater than Heaven! If the Jade Emperor has know- ledge of this, it'll be difficult to preserve my life! Go! Go! Go! I'll go back to the Region Below to be a king." He ran out of the Tushita Palace and, avoiding the former way, left by the West Heavenly Gate, making himself invisible by the magic of body concealment. Lowering the direction of his cloud, he returned to the Flower-Fruit Mountain. There he was greeted by flashing banners and shining spears, for the four mighty commanders and the monster kings of seventy-two caves were engaging in a military exercise. "Little ones," the Great Sage called out loudly, "I have returned!" The monsters dropped their weapons and knelt down, saying, "Great Sage! What laxity of mind! You left us for so long, and did not even once visit us

to see how we were doing." "It's not that long!" said the Great Sage.
"It's not that long!" They walked as they talked, and went deep inside
the cave dwelling. After sweeping the place clean and preparing a
place for him to rest, and after kowtowing and doing homage, the
four mighty commanders said, "The Great Sage has been living for
over a century in Heaven. May we ask what appointment he actually
received?" "I recall that it's been but half a year," said the Great
Sage, laughing. "How can you talk of a century?" "One day in
Heaven," said the commanders, "is equal to one year on Earth." The
Great Sage said, "I am glad to say that the Jade Emperor this time
was more favorably disposed toward me, and he did indeed appoint
me Great Sage, Equal to Heaven. An official residence was built for
me, and two departments—Peace and Quiet, and Serene Spirit—were
established, with bodyguards and attendants in each department.
Later, when it was found that I carried no responsibility, I was asked
to take care of the Garden of Immortal Peaches. Recently the Lady
Queen Mother gave the Grand Festival of Immortal Peaches, but she
did not invite me. Without waiting for her invitation, I went first to
the Jasper Pool and secretly consumed the food and wine. Leaving
that place, I staggered into the palace of Lao Tzu and finished up all
the elixir stored in five gourds. I was afraid that the Jade Emperor
would be offended, and so I decided to walk out of the Heavenly Gate."

The various monsters were delighted by these words, and they
prepared a banquet of fruits and wine to welcome him. A stone bowl
was filled with coconut wine and presented to the Great Sage, who
took a mouthful and then exclaimed with a grimace, "It tastes awful!
"Just awful!" "The Great Sage," said Pêng and Pa, the two commanders, "has grown accustomed to tasting divine wine and food in
Heaven. Small wonder that coconut wine now seems hardly delect-
able. But the proverb says, 'Tasty or not, it's water from home!'"
"And all of you are, 'related or not, people from home!'" said the
Great Sage. "When I was enjoying myself this morning at the Jaspar
Pool, I saw many jars and jugs in the corridor full of the juices of jade,
which you have never savored. Let me go back and steal a few bottles
to bring down here. Just drink half a cup, and each one of you will
live long without growing old." The various monkeys could not
contain their delight. The Great Sage immediately left the cave and,
with one somersault, went directly back to the Festival of Immortal
Peaches, again using the magic of body concealment. As he entered

the doorway of the Palace of the Jaspar Pool, he saw that the wine makers, the grain mashers, the water carriers, and the fire tenders were still asleep and snoring. He took two large bottles, one under each arm, and carried two more in his hands. Reversing the direction of his cloud, he returned to the monkeys in the cave. They held their own Festival of Immortal Wine, with each one drinking a few cups, which incident we shall relate no further.

Now we tell you about the Seven-Gown Immortal Maidens, who did not find a release from the Great Sage's magic of immobilization until a whole day had gone by. Each one of them then took her flower basket and reported to the Queen Mother, saying, "We are delayed because the Great Sage, Equal to Heaven, imprisoned us with his magic." "How many baskets of immortal peaches have you gathered?" asked the Queen Mother. "Only two baskets of small peaches, and three of medium-sized peaches," said the Immortal Maidens, "for when we went to the back of the grove, there was not even half a large one left! We think the Great Sage must have eaten them all. As we went looking for him, he unexpectedly made his appearance and threatened us with violence and beating. He also questioned us about who had been invited to the banquet, and we gave him a thorough account of the last festival. It was then that he bound us with a spell, and we didn't know where he went. It was only a moment ago that we found release and so could come back here."

When the Queen Mother heard these words, she went immediately to the Jade Emperor and presented him with a full account of what had taken place. Before she finished speaking, the group of wine makers together with the various divine officials also came to report: "Someone unknown to us has vandalized the Festival of Immortal Peaches. The juice of jade, the eight dainties, and the hundred delicacies have all been stolen or eaten up." Four royal preceptors then came up to announce, "The Supreme Patriarch of Tao has arrived." The Jade Emperor went out with the Queen Mother to greet him. Having paid his respects to them, Lao Tzu said, "There are, in the house of this old Taoist, some finished Golden Elixir of Nine Turns,[12] which are reserved for the use of Your Majesty during the next Grand Festival of Cinnabar. Strange to say, they have been stolen by some thief, and I have come specifically to make this known to Your Majesty." This report stunned the Jade Emperor. Presently the officials from the Equal to Heaven Residence came to announce, kowtowing, "The Great Sage Sun has not been discharging his duties of late. He went out yesterday and still has not yet returned. Moreover, we do not know where he went." These words gave the Jade Emperor added anxiety. Next came the Great Immortal of Naked Feet, who prostrated himself and said, "Yesterday, in response to the Queen Mother's invitation, your subject was on his way to attend the festival when he met by chance the Great Sage, Equal to Heaven. The Sage said to your subject that Your Majesty had ordered him to send your subject first to the Hall of Perfect Light for a rehearsal of ceremonies before attending the banquet. Your subject followed his direction and duly went to the Hall. But I did not see the dragon chariot and the phoenix carriage of Your Majesty, and therefore hastened to come here to wait upon you." More astounded than ever, the Jade Emperor said, "This fellow now falsifies imperial decrees and deceives my worthy ministers! Let the Divine Minister of Detection quickly locate his whereabouts!"

The minister received his order and left the palace to make a thorough investigation. After obtaining all the details, he returned presently to report, "The person who has so profoundly disturbed Heaven is none other than the Great Sage, Equal to Heaven." He then gave a repeated account of all the previous incidents, and the Jade Emperor was furious. He at once commanded the Four Great Devarājas to assist Devarāja Li and Prince Naṭa. Together, they called up the Twenty-Eight Constellations, the Nine Luminaries, the Twelve Horary Branches, the Fearless Guards of Five Quarters,[13] the Four Temporal Guardians,[14] the Stars of East and West, the Gods of North and South, the Deities of the Five Mountains and the Four Rivers,[15] the Star Spirits of the entire Heaven, and a hundred thousand celestial soldiers. They were ordered to set up eighteen sets of cosmic net, to journey to the Region Below, to encircle completely the Flower-Fruit Mountain, and to capture the rogue and bring him to justice. All the deities immediately alerted their troops and departed from the Heavenly Palace. As they left, this was the spectacle of the expedition:

Yellow with dust, the churning wind concealed the dark'ning sky;
Reddish with clay, the rising fog o'erlaid the dusky world.
Because an impish monkey insulted the Highest Lord,
The saints of all Heaven descended to this mortal Earth.
Those Four Great Devarājas,
Those Fearless Guards of Five Quarters—

Those Four Great Deva Kings made up the main command;
Those Fearless Guards of Five Quarters moved countless troops.
Li, the Pagoda Bearer, gave orders from the army's center,
With the fierce Naṭa as the captain of his vanward forces.
The Star of Rāhu, at the forefront, made the roll call;
The Star of Ketu, noble and tall, brought up the rear;
Sōma, the moon, displayed a spirit most eager;
Āditya, the sun, was all shining and radiant.
Heroes of special talents were the Stars of Five Phases.
The Nine Luminaries most relished a good battle.
The Horary Branches of Tzŭ, Wu, Mao, and Yao—
They were all celestial guardians of titanic strength.
To the east and west, the Five Plagues[16] and the Five Mountains!
To the left and right, the Six Gods of Darkness and the Six Gods of
     Light!
Above and below, the Dragon Gods of the Four Rivers!
And in tightest formation, the Twenty-Eight Constellations![17]
Citrā, Svātī, Viśākhā, and Anurādhā were the captains.
Revatī, Aśvinī, Apabharaṇī, and Kṛttikā knew combat well.
Uttara-Aṣāḍhā, Abhijit, Śravaṇā, Śraviṣṭha, Śatabhiṣā, Pūrva-
     Proṣṭhapada, Uttara-Proṣṭhapada,
Rohiṇī, Mūlabarhaṇī, Pūrva-Aṣāḍhā—every one an able star!
Punarvasu, Tiṣya, Aśleṣā, Maghā, Pūrva-Phalgunī, Uttara-
     Phalgunī, and Hastā—
All brandished swords and spears to show their power.
Stopping the cloud and lowering the mist they came to this mortal
     world
And pitched their tents before the Mountain of Flower and Fruit.
The poem says:
Many are the forms of the changeful Heaven-born Monkey King!
Snatching wine and stealing elixir, he revels in his mountain lair.
Since he has wrecked the Grand Festival of Immortal Peaches,
A hundred thousand soldiers of Heaven now spread the net of God.
Devarāja Li now gave the order for the celestial soldiers to pitch their
tents, and a cordon was drawn so tightly around the Flower-Fruit
Mountain that not even water could escape! Moreover, eighteen sets
of cosmic net were spread out above and below the region, and the
Nine Luminaries were then ordered to go into battle. They led their
troops and advanced to the cave, in front of which they found a

troop of monkeys, both great and small, prancing about playfully. "Little monsters over there," cried one of the Star Spirits in a severe voice, "where is your Great Sage? We are Heavenly deities sent here from the Region Above to subdue your rebellious Great Sage. Tell him to come here quickly and surrender. If he but utters half a 'No,' all of you will be executed." Hastily the little monsters reported inside, "Great Sage, diaster! Disaster! Outside there are nine savage deities who claim that they are sent from the Region Above to subdue the Great Sage."

Our Great Sage was just sharing the Heavenly wine with the four mighty commanders and the monster kings of seventy-two caves. Hearing this announcement, he said in a most nonchalant manner, " 'If you have wine today, get drunk today; mind not the troubles in front of your door!' " Scarcely had he uttered this proverb when another group of imps came leaping and said, "Those nine savage gods are trying to provoke battle with foul words and nasty language." "Don't listen to them," said the Great Sage, laughing. " 'Let us seek today's pleasure in poetry and wine, and cease asking when we may achieve glory or fame.' " Hardly had he finished speaking when still another flock of imps arrived to report, "Father, those nine savage gods have broken down the door, and are about to fight their way in!" "The reckless, witless deities!" said the Great Sage angrily. "They really have no manners! I was not about to quarrel with them. Why are they abusing me to my face?" He gave the order for the One-Horn Demon King to lead the monster kings of seventy-two caves to battle, adding that old Monkey and the four mighty commanders would follow in the rear. The Demon King swiftly led his troops of ogres to go out to fight, but they were ambushed by the Nine Luminaries and pinned down right at the head of the sheet iron bridge.

At the height of the melee, the Great Sage arrived. "Make way!" he yelled, whipping out his iron rod. One wave of it and it was as thick as a rice bowl and about twelve feet long. The Great Sage plunged into battle, and none of the Nine Luminaries dared oppose him. In a moment, they were all beaten back. When they regrouped themselves again in battle formation, the Nine Luminaries stood still and said, "You senseless pi-ma-wên! You are guilty of the ten evils.[18] You first stole peaches and then wine, utterly disrupting the Grand Festival of Immortal Peaches. You also robbed Lao Tzu of his immortal elixir, and then you had the gall to plunder the imperial winery for your personal enjoyment. Don't you realize that you have piled up sin upon sin?" "Indeed," said the Great Sage, "these several incidents did occur! But what do you intend to do now?" The Nine Luminaries said, "We received the golden decree of the Jade Emperor to lead our troops here to subdue you. Submit at once, and spare these creatures from being slaughtered. If not, we shall level this mountain and overturn this cave!" "How great is your magical power, silly gods," retorted the Great Sage angrily, "that you dare to mouth such foolhardy words? Don't go away! Have a taste of old Monkey's rod!" The Nine Luminaries mounted a joint attack, but the Handsome Monkey King was not in the least intimidated. He wielded his golden-hooped rod, parrying left and right, and fought the Nine Luminaries until they were thoroughly exhausted. Every one of them turned around and fled, his weapons trailing behind him. Running into the tent at the center of their army, they said to the Pagoda Bearer Devarāja, "That Monkey King is indeed an intrepid warrior! We cannot withstand him, and have returned defeated." Devarāja Li then ordered the Four Great Devarājas and the Twenty-Eight Constellations to go out together to do battle. Without displaying the slightest panic, the Great Sage also ordered the One-Horn Demon King, the monster kings of seventy-two caves, and the four mighty commanders to range themselves in battle formation in front of the cave. Look at this all-out battle! It was truly terrifying with

The cold, soughing wind,
The dark, dreadful fog.
On one side, the colorful banners fluttered;
On the other, lances and halberds glimmered.
There were row upon row of shining helmets,
And coat upon coat of gleaming armor.
Row upon row of helmets shining in the sunlight
Resembled silver bells whose chimes echoed in the sky;
Coat upon coat of gleaming armor rising clifflike in layers
Seemed like glaciers crushing the earth.
The giant scimitars
Flew and flashed like lightning;
The mulberry-white spears,
Could pierce even mist and cloud!
The crosslike halberds

And tiger-eye lashes
Were arranged like thick rows of hemp;
The green swords of bronze
And four-sided shovels
Crowded together like trees in a dense forest.
Curved bows, crossbows, and stout arrows with eagle plumes,
Short staffs and snakelike lances—all could kill or maim.
That compliant rod, which the Great Sage owned,
Kept tossing and turning in this battle with gods.
They fought till the air was rid of birds flying by;
Wolves and tigers were driven from within the mount;
The planet was darkened by hurtling rocks and stones,
And the cosmos bedimmed by flying dust and dirt.
The clamor and clangor disturbed Heaven and Earth;
The scrap and scuffle alarmed both demons and gods.

Beginning with the battle formation at dawn, they fought until the sun sank down behind the western hills. The One-Horn Demon King and the monster kings of seventy-two caves were all taken captive by the forces of Heaven. Those who escaped were the four mighty commanders and the troop of monkeys, who hid themselves deep inside the Water-Curtain Cave. With his single rod, the Great Sage withstood in midair the Four Great Devarājas, Li the Pagoda Bearer, and Prince Naṭa and battled with them for a long time. When he saw that evening was approaching, the Great Sage plucked a handful of hairs, threw them into his mouth, and chewed them to pieces. He spat them out, crying, "Change!" They changed at once into many thousands of Great Sages, each employing a golden-hooped rod! They beat back Prince Naṭa and defeated the Five Devarājas.

In triumph the Great Sage collected back his hairs and hurried back to his cave. Soon, at the head of the sheet iron bridge, he was met by the four mighty commanders leading the rest of the monkeys. As they kowtowed to receive him they cried three times, sobbing aloud, and then they laughed three times, hee-heeing and ho-hoing. The Great Sage said, "Why do you all laugh and cry when you see me?" "When we fought with the Deva Kings this morning," said the four mighty commanders, "the monster kings of seventy-two caves and the One-Horn Demon King were all taken captive by the gods. We were the only ones who managed to escape alive, and that is why we cried. Now we see that the Great Sage has returned unharmed and triumphant, and so we laugh as well." "Victory and defeat," said the Great Sage, "are the common experiences of a soldier. The ancient proverb says, 'You may kill ten thousand of your enemies, but you will lose three thousand of your allies!' Moreover, those chieftains who have been captured are tigers and leopards, wolves and insects, badgers and foxes, and the like. Not a single member of our own kind has been hurt. Why then should we be disconsolate? Although our adversaries have been beaten back by my magic of body division, they are still encamped at the foot of our mountain. Let us be most vigilant, therefore, in our defense. Have a good meal, rest well, and conserve your energy. When morning comes, watch me perform a great magic and capture some of these generals from Heaven, so that our comrades may be avenged." The four mighty commanders drank a few bowls of coconut wine with the host of monkeys and went to sleep peacefully. We shall speak no more of them.

When those four Devarājas retired their troops and stopped their fighting, each one of the Heavenly commanders came to report his accomplishment. There were those who had captured lions and elephants and those who had apprehended wolves, crawling creatures, and foxes. Not a single monkey monster, however, had been seized. The camp was then secured, a great tent was pitched, and those commanders with meritorious services were rewarded. The soldiers in charge of the cosmic nets were ordered to carry bells and were given passwords. They encircled the Flower-Fruit Mountain to await the great battle of the next day, and each soldier everywhere diligently kept his watch. So this is the situation:

The impish monkey in rebellion disturbs Heaven and Earth.

But the net is spread and open, ready night and day.

We do not know what took place after the next morning, and you must listen to the explanation in the next chapter.

Six

Kuan-yin, attending the banquet, inquires into the affair;
The Little Sage, exerting his power, subdues the Great Sage.

For the moment we shall not tell you about the siege of the gods or
the Great Sage at rest. We speak instead of the Great Compassionate
Deliverer, the Efficacious Bodhisattva Kuan-yin from the Potalaka
Mountain of the South Sea.[1] Invited by the Lady Queen Mother to
attend the Grand Festival of Immortal Peaches, she arrived at the
treasure chamber of the Jasper Pool with her senior disciple, Hui-an.
There they found the whole place desolate and the banquet tables
in utter disarray. Although several members of the Heavenly
pantheon were present, none was seated. Instead, they were all
engaged in vigorous exchanges and discussions. After the Bodhisattva had greeted the various deities, they told her what had
occurred. "Since there will be no festival," said the Bodhisattva, "nor
any raising of cups, all of you might as well come with this humble
cleric to see the Jade Emperor." The gods followed her gladly, and
they went to the entrance to the Hall of Perfect Light. There the
Bodhisattva was met by the Four Heavenly Preceptors and the
Immortal of Naked Feet, who recounted how the celestial soldiers,
ordered by an enraged Jade Emperor to capture the monster, had not
yet returned. The Bodhisattva said, "I would like to have an audience
with the Jade Emperor. May I trouble one of you to announce my
arrival?" The Heavenly Preceptor Ch'iu Hung-chi went at once into
the Treasure Hall of Divine Mists and, having made his report, invited
Kuan-yin to enter. Lao Tzu then took the upper seat with the
Emperor, while the Lady Queen Mother was in attendance behind the
throne.

The Bodhisattva led the crowd inside. After paying homage to the
Jade Emperor, they also saluted Lao Tzu and the Queen Mother. When
each of them was seated, she asked, "How is the Grand Festival of
Immortal Peaches?" "Every year when the Festival has been given,"
said the Jade Emperor, "we have thoroughly enjoyed ourselves. This

year it has been completely ruined by a baneful monkey, leaving us with nothing but an invitation to disappointment." "Where did this baneful monkey come from?" asked the Bodhisattva. "He was born of a stone egg on top of the Flower-Fruit Mountain of the Ao-lai Country at the East Pūrvavideha Continent," said the Jade Emperor. "At the moment of his birth, two beams of golden light flashed immediately from his eyes, reaching as far as the Palace of the Polestar. We did not think much of that, but he later became a monster, subduing the Dragon and taming the Tiger as well as eradicating his name from the Register of Death. When the Dragon Kings and the Kings of the Underworld brought the matter to our attention, we wanted to capture him. The Star of Long Life, however, observed that all the beings of the three regions which possessed the nine apertures could attain immortality. We therefore decided to educate and nurture the talented monkey and summoned him to the Region Above. He was appointed to the post of pi-ma-wên at the imperial stables, but, taking offense at the lowliness of his position, he left Heaven in rebellion. We then sent Devarāja Li and Prince Naṭa to ask for his submission by proclaiming a decree of pacification. He was brought again to the Region Above and was appointed the Great Sage, Equal to Heaven—a rank without compensation. Since he had nothing to do but to wander east and west, we feared that he might cause further trouble. So he was asked to look after the Garden of Immortal Peaches. But he broke the Law and ate all the large peaches from the oldest trees. By then, the banquet was about to be given. As a person without salary he was, of course, not invited; nonetheless, he plotted to deceive the Immortal of Naked Feet and managed to sneak into the banquet by assuming the Immortal's appearance. He finished off all the divine wine and food, after which he also stole Lao Tzu's elixir and took away a considerable quantity of imperial wine for the enjoyment of his mountain monkeys. Our mind has been sorely vexed by this, and we therefore sent a hundred thousand celestial soldiers with cosmic nets to capture him. We haven't yet received today's report on how the battle is faring."

When the Bodhisattva heard this, she said to Disciple Hui-an, "You must leave Heaven at once, go down to the Flower-Fruit Mountain, and inquire into the military situation. If the enemy is engaged, you can lend your assistance; in any event, you must bring back a factual report." The Disciple Hui-an straightened out his attire and mounted the cloud to leave the palace, an iron rod in his hand. When he arrived at the mountain, he found layers of cosmic net drawn tightly and sentries at every gate holding bells and shouting passwords. The encirclement of the mountain was indeed watertight! Hui-an stood still and called out, "Heavenly sentinels, may I trouble you to announce my arrival? I am Prince Mokṣa, second son of Devarāja Li, and I am also Hui-an, senior disciple of Kuan-yin of South Sea. I have come to inquire about the military situation." The divine soldiers of the Five Mountains at once reported this beyond the gate. The consellations Aquarius, Pleiades, Hydra, and Scorpio then conveyed the message to the central tent. Devarāja Li issued a directorial flag, which ordered the cosmic nets to be opened and entrance permitted for the visitor. Day was just dawning in the east as Hui-an followed the flag inside and prostrated himself before the Four Great Devarājas and Devarāja Li. After he had finished his greetings, Devarāja Li said, "My child, where have you come from?" "Your untutored son," said Hui-an, "accompanied the Bodhisattva to attend the Festival of Grand Peaches. Seeing that the festival was desolate and the Jasper Pool laid waste, the Bodhisattva led the various deities and your untutored son to have an audience with the Jade Emperor. The Jade Emperor spoke at length about Father and King's expedition to the Region Below to subdue the baneful monkey. Since no report has returned for a whole day and neither victory nor defeat has been ascertained, the Bodhisattva ordered your untutored son to come here to find out how things stand." "We came here yesterday to set up the encampment," said Devarāja Li, "and the Nine Luminaries were sent to provoke battle. But this fellow made a grand display of his magical powers, and the Nine Luminaries all returned defeated. After that, I led the troops personally to confront him, and the fellow also brought his forces into formation. Our hundred thousand celestial soldiers fought with him until evening, when he retreated from the battle by using the magic of body division. When we recalled the troops and made our investigation, we found that we had captured some wolves, crawling creatures, tigers, leopards, and the like. But we did not even catch half a monkey monster! And today we have not yet gone into battle."

As he was saying all this, someone came from the gate of the camp to report, "That Great Sage, leading his band of monkey monsters, is shouting for battle outside." The Four Devarājas, Devarāja Li, and the prince at once made plans to bring out the troops, when Mokṣa said, "Father King, your untutored son was told by the Bodhisattva to come down here to acquire information. She also told me to give you assistance should there be actual combat. Though I am not very talented, I volunteer to go out now and see what kind of a Great Sage this is!" "Child," said the Devarāja, "since you have studied with the Bodhisattva for several years, you must, I suppose, have some powers! But do be careful!"

Dear prince! Grasping the iron rod with both hands, he tightened up his embroidered garment and leaped out of the gate. "Who is the Great Sage, Equal to Heaven?" he cried. Holding high his compliant rod, the Great Sage answered, "None other than old Monkey here! Who are you that you dare question me?" "I am Mokṣa, the second prince of Devarāja Li," said Mokṣa. "At present I am also the disciple of Bodhisattva Kuan-yin, a defender of the faith before her treasure throne. And my religious name is Hui-an." "Why have you left your religious training at South Sea and come here to see me?" said the Great Sage. "I was sent by my master to inquire about the military situation," said Mokṣa. "Seeing what a nuisance you have made of yourself, I have come specifically to capture you." "You dare to talk so big?" said the Great Sage. "But don't run away! Have a taste of old Monkey's rod!" Mokṣa was not at all frightened and met his opponent squarely with his own iron rod. The two of them stood before the gate of the camp at mid-mountain, and what a magnificent battle they fought!

> Though one rod is pitted against another, the iron's quite different;
> Though this weapon couples with the other, the persons are not
> the same.
> The one called the Great Sage is an apostate primordial immortal;
> The other is Kuan-yin's disciple, truly heroic and proud.
> The all-iron rod, pounded by a thousand hammers,
> Is made by the Six Gods of Darkness and Six Gods of Light.
> The compliant rod fixes the depth of Heaven's river,
> A thing divine ruling the oceans with its magic might.
> The two of them in meeting have found their match;
> Back and forth they battle in endless rounds.
> From this one the rod of stealthy hands,
> Savage and fierce,
> Around the waist stabs and jabs swiftly as the wind;

From the other the rod, doubling as a spear
Driving and relentless,
Lets up not a moment its parrying left and right.
On this side the banners flare and flutter;
On the other the war drums roll and rattle.
Ten thousand celestial fighters circle round and round.
The monkey monsters of a whole cave stand in rows and rows.
Weird fog and dark cloud spread throughout the earth.
The fume and smoke of battle reach even Heaven's Palace.
Yesterday's battle was something to behold.
Still more violent is the contest today.
Envy the Monkey King, for he's truly able:
Mokṣa's defeated—he's fleeing for his life!

Our Great Sage battled Hui-an for fifty or sixty rounds until the prince's arms and shoulders were sore and numb and he could fight no longer. After one final, futile swing of his weapon, he fled in defeat. The Great Sage then gathered together his monkey troops and stationed them securely outside the entrance of the cave. At the camp of the Devarāja, the celestial soldiers could be seen receiving the prince and making way for him to enter the gate. Panting and puffing, he ran in and gasped out to the Four Devarājas, Pagoda Bearer Li, and Naṭa, "That Great Sage! What an ace! Great indeed is his magical power! Your son cannot overcome him and has returned defeated." Shocked by the sight, Devarāja Li at once wrote a memorial to the Throne to request further assistance. The demon king Mahābāli and Prince Mokṣa were sent to Heaven to present the document.

The two of them dared not linger. They crashed out of the cosmic nets and mounted the holy mist and hallowed cloud. In a moment they reached the Hall of Perfect Light and met the Four Heavenly Preceptors, who led them into the Treasure Hall of Divine Mists to present their memorial. Hui-an also saluted the Bodhisattva, who asked him, "What have you found out about the situation?" "When I reached the Flower-Fruit Mountain by your order," said Hui-an, "I opened the cosmic nets by my call. Seeing my father, I told him of my master's intentions in sending me. Father King said, 'We fought a battle yesterday with that Monkey King but managed to take from him only tigers, leopards, lions, elephants, and the like. We did not catch a single one of his monkey monsters.' As we were talking, he again demanded battle. Your disciple used the iron rod to fight him

for fifty or sixty rounds, but I could not prevail against him and
returned to the camp defeated. Thus father had to send the demon
king Mahābāli and your pupil to come here for help." The Bodhisattva
bowed her head and pondered.

We now tell you about the Jade Emperor, who opened the memorial
and found a message asking for assistance. "This is rather absurd!"
he said laughing. "Is this monkey monster such a wizard that not
even a hundred thousand soldiers from Heaven can vanquish him?
Devarāja Li is again asking for help. What division of divine warriors
can we send to assist him?" Hardly he had finished speaking when
Kuan-yin folded her hands and said to him, "Your Majesty, let not your
mind be troubled! This humble cleric will recommend a god who can
capture the monkey." "Which one would you recommend?" said the
Jade Emperor. "Your Majesty's nephew," said the Bodhisattva, "the
Immortal Master of Illustrious Sagacity Erh-lang,[2] who is living at
the mouth of the River of Libations in the Kuan Prefecture and enjoying the incense and oblations offered to him from the Region Below.
In former days he himself slew six monsters. Under his command are
the Brothers of Plum Mountain and twelve hundred plant-headed
deities, all possessing great magical powers. However, he will agree
only to special assignments and will not obey any general summons.
Your Majesty may want to send an edict transferring his troops to
the scene of the battle and requesting his assistance. Our monster will
surely be captured." When the Jade Emperor heard this, he immediately issued such an edict and ordered the demon king Mahābāli to
present it.

Having received the edict, the demon king mounted a cloud and
went straight to the mouth of the River of Libations. It took him less
than half an hour to reach the temple of the Immortal Master.
Immediately the demon magistrates guarding the doors made this
report inside: "There is a messenger from Heaven outside who has
arrived with an edict in his hand." Erh-lang and his brothers came
out to receive the edict, which was read before burning incense. The
edict said:

> The Great Sage, Equal to Heaven, a monstrous monkey from the
> Flower-Fruit Mountain, is in revolt. At the Palace he stole
> peaches, wine, and elixir, and disrupted the Grand Festival of
> Immortal Peaches. A hundred thousand heavenly soldiers with
> eighteen sets of cosmic nets were dispatched to surround the

mountain and capture him, but victory has not yet been secured. We therefore make this special request of our worthy nephew and his sworn brothers to go to the Flower-Fruit Mountain and assist in destroying this monster. Following your success will be lofty elevation and abundant reward.

In great delight the Immortal Master said, "Let the messenger of Heaven go back. I will go at once to offer my assistance with drawn sword." The demon king went back to report, but we shall speak no further of that.

This Immortal Master called together the Six Brothers of Plum Mountain: they were K'ang, Chang, Yao, and Li, the four grand marshals, and Kuo Shên and Chih Chien, the two generals. As they congregated before the court, he said to them, "The Jade Emperor just now sent us to the Flower-Fruit Mountain to capture a monstrous monkey. Let's get going!" Delighted and willing, the brothers at once called out the divine soldiers under their command. With falcons mounted and dogs on leashes, with arrows ready and bows drawn, they left in a violent magic wind and crossed in a moment the great Eastern Ocean. As they landed on the Flower-Fruit Mountain, they saw their way blocked by dense layers of cosmic net. "Divine commanders guarding the cosmic nets, hear us," they shouted. "We are specially assigned by the Jade Emperor to capture the monstrous monkey. Open the gate of your camp quickly and let us through." The various deities conveyed the message to the inside, level by level. The Four Devarājas and Devarāja Li then came out to the gate of the camp to receive them. After they had exchanged greetings, there were questions about the military situation, and the Devarāja gave them a thorough briefing. "Now that I, the Little Sage, have come," said the Immortal Master, laughing, "he will have to engage in a contest of transformations with his adversary. You gentlemen make sure that the cosmic nets are tightly drawn on all sides, but leave the top uncovered. Let me try my hand in this contest. If I lose, you gentlemen need not come to my assistance, for my own brothers will be there to support me. If I win, you gentlemen will not be needed in tying him up either; my own brothers will take care of that. All I need is the Pagoda Bearer Devarāja to stand in midair with his imp-reflecting mirror. If the monster should be defeated, I fear that he may try to flee to a distant locality. Make sure that his image is clearly reflected in the mirror, so that we don't lose him." The Devarājas set themselves up in the four directions, while the Heavenly soldiers all lined up according to their planned formations.

With himself as the seventh brother, the Immortal Master led the four grand marshals and the two generals out of the camp to provoke battle. The other warriors were ordered to defend their encampment with vigilance, and the plant-headed deities were ordered to have the falcons and dogs ready for battle. The Immortal Master went to the front of the Water-Curtain Cave, where he saw a troop of monkeys neatly positioned in an array that resembled a coiled dragon. At the center of the array was the banner bearing the words "The Great Sage, Equal to Heaven." "That audacious monster!" said the Immortal Master. "How dare he assume the rank 'Equal to Heaven'?" "There's no time for praise or blame," said the Six Brothers of Plum Mountain. "Let's challenge him at once!" When the little monkeys in front of the camp saw the Immortal Master, they ran quickly to make their report. Seizing his golden-hooped rod, straightening out his golden cuirass, slipping on his cloud-treading shoes, and pressing down his red-gold cap, the Monkey King leaped out of the camp. He opened his eyes wide to stare at the Immortal Master, whose features were remarkably refined and whose attire was most elegant. Truly, he was a man of

Features most comely and noble mien,
With ears reaching his shoulders and eyes alert and bright.
A cap of the Three Mountains' Phoenix flying crowned his head,
And a pale yellow robe of goose-down he wore on his frame.
His boots of gold threads matched the hoses of coiling dragons.
Eight emblems[3] like flower clusters adorned his belt of jade.
From his waist hung the pellet bow of new moon shape.
His hands held a lance with three points and two blades.
He once axed open the Peach Mountain to save his mother.
He struck with a single pellet two phoenixes of Tsung-lo.
He slew the Eight Monsters, and his fame spread wide;
He formed a chivalric alliance named the Plum Mountain's Seven
    Sages.
A lofty mind, he scorned being a relative of Heaven.
His proud nature led him to live near the River of Libations.
This is the Kind and Magnanimous Sage from the City of Ch'ih;[4]
Skilled in boundless transformations, his name's Erh-lang.

When the Great Sage saw him, he lifted high his golden-hooped rod

with gales of laughter and called out, "What little warrior are you
and where do you come from, that you dare present yourself here to
provoke battle?" "You must have eyes but no pupils," shouted the
Immortal Master, "if you don't recognize me! I am the maternal
nephew of the Jade Emperor, Erh-lang, the King of Illustrious Grace
and Spirit by imperial appointment. I have received my order from
above to arrest you, the rebellious pi-ma-wên ape. Don't you know
that your time has come?" "I remember," said the Great Sage, "that
the sister of the Jade Emperor some years ago became enamored of
the Region Below; she married a man by the name of Yang and had
a son by him. Are you that boy who was reputed to have cleaved
open the Peach Mountain with his ax? I would like to rebuke you
roundly, but I have no grudge against you. I can hit you with this
rod of mine too, but I'd like to spare your life! A little boy like you,
why don't you hurry back and ask your Four Great Devarājas to
come out?" When the Immortal Master heard this, he grew very
angry and shouted, "Reckless ape! Don't you dare be so insolent!
Take a sample of my blade!" Swerving to dodge the blow, the Great
Sage quickly raised his golden-hooped rod to engage his opponent.
What a fine fight there was between the two of them:

Erh-lang, the God of Illustrious Kindness,
And the Great Sage, Equal to Heaven!
The former, haughty and high-minded, defied the Handsome
    Monkey King.
The latter, not knowing his man, would crush a stalwart foe.
Suddenly these two met,
And both desired a match—
They had never known which was the better man;
Today they'll learn who's strong and who's weak!
The iron rod seemed a flying dragon,
And the lance divine a dancing phoenix:
Left and right they struck,
Attacking both front and back.
The Six Brothers of Plum Mountain filled one side with their
    awesome presence,
While the four generals, like Ma and Liu, took command on the
    other side.
All worked as one to wave the flags and beat the drums;
All assisted the battle by cheering and sounding the gong.

Those two sharp weapons sought a chance to hurt,
But the thrusts and parries slacked not one whit.
The golden-hooped rod, that wonder of the sea,
Could change and fly to gain a victory.
A little lag and your life is over!
A tiny slip and your luck runs out!

The Immortal Master fought the Great Sage for more than three hundred rounds, but the result still could not be determined. The Immortal Master, therefore, summoned all his magical powers; with a shake, he made his body a hundred thousand feet tall. Holding with both hands the divine lance of three points and two blades like the peaks that cap the Hua Mountain, this green-faced, saber-toothed figure with scarlet hair aimed a violent blow at the head of the Great Sage. But the Great Sage also exerted his magical power and changed himself into a figure having the features and height of Erh-lang. He wielded a compliant golden-hooped rod that resembled the heaven-supporting pillar on top of Mount K'un-lun to oppose the god Erh-lang. This vision so terrified the marshals, Ma and Liu, that they could no longer wave the flags, and so appalled the generals, Pêng and Pa, that they could use neither scimitar nor sword. On the side of Erh-lang, the Brothers K'ang, Chang, Yao, Li, Kuo Shên, and Chih Chien gave the order to the plant-headed deities to let loose the falcons and dogs and to advance upon those monkeys in front of the Water-Curtain Cave with mounted arrows and drawn bows. The charge, alas, dispersed the four mighty commanders of monkey imps and captured two or three thousand intelligent monsters! Those monkeys dropped their spears and abandoned their armor, forsook their swords and threw away their lances. They scattered in all directions—running, screaming, scuttling up the mountain, or scrambling back to the cave. It was as if a cat at night had stolen upon resting birds: they darted up as stars to fill the sky. The Brothers thus gained a complete victory, of which we shall speak no further.

Now we were telling you about the Immortal Master and the Great Sage who had changed themselves into forms which imitated Heaven and Earth. As they were doing battle, the Great Sage suddenly perceived that the monkeys of his camp were put to rout, and his heart grew faint. He changed out of his magic form, turned around, and fled, dragging his rod behind him. When the Immortal Master saw that he was running away, he chased him with great strides, saying,

"Where you you going? Surrender now, and your life will be spared!"
The Great Sage did not stop to fight anymore but ran as fast as he
could. Near the cave's entrance, he ran right into K'ang, Chang,
Yao, and Li, the four grand marshals, and Kuo Shên and Chih Chien,
the two generals, who were at the head of an army blocking his way.
"Lawless ape!" they cried, "where do you think you're going?"
Quivering all over, the Great Sage squeezed his golden-hooped rod
back into an embroidery needle and hid it in his ear. With a shake
of his body, he changed himself into a small sparrow and flew to
perch on top of a tree. In great agitation, the six Brothers searched all
around but could not find him. "We've lost the monkey monster!
We've lost the monkey monster!" they all cried.

    As they were making all that clamor, the Immortal Master arrived
and asked, "Brothers, where did you lose him in the chase?" "We
just had him boxed in here," said the gods, "but he simply vanished."
Scanning the place with his phoenix eye wide open,[5] Erh-lang at
once discovered that the Great Sage had changed into a small sparrow
perched on a tree. He changed out of his magic form and took off his
pellet bow. With a shake of his body, he changed into a sparrow
hawk with outstretched wings, ready to attack its prey. When the
Great Sage saw this, he darted up with a flutter of his wings; changing
himself into a cormorant, he headed straight for the open sky. When
Erh-lang saw this, he quickly shook his feathers and changed into a
huge ocean crane, which could penetrate the clouds to strike with
its bill. The Great Sage therefore lowered his direction, changed into
a small fish, and dove into a stream with a splash. Erh-lang rushed
to the edge of the water but could see no trace of him. He thought to
himself, "This simian must have gone into the water and changed
himself into a fish, a shrimp, or the like. I'll change again to catch
him." He duly changed into a fish hawk and skimmed downstream
over the waves. After a while, the fish into which the Great Sage had
changed was swimming along with the current. Suddenly he saw a
bird that looked like a green kite though its feathers were not entirely
green, like an egret though it had small feathers, and like an old
crane though its feet were not red. "That must be the transformed
Erh-lang waiting for me," he thought to himself. He swiftly turned
around and swam away after releasing a few bubbles. When Erh-lang
saw this, he said, "The fish that released the bubbles looks like a carp
though its tail is not red, like a perch though there are no patterns

on its scales, like a snake fish though there are no stars on its head, like a bream though its gills have no bristles. Why does it move away the moment it sees me? It must be the transformed monkey himself!" He swooped toward the fish and snapped at it with his beak. The Great Sage shot out of the water and changed at once into a water snake; he swam toward shore and wriggled into the grass along the bank. When Erh-lang saw that he had snapped in vain and that a snake had darted away in the water with a splash, he knew that the Great Sage had changed again. Turning around quickly, he changed into a scarlet-topped gray crane, which extended its beak like sharp iron pincers to devour the snake. With a bounce, the snake changed again into a spotted bustard standing by itself rather stupidly amid the water-pepper along the bank. When Erh-lang saw that the monkey had changed into such a vulgar creature—for the spotted bustard is the basest and most promiscuous of birds, mating indiscriminately with phoenixes, hawks, or crows—he refused to approach him. Changing back into his true form, he went and stretched his bow to the fullest. With one pellet he sent the bird hurtling.

The Great Sage took advantage of this opportunity, nonetheless. Rolling down the mountain slope, he squatted there to change again —this time into a little temple for the local spirit. His wide-open mouth became the entrance, his teeth the doors, his tongue the Bodhisattva, and his eyes the windows. Only his tail he found to be troublesome, so he stuck it up in the back and changed it into a flagpole. The Immortal Master chased him down the slope, but instead of the bustard he had hit he found only a little temple. He opened his phoenix eye quickly and looked at it carefully. Seeing the flagpole behind it, he laughed and said, "It's the ape! Now he's trying to deceive me again! I have seen plenty of temples before but never one with a flagpole behind it. This must be another of that animal's tricks. Why should I let him lure me inside where he can bite me once I've entered? First I'll smash the windows with my fist! Then I'll kick down the doors!" The Great Sage heard this and said in dismay, "How vicious! The doors are my teeth and the windows my eyes. What am I going to do with my eyes smashed and my teeth knocked out?" Leaping up like a tiger, he disappeared again into the air. The Immortal Master was looking all around for him when the four grand marshals and the two generals arrived together. "Elder Brother," they said, "have you caught the Great Sage?" "A moment ago," said the Immortal Master laughing, "the monkey changed into a temple to trick me. I was about to smash the windows and kick down the doors when he vanished out of sight with a leap. It's all very strange! Very strange!" The Brothers were astonished, but they could find no trace of him in any direction. "Brothers," said the Immortal Master, "keep a lookout down here. Let me go up there to find him." He swiftly mounted the clouds and rose up into the sky, where he saw Devarāja Li holding high the imp-reflecting mirror and standing on top of the clouds with Naṭa. "Devarāja," said the Immortal Master, "have you seen the Monkey King?" "He hadn't come up here," said the Devarāja. "I have been watching him in the mirror." After telling them about the duel in magic and transformations and the captivity of the rest of the monkeys, the Immortal Master said, "He finally changed into a temple. Just as I was about to attack him, he got away." When Devarāja Li heard these words, he turned the imp-reflecting mirror all the way around once more and looked into it. "Immortal Master," he said, roaring with laughter. "Go quickly! Quickly! That monkey used his magic of body concealment to escape from the cordon and he's now heading for the mouth of your River of Libations."

We now tell you about the Great Sage, who had arrived at the mouth of the River of Libations. With a shake of his body, he changed into the form of Holy Father Erh-lang. Lowering the direction of his cloud, he went straight into the temple, and the demon magistrates could not tell that he was not the real Ehr-lang. Every one of them, in fact, kowtowed to receive him. He sat down in the middle and began to examine the various offerings; the three kinds of sacrificial meat brought by Li Hu, the votive offering of Chang Lung, the petition for a son by Chao Chia, and the request for healing by Ch'ien Ping. As he was looking at these, someone made the report, "Another Holy Father has arrived!" The various demon magistrates went quickly to look and were terror-stricken, one and all. The Immortal Master asked, "Did a so-called Great Sage, Equal to Heaven, come here?" "We haven't seen any Great Sage," said the demon magistrates. "But another Holy Father is in there examining the offerings." The Immortal Master crashed through the door; seeing him, the Great Sage revealed his true form and said, "There's no need for the little boy to strive anymore! Sun is now the name of this temple!"

The Immortal Master lifted his divine lance of three points and two blades and struck, but the Monkey King with agile body was quick to move out of the way. He whipped out that embroidery needle of his, and with one wave caused it to take on the thickness of a rice bowl. Rushing forward, he engaged Erh-lang face to face. Starting at the door of the temple, the two combatants fought all the way back to the Flower-Fruit Mountain, treading on clouds and mists and shouting insults at each other. The Four Devarājas and their followers were so startled by their appearance that they stood guard with even greater vigilance, while the grand marshals joined the Immortal Master to surround the Handsome Monkey King. But we shall speak of them no more.

We tell you instead about the demon king Mahābāli, who, having requested the Immortal Master and his Six Brothers to lead their troops to subdue the monster, returned to the Region Above to make his report. Conversing with the Bodhisattva Kuan-yin, the Queen Mother, and the various divine officials in the Hall of Divine Mists, the Jade Emperor said, "If Erh-lang has already gone into battle, why has no further report come back today?" Folding her hands, Kuan-yin said, "Permit this humble cleric to invite Your Majesty and the Patriarch of Tao to go outside the South Heavenly Gate, so that you may find out personally how things are faring." "That's a good suggestion," said the Jade Emperor. He at once sent for his imperial carriage and went with the Patriarch, Kuan-yin, the Queen Mother, and the various divine officials to the South Heavenly Gate, where the cortege was met by celestial soldiers and guardians. They opened the gate and peered into the distance; there they saw cosmic nets on every side manned by Heavenly soldiers, Devarāja Li and Naṭa in midair holding high the imp-reflecting mirror, and the Immortal Master and his Brothers encircling the Great Sage in the middle and fighting fiercely. The Bodhisattva opened her mouth and addressed Lao Tzu: "What do you think of Erh-lang, whom this humble cleric recommended? He is certainly powerful enough to have the Great Sage surrounded, if not yet captured. I shall now help him to achieve his victory and make certain that the enemy will be taken prisoner." "What weapon will the Bodhisattva use," asked Lao Tzu, "and how will you assist him?" "I shall throw down my immaculate vase which I use for holding my willow sprig," said the Bodhisattva. "When it hits that monkey, at least it will knock him over, even if it doesn't kill him.

Erh-lang, the Little Sage, will then be able to capture him." "That vase of yours," said Lao Tzu, "is made of porcelain. It's all right if it hits him on the head. But if it crashed on the iron rod instead, won't it be shattered? You had better not raise your hands; let *me* help him win." The Bodhisattva said, "Do you have any weapon?" "I do, indeed," said Lao Tzu. He rolled up his sleeve and took down from his left arm an armlet, saying, "This is a weapon made of red steel, brought into existence during my preparation of elixir and fully charged with theurgical forces. It can be made to transform at will; indestructible by fire or water, it can entrap many things. It's called the diamond cutter or the diamond snare. The year when I crossed the Han-ku Pass, I depended on it a great deal for the conversion of the barbarians, for it was practically my bodyguard night and day. Let me throw it down and hit him." After saying this, Lao Tzu hurled the snare down from the Heavenly Gate; it went tumbling down into the battlefield at the Flower-Fruit Mountain and landed smack on the Monkey King's head. The Monkey King was engaged in a bitter struggle with the Seven Sages and was completely unaware of this weapon which had dropped from the sky and hit him on the crown of his head. No longer able to stand on his feet, he toppled over. He managed to scramble up again and was about to flee, when the Holy Father Erh-lang's small hound dashed forward and bit him in the calf. He was pulled down for the second time and lay on the ground cursing, "You brute! Why don't you go and do your master in, instead of coming to bite old Monkey?" Rolling over quickly, he tried to get up, but the Seven Sages all pounced on him and pinned him down. They bound him with ropes and punctured his breastbone with a knife, so that he could transform no further.

Lao Tzu retrieved his diamond snare and requested the Jade Emperor to return to the Hall of Divine Mists with Kuan-yin, the Queen Mother, and the rest of the Immortals. Down below the Four Great Deva Kings and Deva King Li all retired their troops, broke camp, and went forward to congratulate Erh-lang, saying, "This is indeed a magnificent accomplishment by the Little Sage!" "This has been the great blessing of the Heavenly Devas," said the Little Sage, "and the proper exercise of their divine authority. What have I accomplished?" The Brothers K'ang, Chang, Yao, and Li said, "Elder Brother need have no further discussion. Let us take this fellow up to the Jade Emperor to see what will be done with him." "Worthy

Brothers," said the Immortal Master, "you may not have a personal audience with the Jade Emperor because you have not received any divine appointment. Let the celestial guardians take him into custody. I shall go with the Devarājas to the Region Above to make our report, while all of you make a thorough search of the mountain here. After you have cleaned it out, go back to the River of Libations. When I have our deeds recorded and received our rewards, I shall return to celebrate with you." The four grand marshals and the two generals followed his bidding. The Immortal Master then mounted the clouds with the rest of the deities, and they began their triumphal journey back to Heaven, singing songs of victory all the way. In a little while, they reached the outer court of the Hall of Perfect Light, and the heavenly preceptor went forward to memorialize to the Throne, saying, "The Four Great Devarājas have captured the monstrous monkey, the Great Sage, Equal to Heaven. They await the command of Your Majesty." The Jade Emperor then gave the order that the demon king Mahābāli and the heavenly guardians take the prisoner to the monster execution block, where he was to be cut to small pieces. Alas, this is what happens to

Fraud and impudence, now punished by the Law;
Heroics grand will fade in the briefest time!

We do not know what will become of the Monkey King, and you must listen to the explanation in the next chapter.

Seven

From the Brazier of Eight Trigrams the Great Sage escapes;
Beneath the Five Phases Mountain the Monkey of the Mind[1]
   is stilled.

Fame and fortune,
All predestined;
One must ever shun a guileful heart.
Rectitude and truth,
The fruits of virtue grow both long and deep.
A little presumption brings on Heaven's wrath;
Though yet unseen, it will surely come in time.
If we ask the Lord of the East[2] for reasons why
Such pains and perils now appear,
It's because pride has sought to scale the limits,
Confounding the world's order and perverting the law.

We were telling you about the Great Sage, Equal to Heaven, who was taken by the celestial guardians to the monster execution block, where he was bound to the monster-subduing pillar. They then slashed him with a scimitar, hewed him with an ax, stabbed him with a spear, and hacked him with a sword, but they could not hurt his body in any way. Next, the Star Spirit of South Pole ordered the various deities of the Fire Department to burn him with fire, but that, too, had little effect. The gods of the Thunder Department were then ordered to strike him with thunderbolts, but not a single one of his hairs was destroyed. The demon king Mahābāli and the others therefore went back to report to the Throne, saying, "Your Majesty, we don't know where this Great Sage has acquired such power to protect his body. Your subjects slashed him with a scimitar and hewed him with an ax; we also struck him with thunder and burned him with fire. Not a single one of his hairs was destroyed. What shall we do?" When the Jade Emperor heard these words, he said, "What indeed can we do to a fellow like that, a creature of that sort?" Lao Tzu then came forward and said, "That monkey ate the immortal peaches and drank the imperial wine. Moreover, he stole the divine elixir and ate five gourdfuls of it, both raw and cooked. All this was probably refined in his stomach by the Samādhi fire[3] to form a single solid mass. The union with his constitution gave him a diamond body which cannot be quickly destroyed. It would be better, therefore, if this Taoist takes him away and places him in the Brazier of Eight Trigrams, where he will be smelted by high and low heat. When he is finally separated from my elixir, his body will certainly be reduced to ashes." When the Jade Emperor heard these words, he told the Six Guardians of Darkness and the Six Guardians of Light to release the prisoner and hand him over to Lao Tzu, who left in obedience to the divine decree. Meanwhile, the illustrious Sage Erh-lang was rewarded with a hundred gold blossoms, a hundred bottles of imperial wine, a hundred pellets of elixir, together with rare treasures, lustrous pearls, and brocades, which he was told to share with his brothers. After expressing his gratitude, the Immortal Master returned to the mouth of the River of Libations, and for the time being we shall speak of him no further.

Arriving at the Tushita Palace, Lao Tzu loosened the ropes on the Great Sage, pulled out the weapon from his breastbone, and pushed him into the Brazier of Eight Trigrams. He then ordered the Taoist who watched over the brazier and the page boy in charge of the fire to blow up a strong flame for the smelting process. The brazier, you see, was of eight compartments corresponding to the eight trigrams of Ch'ien, K'an, Kên, Chên, Sun, Li, K'un, and Tui. The Great Sage crawled into the space beneath the compartment which corresponded to the Sun trigram. Now Sun symbolizes wind; where there is wind, there is no fire. However, wind could churn up smoke, which at that moment reddened his eyes, giving them a permanently inflamed condition. Hence they were sometimes called Fiery Eyes and Diamond Pupils.

Truly time passed by swiftly, and the forty-ninth day[4] arrived imperceptibly. The alchemical process of Lao Tzu was perfected, and on that day he came to open the brazier to take out his elixir. The Great Sage at the time was covering his eyes with both hands, rubbing his face and shedding tears. He heard noises on top of the brazier and, opening his eyes, suddenly saw light. Unable to restrain himself, he leaped out of the brazier and kicked it over with a loud crash. He began to walk straight out of the room, while a group of startled fire tenders and guardians tried desperately to grab hold of him. Every

one of them was overthrown; he was as wild as a white brow tiger
in a fit, a one-horn dragon with a fever. Lao Tzu rushed up to clutch
at him, only to be greeted by such a violent shove that he fell head
over heels while the Great Sage escaped. Whipping the compliant
rod out from his ear, he waved it once in the wind and it had the
thickness of a rice bowl. Holding it in his hands, without regard for
good or ill, he once more careened through the Heavenly Palace,
fighting so fiercely that the Nine Luminaries all shut themselves in
and the Four Devarājas disappeared from sight. Dear Monkey
Monster! Here is a testimonial poem for him. The poem says:

> This cosmic being perfectly fused with nature's gifts
> Passes with ease through ten thousand toils and tests.
> Vast and motionless like the One Great Void,
> Perfect and quiescent, he's named The Primal Depth.
> Refined a long while in the brazier, though not of mercurial stuff,[5]
> He's the very immortal, living ever above all things.
> Knowing boundless transformations, he changes still;
> The three refuges and five commandments[6] he all rejects.

Here is another poem:

> Just as light supernal fills the boundless space,
> So does that cudgel serve his master's hand.
> It lengthens or shortens according to the wish of man;
> Upright or recumbent, it grows or shrinks at will.

And another:

> A monkey's transformed body weds the human mind.
> Mind is a monkey—this, the truth profound.
> The Great Sage, Equal to Heaven, is no idle thought.
> For how could the post of pi-ma justly show his gifts?
> The Horse works with the Monkey—this means both Mind and
>   Will
> Must firmly be harnessed and not be ruled without.
> All things return to Nirvāṇa, taking this one course:
> In union with Tathāgata[7] to live beneath twin trees.[8]

This time our Monkey King had no respect for persons great or small;
he lashed out this way and that with his iron rod, and not a single
deity could withstand him. He fought all the way into the Hall of
Perfect Light and was approaching the Hall of Divine Mists, where
fortunately Wang Ling-kuan, aide to the Immortal Master of Adjuvant
Holiness, was on duty. He saw the Great Sage advancing recklessly

and went forward to bar his way, holding high his golden whip.
"Wanton monkey," he cried, "where are you going? I am here, so
don't you dare be insolent!" The Great Sage did not wait for further
utterance; he raised his rod and struck at once, while the Ling-kuan
met him also with brandished whip. The two of them charged into
each other in front of the Hall of Divine Mists. What a fight that was
between

A red-blooded patriot with reputation great,
And a defier of Heaven with notorious name!
The saint and the sinner gladly do this fight,
To test the skills of two warriors brave.
Though the rod is brutal
And the whip is fleet,
How can the hero, upright and just, forbear?
This one is a supreme god of vengeance with thunderous voice;
The other, the Great Sage, Equal to Heaven, a monstrous ape.
The golden whip and the iron rod used by the two
Are both weapons divine from the House of God.
At the Treasure Hall of Divine Mists this day they show their might,
Displaying each his prowess most admirably.
This one brashly seeks to take the Big Dipper Palace.
The other with all his strength defends the sacred realm.
In bitter strife relentless they show their power;
Moving back and forth, whip or rod has yet to score.

The two of them fought for some time, and neither victory nor defeat
could yet be determined. The Immortal Master of Adjuvant Holiness,
however, had already sent word to the Thunder Department, and
thirty-six thunder deities were summoned to the scene. They surrounded the Great Sage and plunged into a fierce battle. The Great
Sage was not in the least intimidated; wielding his compliant rod, he
parried left and right and met his attackers to the front and to the
rear. In a moment he saw that the scimitars, lances, swords, halberds.
whips, maces, hammers, axes, gilt bludgeons, sickles, and spades of
the thunder deities were coming thick and fast. So with one shake of
his body he changed into a creature with six arms and three heads.
One wave of the compliant rod and it turned into three; his six arms
wielded the three rods like a spinning wheel, whirling and dancing
in their midst. The various thunder deities could not approach him
at all. Truly his form was

Tumbling round and round,
Bright and luminous;
A form everlasting, how imitated by men?
He cannot be burned by fire.
Can he ever be drowned in water?
A lustrous pearl of maṇi[9] he is indeed,
Immune to all the spears and the swords.
He could be good;
He could be bad;
Present good and evil he could do at will.
Immortal he'll be in goodness or a Buddha,
But working ill, he's covered by hair and horn.[10]
Endlessly changing he runs amok in Heaven,
Not to be seized by fighting lords or thunder gods.

At the time the various deities had the Great Sage surrounded, but they could not close in on him. All the hustle and bustle soon disturbed the Jade Emperor, who at once sent the Wandering Minister of Inspection and the Immortal Master of Blessed Wings to go to the Western Region and invite the aged Buddha to come and subdue the monster.

The two sages received the decree and went straight to the Spirit Mountain. After they had greeted the Four Vajra-Buddhas and the Eight Bodhisattvas in front of the Treasure Temple of Thunderclap, they asked them to announce their arrival. The deities therefore went before the Treasure Lotus Platform and made their report. Tathāgata at once invited them to appear before him, and the two sages made obeisance to the Buddha three times before standing in attendance beneath the platform. Tathāgata asked, "What causes the Jade Emperor to trouble the two sages to come here?"

The two sages explained as follows: "Some time ago there was born on the Flower-Fruit Mountain a monkey who exercised his magic powers and gathered to himself a troop of monkeys to disturb the world. The Jade Emperor threw down a decree of pacification and appointed him a pi-ma-wên, but he despised the lowliness of that position and left in rebellion. Devarāja Li and Prince Naṭa were sent to capture him, but they were unsuccessful, and another proclamation of amnesty was given to him. He was then made the Great Sage, Equal to Heaven, a rank without compensation. After a while he was given the temporary job of looking after the Garden of Immortal

Peaches, where almost immediately he stole the peaches. He also went to the Jasper Pool and made off with the food and wine, devastating the Grand Festival. Half-drunk, he went secretly into the Tushita Palace, stole the elixir of Lao Tzu, and then left the Celestial Palace in revolt. Again the Jade Emperor sent a hundred thousand Heavenly soldiers, but he was not to be subdued. Thereafter Kuan-yin sent for the Immortal Master Erh-lang and his sworn brothers, who fought and pursued him. Even then he knew many tricks of transformation, and only after he was hit by Lao Tzu's diamond snare could Erh-lang finally capture him. Taken before the Throne, he was condemned to be executed; but, though slashed by a scimitar and hewn by an ax, burned by fire and struck by thunder, he was not hurt at all. After Lao Tzu had received royal permission to take him away, he was refined by fire, and the brazier was not opened until the forty-ninth day. Immediately he jumped out of the Brazier of Eight Trigrams and beat back the celestial guardians. He penetrated into the Hall of Perfect Light and was approaching the Hall of Divine Mists when Wang Ling-kuan, aide to the Immortal Master of Adjuvant Holiness, met and fought with him bitterly. Thirty-six thunder generals were ordered to encircle him completely, but they could never get near him. The situation is desperate, and for this reason, the Jade Emperor sent a special request for you to defend the Throne."

When Tathāgata heard this, he said to the various bodhisattvas, "All of you remain steadfast here in the chief temple, and let no one relax his meditative posture. I have to go exorcise a demon and defend the Throne."

Tathāgata then called Ānanda and Kāśyapa, his two venerable disciples, to follow him. They left the Thunderclap Temple and arrived at the gate of the Hall of Divine Mists, where they were met by deafening shouts and yells. There the Great Sage was being beset by the thirty-six thunder deities. The Buddhist Patriarch gave the dharma-order: "Let the thunder deities lower their arms and break up their encirclement. Ask the Great Sage to come out here and let me ask him what sort of divine power he has." The various warriors retreated immediately, and the Great Sage also threw off his magical appearance. Changing back into his true form, he approached angrily and shouted with ill humor, "What region are you from, monk, that you dare stop the battle and question me?" Tathāgata laughed and said, "I am Śākyamuni, the Venerable One from the Western Region of

Ultimate Bliss. I have heard just now about your audacity, your wildness, and your repeated acts of rebellion against Heaven. Where were you born? When did you learn the Great Art? Why are you so violent and unruly?"

The Great Sage said, "I was
Born of Earth and Heaven, immortal magically fused,
An old monkey hailing from the Flower-Fruit Mount.
I made my home in the Water-Curtain Cave;
I sought friend and teacher to gain the Mystery Great.
Perfected in the many arts of ageless life,
I learned to change in ways boundless and vast.
Too narrow the space I found on that mortal earth;
I set my mind to live in the Green Jade Sky.
In Divine Mists Hall none should long reside,
For king may follow king in the reign of man.
If might is honor, let them yield to me.
Only he is hero who dares to fight and win!"

When the Buddhist Patriarch heard these words, he laughed aloud in scorn. "A fellow like you," he said, "is only a monkey who happens to become a spirit. How dare you be so presumptuous as to want to seize the honored throne of the Exalted Jade Emperor? He began practicing religion when he was very young, and he has gone through the bitter experience of one thousand, seven hundred and fifty kalpas, with each kalpa lasting a hundred and twenty-nine thousand, six hundred years. Figure out yourself how many years it took him to rise to the enjoyment of his great and limitless position! You are merely a beast who has just attained human form in this incarnation. How dare you make such a boast? Blasphemy! This is sheer blasphemy, and it will surely shorten your allotted age. Repent while there's still time and cease your idle talk! Be wary that you don't encounter such peril that you will be cut down in an instant, and all your original gifts will be wasted."

"Even if the Jade Emperor has practiced religion from childhood," said the Great Sage, "he should not be allowed to remain here forever. The proverb says, 'Many are the turns of kingship, and next year the turn will be mine!' Tell him to move out at once and hand over the Celestial Palace to me. That'll be the end of the matter. If not, I shall continue to cause disturbances and there'll never be peace!" "Besides your immortality and your transformations," said the Buddhist

Patriarch, "what other powers do you have that you dare to usurp this hallowed region of Heaven?" "I've plenty of them!" said the Great Sage. "Indeed, I know seventy-two transformations and a life that does not grow old through ten thousand kalpas. I know also how to cloud-somersault, and one leap will take me a hundred and eight thousand miles. Why can't I sit on the Heavenly throne?"

The Buddhist Patriarch said, "Let me make a wager with you. If you have the ability to somersault clear of this right palm of mine, I shall consider you the winner. You need not raise your weapon in battle then, for I shall ask the Jade Emperor to go live with me in the West and let you have the Celestial Palace. If you cannot somersault out of my hand, you can go back to the Region Below and be a monster. Work through a few more kalpas before you return to cause more trouble."

When the Great Sage heard this, he said to himself, snickering, "What a fool this Tathāgata is! A single somersault of mine can carry old Monkey a hundred and eight thousand miles, yet his palm is not even one foot across. How could I possibly not jump clear of it?" He asked quickly, "You're certain that your decision will stand?" "Certainly it will," said Tathāgata. He stretched out his right hand, which was about the size of a lotus leaf. Our Great Sage put away his compliant rod and, summoning his power, leaped up and stood right in the center of the Patriarch's hand. He said simply, "I'm off!" and he was gone—all but invisible like a streak of light in the clouds. Training the eye of wisdom on him, the Buddhist Patriarch saw that the Monkey King was hurtling along relentlessly like a whirligig.

As the Great Sage advanced, he suddenly saw five flesh-pink pillars supporting a mass of green air. "This must be the end of the road," he said. "When I go back presently, Tathāgata will be my witness and I shall certainly take up residence in the Palace of Divine Mists." But he thought to himself, "Wait a moment! I'd better leave some kind of memento if I'm going to negotiate with Tathāgata." He plucked a hair and blew a mouthful of magic breath onto it, crying, "Change!" It changed into a writing brush with extra thick hair soaked in heavy ink. On the middle pillar he then wrote in large letters the following line: "The Great Sage, Equal to Heaven, has made a tour of this place." When he had finished writing, he retrieved his hair, and with a total lack of respect he left a bubbling pool of monkey urine at the base of the first pillar. He reversed his cloud-somersault and went back to where he had started. Standing on Tathāgata's palm, he said, "I left, and now I'm back. Tell the Jade Emperor to give me the Celestial Palace." "You stinking, urinous ape!" scolded Tathāgata. "Since when did you ever leave the palm of my hand?" The Great Sage said, "You are just ignorant! I went to the edge of Heaven, and I found five flesh-pink pillars supporting a mass of green air. I left a memento there. Do you dare go with me to have a look at the place?" "No need to go there," said Tathāgata. "Just lower your head and take a look." When the Great Sage stared down with his fiery eyes and diamond pupils, he found written on the middle finger of the Buddhist Patriarch's right hand the sentence "The Great Sage, Equal to Heaven, has made a tour of this place." A pungent whiff of monkey urine came from the fork between the thumb and the first finger. Astonished, the Great Sage said, "Could this really happen? Could this really happen? I wrote those words on the pillars supporting the sky. How is it that they now appear on his finger? Could it be that he is exercising the magic power of foreknowledge without divination? I won't believe it! I won't believe it! Let me go there once more!"

Dear Great Sage! Quickly he crouched and was about to jump up again, when the Buddhist Patriarch flipped his hand over, and tossed the Monkey King out of the West Heavenly Gate. The five fingers were transformed into the Five Phases of metal, wood, water, fire, and earth. They became, in fact, five connected mountains, named Five-Phases Mountain, which pinned him down with just enough pressure to keep him there. The thunder deities, Ānanda, and Kāśyapa all folded their hands and cried in acclamation:

Wonderful! Wonderful!

Taught to be manlike since hatching from an egg that year,
He set his aim to learn and walk the Way of Truth.
He lived in a lovely region by ten thousand kalpas unmoved.
But one day he changed, dissipating vigor and strength.
Craving high place, he flouted Heaven's dominion;
Mocking sages, he stole pills and upset the great relations.
Evil, full to the brim, now meets its retribution.
We know not when he may hope to find release.

After the Buddhist Patriarch Tathāgata had vanquished the monstrous monkey, he at once called Ānanda and Kāśyapa to return with him to the Western Paradise. At that moment, however, T'ien-p'êng and T'ien-yu, two heavenly messengers, came running out of the Treasure Hall of Divine Mists and said, "We beg Tathāgata to wait a moment, please! Our Lord's grand carriage will arrive momentarily." When the Buddhist Patriarch heard these words, he turned around and waited with reverence. In a moment he did indeed see a chariot drawn by eight colorful phoenixes and covered by a canopy adorned with nine luminous jewels. The entire cortege was accompanied by the sound of wondrous songs and melodies, chanted by a vast celestial choir. Scattering precious blossoms and diffusing fragrant incense, it came up to the Buddha, and the Jade Emperor offered his thanks, saying, "We are truly indebted to your mighty dharma for vanquishing that monster. We beseech Tathāgata to remain for one brief day, so that we may invite the immortals to join us in giving you a banquet of thanks." Not daring to refuse, Tathāgata folded his hands to thank the Jade Emperor, saying, "Your old monk came here at your command, Most Honorable Deva. Of what power may I boast, really? I owe my success entirely to the excellent fortune of Your Majesty and the various deities. How can I be worthy of your thanks?" The Jade Emperor then ordered the various deities from the Thunder Department to send invitations abroad to the Three Pure Ones, the Four Ministers, the Five Elders, the Six Women Officials,[11] the Seven Stars, the Eight Poles, the Nine Luminaries, and the Ten Capitals. Together with a thousand immortals and ten thousand sages, they were to come to the thanksgiving banquet given for the Buddhist Patriarch. The Four Great Imperial Preceptors and the Divine Maidens of Nine Heavens were told to open wide the golden gates of the Jade Capital, the Treasure Palace of Primal Secret, and the Five Lodges of Penetrating Brightness. Tathāgata was asked to be seated high on the Spirit Platform of Seven Treasures, and the rest of the deities were then seated according to rank and age before a banquet of dragon livers, phoenix marrow, juices of jade, and immortal peaches.

In a little while, the Jade-Pure Honorable Divine of the Origin, the Exalted-Pure Honorable Divine of Spiritual Treasures, the Primal-Pure Honorable Divine of Moral Virtue, the Immortal Masters of Five Influences, the Star Spirits of Five Constellations, the Three Ministers, the Four Sages, the Nine Luminaries, the Left and Right Assistants, the Devarāja, and Prince Naṭa all marched in leading a train of flags and canopies in pairs. They were all holding rare treasures and lustrous pearls, fruits of longevity and exotic flowers to be presented to the Buddha. As they bowed before him, they said, "We are most grateful for the unfathomable power of Tathāgata, who has subdued the monstrous monkey. We are grateful, too, to the Most Honorable Deva, who is having this banquet and asked us to come here to offer our thanks. May we beseech Tathāgata to give this banquet a name?" Responding to the petition of the various deities, Tathāgata said, "If a name is desired, let this be called 'The Great Banquet for Peace in Heaven.'" "What a magnificent name!" the various Immortals cried in unison. "Indeed, it shall be the Great Banquet for Peace in Heaven." When they finished speaking, they took their seats separately, and there was the pouring of wine and exchanging of cups, pinning of corsages[12] and playing of zithers. It was indeed a magnificent banquet, for which we have a testimonial poem. The poem says:

That Feast of Peaches Immortal disturbed by the ape
Is now surpassed by this Banquet for Peace in Heaven.
Dragon flags and phoenix chariots stand glowing in halos bright,
As standards and blazing banners whirl in hallowed light.
Sweet are the tunes of immortal airs and songs,
Noble the sounds of panpipes and double flutes of jade.
Incense ambrosial surrounds this assembly of saints.
The world is tranquil. May the Holy Court be praised!

As all of them were feasting happily, the Lady Queen Mother also led a host of divine maidens and immortal singing-girls to come before the Buddha, dancing with light feet. They bowed to him, and she said, "Our Festival of Immortal Peaches was ruined by that monstrous monkey. We are beholden to the mighty power of Tathāgata for the enchainment of this mischievous ape. In the celebration during this Great Banquet for Peace in Heaven, we have little to offer as a token of our thanks. Please accept, however, these few immortal peaches plucked from the large trees by our own hands." They were truly

Half red, half green, and spouting aroma sweet,
Of luscious roots immortal, and ten thousand years old.
Pity those fruits planted at the Wu-ling Spring![13]
How do they equal the marvels of Heaven's home:
Those tender ones of purple veins so rare in the world,
And those of matchless sweetness with pale yellow pits?

They lengthen your age and prolong your life by changing your
   frame.
He who has the luck to eat them will never be the same.
After the Buddhist Patriarch had pressed together his hands to thank
the Queen Mother, she ordered the immortal singing-girls and the
divine maidens to sing and dance. All the immortals at the banquet
applauded enthusiastically. Truly there were
   Whorls of heavenly incense filling the seats,
   And profuse array of divine petals and stems.
   Jade capital and golden arches in what great splendor!
   How priceless, too, the strange goods and rare treasures!
   Every pair had the same age as Heaven.
   Every set increased through ten thousand kalpas.
   Mulberry fields or vast oceans, let them shift and change.
   He who lives here has neither grief nor fear.
The Queen Mother commanded the immortal maidens to sing and
dance, as wine cups and goblets clinked together steadily. After a
little while, suddenly
   A wondrous fragrance came to meet the nose,
   Rousing Stars and Planets in that great hall.
   The gods and the Buddha put down their cups.
   Raising his head, each waited with his eyes.
   There in the air appeared an aged man,
   Holding a most luxuriant long-life plant.
   His gourd had elixir of ten thousand years.
   His book listed names twelve millennia old.
   Sky and earth in his cave knew no constraint.
   Sun and moon were perfected in his vase.[14]
   He roamed the Four Seas in joy serene,
   And made the Ten Islets[15] his tranquil home.
   Getting drunk often at the Peaches Feast
   He woke; the moon shone brightly as of old.
   He had a long head, short frame, and large ears.
   His name: Star of Long Life from South Pole.
After the Star of Long Life had arrived and had greeted the Jade
Emperor, he also went up to thank Tathāgata, saying, "When I first
heard that the baneful monkey was being led by Lao Tzu to the
Tushita Palace to be refined by alchemical fire, I thought peace was

surely secured. I never suspected that he could still escape, and it was fortunate that Tathāgata in his goodness had subdued this monster. When I got word of the thanksgiving banquet, I came at once. I have no other gifts to present to you but these purple agaric, jasper plant, jade-green lotus root, and golden elixir." The poem says:

Jade-green lotus and golden drug are given to Śākya.
Like the sands of Ganges is the age of Tathāgata.
The brocade of the three wains is calm, eternal bliss.[16]
The nine-grade garland is a wholesome, endless life.[17]
In the School Mādhyamika he's the true master,[18]
Whose home is the Heaven both of form and emptiness.[19]
The great Earth and cosmos all call him Lord.
His sixteen-foot diamond body[20] abounds in blessing and life.

Tathāgata accepted the thanks cheerfully, and the Star of Long Life went to his seat. Again there was pouring of wine and exchanging of cups. The Great Immortal of Naked Feet also arrived. After prostrating himself before the Jade Emperor, he too went to thank the Buddhist Patriarch, saying, "I am profoundly grateful for your dharma which subdued the baneful monkey. I have no other things to convey my respect but two magic pears and some fire dates,[21] which I now present to you." The poem says:

Fragrant are the pears and dates of the Naked-Feet Immortal,
Presented to Amitābha, whose count of years is long.
Firm as a hill is his Lotus Platform of Seven Treasures;
Brocadelike is his Flower Seat of Thousand Gold adorned.
No false speech is this—his age equals Heaven and Earth;
Nor is this a lie—his luck is great as the sea.
Blessing and long life reach in him their fullest scope,
Dwelling in that Western Region of calm, eternal bliss.

Tathāgata again thanked him and asked Ānanda and Kāśyapa to put away the gifts one by one before approaching the Jade Emperor to express his gratitude for the banquet. By now, everyone was somewhat tipsy. A Spirit Minister of Inspection then arrived to make the report, "The Great Sage is sticking out his head!" "No need to worry," said the Buddhist Patriarch. He took from his sleeve a tag on which were written in gold letters the words *Oṁ maṇi padme hūṁ*.[22] Handing it over to Ānanda, he told him to stick it on the top of the mountain. This deva received the tag, took it out of the Heavenly Gate, and stuck it tightly on a square piece of rock at the top of the Mountain of Five

Phases. The mountain immediately struck root and grew together at the seams, though there was enough space for breathing and for the prisoner's hands to crawl out and move around a bit. Ānanda then returned to report, "The tag is tightly attached."

Tathāgata then took leave of the Jade Emperor and the deities, and went with the two devas out of the Heavenly Gate. Moved by compassion, he recited a divine spell and called together a local spirit and the Fearless Guards of Five Quarters to stand watch over the Five-Phases Mountain. They were told to feed the prisoner with iron pellets when he was hungry and to give him melted copper to drink when he was thirsty. When the time of his chastisement was fulfilled, they were told, someone would be coming to deliver him. So it is that

The brash, baneful monkey in revolt against Heaven
Is brought to submission by Tathāgata.
He drinks melted copper to endure the seasons,
And feeds on iron pellets to pass the time.
Tried by this bitter misfortune sent from the Sky,
He's glad to be living, though in a piteous lot.
If this hero is allowed to struggle anew,
He'll serve Buddha in future and go to the West.

Another poem says:

Prideful of his power once the time was ripe,
He tamed dragon and tiger, exploiting wily might.
Stealing peaches and wine, he roamed the House of Heaven.
He found trust and favor in the Capital of Jade.
He's now imprisoned, for his evil's full to the brim.
By the good stock[23] unfailing his spirit will rise again.
If he's indeed to escape Tathāgata's hands,
He must await the holy monk from T'ang Court.

We do not know in what month or year hereafter the days of his penance will be fulfilled, and you must listen to the explanation in the next chapter.

Eight

The Sovereign Buddha has made scriptures to impart
  ultimate bliss;
Kuan-yin receives the decree to go up to Ch'ang-an.[1]

> Ask at the site of meditation,
> How it is that even endless exercise
> Often leads only to empty old age!
> Polishing bricks to make a mirror,
> Hoarding snow to use as foodstuff—[2]
> How many young persons are thus deceived?
> A feather swallows the great ocean?
> A mustard seed contains the Sumeru?[3]
> The Golden Dhūta is gently smiling.[4]
> Enlightened, one transcends the ten stages[5] and three vehicles.
> The sluggards must join the four creatures[6] and six ways.[7]
> Who has heard below the Thoughtless Cliff,
> Beneath the Shadowless Tree,
> The cuckoo's one call greeting the dawn of spring?
> Perilous are the roads at Ts'ao-ch'i,[8]
> And dense are the clouds on Chiu-ling;[9]
> Here the voice of any acquaintance is mute.
> The waterfall of ten thousand feet.
> The spreading fivefold leaf of the lotus.
> The incense-draped curtain hanging in an old temple.
> In that hour,
> Once you penetrate to the origin,
> You'll see the three jewels[10] and the Dragon King.

The tune of this tz'ŭ poem is the *Su-wu-man*. We shall now tell you
about the Sovereign Buddha Tathāgata, who took leave of the Jade
Emperor and returned to the Treasure Monastery of Thunderclap.
All the three thousand buddhas, the five hundred arhats, the eight
diamond kings, and the countless bodhisattvas held temple pennants,
embroidered canopies, rare treasures, and immortal flowers, forming
an orderly array before the Spirit Mountain and beneath the two

Śāla Trees to welcome him. Tathāgata stopped his hallowed cloud
and said to them:

I have
With incomparable prajñā[11]
Looked through the three regions.
The fundamental nature of all things
Will finally come to naught.
Equally empty is immateriality,
For nothing of independent nature exists.
The extirpation of the wily monkey,
This event none can comprehend.
Name, birth, death, and origin—
Such are the characteristics of all things.

When he had finished speaking, he beamed forth the śārī light,[12]
which filled the air with forty-two white rainbows, connected end to
end from north to south. Seeing this, the crowd bowed down and
worshiped. In a little while, Tathāgata gathered together the holy
clouds and blessed fog, ascended the lotus platform of the highest
rank, and sat down solemnly. Those three thousand buddhas, five
hundred arhats, eight diamond kings, and four bodhisattvas folded
their hands and drew near. After bowing down, they asked, "The
one who caused disturbance in Heaven and ruined the Peach
Festival, who was he?" "That fellow," said Tathāgata, "was a
baneful monkey born in the Flower-Fruit Mountain. His wickedness
was beyond all bounds and defied description. The divine warriors
of the entire Heaven could not bring him to submission. Though
Erh-lang caught him and Lao Tzu tried to refine him with fire, they
could not hurt him at all. When I arrived, he was just making an
exhibition of his might and prowess in the midst of the thunder deities.
When I stopped the fighting and asked about his antecedents, he said
that he had magic powers, knowing how to transform himself and
how to cloud-somersault, which would carry him a hundred and
eight thousand miles at a time. I made a wager with him to see
whether he could leap clear of my hand. I then grabbed hold of him
while my fingers changed into the Mountain of Five Phases, which
had him firmly pinned down. The Jade Emperor opened wide the
golden doors of the Jade Palace, invited me to sit at the head table,
and gave a Banquet for Peace in Heaven to thank me. It was only a
short while ago that I took leave of the Throne to come back here."

All were delighted by these words. After they had expressed their highest praise for the Buddha, they withdrew according to their ranks; they went back to their several duties and enjoyed the *bhūtatathatā*.[13] Truly it is the scene of

Holy mist encompassing T'ien-chu,[14]
Rainbow light enclosing the Honored One,
Who is called the First in the West,
The King of the Formlessness School.[15]
Here often black apes are seen presenting fruits,
Tailed-deer holding flowers in their mouths,
Blue phoenixes dancing,
Colorful birds singing,
The spirit tortoise boasting of his age,
And the divine crane picking agaric.
They enjoy in peace the Pure Land's Jetavana,[16]
The Dragon Palace, and worlds vast as Ganges' sands.
Every day the flowers bloom;
Every hour the fruits ripen.
They practice silence to return to the Real.
They meditate to reach the fruition right.
They do not die nor are they born.
No growth is there, nor any decrease.
Mist and smoke wraithlike may come and go.
No seasons intrude, nor are years remembered.

The poem says:

All the movements are easy and free;
There is neither fear nor sorrow here.
The fields of Paradise are flat and wide.
This world's not affected by autumn or spring.

As the Buddhist Patriarch lived in the Treasure Monastery of the Thunderclap in the Spirit Mountain, he called together one day the various buddhas, arhats, guardians, bodhisattvas, diamond kings, mendicant monks and nuns and said to them, "We do not know how much time has passed here since I subdued the wily monkey and pacified Heaven, but I suppose at least half a millennium has gone by on Earth. As this is the fifteenth day of the first month of autumn, I have prepared a treasure bowl filled with a hundred varieties of exotic flowers and a thousand kinds of rare fruit. I would like to share them with all of you in celebration of the Feast of the

Ullambana Bowl.[17] How about it?" Every one of them folded his hands and paid obeisance to the Buddha three times to receive the festival. Tathāgata then ordered Ānanda to take the flowers and fruits from the treasure bowl, and Kāśyapa was asked to distribute them. All were thankful, and they presented poems to express their gratitude. The poem of blessing says:

The star of blessing shines brightly before Lokajyeṣṭha,[18]
Who enjoys blessing most enduring and immense.
His boundless virtue and blessing last as long as Earth.
His source of blessing is happily joined to the sky.
His widely planted fields of blessing prosper year to year.
His deep and vast sea of blessing is ever unchanged.
His world's filled with blessing, thus all will be blessed.
May his blessing increase, be boundless, and ever complete.

The poem of wealth says:

His wealth's weighty as a mountain: so phoenixes sing.
His wealth follows the seasons to extol his long life.
He gains in wealth by ten thousand pecks as his body in health.
He enjoys wealth of a thousand bushels as the world peace.
The range of his wealth, reaching to Heaven, is ever safe;
The name of his wealth is like the sea—but purer.
The grace of his wealth reaching afar is by many sought.
The scope of his wealth is boundless, enriching countless lands.

The poem of longevity says:

The Star of Longevity gave gifts to Tathāgata,
From whom light radiates on this place of longevity.
The fruits of longevity fill the bowl with hues divine.
The blooms of longevity, newly plucked, deck the lotus seat.
The poems of longevity, how elegant and finely wrought!
The songs of longevity are scored by most gifted minds.
The life of longevity lengthens to match the sun and moon.
Longevity, like mountain and sea, is longer than both!

After the bodhisattvas had presented their poems, they invited Tathāgata to disclose the origin and elucidate the source. Tathāgata gently opened his benevolent mouth to expound the great dharma and to proclaim the truth. He lectured on the wondrous doctrines of the three vehicles, the five skandhas,[19] and the *Śūraṅgamā Sūtra*. As he did so, celestial dragons were seen circling above and flowers descended like rain in abundance. It was truly thus:

The mind of Zen is bright as the moon of a thousand rivers.

The true nature is pure and spacious as an unclouded sky.

When Tathāgata had finished his lecture, he said to the congregation, "I have watched the Four Great Continents, and the morality of their inhabitants varies from place to place. Those living on the East Pūrvavideha revere Heaven and Earth, and they are straightforward and peaceful. Those on the North Uttarakuru, though they love to destroy life, do so out of the necessity of making a livelihood. Moreover, they are rather dull of mind and lethargic in spirit, and they are not likely to do much harm. Those of our West Aparagodānīya are neither covetous nor prone to kill; they control their humor and temper their spirit. There is, to be sure, no illuminate of the first order, but everyone is certain to attain longevity. Those who reside in the South Jambūdvīpa, however, are prone to practice lechery and delight in evildoing, indulging in much slaughter and strife. Indeed, they are all caught in the treacherous field of tongue and mouth, in the wicked sea of slander and malice. However, I have three baskets of true scriptures which can persuade man to do good." When the various bodhisattvas heard these words, they folded their hands and bowed down. "What are the three baskets of authentic sciptures," they asked, "that Tathāgata possesses?" Tathāgata said, "I have one basket of vinaya, which speaks of Heaven; one basket of śāstras, which tells of the Earth; and one basket of sūtras, which redeems the damned. Altogether the three baskets of scriptures contain thirty-five divisions written in fifteen thousand, one hundred and forty-four scrolls. They are the scriptures for the cultivation of truth; they are the gate to ultimate goodness. I myself would like to send these to the Land of the East; but the creatures in that region are so stupid and so scornful of the truth that they ignore the weighty elements of our Law and mock the true sect of Yoga. Somehow we need a person with power to go to the Land of the East and find a virtuous believer. He will be asked to experience the bitter travail of passing through a thousand mountains and ten thousand waters to come here in quest of the authentic scriptures, so that they may be forever implanted in the east to enlighten the people. This will provide a source of blessings great as a mountain and deep as the sea. Which one of you is willing to make such a trip?" At that moment, the Bodhisattva Kuan-yin came near the lotus platform and paid obeisance three times to the Buddha, saying, "Though your disciple is untalented, she

is willing to go to the Land of the East to find a scripture pilgrim."
Lifting their heads to look, the various buddhas saw that the Bodhisattva had

A mind perfected in the four virtues,[20]
A golden body filled with wisdom,
Fringes of dangling pearls and jade,
Scented bracelets set with lustrous treasures,
Dark hair piled smoothly in a coiled-dragon bun,
And elegant sashes lightly fluttering as phoenix quills.
Her green jade buttons
And white silk robe
Bathed in holy light;
Her velvet skirt
And golden cords
Wrapped by hallowed air.
With brows of new moon shape
And eyes like two bright stars,
Her jadelike face beams natural joy,
And her ruddy lips seem a flash of red.
Her immaculate vase overflows with nectar from year to year,
Holding sprigs of weeping willow green from age to age.
She disperses the eight woes;
She redeems the multitude;
She has great compassion;
Thus she rules on the T'ai Mountain,
And lives at the South Sea.
She saves the poor, searching for their voices,
Ever heedful and solicitous,
Ever wise and efficacious.
Her orchid heart delights in green bamboos;
Her chaste nature loves the wistaria.
She is the merciful ruler of the Potalaka Mountain,
The Living Kuan-yin from the Cave of Tidal Sound.

When Tathāgata saw her, he was most delighted and said to her, "No
other person is qualified to make this journey. It must be the Honorable Kuan-yin of mighty magic powers—she's the one to do it!" "As
your disciple departs for the east," said the Bodhisattva, "do you have
any instructions?" "As you travel," said Tathāgata, "you are to
examine the way carefully. Do not journey high in the air, but remain

at an altitude halfway between mist and cloud so that you can see
the mountains and waters and remember the exact distance. You will
then be able to give close instructions to the scripture pilgrim. Since
he may still find the journey difficult, I shall also give you five talis-
mans." He ordered Ānanda and Kāśyapa to bring out an embroidered
cassock and a nine-ring priestly staff. He said to the Bodhisattva,
"You may give this cassock and this staff to the scripture pilgrim. If
he is firm in his intention to come here, he may put on the cassock
and it will protect him from falling back into the wheel of transmigration. When he holds the staff, it will keep him from meeting
poison or harm." The Bodhisattva bowed low to receive the gifts.
Tathāgata then took out also three fillets and handed them to the
Bodhisattva, saying, "These treasures are called the tightening
fillets, and though they are all alike, their uses are not the same. I
have a separate spell for each of them: the Golden, the Constrictive,
and the Prohibitive Spell. If you encounter on the way any monster
who possesses great magic powers, you must persuade him to learn
to be good and to follow the scripture pilgrim as his disciple. If he is
disobedient, this fillet may be put on his head, and it will strike root
the moment it comes into contact with the flesh. Recite the particular
spell which belongs to the fillet and it will cause the head to swell and
ache so painfully that he will think his brains are bursting. That will
persuade him to come within our fold."

  After the Bodhisattva had bowed to the Buddha and taken her leave,
she called Disciple Hui-an to follow her. This Hui-an, you see, carried
a huge iron rod which weighed a thousand pounds. He followed the
Bodhisattva closely and served her as a powerful bodyguard. The
Bodhisattva made the embroidered cassock into a bundle and placed
it on his back; she hid the golden fillets, took up the priestly staff, and
went down the Spirit Mountain. Lo, this one journey will result in

  A son of Buddha returning to fulfil his original vow.

  The Gold Cicada Elder will clasp the candana.[21]

The Bodhisattva went to the bottom of the hill, where she was
received at the door of the Yü-chên Taoist Temple by the Great
Immortal of Golden Head. The Bodhisattva was presented with tea,
but she did not dare linger long, saying, "I have received the dharma-
decree of Tathāgata to look for a scripture pilgrim in the Land of
the East." The Great Immortal said, "When do you expect the
scripture pilgrim to arrive?" "I'm not sure," said the Bodhisattva.

"Perhaps in two or three years' time he'll be able to get here." So she took leave of the Great Immortal and traveled at an altitude half-way between cloud and mist in order that she might remember the way and the distance. We have a testimonial poem for her which says:

A search throughout ten thousand miles—that goes without saying!
To state who will be found is no easy prediction.
For the seeker of man, has it not been ever like this?
Can it be mere chance that such is the way of my life?
Preaching the Tao with method becomes a vain word
When declaration meets no belief; it's empty preaching.
To find some percipient I would disgorge liver and gall,
Supposing such fated occasion lies indeed ahead.

As the mentor and her disciple journeyed, they suddenly came upon a large body of Weak Water, for this was the region of the Flowing Sand River.[22] "My disciple," said the Bodhisattva, "this place is difficult to cross. The scripture pilgrim will be of temporal bones and mortal stock. How will he be able to get across?" "Teacher," said Hui-an, "how wide do you suppose this river is?" The Bodhisattva stopped her cloud to take a look, and she saw that

In the east it touches the sandy coast;
In the west it joins the barbaric states;
In the south it reaches even Wu-i;[23]
In the north it approaches the Tartars.
Its width is eight hundred miles,
And its length must measure many thousand more.
The water flows as if Earth is heaving its frame.
The current rises like a mountain upraising its back.
Outspread and immense;
Vast and interminable.
The sound of its towering billows reaches distant ears.
The raft of a god cannot come here,
Nor can a leaf of the lotus stay afloat.
Lifeless grass in the twilight drifts along the crooked banks.
Yellow clouds conceal the sun to darken the long dikes.
Where can one find the traffic of merchants?
Has there been ever a shelter for fishermen?
On the flat sand no wild geese descend;

From distant shores comes the crying of apes.
Only the red smartweed flowers know this scene,
Accompanied by the white duckweed's fragile scent.

The Bodhisattva was looking over the river when suddenly a loud splash was heard, and from the midst of the waves leaped an ugly and ferocious monster. He appeared to have

A green, though not too green,
And black, though not too black,
Face of gloomy complexion;
A long, though not too long,
And short, though not too short,
Sinewy body with naked feet.
His gleaming eyes
Shone like two lights beneath the stove.
His mouth, forked at the corners,
Was like a butcher's bloody bowl.
With teeth protruding like swords and knives,
And red hair all disheveled,
He bellowed once and it sounded like thunder,
While his legs sprinted like whirling wind.

Holding in his hands a priestly staff, that fiendish creature ran up the bank and tried to seize the Bodhisattva. He was opposed, however, by Hui-an, who wielded his iron rod, crying, "Stop!" but the fiendish creature raised his staff to meet him. So the two of them engaged in a fierce battle beside the Flowing Sand River which was truly terrifying.

The iron rod of Mokṣa
Displays its power to defend the Law;
The monster-taming staff of the creature
Labors to show its heroic might.
Two silver pythons dance along the river's side.
A pair of godlike monks charge each other on the shore.
This one plies his talents as the forceful lord of Flowing Sand.
That one protects Kuan-yin by strength to attain merit great.
This one churns up foam and stirs up waves.
That one belches fog and spits out wind.
The stirred-up foams and waves darken Heaven and Earth.
The spat-out fog and wind make dim both sun and moon.
The monster-taming staff of this one

Is like a white tiger emerging from the mountain;
The iron rod of that one
Is like a yellow dragon lying on the way.
When used by one,
This weapon spreads open the grass and finds the snake.
When let loose by the other,
That weapon knocks down the kite and splits the pine.
They fight until the darkness thickens
Save for the glittering stars,
And the fog looms up
To obscure both sky and land.
This one, long a dweller in the Weak Water, is uniquely fierce.
That one, newly leaving the Spirit Mountain, seeks his first
    triumph.

Back and forth along the river the two of them fought for twenty or
thirty rounds without either prevailing, when the fiendish creature
stilled the other's iron rod and asked, "What region do you come
from, monk, that you dare oppose me?" "I'm the second son of the
Pagoda Bearer Devarāja," said Mokṣa, "Mokṣa, Disciple Hui-an. I am
serving as the guardian of my mentor, who is looking for a scripture
pilgrim in the Land of the East. What kind of monster are you that
you dare block our way?" "I remember," said the monster, suddenly
recognizing his opponent, "that you used to follow the Kuan-yin of
the South Sea and practice austerities there in the bamboo grove.
How did you get to this place?" "Don't you realize," said Mokṣa, "that
she is my mentor—the one over there on the shore?"

When the monster heard these words, he apologized repeatedly.
Putting away his staff, he allowed Mokṣa to grasp him by the collar
and lead him away. He lowered his head and bowed low to Kuan-yin,
saying, "Bodhisattva, please forgive me and let me submit my
explanation. I am no monster; I am rather the Curtain-Raising
Marshal who waits upon the phoenix chariot of the Jade Emperor at
the Divine Mists Hall. Because I carelessly broke a crystal cup at one
of the Festivals of Immortal Peaches, the Jade Emperor gave me eight
hundred lashes, banished me to the Region Below, and changed me
into my present shape. Every seventh day he sends a flying sword to
stab my breast and side more than a hundred times before it leaves
me. Hence my present wretchedness! Moreover, the hunger and cold
are unbearable, and I am driven every few days to come out of the

waves and find a traveler for food. I certainly did not expect that my ignorance would today lead me to offend the great, merciful Bodhisattva."

"Because of your sin in Heaven," said the Bodhisattva, "you were banished. Yet the slaying of life in your present manner can surely be said to be adding sin to sin. By the decree of Buddha, I am on my way to the Land of the East to find a scripture pilgrim. Why don't you come into my fold, take refuge in good works, and follow the scripture pilgrim as his disciple when he goes to the Western Heaven to ask Buddha for the scriptures? I'll order the flying sword to stop piercing you. At the time when you achieve merit, your sin will be expiated and you will be restored to your former position. How do you feel about that?" "I'm willing," said the monster, "to seek refuge in right action." He said also, "Bodhisattva, I have devoured countless human beings at this place. There have even been a number of scripture pilgrims here, and I ate all of them. The heads of those I devoured I threw into the Flowing Sand, and they sank to the bottom, for such is the nature of this water that not even goose down can float on it. But the skulls of the nine pilgrims floated on the water and would not sink. Regarding them as something unusual, I chained them together with a rope and played with them at my leisure. If this becomes known, I fear that no other scripture pilgrim will want to come this way. Won't it jeopardize my future?"

"Not come this way? How absurd!" said the Bodhisattva. "You may take the skulls and hang them round your neck. When the scripture pilgrim arrives, there will be a use for them." "If that's the case," said the monster, "I'm now willing to receive your instructions." The Bodhisattva then touched the top of his head[24] and gave him the commandments. The sand was taken to be a sign, and he was given the surname "Sha" and the religious name "Wu-ching,"[25] and that was how he entered the Gate of Sand.[26] After he had seen the Bodhisattva on her way, he washed his heart and purified himself; he never took life again but waited attentively for the arrival of the scripture pilgrim.

So the Bodhisattva parted with him and went with Mokṣa toward the Land of the East. They traveled for a long time and came upon a high mountain, which was covered by miasma so foul that they could not ascend it on foot. They were just about to mount the clouds and

pass over it when a sudden blast of violent wind brought into view
another monster of most ferocious appearance. Look at his

Lips curled and twisted like dried lotus leaves;
Ears like rush-leaf fans and hard, gleaming eyes;
Gaping teeth as sharp as a fine steel file's;
A long mouth wide open as a fire pot.
A gold cap is fastened with bands by the cheek.
Straps on his armor seem like scaleless snakes.
He holds a rake—a dragon's out-stretched claws;
From his waist hangs a bow of half-moon shape.
His awesome presence and his prideful mien,
Defy the deities and daunt the gods.

He rushed up toward the two travelers and, without regard for good
or ill, lifted the rake and brought it down hard on the Bodhisattva.
But he was met by Disciple Hui-an, who cried with a loud voice,
"Reckless monster! Desist from such insolence! Look out for my
rod!" "This monk," said the monster, "doesn't know any better!
Look out for my rake!" The two of them clashed together at the foot
of the mountain to discover who was to be the victor. It was a
magnificent battle!

The monster is fierce.
Hui-an is powerful.
The iron rod jabs at the heart;
The muckrake swipes at the face.
Spraying mud and splattering dust darken Heaven and Earth;
Flying sand and hurling rocks scare demons and gods.
The nine-teeth rake,
All burnished,
Loudly jingles with double rings;
The single rod,
Black throughout,
Leaps and flies in both hands.
This one is the prince of a Devarāja;
That one is the spirit of a grand marshal.
This one defends the faith at Potalaka;
That one lives in a cave as a monster.
Meeting this time they rush to fight,
Not knowing who shall lose and who shall win.

At the very height of their battle, Kuan-yin threw down some lotus flowers from midair, separating the rod from the rake. Alarmed by what he saw, the fiendish creature asked, "What region are you from, monk, that you dare to play this 'flower-in-the-eye' trick on me?" "Cursed beast of fleshly eyes and mortal stock!" said Mokṣa. "I am the disciple of the Bodhisattva from South Sea, and these are lotus flowers thrown down by my mentor. Don't you recognize them?" "The Bodhisattva from South Sea?" asked the fiend. "Is she Kuan-yin who sweeps away the three calamities and rescues us from the eight disasters?" "Who else," said Mokṣa, "if not she?" The fiend threw away his muckrake, lowered his head, and bowed, saying, "Venerable brother! Where is the Bodhisattva? Please be so good as to introduce me to her." Mokṣa raised his head and pointed upward, saying, "Isn't she up there?" "Bodhisattva!" the fiend kowtowed toward her and cried with a loud voice, "Pardon my sin! Pardon my sin!"

Kuan-yin lowered the direction of her cloud and came to ask him, "What region are you from, wild boar who has become a spirit or old sow who has become a fiend, that you dare bar my way?" "I am neither a wild boar," said the fiend, "nor am I an old sow! I was originally the Marshal of the Heavenly Reeds in the Heavenly River.[27] Because I got drunk and dallied with the Goddess of the Moon,[28] the Jade Emperor had me beaten with a mallet two thousand times and banished me to the world of dust. My true spirit was seeking the proper home for my next incarnation when I lost my way, passed through the womb of an old sow, and ended up with a shape like this! Having bitten the sow to death and killed the rest of the litter, I took over this mountain ranch and passed my days eating people. Little did I expect to run into the Bodhisattva. Save me, I implore you! Save me!"

"What is the name of this mountain?" said the Bodhisattva. "It's called the Mountain of the Blessed Mound," said the fiendish creature, "and there is a cave in it by the name of Cloudy Paths. There was a Second Elder Sister Luan[29] originally in the cave. She saw that I knew something of the martial art and therefore asked me to be the head of the family, following the so-called practice of 'standing backward in the door.'[30] After less than a year, she died, leaving me to enjoy the possession of her entire cave. I have spent many days and years at this place, but I know no means of supporting myself and I pass the time eating people. I implore the Bodhisattva to pardon my sin." The Bodhisattva said, "There is an old saying: 'If you desire to have a future, act with reverence for the future.' You have already transgressed in the Region Above, and yet you have not changed your violent ways but indulge in the taking of life. Don't you know that both crimes will be punished?" "The future! The future!" said the fiend. "If I listen to you, I might as well feed on the wind! The proverb says, 'If you follow the law of the court, you'll be beaten to death; if you follow the law of Buddha, you'll be starved to death!' Let me go! Let me go! I would much prefer catching a few travelers and munching on the plump and juicy lady of the family. Why should I care about two crimes, three crimes, a thousand crimes, or ten thousand crimes?" "There is a saying," said the Bodhisattva, "'Heaven helps those who have good intentions.' If you are willing to return to the fruits of truth, there will be means to sustain your body. There are five kinds of grain in this world and they all can relieve hunger. Why do you need to pass the time by feeding on human beings?"

When the fiend heard these words, he was like one who wakes from a dream, and he said to the Bodhisattva, "I would very much like to follow the truth. But 'since I have offended Heaven, even my prayers are of little avail.'" "I have received the decree from Buddha to go to the land of the east to find a scripture pilgrim," said the Bodhisattva. "You can follow him as his disciple and make a trip to the Western Heaven; your merit will cancel out your sins, and you will surely be delivered from your calamities." "I'm willing, I'm willing," promised the fiend with enthusiasm. The Bodhisattva then touched his head and gave him the instructions. Pointing to his body as a sign, she gave him the surname "Chu" and the religious name "Wu-nêng."[31] From that moment on, he accepted the commandment to return to the real. He fasted and ate only a vegetable diet, abstaining from the five forbidden viands and the three undesirable foods,[32] and waiting single-mindedly for the scripture pilgrim.

The Bodhisattva and Mokṣa took leave of Wu-nêng and proceeded again halfway between cloud and mist. As they were journeying, they saw in midair a young dragon calling for help. The Bodhisattva drew near and asked, "What dragon are you, and why are you suffering here?" The dragon said, "I am the son of Ao-jun, the Dragon King of the Western Ocean. Because I inadvertently set fire to the palace and burned some of the pearls in it, my father the king memorialized to the Heavenly Court and charged me with grave disobedience. The Jade Emperor hung me in the sky and gave me three hundred lashes, and I shall be executed in a few days. I beg the Bodhisattva to save me."

When Kuan-yin heard these words, she rushed with Mokṣa up to the South Heavenly Gate. She was received by Ch'iu and Chang, the two Divine Preceptors, who asked her, "Where are you going?" "This humble cleric needs to have an audience with the Jade Emperor," said the Bodhisattva. The two Divine Preceptors promptly made the report, and the Jade Emperor left the hall to receive her. After presenting her greetings, the Bodhisattva said, "This humble cleric is journeying by the decree of Buddha to the land of the East to find a scripture pilgrim. On the way I met a mischievous dragon hanging in the sky. I have come specially to beg you to spare his life and grant him to me. He can be a good means of transportation for the scripture pilgrim." When the Jade Emperor heard these words, he at once gave the decree of pardon, ordering the Heavenly sentinels to release the dragon to Bodhisattva. The Bodhisattva thanked the Emperor, while the young dragon also kowtowed to the Bodhisattva to thank her for saving his life and pledged obedience to her command. The Bodhisattva then sent him to live in a deep mountain stream with the instruction that when the scripture pilgrim should arrive, he was to change into a white horse and go to the Western Heaven. The young dragon obeyed the order and hid himself, and we shall speak no more of him for the moment.

The Bodhisattva then led Mokṣa past the mountain, and they headed again toward the Land of the East. They had not traveled long before they suddenly came upon ten thousand shafts of golden light and a thousand layers of radiant vapor. "Teacher," said Mokṣa, "that luminous place must be the Mountain of Five Phases. I can see the tag of Tathāgata imprinted on it." "So beneath this place," said the Bodhisattva, "is where the Great Sage, Equal to Heaven, who disturbed Heaven and the Festival of Immortal Peaches, is being imprisoned." "Yes, indeed," said Mokṣa. The mentor and her disciple ascended the mountain and looked at the tag, on which was inscribed the divine words of *Oṁ maṇi padme hūṁ*. When the Bodhisattva saw this, she could not help sighing, and composed the following poem:

Rueful is the impish monkey who honored not the Law,
Who rashly sought to be a hero in the years past.
With mind puffed up he disrupted the Peach Banquet,
And boldly plundered the Tushita Palace.
He found no worthy rival in ten thousand troops;
Through Heaven's nine spheres he spread his terror wide.
Imprisoned now by Sovereign Tathāgata,
When will he be free again to show his power?

As mentor and disciple were speaking, they disturbed the Great Sage, who called out loudly from the base of the mountain, "Who is up there on the mountain composing verses to reveal my short-comings?" When the Bodhisattva heard those words, she came down the mountain to take a look. There beneath the rocky ledges were the local spirit, the mountain god, and the Heavenly sentinels guarding the Great Sage. They all came and bowed to receive the Bodhisattva, leading her before the Great Sage. She looked and saw that he was pinned down in a kind of stone box: though he could speak, he could not move his body. "You whose name is Sun," said the Bodhisattva, "do you recognize me?" The Great Sage opened wide his fiery eyes and diamond pupils and nodded. "How could I not recognize you?" he cried loudly. "You are the Mighty Deliverer, the Great Com-passionate Bodhisattva Kuan-yin from the Potalaka Mountain of the South Sea. Thank you, thank you for coming to see me! At this place every day is like a year, for not a single acquaintance has ever come to visit me. Where did you come from?" "I have received the decree from Buddha," said the Bodhisattva, "to go to the Land of the East to find a scripture pilgrim. Since I was passing through here, I rested my steps briefly to see you." "Tathāgata deceived me," said the Great Sage, "and imprisoned me beneath this mountain. For over five hundred years already I have not been able to move. I implore the Bodhisattva to show a little mercy and rescue old Monkey!" "Great were your sinful works," said the Bodhisattva. "If I rescue you, I fear that you will again perpetrate violence, and that will be bad indeed." "Now I know the meaning of penitence," said the Great Sage. "So I entreat the Great Compassion to show me the proper path, for I am willing to practice religion." Truly it is that

One wish born in the heart of man
Is known throughout Heaven and Earth.

If vice or virtue lacks reward,

Unjust must be the universe.

When the Bodhisattva heard those words, she was filled with pleasure and said to the Great Sage, "The scripture says, 'When a good word is spoken, an answer will come from beyond a thousand miles; but when an evil word is spoken, there will be opposition from beyond a thousand miles.' If you have such a purpose, wait until I reach the Great T'ang Nation in the Land of the East and find the scripture pilgrim. He will be told to come and rescue you, and you can follow him as a disciple. You shall keep the teachings and hold the rosary to enter our gate of Buddha, so that you may again cultivate the fruits of righteousness. Will you do that?" "I'm willing, I'm willing," said the Great Sage repeatedly. "If you are indeed seeking the fruits of virtue," said the Bodhisattva, "let me give you a religious name." "I have one already," said the Great Sage, "and I'm called Sun Wu-k'ung." "There were two persons before you who came into our faith," said the delighted Bodhisattva, "and their names, too, are built on the word 'Wu.' Your name will agree with theirs perfectly, and that is splendid indeed. I need not give you any more instruction; I must be going." So our Great Sage, with enlightened mind and nature, returned to the Buddhist faith, while our Bodhisattva, with care and diligence, sought the divine monk.

She left the place with Mokṣa and proceeded straight to the east; in a few days they reached Ch'ang-an of the Great T'ang Nation. Forsaking the mist and abandoning the cloud, mentor and disciple changed themselves into two wandering monks covered with scabby sores[33] and went into the city. It was already dusk. As they walked through one of the main streets, they saw a temple of the local spirit. They both went straight in, alarming the spirit and the demon guards, who recognized the Bodhisattva. They kowtowed to receive her, and the local spirit then ran quickly to report to the city's guardian deity, the god of the soil, and the spirits of various temples of Ch'ang-an. When they learned that it was the Bodhisattva, they all came to pay homage, saying, "Bodhisattva, please pardon us for being tardy in our reception." "None of you," said the Bodhisattva, "should let a word of this leak out! I came here by the special decree of Buddha to look for a scripture pilgrim. I would like to stay just for a few days in one of your temples, and I shall depart when the true monk is found." The various deities went back to their own places, but they sent the local spirit off to the residence of the city's guardian deity so that the teacher and the disciple could remain incognito in the spirit's temple. We do not know what sort of scripture pilgrim was found, and so you must listen to the explanation in the next chapter.

Nine

Ch'ên Kuang-jui, going to his post, meets disaster;
Monk River Float, avenging his parents, repays
   their kindness.

We now tell you about the city of Ch'ang-an in the great nation in
Shensi Province which was the place that kings and emperors from
generation to generation had made their capital. Since the periods
of Chou, Ch'in, and Han, flowers in its three counties grew like
brocade, and the eight waters[1] encircled the city. It was truly a land
of great scenic beauty. At this time the emperor T'ai-tsung[2] of the
Great T'ang dynasty was on the throne, and the name of his reign
was Chên-kuan. He had been ruling now for thirteen years, and the
cyclical name of the year was Chi-ssǔ.[3] The whole land was at peace;
people came bearing tributes from eight directions; and the inhabitants of the whole world called themselves his subjects.

One day T'ai-tsung ascended his throne and assembled his civil and
military officials. After they had paid him homage, the prime minister
Wei Chêng[4] left the ranks and came forward to memorialize to the
Throne, saying, "Since the world now is at peace and tranquility
reigns everywhere, we should follow the ancient custom and establish
sites for examinations, so that we may invite worthy scholars to
come here and select those talents who will best serve the work of
administration and government." "Our worthy subject has voiced a
sound principle in his memorial," said T'ai-tsung. He therefore issued
a summons to be proclaimed throughout the empire: in every prefecture, county, and town, those who were learned in the Confucian
classics, who could write with ease and lucidity, and who had passed
the three sessions of examination,[5] regardless of whether they were
soldiers or peasants, were invited to go to Ch'ang-an to take the
imperial examination.

This summons reached the place Hai Chou, where it was seen by
a certain man named Ch'ên O (with the courtesy name of Kuang-jui),
who then went straight home to talk to his mother, whose maiden

name was Chang. "The court," he said, "has sent a yellow summons,[6] declaring in these southern provinces that there will be examinations for the selection of the worthy and the talented. Your child wishes to try out at such an examination, for if I manage to acquire an appointment, or even half a post, I would become more of a credit to my parents, magnify our name, give my wife a title, benefit my son, and bring glory to this house of ours. Such is the aspiration of your son; I wish to tell my mother plainly before I leave." "My son," said she of the Chang family, "an educated person 'learns when he is young, but leaves when he is grown.' You should indeed follow this maxim. But as you go to the examination, you must be careful on the way, and, when you have secured a post, come home quickly." So Kuang-jui gave instructions for his family page to pack his bags, took leave of his mother, and began his journey. When he reached Ch'ang-an, the examination site had just been opened, and he went straight in. He took the preliminary tests, passed them, and went to the court examination, where in three sessions on administrative policy he took first place, receiving the title "chuang-yüan," the certificate of which was signed by the T'ang emperor's own hand. As was the custom, he was led through the streets on horseback for three days.

The procession at one point passed by the house of the chief minister, Yin K'ai-shan, who had a daughter named Wên-chiao, nicknamed Man-t'ang-chiao.[7] She was not yet married, and at this time she was just about to throw down an embroidered ball from high up on a festooned tower in order to select her spouse. It happened that Ch'ên Kuang-jui was passing by the tower down below. When the young maiden saw Kuang-jui's outstanding appearance and knew that he was the recent chuang-yüan of the examinations, she was very pleased. She threw down the embroidered ball, which just happened to hit the black gauze hat of Kuang-jui. Immediately, the lively music of pipes and flutes could be heard throughout the area; scores of maids and serving-girls ran down from the tower, took hold of the bridle of Kuang-jui's horse, and led him into the residence of the chief minister for the wedding. The chief minister and his wife at once came out of their chambers, called together the guests and the master of ceremonies, and gave the girl to Kuang-jui as his bride. Together, they bowed to Heaven and Earth; then husband and wife bowed to each other, before bowing to the father- and mother-in-law.

The chief minister then gave a big banquet and everyone feasted merrily for a whole evening, after which the two of them walked hand in hand into the bridal chamber.

At the fifth watch early next morning, T'ai-tsung took his seat in the Treasure Hall of Golden Chimes as civil and military officials attended the court. T'ai-tsung asked, "What appointment should the new chuang-yüan receive?" The prime minister Wei Chêng said, "Your subject has discovered that within our territory there is a vacancy at Chiang Chou. I beg my Lord to grant him this post." T'ai-tsung at once made him governor of Chiang Chou and ordered him to leave without delay. After thanking the emperor and leaving the court, Kuang-jui went back to the house of the chief minister to inform his wife. He took leave of his father- and mother-in-law and proceeded with his wife to the new post at Chiang Chou.

As they left Ch'ang-an and went on their journey, the season was late spring: a soft wind blew to green the willows, and a fine rain spotted to redden the flowers. As his home was on the way, Kuang-jui returned to his house where husband and wife bowed together to his mother, Lady Chang. "Congratulations, my son," said she of the Chang family, "you even came back with a wife!" "Your child," said Kuang-jui, "relied on the power of your blessing and was able to attain the undeserved honor of chuang-yüan. By imperial command I was making a tour of the streets when, as I passed by the mansion of Chief Minister Yin, I was hit by an embroidered ball. The chief minister kindly gave his daughter to your child to be his wife, and His Majesty appointed him governor of Chiang Chou. I have returned to take you with me to the post." She of the Chang family was delighted and packed at once for the journey.

They had been on the road for a few days when they came to stay at the Inn of Ten Thousand Flowers, kept by a certain Liu Hsiao-erh. She of the Chang family suddenly became ill and said to Kuang-jui, "I don't feel well at all. Let's rest here for a day or two before we journey again." Kuang-jui obeyed. Next morning there was a man outside the inn holding a golden carp for sale, which Kuang-jui bought for a string of coins. He was about to have it cooked for his mother when he saw that the carp was blinking its eyes vigorously. In astonishment, Kuang-jui said, "I have heard that when a fish or a snake blinks its eyes in this manner, that's the sure sign that it's not an ordinary creature!" He therefore asked the fisherman, "Where did you catch this fish?" "I caught it," said the fisherman, "from the River Hung, some fifteen miles from this district." Accordingly, Kuang-jui sent the fish live back to the river and returned to the inn to tell his mother about it. "It is a good deed to release living creatures," said she of the Chang family. "I am very pleased." "We have stayed in this inn now for three days," said Kuang-jui. "The imperial command is an urgent one. Your child intends to leave tomorrow, but he would like to know whether mother has fully recovered." She of the Chang family said, "I'm still not well, and the heat on the journey at this time of year, I fear, will only add to my illness. Why don't you rent a house for me to stay here temporarily and leave me an allowance? The two of you can proceed to your new post. By autumn, when it's cool, you can come fetch me." Kuang-jui discussed the matter with his wife; they duly rented a house for her and left some cash with her, after which they took leave and left.

They felt the fatigue of traveling, journeying by day and resting by night, and they soon came to the crossing of the Hung River, where two boatmen, Liu Hung and Li Piao, took them into their boat. It happened that Kuang-jui was destined in his previous incarnation to meet this calamity, and so he had to come upon these fated enemies of his. After ordering the houseboy to put the luggage on the boat, Kuang-jui and his wife were just about to get aboard when Liu Hung noticed the beauty of Lady Yin, who had a face like a full moon, eyes like autumnal water, a small, cherrylike mouth, and a tiny, willow-like waist. Her features were striking enough to sink fishes and drop wild geese, and her complexion would cause the moon to hide and put the flowers to shame. Stirred to cruelty, he plotted with Li Piao; together they punted the boat to an isolated area and waited until the middle of the night. They killed the houseboy first, and then they beat Kuang-jui to death, pushing both bodies into the water. When the lady saw that they had killed her husband, she made a dive for the water, but Liu Hung threw his arms around her and caught her. "If you consent to my demand," he said, "everything will be all right. If you do not, this knife will cut you in two!" Unable to think of any better plan, the lady had to give her consent for the time being and yielded herself to Liu Hung. The thief took the boat to the south bank, where he turned the boat over to the care of Li Piao. He himself put on Kuang-jui's cap and robe, took his credentials, and proceeded with the lady to the post at Chiang Chou.

We should now tell you that the body of the houseboy killed by Liu Hung drifted away with the current. The body of Ch'ên Kuang-jui, however, sank to the bottom of the water and stayed there. A yakṣa on patrol at the mouth of the Hung River saw it and rushed into the Dragon Palace. The Dragon King was just holding court when the yakṣa entered to report, saying, "A scholar has been beaten to death at the mouth of the Hung River by some unknown person, and his body is now lying at the bottom of the water." The Dragon King had the corpse brought in and laid before him. He took a careful look at it and said, "But this man was my benefactor! How could he have been murdered? As the common saying goes, 'Kindness should be paid by kindness.' I must save his life today so that I may repay the kindness of yesterday." He at once issued an official dispatch, sending a yakṣa to deliver it to the municipal deity and local spirit of Hung-chou, and asked for the soul of the scholar so that his life might be saved. The municipal deity and the local spirit in turn ordered the little demons to hand over the soul of Ch'ên Kuang-jui to the yakṣa, who led the soul back to the Water Crystal Palace for an audience with the Dragon King.

"Scholar," asked the Dragon King, "what is your name? Where did you come from? Why did you come here, and for what reason were you beaten to death?" Kuang-jui saluted him and said, "This minor student is named Ch'ên O, and my courtesy name is Kuang-jui. I am from the Hung-nung district of Hai Chou. As the unworthy chuang-yüan of the recent session of examination, I was appointed by the court to be governor of Chiang Chou, and I was going to my post with my wife. When I took a boat at the river, I did not expect the boatman, Liu Hung, to covet my wife and plot against me. He beat me to death and tossed out my body. I beg the Great King to save me." Hearing these words, the Dragon King said, "So, that's it! Good sir, the golden carp that you released earlier was myself. You are my benefactor. You may be in dire difficulty at the moment, but is there any reason why I should not come to your asistance?" He therefore laid the body of Kuang-jui to one side, and put a preservative pearl in his mouth so that his body would not deteriorate but be reunited with his soul to avenge himself in the future. He also said,

"Your true soul may remain temporarily in my Water Bureau as an officer." Kuang-jui kowtowed to thank him, and the Dragon King prepared a banquet to entertain him, but we shall say no more about that.

We now tell you that Lady Yin hated the bandit Liu so bitterly that she wished she could eat his flesh and sleep on his skin! But because she was with child and did not know whether it would be a boy or a girl, she had no alternative but to yield reluctantly to her captor. In a little while they arrived at Chiang Chou; the clerks and the lictors all came to meet them, and all the subordinate officials gave a banquet for them at the governor's mansion. Liu Hung said, "Having come here, a student like me is utterly dependent on the support and assistance of you gentlemen." "Your Honor," replied the officials, "is first in the examinations and a major talent. You will, of course, regard your people as your children; your public declarations will be simple as your settlement of litigation is fair. We subordinates are all dependent on your leadership, so why should you be unduly modest?" When the official banquet ended, the people all left.

Time passed by swiftly. One day, Liu Hung went far away on official business, while Lady Yin at the mansion was thinking of her mother-in-law and her husband and sighing in the garden pavilion. Suddenly she was seized by tremendous fatigue and sharp pains in her belly. Falling unconscious to the ground, she gave birth to a son. Presently she heard someone whispering in her ear: "Man-t'ang-chiao, listen carefully to what I have to say. I am the Star Spirit of South Pole, who sends you this son by the express command of the Bodhisattva Kuan-yin. One day his name will be known far and wide, for he is not to be compared with an ordinary mortal. But when the bandit Liu returns, he will surely try to harm the child, and you must take care to protect him. Your husband has been rescued by the Dragon King; in the future both of you will meet again even as son and mother will be reunited. A day will come when wrongs will be redressed and crimes punished. Remember my words! Wake up! Wake up!" The voice ceased and departed. The lady woke up and remembered every word; she clasped her son tightly to her but could devise no plan to protect him. Liu Hung then returned and wanted to have the child killed by drowning the moment he saw him. The lady said, "Today it's late already. Allow him to live till tomorrow and then have him thrown into the river."

It was fortunate that Liu Hung was called away by urgent business the next morning. The lady thought to herself: "If this child is here when that bandit returns, his life is finished! I might as well abandon him now to the river, and let life or death take its own course. Perhaps Heaven, taking pity on him, will send someone to his rescue and to have him cared for. Then we may have a chance to meet again." She was afraid, however, that future recognition would be difficult; so she bit her finger and wrote a letter with her blood, stating in detail the names of the parents, the family history, and the reason for the child's abandonment. She also bit off a little toe from the child's left foot to establish a mark of his identity. Taking one of her own inner garments she wrapped the child and took him out of the mansion when no one was watching. Fortunately the mansion was not far from the river. Reaching the bank, the lady burst into tears and wailed long and loud. She was about to toss the child into the river when she caught sight of a plank floating by the river bank. At once she prayed to Heaven, after which she placed the child on the plank and tied him securely to it with some rope. She fastened the letter written in blood to his chest, pushed the plank out into the water, and let it drift away. With tears in her eyes, the lady went back to the mansion, but we shall say no more of that.

Now we shall tell you about the boy on the plank, which floated with the current until it came to a standstill just beneath the Temple of the Golden Mountain. The abbot of this temple was called Monk Fa-ming. In the cultivation and comprehension of truth, he had attained already the wondrous secret of immortality. He was sitting in meditation when all at once he heard a baby crying. Moved by this, he went quickly down to the river to have a look, and discovered the baby lying there on a plank at the edge of the water. Hurriedly the abbot lifted him out of the water. When he read the letter in blood fastened to his chest, he found out about the child's origin. He then gave him the baby name River Float and arranged for someone to nurse and care for him, while he himself kept the letter written in blood safely hidden. Time passed by like an arrow, and the seasons like a weaver's shuttle; River Float soon reached his eighteenth year. The abbot had his hair shaved and asked him to join in the practice of austerities, giving him the religious name Hsüan-tsang. Having had his head touched and having received the prohibitions, Hsüan-tsang pursued the Way with great determination.

One day in late spring, the various monks gathered in the shade of pine trees were discussing the canons of Zen and debating the fine points of the mysteries. One feckless monk, who happened to have been completely outwitted by Hsüan-tsang's questions, cried in great anger, "You damnable beast! You don't even know your own name, and you are ignorant of your own parents! Why are you still hanging around here playing tricks on people?" When Hsüan-tsang heard such language of rebuke, he went into the temple and knelt before the master, saying with tears flowing from his eyes, "Though a human being born into this world receives his natural endowments from the forces of yin and yang and from the Five Phases, he is always nurtured by his parents. How can there be a person in this world who has no father or mother?" Repeatedly and piteously he begged for the names of his parents. The abbot said, "If you truly wish to seek your parents, you may follow me to my cell." Hsüang-tsang duly followed him to his cell, where, from the top of a heavy crossbeam, the abbot took down a small box. Opening the box, he took out a letter written in blood and an inner garment and gave them to Hsüan-tsang. Only after he had unfolded the letter and read it did Hsüang-tsang learn the names of his parents and understand in detail the wrongs that had been done them.

When Hsüan-tsang had finished reading, he fell weeping to the floor, saying, "How can anyone be worthy to bear the name of man if he cannot avenge the wrongs done to his parents? For eighteen years, I have been ignorant of my true parents, and only this day have I learned that I have a mother! And yet, would I have even reached this day if my master had not saved me and cared for me? Permit your disciple to go seek my mother. Thereafter, I will rebuild this temple with an incense bowl on my head,[8] and repay the profound kindness of my teacher." "If you desire to seek your mother," said the master, "you may take this letter in blood and the inner garment with you. Go as a mendicant monk to the private quarters at the governor's mansion of Chiang Chou. You will then be able to meet your mother."

Hsüan-tsang followed the words of his master and went to Chiang Chou as a mendicant monk. It happened that Liu Hung was out on business, for Heaven had planned that mother and child should meet. Hsüan-tsang went straight to the door of the private quarters of the governor's mansion to beg for alms. Lady Yin, you see, had had a dream the night before in which she saw a waning moon become full again. She thought to herself, "I have no news from my mother-in-law; my husband was murdered by this bandit; my son was thrown into the river. If by chance someone rescued him and had him cared for, he must be eighteen by now. Perhaps Heaven wished us to be reunited today. Who can tell?" As she was pondering the matter in her heart, she suddenly heard someone reciting the scriptures outside her residence and crying repeatedly, "Alms! Alms!" At a convenient moment, the lady slipped out and asked him, "Where did you come from?" "Your poor monk," said Hsüan-tsang, "is the disciple of Fa-ming, abbot of the Temple of the Golden Mountain." "So you are the disciple of the abbot of that temple?" She asked him into the mansion and served him some vegetables and rice. Watching him closely, she noticed that in speech and manner he bore a remarkable resemblance to her husband. The lady sent her maid away and then asked, "Young master! Did you leave your family as a child or when you grew up? What are your given name and your surname? Do you have any parents?" "I did not leave my family when I was young," replied Hsüan-tsang, "nor did I do so when I grew up. To tell you the truth, I have a wrong to avenge great as the sky, an enmity deep as the sea. My father was a murder victim, and my mother was taken by force. My master the abbot Fa-ming told me to seek my mother in the governor's mansion of Chiang Chou." "What is your mother's surname?" asked the lady. "My mother's surname is Yin," said Hsüan-tsang, "and her given name is Wên-chiao. My father's surname is Ch'ên, and his given name is Kuang-jui. My nickname is River Float, but my religious name is Hsüan-tsang." "I am Wên-chiao," said the lady, "but what proof have you of your identity?" When Hsüan-tsang heard that she was his mother, he fell to his knees and wept most grievously. "If my own mother doesn't believe me," he said, "you may see the proof in this letter written in blood and this inner garment." Wên-chiao took them in her hands, and one look told her that they were the real things. Mother and child embraced each other and wept.

Lady Yin then cried, "My son, leave at once!" "For eighteen years I have not known my true parents," said Hsüan-tsang, "and I've seen my mother for the first time only this morning. How could your son bear so swift a separation?" "My son," said the lady, "leave at once, as if you were on fire! If that bandit Liu returns, he will surely take your life. I shall pretend to be ill tomorrow and say that I must go to your temple and fulfill a vow I made in a previous year to donate a hundred pairs of monk shoes. At that time I shall have more to say to you." Hsüan-tsang followed her bidding and bowed to take leave of her.

We were speaking of Lady Yin, who, having seen her son, was filled with both anxiety and joy. The next day, under the pretext of being sick, she lay on her bed and would take neither tea nor rice. Liu Hung returned to the mansion and questioned her. "When I was young," said Lady Yin, "I vowed to donate a hundred pairs of monk shoes. Five days ago, I dreamed that a monk demanded those shoes of me, holding a knife in his hand. From then on, I did not feel well." "Such a small matter!" said Liu Hung. "Why didn't you tell me earlier?" He at once went up to the governor's hall and gave the order to his stewards Wang and Li that a hundred families of the city were each to bring in a pair of monk shoes within five days. The families obeyed and completed their presentations. "Now that we have the shoes," said Lady Yin to Liu Hung, "what kind of temple do we have nearby that I can go to fulfill my vow?" Liu Hung said, "There is a Temple of the Golden Mountain here in Chiang Chou as well as a Temple of the Burned Mountain. You may go to whichever one you choose." "I have long heard," said the lady, "that the Temple of the Golden Mountain is a very good one. I shall go there." Liu Hung at once gave the order to his stewards Wang and Li to prepare a boat. Lady Yin took a trusted companion with her and boarded the boat. The boatmen poled it away from the shore and headed for the Temple of the Golden Mountain.

We now tell you about Hsüan-tsang, who returned to the temple and told the abbot Fa-ming what had happened. The next day, a young housemaid arrived to announce that her mistress was coming to the temple to fulfill a vow she had made. All the monks came out of the temple to receive her. The lady went straight inside to worship the Bodhisattva and to give a great vegetarian banquet. She ordered the housemaid to put the monk shoes and stockings in trays and have them brought into the main ceremonial hall. After the lady had again worshiped with extreme devoutness, she asked the abbot Fa-ming to distribute the gifts to the various monks before they dispersed. When Hsüan-tsang saw that all the monks had left and that there was no one else in the hall, he drew near and knelt down. The lady asked him to remove his shoes and stockings, and she saw that there was, indeed, a small toe missing from his left foot. Once again, the two of them embraced and wept. They also thanked the abbot for his kindness in fostering the youth. Fa-ming said, "I fear that the present meeting of mother and child may become known to that wily bandit. You must leave speedily so that you may avoid any harm." "My son," the lady said, "let me give you an incense ring. Go to Hung Chou, about fifteen hundred miles northwest of here, where you will find the Ten Thousand Flowers Inn. Earlier we left an aged woman there whose maiden name is Chang and who is the true mother of your father. I have also written a letter for you to take to the capital of the T'ang emperor. To the left of the Golden Palace is the house of Chief Minister Yin, who is the true father of your mother. Give my letter to your maternal grandfather, and ask him to request the T'ang emperor to dispatch men and horses to have this bandit arrested and executed, so that your father may be avenged. Only then will you be able to rescue your old mother. I dare not linger now, for I fear that that knave may be offended by my returning late." She went out of the temple, boarded the boat, and left.

Hsüan-tsang returned weeping to the temple. He told his master everything and bowed to take leave of him immediately. Going straight to Hung Chou, he came to the Ten Thousand Flowers Inn and addressed the innkeeper, Liu Hsiao-erh, saying, "In a previous year there was an honored guest here by the name of Ch'ên, whose mother remained at your inn. How is she now?" "Originally," said Liu Hsiao-erh, "she stayed in my inn. Afterwards she went blind, and for three or four years did not pay me any rent. She now lives in a dilapidated potter's kiln near the Southern Gate, and every day she goes begging on the streets. Once that honored guest had left, he was gone for a long time, and even now there is no news of him whatever. I can't understand it."

When Hsüan-tsang had heard this, he went at once to the dilapidated potter's kiln at the Southern Gate and found his grandmother. The grandmother said, "Your voice sounds very much like that of my son Ch'ên Kuang-jui." "I'm not Ch'ên Kuang-jui," said Hsüantsang, "only his son! Lady Wên-chiao is my mother." "Why didn't your father and mother come back?" asked the grandmother. "My father was beaten to death by bandits," said Hsüan-tsang, "and one of them forced my mother to be his wife." "How did you know where to find me?" asked the grandmother. "It was my mother," answered Hsüan-tsang, "who told me to seek my grandmother. There's a letter from mother here and there's also an incense ring." The grandmother took the letter and the incense ring and wept without restraint. "For merit and reputation," she said, "my son came to this! I thought that he had turned his back on righteousness and had forgotten parental kindness. How should I know that he was murdered! Fortunately, Heaven remembered me at least in pity, and this day a grandson has come to seek me out." "Grandmother," asked Hsüan-tsang, "how did you go blind?" "Because I thought so often about your father," said the grandmother. "I waited for him daily, but he did not return. I wept until I was blind in both eyes." Hsüan-tsang knelt down and prayed to Heaven, saying, "Have regard of Hsüan-tsang who, at the age of eighteen, has not yet avenged the wrong done to his parents. By the command of my mother, I came this day to find my grandmother. If Heaven would take pity on my sincerity, grant that the eyes of my grandmother regain their sight." When he finished his petition, he licked the eyes of his grandmother with the tip of his tongue. In a moment, both eyes were licked open and they were as of old. When the grandmother saw the youthful monk, she said, "You're indeed my grandson! Why, you are just like my son Kuang-jui!" She felt both happy and sad. Hsüan-tsang led the grandmother out of the kiln and went back to Liu Hsiao-erh's inn, where he rented a room for her to stay. He also gave her some money, saying, "In a little more than a month's time, I'll be back."

Taking leave of his grandmother, he went straight to the capital and found his way to the house of the chief minister Yin on the eastern street of the imperial city. He said to the porter, "This little monk is a kinsman who has come to visit the chief minister." The porter made the report to the chief minister, who said, "I'm not related to any monk!" But his wife said, "I dreamed last night that my daughter Man-t'ang-chiao came home. Could it be that our son-in-law has sent us a letter?" The chief minister therefore had the little monk shown to the living room. When he saw the chief minister and his wife, he fell weeping to the floor. Taking a letter from within the folds of his robe, he handed it over to the chief minister. The chief minister opened it, read it from beginning to end, and wept without restraint. "Your Excellency, what is the matter?" asked his wife. "This monk," said the chief minister, "is our grandson. Our son-in-

law, Ch'ên Kuang-jui, was murdered by bandits, and Man-t'ang-
chiao was made the wife of the murderer by force." When the wife
heard this, she too wept inconsolably. "Let our lady restrain her
grief," said the chief minister. "Tomorrow morning I shall present a
memorial to our Lord. I shall lead the troops myself to avenge our
son-in-law."

Next day, the chief minister went into court to present his memorial
to the T'ang emperor, which read:

The son-in-law of your subject, the chuang-yüan Ch'ên Kuang-jui,
was proceeding to his post at Chiang Chou with members of his
family. He was beaten to death by the boatman Liu Hung, who
then took our daughter by force to be his wife. He pretended to
be the son-in-law of your subject and usurped his post for many
years. This is indeed a shocking and tragic incident. I beg Your
Majesty to dispatch horses and men at once to exterminate the
bandits.

The T'ang emperor saw the memorial and became exceedingly angry.
He immediately called up sixty thousand imperial soldiers and
ordered the chief minister Yin to lead them forth. The chief minister
took the decree and left the court to make the roll call for the troops
at the barracks. They proceeded immediately toward Chiang Chou,
journeying by day and resting by night, and they soon reached the
place. Horses and men pitched camps on the north shore, and that
very night, the chief minister summoned with golden tablets⁹ the
Subprefect and County Judge of Chiang Chou to his camp. He explained to the two of them the reason for the expedition and asked
for their military assistance. They then crossed the river and, before
the sky was light, had the mansion of Liu Hung completely surrounded. Liu Hung was still in his dreams when at the shot of a single
cannon and the unisonous roll of drums, the soldiers broke into the
private quarters of the mansion. Liu Hung was seized before he could
offer any resistance. The chief minister had him and the rest of the
prisoners bound and taken to the field of execution, while the rest of
the soldiers pitched camp outside the city.

Taking a seat in the great hall of the mansion, the chief minister
invited the lady to come out to meet him. She was about to do so but
was overcome by shame at seeing her father again, and wanted to
hang herself right there. Hsüan-tsang learned of this and rushed
inside to save his mother. Falling to his knees, he said to her, "Your

son and his grandfather led the troops here to avenge father. The bandit has already been captured. Why does mother want to die now? If mother were dead, how could your son possibly remain alive?" The chief minister also went inside to offer his consolation. "I have heard," said the lady, "that a woman follows her spouse to the grave. My husband was murdered by this bandit, causing me dreadful grief. How could I yield so shamefully to the thief? The child I was carrying—that was my sole lease on life which helped me bear my humiliation! Now that my son is grown and my old father has led troops to avenge our wrong, I who am the daughter have little face left for my reunion. I can only die to repay my husband!" "My child," said the chief minister, "you did not alter your virtue according to prosperity or adversity. You had no choice! How can this be regarded as shame!" Father and daughter embraced, weeping; Hsüan-tsang, too, could not contain his emotion.

Wiping away his tears, the chief minister said, "The two of you must sorrow no more. I have already captured the culprit, and I must now dispose of him." He got up and went to the execution site, and it happened that the Subprefect of Chiang Chou had also apprehended the pirate, Li Piao, who was brought by sentinels to the same place. Highly pleased, the chief minister ordered Liu Hung and Li Piao to be flogged a hundred times with large canes. Each signed an affidavit, giving a thorough account of the murder of Ch'ên Kuang-jui. First Li Piao was nailed to a wooden ass, and after it had been pushed to the market place, he was cut to pieces and his head exposed on a pole for all to see. Liu Hung was then taken to the crossing at the Hung River, to the exact spot where he had beaten Ch'ên Kuang-jui to death. The chief minister, the lady, and Hsüan-tsang all went to the bank of the river, and as libations they offered the heart and liver of Liu Hung which had been gouged out from him live. Finally, an essay eulogizing the deceased was burned.

Facing the river the three persons wept without restraint, and their sobs were heard down below in the water region. A yakṣa patrolling the waters brought the essay in its spirit form to the Dragon King, who read it and at once sent a turtle marshal to fetch Kuang-jui. "Sir," said the king, "congratulations! Congratulations! At this moment, your wife, your son, and your father-in-law are offering sacrifices to you at the bank of the river. I am now letting your soul go so that you may return to life. We are also presenting you with a pearl of wish fulfillment,[10] two rolling-pan pearls,[11] ten bales of mermaid silk,[12] and a jade belt with lustrous pearls. Today you will enjoy the reunion of husband and wife, mother and son." After Kuang-jui had given thanks repeatedly, the Dragon King ordered a yakṣa to escort his body to the mouth of the river and there to return his soul. The yakṣa followed the order and left.

We tell you now about Lady Yin, who, having wept for some time for her husband, would have killed herself again by plunging into the water if Hsüan-tsang had not desperately held on to her. They were struggling pitifully when they saw a dead body floating toward the river bank. The lady hurriedly went forward to look at it. Recognizing it as her husband's body, she burst into even louder wailing. As the other people gathered around to look, they suddenly saw Kuang-jui unclasping his fists and stretching his legs. The entire body began to stir, and in a moment he clambered up to the bank and sat down, to the infinite amazement of everyone. Kuang-jui opened his eyes and saw Lady Yin, the chief minister Yin, his father-in-law, and a youthful monk, all weeping around him. "Why are you all here?" said Kuang-jui. "It all began," said Lady Yin, "when you were beaten to death by bandits. Afterwards your unworthy wife gave birth to this son, who is fortunate enough to have been brought up by the abbot of the Golden Mountain Temple. The abbot sent him to meet me, and I told him to go seek his maternal grandfather. When father heard this, he made it known to the court and led troops here to arrest the bandits. Just now we took out the culprit's liver and heart live to offer to you as libations, but I would like to know how my husband's soul is able to return to give him life." Kuang-jui said, "That's all on account of our buying the golden carp, when you and I were staying at the Inn of Ten Thousand Flowers. I let that carp go, not knowing that it was none other than the Dragon King of this place. When the bandits pushed me into the river thereafter, he was the one who came to my rescue. Just now he was also the one who gave me back my soul as well as many precious gifts, which I have here with me. I never even knew that you had given birth to this boy, and I am grateful that my father-in-law has avenged me. Indeed, bitterness has passed and sweetness has come! What unsurpassable joy!"

When the various officials heard about this, they all came to tender their congratulations. The chief minister then ordered a great banquet to thank his subordinates, after which the troops and horses on the very same day began their march homeward. When they came to the Inn of Ten Thousand Flowers, the chief minister gave order to pitch camp. Kuang-jui went with Hsüan-tsang to the Inn of Liu to seek the grandmother, who happened to have dreamed the night before that a withered tree had blossomed. Magpies behind her house were chattering incessantly also. She thought to herself, "Could it be that my grandson is coming?" Before she had finished talking to herself, father and son arrived together. The youthful monk pointed to her and said, "Isn't this my grandmother?" When Kuang-jui saw his aged mother, he bowed in haste; mother and son embraced and wept without restraint for a while. After recounting to each other what had happened, they paid the innkeeper his bill and set out again for the capital. When they reached the chief minister's residence, Kuang-jui, his wife, and his mother all went to greet the chief minister's wife, who was overjoyed. She ordered her servants to prepare a huge banquet to celebrate the occasion. The chief minister said, "This banquet today may be named the Festival of Reunion, for truly our whole family is rejoicing."

Early next morning, the T'ang emperor held court, during which time the chief minister Yin left the ranks to give a careful report on what had taken place. He also recommended that a talent like Kuang-jui's be used in some important capacity. The T'ang emperor approved the memorial, and ordered that Ch'ên O be promoted to Subchancellor of the Grand Secretariat so that he could accompany the court and carry out its policies. Hsüan-tsang, determined to follow the way of Zen, was sent to practice austerities at the Temple of Infinite Blessing. Some time after this, Lady Yin calmly committed suicide after all, and Hsüan-tsang went back to the Golden Mountain Temple to repay the kindness of abbot Fa-ming. We do not know how things went thereafter, and so you must listen to the explanation in the next chapter.

Ten

The Old Dragon King, in foolish schemes, transgresses
   Heaven's decrees;
Prime Minister Wei sends a letter to an official
   of the dead.

For the time being, we shall make no mention of Kuang-jui serving in his post and Hsüan-tsang practicing austerities. We tell you now about two worthies who lived on the banks of the river Ching outside the city of Ch'ang-an: a fisherman by the name of Chang Shao and a woodman by the name of Li Ting.[1] The two of them were scholars who had passed no official examination, mountain folks who knew how to read. One day in the city of Ch'ang-an, after they had sold the wood on the one's back and the carp in the other's basket, they went into a small inn and drank until they were slightly tipsy. Each carrying a bottle, they followed the bank of the Ching River and walked slowly back. "Brother Li," said Chang Shao, "in my opinion those who strive for fame will lose their lives on account of fame; those who live in quest of fortune will perish because of riches; those who have titles sleep embracing a tiger; and those who receive official favors walk with snakes in their sleeves. When you think of it, their lives cannot compare with our carefree existence, close to the blue mountains and fair waters. We cherish poverty and pass our days without having to quarrel with fate." "Brother Chang," said Li Ting, "there's a great deal of truth in what you say. But your fair waters cannot match my blue mountains." "On the contrary," said Chang Shao, "your blue mountains cannot match my fair waters, in testimony of which I offer a tz'ŭ poem to the tune of *Tieh-lien-hua*.[2] The poem says:
   On ten thousand miles of misty waters in a tiny boat
   I lean to the silent, solitary sail,
   Surrounded by the sound of the mermaid-fish.
   My mind cleansed, my care purged, for here's little wealth or fame;
   I pick in leisure the stems of bulrushes and reeds.
   To count the seagulls: there's a joy to be told!

At willowed banks and reeded bays
My wife and children join my laughter gay.
I sleep most soundly as wind and wave recede;
No shame, no glory, nor any misery."
Li Ting said, "Your fair waters are not as good as my blue mountains.
I also have as testimony a tz'ŭ poem to the tune of *Tieh-lien-hua*. The
poem says:
    In one pine-seeded corner of a forest dense,
    I listen wordless to the oriole
    With its deft tongue like a tuneful pipe.
    Pale reds and bright greens announce the warmth of spring;
    Summer comes abruptly; so passes time.
    Then autumn arrives (for it's an easy change)
    With fragrant golden flowers
    Most worthy of our joy;
    And cold winter enters, swift as a finger snaps.
    Ruled by no one, I'm free in all four seasons."
The fisherman said, "Your blue mountains are not as good as my
fair waters, which offer me some fine things to enjoy. As testimony I
have here a tz'ŭ poem to the tune of *Chê-ku-t'ien*:
    The fairyland cloud and water do surely suffice:
    Boat adrift; oars accumbent; there's at once my home.
    I split fresh fishes alive and cook the green turtles;
    I then steam purple crabs and boil red shrimps;
    The green reed-shoots,
    The water-plant sprouts;
    Even better are the 'chicken heads,'[3] the water caltrops,
    The lotus roots, old or young, the tender celery leaves,
    The arrowheads, the white caltrops, and the niao-ying flowers."
The woodman said, "Your fair waters are not as good as my blue
mountains, which offer me some fine things to enjoy. As testimony I
too have a tz'ŭ poem to the tune of *Chê-ku-t'ien*:
    On tall, craggy peaks touching the edge of the sky,
    A grass house or a straw hut makes up my home.
    Salted fowls and smoked geese surpass turtles or crabs;
    Hares, antelopes, and deer best fishes or shrimps.
    The scented ch'un leaves;[4]
    The yellow lien sprouts;[5]

Even better are the bamboo shoots and mountain tea;
Purple plums, red peaches, prunes and apricots ripe,
Sweet pears, sour dates, and the cassia flowers."

The fisherman said, "Your blue mountains are truly not as good as
my fair waters. I have another tz'ŭ poem to the tune of *T'ien-hsien-tzŭ*:

One leaflike boat goes wherever I choose to stay.
I fear not ten thousand folds of wave or mist.
I drop hooks and cast nets to catch fresh fish:
Without sauce or fat,
It's tastier yet.
Old wife and young son complete my home.
When fishes are plenty, I go to Ch'ang-an marts
And trade them for wine I drink till I'm drunk.
A coir coat's my cover, on autumnal stream I lie;
Snoring, asleep;
No fret or care.
Not for me the glory or the pomp of man."

The woodman said, "Your fair waters are still not as good as my blue
mountains. I too have a poem to the tune of *T'ien-hsien-tzŭ*:

A few straw huts built beneath a hill.
Pines, orchids, plums, bamboos—lovable all!
Passing groves and climbing mountains I seek dried woods.
With none to chide,
I sell as I wish—
How much, how little, depends on my yield.
I use the money to buy wine as I please.
Earthen crocks and clay flagons both put me at ease!
Sodden with wine, in the pine shade I lie:
No anxious thoughts;
No gain or loss;
No care for this world's failure or success."

The fisherman said, "Brother Li, your mountain life is not as pleasing
as my existence on the waters. As testimony, I have a tz'ŭ poem to
the tune of *Hsi-chiang-yüeh*:[6]

Dense flowers of red smartweeds glow in the moonlight;
Tousled leaves of yellow rushes shake in the wind.
The blue sky, clean and distant—an empty Ch'u River;
Drawing in my lines, I stir a deep pool of stars.

In rank and file big fishes enter the net.
In groups and teams small perches swallow the hooks.
Their taste is special when they're thus caught and cooked.
My boisterous laugh presides over rivers and lakes."
The woodman says, "Brother Chang, your life on the waters is not as
pleasing as my existence in the mountains. As testimony, I also have
a tz'ŭ poem to the tune of *Hsi-chiang-yüeh*:
    Dead leaves and parched creepers choking the road;
    Snapped poles and aged bamboos crowding the hill;
    Dried tendrils and sedges in disheveled growth
    I break and take, my ropes trussing the load.
    The trunks of willow emptied by insects,
    The branches of pine clipped off by wind,
    I gather and stockpile, ready for winter's cold;
    To change them for wine or money is my own choice."
The fisherman said, "Though your life in the mountains is not bad,
it is still not as charming and graceful as mine is on the fair waters.
As testimony, I have a tz'ŭ poem to the tune of *Lin-chiang-hsien*:
    The falling tide will move my single boat away;
    I rest my oars, my song comes with the night.
    The coir coat, the waning moon—how charming they are!
    No seagull is startled from sleep
    As rosy clouds spread in the sky.
    At reed-filled islets undisturbed I sleep
    And there remain even when the sun is high.
    I work according to my own plans and desires.
    Vassals tending court in nocturnal cold,
    How do they match my free and easy mind?
The woodman said, "The charm and grace of your fair waters cannot
be compared with those of my blue mountains. I too have a testimony
to the tune of *Lin-chiang-hsien*:
    On frosted paths in autumn's height I leave, dragging my ax;
    In night's cool returning I bear my load.
    More wondrous indeed the wild blooms stuck to my temples!
    Brushing clouds aside I find my way home;
    Waiting for the moon I call open my gate.
    My rustic wife and young son meet me with merry smiles;
    On straw bed and wooden pillow I then recline.

    Steamed pears and cooked millets are soon prepared.

    The brew newly mellowed in the urn

    Will truly expand my charming thoughts!"

The fisherman said, "All these things in our poems have to do with our livelihood, the occupations with which we support ourselves. But your life is not as good as those leisurely moments of mine, for which I have as testimony a shih poem. The poem says:

    Idly I watch the blue sky and the white cranes fly.

    My boat's moored by the stream, my door's half-closed.

    Beneath the sail I teach my son to twist the fishing threads;

    I stop the oars to dry with my wife the nets in the sun.

    My mind's composed: I know then the water too is calm.

    My self's secure: I feel then even the wind is light.

    I freely don my green coir coat and bamboo hat;

    It's better than wearing a court robe or purple sash."

The woodman said, "Your leisurely moments are not as good as mine, for which I also have a shih poem as a testimony. The poem says:

    Idly I watch the billowy white clouds fly,

    Or sit alone in my straw hut closing my bamboo gate.

    In leisure I open some books to teach my son;

    At times I face my guest and play encircling chess.[7]

    Excited, I stroll with my cane to sing on floral paths.

    Aroused, I climb green mountains, lute in hand.

    Straw sandals, hemp sashes, and coarse cloth quilts—

    They beat silk garments if your heart is free!"

Chang Shao said, "Li Ting, the two of us indeed are

    'Fortunate to have light songs for our amusement,

    Needless of castanets or flasks of gold.'[8]

But the poems we have recited thus far are occasional pieces, hardly anything unusual. Why don't we attempt a long poem in the linking-verse manner,[9] and see how fares the conversation between the fisherman and the woodman?" Li Ting said, "That's a marvelous proposal, Brother Chang! Please begin."

    My boat rests on the green water, on the mist and wave.[10]

    My home's on deep mountains and deserted plains.

    I love most the streams and bridges as spring tide swells.

    I care most for ridges veiled by the clouds of dawn.

    My fresh carps from Lung-mên are often cooked.[11]

My dried woods, worm-rotted, are daily burned.
Hooks and nets a-plenty can support my old age.
Both pole and rope will see me to the end.
I lie in a small boat and watch wild geese fly.
I lie on grassy paths and hear wild swans cry.
I have no stake in the fields of mouth and tongue.
Through seas of scandal I've not made my way.
Hung-dried beside the stream, my net's like brocade.
Polished anew on rocks, my ax is a fine blade.
Beneath the bright moon of autumn I often fish alone.
In lonely spring mountains I meet no one.
Fishes, when plentiful, are traded for wine to drink with my wife.
I exchange surplus firewood for a bottle to consort with my sons.
I sing, I pour freely after my heart's desire.
In songs and sighs I have none to restrain me.
Calling elder and younger brothers, I invite fellow boatmen.
We mix with friends and neighbors, with old men of the wilds.
We make rules and play games, oft exchanging cups.
We break words apart and remake them for passing the mugs.
Cooked shrimps, boiled crabs—these are my daily feasts.
I'm daily regaled with smoked fowls and fried ducks.
My unlettered spouse makes tea with languid ease.
My mountain wife cooks rice in leisurely pace.
When dawn comes, I lift my rod to stir the gentle waves.
When the sun rises, I pole my wood to cross the great roads.
I wear my coir coat to catch live carps after the rain.
I brandish my ax to cut dried pines before the wind.
Covering my tracks and fleeing the world I act like a fool.
Hiding my name and surname I pretend to be deaf and dumb.
Chang Shao said, "Brother Li, just now I presumed to take the lead
and began with the first line of the poem. Why don't you begin this
time and I shall follow you."
A rustic man, feigning madness, loves the wind and moon.
An old fellow leaves his pride to the streams and lakes.
My portion is leisure, I seek laxity and ease.
Shunning slander and gossip, I cherish my peace.
In moonlit nights I sleep snugly in a straw hut.
When the sky dims, I'm shrouded by my light coir coat.
Untouched by life's joys or sorrows I befriend pines and plums.

I'm pleased to keep company with egrets and gulls.
I've no plans for fame and fortune in my heart.
My ears haven't heard the din of spears and drums.
At all times I pour the fragrant, unstrained wine.
Three times a day I dine on vegetable broth.
My livelihood consists in two bundles of wood.
My trade is my pole with hooks and threads.
Calmly I call my young son to sharpen our ax.
At peace I tell my small rogue to mend our nets.
I love to watch the green willows when spring comes.
In warm weather I'm glad to see the rushes and reeds.
To flee the heat of summer I plant new bamboos.
I pick young lotus to cool myself in June.
When Frost Descends[12] the fatted fowls are often slain.
By Double Ninth[13] I shall have cooked the king-size crabs.
When winter comes I sleep soundly though the sun is high.
Under the tall, hazy sky I feel no sultry heat.
Throughout the year I roam freely in the hills.
In the four seasons I plow the lakes without restraint.
Gathering my wood, I share the immortals' fun.
Lowering my line, I'm not like a worldly man.
Radiant and fragrant are the wild blooms at my door.
Tranquil's the green water at the head of my boat.
Content, I'm not seeking the three ministers' seat.[14]
My mind's composed and strong as a ten-mile city.
The city, though tall, must guard against a siege.
The ministers, though high-ranked, must heed the call.[15]
To take pleasure in hills and waters is truly rare.[16]
We thank Heaven and Earth, and all the gods!

The two of them thus recited poems and songs and composed linking-verses. Arriving at the place where their ways parted, they bowed to take leave of each other. "Elder Brother Li," said Chang Shao, "take care as you go on your way. When you climb the mountains, be wary of the tiger. If you were harmed, I would find, as the saying goes, 'one friend missing on the street tomorrow.'" When Li Ting heard these words, he grew very angry saying, "What a scoundrel you are! Good friends would even die for each other! But you, why do you say such unlucky things to me? If I'm to be harmed by a tiger, your boat will surely capsize in the river." "I'll never capsize my boat in the river," said Chang Shao. " 'As there are unexpected storms in the sky,' " said Li Ting, " 'so there is sudden weal or woe on earth.'[17] What makes you so sure that you won't have an accident?" "Elder Brother Li," said Chang Shao, "you say this because you have no idea what may befall you in your business, whereas I can predict what'll happen in my kind of business. And I assure you that I won't have any accident." "The kind of living you pick up on the waters," said Li Ting, "is an exceedingly treacherous business. You have to take chances all the time. How can you be so certain about your future?" "Here's something you don't know about," said Chang Shao. "In this city of Ch'ang-an, there's a fortune teller who plies his trade on the West Gate Street. Every day I give him a golden carp as a present, and he consults the sticks in his sleeve for me. I follow his instructions when I lower my nets, and I've never missed in a hundred times. Today I went again to buy his prediction; he told me to set my nets at the east bend of the Ching River and to cast my line from the west bank. I know I'll come back with a fine catch of fishes and shrimps. When I go up to the city tomorrow, I'll sell my catch and buy some wine, and then I'll get together with you again, old brother." The two men then parted.

But there is a proverb: "What is said on the road is heard in the grass." For you see, it happened that a yakṣa on patrol in the Ching River overheard the part of the conversation about not having missed a hundred times. He dashed back to the Water Crystal Palace and hastily reported to the Dragon King, shouting, "Disaster! Disaster!" "What sort of disaster?" asked the Dragon King. "Your subject," said the yakṣa, "was patrolling the river and overheard a conversation between a woodman and a fisherman. Before they parted, they said something terrible. According to the fisherman, there is a fortune teller on West Gate Street in the City of Ch'ang-an who is most accurate in his calculations. Everyday the fisherman gives him a carp, and he then consults the sticks in his sleeve, with the result that the fisherman has not missed once in a hundred times when he casts his line! If such accurate calculations continue, will not all our water kin be exterminated? Where will you find any more inhabitants for the watery region who will toss and leap in the waves to enhance the majesty of the Great King?" The Dragon King became so angry that he wanted to take the sword and go at once up to Ch'ang-an to slay the fortune teller. But his Dragon sons and grandsons, the shrimp

and crab ministers, the samli counselor, the perch Subdirector of the
Minor Court, and the carp President of the Board of Civil Office all
came from the side and said to him, "Let the Great King restrain his
anger. The proverb says, 'Don't believe everything you hear.' If the
Great King goes forth like this, the clouds will accompany you and
the rains will follow you. We fear that the people of Ch'ang-an will
be terrified and Heaven will be offended. Since the Great King has
the power to appear or disappear suddenly and to transform into
many shapes and sizes, let him change into a scholar. Then go to the
city of Ch'ang-an and investigate the matter. If there is indeed such
a person, you can slay him without delay; but if there is no such
person, there is no need then to harm innocent people." The Dragon
King accepted their suggestion; he abandoned his sword and dismissed the clouds and the rains. Reaching the river bank, he shook
his body and changed into a white-robed scholar, truly with

Features most virile,
A stature towering;
A stride most stately—
So orderly and firm.
His speech exalts K'ung and Mêng;[18]
His manner embodies Chou and Wên.[19]
He wears a silk robe of the color of jade;
His casual head-wrap's shaped like the letter one.[20]

Coming out of the water, he strode to the West Gate Street in the
city of Ch'ang-an, There he found a noisy crowd surrounding someone who was saying in a lofty and self-assured manner, "Those born
under the Dragon will follow their fate; those under the Tiger will
collide with their physiognomies.[21] The branches Yin, Ch'ên, Szu,
and Hai may be said to fit into the grand scheme, but I fear your
birthday may clash with the Planet Jupiter." When the Dragon King
heard this, he knew that he had come upon the fortune teller's place.
He walked up to it, pushed the people aside and peered inside. He saw

Four walls of exquisite writings;
A room full of brocaded paintings;
Smoke unending from the treasure duck;[22]
And such pure water in a porcelain vase.
On both sides are mounted Wang Wei's paintings;
High above his seat hangs the Kuei-ku form.[23]
The Tuan-ch'i[24] ink slab,

The golden smoke ink,
Both match the great brush of frostiest hair;
The crystal balls,
Kuo P'u's[25] numbers,
Neatly face new classics of soothsaying.
He knows the hexagrams well;
He's mastered the eight trigrams;
He perceives the laws of Heaven and Earth;
He discerns the ways of demons and gods.
One tray before him fixes the cosmic hours;
His mind clearly orders all planets and stars.
Truly those things to come
And those things past
He beholds as in a mirror;
Which house will rise
And which will fall
He foresees like a god.
He knows evil and decrees the good;
He prescribes death and predicts life.
His pronouncements quicken the wind and rain;
His brush alarms both spirits and gods.
His shop sign has letters to declare his name;
This divine diviner, Yüan Shou-ch'êng.

Who was this man? He was actually the uncle of Yüan T'ien-kang, president of the Imperial Board of Astronomy in the present dynasty. The gentleman was truly a man of extraordinary appearance and elegant features; his name was known throughout the great country and his art was considered the highest in Ch'ang-an. The Dragon King went inside the door and met the Master; after exchanging greetings, he was invited to take the seat of honor while a boy served him tea. The Master asked, "What would you like to know?" The Dragon King said, "Please forecast the weather." The Master consulted his sticks and made his judgment:

Mists hide the treetops
Clouds veil the hill.
If you want rain tomorrow
You shall have your fill.[26]

"At what hour will it rain tomorrow, and how much rain will there be?" said the Dragon King. "At the hour of the Dragon the clouds will gather," said the Master, "and thunder will be heard at the hour of the Serpent. Rain will come at the hour of the Horse and reach its limit at the hour of the Sheep.[27] There will be altogether three feet. three inches, and forty-eight drops of rain." "You had better not be joking now," said the Dragon King, laughing. "If it rains tomorrow and if it is in accordance with the time and the amount you prophesied, I shall present you with fifty taels of gold as my thanks. But if it does not rain, or if the amount and the hours are incorrect, I tell you truly that I shall come and break your front door to pieces and tear down your shop sign. You will be chased out of Ch'ang-an at once so that you may no longer seduce the multitude." "You may certainly do that," said the Master amiably. "Good-bye for now. Please come again tomorrow after the rain."

The Dragon King took leave and returned to his water residence. He was received by various aquatic deities, who asked, "How was the Great King's visit to the soothsayer?" "Yes, yes, yes," said the Dragon King, "there is indeed such a person, but he's a garrulous fortune teller. I asked him when it would rain, and he said tomorrow; I asked him again about the time and the amount, and he told me that clouds would gather at the hour of the Dragon, thunder would be heard at the hour of the Serpent, rain would come at the hour of the Horse and would reach its limit at the hour of the Sheep. Altogether there would be three feet, three inches, and forty-eight drops of water. I made a wager with him: if it is as he said, I'll reward him with fifty taels of gold. If there is the slightest error, I'll break down his shop and chase him away, so that he will not be permitted to seduce the multitude at Ch'ang-an." "The Great King is the supreme commander of the eight rivers," said the water kin laughing, "the great Dragon Deity in charge of rain. Whether there is going to be rain or not, only the Great King knows that. How dare he speak so foolishly? That soothsayer is sure to lose!"

While the Dragon sons and grandsons were laughing at the matter with the fish and crab officials, a voice was heard suddenly in midair announcing, "Dragon King of the Ching River, receive the imperial command." They raised their heads to look and saw a golden-robed guardian holding the decree of the Jade Emperor and heading straight for the water residence. The Dragon King hastily straightened out his attire and burned incense to receive the decree. After he had made his delivery, the guardian rose into the air and left. The Dragon King opened the decree, which said:

> We bid the Eight-Rivers Prince
> To call up thunder and rain;
> Pour out tomorrow your grace
> To benefit Ch'ang-an's race.

The instructions regarding the hours and the amount of rain written on the decree did not even differ in the slightest from the soothsayer's prediction. So overwhelmed was the Dragon King that his spirit left him and his soul fled, and only after a while did he regain consciousness. He said to his water kinsmen, "There is indeed an intelligent creature in the world of dust! How well he comprehends the laws of Heaven and Earth! I'm bound to lose to him!" "Let the Great King calm himself," said the samli counselor. "Is it so difficult to get the better of the fortune teller? Your subject here has a little plan which will silence that fellow for good." When the Dragon King asked what the plan was, the counselor said, "If the rain tomorrow misses the timing and the amount specified by a mere fraction, it will mean that his prediction is not accurate. Won't you have won? What's there to stop you then from tearing up his shop sign and putting him on the road?" The Dragon King took his counsel and stopped worrying.

The next day he ordered the Duke of Wind, the Lord of Thunder, the Boy of Clouds, and the Mother of Lightning to go with him to the sky above Ch'ang-an. He waited until the hour of the Serpent before spreading the clouds, the hour of the Horse before letting go the thunder, the hour of the Sheep before releasing the rain, and only by the hour of the Monkey[28] did the rain stop. There were only three feet and forty drops of water, since the times were altered by an hour and the amount was changed by three inches and eight drops.

After the rain, the Dragon King dismissed his followers and came down from the clouds, transformed once again into a scholar dressed in white. He went to the West Gate street and crashed into Yüan Shou-ch'êng's shop. Without a word of explanation, he began to smash the shop sign, the brushes, and the ink slab to pieces. The Master, however, sat on his chair and remained unmoved; so the Dragon King unhinged the door and threatened to hit him with it, crying, "You're nothing but a bogus prophet of good and evil, an imposter who deludes the minds of the people! Your predictions are incorrect; your words are patently false! What you told me about the time and quantity of today's rain was utterly inaccurate. And yet you dare sit so smugly and so high on your seat? Leave here at once before you are executed!" Still Yüan Shou-ch'êng was not at all intimidated. He lifted up his head and laughed scornfully. "I'm not afraid!" he said. "Not in the least! I'm not guilty of death, but I fear that you have committed a mortal crime. You can fool other people, but you can't fool me! I recognize you all right: you are not a white-robed scholar but the Dragon King of the Ching River. By altering the times and holding back the quantity of rain, you have disobeyed the decree of the Jade Emperor and transgressed the law of Heaven. On the dragon execution block you won't escape the knife! And here you are, railing at me!" When the Dragon King heard these words, his heart trembled and his hair stood on end. He dropped the door quickly, tidied his clothes, and knelt before the Master saying, "I beg the Master not to take offense. My previous words were spoken in jest; little did I realize that my prank would turn out to be such a serious crime. Now I have indeed transgressed the law of Heaven. What am I to do? I beseech the Master to save me. If you won't, I'll never let you go!" "I can't save you," said Shou-ch'êng. "I can only point out to you what may be a way of life." "I'm willing to be instructed," said the Dragon. The Master said, "You are to be executed tomorrow by the human judge, Wei Chêng, at the third quarter past the hour of noon. If you want to preserve your life, you must go quickly to plead your case before the present emperor T'ang T'ai-tsung, for Wei Chêng is the prime minister before his throne. If you can win the emperor's favor, you'll be spared." Hearing this, the Dragon took leave with tears in his eyes. Soon the red sun sank down and the moon arose. You see

> Smoke thickens on purple mountains as weary crows return;
> And travelers on distant journeys head for the inns.
> Young wild geese at river crossings rest on the sand.
> The silver stream[29] appears
> To hasten the time floats.[30]
> Lights flicker in a lonely village from dying flames;
> Wind sweeps the burner, clearing the Taoist yard of smoke.
> A man fades away in the butterfly dream.[31]
> The moon moves floral shadows up the garden's rails.
> The stars are rife

As water clocks strike;
So swiftly the gloom deepens that it's midnight.
Our Dragon King of the Ching River did not even return to his water home; he waited in the air until it was about the hour of the Rat,[32] when he descended from the clouds and mists and came to the gate of the palace. At this time the T'ang emperor was just having a dream about taking a walk outside the palace in the moonlight, beneath the shades of flowers. The Dragon suddenly assumed the form of a human being and went up to him. Kneeling, he cried out, "Your Majesty, save me, save me!" "Who are you?" asked T'ai-tsung. "We would be glad to save you." "Your Majesty is the true dragon," said the Dragon King, "but I am an accursed one. Because I have disobeyed the decree of Heaven, I am to be executed by a worthy subject of Your Majesty, the human judge Wei Chêng. I have therefore come here to plead with you to save me." "If Wei Chêng is to be the executioner," said T'ai-tsung, "we can certainly save you. You may leave and not worry." The Dragon King was delighted and left after expressing his gratitude.

We tell you now about T'ai-tsung, who, having awakened, was still turning over in his mind what he had dreamed about. Soon it was three-fifths past the hour of the fifth watch, and T'ai-tsung held court for his ministers, both civil and martial. You see

Smoke shrouding the phoenix arches;
Incense clouding the dragon domes;
Light shimmering as the silk screens move;
Clouds brushing the feathered flags,[33]
Rulers and lords harmonious as Yao and Shun;[34]
Rituals and music solemn as Han's and Chou's.
The attendant lamps,
The court-maiden fans
Show their colors in pairs;
From peacock screens
And unicorn halls
Light radiates everywhere.
Three cheers for long life!
A wish for reign everlasting!
When a whip cracks three times,
The caps and robes will bow to the Crown.
Brilliant the palatial blooms, endued by Heaven's scent;

Pliant the bank willows, sung and praised by court music.
The screens of pearl,
The screens of jade,
Are drawn high by golden hooks;
The dragon-phoenix fan,
The mountain-river fan,[35]
Rest on top of the royal carriage.
The civil lords are noble and refined;
The martial lords, strong and valiant.
The imperial path divides the ranks;
The vermilion court aligns the grades.
The golden seal and purple sashes bearing the three signs[36]
Will last for millions of years as Heaven and Earth.

After the ministers had paid their homage, they all went back to standing in rows according to their rank. The T'ang emperor opened his dragon eyes to look at them one by one: among the civil officials were Fang Hsüan-ling, Tu Ju-hui, Hsü Shih-chi, Hsü Ching-tsung, and Wang Kuei; and among the military officials were Ma San-pao, Tuan Chih-hsien, Yin K'ai-shan, Ch'êng Yao-chin, Liu Hung-chi, Hu Ching-tê, and Ch'in Shu-pao. Each one of them was standing there in a most solemn manner, but the prime minister Wei Chêng was not to be seen anywhere. The T'ang emperor asked Hsü Shih-chi to come forward and said to him, "We had a strange dream last night: there was a man who paid homage to us, calling himself the Dragon King of the Ching River. He said that he had disobeyed the command of Heaven and was supposed to be executed by the human judge Wei Chêng. He implored us to save him, and we gave our consent. Today only Wei Chêng is absent from the ranks. Why is that?" "This dream may indeed come true," answered Shih-chi, "and Wei Chêng must be summoned to court immediately. Once he arrives, let Your Majesty keep him here for a whole day and not permit him to leave. After this day, the dragon in the dream will be saved." The T'ang emperor was most delighted; he gave the order at once to have Wei Chêng summoned to court.

We speak now of prime minister Wei Chêng, who studied the movement of the stars and burned incense at his home that evening. He heard the cries of cranes in the air and saw there a Heavenly messenger holding the golden decree of the Jade Emperor, which ordered him to execute in his dream the old dragon of the Ching

River at precisely the third quarter past the noon hour. Having thanked the Heavenly grace, our prime minister prepared himself in his residence by bathing himself and abstaining from food; he was also sharpening his magic sword and exercising his spirit, and therefore he did not attend court. He was terribly flustered when he saw the royal officer on duty arriving with the summons. Not daring, however, to disobey the emperor's command, he had to dress quickly and follow the summons into court, kow-towing and asking for pardon before the throne. The T'ang emperor said, "We pardoned indeed our worthy subject." At that time the various ministers had not yet retired from the court, and only after Wei Chêng's arrival was the curtain drawn up for the court's dismissal. Wei Chêng alone was asked to remain; he rode the golden carriage with the emperor to enter the chamber for relaxation, where he discussed with the emperor tactics for making the empire secure and other affairs of state. When it was just about midway between the hour of the Serpent and the hour of the Horse, the emperor asked the royal attendants to bring out a large chess set, saying, "We shall have a game with our worthy subject." The various concubines took out the chessboard and set it on the imperial table. After expressing his gratitude, Wei Chêng set out to play chess with the T'ang emperor, both of them moving the pieces step by step into positions. It was completely in accordance with the instruction of the *Chess Classic*:

> The way of chess exalts discipline and caution; the most powerful pieces should remain in the center, the weakest ones at the flanks, and the less powerful ones at the corners. This is a familiar law of the chess player. The law says: "You should rather lose a piece than an advantage. When you strike on the left, you must guard your right; when you attack in the rear, you must watch your front. Only when you have a secure front will you also have a rear, and only if you have a secure rear will you maintain your front. The two ends cannot be separated, and yet both must remain flexible and not be encumbered. A broad formation should not be too loose, while a tight position should not be constricted. Rather than clinging on to save a single piece, it is better to sacrifice it in order to win; rather than moving without purpose, it is better to remain stationary in order to be self-supportive. When your adversary outnumbers you, your first concern is to survive; when you outnumber your adversary, you must strive

to exploit your force. He who knows how to win will not prolong
his fight; he who is a master of positions will not engage in direct
combat; he who knows how to fight will not suffer defeat; and
he who knows how to lose will not panic. For chess begins with
proper engagement but ends in unexpected victory. If your enemy,
even without being threatened, is bringing up his reinforcement,
it is a sign of his intention to attack; if he deserts a small piece
without trying to save it, he may be stalking a bigger piece. If
he moves in a casual manner, he is a man without thoughts;
response without thought is the way to defeat. The *Book of Odes*
says: 'Approach with extreme caution as if facing a deep
canyon.' Such is the meaning thereof."

The poem says:

The chessboard is the earth; the pieces form the sky;
The colors are light and dark[37] as the whole universe.
When the playing reaches that skillful, subtle stage,
Praise with laughter the Chess Immortal of old.[38]

The two of them, emperor and subject, played chess until three
quarters past the noon hour, but the game was not yet finished.
Suddenly Wei Chêng put his head on the table and fell fast asleep.
T'ai-tsung laughed and said, "Our worthy subject truly has worn
himself out for the state and exhausted his strength on behalf of the
empire. He has therefore fallen asleep in spite of himself." T'ai-tsung
allowed him to sleep on and did not arouse him. In a little while,
Wei Chêng awoke and prostrated himself on the ground saying, "Your
subject deserves ten thousand deaths! Your subject deserves ten
thousand deaths! Just now I lost consciousness for no reason at all.
I beg Your Majesty's pardon for such insult against the emperor."
"What insult is there?" said T'ai-tsung. "Arise! Let us forget the old
game and start a new one instead." Wei Chêng expressed his
gratitude; he had his hand on a piece when a loud clamor was heard
outside the gate. It was occasioned by the ministers Ch'in Shu-pao
and Hsü Mou-kung, who arrived with a dragon head dripping with
blood. Throwing it in front of the emperor they said, "Your Majesty,
we have seen seas turn shallow and rivers run dry, but a thing as
strange as this we have never even heard of." T'ai-tsung arose with
Wei Chêng and said, "Where did this thing come from?" "South of
the Thousand-Step Corridor," said Shu-pao and Mou-kung, "at the
crossroads, this dragon head fell from the clouds. Your lowly subjects

dare not withhold it from you." In alarm, the T'ang emperor asked
Wei Chêng, "What's the meaning of this?" Turning to kowtow to
him, Wei Chêng said, "This dragon was executed just now by your
subject in his dream." When the T'ang emperor heard this, he was
seized with fear and said, "When our worthy minister was sleeping,
I did not see any movement of body or limb, nor did I perceive any
scimitar or sword. How could you have executed this dragon?" Wei
Chêng replied, "My lord, although

My body was before my master,
I left Your Majesty in my dream;
My body before my master faced the unfinished game,
With dim eyes fully closed;
I left Your Majesty in my dream to ride the blessed cloud,
With spirit most eager and alert.
That dragon on the dragon execution block
Was bound up there by celestial hosts.
Your subject said,
'For breaking Heaven's law,
You are worthy of death.
Now by Heaven's command,
I end your wretched life.'
The dragon listened in grief;
Your subject bestirred his spirit;
The dragon listened in grief,
Retrieving claws and scales to await his death;
Your subject bestirred his spirit,
Lifting robe and taking step to hold high his blade.
With one loud crack the knife descended;
And thus the head of the dragon fell from the sky."

When T'ai-tsung heard these words, he was filled with both sadness
and delight. The delight was caused by his pride in having a minister as
good as Wei Chêng. If he had worthies of this kind in his court, he
thought, need he worry about the security of his empire? He was
saddened, however, by the fact that he had promised in his dream to
save the dragon, and he had not anticipated that the creature would
be killed in this manner. He had to force himself to give the order to
Shu-pao that the dragon head be hung on display at the market, so
that the populace of Ch'ang-an might be informed. Meanwhile, he
rewarded Wei Chêng, after which the various ministers dispersed.

That night he returned to his palace in deep depression; he kept remembering the dragon in the dream crying and begging for his life. Little did he expect that the turn of events would be such that the dragon still could not escape calamity. Having thought about the matter for a long time, he became physically and mentally drained. At about the hour of the second watch, the sound of weeping was heard outside the door of the palace, and T'ai-tsung became even more fearful. He was sleeping fitfully when he saw our Dragon King of the Ching River holding his head dripping with blood in his hand, and crying in a loud voice: "T'ang T'ai-tsung! Give me back my life! Give me back my life! Last night you were full of promises to save me. Why did you order a human judge in the daytime to have me executed? Come out, come out! I am going to argue this case with you before the King of the Underworld." He seized T'ai-tsung and would neither let go nor desist from his protestation. T'ai-tsung could not say a word; he could only struggle until perspiration covered his entire body. Just at the moment when it seemed that nothing could separate them, fragrant clouds and colourful mists appeared from the south. A Taoist priestess came forward and waved a willow twig. That headless dragon, still mourning and weeping, left at once toward the northwest. For you see, this was none other than the Bodhisattva Kuan-yin, who by the decree of Buddha was seeking a scripture pilgrim in the Land of the East. She was staying in the temple of the local spirit at the city of Ch'ang-an when she heard in the night the weeping of demons and the crying of spirits. So she came specially to drive the accursed dragon away and to rescue the emperor. That dragon went directly to the court of the Underworld to file suit, of which we shall say no more.

We now tell you about T'ai-tsung who, when he awoke, could only yell, "Ghost! Ghost!" He so terrified the queens of three palaces, the concubines of six chambers, and the attending eunuchs that they remained sleepless for the entire night. Soon it was the fifth watch, and all the officials of the court, both civil and military, were waiting for an audience outside the gate. They waited until dawn, but the emperor did not appear, and every one of them became fearful and restless. Only after the sun was high in the sky did a proclamation come out saying, "We are not feeling too well. The ministers are excused from court." Five or six days went by swiftly, and the various officials were so anxious that they were about to enter the court without summons and inquire after the Throne. Just then the queen mother gave the order to have the physician brought into the palace, and so the multitude waited at the gate of the court for some news. In a little while, the physician came out and he was questioned by them about the emperor's illness. "The pulse of His Majesty is irregular," said the physician, "for it is weak as well as rapid. He blabbers about seeing ghosts. I also perceive that there were ten movements and one rest, but there is no breath left in his viscera. I am afraid that he will pass away within seven days." When the various ministers heard this statement, they paled with fright.

In this state of alarm, they again heard that T'ai-tsung had summoned Hsü Mou-kung, Hu-kuo Kung, and Yü-ch'ih Kung to appear before him. The three ministers hurried into the auxiliary palace, where they prostrated themselves. Speaking somberly and with great effort, T'ai-tsung said, "My worthy subjects, since the age of nineteen I have been leading my army in expeditions to the four corners of the Earth. I have experienced much hardship throughout the years, but I have never encountered any kind of strange or weird thing. This day, however, I have seen ghosts!" "When you established your empire," said Yü-ch'ih Kung, "you had to kill countless people. Why should you fear ghosts?" "You may not believe it," said T'ai-tsung, "but outside this bedroom of mine at night, there are bricks thrown and spirits screaming to a degree that is truly unmanageable. In the daytime it's not too bad, but it's intolerable at night!" "Let Your Majesty be relieved," said Shu-pao, "for this evening your subject and Ching-tê[39] will stand guard at the palace gate. We shall see what sort of ghostly business there is." T'ai-tsung agreed to the proposal and Mou-kung and the other ministers retired after expressing their gratitude.

That evening the two ministers, in full battle dress and holding golden bludgeon and battle-ax, stood guard outside the palace gate. Dear generals! Look how they are attired:

They wore on their heads bright glimmering golden helmets,
And on their bodies cuirasses of dragon scales.
Their jeweled breastplates glow like hallowed clouds;
With lion knots tightly drawn,
And silk sashes newly spun.
This one had phoenix eyes staring into the sky to frighten the
    stars;

The other had brown eyes glowering like lightning and shining
  like the moon.
They were once warriors of greatest merit;
But now they became for all time the guardians of the gates,
In all ages the protectors of the home.[40]

The two generals stood beside the door for the entire night and did
not see the slightest disturbance. That night T'ai-tsung rested peacefully in the palace; when morning came he summoned the two
generals before him and thanked them profusely, saying, "Since
falling ill, I haven't been able to sleep for days, and only last night
did I manage to get some rest because of your presence. Let our
worthy ministers retire now for some rest so that we may count on
your protection once again at night." The two generals left after
expressing their gratitude, and for the following two or three nights
their standing guard brought continued peace. However, the royal
appetite diminished and the illness became more severe. T'ai-tsung,
moreover, could not bear to see the two generals overworked. So
once again he called Shu-pao, Ching-tê, the ministers Tu and Fang
into the palace, saying to them, "Though I got some rest these past
two days, I have imposed on the two generals the hardship of staying
up all night. I wish to have portraits made of both of them by a skilled
painter and have these pasted on the door, so that the two generals
will be spared any further labor. How about it?" The various
ministers obeyed; they selected two portrait painters, who made
pictures of the two generals in their proper battle attire. The portraits
were then mounted near the gate, and no incident occurred during
the night.

So it was for two or three days, until the loud rattling of bricks and
tiles was again heard at the rear gate of the palace. At dawn the
emperor called together the various ministers, saying to them, "For
the past few days there have been, happily, no incidents at the front
of the palace, but last night the noises at the back door were such
that they nearly frightened me to death." Mou-kung stepped forward
and said, "The disturbances at the front door were driven off by
Ching-tê and Shu-pao. If there is disturbance at the rear gate, then
Wei Chêng ought to stand guard." T'ai-tsung approved the suggestion and ordered Wei Chêng to guard the rear door that night.
Accepting the charge, Wei donned his full court regalia that evening;
holding the sword with which he had slain the dragon, he stood in

attention before the rear gate of the palace. What splendid heroic stature! Look how he is attired:

A turban of green satin swathed his brow;
On his brocaded robe a jade belt hung from his waist;
The sleeves of his crane-skinned gown floated in the wind like drifting snow,
He surpassed even the divine figures of Lü and Shu.[41]
His feet were shod in black boots supple and smooth;
In his hands was a sharp blade, fierce and keen.
With glaring eyes he looked all around.
What goblin or demon would dare approach?

A whole night went by and no ghost appeared. But though there were no incidents at either the front or the rear gate, the emperor's condition worsened. One day the queen mother sent for all the ministers to discuss funeral arrangements. T'ai-tsung himself also summoned Hsü Mou-kung to his bedside to entrust to him the affairs of state, committing the crown prince to the minister's care as Liu Pei did to Chu-Ko Liang.[42] When he had finished speaking, he bathed and changed his garments, waiting for his time to come.

Wei Chêng then stepped out from the side and tugged the royal garment with his hand, saying, "Let Your Majesty be relieved. Your subject knows something which will guarantee long life for Your Majesty." "My illness," said T'ai-tsung, "has reached the irremediable stage; my life is in danger. How can you preserve it?" "Your subject has a letter here," said Wei, "which I submit to Your Majesty to take with you to Hell and give to the Judge of the Underworld, Ts'ui Chüeh." "Who is Ts'ui Chüeh," asked T'ai-tsung. "Ts'ui Chüeh," said Wei, "was the subject of the deceased emperor, your father; at first he was the district magistrate of Tzu-chou, and subsequently he was promoted to vice-president of the Board of Rites. When he was alive, he was an intimate friend and sworn brother of your subject. Now that he is dead, he has become a judge in the capital of the Underworld, having in his charge the chronicles of life and death in the region of darkness. He meets with me frequently, however, in my dreams. If you go there presently and hand this letter to him, he will certainly remember his obligation toward your lowly subject and allow Your Majesty to return here. Surely your soul will return to the human world, and your royal countenance will once more grace the capital." When T'ai-tsung heard these words, he took the letter in his hands and put it in his sleeve; with that, he closed his eyes and died. Those queens and concubines from three palaces and six chambers, the crown prince and the two rows of civil and military officials, all put on their mourning garb to mourn him, as the imperial coffin lay in state at the Hall of the White Tiger, but we shall say no more about that. We do not know how the soul of T'ai-tsung came back, and so you must listen to the explanation in the next chapter.

Eleven

Having toured the underworld, T'ai-tsung returns
   to life;

Having presented melons and fruits, Liu Ch'üan
   marries again.

The poem says:
   A hundred years pass by like a flowing stream;
   The work of a lifetime is only froth and foam.
   Yesterday's face had the glow of peaches,
   But today's temples are touched by flakes of snow.
   Even termites disband—such is life's illusion![1]
   The cuckoo calls gravely, you must soon turn back.[2]
   Good works in secret may always prolong life;
   Virtue needs no pity, for Heaven will mind its own.

We now tell you about T'ai-tsung, whose soul drifted out of the Tower of Five Phoenixes. Everything was blurred and indistinct. It seemed to him that a company of imperial guardsmen was inviting him to a hunting party, to which T'ai-tsung gladly gave his consent and went off with them. They had journeyed for a long time when suddenly all the men and horses vanished from sight. He was left alone, walking the deserted fields and desolate plains. As he was anxiously trying to find his way back, he heard someone from beyond calling in a loud voice: "Great T'ang Emperor, come over here! Come over here!" T'ai-tsung heard this and looked up. He saw that the man had

   A black gauze cap on his head;
   Rhinoceros' horns around his waist.[3]
   Soft bands dangled from the black gauze hat on his head;
   Golden buckles enhanced the rhinoceros' horns around his waist.
   He held an ivory tablet shrouded by blessed mist;
   He wore a silk robe encircled by holy light.
   On his feet was a pair of white-soled boots
   To walk the clouds and climb the fog;
   He carried near his heart a book of life and death,
   Which determined one's fate.
   His hair, loose and luxuriant, haloed his head;

His beard floated and danced around his jaws.
He was once a T'ang prime minister;
Now he handled cases to serve the King of Hades.

T'ai-tsung walked toward him, and the man, kneeling at the side of
the road, said to him, "Your Majesty, please pardon your subject for
neglecting to meet you at a greater distance." "Who are you," asked
T'ai-tsung, "and for what reason did you come to meet me?" The
man said, "Half a month ago, your lowly subject met in the Halls of
Darkness the Dragon Ghost of the Ching River, who was filing suit
against Your Majesty for having him executed after promising to save
him. So the great king Ch'in-Kuang of the first chamber immediately
sent demon messengers to arrest you and bring you to trial before the
Three Tribunes. Your subject learned of this and therefore came here
to receive you. I did not expect to come late today, and I beg you to
forgive me." "What is your name," said T'ai-tsung, "and what is
your rank?" "When your lowly subject was alive," said that man,
"he served on Earth before the previous emperor as the district
magistrate of Tz'u-chou. Afterwards I was appointed vice-president of
the Board of Rites. My surname is Ts'ui and my given name is
Chüeh. In the Region of Darkness I hold a judgeship in the Capital of
Death." T'ai-tsung was very glad; he went forward and held out his
royal hands to raise the man up, saying, "I am sorry to have incon-
venienced you. Wei Chêng, who serves before my throne, has a letter
for you. I'm glad that we have a chance to meet here." The judge
expressed his gratitude and asked where the letter was. T'ai-tsung
took it out of his sleeve and handed it over to Ts'ui Chüeh, who
received it, bowing, and then opened it and read:

> Your unworthily beloved brother Wei Chêng sends with bowed
> head this letter to the Great Judge, my sworn brother the
> Honorable Mr. Ts'ui. I recall our former goodly society, and both
> your voice and your countenance seem to be present with me.
> Several years have hastened by since I last heard your lofty
> discourse. I could only prepare a few vegetables and fruits to offer
> to you as sacrifices during the festive times of the year, though
> I do not know whether you have enjoyed them or not. I am
> grateful, however, that you have not forgotten me, and that you
> have revealed to me in my dreams that you, my elder brother,
> have ascended to an even higher office. Unfortunately, the worlds
> of Light and Darkness are separated by a gulf wide as the

heavens, so that we cannot meet face to face. The reason that
I am writing you now is the sudden demise of my emperor, the
accomplished T'ai-tsung, whose case, I suppose, will be reviewed
by the Three Tribunes, so that he will certainly be given the
opportunity to meet you. I earnestly beseech you to remember
our friendship while you were living and grant me the small
favor of allowing His Majesty to return to life. This will be a very
great favor to me, for which I thank you once more.

After reading the letter, the judge said with great delight, "The
execution of the old dragon the other day by the human judge Wei
is already known to your subject, who greatly admires him for this
deed. I am, moreover, indebted to him for looking after my children.
Since he has written such a letter now, Your Majesty need have no
further concern. Your lowly subject will make certain that you will
be returned to life, to ascend once more your throne of jade." T'ai-
tsung thanked him.

As the two of them were speaking, they saw in the distance two
young boys in blue robes holding banners and flags and calling out,
"The King of the Underworld has an invitation for you." T'ai-tsung
went forward with Judge Ts'ui and the two boys. He suddenly saw a
huge city, and on a large plaque above the city gate was the inscription in gold letters, "The Region of Darkness, The Gate of Spirits."
Waving the banners, the blue robes led T'ai-tsung into the city. As
they walked along, they saw at the side of the street the emperor's
predecessor Li Yüan, his elder brother Chien-ch'êng, and his deceased
brother Yüan-chi, who came toward them, shouting, "Here comes
Shih-min! Here comes Shih-min!" The brothers clutched at T'ai-
tsung and began beating him and threatening vengeance.[4] Having
no place to dodge, the emperor fell into their clutch; and only when
Judge Ts'ui called a blue-faced, hook-tusked demon to drive them
away could he escape and continue his journey.

They had traveled no more than a few miles when they arrived at
a towering edifice with green tiles. This building was truly magnificent.
You see

Lightly ten thousand folds of colored mists pile high;
Dimly a thousand strands of crimson brume appear.
Heads of wild beasts rear up from the eaves aglow.
Lambent roof tiles in pairs rise in tiers of five.
Rows of red-gold nails bore deeply into doors;

Crosswise, white jade slabs form the sills.
Windows near the lights release luminous smoke.
The screens, the curtains, flash like fiery bolts.
High-rising towers reach to the blue sky.
Criss-crossing hallways join the treasure rooms.
Fragrant clouds from ornate ting[5] line the royal robes;
Fires of scarlet silk lanterns brighten the portals' leaves.
On the left, hordes of fierce Bull-heads stand;
On the right, gangs of gruesome Horse-faces hover.
To greet the dead, to guide the ghosts, the gold placards turn;
To lead the souls, to call the spirits, the white silk descends.
It bears this name: The Central Gate of Hell,
The Hall of Darkness of the Princes of Hades.

As T'ai-tsung was looking at the place, there came from within the tinkling of girdle jade, the mysterious fragrance of divine incense, and two pairs of torch candles followed by the Ten Kings of the Underworld coming down the steps. The Ten Kings were: King Ch'in-Kuang, King of the Beginning River, King of the Sung Emperor, King of Avenging Ministers, King Yama, King of Equal Ranks, King of the T'ai Mountain, King of City Markets, King of Complete Change, and King of the Turning Wheel. Coming out of the Treasure Hall of Darkness, they bowed to receive T'ai-tsung, who, feigning modesty, declined to lead the way. The Ten Kings said, "Your Majesty is the emperor of men in the World of Light, whereas we are but the kings of spirits in the World of Darkness. Such are indeed our appointed stations, so why should you defer to us?" "I'm afraid that I have offended all of you," said T'ai-tsung, "so how can I dare to speak of observing the etiquette of ghosts and men, of Light and Darkness?" Only after much protestation did T'ai-tsung proceed into the Hall of Darkness. After he had greeted the Ten Kings properly, they sat down according to the places assigned to hosts and guests.

After a little while, King Ch'in-Kuang folded his hands in front of him and came forward, saying, "The Dragon Spirit of the Ching River accuses Your Majesty of having him slain after promising to save him. Why?" "I did promise him that nothing would happen," said T'ai-tsung, "when the old dragon appealed to me in my dream at night. He was guilty, you know, and was condemned to be executed by the human judge Wei Chêng. It was to save him that I invited Wei Chêng to play chess with me, not anticipating that Wei Chêng could have performed the execution in his dream! That was indeed a miraculous stratagem devised by the human judge, and, after all, the dragon was also guilty of a mortal offense. I fail to see how I am to blame." When the Ten Kings heard these words, they replied, bowing, "Even before that dragon was born, it was already written on the Book of Death held by the Star of South Pole that he should be slain by a human judge. We have known this all along, but the dragon lodged his complaint here and insisted that Your Majesty be brought down so that his case might be reviewed by the Three Tribunes. We have already sent him on his way to his next incarnation through the Wheel of Transmigration. We regret, however, that we have caused Your Majesty the inconvenience of this journey, and we beg your pardon for pressing you to come here." When they had finished speaking, they ordered the judge in charge of the Books of Life and Death to bring out the records quickly so that they could ascertain what the allotted time of the emperor was to be. Judge Ts'ui went at once to his chamber and examined, one by one, the ages preordained for all the kings in the world that were inscribed in the books. Startled when he saw that the Great T'ang Emperor T'ai-tsung of the South Jambūdvīpa Continent was destined to die in the thirteenth year of the period Chên-kuan, he swiftly dipped his big brush in thick ink and added two strokes before presenting the book. The Ten Kings took one look and saw that "thirty-three years" was written beneath the name T'ai-tsung. They asked in alarm: "How long has it been since Your Majesty was enthroned?" "It has been thirteen years," said T'ai-tsung. "Your Majesty need have no worry," said King Yama, "for you still have twenty years of life. Now that your case has been clearly reviewed, we can send you back to the World of Light." When T'ai-tsung heard this, he bowed to express his gratitude as the Ten Kings ordered Judge Ts'ui and Grand Marshal Chu to accompany him back to life.

T'ai-tsung walked out of the Hall of Darkness and asked, saluting the Ten Kings once again, "What's going to happen to those living in my palace?" "Everyone will be safe," said the Ten Kings, "except your younger sister. It appears that she will not live long." "When I return to the World of Light," said T'ai-tsung, bowing again to thank them, "I have very little that I can present you as a token of my gratitude. Perhaps I can send you some melons or other kinds of fruit?" Delighted, the Ten Kings said, "We have eastern and western melons here, but we lack southern melons."[6] "The moment I get back," said T'ai-tsung, "I shall send you some." They bowed to each other with hands folded, and parted.

The marshal took the lead, holding a flag for guiding souls, while Judge Ts'ui followed behind to protect T'ai-tsung. They walked out of the Region of Darkness, and T'ai-tsung saw that it was not the same road. He asked the judge, "Are we going on the wrong way?" "No," said the judge, "for this is how it is in the Region of Darkness: there is a way for you to come, but there is no way out. Now we must send Your Majesty off from the region of the Wheel of Transmigration, so that you can make a tour of Hell as well as be sent on your way to reincarnation." T'ai-tsung had little alternative but to follow their lead.

They had gone only a few miles when they came upon a tall mountain. Dark clouds touched the ground around it, and black mists shrouded the sky. "Mr. Ts'ui," said T'ai-tsung, "what mountain is this?" The judge said, "It's the Mountain of Perpetual Shade in the Region of Darkness." "How can we go there?" asked T'ai-tsung fearfully. "Your Majesty need not worry," said the judge, "for your subjects are here to guide you." Shaking and quaking, T'ai-tsung followed the two of them and ascended the slope. He raised his head to look around and saw that

Its shape was both craggy and curvate,
And its form was even more tortuous.
Rugged like the Shu peaks;[7]
Tall like the Lu summits;[8]
It was not a famed mountain in the World of Light,
But a treacherous place in the Region of Darkness.
Thickets of thorns sheltered monsters;
Tiers of stone ridges harbored demons.
No sound of fowl or beast came to one's ears;
Only ghosts or griffins walked before one's eyes.
The howling cold wind;
The endless black mist;
The howling cold wind was the huffing of infernal hosts;
The endless black mist was the puffing of demonic troops.
There was no scenic splendor though one looked high and low;
All was desolation when one stared left and right.
At that place there were mountains

And peaks,
And summits,
And caves,
And streams;
Only no grass grew on the mountains;
No peaks punctured the sky;
No travelers scaled the summits;
No clouds ever entered the caves;
No water flowed in the streams.
They were all specters on the shores,
And bogies beneath the cliffs.
The phantoms huddled in the caves,
And lost souls hid on the floors of streams.
All around the mountain,
Bull-heads and Horse-faces wildly clamored;
Half hidden and half in sight,
Hungry ghosts[9] and needy souls frequently wept.
The judge in quest of souls,
In haste and fury delivered his summons;
The guard who chased the spirits,
Snorted and shouted to present his papers.
The Swift of Foot:
A boiling cyclone!
The Soul Snatcher:
A spreading dark mist!

Had he not trusted in the judge's protection, T'ai-tsung would have never made it across this Mountain of Perpetual Shade.

As they proceeded, they came to a place where there were many halls and chambers; everywhere they turned, melancholy cries blasted their ears and grotesque sights struck terror in their hearts. "What is this place?" asked T'ai-tsung again. "The Eighteenfold Hell behind the Mountain of Perpetual Shade," said the judge. "What is that?" said T'ai-tsung. The judge replied, "Listen to what I have to say:

The Hell of the Rack,
The Hell of Gloomy Guilt,
The Hell of the Fiery Pit:
All such sorrow,
All such desolation,

Are caused by a thousand sins committed in the life before;
They all come to suffer after they die.
The Hell of Hades,
The Hell of Tongue-Pulling,
The Hell of Skin-Shredding:
All those weeping and wailing,
All those pining and mourning,
Await the traitors, the rebels, and the Heaven baiters;
He of Buddha-mouth and serpent-heart will end up here.
The Hell of Grinding,
The Hell of Pounding,
The Hell of Crushing;
With frayed skin and torn flesh,
Gaping mouths and grinding teeth,
These are they who cheat and lie to work injustice,
Who fawn and flatter to deceive.
The Hell of Ice,
The Hell of Mutilation,
The Hell of Evisceration:
With grimy face and matted hair,
Knitted brow and doleful look,
These are they who fleece the simple with weights unjust,
And so bring ruin upon themselves.
The Hell of Boiling Oil,
The Hell of Grim Darkness,
The Hell of the Sword Mountain:
They shake and quake;
They sorrow and pine:
For oppressing the righteous by violence and fraud
They now must cower in their lonely pain.
The Hell of the Pool of Blood,
The Hell of Avīci,[10]
The Hell of Scales and Weights:
All the skins peeled and bones exposed,
The limbs cut and the tendons severed,
Are caused by murder stemming from greed,
The taking of life of both humans and beasts.
Their fall has no reversal in a thousand years—
Eternal perdition without release.

Each is firmly bound and tightly tied,
Shackled by both ropes and cords.
The slightest move brings on the Red-hair demons,
The Black-face demons,
With long spears and sharp swords;
The Bull-head demons
The Horse-face demons
With iron spikes and bronze gavels,
They strike till faces contort and blood flows down;
But cries to Earth and Heaven find no response.
So it is that man should not betray his own conscience,
For gods are knowing; whom will they overlook?
Vice and virtue will get their due in the end—
A matter of payment early or late."

When T'ai-tsung heard these words, he was terror-stricken.

They went on for a little while and came upon a group of demon soldiers, each holding banners and flags and kneeling beside the road. "The Guards of the Bridges have come to receive you," they said. The judge ordered them to make way and proceeded to lead T'ai-tsung across a golden bridge. Looking to one side, T'ai-tsung saw another silver bridge, on which there were several travelers who seemed to be persons of principle and rectitude, justice and honesty. They too were led by banners and flags. On the other side was another bridge, with icy wind churning around it and bloody waves seething below. The continuous sound of weeping and wailing could be heard. "What is the name of that bridge?" asked T'ai-tsung. "Your Majesty," said the judge, "it is the Bridge with No Alternative.[11] When you reach the World of Light, you must have this recorded for posterity. For below the bridge there is nothing but

A vast body of surging water;
A strait and treacherous path;
Like bales of raw silk flowing down the Long River,
Or the Pit of Fire floating up to Earth,
This cold air, oppressive, this bone-piercing chill;
This foul stench both irksome and nauseous.
The waves roll and swirl;
No boat comes or goes to ferry men across;
With naked feet and tangled hair
Those moving here and there are all damned spirits.

The bridge is a few miles long
But only three spans wide.
Its height measures a hundred feet;
Below, a thousand fathoms deep.
On top are no railways for hands to hold;
Beneath you have man-seizing savage fiends
Who, bound by cangues and locks,
Will fight to flee the perilous stream.
Look at those ferocious guardians beside the bridge
And those damned souls in the river—how truly wretched!
On branches and twigs
Clothes of green, red, yellow, and purple silk hang;
Below the precipice
Strumpets crouch for having abused their own in-laws.
Iron dogs and brass serpents will strive to feed on them.
Their fall's eternal—there is no way out."
The poem says:
Demons and ghosts are often heard wailing.
The waves of blood are ten thousand feet high.
Horse-faces and Bull-heads by countless scores
Stand guard most fiercely by this Nai-ho Bridge.
While T'ai-tsung and his guides were speaking, the several Guardians
of the Bridge went back to their station. Terrified by his vision,
T'ai-tsung could only nod his head in silent horror. He followed the
judge and the Grand Marshal across the River of No Alternative and
the bitter Realm of the Bloody Bowl. Soon they arrived at the City of
the Dead, where clamoring voices were heard proclaiming distinctly,
"Li Shih-min has come! Li Shih-min has come!" When T'ai-tsung
heard all this shouting, his heart shook and his gall quivered. Then
he saw a throng of spirits, some with backs broken by the rack, some
with severed limbs, and some headless, who barred his way and
shouted together, "Give us back our lives! Give us back our lives!"
In terror T'ai-tsung tried desperately to flee and hide, at the same time
crying, "Mr. Ts'ui, save me! Mr. Ts'ui, save me!" "Your Majesty,"
said the judge, "these are the spirits of various princes and their
underlings, of brigands and robbers from sundry places. Through
works of injustice, both theirs and others', they perished and are now
cut off from salvation because there is none to receive them or care
for them. Since they have no money or belongings, they are ghosts

abandoned to hunger and cold. Only if Your Majesty can give them some money will I be able to offer you deliverance." "I came here," said T'ai-tsung, "with empty hands. Where can I get money?" "Your Majesty," said the judge, "there is in the World of the Living a man who has deposited great sums of gold and silver in our Region of Darkness. You can use your name for a loan, and your lowly judge will serve as your voucher; we shall borrow a roomful of money from him and distribute it among the hungry ghosts. You will then be able to get past them." "Who is this man?" asked T'ai-tsung. "He's a man from the K'ai-fêng District in Honan Province," said the judge. "His given name is Liang and his surname is Hsiang. He has thirteen rooms of gold and silver down here. If Your Majesty borrows from him, you can repay him when you return to the World of Light." Highly pleased and more than willing to use his name for the loan, T'ai-tsung at once signed a note for the judge. He borrowed a roomful of gold and silver, and the grand marshal was asked to distribute the money among the ghosts. The judge also instructed them, saying, "You may divide up these pieces of silver and gold among yourselves and use them accordingly. Let the Great T'ang Father pass, for he still has a long time to live. By the solemn word of the Ten Kings I am accompanying him to return to life. When he reaches the world of the living, he has been instructed to hold a Grand Mass of Land and Water for your salvation.[12] So don't start any more trouble." When the ghosts heard these words and received the silver and gold, they obeyed and turned back. The judge ordered the grand marshal to wave the flag for guiding souls, and led T'ai-tsung out of the City of the Dead. They set out again on a broad and level path, leaving quickly with light, airy steps.

They traveled for a long time and arrived at the junction of the Sixfold Path of Transmigration. They saw some people riding the clouds wearing embroidered capes, and some with Taoist amulets of gold fish dangling from their waists; there were in fact monks, nuns, Taoists, and secular persons, and all varieties of beasts and fowls, ghosts and spirits. In an unending stream they all ran beneath the Wheel of Transmigration to enter each into a predestined path. "What is the meaning of this?" asked the T'ang emperor. "Your Majesty," said the judge, "as your mind is enlightened to perceive that the Buddha-nature is immanent in all things, you must remember this and proclaim it in the World of the Living. This is called the Sixfold Path of Transmigration. Those who perform good works will ascend to the way of the immortals; those who remain patriotic to the end will advance to the way of nobility; those who practice filial piety will be born again into the way of blessing; those who are just and honest will enter once more into the way of humans; those who cherish virtue will proceed to the way of riches; those who are vicious and violent will fall back into the way of demons." When the T'ang emperor heard this, he nodded his head and sighed, saying,

Ah, how truly good is goodness!
To do good will never bring illness!
Let kindness always be your aim.
On charity don't shut your door.
Allow no evil thoughts to rise.
Be certain to cut down mischief.
Don't say there's no retribution,
For gods have their disposition.

The judge accompanied the T'ang emperor up to the very entrance to the way of nobility before he prostrated himself and called out, "Your Majesty, this is where you must proceed, and here your humble judge will take leave of you. I am asking Grand Marshal Chu to accompany you a little further." The T'ang emperor thanked him, saying, "I'm sorry, sir, that you have had to travel such great distance on my account." "When Your Majesty returns to the World of Light," said the judge, "be very certain that you celebrate the Grand Mass of Land and Water so that those wretched, homeless souls may be delivered. Please do not forget! Only if there is no murmuring for vengeance in the Region of Darkness will there be the prosperity of peace in your World of Light. If there are any wicked ways in your life, you must change them one by one, and you must teach your subjects far and wide to do good. You may be assured then that your empire will be firmly established, and that your fame will go down to posterity." The T'ang emperor promised to grant each one of the judge's requests.

Having parted from Judge Ts'ui, he followed Grand Marshal Chu and entered the gate. The grand marshal saw inside a black-maned bay horse complete with rein and saddle. Lending the emperor assistance from left and right, he quickly helped him mount it. The horse shot forward like an arrow, and soon they reached the bank of the Wei River, where a pair of golden carps could be seen frolicking on top of the waves. Pleased by what he saw, the T'ang emperor reined in his horse and stopped to watch. "Your Majesty," said the grand marshal, "let's hurry and get you back into your city while there is still time." But the emperor persisted in his indulgence and refused to go forward. The grand marshal grabbed one of his legs and shouted, "You still won't move? What are you waiting for?" Making a loud splash, he was pushed off his horse into the Wei River; he thus left the Region of Darkness and returned to the World of Light.

We shall now tell you about those who served before the Throne in the T'ang dynasty. Hsü Mou-kung, Ch'in Shu-pao, Hu Ching-tê, Tuan Chih-hsien, Ma San-pao, Ch'êng Yao-chin, Kao Shih-lien, Li Shih-chi, Fang Hsüan-ling, Tu Ju-hui, Hsiao Yü, Fu I, Chang Tao-yüan, Chang Shih-hêng, and Wang Kuei constituted the two groups of civil and military officials. They gathered with the crown prince of the Eastern Palace, the queen, the ladies of the court, and the chief steward in the Hall of the White Tiger for the imperial mourning. At the same time, they were talking about issuing the obituary proclamation for the whole empire and crowning the prince as emperor. From one side of the hall, Wei Chêng stepped forward and said, "All of you, please refrain from doing anything hasty. If you alarm the various districts and cities, you may bring about something undesirable and unexpected. Let's wait here for another day, for our lord will surely come back to life." "What nonsense you are talking, Prime Minister Wei," said Hsü Ching-tsung, coming from below, "for the ancient proverb says, 'Just as spilled water cannot be retrieved, so a dead man can never return!' Why do you mouth such empty words to vex our minds? What reason do you have for this?" "To tell you the truth, Mr. Hsü," said Wei Chêng, "I have been instructed since my youth in the arts of immortality. My calculations are most accurate, and I promise you that His Majesty will not die."

As they were talking, they suddenly heard a loud voice crying in the coffin, "You've drowned me! You've drowned me!" It so startled the civil and military officials, and so terrified the queen and the ladies, that every one of them had

A face yellow as autumnal mulberry leaves,
A body limp as the willow of early spring.
The legs of the crown prince buckled,
He could not hold the mourning staff to finish his rites.

The soul of the steward left him,
He could not wear the mourning cap to show his grief.
The matrons collapsed;
The ladies pitched sideways;
The matrons collapsed
Like weak hibiscus blasted by savage wind.
The ladies pitched sideways
Like lilies overwhelmed by sudden rain.
The petrified lords,
Their bones and tendons feeble,
Trembled and shook,
All dumb and awe-struck.
The whole White-Tiger Hall was like a bridge with broken beams;
The funeral stage resembled a temple wrecked.

Every person attending the court ran away, and no one dared approach the coffin. Only the upright Hsü Mou-kung, the rational Prime Minister Wei, the courageous Ch'in Ch'iung, and the impulsive Ching-tê came forward and took hold of the coffin. "Your Majesty," they cried, "if there's something bothering you, tell us about it. Don't play ghost and terrify your relatives!" But Wei Chêng said, "He's not playing ghost. His Majesty is coming back to life! Get some tools, quick!" They opened the top of the coffin and saw indeed that T'ai-tsung was sitting up inside, still shouting, "You've drowned me! Who bailed me out?" Mou-kung and the rest of them went forward to lift him up, saying, "Don't be afraid, Your Majesty, and wake up. Your subjects are here to protect you." Only then did the T'ang emperor open his eyes and say, "How I suffered just now! I barely escaped attack by spiteful demons from the Region of Darkness, only to encounter death by drowning!" "Have no fear, Your Majesty," said the ministers. "What kind of calamity occurred in the water?" "I was riding a horse," the T'ang emperor said, "when we came near the Wei River where two fishes were playing. That deceitful Grand Marshal Chu pushed me off my horse into the river, and I was almost drowned." "His Majesty is still not entirely free from the influences of the dead," said Wei Chêng. He quickly ordered from the imperial dispensary medicinal broth designed to calm his spirit and fortify his soul. They also prepared some rice gruel, and only after taking such nourishments once or twice did he become his old self again, fully regaining his living senses. A quick calculation revealed that the

T'ang emperor had been dead for three days and nights and then returned to life to rule again. We have thus a testimonial poem:

From ancient times how often the world changed!
History is full of kingdoms' rise and fall.
Countless the wonders of Chou, Han, and Tsin—
Which could compare with this resurrection?

By then it was dusk; the various ministers withdrew after they had seen the emperor retire.

Next day, they took off their mourning garb and changed into their court attire: everyone had on his red robe and black cap, his purple sash and gold medal, waiting outside the gate to be summoned to court. We now tell you about T'ai-tsung, who, having received the medicine prescribed for calming his spirit and fortifying his soul, and having taken the rice broth several times, was carried into his bed-chamber by his attendants. He slept soundly that whole night, and when he arose at dawn, his spirit was fully revived. Look how he was attired:

He donned a tall, royal cap;
He wore a dark ocher robe;
He put on a belt of green jade from Blue Mountain;
He trod a pair of empire-building carefree boots.
His stunning looks
Surpassed anyone in court;
With power to spare
He resumed his reign.
What a great T'ang emperor of justice and truth,
The Majestic Li who rose again from the dead!

The T'ang emperor went up to the Treasure Hall of the Golden Carriage and gathered together the two groups of civil and military officials, who, after shouting "Long live the emperor" three times, stood in attention according to rank and file. Then this announcement was heard: "If there is any business, come forth and make your memorial; if there is no business, you are dismissed from court." From the east came Hsü Mou-kung, Wei Chêng, Wang Kuei, Tu Ju-hui, Fang Hsüan-ling, Yüan T'ien-kang, Li Ch'un-fêng and Hsü Ching-tsung; and from the west came Yin K'ai-shan, Liu Hung-chi, Ma San-pao, Tuan Chih-hsien, Ch'êng Yao-chin, Ch'in Shu-pao, Hu Ching-tê, and Hsüeh Jen-kuei; they all went forward and prostrated themselves before the steps of white jade. "Your Majesty," they said, "may we inquire how you awoke from your slumber which lasted for so long?" "On that day, after we had received the letter from Wei Chêng," said T'ai-tsung, "we felt that our soul had departed from these halls, having been invited by the imperial guardsmen to join a hunting party. As we were traveling, the men and horses both disappeared, whereupon my father, the former emperor, and my deceased brothers came to hassle us. We would not have been able to escape them had it not been for the arrival of someone in black cap and robe; this man happened to be the judge Ts'ui Chüeh, who managed to send my deceased brothers away. We handed Wei Chêng's letter over to him, and as he was reading it, some boys in blue came to lead us with flags and banners to the Hall of Darkness, where we were met by the Ten Kings of the Underworld. They told us of the Ching River Dragon, who accused us of having him slain after promising to save him. We in turn explained to them what happened, and they assured us that our case had been jointly reviewed by the Three Tribunes. Then they asked for the Chronicles of Life and Death to examine what was to be our allotted age. Judge Ts'ui presented his books, and King Yama, after checking them, said that Heaven had assigned us a portion of thirty-three years. Since we had ruled for only thirteen years, we were entitled to twenty more years of living. So Grand Marshal Chu and Judge Ts'ui were ordered to send us back here. We took leave of the Ten Kings and promised to thank them with gifts of melons and other fruits. After our departure from the Hall of Darkness, we encountered in the Underworld all those who were treasonous to the state and disloyal to their parents, those who practiced neither virtue nor righteousness, those who squandered the five grains, those who cheated openly or in secret, those who indulged in unjust weights and measurements—in sum, the rapists, the thieves, the liars, and hypocrites, the wantons, the deviates, the connivers, and the lawbreakers. They were all suffering from various tortures by grinding, burning, pounding, sawing, frying, boiling, hanging, and skinning. There were tens of thousands of them, and we could not make an end of this ghastly sight. Thereafter we passed by the City of the Dead, filled with the souls of brigands and bandits from all over the Earth, who came to block our path. Fortunately, Judge Ts'ui was willing to vouch for us, and we could then borrow a roomful of gold and silver from Old Man Hsiang of Honan to buy off the spirits before we could proceed once more. We finally parted after Judge Ts'ui had repeatedly instructed us that when we returned to the World of Light we were to celebrate a Grand Mass of Land and Water for the salvation of those orphaned spirits. After leaving the Sixfold Path of Transmigration, Grand Marshal Chu asked us to mount a horse so swift it seemed to be flying, and brought me to the bank of the Wei River. As we were enjoying the sight of two fishes playing in the water, he grabbed our legs and pushed us into the river. Only then did we come back to life." When the various ministers heard these words, they all praised and congratulated the emperor. A notice was also sent out to every town and district in the empire, and all the officials presented gratulatory memorials, which we shall mention no further.

We shall now tell you about T'ai-tsung, who proclaimed a general amnesty for the prisoners in the empire. Moreover, he asked for an inventory of those convicted of capital crimes, and the judge from the Board of Justice submitted some four hundred names of those awaiting death by beheading or hanging. T'ai-tsung granted them one year's leave to return to their families, so that they could settle their affairs and put their property in order before going to the marketplace to receive their just deserts. The prisoners all thanked him for such grace before departing. After issuing another edict for the care and welfare of orphans, T'ai-tsung also released some three thousand court maidens and concubines from the palace and married them off to worthy military officers. From that time on, his reign was truly a virtuous one, to which we have a testimonial poem:

Great is the virtue of the Great T'ang Ruler!
Surpassing Sage Kings,[13] he makes his people prosper.
Five hundred convicts may now leave the prison;
Three thousand maidens find release from the palace.
The empire's officials all wish him long life.
The ministers at court all give him high praise.
Such good heart, once stirred, the Heavens should bless,
And pass such weal to seventeen generations.

After releasing the court maidens and convicts, T'ai-tsung also issued another proclamation to be posted throughout the empire. The proclamation read:

The cosmos, though vast,
Is brightly surveyed by the sun and the moon;
The world, though immense,

Approves not villains in Heaven or on Earth.
If your intent is trickery,
Even this life will bring retribution;
If your giving exceeds receiving,
There's blessing not only in the life hereafter.
A thousand clever designs
Are not as living according to one's duties;
Ten thousand men of violence
Cannot compare with one frugal and content.
If you're bent on good works and mercy,
Need you read the sūtras with diligence?
If you intend to harm others,
Even the learning of Buddha is vain!

From that time on, there was not a single person in the empire who did not practice virtue. Meanwhile, another notice was posted asking for a volunteer to take the melons and other fruits to the Region of Darkness. At the same time, a roomful of gold and silver from the treasury was sent with the Imperial Duke of Khotan, Hu Ching-tê, to the K'ai-fêng District of Honan so that the debt to Hsiang Liang could be repaid. After the notice had been posted for some days, a worthy came forth to volunteer his life for the mission. He was originally from Chün Chou; his surname was Liu and his given name Ch'üan, and he belonged to a family of great wealth. The reason he came forward was that his wife, Li Ts'ui-lien, happened to have given a gold hairpin from her head, by way of alms, to a monk in front of their house. When Liu Ch'üan chided her for her indiscretion in flaunting herself outside their home, Li became so upset that she promptly hanged herself, leaving behind her a pair of young children, who wept piteously day and night. Liu Ch'üan was so filled with remorse by the sight of them that he was willing to leave life and property to take the melons to hell. He therefore took down the royal notice and came to see the T'ang emperor. The emperor ordered him to go to the Lodge of the Golden Pavilion, where a pair of southern melons were put on his head, some money in his sleeve, and some medicine in his mouth.

So Liu Ch'üan died by taking poison. His soul, still bearing the fruits on his head, arrived at the Gate of Spirits. The demon guardian at the door shouted, "Who are you, that you dare to come here?" "By the imperial command of the great T'ang emperor T'ai-tsung," said Liu Ch'üan, "I came here especially to present melons and other fruits for the enjoyment of the Ten Kings of the Underworld." The demon guardian received him amiably and led him to the Treasure Hall of Darkness. When he saw King Yama, he presented the melons saying, "By order of the T'ang emperor, I came from afar to present these melons as a token of thanks for the gracious hospitality of the Ten Kings." Highly pleased, King Yama said, "That Emperor T'ai-tsung is certainly a man of his word!" He accepted the melons and proceeded to ask the messenger about his name and his home. "Your humble servant," said Liu Ch'üan, "resided originally in Chün Chou; my surname is Liu and my given name is Ch'üan. Because my wife hanged herself, leaving no one to care for our children, I decided to leave home and children and sacrifice my life for the country by helping my emperor to take these melons here as a thank-offering." When the Ten Kings heard these words, they asked at once for Li, the wife of Liu Ch'üan; she was brought in by the demon guardian, and wife and husband had a reunion before the Hall of Darkness. They conversed about what had happened and also thanked the Ten Kings for this meeting. King Yama, moreover, examined the Books of Life and Death and found that both husband and wife were supposed to live to a ripe old age. He quickly ordered the demon guardian to take them back to life, but the guardian said, "Since Li Ts'ui-lien has been back in the World of Darkness for many days, her body no longer exists. To whom should her soul attach herself?" "The emperor's sister, Li Yü-ying," said King Yama, "is destined to die very soon. Borrow her body right away so that this woman can return to life." The demon guardian obeyed the order and led Liu Ch'üan and his wife out of the Region of Darkness to return to life. We do not know how the two of them returned to life, and you must listen to the explanation in the next chapter.

Twelve

The T'ang emperor, firm in sincerity, convenes the
   Grand Mass;
Kuan-yin, revealing herself, converts Gold Cicada.

We were telling you about the demon guardian who was leading Liu
Ch'üan and his wife out of the Region of Darkness. Accompanied by
a swirling dark wind, they went directly back to Ch'ang-an of the
great nation. The demon pushed the soul of Liu Ch'üan into the
Golden Court Pavilion Lodge, but the soul of Ts'ui-lien was brought
into the inner court of the royal palace. Just then the Princess Yü-ying
was walking beneath the shadows of flowers along a path covered
with green moss. The demon guardian crashed right into her and
pushed her to the ground; her living soul was snatched away and the
soul of Ts'ui-lien was pushed into Yü-ying's body instead. The demon
guardian then returned to the Region of Darkness, and we shall say
no more about that.

   We now tell you that the maidservants of the palace, both young
and old, when they saw that Yü-ying had fallen and died, ran quickly
to the Hall of the Golden Chimes and reported the incident to the
queen, saying, "The princess has fallen and died!" Horrified, the
queen reported it to T'ai-tsung. When T'ai-tsung heard the news,
he nodded, sighing, and said, "So this has come to pass indeed! We
did ask the King of Darkness whether the old and young of our family
would be safe or not. He said, 'They will all be safe, but I fear that
your royal sister will not live long.' Now his word is fulfilled." All the
inhabitants of the palace came to mourn her, but when they reached
the spot where she had fallen, they saw that the princess was breathing. "Stop weeping! Stop weeping!" said the T'ang emperor. "Don't
startle her!" He went forward and lifted her head with the royal hand,
crying out, "Wake up, royal sister!" Our princess suddenly turned
over and cried, "Husband, walk slowly! Wait for me!" "Sister," said
T'ai-tsung, "we are all here." Lifting her head and opening her eyes
to look around, the princess said, "Who are you that you dare touch
me?" "This is your royal brother," said T'ai-tsung, "and your sister-

in-law." "Where do I have any royal brother and sister-in-law?" asked the princess. "My family is Li, and my maiden name is Li Ts'ui-lien. My husband's surname is Liu and his given name is Ch'üan; both of us are from Chün Chou. Because I pulled a golden hairpin to give to a monk outside our home as alms three months ago, my husband rebuked me for walking indiscreetly out of our doors and thus violating the etiquette appropriate to a woman. He scolded me, and I became so enraged that I hanged myself with a white silk cord, leaving behind a pair of children who wept night and day. On account of my husband, who was sent by the T'ang emperor to the Region of Darkness to present melons, King Yama took pity on us and allowed us both to return to life. He was walking ahead; I could not keep up with him, tripped, and fell. How rude you all are! Not knowing my name, how dare you touch me!" When T'ai-tsung heard these words, he said to his attendants, "I suppose my sister was knocked senseless by the fall. She's babbling!" He ordered that Yü-ying be helped into the palace and medicine be brought in from the court dispensary.

As the T'ang emperor went back to the court, one of his assistants came forward to report, saying, "Your Majesty, the man Liu Ch'üan, who went to present the melons, has returned to life. He is now outside the gate, awaiting your order." Greatly startled, the T'ang emperor at once gave the order for Liu Ch'üan to be brought in, who then prostrated himself before the red-lacquered courtyard. T'ai-tsung asked him, "How did the presentation of melons come off?" "Your subject," said Liu Ch'üan, "bore the melons on his head and went straight to the Gate of Spirits. I was led to the Hall of Darkness, where I met the Ten Kings of the Underworld. I presented the melons and spoke at length about the sincere gratitude of my lord. King Yama was most delighted, and he complimented Your Majesty profusely, saying, 'That T'ai-tsung emperor is indeed a man of virtue and a man of his word.'" "What did you happen to see in the Region of Darkness?" asked the T'ang emperor. "Your subject did not travel far," said Liu Ch'üan, "and I did not see much. I only heard King Yama questioning me on my native village and my name. Your subject therefore gave him a full account of how I abandoned home and children because of my wife's suicide and volunteered for the mission. He quickly sent for a demon guardian, who brought in my wife, and we were reunited at the Hall of Darkness. Meanwhile, they also examined the Books of Life and Death and told us that we both should live to a ripe old age. The demon guardian was dispatched to see us back to life. Your subject walked ahead, but my wife fell behind. I am grateful that I am now returned to life, but I do not know where my wife has gone." Alarmed, the T'ang emperor asked, "Did King Yama say anything about your wife?" "He didn't say much," said Liu Ch'üan. "I only heard the demon guardian's exclamation that Li Ts'ui-lien had been dead for so long that her body no longer existed. King Yama said, 'The royal sister, Li Yü-ying, should die shortly. Let Ts'ui-lien borrow the body of Yü-ying so that she may return to life.' Your subject has no knowledge of who that royal sister is and where she resides, nor has he made any attempt to locate her."

When the T'ang emperor heard this report, he was filled with delight and said to the many officials around him, "When we took leave of King Yama, we questioned him with regard to the inhabitants of the palace. He said that the old and the young would all be safe, though he feared that our sister would not live long. Just now our sister Yü-ying fell dying beneath the flowers. When we went to her assistance, she regained her consciousness momentarily, crying, 'Husband, walk slowly! Wait for me!' We thought that her fall had knocked her senseless, as she was babbling like that. But when we questioned her carefully, she said exactly what Liu Ch'üan now tells us." "If Her Royal Highness passed away momentarily, only to say these things after she regained consciousness," said Wei Chêng, "this means that there is a real possibility that Liu Ch'üan's wife has returned to life by borrowing another person's body. Let us invite the princess to come out, and see what she has to tell us." "We just asked the court dispensary to send in some medicine," said the T'ang emperor, "and we don't know what's happening." Some ladies of the court were sent to fetch the princess, and they found her inside, screaming, "Why do I need to take any medicine? How can this be my house? Ours is a clean, cool house of tiles; it's not like this one, yellow as if it has jaundice, and with such gaudy appointments! Let me out! Let me out!"

She was still shouting when four or five ladies and two or three eunuchs took hold of her and led her outside to the court. The T'ang emperor said, "Do you recognize your husband?" "What are you talking about?" said Yü-ying. "The two of us were pledged to each other since childhood as husband and wife. I bore him a boy and a girl. How could I not recognize him?" The T'ang emperor asked one of the palatial officials to help her go down from the Treasure Hall. The princess went right before the steps of white jade, and when she saw Liu Ch'üan, she grabbed him, saying, "Husband, where have you been? You didn't even wait for me! I tripped and fell, and then I was surrounded by all these crazy people, talking nonsense! What do you have to say to this?" Liu Ch'üan heard that she was speaking like his wife, but the person he saw certainly did not resemble her, and he dared not acknowledge her to be his own. The T'ang emperor said,

Indeed,
Men have seen mountains cracking, or the gaping of earth;
But none has seen the living exchanged for the dead!

What a just and kindly ruler! He took his sister's toilet boxes, garments, and jewelry and bestowed them all on Liu Ch'üan; it was as if the man was provided with a dowry. He was, moreover, exempted forever from having to engage in any compulsory service to the Crown, and was told to take the royal sister back to his home. So, husband and wife together expressed their gratitude before the steps and returned happily to their village. We have a poem in testimony:

Man lives and dies, foreordained by fate.
How long, how short—each has his span of years.
Liu Ch'üan presented melons and returned to life.
Taking someone's body, Li Ts'ui-lien revived.

The two of them took leave of the emperor, went directly back to Chün Chou, and saw that both house and children were in good order. They never ceased thereafter to proclaim the rewards of virtue, but we shall speak of them no further.

We now tell you about Yü-ch'ih Kung, who took a huge load of gold and silver and went to see Hsiang Liang at the K'ai-fêng District in Honan. It turned out that the man made his living by selling water, while his wife, whose surname was Chang, sold pottery in front of their home. Whatever money they made, they kept only enough for their subsistence, giving all the rest either as alms to the monks or as gifts to the dead by purchasing paper money and burning it. They thus built up enormous merit; for though they were poor folks in the World of Light, they were, in fact, leading citizens for whom jade and gold were laid up in the other world. When Yü-ch'ih Kung came to their door with the gold and silver, Papa Hsiang and Mama Hsiang were terror-stricken. And when they also saw the district officials with their horses and carriages assembling outside their thatched hut, the aged couple were dumbfounded. They knelt on the floor and kowtowed without ceasing. "Old folks, please arise," said Yü-ch'ih Kung. "Though I am an imperial official, I came here with this gold and silver to repay you by order of my king." Shaking and quaking, the man said, "Your lowly servant has never lent money to others. How dare we accept such inexplicable wealth?" "I have found out," said Yü-ch'ih Kung, "that you are indeed a poor fellow. But you have also given alms to feed the monks. Whatever exceeds your necessities you have used to purchase paper money, which you burned in dedication to the Region of Darkness. You have thus accumulated a vast fortune down below. Our emperor, T'ai-tsung, returned to life after being dead for three days; he borrowed a roomful of gold and silver from you while he was in the Region of Darkness, and we are returning the exact sum to you. Please count your money accordingly so that we may make our report back to the emperor." Hsiang Liang and his wife, however, remained adamant. They raised their hands to Heaven and cried, "If your lowly servants accepted this gold and silver, we should die quickly. We might have been given credit for burning paper cash, but this is a secret unknown to us. Moreover, what evidence do we have that our Father, His Majesty, borrowed our money in some other world? We simply dare not accept this." "His Majesty told us," said Yü-ch'ih Kung, "that he received the loan from you because Judge Ts'ui vouched for him, and he could bear testimony. So please accept this." "Even if I were to die," said Hsiang Liang, "I could not accept the gift."

Seeing that they persisted in their refusal, Yü-ch'ih Kung had no alternative but to send someone back to report to the Throne. When T'ai-tsung saw the report and learned that Hsiang Liang had refused to accept the gold and silver, he said, "They are truly virtuous elders!" He issued a decree at once that Hu Ching-tê should use the money to erect a temple, to build a shrine, and to support the religious services that would be performed in them. The old couple, in other words, would be repaid in this manner. The decree went out to Ching-tê, who, having expressed his gratitude, facing the capital, proclaimed its content for all to know. He used the money to purchase a lot of about fifty acres not needed either by the military authorities or the people. A temple was erected on this piece of land and named the Royal Hsiang-Kuo Temple.[1] To the left of it there was also a shrine dedicated to Papa and Mama Hsiang, with a stone inscription stating that the buildings were erected under the supervision of Yü-ch'ih Kung. This is the Great Hsiang-Kuo Temple still standing today.

The work was finished and reported; T'ai-tsung was exceedingly pleased. He then gathered many officials together in order that a public notice be issued to invite monks for the celebration of the Grand Mass of Land and Water, so that those orphaned souls in the Region of Darkness might find salvation. The notice went throughout the empire, and officials of all regions were asked to recommend monks illustrious for their holiness to go to Ch'ang-an for the Mass. In less than a month's time, the various monks from the empire had arrived. The T'ang emperor ordered the court historian, Fu I, to select an illustrious priest to take charge of the ceremonies. When Fu I received the order, however, he presented a memorial to the Throne which attempted to dispute the worth of Buddha.[2] The memorial said:

The teachings of the Western Territory deny the relations of ruler and subject, of father and son. With the doctrines of the Three Ways and the Sixfold Path, they beguile and seduce the foolish and the simpleminded. They emphasize the sins of the past in order to ensure the felicities of the future. By chanting in Sanskrit, they seek a way of escape. We submit, however, that birth, death, and the length of one's life are ordered by nature; but the conditions of public disgrace or honor are determined by human volition. These phenomena are not, as some philistines would now maintain, ordained by Buddha. The teachings of Buddha did not exist in the time of the Three Kings and the Five Emperors, and yet those rulers were wise, their subjects loyal, and their reigns long-lasting. It was not until the period of Ming Ti in the Han dynasty that the worship of foreign gods was established,[3] but this meant only that priests of the Western Territory were permitted to propagate their faith. The event, in fact, represented a foreign intrusion in China, and the teachings are hardly worthy to be believed.

When T'ai-tsung saw the memorial, he had it distributed among the various officials for discussion. At that time the prime minister Hsiao Yü came forward and prostrated himself to address the Throne, saying, "The teachings of Buddha, which have flourished in several previous dynasties, seek to exalt the good and to restrain what is evil. In this way they are covertly an aid to the nation, and there is no reason why they should be rejected. For Buddha after all is also a sage, and he who spurns a sage is himself lawless. I urge that the dissenter be severely punished."

Taking up the debate with Hsiao Yü, Fu I contended that propriety had its foundation in service to one's parents and ruler. Yet Buddha forsook his parents and left his family; indeed, he defied the Son of Heaven all by himself, just as he used an inherited body to rebel against his parents. Hsiao Yü, Fu I went on to say, was not born in the wilds, but by his adherence to this doctrine of parental denial, he confirmed the saying that an unfilial son had in fact no parents. Hsiao Yü, however, folded his hands in front of him and declared, "Hell was established precisely for people of this kind." T'ai-tsung thereupon called on the Lord High Chamberlain, Chang Tao-yüan, and the President of the Grand Secretariat, Chang Shih-hêng, and asked how efficacious the Buddhist exercises were in the procurement of blessings. The two officials replied, "The emphasis of Buddha is on purity, benevolence, compassion, the proper fruits, and the unreality of things. It was Emperor Wu of the Northern Chou dynasty who set the Three Religions in order.[4] The Ch'an Master, Ta Hui, also had extolled those concepts of the dark and the distant. Generations of people revered such saints as the Fifth Patriarch, who became man,[5] or the Bodhidharma, who appeared in his sacred form; none of them proved to be inconspicuous in grace and power. Moreover, it has been held since antiquity that the Three Religions are most honorable, not to be destroyed or abolished. We beseech, therefore, Your Majesty to exercise your clear and sagacious judgment." Highly pleased, T'ai-tsung said, "The words of our worthy subjects are not unreasonable. Anyone who disputes them further will be punished." He thereupon ordered Wei Chêng, Hsiao Yü, and Chang Tao-yüan to invite the various Buddhist priests to prepare the site for the Grand Mass and to select from among them someone of great merit and virtue to preside over the ceremonies. All the officials then bowed their heads to the ground to thank the emperor before withdrawing. From that time also came the law that any person who denounces a monk or Buddhism will have his arms broken.

Next day the three court officials began the process of selection at the Mountain-River Platform, and from among the priests gathered there they chose an illustrious monk of great merit. Who is this person, you ask.

Gold Cicada was his former divine name.
As heedless he was of the Buddha's talk,
He had to suffer in this world of dust,
To fall in the net by being born a man.
He met misfortune as he came to Earth,
And evildoers even before his birth.
His father: Ch'ên, a chuang-yüan from Hai Chou.
His mother's sire: chief of this dynasty's court.
Fated by his natal star to fall in the stream,
He followed tide and current, chased by mighty waves.
At Gold Mountain, the island, he had great fortune;
For the abbot, Ch'ien-an, raised him up.
He met his true mother at age eighteen,
And called on her father at the capital.
A great army was sent by Chief K'ai-shan
To stamp out the vicious crew at Hung Chou.
The chuang-yüan Kuang-jui escaped his doom:
Son united with sire—how worthy of praise!
They saw the king to receive his favor;
Their names resounded in Ling-yen Tower.[6]
Declining office, he wished to be a monk,
To seek at Hung-fu Temple the Way of Truth,
A former child of Buddha, nicknamed River Float.
His religious name was Ch'ên Hsüan-tsang.

So that very day the multitude selected the priest Hsüan-tsang, a man who had been a monk since childhood, who maintained a vegetarian diet, and who had received the commandments the moment he left his mother's womb. His maternal grandfather was Yin K'ai-shan, one of the chief army commanders of the present dynasty. His father, Ch'ên Kuang-jui, had taken the prize of chuang-yüan and was appointed Grand Secretary of the Wen-yüan Chamber. Hsüan-tsang, however, had no love for glory or wealth, being dedicated wholly to the pursuit of nirvāna. Their investigations revealed that he had an excellent family background and the highest moral character. Not one of the thousands of classics and sūtras he had failed to master; none of the Buddhist chants and hymns was unknown to him.

The three officials led Hsüan-tsang before the Throne. After going through elaborate court ritual, they bowed to report, "Your subjects, in obedience to your holy decree, have selected an illustrious monk

by the name of Ch'ên Hsüan-tsang." Hearing the name, T'ai-tsung
thought silently for a long time and said, "Can Hsüan-tsang be the
son of Grand Secretary Ch'ên Kuang-jui?" Child River Float kowtowed and replied, "That is indeed your subject." "This is a most
appropriate choice," said T'ai-tsung, delighted. "You are truly a monk
of great virtue and devotion. We therefore appoint you the Grand
Expositor of the Faith, Supreme Vicar of Priests." Hsüan-tsang
touched his forehead to the ground to express his gratitude and to
receive his appointment. He was given, furthermore, a cassock of
knitted gold and five colors, a Vairocana hat,[7] and the instruction
diligently to seek out all worthy monks and to rank all these ācāryas[8]
in order. They were to follow the imperial decree and proceed to the
Temple of Transformation,[9] where they would begin the ceremony
after selecting a propitious day and hour.

Hsüan-tsang bowed again to receive the decree and left. He went
to the Temple of Transformation and gathered many monks together;
they made ready the beds, built the platforms, and rehearsed the
music. A total of one thousand two hundred worthy monks, young
and old, were chosen, who were further separated into three divisions,
occupying the rear, middle, and front portions of the hall. All the
preparations were completed and everything was put in order before
the Buddhas. The third day of the ninth month of that same year was
selected as the lucky day, when a Grand Mass of Land and Water
lasting forty-nine days (in accordance with the number seven times
seven) would begin. A memorial was presented to T'ai-tsang, who
went with all his relatives and officials, both civil and military, to the
mass on that day to burn incense and listen to the lecture. We have a
poem as testimony. The poem says:

When the year-star of Chên-kuan reached thirteen,
The king called his people to hear the Sacred Books.
The boundless Law was performed at a plot of truth;
Cloud, fog, and light filled the Great Promise Hall.
By grace and the king's edict they met at this grand temple;
Gold Cicada cast his shell, changed by the bounteous West.
He spread wide the good works to save the damned,
And held fast his faith to preach the Three Modes of Life.[10]

In the thirteenth year of the Chên-kuan period, when the year stood
at chi-ssŭ and the ninth month at chia-hsü, on the third day and at
the auspicious hour of kuei-mao, Ch'ên Hsüan-tsang, the Great

Expositor-Priest, gathered together one thousand two hundred illustrious monks. They met at the Temple of Transformation in the city
of Ch'ang-an to expound the various holy sūtras. After holding court
early that morning, the emperor led many officials both military and
civil and left the Treasure Hall of Golden Chimes by phoenix carriages
and dragon chariots. They came to the temple to listen to the lectures
and raise incense. How does the imperial cortege appear? Truly it
comes with

A sky full of blessed air
And ten thousand shafts of hallowed light.
The favorable wind blows gently;
The omnific sun shines brightly.
A thousand lords with girdle-jade walk in front and rear.
The many flags of guardsmen stand both left and right.
Those holding gilt bludgeons,
And halberds and axes,
March in pairs and pairs;
The red silk lanterns,
The royal incense urn,
Move in solemnity.
The dragons fly and the phoenixes dance;
The falcons soar and the eagles take wing.
Most holy is the king and upright;
Most principled are the lords and true.
They increase our bliss by a thousand years, surpassing Yü
    and Shun;
They secure peace of ten thousand ages, rivaling Yao and T'ang.
We also see the curve-handled umbrella,
And robes with rolling dragons—
Their glare lighting up each other;
The jade joined-rings,
The phoenix fans,
Waving through holy mist.
Those caps of pearls and belts of jade;
The purple sashes and medals of gold.
A thousand rows of soldiers protect the Throne;
Two lines of marshals uphold the carriage.
This emperor, cleansed and sincere, bows to the Buddha,
Glad to raise incense and seek virtue's fruit.

The grand cortege of the T'ang emperor soon arrived in front of the temple. The emperor ordered a halt to the music, left the carriages, and led many officials in the worship of Buddha by taking up burning incense sticks in their hands. After bowing three times holding the incense, they raised their heads and looked around them. This was indeed a splendid religious hall. You see

Dancing flags and banners;
Bright, gleaming sunshades.
Dancing flags and banners
Fill the air with strands of flashing colored mists.
Bright, gleaming sunshades
Glow in the sun as fiery bolts.
Imposing, the gold image of Lokajyeṣṭha;[11]
Most awesome, the jade features of the Arhats.
Divine flowers fill the vases.
Sandal wood incense burn in the urns.
The divine flowers filling the vases
Adorn the temple with a brilliant forest of brocade.
The sandalwood incense burning in the urns
Covers the clear sky with waves of fragrant clouds.
Piled high on red trays are fruits in season.
On colored counters, mounds of cakes and sweets rest.
Rows of noble priests chant the holy sūtras
To save from their afflictions those orphaned souls.

T'ai-tsung and his officials each lifted the incense; they also worshiped the golden body of the Buddha and paid homage to the Arhats. Thereafter, the Master of the Law, Ch'ên Hsüan-tsang, the Grand Expositor of the Faith, led the various monks to greet the T'ang emperor. After the ceremony, they went back to their seats according to their rank and station. The priest then presented T'ai-tsung with the proclamation for the deliverance of the orphaned souls. It read:

The supreme virtue is vast and endless, for Buddhism is
founded upon nirvāṇa. The spirit of the pure and the clean
circulates freely and flows everywhere in the Three Regions.
There are a thousand changes and ten thousand transformations,
all regulated by the forces of yin and yang. Boundless and vast
indeed are the substance, the function, the true nature, and the
permanence of such phenomena. But look at those orphaned

souls, how worthy they are of our pity and commiseration! Now by the holy command of T'ai-tsung, we have selected and assembled various priests, who will engage in meditation and in the proclamation of the Law. Flinging wide the gates of salvation and setting in motion many vessels of mercy, we would deliver you, the multitudes, from the Sea of Woe and save you from perdition and from the Sixfold Path. You will be led to return to the way of truth and to enjoy the bliss of Heaven. Whether it be by motion, rest, or nonactivity, you will be united with, and become, pure essences. Therefore make use of this noble occasion, for you are invited to the pleasures of the celestial city. Take advantage of our Grand Mass so that you may find release from Hell's confinement, ascend quickly and freely to ultimate bliss, and travel without restraint in the Region of the West.

The poem says:

An urn of immortal incense.
Some scrolls of salvific power.
As we proclaim this boundless Law,
Receive now Heaven's endless grace.
All your guilt and crime abolished,
You lost souls may leave your prison.
May our nation be firmly blessed
With peace long and all-embracing.

Highly pleased by what he read, T'ai-tsung said to the monks, "Be firm, all of you, in your devotion, and do not slack in your service to Buddha. After the achievement of merit and after each has received his blessing, we shall reward you handsomely. Be assured that you will not have labored in vain." The twelve hundred monks all touched their foreheads to the ground to express their gratitude. After the three vegetarian meals of the day, the T'ang emperor returned to the palace to wait for the formal celebration of the mass seven days hence, when he would again be invited to raise incense. As dusk was about to fall, the various officials all retired. What sort of evening was this? Look at

The long stretch of clear sky and twilight dimming,
And few specks of jackdaw returning late to their perch.
People grow quiet, the city's filled with lights—
A time for stillness, as ch'an monks[12] will meditate.

We have told you about the scenery of the night. The next morning the Master of the Law again ascended his seat and gathered the monks to recite their sūtras, but we shall say no more about that.

We shall now tell you about the Bodhisattva Kuan-yin of the Potalaka Mountain in the South Sea, who, since receiving the command of Tathāgata, was searching in the city of Ch'ang-an for a worthy person to be the seeker of scriptures. For a long time, however, she did not encounter anyone truly virtuous. Then she learned that T'ai-tsung was extolling merit and virtue and selecting illustrious monks to hold the Grand Mass. When she discovered, moreover, that the chief priest and celebrant was the monk Child River Float, who was a child of Buddha born from paradise and who happened also to be the very elder whom she had sent to this incarnation, the Bodhisattva was exceedingly pleased. She immediately took the treasures bestowed by Buddha and carried them out with Mokṣa to sell them on the main streets of the city. "What were these treasures?" you ask. There were the embroidered cassock with rare jewels and the nine-ring priestly staff. But she kept hidden the Golden, the Constrictive, and the Prohibitive Fillets for use in a later time, putting up for sale only the cassock and the priestly staff.

Now in the city of Ch'ang-an there was one of those foolish monks who had not been selected to participate in the Grand Mass but who happened to possess a few strands of pelf. Seeing the Bodhisattva, who had changed herself into a monk covered with scabs and sores, bare-footed and bare-headed, dressed in rags, and holding up for sale the glowing cassock, he approached and asked, "You filthy monk, how much do you want for your cassock?" "The price of the cassock," said the Bodhisattva, "is five thousand taels of silver; for the staff, two thousand." The foolish monk laughed and said, "This filthy monk is mad! A lunatic! You want seven thousand taels of silver for two such common articles? They are not worth that much even if wearing them would make you immortal or turn you into a buddha. Take them away! You'll never be able to sell them!" The Bodhisattva did not bother to argue with him; she walked away and proceeded on her journey with Mokṣa. After a long while, they came to the Eastern Flower Gate and ran right into the chief minister Hsiao Yü, who was just returning from court. His outriders were shouting to clear the streets, but the Bodhisattva boldly refused to step aside. She stood on the street holding the cassock and met the chief minister head on. The chief minister pulled in his reins to look at this bright, luminous cassock, and asked his subordinates to inquire about the price of the garment. "I want five thousand taels for the cassock," said the Bodhisattva, "and two thousand for the staff." "What is so good about them," said Hsiao Yü, "that they should be so expensive?" "This cassock," said the Bodhisattva, "has something good about it, and something bad too. For some people it may be very expensive, but for others it may cost nothing at all." "What's good about it," asked Hsiao Yü, "and what's bad about it?" "He who wears my cassock," said the Bodhisattva, "will not fall into perdition, will not suffer in Hell, will not encounter violence, and will not meet tigers and wolves. That's how good it is! But if the person happens to be a foolish monk who relishes pleasures and rejoices in iniquities, or a priest who obeys neither the dietary laws nor the commandments, or a worldly fellow who attacks the sūtras and slanders the Buddha, he will never even get to see my cassock. That's what's bad about it!" The chief minister asked again, "What do you mean, it will be expensive for some and not expensive for others?" "He who does not follow the Law of Buddha," said the Bodhisattva, "or revere the Three Jewels, will be required to pay seven thousand taels if he insists on buying my cassock and my staff. That's how expensive it'll be! But if he honors the Three Jewels, rejoices in doing good deeds, and obeys our Buddha, he is a person worthy of these things. I shall willingly give him the cassock and the staff to establish an affinity of goodness with him. That's what I meant when I said that for some it would cost nothing."

When Hsiao Yü heard these words, his face could not hide his pleasure, for he knew that this was a good person. He dismounted at once and greeted the Bodhisattva ceremoniously, saying, "Your Holy Eminence, please pardon whatever offense Hsiao Yü might have caused. Our great T'ang emperor is a most religious person, and all the officials of his court are like-minded. In fact, we have just begun a Grand Mass of Land and Water, and this cassock will be most appropriate for the use of Ch'ên Hsüan-tsang, the Grand Expositor of the Faith. Let me go with you to have an audience with the Throne."

The Bodhisattva was happy to comply with the suggestion. They turned around and went into the Eastern Flower Gate. The Custodian of the Yellow Door went inside to make the report, and they were summoned to the Treasure Hall, where Hsiao Yü and the two monks covered with scabs and sores stood below the steps. "What does Hsiao Yü want to report to us?" asked the T'ang emperor. Prostrating himself before the steps, Hsiao Yü said, "Your subject going out of the Eastern Flower Gate met by chance these two monks, selling a cassock and a priestly staff. I thought of the priest, Hsüan-tsang, who might wear this garment. For this reason, we asked to have an audience with Your Majesty." Highly pleased, T'ai-tsung asked for the price of the cassock. The Bodhisattva and Mokṣa stood at the foot of the steps but did not bow at all. When asked the price of the cassock, the Bodhisattva replied, "Five thousand taels for the cassock and two thousand for the priestly staff." "What's so good about the cassock," said T'ai-tsung, "that it should cost so much?" The Bodhisattva said:

Of this cassock,
A dragon which wears but one shred
Will miss the woe of being devoured by the great roc;
Or a crane on which one thread is hung
Will transcend this world and reach the place of the gods.
Sit in it:
Ten thousand gods will salute you!
Move with it:
Seven Buddhas will follow you![13]
This cassock was made of silk drawn from ice silkworms[14]
And threads spun by skilled craftsmen.
Immortal girls did the weaving;
Divine maidens helped at the loom.
Bit by bit, the parts were sewn and embroidered.
Stitch by stitch, it arose—a brocade from the heddle,
Its pellucid weave finer than ornate blooms.
Its colors, brilliant, emit precious light.
Wear it, and crimson mist will surround your frame.
Doff it, and see the colored clouds take flight.
Outside the Three Heavens' door its primal light was seen;
Before the Five Mountains its magic aura grew.
Inlaid are layers of lotus from the West,
And hanging pearls shine like planets and stars.
On four corners are pearls which glow at night;
On top stays fastened an emerald.
Though lacking the all-seeing primal form,
It's held by Eight Treasures all aglow.

This cassock
You keep folded at leisure;
You wear it to meet sages.
When it's kept folded at leisure,
Its rainbowlike hues cut through a thousand wrappings.
When you wear it to meet sages,
All Heaven takes fright—both demons and gods!
On top are the ṛddhi pearl,
The māṇi pearl,
The dust-clearing pearl,
The wind-stopping pearl.
There are also the red cornelian,
The purple coral,
The luminescent pearl,[15]
The Śāriputra.
They rob the moon of its whiteness;
They match the sun in its redness.
In waves its divine aura imbues the sky;
In flashes its brightness lifts up its perfection.
In waves its divine aura imbues the sky,
Flooding the Gate of Heaven.
In flashes its brightness lifts up its perfection,
Lighting up the whole world.
Shining upon the mountains and the streams,
It wakens tigers and leopards;
Lighting up the isles and the seas,
It moves dragons and fishes.
Along its edges hang two chains of melted gold,
And joins the collars a ring of snow-white jade.
The poem says:
The august Three Jewels, this venerable Truth—
It judges all Four Creatures on the Sixfold Path.
The mind enlightened knows and holds God's Law and man's;
The soul illumined can transmit the lamp of wisdom.
The solemn guard of one's body is Vajradhātu;[16]
Like ice in a jade pitcher is the purified mind.
Since Buddha caused this cassock to be made,
Which of ten thousand kalpas can harm a monk?
When the T'ang emperor, who was up in the Treasure Hall, heard

these words, he was highly pleased. "Tell me, priest," he asked again, "What's so good about the nine-ring priestly staff?" "My staff," said the Bodhisattva, "has on it

Nine joined-rings made of iron and set in bronze,
And nine joints of vine immortal ever young.
When held, it scorns the sight of aging bones;[17]
It leaves the mount to return with fleecy clouds.
It roamed through Heaven with the Fifth Patriarch;
It broke Hell's gate when Lo Po sought his mother.[18]
Not soiled by the filth of this red-dust world,
It gladly follows the god-monk up Yü Shan."[19]

When the T'ang emperor heard these words, he gave the order to have the cassock spread open so that he might examine it carefully from top to bottom. It was indeed a marvelous thing! "Venerable Elder of the Great Law," he said, "we shall not deceive you. At this very moment we have exalted the Religion of Mercy and planted abundantly in the fields of blessing. You may see many priests assembled in the Temple of Transformation to perform the Law and the sūtras. In their midst is a man of great merit and virtue, whose religious name is Hsüan-tsang. We wish, therefore, to purchase these two treasure objects from you to give them to him. How much do you really want for these things?" Hearing these words, the Bodhisattva and Mokṣa folded their hands and gave praise to the Buddha. "If he is a man of virtue and merit," she said to the Throne, bowing, "this humble cleric is willing to give them to him. I shall not accept any money." She finished speaking and turned at once to leave. The T'ang emperor quickly asked Hsiao Yü to hold her back. Standing up in the Hall, he bowed low before saying, "Previously you claimed that the cassock was worth five thousand taels of silver, and the staff two thousand. Now that you see we want to buy them, you refuse to accept payment. Are you implying that we would bank on our position and take your possession by force? That's absurd! We shall pay you according to the original sum you asked for; please do not refuse it." Raising her hands for a salutation, the Bodhisattva said, "This humble cleric made a vow before, stating that anyone who reveres the Three Treasures, rejoices in virtue, and submits to our Buddha will be given these treasures free. Since it is clear that Your Majesty is eager to magnify virtue, to rest in excellence, and to honor our Buddhist faith by having an illustrious monk proclaim the

Great Law, it is my duty to present these gifts to you. I shall take no money for them. They will be left here and this humble cleric will take leave of you." When the T'ang emperor saw that she was so insistent, he was very pleased. He ordered the Court of Banquets to prepare a huge vegetarian feast to thank the Bodhisattva, who firmly declined that also. She left amiably and went back to her hiding place at the Temple of the Local Spirit, which we shall mention no further.

We tell you now about T'ai-tsung, who held a noon court and asked Wei Chêng to summon Hsüan-tsang to an audience. That Master of the Law was just leading the monks in chanting sūtras and reciting geyas.[20] When he heard the emperor's decree, he left the platform immediately and followed Wei Chêng to come before the Throne. "We have greatly troubled our Master," said T'ai-tsung, "to render exemplary good works, for which we have hardly anything to offer you in thanks. This morning Hsiao Yü came upon two monks who were willing to present us with a brocaded cassock with rare treasures and a nine-ring priestly staff. We therefore call specially for you so that you may receive them for your enjoyment and use." Hsüan-tsang kowtowed to express his thanks. "If our Master of the Law is willing," said T'ai-tsung, "please put the garment on for us to have a look." The priest accordingly shook open the cassock and draped it on his body, holding the staff in his hands. As he stood before the steps, ruler and subjects were all delighted. Here was a true child of Tathāgata! Look at him:

His looks imposing, how elegant and fine!
This robe of Buddha fits him like a glove!
Its splendor, most lustrous, spills over the world;
Its radiant colors imbue the universe.
Up and down are set rows of shining pearls.
Back and front, layers of golden cords are threaded.
Brocade gilds the robe's edges all around,
With patterns embroidered most varied and rare.
The frogs, thread-made, are shaped Eight Treasures like.
A gold ring joins the collars with velvet loops.
It shows on top and bottom Heaven's ranks,
And stars, great and small, are placed left and right.
Great is the fortune of Hsüan-tsang, the priest,
Now most deserving of this precious thing.
He seems a living arhat from the West,

Or even better than its true elite.
Holding his staff, with all its nine rings clanging;
Benevolent in the Vairocana hat,
He's a true child of Buddha, it's no idle tale!
Nor is it false that he the Bodhi matched.

The various officials, both civil and military, stood before the steps and shouted "Bravo!" T'ai-tsung could not have been more pleased, and he told the Master of the Law to keep his cassock on and the staff in his hands. Two regiments of honor guards were ordered to accompany him along with many other officials. They left the gate of the court and proceeded on the main streets toward the temple, and the whole entourage gave the impression that a chuang-yüan was making a tour of the city. The procession was a stirring sight indeed! The merchants and tradesmen in the city of Ch'ang-an, the princes and noblemen, the men of ink and letters, the grown men and the little girls—all vied to get a good view. Everyone exclaimed, "What a priest! He is truly a living arhat descended to Earth, a live bodhisattva coming to the world!" Hsüan-tsang went right to the temple where he was met by all the monks leaving their seats. The moment they saw him wearing that cassock and holding the staff, they all said that King Kṣitigarbha had arrived![21] Everyone bowed to him and waited on him left and right. Going up to the main hall, Hsüan-tsang lighted incense to honor the Buddha, after which he spoke of the emperor's favor to the multitude. Thereafter, each went back to his assigned seat, and soon the fiery orb sank westward. So it was

Sunset, and mist hid trees and grasses,
As the capital's first chimes rang out.
Chêng-chêng they struck thrice, and human traffic ceased;
Main streets and alleys soon grew quiet.
Though lights burned bright at First Temple,
The lone hamlet was noiseless and still.
The monk in silence tended the sūtras yet—
Ready to tame demons, to train his spirit.

Time went by like the snapping of fingers, and the formal celebration of the Grand Mass on the seventh day was to take place. Hsüan-tsang presented the T'ang emperor with a memorial, inviting him to raise the incense. News of these good works was circulating throughout the empire. Upon receiving the notice, T'ai-tsung sent for his carriage and

led many of his officials, both civil and military, as well as his
relatives and the ladies of the court, to the temple. All the people of
the city—young and old, nobles and plebeians—went along also to
hear the preaching. At the same time, the Bodhisattva said to Mokṣa,
"Today is the formal celebration of the Grand Mass, the first seventh
of seven such occasions. It's about time for you and me to join the
crowd. First, we want to see how the mass is going; second, we want
to find out whether Gold Cicada is worthy of my treasures; and third,
we can discover what division of Buddhism he is preaching about."
The two of them thereupon went to the temple; and so it is that,
having affinity, one will meet old acquaintances, as perfection returns
to this holy site. As they walked inside the temple to look around, they
discovered that such a place in the capital of a great nation indeed
surpassed the Ṣaḍ-varṣa,²² or even the Jetavana²³ Garden of the
Śrāvastī. It was truly a lofty temple of Caturdiśaḥ,²⁴ resounding with
divine music and Buddhist chants. Our Bodhisattva went directly to
the side of the platform of many treasures and beheld a form truly
resembling the enlightened Gold Cicada. The poem says:

All things were pure with not a spot of dust.
Hsüan-tsang of the Great Law sat high on stage.
Lost souls, redeemed, approached the place unseen;
The city's highborn came to hear the Law.
You give when time's ripe: this intent's far-reaching.
You die as you please, the Canon door's open.
As they heard him rehearse the Boundless Law,
Young and old were glad and comforted.

Another poem says:

Since she made a tour of this sanctuary,
She met a friend unlike all other men.
They spoke of the present and of countless things—
Of merit and trial in this world of dust.
The cloud of Law extends to shroud the hills;
The net of Truth spread wide to fill all space.
Examine your lives and return to Good,
For Heaven's grace is rife as falling blooms.

On the platform, that Master of the Law recited for a while the *Sūtra
of Life and Deliverance for the Dead*; he then lectured for a while on the
Heavenly Treasure Chronicle for Peace in the Nation, after which he

preached for a while on the *Scroll on Merit and Self-Cultivation*.²⁵ The
Bodhisattva drew near and thumped her hands on the platform,
calling out in a loud voice, "Hey, monk! You only know how to talk
about the teachings of the Little Vehicle. Don't you know anything
about the Great Vehicle?" When Hsüan-tsang heard this question,
he was filled with delight. He turned and leaped down from the platform, raised his hands and saluted the Bodhisattva, saying, "Venerable Teacher, please pardon your pupil for much disrespect. I only
know that the priests who came before me all talk about the teachings of the Little Vehicle. I have no idea what the Great Vehicle
teaches." "The doctrines of your Little Vehicle," said the Bodhisattva,
"cannot save the damned by leading them up to Heaven; they can
only mislead and confuse mortals. I have in my possession Tripitaka,
three collections of the Great Vehicle Laws of Buddha, which are able
to send the lost to Heaven, to deliver the afflicted from their sufferings,
to fashion ageless bodies, and to break the cycles of coming and
going."

As they were speaking, the officer in charge of incense and the
inspection of halls went to report to the emperor, saying, "The Master
was just in the process of lecturing on the wondrous Law when he
was pulled down by two scabby mendicants, babbling some kind of
nonsense." The king ordered them to be arrested, and the two monks
were taken by many people and pushed into the hall in the rear.
When the monk saw T'ai-tsung, she neither raised her hands nor
made a bow; instead, she lifted her face and said, "What do you want
of me, Your Majesty?" Recognizing her, the T'ang emperor said,
"Aren't you the monk who brought us the cassock the other day?"
"I am," said the Bodhisattva. "If you have come to listen to the
lecture," said T'ai-tsung, "you may as well take some vegetarian food.
Why indulge in this wanton discussion with our Master and disturb
the lecture hall, delaying our religious service?" "What that Master
of yours was lecturing on," said the Bodhisattva, "happens to be the
teachings of the Little Vehicle, which cannot lead the lost up to
Heaven. In my possession is the Tripitaka, the Great Vehicle Law of
Buddha, which is able to save the damned, deliver the afflicted, and
fashion the indestructible body." Delighted, T'ai-tsung asked eagerly,
"Where is your Great Vehicle Law of Buddha?" "At the place of our
lord, Tathāgata," said the Bodhisattva, "in the Great Temple of
Thunderclap, located in India of the Great Western Heaven. It can

untie the knot of a hundred enmities; it can dispel unexpected misfortunes." "Can you remember any of it?" said T'ai-tsung. "Certainly," said the Bodhisattva. T'ai-tsung was overjoyed and said, "Let
the Master lead this monk to the platform to begin a lecture at once."

Our Bodhisattva led Mokṣa and flew up onto the high platform.
She then rose up into the air, treading on hallowed clouds, and
revealed her true salvific form holding the pure vase with the willow
branch. At her left stood the virile figure of Mokṣa carrying the rod.
The T'ang emperor was so overcome that he bowed to the sky and
worshiped, as civil and military officials all knelt on the ground and
burned incense. Throughout the temple, there was not one of the
monks, nuns, Taoists, secular persons, scholars, craftsmen, and
merchants, who did not bow down and exclaim, "Dear Bodhisattva!
Dear Bodhisattva!" We have a song as a testimony. They saw only

Auspicious mist in diffusion
And dharmakāya[26] veiled by holy light.
In the bright air of ninefold Heaven
A womanly True One appeared.
That Bodhisattva
Wore on her head a cap
Fastened by leaves of gold
And set with flowers of jade,
With tassels of dangling pearls,
All aglow with golden light.
On her body she had
A robe of fine blue silk,
Lightly colored
And simply fretted
By circling dragons
And soaring phoenixes.
Down in front was hung
A pair of fragrant girdle-jade,
Which glowed with the moon
And danced with the wind,
Overlaid with precious pearls
And with imperial jade.
Around her waist was tied
An embroidered velvet skirt
Of ice-worm silk

And piped in gold,
In which she topped the colored clouds
And crossed the jasper sea.
Before her she led
A cockatoo with red beak and yellow plumes,
Which had roamed the Eastern Ocean
And throughout the world
To foster deeds of mercy and filial piety.
She held in her hands
A grace-dispensing and world-sustaining precious vase,
In which was planted
A twig of pliant willow,
That could moisten the blue sky,
And sweep aside all evil—
All clinging fog and smoke.
Her jade rings joined the embroidered loops,
And gold lotus grew thick beneath her feet.
In three days how often she came and went:
This very Kuan-shih-yin[27] who saves from pain and woe.

So pleased by the vision was T'ang T'ai-tsung that he forgot about his empire; so enthralled were the civil and military officials that they completely disregarded the etiquette of the court. Everyone was chanting, "Namo[28] Bodhisattva Kuan-shih-yin!" T'ai-tsung at once gave the order for a skilled painter to sketch the true form of the Bodhisattva. No sooner had he spoken than a certain Wu Tao-tzu was selected, who could portray gods and sages and was a master of the noble perspective and lofty vision. (This man, in fact, was the one who would later paint the portraits of meritorious officials in the Ling-yen Tower.) Immediately he opened up his magnificent brush to record the true form. The hallowed clouds of the Bodhisattva gradually drifted away, and in a little while the golden light disappeared. From midair came floating down a slip of paper on which were plainly written several lines in the style of the *sung*:[29]

We greet the great Ruler of T'ang
With scripts most sublime of the West.
The way: a hundred and eight thousand miles.
Seek earnestly this Mahāyāna.[30]
These Books, when they reach your fair state,
Can redeem damned spirits from Hell.

If someone is willing to go,

He'll become a Buddha of gold.

When T'ai-tsung saw the *sung*, he said to the various monks: "Let's stop the mass. Wait until I have sent someone to bring back the scriptures of the Great Vehicle. We shall then renew our sincere effort to cultivate the fruits of virtue." Not one of the officials disagreed with the emperor, who then asked in the temple, "Who is willing to accept our commission to seek scriptures from Buddha in the Western Heaven?" Hardly had he finished speaking when the Master of the Law stepped from the side and saluted him, saying, "Though your poor monk has no talents, he is ready to perform the service of a dog and a horse. I shall seek these true scriptures on behalf of your Majesty, that the empire of our king may be firm and everlasting." The T'ang emperor was highly pleased. He went forward to raise up the monk with his royal hands, saying, "If the Master is willing to express his loyalty this way, undaunted by the great distance or by the journey over mountains and streams, we are willing to become bond brothers with you." Hsüan-tsang touched his forehead to the ground to express his gratitude. Being indeed a righteous man, the T'ang emperor went at once before Buddha's image in the temple and bowed to Hsüan-tsang four times, addressing him as "Our brother and holy monk." Deeply moved, Hsüan-tsang said, "Your Majesty, what ability and what virtue does your poor monk possess that he should merit such affection from your Heavenly Grace? I shall not spare myself in this journey, but I shall proceed with all diligence until I reach the Western Heaven. If I do not attain my goal, or the true scriptures, I shall not return to our land even if I have to die. I would rather fall into eternal perdition in Hell." He thereupon lifted the incense before Buddha and made that his vow. Highly pleased, the T'ang emperor ordered his carriage back to the palace to wait for the auspicious day and hour, when official documents could be issued for the journey to begin. And so the Throne withdrew as everyone dispersed.

Hsüan-tsang also went back to the Temple of Great Blessing. The many monks of that temple and his several disciples, who had heard about the quest for the scriptures, all came to see him. They asked, "Is it true that you have vowed to go to the Western Heaven?" "It is," said Hsüan-tsang. "O Master," one of his disciples said, "I have heard people say that the way to the Western Heaven is long, filled

with tigers, leopards, and all kinds of monsters. I fear that there will
be departure but no return for you, as it will be difficult to safeguard
your life." "I have already made a great vow and a profound
promise," said Hsüan-tsang, "that if I do not acquire the true scriptures, I shall fall into eternal perdition in Hell. Since I have received
such grace and favor from the king, I have no alternative but to
serve my country to the utmost of my loyalty. It is true, of course,
that I have no knowledge of how I shall fare on this journey or
whether good or evil awaits me." He said to them again, "My
disciples, after I leave, wait for two or three years, or six or seven
years. If you see the branches of the pine trees within our gate
pointing eastward, you will know that I am about to return. If not,
I shall not be coming back." The disciples all committed his words
firmly to memory.

The next morning T'ai-tsung held court and gathered all the
officials together. They wrote up the formal rescript stating the intent
to acquire scriptures and stamped it with the seal of free passage. The
President of the Imperial Board of Astronomy then came with the
report, "Today the positions of the planets are especially favorable
for men to make a journey of great length." The T'ang emperor was
most delighted. Thereafter the Custodian of the Yellow Gate also made
a report, saying, "The Master of the Law awaits your pleasure outside the court." The emperor summoned him up to the treasure hall
and said, "Royal Brother, today is an auspicious day for the journey,
and your rescript for free passage is ready. We also present you with
a bowl made of purple gold for you to collect alms on your way. Two
attendants have been selected to accompany you, and a horse will be
your means of travel. You may begin your journey at once." Highly
pleased, Hsüan-tsang expressed his gratitude and received his gifts,
not displaying the least desire to linger. The T'ang emperor called for
his carriage and led many officials outside the city gate to see him off.
The monks in the Temple of Great Blessing and the disciples were
already waiting there with Hsüan-tsang's winter and summer clothing. When the emperor saw them, he ordered the bags to be packed
on the horses first, and then asked an officer to bring a pitcher of
wine. T'ai-tsung lifted his cup to toast the pilgrim saying, "What is
the byname of our Royal Brother?" "Your poor monk," said Hsüan-
tsang, "is a person who has left the family. He dares not assume a
byname." "The Bodhisattva said earlier," said T'ai-tsung, "that there

were three collections of scriptures in the Western Heaven. Our Brother can take that as a byname and call himself Tripitaka. How about it?" Thanking him, Hsüan-tsang accepted the wine and said, "Your Majesty, wine is the first prohibition of priesthood. Your poor monk has practiced abstinence since birth." "Today's journey," said T'ai-tsung, "is not to be compared with any ordinary event. Please drink one cup of this vegetarian wine, and accept our good wishes that go along with the toast." Hsüan-tsang dared not refuse; he took the wine and was about to drink, when he saw T'ai-tsung stoop down to scoop up a handful of dirt with his fingers and sprinkle it in the wine. Tripitaka had no idea what this gesture meant. "Dear Brother," said T'ai-tsung, laughing, "how long will it take you to come back from this trip to the Western Heaven?" "Probably in three years time," said Tripitaka, "I'll be returning to our noble nation." "The years are long and the journey is great," said T'ai-tsung. "Drink this, Royal Brother, and remember: Treasure a handful of dirt from your home, but love not ten thousand taels of foreign gold." Then Tripitaka understood the meaning of the handful of dirt sprinkled in his cup; he thanked the emperor once more and drained the cup. He went out of the gate and left, as the T'ang emperor returned in his carriage. We do not know what will happen to him on this journey, and you must listen to the explanation in the next chapter.

Thirteen

In the Den of Tigers, the Gold Star brings deliverance;
At Double-Fork Ridge, Po-ch'in detains the monk.

The rich T'ang ruler issued a decree,
Deputing Hsüan-tsang to seek the source of Zen.
He bent his mind to find the Dragon Den,
Firmly resolved to climb the Vulture Peak.[1]
Through how many states did he roam beyond his own?
Through clouds and hills he passed ten thousand times.
He now leaves the Throne to go to the West;
He'll keep law and faith to reach the Great Void.

We shall now tell you about Tripitaka, who, on the third day before
the fifteenth of the ninth month in the thirteenth year of the period
Chên-kuan, was sent off by the T'ang emperor and many officials
from outside the gate of Ch'ang-an. For a couple of days his horse
trotted without ceasing, and soon they reached the Temple of the
Law Gate. The abbot of that temple led some five hundred monks on
both sides to receive him and took him inside. As they met, tea was
served, after which a vegetarian meal was presented. Soon after the
meal, dusk fell, and thus

Shadows moved to the Star River's nearing pulse;
The moon was bright with not a speck of dust.
The wild geese called from the distant sky,
And washing flails beat from nearby homes.
As birds returned to perch on withered trees,
The Zen monks conversed in their Sanskrit tones.
On rush mats placed upon a single bunk,
They sat until halfway through the night.

Beneath the lamps the various monks discussed Buddhist doctrines
and the purpose of seeking scriptures in the Western Heaven. Some
pointed out that the waters were wide and the mountains very high;
others mentioned that the roads were crowded with tigers and
leopards; still others maintained that the precipitous peaks were

difficult to scale; and another group insisted that the vicious monsters were hard to subdue. Tripitaka, however, kept his mouth shut tightly, but he pointed with his finger to his own heart and nodded his head several times. Not perceiving what he meant, the various monks folded their hands and asked, "Why did the Master of the Law point to his heart and nod his head?" "When the mind is active," Tripitaka replied, "all kinds of māra come into existence; when the mind is extinguished, all kinds of māra will be extinguished.[2] This disciple has already made an important vow before Buddha in the Temple of Transformation, and he has no alternative but to fulfill it with his whole heart. If I go, I shall not turn aside until I have reached the Western Heaven, seen Buddha, and acquired the scriptures so that the Wheel of the Law will be turned to us[3] and the kingdom of our lord will be secured forever." When the various monks heard this statement, everyone congratulated and commended him, saying, "A loyal and valiant master!" They praised him unceasingly as they escorted him to bed.

Soon the bamboos struck down the setting moon,[4] and the cocks crew to gather the clouds of dawn. The various monks arose and prepared some tea and the morning meal. Hsüan-tsang put on his cassock and went to worship Buddha in the main hall. "Your disciple, Ch'ên Hsüan-tsang," he said, "is on his way to seek scriptures in the Western Heaven. But my fleshly eyes are dim and unperceptive and do not recognize the true form of the living Buddha. Now I wish to make a vow: that throughout this journey I shall burn incense whenever I come upon a temple, I shall worship Buddha whenever I meet a Buddha, and I shall sweep a pagoda whenever I reach a pagoda. May our Buddha be merciful and soon reveal to me his Diamond Body sixteen feet tall.[5] May he grant me the true scriptures so that they may be preserved in the Land of the East."

He finished his prayer and went back to the hall for the vegetarian meal, after which his two attendants made ready the saddle and urged him to begin his journey. Going out of the temple's gate, Tripitaka took leave of the monks, who grieved to see him go. They accompanied him for ten miles before turning back, tears in their eyes, as Tripitaka proceeded directly toward the West. It was the time of late autumn. You see

Trees growing bare in hamlets as rush petals break;
From every maple column the red leaves fall.

Few are the trekkers through paths of mist and rain.
The fair chrysanthemums,
The sharp mountain rocks,
Cold streams and cracked lilies all make one sad.
Snow falls from a frosty sky on reeds and rushes.
One duck at dusk descends in the distant void.
Clouds over the wilds move through the gathering gloom.
The swallows depart;
The wild geese appear—
Their cries, though loud, are halting and forlorn.

After traveling for several days, master and disciples arrived at the city of Kung Chou. They were met at once by the various municipal officials of that city, where they spent the night. The next morning they set off again, taking food and drink along the way, resting by night and journeying by day. In two or three days, they arrived at the District of Ho Chou, which formed the border of the Great T'ang Empire. When the garrison commander of the border as well as the local monks and priests heard that the Master of the Law, a bond brother of the emperor, was on his way to the Western Heaven to see Buddha by royal commission, they received the travelers with due reverence. Some chief priests then invited them to spend the night at Fu-yüan Temple, where every resident cleric came to pay respect to the pilgrims. Dinner was served, after which the two attendants were told to feed the horses well, for the master wanted to leave before dawn. At the first crowing of the cock, he called for his attendants and aroused the monks of that temple. They hastened to prepare tea and breakfast, after which the pilgrims departed from the border.

As he was somewhat impatient to get going, the Master arose a trifle too early. The fact is that this was late autumn, when cocks crow rather early—at about the time of the fourth watch. Facing the clear frost and the bright moon, the three of them (the horse made up the fourth member of the team) journeyed for some twenty or thirty miles, when they came upon a mountain range. It soon became exceedingly difficult for them to find their way. As they had to poke around in the grass to look for a path, they began to worry that they might be heading in the wrong direction. In that very anxious moment, they suddenly tripped; all three of them as well as the horse tumbled into a deep pit. Tripitaka was terrified; his companions all shook with fear. They were still trembling when they heard voices shouting, "Seize them! Seize them!" A violent wind swept by, and a mob of fifty or sixty ogres appeared, who seized Tripitaka with his companions and hauled them out of the pit. Quivering and shivering, the Master of the Law stole a glance around and saw a ferocious Monster King seated up on high. Truly he had

A figure most awesomely bold,
A face most distinctly fierce.
Light flashed from his lightninglike eyes;
All quaked at his thunderous voice.
His sawlike teeth jutted outward,
Like fangs they emerged from his jaws.
Brocade wrapped his body around,
And coiling stripes covered his spine.
They saw flesh through sparse, steely whiskers.
Keen-edged were his claws like sharp swords.
Even Huang Kung[6] of Tung Hai would fear
This white-browed King of South Mountain.

Tripitaka was so frightened that his spirit left him, while the bones of his followers grew weak and their tendons turned numb. The Monster King shouted for them to be bound, and the various ogres tied up all three of them with ropes. They were being prepared to be eaten when a clamor was heard outside the camp. Someone came in to report: "The Bear Mountain Lord and the Steer Hermit have arrived." Hearing this, Tripitaka looked up. The first one to come in was a swarthy fellow. "How did he look?" you ask.

He seemed valiant and courageous,
With body both tough and brawny.
His great strength could ford the waters.
He prowled the woods, flaunting his power.
Ever a good omen in dreams,[7]
He showed now his forceful features.
He could break or climb the green trees,
And predicted when winter was near.
Truly he was most clever.
Hence Mountain Lord was his name.

Following behind him was another husky fellow. "How did he look?" you ask.

A cap of twin horns rugged,
And a humpback most majestic.

His green robe showed his calm nature,
He walked with a slumberous gait.
He came from a father named Bull;
His mother's name proper was Cow.
A great boon to people who plowed,
He was thus called the Steer Hermit.

The two creatures swaggered in, and the Monster King hurried out to receive them. The Bear Mountain Lord said, "You are in top form, General Yin. Congratulations! Congratulations!" "General Yin looks better than ever," said the Steer Hermit. "It's marvelous! It's marvelous!" "And you two gentlemen, how have you been these days?" asked the Monster King. "Just maintaining my idleness," said the Mountain Lord. "Just keeping up with the times," said the Hermit. After these exchanges, they sat down to chat some more.

Meanwhile, one of Tripitaka's attendants was bound so tightly that he began to moan pitifully. "How did these three get here?" asked the swarthy fellow. "They practically presented themselves at the door!" said the Monster King. "Can they be used for the guests' dinner?" asked the Hermit, laughing. "By all means!" said the Monster King. "Let's not finish them all up," said the Mountain Lord. "We'll dine on two of them and leave one over." The Monster King agreed. He called his subordinates at once to have the attendants eviscerated and their carcasses carved up; their heads, hearts, and livers were to be presented to the guests, the limbs to the host, and the remaining portions of flesh and bone to the rest of the ogres. The moment the order was given, the ogres pounced on the attendants like tigers preying on sheep; munching and crunching, they devoured them in no time at all. The priest nearly died of fear, for this, you see, was his first bitter ordeal since his departure from Ch'ang-an.

As he was nursing his horror, light began to grow in the east. The two monsters did not retire until dawn. Saying, "We're beholden to your generous hospitality today. Permit us to repay in kind in another time," they left together. Soon the sun rose high in the sky, but Tripitaka was still in a stupor, unable to discern which way was north, south, east, or west. In that half-dead condition, he suddenly saw an old man approaching, holding a staff in his hands. Walking up to Tripitaka, the man waved his hands and all the ropes snapped. He then blew on Tripitaka, and the monk began to revive. Falling on the ground, he said, "I thank the aged father for saving the life of this poor monk!" "Get up," the old man said, returning his salute, "have you lost anything?" "The followers of your poor monk," said Tripitaka, "have been eaten by the monsters. I have no idea where my horse is or my luggage." "Isn't that your horse over there with the two bundles?" asked the old man, pointing with his staff. Tripitaka turned around and discovered that his belongings had indeed remained untouched. Somewhat relieved, he asked the old man, "Aged father, what is this place? How do you happen to be here?" "It is called the Double-Fork Ridge, a place infested with tigers and wolves. How did you manage to get here?" "At the first crow of the cock," said Tripitaka, "your poor monk left the District of Ho Chou. Little did I realize that we had risen too early, and we lost our way tramping through fog and dew. We came upon this Monster King so exceedingly ferocious that he captured me and my two followers. There was also a swarthy fellow called the Bear Mountain Lord and a husky fellow called the Steer Hermit. They arrived and addressed the Monster King as General Yin. All three of them devoured my two followers and retired only at dawn. I have no idea where I accrued the fortune and merit that caused the aged father to rescue me here." "That Steer Hermit," said the old man, "is a wild bull spirit; the Mountain Lord, a bear spirit; and General Yin, a tiger spirit. The various ogres are all demons of mountains and trees, spirits of strange beasts and wolves. Because of the primal purity of your nature, they cannot devour you. Follow me now, and I shall lead you on your way." Tripitaka could not be more thankful. Fastening the bundles on the saddle and leading his horse, he followed the old man out of the pit and walked toward the main road. He tied the horse to the bushes beside the path and turned to thank the aged father. At that moment a gentle breeze swept by, and the old man rose into the air and left, riding on a white crane with a crimson head. As the wind subsided, a slip of paper fluttered down, with four lines of verse written on it:

I am the Planet Venus from the West,

Who came to save you by special request,

Some pupils divine will come to your aid.

Blame not the scriptures for hardships ahead.

When Tripitaka read this, he bowed toward the sky saying, "I thank the Gold Star for seeing me through this ordeal." After that, he led his horse off again on his lonely and melancholy journey. On this ridge truly you have

Cold and soughing, the wind of the rain forest;
Purling and gurgling, the water of the brooklets;
Fragrant and musky, wild flowers in bloom;
In clutters and clumps, rough rocks piled high;
Chattering and clattering, the apes and the deer;
In rank and file, the musk and the fallow deer.
Chirping and cooing, birds frequently call.
Silent and still, not one man is in sight.
That master
Shivers and quivers to his anxious mind.
This dear horse,
Scared and nervous, can barely raise his legs.

Ready to abandon his body and sacrifice his life, Tripitaka started up that rugged mountain. He journeyed for half a day, but not a single human being or dwelling was in sight. He was gnawed by hunger and disheartened by the rough road. In that desperate moment, he saw two fierce tigers growling in front of him and several huge snakes circling behind him; vicious creatures appeared on his left and strange beasts on his right. As he was all by himself, Tripitaka had little alternative but to submit himself to the will of Heaven. As if to complete his helplessness, his horse's back was sagging and its legs were buckling; it went to its knees and soon lay prostrate on the ground. He could budge it neither by beating nor by tugging. With hardly an inch of space to stand on, our Master of the Law was in the depths of despair, thinking that certain death would be his fate.

We can tell you, however, that though he was in danger, help was on its way. For just as he thought he was about to expire, the vicious creatures began to scatter and the monstrous beasts fled; the fierce tigers vanished and the huge snakes disappeared. When Tripitaka looked further ahead, he saw a man coming over the mountain slope with a steel trident in his hands and bow and arrows at his waist. He was indeed a valiant figure! Look at him:

He had on his head a cap
Of leopard skin, spotted and artemisia-white;
He wore on his body a robe
Of lamb's wool with dark silk brocade.
Around his waist was tied a lion king belt,[8]
And on his feet he wore tall boots of suede.
His eyes were staring like those of a hanged man.

With wild beard, he looked like a fierce god!
A bow and poisoned arrows hung on him.
He held a huge trident of the finest steel.
His voice like thunder appalled the mountain cats,
And wild pheasants trembled at his truculence.

When Tripitaka saw him draw near, he knelt at the side of the path and called out, his hands clasped in front of him, "Great king, save me! Great king, save me!" The fellow came up to Tripitaka and put down his trident. Raising up the monk with his hands, he said, "Don't be afraid, Elder, for I'm not a wicked man. I'm a hunter living in this mountain; my surname is Liu and my given name is Po-ch'in. I also go by the nickname of Senior Guardian of the Mountain. I came here to find some animals to eat, not expecting to run into you. I hope I didn't scare you." "Your poor monk," said Tripitaka, "is a cleric who has been sent by his Majesty, the T'ang emperor, to seek scriptures from Buddha in the Western Heaven. When I arrived here a few moments ago, I was surrounded by tigers, wolves, and snakes, so that I could not proceed. But when the creatures saw you coming they all scattered, and you have thus saved my life. Many thanks! Many thanks!" "Since I live here and my livelihood depends on killing a few tigers and wolves," said Po-ch'in, "or catching a few snakes and reptiles, I usually frighten the wild beasts away. If you have come from the T'ang empire, you are actually a native here, for this is still T'ang territory and I am a T'ang subject. You and I both live off the land belonging to the king, so that we are in truth citizens of the same nation. Don't be afraid. Follow me. You may rest your horse at my place, and I shall see you off in the morning." Tripitaka was filled with delight when he heard these words, and he led his horse to follow the hunter.

They passed the slope and again heard the howling of the wind. "Sit here, Elder," said Po-ch'in, "and don't move. The sound of that wind tells me that a mountain cat is approaching. I'll take him home so that I can make you a meal of him." When Tripitaka heard this, his heart hammered and his gall quivered and he became rooted to the ground. Grasping his trident, that Guardian strode forward and came face to face with a great striped tiger. Seeing Po-ch'in, he turned and fled. Like a crack of thunder, the Guardian bellowed, "Cursed beast! Where will you flee?" When the tiger saw him pressing near, he turned with flailing claws to spring at him, only to be met by the

Guardian with uplifted trident. Tripitaka was so terrified that he lay
paralyzed on the grass. Since leaving his mother's belly, when had
he ever witnessed such violent and dangerous goings-on? The
Guardian went after that tiger to the foot of the slope, and it was a
magnificent battle between man and beast. You see
Raging resentment,
And churning whirlwind.
In raging resentment
The mighty Guardian's hair pushed up his cap;
Like churning whirlwind
The striped prince belched dust, displaying his strength.
This one bared its teeth and wielded its paws;
That one stepped sideways, yet turning to fight.
The trident reached skyward, reflecting the sun.
The striped tail stirred up both fog and cloud.
This one stabbed madly at the breast of his foe;
That one, facing him would swallow him whole.
Stay away and you may live out your years.
Join the fray and you'll meet Yama, the king!
You hear the roar of the striped prince
And the harsh cries of the Guardian.
The roar of the striped prince
Shook mountains and streams to terrify birds and beasts;
The harsh cries of the Guardian
Unlocked the heavens to make the stars appear.
The gold eyeballs of this one protruded,
And wrath burst from the bold heart of that one.
Lovable was Liu the Mountain Guardian;
Praiseworthy was this king of the wild beasts.
So tiger and man fought, each craving life—
A little slower, and one forfeits his soul!
The two of them fought for about an hour, and as the paws of the
tiger began to slow and his torso to slacken, he was downed by the
Guardian's trident stabbing him through the chest. A pitiful sight it
was! The points of the trident pierced the heart, and at once the
ground was covered with blood. The Guardian then dragged the
beast by the ear up the road. What a man! He hardly panted, nor did
his face change color. He said to Tripitaka, "We're lucky! We're
lucky! This mountain cat should be sufficient for a day's food for the

elder." Applauding him unceasingly, Tripitaka said, "The Guardian is truly a mountain god!" "What ability do I have," said Po-ch'in, "that I merit such acclaim? This is really the good fortune of the father. Let's go. I'd like to skin him quickly so that I can cook some of his meat to entertain you." He held the trident in one hand and dragged the tiger with the other, leading the way while Tripitaka followed him with his horse. They walked together past the slope and all at once came upon a mountain village, in front of which

Old trees soared skyward,
And roads were filled with wild creepers.
In countless canyons the wind was cool;
On many ridges were strange sounds and sights.
One path's wild blooms, whose scent clung to one's body;
A few poles of bamboo and what memorable green!
The portal of grass,
The wattle-fenced yard—
A picture to paint or sketch.
The stone-slab bridge,
The white-earth walls—
How charming indeed, and rare!
Now in the wistful face of autumn,
The air was cool and brisk,
By the wayside yellow leaves fell;
Over the peaks the white clouds drifted.
In thinly-grown woods the wild fowls twittered,
And young dogs yelped outside the village gate.

When Po-ch'in reached the door of his house, he threw down the dead tiger and called, "Little ones, where are you?" Out came three or four houseboys, all rather unattractive and mean-looking, who hauled the tiger inside. Po-ch'in told them to skin it quickly and prepare it for the guest. He then turned around to welcome Tripitaka into his dwelling, and as they greeted each other, Tripitaka thanked him again for the great favor of saving his life. "We are fellow countrymen," said Po-ch'in, "and there's little need for you to thank me." After they had sat down and drunk tea, an old woman with someone who appeared to be her daughter-in-law came out to greet Tripitaka. "This is my mother, and this my wife," said Po-ch'in. "Pray ask your parent to take the honored seat," said Tripitaka, "and let your poor monk pay his respects." "Father is a guest coming from great distance," said the old woman. "Please relax and don't stand on ceremony." "Mother," said Po-ch'in, "he has been sent by the T'ang emperor to seek scriptures from Buddha in the Western Heaven. He met your son just now at the ridge. Since we are fellow countrymen, I invited him to the house to rest his horse. Tomorrow I shall see him on his way." When she heard these words, the old woman was very pleased. "Good! Good! Good!" she said. "The timing couldn't be better, even if we had planned to invite him. For tomorrow happens to be the anniversary of your late father's death. Let us invite the elder to perform some good deeds and recite an appropriate passage of scripture. We shall see him off day after tomorrow." Although he was a tiger slayer, a so-called "Guardian of the Mountain," our Liu Po-ch'in had a good deal of filial feeling for his mother. When he heard what she said, he immediately wanted to prepare the incense and the paper money, so that Tripitaka might be asked to stay.

As they talked, the sky began to darken. The servants brought chairs and a table and set out several dishes of well-cooked tiger meat, steaming hot. Po-ch'in invited Tripitaka to begin, telling him that rice would follow. "O dear!" said Tripitaka, his hands folded. "To tell you the truth, I have been a monk since leaving my mother's womb, and I have never eaten any meat." Hearing this, Po-ch'in reflected a while. He then said, "Elder, for generations this humble family has never kept a vegetarian diet. We could, I suppose, find some bamboo shoots and wood ears and prepare some dried vegetables and bean cakes, but they would all be cooked with the fat of deer or tigers. Even our pots and pans are grease-soaked! What am I to do? I must ask the elder's pardon." "Don't fret," said Tripitaka. "Enjoy the food yourself. Even if I were not to eat for three or four days, I could bear the hunger. But I dare not break the dietary commandment." "Suppose you starve to death," said Po-ch'in, "what then?" "I am indebted to the Heavenly kindness of the Guardian," said Tripitaka, "for saving me from the packs of tigers and wolves. Starving to death is better than being food for a tiger."

When Po-ch'in's mother heard this, she cried, "Son, stop such idle talk with the elder. Let me prepare a vegetarian dish to serve him." "Where would you get such a dish?" said Po-ch'in. "Never mind. I'll fix it," said his mother. She asked her daughter-in-law to take down

a small cooking pan and heat it until much of the grease had burned
off. They washed and scrubbed the pan again and again and then
put it back on the stove and boiled some water in it. Taking some elm
leaves from the mountain, they made soup with it, after which they
cooked some rice with yellow millet mixed with Indian corn. They
also prepared two bowls of dried vegetables and brought it all out to
the table. "Elder," the aged mother said to Tripitaka, "please have
some. This is the cleanest and purest food that my daughter-in-law
and I have ever prepared." Tripitaka left his seat to thank her before
sitting down again. Po-ch'in removed himself to another place; dishes
and bowls full of unsauced and unsalted tiger meat, musk-deer meat,
serpent meat, fox flesh, rabbit, and strips of cured venison were set
before him. To keep Tripitaka company, he sat down and was about
to pick up his chopsticks when he saw Tripitaka fold his hands and
begin to recite something. Startled, Po-ch'in dared not touch his
chopsticks; he jumped up instead and stood to one side. Having
uttered no more than a few phrases, Tripitaka said to him, "Please
eat." "You are a priest who likes to recite short scriptures," said
Po-ch'in. "That was not scripture," said Tripitaka, "only a prayer to
be said before meals." "You people who leave your families," said
Po-ch'in, "are particular about everything! Even for a meal you have
to mumble something!"

They ate their dinner and the dishes and bowls were taken away.
Evening was setting in when Po-ch'in led Tripitaka out of the main
hall to go for a walk at the back of the dwelling. They passed through
a corridor and arrived at a straw shed. Pushing open the door, they
walked inside, where they found several heavy bows and some
quivers of arrows hanging on the walls. Two pieces of tiger skin,
stinking and blood-stained, were draped across the cross beams, and
a number of spears, knives, tridents, and rods were stuck into the
ground at one corner. There were two seats in the middle of the shed,
and Po-ch'in invited Tripitaka to sit for a moment. Seeing that the
place was so gruesome and putrid, Tripitaka dared not linger. They
soon left the shed and walked further back to a huge garden, where
there seemed to be no end of thick clumps of chrysanthemum piling
their gold and stands of maple hoisting their crimson. With a loud
rustle, more than a dozen fat deer and a large herd of musk deer
jumped out. Calm and mild-mannered, they were not at all frightened

at the sight of human beings. Tripitaka said, "You must have tamed these animals." "Like the people in your city of Ch'ang-an," said Po-ch'in, "where the affluent store up wealth and treasures and the landlords gather rice and grain, so we hunters must keep some of these wild beasts to prepare against dark days. That's all!" As they walked and conversed, it grew dark, and they returned to the house to rest.

As soon as the members of the family, young and old, arose next morning, they went to prepare vegetarian food to serve to the priest, who was then asked to begin his recitations. Having first washed his hands, the priest went to the ancestral hall with the Guardian to burn incense. Only after he had bowed to the house shrine did Tripitaka beat on his wooden fish and recite first the true sentences for the purification of the mouth, and then the divine formula for the purification of mind and body. He went on to the *Sūtra for the Salvation of the Dead*, after which Po-ch'in requested him to compose in writing a specific prayer for the deliverance of the deceased. He then took up the *Diamond Sūtra* and the *Kuan-yin Sūtra*, each of which was given a loud and clear recitation. After lunch, he recited several sections from the *Lotus Sūtra* and the *Amitāyus Sūtra*, before finishing with the *Peacock Sūtra* and a brief recounting of the story of Buddha healing a bhikṣu.[9] Soon it was evening again. All kinds of incense were burned together with the various paper horses, images of the deities, and the prayer for the deliverance of the deceased. The Buddhist service was thus completed, and each person retired.

We shall now tell you about the soul of Po-ch'in's father, verily a ghost redeemed from perdition, who came to his own house and appeared to all the members of his family in a dream. "It was difficult," he said, "for me to escape my bitter ordeals in the Region of Darkness, and for a long time I could not attain salvation. Fortunately, the holy monk's recitations have now expiated my sins. King Yama has ordered someone to send me to the rich land of China, where I may assume my next incarnation in a noble family. All of you, therefore, must take care to thank the elder, and see that you are not negligent in any way. Now I leave you." So it is that,

There is, in all things, a solemn purpose:
To save the dead from perdition and pain.
When the whole family awoke from the dream, the sun was already

rising in the east. The wife of Po-ch'in said, "Guardian, I dreamed last night that father came to the house. He said that it was difficult for him to escape his bitter ordeals in the Region of Darkness, and that for a long time he could not attain salvation. Fortunately, the holy monk's recitations have now expiated his sins, and King Yama has ordered someone to send him to the rich land of China where he may assume his next incarnation in a noble family. He told us to take care to thank the elder and not be negligent in any way. After he had finished speaking, he drifted away, despite my plea for him to stay. I woke up and it was all a dream!" "I had a dream also," said Po-ch'in, "one exactly like yours! Let's get up and talk to mother about this." The two of them were about to do so when they heard the old mother calling, "Po-ch'in, come here. I want to talk to you." They went in and found the mother sitting up in bed. "Son," she said, "I had a happy dream last night. I dreamed that your father came to the house saying that, thanks to the redemptive work of the elder, his sins had been expiated. He is on his way to the rich land of China, where he will assume his next incarnation in a noble family." Husband and wife laughed uproariously. Po-ch'in said, "Your daughter-in-law and I both had this dream, and we were just coming to tell you. Little did we expect that mother's call also had to do with this dream." They therefore called on every member of the family to express their gratitude and prepare the monk's horse for travel. They came bowing before the priest and said, "We thank the elder for providing life and deliverance for our deceased father, for which we can never repay you sufficiently." "What has this poor monk accomplished," said Tripitaka, "that merits such gratitude?"

Po-ch'in gave a thorough account of the dream that the three of them had had, and Tripitaka was also very pleased. A vegetarian meal was again served, and a tael of silver was presented as a token of their gratitude. Tripitaka refused to accept so much as a penny, though the whole family begged him earnestly. He only said, "If, in compassion, you can escort me on the first part of my way, I shall ever be grateful for such kindness." Po-ch'in and his mother and wife had little alternative but hastily to prepare some biscuits from un-refined flour, which Tripitaka was glad to accept. Po-ch'in was told to escort him as far as possible. Obeying his mother's bidding, the Guardian also ordered several houseboys to join them, each bringing hunting equipment and weapons. They walked to the main road, and there seemed to be no end to the scenic splendor of the mountains and peaks.

When they had traveled for half a day, they came upon a huge mountain so tall and rugged that it truly seemed to touch the blue sky. In a little while the whole company reached the foot of the mountain, and the Guardian began to ascend it as if he were walking on level ground. Halfway up, Po-ch'in turned around and stood still at the side of the road, saying, "Elder, please go on yourself. I must now take leave of you and turn back." When Tripitaka heard these words, he rolled down from his saddle and said, "I beg you to escort me a little further." "You do not realize, Elder," said Po-ch'in, "that this mountain is called the Mountain of Two Frontiers; the eastern half belongs to our great T'ang domain, but the western half is the territory of the Tartars. The tigers and wolves over there are not my subjects, nor should I cross the border. You must proceed by yourself." Tripitaka became fearful; he stretched out his hands and clutched at the sleeves of the hunter, tears pouring from his eyes. It was at this tender moment of farewell that there came from beneath the mountain a thunderous voice crying, "My master has come! My master has come!" Tripitaka was dumbfounded, and Po-ch'in trembled. We do not know who was crying, and you must listen to the explanation in the next chapter.

Fourteen

The Monkey of the Mind returns to the Right;
All the Six Robbers[1] vanish from sight.

The Mind is the Buddha and the Buddha is Mind;
Both Mind and Buddha are important things.
If you perceive there's neither Mind nor Thing,
Yours is the dharmakāya of True Mind.
The dharmakāya
Has no shape or form:
One pearllike radiance holding myriad things.
The bodiless body is the body true,
And real form is that form which has no form.
There's no form, no void, no no-emptiness;
No coming, no leaving, no pariṇāmanā;[2]
No contrast, no sameness, no being or nonbeing;
No giving, no taking, no hopeful craving.
Light efficacious is in and out the same.
Buddha's whole realm is in a grain of sand.
A grain of sand the chiliocosm holds;
One mind or body's like ten thousand things.
To know this you must grasp the No-mind Spell;
Unclogged and taintless is the karma pure.
Do not the many acts of good or ill:
This is true submission to Śākyamuni.

We were telling you about Tripitaka and Po-ch'in, who, in fear and alarm, again heard the cry: "My Master has come!" The various houseboys said, "It must be the old ape in that stone box beneath the mountain who is shouting." "It's he! It's he!" said the Guardian. Tripitaka asked, "Who is this old ape?" "The ancient name of this mountain," said the Guardian, "was the Mountain of Five Phases. It was changed to the Mountain of the Two Frontiers as a result of our great T'ang ruler's western campaigns to secure his empire. A few years ago, I heard from my elders that during the time when Wang

Mang usurped the throne of the Han emperor,[3] this mountain fell from Heaven with a divine monkey clamped beneath it. He feared neither heat nor cold, and he took neither food nor drink. He had been watched and guarded by the spirits of the Earth, who fed him iron balls when he was hungry and juices of bronze when he was thirsty. He has lasted from that time until now, surviving both cold and hunger. He must be the one who is making all this noise. Don't be afraid, Elder. Let's go down the mountain to take a look."

Tripitaka had to agree and led his horse down the mountain. They had traveled only a few miles when they came upon a stone box in which there was indeed a monkey who, with his head sticking out, was waving his hands wildly and saying, "Master, why have you taken so long to get here? Welcome! Welcome! Get me out, and I'll protect you on your way to the Western Heaven!" The priest went forward to look at him closely. "How does he look?" you ask.

A pointed mouth and hollow cheeks;
Two diamond pupils and fiery eyes.
Lichens had piled on his head;
Wisteria grew in his ears.
At his temples there was more green grass than hair;
Beneath his chin, moss instead of a beard.
With mud on his brow,
And earth in his nose,
He looked most desperate!
His fingers coarse
And calloused palms
Were caked in filth and dirt!
Luckily, his eyes could still roll about,
And the apish tongue, articulate.
Though in speech he had great ease,
His body he could not move.
He was the Great Sage Sun of five hundred years ago.
Today his ordeal ends, he leaves the net of Heaven.

Undeniably a courageous person, that Guardian Liu went up to the creature and pulled away some of the grass at his temples and some of the moss beneath his chin. He asked, "What do you have to say?" "Nothing to you," said the monkey, "but ask that master to come up here. I have a question for him." "What's your question?" asked

Tripitaka. "Are you someone sent by the great king of the Land of the East to go seek scriptures in the Western Heaven?" asked the monkey. "I am," said Tripitaka. "Why do you ask?" "I am the Great Sage, Equal to Heaven," said the monkey, "who greatly disturbed the Heavenly Palace five hundred years ago. Because of my sin of rebellion and disobedience, I was imprisoned here by the Buddha. Some time ago, a certain Bodhisattva Kuan-yin had received the decree of Buddha to go to the Land of the East in quest of a scripture pilgrim. I asked her to give me some help, and she persuaded me not to engage again in violence. I was told to believe in the Law of Buddha, and faithfully to protect the scripture pilgrim on his way to worship Buddha in the West, for there would be a goodly reward reserved for me when such merit is achieved. I have therefore been maintaining my vigilance night and day, waiting for the Master to come to rescue me. I'm willing to protect you in your quest of scriptures and become your disciple."

When Tripitaka heard these words, he was filled with delight and said, "Though you have this good intention, because of the Bodhisattva's instruction, of entering our Buddhist fold, I have neither ax nor drill. How can I free you?" "No need for ax or drill," said the monkey. "If you are willing to rescue me, I'll be able to get out." Tripitaka said, "I'm willing, but how can you get out?" "On top of this mountain," said the monkey, "there is a tag stamped with the golden letters of our Buddha Tathāgata. Go up there and lift up the tag. Then I'll come out." Tripitaka agreed, and turned to Po-ch'in, imploring him, "Guardian, come with me up the mountain." "Do you think he's speaking the truth?" asked Po-ch'in. "It's the truth!" the monkey shouted. "I dare not lie!"

Po-ch'in had no choice but to call his houseboys to lead the horses. He himself supported Tripitaka with his hands, and they again started up the tall mountain. Tugging at creepers and vines, they finally arrived at the highest peak, where they beheld ten thousand shafts of golden light and a thousand folds of hallowed air. There was a huge square slab of stone, on which was taped a seal with the golden letters, Oṁ maṇi padme hūṁ. Tripitaka approached the stone and knelt down; he looked at the golden letters and kowtowed several times to the stone. Then, facing the West, he prayed: "Your disciple, Ch'ên Hsüan-tsang, was specifically commanded to seek scriptures from you. If it is so ordained that he should be my disciple, let me lift up those golden letters so that the divine monkey may find release and join me at the Spirit Mountain. If he is not predestined to be my disciple, if he is only a cruel monster trying to deceive me and to bring misfortune to our enterprise, let me not lift up this tape." He kow-towed again after he had prayed. Going forward, with the greatest of ease he took down the golden letters. A fragrant wind swept by immediately and blew the tag out of his hands into the air as a voice called out, "I am the prison guard of the Great Sage. Today his ordeal is completed, and my colleagues and I are returning this seal to Tathāgata." Tripitaka, Po-ch'in, and their followers were so terrified that they fell on the ground and bowed toward the sky. They then descended from the tall mountain and came back to the stone box, saying to the monkey, "The tag has been lifted. You may come out." Delighted, the monkey said, "Master, you had better walk away from here so that I can come out. I don't want to frighten you."

When Po-ch'in heard this, he led Tripitaka and the rest of the company to walk back eastward for five or six miles. Again they heard the monkey yelling, "Further still! Further still!" So Tripitaka and the others went still further until they had left the mountain. Then came a crash so loud that it was as if the mountain was cracking and the earth splitting wide open; everyone was awe-struck. The next moment the monkey was already in front of Tripitaka's horse; completely naked, he knelt down and cried, "Master, I'm out!" He bowed four times toward Tripitaka, and then, jumping up, he said to Po-ch'in respectfully, "I thank Elder Brother for taking the trouble of escorting my master. I'm grateful also for your shaving the grass from my face." Having thanked him, he went at once to put the luggage in order so that it could be tied onto the horse's back. When the horse saw him, its torso slackened and its legs stiffened. In fear and trembling, it could hardly stand up. For you see, that monkey had been a pi-ma-wên, who used to look after dragon horses in the celestial stables. His authority was such that horses of Earth inevitably would fear him when they saw him.

When Tripitaka saw that the monkey was truly a person of good intentions, someone who truly resembled those who had embraced the Buddhist faith, he called to him, "Disciple, what is your surname?" "My surname is Sun," said the Monkey King. "Let me give you a

religious name," said Tripitaka, "so that it will be convenient to
address you." "This noble thought of the master is deeply appre-
ciated," said the Monkey King, "but I already have a religious name.
I'm called Sun Wu-k'ung." "It exactly fits the emphasis of our
denomination," said Tripitaka, delighted. "But look at you, you look
rather like a little dhūta.⁴ Let me give you a nickname and call you
Pilgrim Sun.⁵ How's that?" "Good! Good!" said Wu-k'ung. So from
then on, he was also called Pilgrim Sun.

When Po-ch'in saw that Pilgrim Sun was definitely preparing to
leave, he turned to speak respectfully to Tripitaka, saying, "Elder,
you are fortunate to have made an excellent disciple here. Congratulations! This person should be most fit to accompany you. I must take
leave of you now." Bowing to thank him, Tripitaka said, "I cannot
thank you enough for all your kindness. Please be certain to thank
your dear mother and wife when you return to your house. I have
caused you all great inconvenience, and I shall thank you again on
my way back." Po-ch'in returned his salutation, and they parted.

We shall now tell you about Pilgrim Sun, who asked Tripitaka to
mount his horse. He himself, completely naked, carried the luggage
on his back and led the way. In a little while, as they were passing
the Mountain of Two Frontiers, they saw a fierce tiger approaching,
growling and waving its tail. Tripitaka, sitting on his horse, became
alarmed, but Pilgrim, walking at the side of the road, was delighted.
"Don't be afraid, Master," he said, "for he's here to present me with
some clothes." He put down the luggage and took a tiny needle out
of his ears. One wave of it facing the wind, and it became an iron rod
with the thickness of a rice bowl. He held it in his hands and laughed,
saying, "I haven't used this precious thing for over five hundred
years! Today I'm taking it out to bag a little garment for myself."
Look at him! He strode right up to the tiger, crying, "Cursed beast!
Where do you think you're going?" Crouching low, the tiger lay down
on the dust and dared not move. Pilgrim Sun aimed the rod at its
head, and one stroke caused its brain to burst out like ten thousand
red petals of peach blossoms, and the teeth to fly out like so many
pieces of white jade. So terrified was our Ch'ên Hsüan-tsang that he
fell off his horse. "O God! O God!" he cried, biting his fingers. "When
Guardian Liu overcame that striped tiger the other day, he had to do
battle with him for almost half a day. But without even fighting

today, Sun Wu-k'ung reduces the tiger to pulp with one blow of his rod. How true is the saying, 'For the strong, there's always someone stronger!'"

"Master," said Pilgrim as he returned dragging the tiger, "sit down for a while, and wait till I have stripped him of his clothes. When I put them on, we'll start off again." "Where does he have any clothes?" said Tripitaka. "Don't mind me, Master," said Pilgrim, "I have my own plan." Dear Monkey King! He pulled off one strand of hair and blew a mouthful of magic breath onto it, crying, "Change!" It changed into a sharp, curved knife, with which he ripped open the tiger's chest. Slitting the skin straight down, he then ripped it off in one piece. He chopped away the paws and the head, cutting the skin into one square piece. He picked it up and tried it for size, and then said, "It's a bit too large; one piece can be made into two." He took the knife and cut it again into two pieces; he put one of these away and wrapped the other around his waist. Ripping off a strand of rattan from the side of the road, he firmly tied on this covering for the lower part of his body. "Master," he said, "let's go! Let's go! When we reach someone's house, we will have sufficient time to borrow some threads and a needle to sew this up." He gave his iron rod a squeeze and it changed back into a tiny needle, which he stored in his ear. Throwing the luggage on his back, he asked his Master to mount the horse.

As they set off, the monk asked him, "Wu-k'ung, how is it that the iron rod you used to slay the tiger has disappeared?" "Master," said Pilgrim laughing, "you have no idea what that rod of mine really is. It was acquired originally from the Dragon Palace in the Eastern Ocean. It's called the Precious Divine Iron for Guarding the Heavenly River, and another name of it is the Compliant Golden-Hooped Rod. At the time when I revolted against Heaven, I depended on it a great deal; for it could change into any shape or form, great or small, according to my wish. Just now I had it changed into a tiny embroidery needle, and it's stored that way in my ear. When I need it, I'll take it out." Secretly pleased by what he heard, Tripitaka asked again: "Why did that tiger become completely motionless when it saw you? How do you explain the fact that it simply let you hit it?" "To tell you the truth," said Wu-k'ung, "even a dragon, let alone this tiger, would behave itself if it saw me! I, old Monkey, possess the ability to subdue dragons and tame tigers, and the power to overturn rivers and stir up oceans. I can look at a person's countenance and discern his character; I can listen merely to sounds and discover the truth. If I want to be big, I can fill the universe; if I want to be small, I can be smaller than a piece of hair. In sum, I have boundless ways of transformation and incalculable means of becoming visible or invisible. What's so strange, then, about my skinning a tiger? Wait till we come to some real difficulties—you'll see my talents then!" When Tripitaka heard these words, he was more relieved than ever and urged his horse forward. So master and disciple, the two of them, chatted as they journeyed, and soon the sun sank in the west. You see

Soft glow of the fading twilight,
And distant clouds slowly returning.
On every hill swells the chorus of birds;
In flocks they seek shelter in the woods.
Wild beasts in couples and pairs,
In packs and groups they trek homeward.
The new moon, hooklike, breaks the spreading gloom,
With ten thousand stars luminous.

Pilgrim said, "Master, let's move along, for it's getting late. There are dense clumps of trees over there, and I suppose there must be a house or village too. Let's hurry over there and ask for lodging." Urging his horse forward, Tripitaka went straight up to a house and dismounted. Pilgrim threw down the bag and went to the door, crying, "Open up! Open up!" An old man came to the door, leaning on a cane. When he pulled open the creaking door, he was panic-stricken by the hideous appearance of Pilgrim, who had the tiger skin around his waist and looked like a thunder god. He began to shout, "A ghost! A ghost!" and other such foolish words. Tripitaka drew near and took hold of him, saying, "Old Patron, don't be afraid. He is my disciple, not a ghost." Only when he looked up and saw the handsome features of Tripitaka did the old man stand still. "Which temple are you from," he asked, "and why are you bringing such a nasty character to my door?" "I am a poor monk from the T'ang court," said Tripitaka, "on my way to seek scriptures from Buddha in the Western Heaven. We were passing through here and it was getting late; that is why we made so bold as to approach your great mansion and beg you for a night's lodging. We plan to leave tomorrow before it's light, and we beseech you not to deny our request." "Though you may be a T'ang man," the old man said, "that nasty character is certainly no T'ang man!" "Old fellow!" cried Wu-k'ung in a loud voice, "you really can't see, can you? The T'ang man is my master, and I am his disciple. Of course, I'm no sugar man[6] or honey man! I am the Great Sage, Equal to Heaven! The members of your family should recognize me. Moreover, I have seen you before." "Where have you seen me before?" "When you were young," said Wu-k'ung, "didn't you gather firewood before my eyes? Didn't you haul vegetables before my face?" The old man said, "That's nonsense! Where did you live? And where was I, that I should have gathered firewood and hauled vegetables before your eyes?" "Only my son would talk nonsense!" said Wu-k'ung. "You really don't recognize me! Take a closer look! I am the Great Sage in the stone box of this Mountain of Two Frontiers." "You do look somewhat like him," said the old man, half recognizing the figure before him, "but how did you get out?" Wu-k'ung thereupon gave a thorough account of how the Bodhisattva had converted him and how she had asked him to wait for the T'ang monk to lift the tag for his deliverance.

After that, the old man bowed deeply and invited Tripitaka in, calling for his aged wife and his children to come out and meet the guests. When he told them what had happened, everyone was delighted. Tea was then served, after which the old man asked Wu-k'ung, "How old are you, Great Sage?" "And how old are you?" said Wu-k'ung. "I have lived foolishly for a hundred and thirty years!" said the old man. "You are still my great-great-great-great-grandson!" said Pilgrim. "I can't remember when I was born, but I have spent over five hundred years underneath this mountain." "Yes, yes," said the old man. "I remember my great-grandfather saying that when this mountain dropped from the sky, it had a divine ape clamped underneath it. To think that you should have waited until now for your freedom! When I saw you in my childhood, you had grass on your head and mud on your face; but I wasn't afraid of you then. Now without mud on your face and grass on your head, you seem a bit thinner. And with that huge piece of tiger skin draped around your waist, what great difference is there between you and a demon?"

When the members of his family heard this remark, they all roared with laughter. Being a rather decent fellow, that old man at once ordered a vegetarian meal to be prepared. Afterwards Wu-k'ung said, "What is your family name?" "Our humble family," said the old man, "goes by the name of Ch'ên." When Tripitaka heard this, he left his seat to salute him, saying, "Old Patron, you and I share the same illustrious ancestors." "Master," said Pilgrim, "your surname is T'ang. How can it be that you and he share the same illustrious ancestors?" Tripitaka said, "The surname of my secular family is also Ch'ên, and I come from the Chü-hsien Village, in the Hung-nung District of Hai Chou in the T'ang domain. My religious name is Ch'ên Hsüan-tsang. Because our Great T'ang Emperor T'ai-tsung made me his brother by decree, I took the name Tripitaka and used T'ang as my surname. Hence I'm called the T'ang monk." The old man was very pleased to hear that they had the same surname.

"Old Ch'ên," said Pilgrim, "I must trouble your family some more, for I haven't taken a bath for five hundred years! Please go and boil some water so that my master and, I his disciple, can wash ourselves. We shall thank you all the more when we leave." The old man at once gave the order for water to be boiled and basins to be brought in with several lamps. As master and disciple sat before the lamps after their baths, Pilgrim said, "Old Ch'ên, I still have one more favor to ask of you. Can you lend me a needle and some thread?" "Of course, of course," said the old man. One of the amahs was told to fetch the needle and thread, which were then handed over to the Pilgrim. Pilgrim, you see, had the keenest sight; he noticed that Tripitaka had taken off a shirt made of white cloth and had not put it on again after his bath. Pilgrim grabbed it and put it on himself. Taking off his tiger skin, he sewed the hems together using a "horse-face fold"[7] and fastened it round his waist again with the strand of rattan. He paraded in front of his master saying, "How does old Monkey look today compared with the way he looked yesterday?" "Very good," said Tripitaka, "very good! Now you do look like a pilgrim! If you don't think that the shirt is too worn or old, you may keep it." "Thanks for the gift!" said Wu-k'ung respectfully. He then went out to find some hay to feed the horse, after which master and disciple both retired with the old man and his household.

Next morning Wu-k'ung arose and woke up his master to get ready for the journey. Tripitaka dressed himself while Wu-k'ung put their luggage in order. They were about to leave when the old man brought

in washing water and some vegetarian food, and so they did not set
out until after the meal. Tripitaka rode his horse with Pilgrim leading
the way; they journeyed by day and rested by night, taking food and
drink according to their needs. Soon it was early winter. You see

Frost-blighted maples and the wizened trees;
Few verdant pine and cypress still on the ridge.
Budding plum blossoms spread their gentle scent.
The brief, warm day—
A Little Spring gift![8]
But dying lilies yield to the lush wild tea.
A cold bridge struggles against an old tree's bough,
And gurgling water flows in the winding brook.
Gray clouds, snow-laden, float throughout the sky.
The strong, cold wind
Tears at the sleeve!
How does one bear this chilly might of night?

Master and disciple had traveled for some time when suddenly six
men jumped out from the side of the road with much clamor, all
holding long spears and short swords, sharp blades and strong bows.
"Stop, monk!" they cried. "Leave your horse and drop your bag at
once, and we'll let you pass on alive!" Tripitaka was so terrified that
his soul left him and his spirit fled; he fell from his horse, unable to
utter a word. But Pilgrim lifted him up, saying, "Don't be alarmed,
Master. It's nothing really, just some people coming to give us clothes
and a travel allowance!" "Wu-k'ung," said Tripitaka, "you must be
a little hard of hearing! They told us to leave our bag and our horse,
and you want to ask them for clothes and a travel allowance?" "You
just stay here and watch our belongings," said Pilgrim, "and let old
Monkey confront them. We'll see what happens." Tripitaka said,
"Even a good punch is no match for a pair of fists, and two fists can't
cope with four hands! There are six big fellows over there, and you
are such a tiny person. How can you have the nerve to confront
them?"

As he always had been audacious, Pilgrim did not wait for further
discussion. He walked forward with arms folded and saluted the six
men, saying, "Sirs, for what reason are you blocking the path of this
poor monk?" "We are kings of the highway," said the men, "philan-
thropic mountain lords. Our fame has long been known, though you

seem to be ignorant of it. Leave your belongings at once, and you will be allowed to pass. If you but utter half a no, you'll be chopped to pieces!" "I have been also a great hereditary king and a mountain lord for centuries," said Pilgrim, "but I have yet to learn of your illustrious names." "So you really don't know!" one of them said. "Let's tell you then: one of us is named Eye that Sees and Delights; another, Ear that Hears and Rages; another Nose that Smells and Loves; another, Tongue that Tastes and Desires; another, Mind that Perceives and Covets; and another, Body that Bears and Suffers." "You are nothing but six hairy brigands," said Wu-k'ung laughing, "who have failed to recognize in me a person who has left the family, your proper master. How dare you bar my way? Bring out the treasures you have stolen so that you and I can divide them into seven portions. I'll spare you then!" Hearing this, the robbers all reacted with rage and amusement, covetousness and fear, desire and anxiety. They rushed forward crying, "You reckless monk! You haven't a thing to offer us, and yet you want us to share our loot with you!" Wielding spears and swords, they surrounded Pilgrim and hacked away at his head seventy or eighty times. Pilgrim stood in their midst and behaved as if nothing were happening. "What a monk!" said one of the robbers. "He really does have a hard head!" "Passably so!" said Pilgrim laughing. "But your hands must be getting tired from all that exercise; it's about time for old Monkey to take out his needle for a little entertainment." "This monk must be an acupuncture man in disguise," said the robber. "We're not sick! What's all this about using a needle?"

Pilgrim reached into his ear and took out a tiny embroidery needle; one wave of it in the wind and it became an iron rod with the thickness of a rice bowl. He held it in his hands, saying, "Don't run! Let old Monkey try his hand on you with this rod!" The six robbers fled in all directions, but with great strides he caught up with them and rounded all of them up. He beat every one of them to death, stripped them of their clothes, and seized their valuables. Then Pilgrim came back smiling broadly and said, "You may proceed now, Master. Those robbers have been exterminated by old Monkey." "That's a terrible thing you have done!" said Tripitaka. "They may have been strong men on the highway, but they would not have been sentenced to death even if they had been caught and tried. If you have such abilities, you should have chased them away. Why did you slay them all? How can you be a monk when you take life without cause? We who have left the family should 'Keep ants out of harm's way when we sweep the floor, and put shades on lamps for the love of moths.' How can you kill them just like that, without regard for black or white? You showed no mercy at all! It's a good thing that we are here in the mountains, where any further investigation will be unlikely. But suppose someone offends you when we reach a city and you act with violence again, hitting people indiscriminately with that rod of yours, would I be able to remain innocent and get away scot-free?" "Master," said Wu-k'ung, "if I hadn't killed them, they would have killed you!" Tripitaka said, "As a priest, I would rather die than practice violence. If I were killed, there would be only one of me, but you slaughtered six persons. How can you justify that? If this matter were brought before a judge, and even if your old man were the judge, you certainly would not be able to justify your action." "To tell you the truth, Master," said Pilgrim, "when I, old Monkey, was king on the Flower-Fruit Mountain five hundred years ago, I killed I don't know how many people. I would not have been a Great Sage, Equal to Heaven, if I had lived by what you are saying." "It's precisely because you had neither scruples nor self-control," said Tripitaka, "unleashing your waywardness on Earth and perpetrating outrage in Heaven, that you had to undergo this ordeal of five hundred years. Now that you have entered the fold of Buddhism, if you still insist on practicing violence and indulge in the taking of life as before, you are not worthy to be a monk, nor can you go to the Western Heaven. You're wicked! You're just too wicked!"

Now this monkey had never in all his life been able to tolerate scolding. When he heard Tripitaka's persistent reprimand, he could not suppress the flames leaping up in his heart. "If that's what you think," he said, "if you think I'm not worthy to be a monk, nor can I go to the Western Heaven, you needn't bother me further with your nagging! I'll leave and go back!" Before Tripitaka had time to reply, Pilgrim was already so enraged that he leaped into the air, crying only, "Old Monkey's off!" Tripitaka quickly raised his head to look, but the monkey had already disappeared, trailed only by a swishing sound fast-fading toward the East. Left by himself, the priest could only shake his head and sigh, "That fellow! He's so unwilling to be taught! I only said a few words to him. How could he vanish without a trace and go back just like that? Well! Well! Well! It must be also that I am destined not to have a disciple or any other companion, for now I couldn't even call him or locate him if I wanted to. I might as well go on by myself!" So, he was prepared to

Lay down his life and go toward the West,
To be his own master and on none rely.

The priest had little alternative but to pack up his bag and put it on the horse, which he did not even bother to mount. Holding his staff in one hand and the reins in the other, he set off sadly toward the West. He had not traveled far when he saw an old woman before him on the mountain road, holding a silk garment and a cap with a floral design. When Tripitaka saw her approach, he hastened to pull his horse aside for her to pass. "Elder, where do you come from," asked the old woman, "and why are you walking here all by yourself?" Tripitaka said, "Your child was sent by the Great King of the Land of the East to seek true scriptures from the living Buddha in the Western Heaven." "The Buddha of the West," said the old woman, "lives in the Great Temple of Thunderclap in the territory of India, and the journey there is a hundred and eight thousand miles long. You are all by yourself, with neither a companion nor a disciple. How can you possibly think of going there?" "A few days ago," said Tripitaka, "I did pick up a disciple, a rather unruly and headstrong character. I scolded him a little, but he refused to be taught, and disappeared." The old woman said, "I have here a silk shirt and a flower cap inlaid with gold, which used to belong to my son. He had been a monk for only three days when unfortunately he died. I have just finished mourning him at the temple, where I was given these things by his master to be kept in his memory. Father, since you have a disciple, I'll give the shirt and the cap to you." "I'm most grateful for your lavish gifts," said Tripitaka, "but my disciple has left. I dare not take them." "Where did he go?" said the old woman. Tripitaka said, "I heard a swishing sound heading toward the East." "My home is not too far away in the east," said the old woman, "and he may be going there. I have a spell which is called the True Words for Controlling the Mind, or the Tight-Fillet Spell. You must memorize it secretly; commit it firmly to your memory, and don't let anyone learn of it. I'll try to catch up with him and persuade him to come back and follow you. When he returns, give him the shirt and the cap to wear; and if he again refuses to obey you, recite the spell silently. He will not dare do violence or leave you again."

On hearing these words, Tripitaka bowed his head to thank her. The old woman changed herself into a shaft of golden light and vanished toward the east. Then Tripitaka realized that it was the Bodhisattva Kuan-yin who had taught him the True Words; he hurriedly picked up a few pinches of earth with his fingers and scattered them like incense, bowing reverently toward the East. He then took the shirt and the cap and hid them in his bag. Sitting beside the road, he began to recite the True Words for Controlling the Mind. After a few times, he knew it thoroughly by heart, but we shall speak no more of him for the time being.

We now tell you about Wu-k'ung, who, having left his master, headed straight toward the Eastern Ocean with a single cloud-somersault. He stopped his cloud, opened up a path in the water, and went directly to the Water Crystal Palace. Learning of his arrival, the Dragon King came out to welcome him. After they had exchanged greetings and sat down, the Dragon King said, "I heard recently that the ordeal of the Great Sage had been completed, and I apologize for not having congratulated you yet. I suppose you have again taken occupancy in your immortal mountain and returned to the ancient cave." "I was so inclined," said Wu-k'ung, "but I became a monk instead." "What sort of a monk?" said the Dragon King. "I was indebted to the Bodhisattva of South Sea," said Pilgrim, "who persuaded me to do good and seek the truth. I was to follow the T'ang monk from the Land of the East to go worship Buddha in the West. Since entering the fold of Buddhism, I was given also the name 'Pilgrim.'" "That is indeed praiseworthy!" said the Dragon King. "You have, as we say, left the wrong and followed the right; you have been created anew by setting your mind on goodness. But if that's the case, why are you not going toward the West, but are returning eastward instead?" Pilgrim laughed and said, "That T'ang monk knows nothing of human nature! There were a few ruffians who wanted to rob us, and I slew them all. But that T'ang monk couldn't stop nagging me, telling me over and over how wrong I was. Can you imagine old Monkey putting up with that sort of tedium? I just left him! I was on my way back to my mountain when I decided to come visit you and ask for a cup of tea." "Thanks for coming!

Thanks for coming!" said the Dragon King. At that moment, the Dragon sons and grandsons presented them with aromatic tea.

When they had finished the tea, Pilgrim happened to turn around and saw hanging behind him on the wall a painting of the presentation of shoes at I Bridge. "What's this all about?" asked Pilgrim. The Dragon King said, "The incident depicted in the painting took place some time after you were born, and you may not recognize what it was, the threefold presentation of shoes at I Bridge." "What do you mean by the threefold presentation of shoes?" asked Pilgrim. "The immortal in the painting," said the Dragon King, "was named Huang Shih-kung, and the young man kneeling in front of him was called Chang Liang.[9] Shih-kung was sitting on the I Bridge when suddenly one of his shoes fell off and dropped under the bridge. He asked Chang Liang to fetch it, and the young man quickly did so, putting it back on for him as he knelt there. This happened three times. Since Chang Liang did not display the slightest sign of pride or impatience, he won the affection of Shih-kung, who imparted to him that night a Heavenly book and told him to support the house of Han. Afterwards, Chang Liang 'made his plans sitting in a military tent to achieve victories a thousand miles away.'[10] When the Han dynasty was established, he left his post and went into the mountains, where he followed the Taoist Red Pine Seed[11] and became enlightened in the way of immortality. Great Sage, if you do not accompany the T'ang monk, if you are unwilling to exercise diligence or to accept instruction, you will remain a bogus immortal after all. Don't think that you'll ever acquire the Fruits of Truth." Wu-k'ung listened to these words and fell silent for some time. The Dragon King said, "Great Sage, you must make the decision yourself. It's unwise to allow momentary comfort to jeopardize your future." "Not another word!" said Wu-k'ung. "Old Monkey will go back to accompany him, that's all!" Delighted, the Dragon King said, "If that's your wish, I dare not detain you. Instead, I ask the Great Sage to show his mercy at once and not permit his master to wait any longer." When Pilgrim heard this exhortation to leave, he bounded right out of the oceanic region; mounting the cloud, he left the Dragon King.

On his way he ran right into the Bodhisattva of South Sea. "Sun Wu-k'ung," said the Bodhisattva, "why did you not listen to me and accompany the T'ang monk? What are you doing here?" Pilgrim was so taken aback that he saluted her on top of the clouds. "I'm most grateful for the kind words of the Bodhisattva," he said. "A monk from the T'ang court did appear, lifted the seal, and saved my life. I became his disciple, but he blamed me for being too violent. I walked out on him for a little while, but I'm going back right now to accompany him." "Go quickly then," said the Bodhisattva, "before you change your mind again." They finished speaking and each went on his way.

In a moment, our Pilgrim saw the T'ang monk sitting dejectedly at the side of the road. He approached him and said, "Master, why are you not on the road? What are you doing here?" "Where have you been?" said Tripitaka, looking up. "Your absence has forced me to sit here and wait for you, not daring to walk or move." Pilgrim said, "I just went to the home of the old Dragon King at the Eastern Ocean to ask for some tea." "Disciple," said Tripitaka, "those who have left the family should not lie. It was less than an hour since you left me, and you claim to have had tea at the home of the Dragon King?" "To tell you the truth," said Pilgrim, laughing, "I know how to cloud-somersault, and a single somersault will carry me a hundred and eight thousand miles. That's why I can go and return in no time at all." Tripitaka said, "Because I spoke to you a little sharply, you were offended and left me in a rage. With your ability, you could go and ask for some tea, but a person like me has no other prospect but to sit here and endure hunger. Do you feel comfortable about that?" "Master," said Pilgrim, "if you're hungry, I'll go beg some food for you." "There's no need to beg," said Tripitaka, "for I still have in my bag some dried goods given to me by the mother of Guardian Liu. Fetch me some water in that bowl; I'll eat some food and we can start out again."

Pilgrim went to untie the bag and found some biscuits made of unrefined flour, which he took out and handed over to the master. He then saw light glowing from a silk shirt and a flower cap inlaid with gold. "Did you bring this garment and cap from the Land of the East?" he asked. "I wore these in my childhood," said Tripitaka unthinkingly. "If you wear the hat, you'll know how to recite scriptures without having to learn them; if you put on the garment, you'll know how to perform ceremonies without having to practice them." "Dear Master," said Pilgrim, "let me put them on." "They may not fit you," said Tripitaka, "but if they do, you may wear them." Pilgrim thereupon took off his old shirt made of white cloth and put on the silk shirt, which seemed to have been made especially for him. Then he put on the cap as well. When Tripitaka saw that he had put on the cap, he stopped eating the dried goods and began to recite the Tight-Fillet Spell silently. "Oh, my head!" cried Pilgrim. "It hurts! It hurts!" The master went through the recitation several times without ceasing, and the pain was so intense that Pilgrim was rolling on the ground, his hands gripping the flower cap inlaid with gold. Fearing that he might break the gold fillet, Tripitaka stopped reciting and the pain ceased. Pilgrim touched his head with his hand and felt that it was tightly bound by a thin metal band; it could be neither pulled off nor ripped apart, for it had, as it were, taken root on his head. Taking the needle out of his ear, he rammed it inside the fillet and started prying madly. Afraid that he might break the fillet with his prying, Tripitaka started his recitation again, and Pilgrim's head began to hurt once more. It was so painful that he did cartwheels and somersaults; his face and even his ears turned red; his eyes bulged; and his body grew weak. When the master saw his appearance, he was moved to break off his recitation, and the pain stopped as before. "My head," said Pilgrim, "the master has put a spell on it." "I was just saying the Tight-Fillet Sūtra," said Tripitaka. "Since when did I put a spell on you?" "Recite it some more and see what happens," said Pilgrim. Tripitaka accordingly began to recite, and the Pilgrim immediately started to hurt. "Stop! Stop!" he cried. "I hurt the moment you begin to recite. How do you explain that?" "Will you listen now to my instructions?" said Tripitaka. "Yes, I will," said Pilgrim. "And never be unruly again?" "I dare not," said Pilgrim.

Although he said that with his mouth, Pilgrim's mind was still devising evil. One wave of the needle and it had the thickness of a rice bowl; he aimed it at the T'ang monk and was about to slam it down on him. The priest was so startled that he went through the recitation two or three more times. Falling to the ground, the monkey threw away the iron rod and could not even raise his hands. "Master," he said, "I've learned my lesson! Stop! Please stop!" "How dare you be so reckless," said Tripitaka, "that you should want to strike me?" "I wouldn't dare strike you," said Pilgrim, "but let me ask you something. Who taught you this magic?" "It was an old woman," said Tripitaka, "who imparted it to me a few moments ago." Growing very angry, Pilgrim said, "You needn't say anything more! The old woman had to be that Kuan-shih-yin! Why did she

want me to suffer like this? I'm going to South Sea to beat her up!"
"If she had taught me this magic," said Tripitaka, "she had to know
it even before I did. If you go looking for her, and she starts her
recitation, won't you be dead?" Pilgrim saw the logic of this and
dared not remove himself. Indeed, he had no alternative but to kneel
in contrition and plead with Tripitaka, saying, "Master, this is her
method of controlling me, allowing me no alternative but to follow
you to the West. I'll not go to bother her, but you must not regard
this spell as a plaything for frequent recitation either! I'm willing to
accompany you without ever entertaining the thought of leaving
again." "If that's so," said Tripitaka, "help me onto the horse and
let's get going." At that point, Pilgrim gave up all thoughts of disobedience or rebellion. Eagerly he tugged at his silk shirt and went to
gather the luggage together, and they headed again toward the
West. We do not know what is to be told after their departure, and
you must listen to the explanation in the next chapter.

Fifteen

At Serpent Coil Mountain, many gods give secret
    protection;
At Eagle Grief Stream the Horse of the Will is held
    and reined.

We were telling you about Pilgrim, who ministered to the T'ang monk faithfully as they journeyed westward. They traveled for several days under the frigid sky of midwinter; a cold wind was blowing fiercely, and slippery icicles hung everywhere. They passed hanging cliffs and precipices along their dangerous path; they scaled peak after peak of a treacherous range. As Tripitaka was riding along on his horse, his ears caught the distant sound of a torrent. He turned to ask: "Wu-k'ung, where is that sound coming from?" Pilgrim said, "The name of this place, I recall, is Serpent Coil Mountain, and there is an Eagle Grief Stream in it. I suppose that's where it's coming from." Before they had finished their conversation, they arrived at the bank of the stream. Tripitaka reined in his horse and looked around. He saw

A bubbling cold stream flowing through the clouds,
Its limpid current reddened by the sun.
Its voice in the night rain reached quiet vales.
Its colors glowed with the dawn to fill the air.
Wave after wave—like flying chips of jade;
Its deep roar resonant as the clear wind.
It flowed to join one boundless spread of tide and smoke,
Where gulls were lost with egrets, but no fisher bode.

Master and disciple were looking at the stream, when there was a loud splash in midstream and a dragon emerged. Churning the waters, it darted toward the bank and headed straight for the priest. Pilgrim was so startled that he threw away the luggage, hauled the master off his horse, and turned to flee with him at once. The dragon could not catch up with them, but it swallowed the white horse, harness and all, with one gulp before losing itself again in the water. Pilgrim carried his master to high ground and left the priest seated there; then he returned to fetch the horse and the luggage. The load of bags was still there, but the horse was nowhere to be seen. Placing the luggage in front of his master, he said, "Master, there's not a trace of that cursed dragon, which has frightened away our horse." "Disciple," said Tripitaka, "how can we find the horse again?" "Relax! Relax!" said Pilgrim. "Let me go and have a look!"

He whistled once and leaped up into the air. Shading his fiery eyes and diamond pupils with his hand, he peered in all four directions, but there was not the slightest trace of the horse. Dropping down from the clouds, he made his report, saying, "Master, our horse must have been eaten by that dragon. It's nowhere to be seen!" "Disciple," said Tripitaka, "how big a mouth does that creature have that he can swallow a horse, harness and all? It must have been frightened away instead, probably still running loose somewhere in the valley. Please take another look." Pilgrim said, "You really have no conception of my ability. This pair of eyes of mine in daylight can discern good and evil within a thousand miles; at that distance, I can even see a dragonfly when it spreads its wings. How can I possibly miss something as big as a horse?" "If it has been eaten," said Tripitaka, "how am I to proceed? Pity me! How can I walk through those thousand hills and ten thousand waters?" As he spoke, tears began to fall like rain. When Pilgrim saw him crying, he was infuriated and began to shout: "Master, stop behaving like a namby-pamby! Sit here! Just sit here! Let old Monkey find that creature and ask him to give us back our horse. That'll be the end of the matter." Clutching at him, Tripitaka said, "Disciple, where do you have to go to find him? Wouldn't I be hurt if he should appear from somewhere after you are gone? How would it be then if both man and horse should perish?" At these words, Pilgrim became even more enraged. Bellowing like thunder he said, "You're a weakling! Truly a weakling! You want a horse to ride on, and yet you won't let me go. You want to sit here and grow old, watching our bags?"

As he was yelling angrily like this, he heard someone calling out in midair: "Great Sage Sun, don't be annoyed. And stop crying, Royal Brother of T'ang. We are a band of deities sent by the Bodhisattva Kuan-yin to give secret protection to the scripture pilgrim." Hearing this, the priest hastily bowed to the ground. "Which divinities are you?" asked Pilgrim. "Tell me your names, so that I can check you off the roll." "We are the Six Gods of Darkness and the Six Gods of light," they said, "the Guardians of Five Points, the Four Sentinels, and the Eighteen Protectors of Monasteries. Every one of us waits upon you in rotation." "Which one of you will begin today?" asked Pilgrim. "The Gods of Darkness and Light will begin," they said, "to be followed by the Sentinels and the Protectors. We Guardians of Five Points, with the exception of the Golden-Headed Guardian, will be here somewhere night and day." "That being the case," said Pilgrim, "those not on duty may retire, but the Six Gods of Darkness, the Day Sentinel, and the Guardians should remain to protect my master. Let old Monkey go find that cursed dragon in the stream and ask him for our horse." The various deities obeyed. Only then did Tripitaka feel somewhat relieved; he sat on the cliff and told Pilgrim to be careful. "Just don't worry," said Pilgrim. Dear Monkey King! He tightened the belt around his silk shirt, hitched up his tiger-skin skirt, and went straight toward the gorge of the stream holding the golden-hooped iron rod. Standing halfway between cloud and fog, he cried loudly on top of the water, "Lawless lizard! Give me back my horse! Give me back my horse!"

We now tell you about the dragon, who, having eaten the white horse of Tripitaka, was lying on the bottom of the stream, subduing his spirit and cultivating his nature. When he heard someone demanding the horse with abusive language, however, he could not restrain the fire leaping up in his heart and he jumped up quickly. Churning the waves, he darted out of the water, saying, "Who dares to insult me here with his big mouth?" Pilgrim saw him and cried ferociously, "Don't run away! Give me back my horse!" Wielding his rod, he aimed at the beast's head and struck, while the dragon attacked with open jaws and dancing claws. The battle between the two of them before the stream was indeed a fierce one. You see

The dragon extending sharp claws;
The monkey lifting his rod.
The whiskers of this one hung like white jade threads;
The eyes of that one shone like red-gold lamps.
The mouth beneath the whiskers of that one belched colored mists;
The iron rod in the hands of this one moved like a fierce wind.
That one was a cursed son who brought his parents grief;
This one was a monster who defied the gods on high.
Both had to suffer because of their plight.
They now want to win, so each displays his might.

Back and forth, round and round, they fought for a long time, until the dragon grew weak and could fight no longer. He turned and darted back into the water; plunging to the bottom of the stream, he refused to come out again. The Monkey King heaped insult upon insult, but the dragon only pretended to be deaf.

Pilgrim had little choice but to return to Tripitaka, saying, "Master, that monster made his appearance as a result of my tongue-lashing. He fought with me for a long time before taking fright and running. He's hiding in the water now and refuses to come out again." "Do you know for certain that it was he who ate my horse?" said Tripitaka. "Look at the way you talk!" said Pilgrim. "If he hadn't eaten it, would he be willing to face me and answer me like that?" "The time you killed the tiger," said Tripitaka, "you claimed that you had the ability to tame dragons and subdue tigers. Why can't you subdue this one today?" Now the monkey had a rather low tolerance for any kind of provocation. This single taunt of Tripitaka so aroused him that he said, "Not one word more! Let me go and show him who is master!"

With great leaps, our Monkey King bounded right to the edge of the stream. Using his magic of overturning seas and rivers, he transformed the clear, limpid water of the Eagle Grief Stream into the muddy currents of the Yellow River during high tide. The cursed dragon in the depth of the stream could neither sit nor lie still for a single moment. He thought to himself: "Just as 'Blessing never repeats itself, so misfortune never comes singly!' It has been barely a year since I escaped execution by Heaven and came to bide my time here; and now I have to run into this wretched monster who is trying to do me harm." Look at him! The more he thought about the matter, the more irritated he became. Unable to withstand it any longer, he gritted his teeth and leaped out of the water, crying, "What kind of monster are you, and where do you come from, that you want to oppress me like this?" "Never mind where I come from," said Pilgrim. "Just return the horse, and I'll spare your life." "I've swallowed your horse into my stomach," said the dragon, "so how am I to throw it up? What are you going to do if I can't return it to you?" Pilgrim said, "If you don't give back the horse, just watch for this rod. Only when your life is made a payment for my horse will there be an end to this matter!" The two of them again waged a bitter struggle below the mountain ridge. After a few rounds, however, the little dragon just could not hold out any longer; shaking his body, he changed himself into a tiny water snake and wriggled into the marshes.

The Monkey King came rushing up with his rod and parted the grass to look for the snake, but there was not a trace of it. He was so exasperated that the spirits of the Three Worms in his body exploded[1] and smoke began to appear from his seven apertures. He recited a spell beginning with the letter *oṁ* and summoned the local spirit and the mountain god of that region. The two of them knelt before him, saying, "The local spirit and the mountain god have come to see you." "Stick out your shanks," said Pilgrim, "and I'll greet each of you with five strokes of my rod just to relieve my feelings." "Great Sage," they pleaded, "please be more lenient and allow your humble subjects to tell you something." "What have you got to say?" said Pilgrim. "The Great Sage has been in captivity for a long time," said the two deities, "and we had no knowledge of when you were released. That's why we have not been here to receive you, and we beg you to pardon us." "All right," said Pilgrim, "I won't hit you. But let me ask you something. Where did that monstrous dragon in the Eagle Grief Stream come from, and why did he devour my master's white horse?" "We have never known the Great Sage to have a master," the two deities said, "for you have always been a first-rank primordial immortal who submits neither to Heaven nor to Earth. What do you mean by your master's horse?" Pilgrim said, "Of course you didn't know about this. Because of my contemptuous behavior toward Heaven, I had to suffer for this five hundred years. I was converted by the kindly persuasion of Bodhisattva Kuan-yin, who had the true monk from the T'ang court rescue me. As his disciple, I was to follow him to the Western Heaven to seek scriptures from Buddha. We passed through this place, and my master's white horse was lost."

"So, that's how it is!" said the two deities. "There has never been anything evil about this stream, except that it is both broad and deep, and its water is so clear that you can see right to the bottom. Large fowls such as crows or eagles are hesitant to fly over it; for when they see their own reflections in the clear water, they are prone to mistake them for other birds of their own flock and throw themselves into the stream. Whence the name, the Steep Eagle Grief Stream. Some years ago, on her way to look for a scripture pilgrim, Bodhisattva Kuan-yin rescued a dragon and sent him here. He was told to wait for the scripture pilgrim and was forbidden to do any evil or violence. Only when he is hungry is he permitted to come up to the banks to feed on birds or antelopes. How could he be so ignorant as to offend the Great Sage!" Pilgrim said, "At first, he wanted to have a contest of strength with me and managed only a few bouts. Afterwards he would not come out even when I abused him. Only when I used the magic of overturning seas and rivers and stirred up the water did he appear again, and then he still wanted to fight. He really had no idea how heavy my rod was! When finally he couldn't hold out any longer, he changed himself into a water snake and wriggled into the grass. I rushed up there to look for him, but there was no trace of him." "You may not know, Great Sage," said the local spirit, "that there are countless holes and crevices along these banks, through which the stream is connected with its many tributaries. The dragon could have crawled into any one of these. But there's no need for the Great Sage to get angry trying to look for him. If you want to capture this creature, all you need do is to ask Kuan-shih-yin to come here; then he'll certainly surrender."

When Pilgrim heard this, he called the mountain god and the local spirit to go with him to see Tripitaka to give an account of what had happened. "If you need to send for the Bodhisattva," said Tripitaka, "when will you be able to return? How can this poor monk endure the cold and hunger?" He had hardly finished speaking when the Golden-Headed Guardian called out from midair, "Great Sage, you needn't leave. Your humble subject will go fetch the Bodhisattva." Pilgrim was very pleased, shouting, "Thanks for taking all that trouble! Go quickly!" The Guardian mounted the clouds swiftly and headed straight for South Sea; Pilgrim asked the mountain god and the local spirit to protect his master and the Day Sentinel to find some vegetarian food, while he himself went back to patrol the stream, and we shall say no more of that.

We now tell you about the Golden-Headed Guardian, who mounted the clouds and soon arrived at South Sea. Descending from the auspicious light, he went straight to the purple bamboo grove of the Potalaka Mountain, where he asked the various deities in golden armor and Mokṣa to announce his arrival. The Bodhisattva said, "What have you come for?" "The T'ang monk lost his horse at the Eagle Grief Stream of the Serpent Coil Mountain," said the Guardian, "and the Great Sage Sun was placed in a terrible dilemma. He questioned the local deities, who claimed that a dragon sent by the Bodhisattva to that stream had eaten it. The Great Sage, therefore, sent me to request the Bodhisattva to go and subdue that cursed dragon, so that he might get back .his horse." Hearing this, the Bodhisattva said, "That creature was originally the son of Ao-jun of the Western Ocean. Because in his carelessness he set fire to the palace and destroyed the luminous pearls hanging there, his father accused him of subversion, and he was condemned to die by the Heavenly Tribunal. It was I who personally sought pardon from the Jade Emperor for him, so that he might serve as a means of transportation for the T'ang monk. I can't understand how he could swallow the monk's horse instead? But if that's what happened, I'll have to get over there myself." The Bodhisattva left her lotus platform and went out of the divine cave. Mounting the auspicious luminosity with the Guardian, she crossed the South Sea. We have a testimonial poem which says:

Buddha proclaimed the Tripitaka Supreme,
Which the Goddess declared throughout Ch'ang-an:
Those great, wondrous truths could reach Heaven and Earth;
Those wise, true words could save the spirits damned.
They caused Gold Cicada to cast again his shell.
They moved Hsüan-tsang to mend his ways anew.
By blocking his path at Eagle Grief Stream,
The dragon son came home[2] in a horse's form.

The Bodhisattva and the Guardian soon arrived at the Serpent Coil Mountain. They stopped the hallowed clouds in midair and saw Pilgrim Sun down below, shouting abuses at the bank of the stream. The Bodhisattva asked the Guardian to fetch him. Lowering his clouds, the Guardian went past Tripitaka and headed straight for the edge of the stream, saying to Pilgrim, "The Bodhisattva has arrived." When Pilgrim heard this, he jumped quickly into the air and yelled at her: "You, so-called Teacher of the Seven Buddhas and the Founder of the Faith of Mercy! Why did you have to use your tricks to harm me?" "You impudent stableman, ignorant red-buttocks!" said the Bodhisattva. "I went to considerable effort to find a scripture pilgrim, whom I carefully instructed to save your life. Instead of thanking me, you are finding fault with me!" "You saved me all right!" said Pilgrim. "If you truly wanted to release me, you should have allowed me to have a little fun with no strings attached. When you met me the other day above the ocean, you could have chastened me with a few words, telling me to serve the T'ang monk with diligence, and that would have been enough. Why did you have to give him a flower cap, and have him deceive me into wearing it so that I would suffer? Now the fillet has taken root on old Monkey's head. And you even taught him this so-called 'Tight-Fillet Spell' which he recites again and again, causing endless pain in my head! You haven't harmed me, indeed!" The Bodhisattva laughed and said, "O, Monkey! You are neither attentive to admonition nor willing to seek the fruit of truth. If you are not restrained like this, you'll probably mock the authority of Heaven again without regard for good or ill. If you create troubles as you did before, who will be able to control you? It's only through this bit of adversity that you will be willing to enter our gate of Yoga." "All right," said Pilgrim, "I'll consider the matter my hard luck. But why did you take that condemned dragon and send him here so that he could become a spirit and swallow my master's horse? It's your fault, you know, if you allow an evildoer to perpetrate his villainies some more!" "I went personally to plead with the Jade Emperor," said the Bodhisattva, "to have the dragon stationed here so that he could serve as a means of transportation for the scripture pilgrim. Those mortal horses from the Land of the East, do you think that they could walk through ten thousand waters and a thousand hills? How could they possibly hope to reach the Spirit Mountain, the land of Buddha? Only a dragon-horse could make that journey!" "But right now he's so terribly afraid of me," said Pilgrim, "that he refuses to come out of his hiding place. What can we do?" The Bodhisattva said to the Guardian, "Go to the edge of the stream and say, 'Come out, Third Prince Jade Dragon of the Dragon-king Ao-jun. The Bodhisattva from South Sea is here.' He'll come out then."

The Guardian went at once to the edge of the stream and called out twice. Churning the waters and leaping across the waves, the little dragon appeared and changed at once into the form of a man. He stepped on the clouds and rose up into the air; saluting the Bodhisattva, he said, "I thank the Bodhisattva again for saving my life. I've waited here a long time, but I've heard no news of the scripture pilgrim." Pointing to Pilgrim, the Bodhisattva said, "Isn't he the eldest disciple of the scripture pilgrim?" When he saw him, the little dragon said, "Bodhisattva, he's my adversary. I was hungry yesterday and ate his horse. We fought over that, but he took advantage of his superior strength and defeated me; in fact, he so abused me that I dared not show myself again. But he has never mentioned a word about scripture seeking." "You didn't bother to ask my name," said Pilgrim. "How did you expect me to tell you anything?" The little dragon said, "Didn't I ask you, 'What kind of a monster are you and where do you come from?' But all you did was shout, 'Never mind where I come from; just return my horse!' Since when did you utter even half the word 'T'ang?'" "That monkey," said the Bodhisattva, "is always relying on his own abilities! When has he ever given any credit to other people? When you set off this time, remember that there are others who will join you. So when they ask you, by all means mention first the matter of scripture seeking; they will submit to you without causing you further trouble."

Pilgrim received this word of counsel amiably. The Bodhisattva went up to the little dragon and plucked off the shining pearls hanging around his neck. She then dipped her willow branch into the sweet dew in her vase and sprinkled it all over his body; blowing a mouthful of magic breath on him, she cried, "Change!" The dragon at once changed into a horse with hair of exactly the same color and quality as that of the horse he had swallowed. The Bodhisattva then told him, "You must overcome with utmost diligence all the cursed barriers. When your merit is achieved, you will no longer be an ordinary dragon; you will acquire the true fruit of a golden body." Holding the bit in his mouth, the little dragon humbly accepted the instruction. The Bodhisattva told Wu-k'ung to lead him to Tripitaka, saying, "I'm returning across the ocrean." Pilgrim took hold of her and refused to let go, saying, "I'm not going on! I'm not going on! The road to the West is so treacherous! If I have to accompany this ordinary monk, when will I ever get there? If I have to endure all these miseries, I may well lose my life. What sort of merit do you think I'll achieve? I'm not going! I'm not going!"

"In years past, before you reached the way of humanity," said the Bodhisattva, "you were most eager to seek enlightenment. Now that you have been delivered from the chastisement of Heaven, how could you become slothful again? The truth of nirvāṇa in our teaching can never be realized without faith and perseverance. If on your journey you should come across any danger that threatens your life, I give you permission to call on Heaven, and Heaven will respond; to call on Earth, and Earth will prove efficacious. In the event of extreme difficulty, I myself will come to rescue you. Come closer, and I shall endow you with one more power." Plucking three leaves from her willow branch, the Bodhisattva placed them at the back of Pilgrim's head, crying, "Change!" They changed at once into three hairs with life-saving power. She said to him: "When you find yourself in a helpless and hopeless situation, you may use these according to your needs, and they will deliver you from your particular affliction." After Pilgrim had heard all these kind words, he thanked the Bodhisattva of Great Mercy and Compassion. With scented wind and colored mists swirling around her, the Bodhisattva returned to Potalaka.

Lowering the direction of his cloud, Pilgrim tugged at the mane of the horse and led him to Tripitaka, saying, "Master, we have a horse!" Highly pleased by what he saw, Tripitaka said, "Disciple, how is it that the horse has grown a little fatter and stronger than before? Where did you find him?" "Master, you are still dreaming!" said Pilgrim. "Just now the Golden-Headed Guardian managed to bring the Bodhisattva here, and she transformed the dragon of the stream into our white horse. Except for the missing harness, the colour and hair are all the same, and old Monkey has pulled him here." "Where is the Bodhisattva?" said Tripitaka, greatly surprised. "Let me go and thank her." "By this time," said Pilgrim, "the Bodhisattva has probably arrived at South Sea; there's no need to bother about that." Picking up a few pinches of earth with his fingers and scattering them like incense, Tripitaka bowed reverently toward the South. He then got up and prepared to leave again with Pilgrim.

Having dismissed the mountain god and the local spirit and given instructions to the Guardians and the Sentinels, Pilgrim asked his master to mount. Tripitaka said, "How can I ride a horse without harness? Let's find a boat to cross this stream, and then we can decide what to do." "This master of mine is truly impractical!" said Pilgrim. "In the wilds of this mountain, where will you find a boat? Since the horse has lived here for a long time, he must know the water's condition. Just ride him like a boat and we'll cross over." Tripitaka had no choice but to follow his suggestion and climbed onto the bare-backed horse; Pilgrim took up the luggage and they arrived at the edge of the stream. Then they saw an old fisherman punting downstream toward them in an old wooden raft. When Pilgrim caught sight of him, he waved his hands and called out: "Old fisher-man, come here! Come here! We come from the Land of the East to seek scriptures. It's difficult for my master to cross, so please take us over." When the fisherman heard these words, he quickly punted the raft up to the bank. Asking his master to dismount, Pilgrim helped Tripitaka onto the raft before he embarked the horse and the luggage. That old fisher punted the raft away, and like an arrow in the wind, they crossed the steep Eagle Grief Stream swiftly and landed on the western shore. Tripitaka told Pilgrim to untie a bag and take out a few T'ang pennies to give to the old fisherman. With a shove of his pole, the old fisherman pulled away, saying, "I don't want any money." He drifted downstream and soon disappeared from sight. Feeling very much obliged, Tripitaka kept folding his hands to express his gratitude. "Master," said Pilgrim, "you needn't be so solicitous. Don't you recognize him? He is the Water God of this stream. Since he didn't come to pay his respects to old Monkey, he was about to get a beating. It's enough that he is now spared from that. Would he dare take any money!" The Master was only half-believing him when he climbed onto the bare-backed horse once again; following Pilgrim, he went up to the main road and set off again toward the West. It would be like this that they

Through the vast Thusness[3] reach the other shore,
And climb with hearts unfeigned the Spirit Mount.

Master and disciple journeyed on, and soon the fiery sun sank westward as the sky gradually darkened. You see

Clouds hazy and aimless,
A mountain moon dim and gloomy.
The sky, all frost-colored, makes you cold;
The wind, howling around, pierces your body.
One bird is lost midst the pale, wide sand bars,
As twilight glows where the distant hills are low.
A thousand trees roar in the sparse woodland;
A lonely ape cries on a peak barren.
No traveler is seen on this long road
When boats from afar return for the night.

As Tripitaka, riding his horse, peered into the distance, he suddenly saw something like a hamlet beside the road. "Wu-k'ung," he said, "there's a house ahead of us. Let's ask for lodging there and travel again tomorrow." Raising his head to take a look, Pilgrim said, "Master, it's no ordinary house." "Why not?" said Tripitaka. "If it were an ordinary house," said Pilgrim, "there would be no flying fishes or reclining beasts decorating the ridge of its roof. That must be a temple or a monastery." While they were speaking, master and disciple arrived at the gate of the building. Dismounting, Tripitaka saw on top of the gate three large words: Li-Shê Shrine. They walked inside, where they were met by an old man with some beads hanging around his neck. He came forward with hands folded, saying, "Master, please take a seat." Tripitaka hastily returned his salutation and then went to the main hall to bow to the holy images. The old man called a youth to serve tea, after which Tripitaka asked him, "Why is this shrine named Li-Shê?" The old man said, "This region belongs to the Hamil Kingdom of the western barbarians. There is a village behind the shrine, which was built from the piety of all its families. The Li refers to the land owned by the whole village, and the Shê is the God of the Soil. During the days of spring sowing, summer plowing, autumn harvesting, and winter storing, each of the families would bring the three beasts,[4] flowers and fruits to sacrifice at the shrine, so that they might be blessed with good luck in all four seasons, a rich harvest of the five grains, and prosperity in raising the six domestic creatures."[5] When Tripitaka heard these words, he nodded his head to show his approval, saying, "This is truly like the proverb: 'Even three miles from home there are customs entirely distinct.' The families in our region do not practice such good works." Then the old man asked, "Where is the honorable home of the master?" "Your poor monk," said Tripitaka, "happens to have been sent by the royal decree from the Great T'ang Nation in the East to go to seek scriptures from Buddha in the Western Heaven. It was getting rather late when I passed your esteemed edifice. I therefore came to your holy shrine to ask for a night's lodging. I'll leave as soon as it gets light." The old man was delighted and kept saying, "Welcome! Welcome!" He called the youth again to prepare a meal, which Tripitaka ate with gratitude.

As usual, Pilgrim was extremely observant. Noticing a rope for hanging laundry tied under the eaves, he walked over to it and pulled at it until it snapped in two. He then used the piece of rope to tie up the horse. "Where did you steal this horse?" said the old man laughing. "Old man," said Pilgrim angrily, "watch what you are saying! We are holy monks going to worship Buddha. How could we steal horses?" "If you didn't steal it," said the old man laughing, "why is there no saddle or rein, so that you have to rip up my clothesline?"

"This rascal is always so impulsive," said Tripitaka apologetically. "If you wanted to tie up the horse, why didn't you ask the old gentleman properly for a rope? Why did you have to rip up his clothesline? Sir, please don't be angry! Our horse, to tell you the truth, is not a stolen one. When we approached the Eagle Grief Stream yesterday from the east, I had a white horse complete with harness. Little did we anticipate that there was a condemned dragon in the stream who had become a spirit, and who swallowed my horse in one gulp, harness and all. Fortunately, my disciple has some talents, and he was able to bring the Bodhisattva Kuan-yin to the stream to subdue the dragon. She told him to assume the form of my original white horse, so that he could carry me to worship Buddha in the Western Heaven. It has barely been one day since we crossed the stream and arrived at your holy shrine. We haven't had time to look for a harness."

"Master, you needn't worry," said the old man. "An old man like me loves to tease, but I had no idea your esteemed disciple was so serious about everything! When I was young, I had a little money, and I too loved to ride. But over the years I had my share of misfortunes: deaths in the family and fires in the household have not left me much. Thus I am reduced to being a caretaker here in the shrine, looking after the fires and incense, and dependent on the goodwill of the patrons in the village back there for a living. I still have in my possession a harness which I have always cherished, and which even in this poverty I couldn't bear to sell. But since hearing your story, how even the Bodhisattva delivered the divine dragon and made him change into a horse to carry you, I feel that I must not withhold from giving either. I shall bring the harness tomorrow and present it to the master, who, I hope, will be pleased to accept it." When Tripitaka heard this, he thanked him repeatedly. Before long, the youth brought in the evening meal, after which lamps were lit and the beds prepared. Everyone then retired.

Next morning, Pilgrim arose and said, "Master, that old caretaker promised last night to give us the harness. Ask him for it. Don't spare him." He had hardly finished speaking when the old man came in with a saddle, together with pads, reins, and the like. Not a single item needed for riding a horse was lacking. He set them down in the corridor, saying, "Master, I am presenting you with this harness." When Tripitaka saw it, he accepted it with delight and asked Pilgrim to try the saddle on the horse. Going forward, Pilgrim took up the

accoutrements and examined them piece by piece. They were indeed
some magnificent articles, for which we have a testimonial poem.
The poem says:

The carved saddle shines with studs of silver stars.
The precious seat glows with bright threads of gold.
The pads are stacks of fine-spun woolen quilts.
The reins are three bands of purple cords of silk.
The bridle's leather straps are shaped like flowers.
The flaps have gold-etched forms of dancing beasts.
The rings and bit are made of finest steel.
And waterproof tassels hang on both sides.

Secretly pleased, Pilgrim put the saddle on the back of the horse, and
it seemed to have been made to measure. Tripitaka bowed to thank
the old man, who hastily raised him up, saying, "It's nothing! What
do you need to thank me for?" The old man did not ask them to stay
any longer; instead, he urged Tripitaka to mount. The priest came
out of the gate and climbed into the saddle, while Pilgrim followed,
hauling the luggage. The old man then took a whip out from his
sleeve, with a handle of rattan wrapped in strips of leather, and the
strap knitted with cords made of tiger ligaments. He stood by the side
of the road and presented it with hands uplifted, saying, "Holy Monk,
I have a whip here which I may as well give you." Tripitaka accepted
it on his horse, saying, "Thanks for your donation! Thanks for your
donation!"

Even as he was saying this, the old man vanished. The priest
turned around to look at the Li-Shê Shrine, but it had become just a
piece of level ground. From the sky came a voice saying, "Holy
Monk, I'm sorry not to have given you a better reception! I am the
local spirit of Potalaka Mountain, who was sent by the Bodhisattva
to present you with the harness. You two must journey to the West
with all diligence. Do not be slothful in any moment." Tripitaka was
so startled that he fell off his horse and bowed toward the sky, saying,
"Your disciple is of fleshly eyes and mortal stock, and he does not
recognize the holy visage of the deity. Please forgive me. I beseech
you to convey my gratitude to the Bodhisattva." Look at him! All he
could do was to kowtow toward the sky without bothering to count
how many times! By the side of the road the Great Sage Sun reeled
with laughter, the Handsome Monkey King broke up with hilarity.
He came up and tugged at his master, saying, "Master, get up! He is

long gone! He can't hear you, nor can he see your kowtowing. Why keep up this adoration?" "Disciple," said the priest, "when I kowtowed like that, all you could do was to stand snickering by the side of the road, with not even a bow. Why?" "You wouldn't know, would you?" said Pilgrim. "For playing a game of hide-and-seek like that with us, he really deserves a beating! But for the sake of the Bodhisattva, I'll spare him—and that's something already! You think he dares accept a bow from old Monkey? Old Monkey has been a hero since his youth, and he doesn't know how to bow to people! Even when I saw the Jade Emperor and Lao Tzu, I just gave them my greeting, that's all!" "Blasphemy!" said Tripitaka. "Stop this idle talk! Let's get going without further delay." So the priest got up and prepared to set off again toward the West.

After leaving that place, they had a peaceful journey for two months, for all they met were barbarians, Muslims, tigers, wolves, and leopards. Time went by swiftly, and it was early spring again. You could see jade green gilding the mountain forest, and green sprouts of grass appearing; the plum blossoms were all fallen and the willow-leaves gently budding. As master and disciple were admiring this scenery of spring, they saw the sun sinking westward again. Reining the horse, Tripitaka peered into the distance and saw at the fold of the hill the shadow of buildings and the dark silhouette of towers. "Wu-k'ung," said Tripitaka, "look at the buildings over there. What sort of place is that?" Stretching his neck to look, Pilgrim said, "It has to be either a temple or a monastery. Let's move along and ask for lodging over there." Tripitaka was glad to follow this suggestion and urged his dragon-horse forward. We do not know what sort of place they arrived at, and you must listen to the explanation in the next chapter.

Sixteen

At Kuan-yin Hall the monks plot for the treasure;
At Black Wind Mountain the monster steals the cassock.

We were telling you about the disciple and master, who urged the horse forward and arrived at the front gate of the building. They saw that it was indeed a monastery with

Tiers of towers and turrets,
And rows of quiet chambers.
Above the temple gate
Hung the august panoply of colored nimbus;
Before the Hall of Five Blessings
Whirled a thousand strands of bright red mists.
Two rows of pines and bamboos;
One grove of juniper and cypress;
Two rows of pines and bamboos
Revealed their fair virtue unspoiled by time;
One grove of juniper and cypress
Displayed its chaste beauty in comely hues.
They saw also the tall belltower,
The pagoda rugged,
Monks in silent meditation
And birds on trees gently cooing.
A dustless seclusion was the real seclusion,
For the quiescence of Tao was truly quiescent.

The poem says:

This temple, like Jetavana,[1] hidden in a jade-green grove:
Its scenic splendor surpasses even the Ṣaḍ-varṣa.[2]
The pure land among mankind is rare indeed,
For this world's famed mountains are mostly held by monks.

The priest dismounted, and Pilgrim laid down his load. They were about to walk through the gate when a monk came out. "How does he look?" you ask.

He wore a hat pinned to the left

And a robe most spotlessly pure.
Two brass rings hung from his ears;
A silk sash was wrapped round his waist.
His straw sandals moved sedately;
His hands carried a wooden fish.
His mouth recited constantly
The Wisdom he sought most humbly.

When Tripitaka saw him, he stood waiting by the gate and saluted with his palms pressed together in front of him. The monk returned the greeting at once and said laughing, "I'm sorry, but I don't know you!" He then asked: "Where do you come from? Please come in for some tea." "Your disciple," said Tripitaka, "has been sent by royal decree from the Land of the East to go to seek scriptures from Buddha in the Temple of Thunderclap. It was getting late when we arrived here, and we would like to ask for a night's lodging in your fair temple." "Please take a seat inside," said the monk. Only then did Tripitaka call Pilgrim to lead the horse inside. When the monk caught sight of Pilgrim's face, he became somewhat afraid and asked: "What's that thing leading the horse?" "Speak softly!" said Tripitaka. "He's easily provoked! If he hears you referring to him as a thing, he'll get mad. He happens to be my disciple." With a shiver, the monk bit his finger and said, "Such a hideous creature, and you made him your disciple!" Tripitaka said, "You can't tell by mere appearance. He may be ugly, but he is very useful."

That monk had little choice but to accompany Tripitaka and Pilgrim as they entered the temple gate. Inside, above the main hall's entrance, the words "Kuan-yin Zen Hall" were written in large letters. Highly pleased, Tripitaka said, "This disciple has repeatedly benefited from the holy grace of the Bodhisattva, though he has had no opportunity to thank her. Now that we are at this Zen hall, it is as if we are meeting the Bodhisattva personally, and it is most proper that I should offer my thanks." When the monk heard this, he told one of the Taoist attendants to open wide the door of the hall and invited Tripitaka to worship. Pilgrim tied up the horse, dropped his luggage, and went with Tripitaka up the hall. Stretching his back and then flattening himself on the ground, Tripitaka kowtowed to the golden image as the monk went to beat the drum, and Pilgrim began to strike the bell. Prostrating himself before the seat of the deity, Tripitaka poured out his heart in prayer. When he finished, the monk stopped the drum, but Pilgrim continued to strike the bell without ceasing. Now rapidly, now slowly, he persisted for a long time. The Taoist said, "The service is over. Why are you still striking the bell?" Only then did Pilgrim throw away the hammer and say, laughing, "You wouldn't know this! I'm just living by the proverb: 'If you are a monk for a day, strike then the bell for a day!'" By then, the monks young and old of the monastery and the elders of upper and lower chambers were all aroused by the unruly sound of the bell. They rushed out together crying, "Who is the maniac fooling with the bell?" Pilgrim leaped out of the hall and shouted, "Your Grandpa Sun sounded it to amuse himself!" The moment the monks saw him, they were so frightened that they tumbled and rolled on the ground. Crawling around, they said, "Father Thunder!" "He's only my great-grandson!" said Pilgrim. "Get up, get up! Don't be afraid. We are noble priests who have come from the Great T'ang Nation in the east." The various monks then bowed courteously to him, and when they saw Tripitaka, they were even more reassured. One of the monks, who was the abbot of the monastery, said, "Let the holy fathers come to the living room in the back so that we may offer them some tea." Untying the reins and leading the horse, they picked up the luggage and went past the main hall to the back of the monastery, where they sat down in orderly rows.

After serving tea, the abbot prepared a vegetarian meal, although it was still rather early for dinner. Tripitaka had not finished thanking him when an old monk emerged from the rear, supported by two boys. Look how he was attired:

He wore on his head a Vairocana hat
Topped by a precious, shining cat's-eye stone;
He wore on his body a brocaded woolen frock,
Piped brilliantly in gold and kingfisher feathers.
A pair of monk shoes on which Eight Treasures were set,
And a priestly staff encased with starry gems.
His face full of wrinkles,
He looked like the Old Witch of Li Mountain;
His eyes were dim-sighted,
Though he seemed a Dragon King of the Eastern Ocean.
Wind stabbed his mouth for his teeth were fallen,
And palsy had made crooked his aged back.

The various monks said, "The Patriarch is here." Tripitaka bowed to receive him, saying, "Old Abbot, your disciple bows to you." The old monk returned the gesture, and they were both seated. "Just now I heard the little ones announcing," said the old monk, "that venerable fathers from the T'ang court have arrived from the east. I came out specifically to meet you." "Without knowing any better," said Tripitaka, "we intruded into your esteemed temple. Please pardon us!" "Please, please!" said the old monk. "May I ask the holy father what the distance is between here and the Land of the East?" "Since leaving the outskirts of Ch'ang-an," said Tripitaka, "I traveled for some five thousand miles before passing the Mountain of Two Frontiers, where I picked up a little disciple. Moving on, we passed through the Hamil Kingdom of the western barbarians, and in two months we had traveled another five or six thousand miles. Only then did we arrive at your noble region." "Well, you have covered the distance of ten thousand miles," said the old monk. "This disciple truly has spent his life in vain, for he has not even left the door of the temple. I have, as the saying goes, 'sat in the well to look at the sky.' A veritable piece of dead wood!"

Then Tripitaka asked: "What is the honorable age of the Old Abbot?" "Foolishly I have reached my two hundred and seventieth year," said the old monk. When Pilgrim heard this, he said, "You are only my descendant of the ten-thousandth generation!" "Careful!" said Tripitaka, looking at him sternly. "Don't offend people with your brashness!" "And you, Elder," asked the old monk, "how old are you?" "I dare not tell," said Pilgrim. That old monk thought that it was just a foolish remark; he paid no further attention, nor did he ask again. Instead, he called for tea to be served, and a young cleric brought out a tray made of milk-white jade on which there were three cloisonné cups with gold edges. Another youth brought out a white copper pot and poured three cups of scented tea, truly more colorful than camellia buds and more fragrant than cassia flowers. When Tripitaka saw these, he could not cease making compliments, saying, "What marvelous things! What marvelous things! A lovely drink, indeed, and lovely utensils!" "Most disgraceful stuff!" said the old monk. "The holy father resides in the heavenly court of a great nation, and he has witnessed all kinds of rare treasures. Things like these are not worthy of your praise. Since you have come from a noble state, do you have any precious thing which you can show me?" "It's pathetic!" said Tripitaka. "We have no precious thing in the Land of the East; and even if we had, I could not bring it with me because of the distance."

From the side, Pilgrim said, "Master, I saw a cassock the other day in our bag. Isn't that a treasure? Why not take it out and show it to him?" When the other monks heard him mentioning a cassock, they all began to snicker. "What are you laughing at?" asked Pilgrim. The abbot said, "To say that a cassock is a treasure, as you just did, is certainly laughable. If you want to talk about cassocks, priests like us would possess more than twenty or thirty such garments. Take the case of our Patriarch, who has been a monk here for some two hundred and fifty years. He has over seven hundred of them!" He then made the suggestion: "Why not take them out for these people to see?" That old monk certainly thought it was his show this time! He asked the Taoists to open up the storage room and the dhūtas to bring out the chests. They brought out twelve of them and set them down in the courtyard. The padlocks were unlocked; clothes racks were set up on both sides; and ropes were strung all around. One by one, the cassocks were shaken loose and hung up for Tripitaka to see. It was truly a roomful of embroidery, four walls of exquisite silk!

Glancing at them one by one, Pilgrim saw that they were all pieces of fine silk intricately woven and delicate embroidery splashed with gold. He laughed and said, "Fine! Fine! Fine! Now pack them up! Let's take ours out for you to look at." Pulling Pilgrim aside, Tripitaka said softly, "Disciple, don't start a contest of wealth with other people. You and I are strangers away from home, and this may be a mistake!" "Just a look at the cassock," said Pilgrim, "how can that be a mistake?" "You haven't considered this," said Tripitaka. "As the ancients declared, 'The rare object of art should not be exposed to the covetous and deceitful person.' For once he sees it, he will be tempted; and once he is tempted, he will plot and scheme. If you are timid, you may end up with yielding to his every demand; otherwise, injury and loss of life may result, and that's no small matter." "Relax! Relax!" said Pilgrim. "Old Monkey will assume all responsibility!" Look at him! He did not permit any further discussion! Darting away, he untied the bag, and brilliant rays already came flashing through the two layers of oil-paper in which the garment was wrapped. He discarded the paper and took out the cassock. As he shook it loose, a crimson light flooded the room and glorious air filled the courtyard. When the various monks saw it, none could suppress the admiration in his heart and the praise on his lips. It was truly a magnificent cassock! It has hanging on it

Sparkling pearls—marvelous in every way—
And Buddha's treasures in each aspect rare.
Up and down spreads grapevine[3] weave on gorgeous silk;
On every side are hems of fine brocade.
Put it on, and goblins will then be slain.
Step into it, and demons will flee to Hell.
It's made by those hands of gods incarnate;
He who's not a true monk dares not wear it.

When the old monk saw a treasure of such quality, he was, indeed, moved to villainy. Walking forward, he knelt down before Tripitaka, and tears began to fall from his eyes. "This disciple truly has no luck," he said. "Old Abbot," said Tripitaka raising him up, "what do you mean?" "It was already getting late," he said, "when the venerable father spread this treasure out. But my eyes are dim and I can't see clearly. Isn't this my misfortune?" "Bring out the lamps," said Tripitaka, "and you can take a better look." The old monk said, "The treasure of the father is already dazzling; if we light the lamps, it will become much too bright for my eyes, and I'll never be able to see it properly." "How would you like to see it?" said Pilgrim. "If the venerable father is inclined to be gracious," said the old monk, "please permit me to take it back to my room, where I can spend the night looking at it carefully. Tomorrow I shall return it to you before you continue your journey to the west. How would that be?" Startled, Tripitaka began to complain to Pilgrim, saying, "It's all your doing! It's all your doing!" "What are you afraid of?" said Pilgrim laughing. "Let me wrap it up and he can take it away. If there's any mishap, old Monkey will take care of it." Tripitaka could not stop him; he handed the cassock over to the monk, saying, "You may look at it, but you must give it back tomorrow morning, just as it is. Don't spoil or damage it in any way!" The old monk was very pleased. After telling the young cleric to take the cassock inside, he gave instructions for the various monks to sweep out the Zen hall in front. Two rattan beds were sent for and the bedding was prepared, so that the two travelers could rest. He gave further instructions for sending them off with breakfast in the morning, after which everyone left. Master and disciple closed up the hall and slept, and we shall say no more of that.

We shall now tell you about the old monk, who had got hold of the cassock by fraud. He took it beneath the lamps in the back room and, sat in front of it, bawling. The chief priest of the monastery was so startled that he dared not retire first. The young cleric, not knowing the reason for the weeping, went to report to the other monks, saying, "The aged father has been crying, and it's now the second watch and he still hasn't stopped." Two grand-disciples, who were his favorites, went forward to ask him, saying, "Grand-master, why are you crying?" "I'm crying over my ill luck," said the old monk, "for I cannot look at the treasure of the T'ang monk." One of the little monks said, "The aged father is becoming a little senile! The cassock is placed right before you. All you have to do is to untie the package and look at it. Why do you have to cry?" "But I can't look at it for long," said the old monk. "I'm two hundred and seventy years old, and yet I have bargained in vain for those several hundred cassocks. What must I do to acquire that one cassock of his? How can I become the T'ang monk himself?" "The grand-master is erring," said the little monk. "The T'ang monk is a mendicant who had to leave his home and country. You are enjoying the benefits of old age here, and that should be sufficient. Why do you want to be a mendicant like him?" The old monk said, "Though I'm relaxing at home and enjoying my declining years, I have no cassock like his to put on. If I can put it on for just one day, I'll die with my eyes shut, for then I shall not have been a monk in vain in this World of Light." "What nonsense!" said another monk. "If you want to put it on, what's so difficult about that? Tomorrow we will ask them to stay for one more day, and you can wear it the whole day; and if that's not enough, we'll detain them for ten days so that you can wear the cassock all that time. That will be the end of the matter. Why do you have to cry like this?" "Even if they were to be detained for a whole year," said the old monk, "I would only be able to wear it for one year. That's not long-lasting! The moment they want to leave, we will have to return it. How can we make it last?"

As they were speaking, one of the little monks, whose name was Great Wisdom, spoke up: "Aged Father, if you want it to last, that's easy too!" When the old monk heard that, he brightened up. "My son," he said, "what profound thoughts do you have?" Great Wisdom said, "The T'ang monk and his disciple are travelers and are subjected to a lot of stress and strain. So they are fast asleep now. I suppose a few of us who are strong could take up knives and spears, break open the Zen hall, and kill them. We could bury them in the back yard, and only those of us within the family would know about it. We could also take over the white horse and the luggage, but the cassock could be kept as an heirloom. Now, isn't this a plan made to last through posterity?" When the old monk heard this, he was filled with delight. Wiping away his tears, he said, "Good! Good! Good! This plan is absolutely marvelous!" He asked at once for knives and spears.

There was in their midst another little monk, whose name was Big Plan, who was the younger classmate of Great Wisdom. Coming forward, he said, "That plan is no good! If you want to kill them, you must first assess the situation. It's easy to take care of the one with the white face, but the hairy face presents more difficulty. If for some reason you are unable to slay him, you might bring disaster upon yourselves. I have a plan which does not call for knives or spears. How do you feel about this?" "My son," said the old monk, "what sort of plan do you have?" "In the opinion of your little grandson," said Big Plan, "we can call up all the resident heads, both senior and junior, in the eastern wing of this monastery, asking each person and his group to bring a bundle of dried firewood. We'll sacrifice the three rooms of the Zen hall and set fire to them; the people inside will be barred from all exits. Even the horse will be burned with them! If the families who live in front of the temple or behind it should see the fire, we can say that they caused it by their carelessness and burned down our Zen hall. Those two monks will surely be burned to death, but no one will know any better. After that, won't we have the cassock as our heirloom?" When the monks heard this, they were all delighted. "Better! Better! Better! This plan is even more marvelous! More marvelous!" they all said. They sent for the resident heads at once to bring firewood. Alas, this single plan will have the result of

A venerable old monk ending his life,
And the Kuan-yin Zen Hall reduced to dust.

That monastery, you see, had over seventy suites and some two hundred monks reside there. Hordes of them went to fetch firewood, which they stacked around the Zen hall until it was completely surrounded. They then made plans to light the fire, but we shall say no more of that.

We must now tell you about Tripitaka and his disciple, who had already gone to rest. That Pilgrim, however, was a spiritual monkey; though he lay down, he was only exercising his breath to nourish his spirit, with his eyes half-closed. Suddenly he heard people running around outside and the crackling of firewood in the wind. "This is a time for quietness," he said to himself, his suspicion fully aroused, "so why do I hear people walking about? Could they be thieves plotting against us?" Whirling around, he leaped up, and would have opened the door to look outside, had he not been afraid of waking his master. Look at him display his abilities! With one shake of his body he changed into a bee. Truly he had

A sweet mouth and a vicious tail;
A small waist and a light body.
He cut through flowers and willow like a dart;
He sought like a meteor the scented pollen.
His light, tiny body could bear much weight.
His thin wings buzzing could ride the wind.
Descending from rafters and beams,
He crawled out to get a clear view.

He then saw that the various monks were hauling hay and carrying firewood; surrounding the Zen hall, they were about to light the fire. "What my master said has really come true!" said Pilgrim, smiling to himself. "Because they wanted to take our lives and rob us of our cassock, they were moved to such treachery. I suppose I could use my rod to attack them, but I'm afraid they wouldn't be able to withstand it. A little beating, and they would all be dead! Then Master would blame me for acting violently again. O, let it be! I shall see to it that the engineer is hoisted with his own petard[4] so that they won't be able to live here anymore." Dear Pilgrim! With a single somersault, he leaped straight up to the South Heavenly Gate. He so startled the divine warriors P'ang, Liu, Kou, and Pi that they bowed, and so alarmed Ma, Chao, Wên, and Kuan that they bent low. "Good Heavens!" they cried. "That character who disrupted Heaven is here again!" "No need to stand on ceremony, all of you!" said Pilgrim, waving his hand. "And don't be alarmed! I came to find Virūpākṣa, the Broad-Eyed Devarāja."

Before he had finished speaking, the Devarāja arrived and greeted Pilgrim, saying, "It's been a long time! I heard some time ago that the Bodhisattva Kuan-yin asked the Jade Emperor for the services of the Four Sentinels, the Six Gods of Light and Darkness, and the Guardians to protect the T'ang monk as he goes in quest of scriptures in the Western Heaven. She also said that you had become his disciple. How do you have the leisure to be here today?" "Don't mention leisure!" said Pilgrim. "The T'ang monk met some wicked people on his journey, who are about to have him burned up. It's an extreme emergency, and that's why I've come to borrow your Fire-Repelling Cover to save him. Bring it to me quickly; I'll return it the moment I'm finished with it." "You are wrong," said the Devarāja. "If wicked people are starting a fire, you should go find water to save him. Why do you want the Fire-Repelling Cover?" Pilgrim said, "You have no idea what's behind this. If I find water to save him, the fire won't burn, and that will benefit our enemies instead. I want this cover so that only the T'ang monk will be protected from harm. I don't care about the rest! Let them burn! Quickly! Quickly! A little delay, and it may be too late! You will botch up my affairs down below!" "This monkey is still plotting with an evil mind," said the Devarāja, laughing. "After looking out for himself, he is not worried about other people." "Hurry!" said Pilgrim. "Stop wagging your tongue, or you'll upset my great enterprise!" The Devarāja dared not refuse and gave Pilgrim the cover.

Pilgrim took it and descended through the clouds to the roof of the Zen hall, where he covered up the T'ang monk, the white horse, and the luggage. He himself then went to sit on the roof of the back room occupied by the old monk in order to guard the cassock. As he saw the people lighting the fire, he pressed his fingers together to make a magic sign and recited a spell. Facing the ground to the southwest, he took a deep breath and then blew it out. At once a strong wind arose and whipped the fire into a mighty blaze. What a fire! What a fire! You see

Rolling black smoke;
Vaulting red flames.
With rolling black smoke
All the stars vanish from the vast sky;
With vaulting red flames
The earth's lit up, made crimson for a thousand miles.
At the beginning,
What gleaming snakes of gold!
Soon thereafter,

What imposing bloody horses!
The Three Southern Forces display their might.
The Great God of Fire reveals his power.
When dried wood burns in such fire intense,
Why speak of Sui-jên[5] drilling fire from wood?
When colored flames shoot out of hot-oiled doors,
They match even the opened oven of Lao Tzu.
This is how fire rages ruthlessly,
Though no worse than such intended fraud
As not suppressing misdeeds
And abetting violence.
The wind sweeps the fire
And flames fly up for some eight thousand feet;
The fire's helped by the wind,
So ashes burst beyond the NineFold Heaven.
P'ing-p'ing, p'ang-p'ang,
They sound like those firecrackers at year's end.
P'o-p'o, la-la,
They're like the roar of cannons in the camps.
It burns till the Buddha's image cannot flee from the scene,
And the Temple Guardians have no place to hide.
It's like the Red Cliff Campaign in the night,[6]
Surpassing the fire at O-P'ang Palace.[7]

As the saying goes, "One little spark of fire can burn ten thousand acres." In a moment, the strong wind and the raging fire made the entire Kuan-yin Hall glowing red. Look at all those monks! They began to bring out the chests and carry out the drawers, to grab for tables and snatch up pots. A loud wailing filled the whole courtyard. Pilgrim Sun, however, stood guard at the back while the Fire-Repelling Cover securely screened off the Zen hall at the front. The rest of the place was completely lit up; truly the sky was illuminated by brilliant red flames, and bright gold light shone through the walls.

No one knew, however, that when the fire had begun, it had caught the attention of a mountain monster. For, about twenty miles due south of this Kuan-yin Hall there was a Black Wind Mountain, where there was also a Black Wind Cave. A monster in the cave, who happened to turn over in his sleep, noticed that his windows were lit up. He thought that dawn had broken, but when he arose and took another look, he saw instead the brilliant glow of fire burning in the north. Astonished, the monster said, "Good Heavens! There must be a fire in the Kuan-yin Hall. Those monks are so careless! Let me see if I can help them a little!" Dear monster! He rose with his cloud and went at once to the place of fire and smoke, where he discovered that the halls front and back were entirely empty while the fire in the corridors on both sides was raging. With great strides he ran inside and was about to call for water when he saw that there was no fire in the back room. Someone, however, was sitting on the roof whipping up the wind. He began to perceive what was happening and ran quickly inside to look around. In the living room of the old monk, he saw on the table colorful radiance emitted by a package wrapped in a blue blanket. He untied it and discovered that it was a cassock of silk brocade, a rare Buddhist treasure. Thus it is how wealth moves the mind of man! He neither attempted to put out the fire nor called for water. Snatching up the cassock, he committed robbery by taking advantage of the confusion and at once turned his cloud back toward the mountain cave.

The fire raged on until the time of the fifth watch before burning itself out. Look at those monks: weeping and wailing, they went with empty hands and naked bodies to rummage about in the ashes, trying desperately to salvage a scrap or two of metal or valuables. Some attempted to erect a temporary shelter along the walls, while others amid the rubble tried to build a makeshift oven so that rice could be cooked. They were all howling and complaining, but we shall say no more about that.

Now we shall tell you about Pilgrim, who, taking the Fire-Repelling Cover, sent it up to the South Heavenly Gate with one somersault. He handed it back to the Broad-Eyed Devarāja, saying, "Thanks so much for lending it to me!" The Devarāja took it back and said, "The Great Sage is very honest. I was a little worried that if you did not return my treasure, I would have a hard time finding you. I'm glad you brought it right back." "Do you think that old Monkey is the sort of person who steals openly?" said Pilgrim. "As the saying goes, 'Return what you borrow, and again you may borrow!'" "I haven't seen you for a long time," said the Devarāja, "and I would like to invite you to spend some time at my palace. How about it?" Pilgrim said, "Old Monkey can't do what he did before, 'squatting on a rotted bench and dispensing lofty discourse.' Now that I have to protect the T'ang monk, I haven't a moment's leisure. Give me a rain check!" He took leave of the Devarāja quickly and dropped down from the clouds. As the sun arose, he arrived at the Zen hall, where with one shake of his body he changed again into a bee. When he flew inside and resumed his original form, he saw that his master was still sleeping soundly.

"Master," cried Pilgrim, "it's dawn. Get up." Only then did Tripitaka awake; he turned around, saying, "Yes, indeed!" Putting on his clothes, he opened the door and went out. As he raised his head, he saw crumbling walls and seared partitions; the towers, the terraces, and the buildings had all disappeared. "Ah!" he cried, greatly shaken. "How is it that the buildings are all gone? Why are there only scorched walls?" "You are still dreaming!" said Pilgrim. "They had a fire here last night." "Why didn't I know about it?" said Tripitaka. "It's old Monkey who safeguarded the Zen hall," said Pilgrim. "When I saw that Master was sound asleep, I did not disturb you." "If you had the ability to safeguard the Zen hall," said Tripitaka, "why didn't you put out the fire in the other buildings?" "So that you may learn the truth," said Pilgrim laughing, "just as you predicted it yesterday. They fell in love with our cassock and made plans to have us burned to death. If old Monkey had been less alert, we would have been reduced to bone and ashes by now!" When Tripitaka heard these words, he was alarmed and asked, "Was it they who set the fire?" "Who else?" said Pilgrim. "Could it be," asked Tripitaka, "that they mistreated you, and you did this?" Pilgrim said, "Is old Monkey the sort of wretch that would indulge in such sordid business? It really was they who set the fire. When I saw how malicious they were, I admit I did not help them put the fire out. I did, however, manage to provide them with a little wind!" "My God! My God!" said Tripitaka. "When a fire starts, you should get water. How could you provide wind instead?" "You must have heard," said Pilgrim, "what the ancients said: 'If a man has no desire to harm a tiger, a tiger has no intention of hurting a man.' If they hadn't played with fire, would I have played with wind?" "Where's the cassock?" said Tripitaka. "Has it been burned?" "Not at all!" said Pilgrim. "It hasn't been burned, for the fire didn't reach the living quarters of the old monk where the cassock was placed." "I don't care!" said Tripitaka, his resentment rising. "If there's the slightest damage, I'm going to recite that little something and you'll be dead!" "Master!" cried Pilgrim with alarm, "don't start your recitation! I'll

find the cassock and return it to you, and that'll be the end of the
matter. Let me go fetch it so that we can start on our journey."
Tripitaka led the horse while Pilgrim took up the load of luggage.
They left the Zen hall and went to the room at the rear.

We now tell you about those monks, who were still grieving when
they suddenly saw master and disciple approaching with the horse
and the luggage. Scared out of their wits, they all said, "The wronged
souls have come to seek vengeance!" "What wronged souls are seeking vengeance?" shouted Pilgrim. "Give back my cassock quickly!"
All the monks fell to their knees at once, saying as they kowtowed,
"Holy Fathers! Just as a wrong implies an enemy, so a debt has its
proper creditor! If you seek vengeance, please understand that we
had nothing to do with this. It was the old monk who plotted with
Big Plan against you. Don't make us pay for your lives!" "You damnable beasts!" cried Pilgrim angrily. "Who wants you to pay with your
lives? Just give me back the cassock and we'll be going." Two of the
monks who were less timid said to him: "Father, you were supposed
to be burned to death in the Zen hall, and yet now you come to
demand the cassock. Are you indeed a man, or are you a ghost?"
"This bunch of accursed creatures!" said Pilgrim laughing. "Where
was the fire? Go to the front and look at the Zen hall. Then you can
come back and talk." The monks got up and went to the front to look;
not even half an inch of the door, the window, or the screen outside
the Zen hall was scorched. One and all were awe-struck and became
convinced that Tripitaka was a divine monk, and Pilgrim a celestial
guardian. They all went forward to kowtow to them, saying, "We
have eyes but no pupils, and therefore we did not recognize True Men
descending to Earth. Your cassock is at the residence of the old
Patriarch at the back." Tripitaka was deeply saddened by the rows of
crumbling walls and damaged partitions which they went past before
arriving at the Patriarch's chambers, which were indeed untouched
by fire. The monks dashed in, crying, "Aged Father, the T'ang monk
must be a god. He hasn't been burned to death, though we have hurt
ourselves. Let's take the cassock quickly and give it back to him."

But the fact of the matter is that the old monk could not find the
cassock. In addition, most of the buildings in his monastery had been
ruined, and he was, of course, terribly distressed. When he heard the
monks calling, how could he have the courage to reply? Feeling
utterly helpless and incapable of solving his dilemma, he bent forward,

took several great strides, and rammed his head into the wall. How pitiful! The impact made

The brain burst, the blood flow, and his soul disperse;
His head stained the sand as his breathing stopped.

We have a poem as a testimony, which says:

So lamentable is this blind old monk!
In vain he lives among men to such old age.
He wants the cassock forever to keep,
Not knowing how uncommon is Buddha's gift.
If you think what endures can come with ease,
Yours will be sure failure and certain grief.
Big Plan, Great Wisdom, of what use are they?
To gain by others' loss—what empty dreams!

Shocked to tears, the monks cried, "The Patriarch has killed himself. And we can't find the cassock. What shall we do?" "It must have been you who stole it and hid it," said Pilgrim. "Come out, all of you! Give me a complete list of your names and let me check you off the roll one by one." The head residents of all the upper and lower chambers made a thorough accounting of all the monks, the dhūtas, the young novices, and the Taoists in two scrolls, and presented Pilgrim with some two hundred and thirty names. Asking his master to take a seat in the middle, Pilgrim went through the roll and examined the monks one by one. Every person had to loosen his clothes to be searched thoroughly, but there was no cassock. They then went to hunt through the trunks and chests that had been salvaged from the fire, but again there was not the slightest trace of the garment. In dismay, Tripitaka became more and more embittered toward Pilgrim until he began reciting the spell as he sat there. Falling at once to the ground, Pilgrim gripped his head with his hands, hardly able to bear the pain. "Stop the recitation! Stop the recitation!" he cried. "I'll find the cassock." Terrified by what they saw, the various monks went forward and knelt down to plead with Tripitaka, who only then stopped his recitation. Pilgrim leaped straight up and whipped out his rod from his ear. He would have struck at the monks, had not Tripitaka shouted for him to halt, crying, "Monkey! Aren't you afraid of your headache? Do you still want to behave badly? Don't move, and don't hurt people! Let me question them further." The monks kowtowed and begged Tripitaka, saying, "Father, please spare us. Truly we did not see your cassock. It was entirely the fault of that old devil! After he got your cassock last night, he started crying until very late; he didn't even bother to look at it, for all he had on his mind was how he might keep it permanently as an heirloom. That was why he made plans to have you burned to death, but after the fire started, a violent wind arose also. Every one of us was only concerned with putting out the fire and trying to save something. We have no idea where the cassock has gone."

Angrily Pilgrim walked into the Patriarch's room, pulled out the corpse of the old man rammed to death, and stripped him naked. The body was examined carefully, but the treasure was nowhere to be seen. Even if they had dug up three feet of the ground in that room, there would have been not a trace of it. Pilgrim thought silently for a while and then asked: "Is there any monster around here who has become a spirit?" "If father hadn't asked," said the abbot, "he would have never known about this. Southeast of us there is a Black Wind Mountain, in which there is a Black Wind Cave. In the cave is a Black Great King, with whom this deceased old fellow of ours used to discuss the Tao frequently. He is the only monster spirit around here." "How far is the mountain from here?" asked Pilgrim. "Only twenty miles," said the abbot. "That peak which you can see right now is where it is." Pilgrim laughed and said, "Relax, Master! No need for further discussion; it must have been stolen by the black monster." "That place is about twenty miles away," said Tripitaka. "How can you be so sure that it was he?" "You didn't see last night's fire," said Pilgrim, "when its light illuminated great distances, and its brightness penetrated the Threefold Heaven. Not just for twenty miles, but for two hundred miles around it could be seen. I have no doubt that he saw the brilliant glow of the fire and used that opportunity to come here secretly. When he saw that our cassock was a treasure, he grabbed it in the confusion and left. Let old Monkey go find him." "Who will care for me while you are gone?" asked Tripitaka. "You can relax," said Pilgrim. "You have in secret the protection of the gods; and in the open, I shall make sure that the monks wait on you." He then called the monks over, saying, "A few of you can go and bury that old devil, while the others can wait on my master and watch our white horse." The monks at once agreed. Pilgrim said again, "Don't give me any casual reply now, only to grow slack in your service after I'm gone. Those who wait on my master must be cheerful and pleasant; those who look after the white horse must take care that water and hay are fed in proper proportions. If there's the slightest mistake, you can count on meeting this rod. Now watch!'' He whipped out his rod and aimed it at the seared bricked wall; with one stroke, not only did he pulverize the wall, but the impact was so great that it caused seven or eight more walls to collapse. When the various monks saw this, they were all paralyzed with fear. They knelt to kowtow with tears flowing from their eyes and said, "Father, please be assured that we shall be most diligent in caring for the holy father after you are gone. We wouldn't dream of slacking in any way.''

Dear Pilgrim! He swiftly mounted the cloud-somersault and went straight to the Black Wind Mountain to look for the cassock. Thus it was that

Truth-seeking Gold Cicada left Ch'ang-an.[8]
With gifts he went westward, passing blue-green hills.
There were wolves and tigers as he walked along,
Though merchants or scholars were rarely seen.
One foolish monk's envy abroad he met;
His refuge solely was the Great Sage's might.
The fire grew; the wind came and wrecked the Zen hall.
A Black Bear at night stole the embroidered robe.

We do not know whether Pilgrim found the cassock or not, or whether the outcome of his search was good or bad; so you must listen to the explanation in the next chapter.

Seventeen

Pilgrim Sun greatly disturbs the Black Wind Mountain;
Kuan-shih-yin brings to submission the Bear Monster.

We now tell you that when Pilgrim Sun somersaulted into the air, he so terrified the monks, the dhūtas, the young novices, and the Taoists at the Kuan-yin Hall that every person bowed to the sky, saying, "O, Father! So you are actually an incarnate deity who knows how to ride the fog and sail with the clouds! No wonder fire cannot harm you! That ignorant old carcass of ours—how despicable he was! He used all his intelligence only to bring disaster on his own head." "Please rise, all of you," said Tripitaka; "there's no need for regret. Let's hope that he'll find the cassock, and everything will be all right. But if not, I would fear for your lives; for that disciple of mine has a bad temper, and I'm afraid that none of you will escape him." When the monks heard this, they were all panic-stricken; they pleaded with Heaven for the cassock to be found so that their lives would be preserved, but we shall say no more about them for the moment.

We were telling you about the Great Sage Sun. Having leaped up into the air, he gave one twist of his torso and arrived at once at the Black Wind Mountain. Stopping his cloud, he looked carefully and saw that it was indeed a magnificent mountain, especially in this time of spring. You see

Many streams aggressively flowing,
And countless cliffs vying for beauty.
The birds call but no man is seen;
Though flowers fall, the tree's yet scented.
The rain passes, the sky's one moist sheet of blue;
The wind comes, the pines rock like screens of jade.
The mountain grass sprouts,
The wild flowers bloom
On hanging cliffs and high ranges.
The wisteria grows,
The handsome trees bud

On rugged peaks and flat plateaus.
You don't even meet a recluse.
Where can you find a woodsman?
By the stream the cranes drink in pairs;
On the rocks wild apes madly play.
Augustly the branches spread their luscious green,
Basking their splendor in bright mountain mist.

Pilgrim was enjoying the scenery when suddenly he heard voices coming from beyond a lovely grass meadow. With light, stealthy steps, he inched forward and hid himself beneath a cliff to have a peep. He saw three monsters sitting on the ground: a swarthy fellow in the middle, a Taoist to the left, and a white-robed scholar to the right. They were in the midst of an animated conversation, discussing how to establish the *ting* and the oven, how to knead the cinnabar and refine the mercury, the topics of white snow and yellow sprout[1] —all esoteric doctrines of heterodox Taoism. As they were speaking, the swarthy fellow said laughing, "The day after tomorrow will be the date of my mother's labor. Will you two gentlemen pay me a visit?" "Every year we celebrate the Great King's birthday," said the white-robed scholar, "How could we think of not coming this year?" "Last night I came upon a treasure," said the swarthy fellow, "which may be called a brocaded robe of Buddha. It's a most attractive thing, and I think I'm going to use it to enhance my birthday. I plan to give a large banquet, starting tomorrow, and to invite all our Taoist friends of various mountains to celebrate this garment. We shall call the party the Festival of the Buddha Robe. How about that?" "Marvelous! Marvelous!" said the Taoist, laughing. "First I'll come to the banquet tomorrow, and then I'll bring you good wishes on your birthday the day after." When Pilgrim heard them speaking about a robe of Buddha, he was certain that they were referring to his own treasure. Unable to suppress his anger, he leaped clear of his hiding place and raised high the golden-hooped rod with both hands, shouting, "You larcenous monsters! You stole my cassock. What Festival of the Buddha Robe do you think you are going to have? Give it back to me at once, and don't try to run away!" Wielding his rod, he struck at their heads. In panic, the swarthy fellow fled by riding the wind, and the Taoist escaped by mounting the clouds. The white-robed scholar, however, was killed by one stroke of the rod, and he turned out to be the spirit of a white-spotted snake when Pilgrim pulled his body over for closer examination. He picked up the corpse again and broke it into several pieces before proceeding deep into the mountain to look for the swarthy fellow. Passing pointed peaks and rugged ridges, he found himself in front of a hanging cliff with a cave dwelling below it. You see.

Mist and smoke abundant,
Cypress and pine umbrageous.
Mist and smoke abundant, their hues surround the door;
Cypress and pine umbrageous, their green entwines the gate.
Flat, dried wood supports a bridge.
Wisterias coil round the ridge.
Birds carrying red petals reach the cloudy gorge.
And deer tread on florets to comb the rocky flats.
Before that door the flowers bloom with the season
As the wind wafts their fragrance.
Atop the dyke-shading willows the oriole sings;
Over the sweet peach by the bank the butterfly flits.
This rustic spot, though not most worthy of acclaim,
Approximates still the beauty of Mount P'êng-lai.[2]

Pilgrim went to the door and found that the two stone doors were tightly closed. On top of the door was a stone tablet, on which was plainly written in large letters, "Black Wind Mountain, Black Wind Cave." He lifted his rod to beat at the door, crying, "Open the door!" A little demon who stood guard at the door came out and asked: "Who are you, that you dare beat at our immortal cave?" "You damnable beast!" scolded Pilgrim. "What sort of a place is this, that you dare assume the title of 'immortal'? Is the word 'immortal' for you to use? Hurry inside and tell that swarthy fellow to bring out your venerable father's cassock at once. Then I may spare the lives of the whole nest of you." The little demon ran swiftly inside and reported: "Great King! You won't have a Festival of the Buddha Robe. There's a monk with a hairy face and a thunder-god mouth outside demanding the cassock." That swarthy fellow, after being chased by Pilgrim from the grass meadow, had just managed to reach the cave. He had not even been able to sit down when he again heard this announcement, and he thought to himself: "I wonder where this fellow came from, so arrogant that he dared show up making demands at my door!" He asked for his armor, and, after putting it on, he walked outside holding a lance with black tassels. Pilgrim stood on

one side of the gate, holding his iron rod and glaring. The monster
indeed cut a formidable figure:

A bowl-like helmet of dark burnished steel;
A black-gold cuirass that shone most bright.
A black silk robe with wide wind-bagging sleeves,
And dark green sashes with long, long tassels.
He held in his hands a black-tasseled lance.
He wore on his feet two black-leather boots.
His eyes' golden pupils like lightning flashed.
He was thus in this mountain the Black Wind King.

"This fellow," said Pilgrim smiling to himself, "looks exactly like a
kiln worker or a coalminer. He must scrub charcoal here for a living!
How did he get to be black all over?" The monster called out in a
loud voice: "What kind of a monk are you that you dare to be so
impudent around here?" Rushing up to him with his iron rod,
Pilgrim roared: "No idle conversation! Return the cassock of your
venerable grandfather at once!" "What monastery are you from,
bonze?" asked the monster, "and where did you lose your cassock
that you dare show up at my place and demand its return?" "My
cassock," said Pilgrim, "was stored in the back room of the Kuan-yin
Hall due north of here. Because of the fire there, you committed
robbery by taking advantage of the confusion; after making off with
the garment, you even wanted to start a Festival of the Buddha Robe
to celebrate your birthday. Do you deny this? Give it back to me
quickly, and I'll spare your life. If you but mutter half a 'no,' I'll overturn the Black Wind Mountain and level the Black Wind Cave. Your
whole cave of demons will be pulverized!"

When the monster heard these words, he laughed scornfully and
said, "You audacious creature! You yourself set the fire last night,
for you were the one who summoned the wind on top of the roof. I
took the cassock all right, but what are you going to do about it?
Where do you come from, and what is your name? What ability do
you have, that you dare mouth such reckless words?" Pilgrim said,
"So you don't recognize your venerable grandfather! He is the
disciple of the Master of the Law, Tripitaka, who happens to be the
brother of the Throne in the Great T'ang Nation. My surname is Sun,
and my given name is Wu-k'ung Pilgrim. If I tell you my abilities,
you'll be frightened out of your wits and die right on the spot!" "I

won't," said the monster. "Tell me what abilities you have." "My
son," said Pilgrim, laughing, "brace yourself! Listen carefully!
    Great since my youth was my magic power;
    I changed with the wind to display my might.
    Long I trained my nature and practiced Truth
    To flee the wheel of karma with my life.
    With mind sincere I always sought the Way;
    Seedlings of herbs I plucked on Mount Ling-t'ai.[3]
    There was an old immortal in that mountain.
    His age: a hundred and eight thousand years!
    He became my master most solemnly
    And showed me the way to longevity,
    Saying that in my body were physic and pills
    Which one would work in vain to seek outside.
    He gave me those high secrets of the gods;
    With no foundation I would have been lost.
    My inner light relumed, I sat in peace
    As sun and moon mated within my body.[4]
    I thought of nothing, all my desires gone;
    My body strengthened, my six senses cleansed.
    From age back to youth was an easy boon;
    To join the sages was no distant goal.
    Three years without leaks[5] made a godlike frame,
    Immune to sufferings known to mortal men.
    I played through the Ten Islets and the Three Isles,
    Making the rounds at Heaven's very edge.
    I lived like that for some three hundred years,
    Though not yet ascended to the Ninefold Heaven.
    Taming sea dragons brought me treasure true:
    The golden-hooped rod I did find below.
    As field marshal at the Flower-Fruit Mount,
    Monsters I gathered at Water-Curtain Cave.
    Then the Jade Emperor gave to me the name,
    Equal to Heaven—such, the rank most high.
    Thrice I caused havoc in Divine Mists Hall;
    Once I purloined the peaches from Wang-mu.
    Thus came a hundred thousand men divine
    To curb me with their rows of spears and swords.

The Devarāja was beaten back to Heaven,
While Naṭa in pain led his troops and fled.
Hsien-shêng Master[6] knew transformations well;
I waged a contest with him and I fell.
Lao Tzu, Kuan-yin, and the Jade Emperor
All watched the battle at South Heaven Gate.
When Lao Tzu decided to lend his help,
Erh-lang brought me to the Heavenly judge.
To the monster-routing pillar I was tied;
The gods were told to have my head cut off.
Failing to harm me with either sledge or sword,
They sought to burn me with fierce thunderclaps.
What skills indeed did this old Monkey have,
Who was not even half a whit afraid!
Into Lao Tzu's brazier they sent me next,
To have me slowly cooked by fire divine.
The day the lid was opened, I jumped out,
And ran through Heaven brandishing a rod.
Back and forth I prowled with none to stop me,
Making havoc through all thirty-six Heavens.
Then Tathāgata revealed his power:
Under the Wu-hsing Mountain[7] he clamped my body,
And there I squirmed for a full five hundred years
Till by luck Tripitaka left the T'ang Court.
Yielded to Truth, I now go to the West
To see Jade Eyebrows[8] at Great Thunderclap.
Go and ask in the four corners of the universe:
You'll learn I'm the famous ranking daimon of all times!''

When the monster heard these words, he laughed and said, "So you are the pi-ma-wên who disturbed the Celestial Palace?" What most annoyed Pilgrim was when people called him pi-ma-wên. The moment he heard that name, he lost his temper. "You monstrous rogue!" he shouted. "You would not return the cassock you stole, and yet you dare insult this holy monk. Don't run away! Watch this rod!" The swarthy fellow jumped aside to dodge the blow; wielding his long lance, he went forward to meet his opponent. That was some battle between the two of them:

The compliant rod,
The black-tasseled lance.

Two men display their power before the cave:
Stabbing at the heart and face;
Striking at the head and arm.
This one proves handy with a death-dealing rod;
That one tilts the lance for swift, triple jabs.
The "white tiger climbing the mountain" extends his paws;
The "yellow dragon lying on the road"⁹ turns his back.
With colored mists flying
And bright flashes of light,
The strength of two godlike monsters is yet to be tried.
One is the truth-seeking, Equal-to-Heaven Sage;
One is the Great Black King who became a spirit.
The reason for this battle waged in the hills:
It's the cassock for which each one now aims to kill!

That monster fought with Pilgrim for more than ten rounds. They fought until about noon, but the battle was a draw. Using his lance to halt the rod for a moment, the swarthy fellow said, "Pilgrim Sun, let us put away our weapons for the time being. Let me have some lunch first, and then I'll wage a further contest with you." "Accursed beast!" said Pilgrim. "You want to be a hero? Which hero wants to eat after fighting for merely half a day? Consider old Monkey, who was imprisoned beneath the mountain for altogether five hundred years and he hadn't even tasted a drop of water. So, what's this about being hungry? Don't give me any excuses and don't run away! Give me back my cassock, and I'll allow you to go and eat." But that monster only managed to throw one more feeble thrust with his lance before dashing into the cave and shutting his stone doors. He dismissed his little demons and made preparations for the banquet, writing out invitation cards to the monster kings of various mountains, but we shall say no more about that.

We must tell you that Pilgrim had no success in breaking down the door and so had to return to the Kuan-yin Hall. The monks of that monastery had already buried the old monk, and they were all gathered in the back room to minister to the T'ang monk, serving him lunch soon after he had finished breakfast. As they were scurrying about fetching soup and hauling water, Pilgrim was seen descending from the sky. The monks bowed courteously and received him into the back room to see Tripitaka. "Wu-k'ung," said Tripitaka, "so you've returned. How is the cassock?" "At least I found the real culprit," said Pilgrim. "It was a good thing that we did not punish these monks, for the monster of Black Wind Mountain did steal it. I went secretly looking for him, and saw him seated on a beautiful grass meadow having a conversation with a white-robed scholar and an old Taoist. He was, in a sense, making a confession without being tortured, saying something about the day after tomorrow being his birthday, when he would invite all the other griffins for the occasion. He also mentioned that he had found an embroidered Buddha robe last night, in celebration of which he was planning to throw a large banquet, calling it the Festival of the Buddha Robe. Old Monkey rushed up to them and struck out with his rod; the swarthy fellow changed into the wind and left, and the Taoist also disappeared. The white-robed scholar, however, was killed, and he turned out to be a white-spotted snake who had become a spirit. I quickly chased the swarthy fellow to his cave and demanded that he come out to fight. He had already admitted that he took the cassock, but we fought to a draw after half a day of battle. The monster returned to his cave because he wanted to eat; he closed his stone doors tightly and refused to fight anymore. I came back to see how you were and to make this report to you. Since I know the whereabouts of the cassock, I'm not worried about his unwillingness to give it back to me."

When the various monks heard this, some of them folded their hands while others kowtowed, all chanting, "Namo Amitābha! Now that the whereabouts of the cassock is known, we have a claim to our lives again." "Don't be jubilant yet," said Pilgrim, "for I have not yet recovered it, nor has my master left. Wait until we have the cassock so that my master can walk peacefully out of this door before you start cheering. If there's the slightest mishap, old Monkey is no customer to be provoked, is he? Have you served some good things to my master? Have you given our horse plenty of hay?" "We have, we have, we have!" cried the monks hastily. "Our service to the holy monk has not slackened in the least!" "You were gone only half a day," said Tripitaka, "and I have been served tea three times and have had two vegetarian meals. They didn't dare slight me. You should therefore make a great effort to get back the cassock." "Don't rush!" said Pilgrim. "Since I know where he is, I shall certainly capture this fellow and return the garment to you. Relax! Relax!"

As they were speaking, the abbot brought in some more vegetarian dainties to serve to the holy monk Sun. Pilgrim ate some and left at once on the hallowed cloud to search for the monster. As he was traveling, he saw a little demon approaching from the main road, who had a box made of peartree wood wedged between his left arm and his body. Suspecting that something important was inside the box, Pilgrim raised his rod and brought it down hard on the demon's head. Alas, the demon could not take such a blow! He was instantly reduced to a meat patty, which Pilgrim tossed to the side of the road. When he opened the box, there was indeed an invitation slip, on which was written:

Your student-servant, the Bear, most humbly addresses the Exalted Aged Dean of the Golden Pool. For the gracious gifts you have bestowed on me on several occasions I am profoundly grateful. I regret that I was unable to assist you last night when you were visited by the God of Fire, but I suppose that Your Holy Eminence has not been adversely affected in any way. Your student by chance has acquired a Buddha robe, and this occasion calls for a festive celebration. I have therefore prepared with care some fine wine for your enjoyment, with the sincere hope that Your Holy Eminence will be pleased to give us a visit. This invitation is respectfully submitted two days in advance.

When Pilgrim saw this, he roared with laughter, saying, "That old carcass! He didn't lose anything by his death! So he was the ally of a monster! Small wonder that he lived to his two hundred and seventieth year! That monster, I suppose, must have taught him some little magic like feeding on his breath, and that's how he enjoys such longevity. I can still remember how he looks. Let me change myself into that monk and go to the cave to see where my cassock is located. If I can manage it, I'll take it back without wasting my energy." Dear Great Sage! He recited a spell, faced the wind, and changed at once into an exact semblance of that old monk. Putting away his iron rod, he strode to the cave, crying, "Open the door!" When the little demon who stood at the door saw such a figure, he quickly made his report inside: "Great King, the Elder of the Golden Pool has arrived." Greatly surprised, the monster said, "I just sent a little one to deliver an invitation to him, but he could not possibly have reached his destination even at this moment. How could the old monk arrive so quickly? I suppose the little one did not run into him on the way, but Pilgrim Sun must have asked him to come here for the cassock. You, steward, hide the cassock! Don't let him see it!"

Walking through the front door, Pilgrim saw in the courtyard pines and bamboos sharing their green, peaches and plums competing in their glamor; flowers were blooming everywhere, and the air was heavy with the scent of orchids. It was, in truth, a heavenly cave dwelling. He saw, moreover, a parallel couplet mounted on both sides of the second doorway which read:

A retreat deep in the mountains without worldly cares.

A divine cave secluded—what joy serene.

Pilgrim said to himself, "This monster is one who withdraws from the dirt and the dust, one who knows his fate." He walked through the door and proceeded further; when he passed through the third doorway, he saw carved beams with elaborate ornaments and large windows brightly decorated. Then the swarthy fellow appeared, wearing a casual jacket made of fine dark-green silk, topped by a crow-green cape of figured damask; he wore a head-wrap of black cloth and was shod in a pair of black suede boots. When he saw Pilgrim entering, he tidied his clothes and went down the steps to receive him, saying, "Golden Pool, old friend, we haven't seen each other for days. Please take a seat! Please take a seat!" Pilgrim greeted him ceremoniously, after which, they sat down and drank tea. After tea, the monster bowed low and said, "I just sent you a brief note, humbly inviting you to visit me the day after tomorrow. Why does my old friend grant me that pleasure today, already?" "I was just coming to pay my respects," said Pilgrim, "and I did not anticipate meeting your kind messenger. When I saw that there was going to be a Festival of the Buddha Robe, I came hurriedly, hoping to see the garment." "My old friend may be mistaken," said the monster laughing. "This cassock originally belonged to the T'ang monk, who was staying at your place. Why would you want to look at it here, since you must surely have seen it before?" "Your poor monk," answered Pilgrim, "did borrow it, but he did not have the opportunity last night to examine it before it was taken by the Great King. Moreover, our monastery, including all our belongings, was destroyed by fire, and the disciple of that T'ang monk was rather bellicose about the matter. In all that confusion, I couldn't find the cassock anywhere, not knowing that the Great King in his good fortune found it. That is why I came specially to see it."

As they were speaking, one of the little demons out on patrol came back to report: "Great King, disaster! The junior officer who went to deliver the invitation was beaten to death by Pilgrim Sun and left by the wayside. Our enemy followed the clue and changed himself into the Golden Pool Elder so that he could obtain the Buddha robe by fraud." When the monster heard that, he said to himself, "I was wondering already why he came today, and in such a hurried manner too! So, it's really he!" Leaping up, he grabbed his lance and aimed it at Pilgrim. Whipping out the rod from his ear, Pilgrim assumed his original form and parried the lance. They rushed from the living room to the front courtyard, and from there they fought their way out to the front door. The monsters in the cave were frightened out of their wits; young and old in that household were horror-stricken. This fierce contest before the mountain was even unlike the last one. What a fight!

This Monkey King boldly posed as a monk;
That swarthy man wisely concealed the robe.
Back and forth went their clever repartee,
Adapting to each instant perfectly.
He would see the cassock but had no means:
This runic treasure, what a mystery true!
The small imp on patrol announced mishap;
The old fiend in anger revealed his power.
They fought their way out of the Black Wind Cave,
The rod and the lance forced a trial by might.
The rod checked the lance, making loud noises;
The lance met the rod, causing sparks to fly.
The changes of Wu-k'ung, all unknown to men;
The monster's magic skills, so rare on earth.
This one wanted for his birthday fete a Buddha robe.
Would that one with no cassock go home in peace?
The bitter fight this time seemed without end.
Even a live Buddha descending could not break them up!

From the entrance of the cave the two of them fought up to the peak of the mountain, and from the peak of the mountain they fought their way up to the clouds. Belching wind and fog, kicking up sand and rocks, they fought till the red sun sank toward the west, but neither of them could gain the upper hand. The monster said, "Hey, Sun! Stop for a moment! It's getting too late to fight any more. Go away! Come back tomorrow morning, and we'll decide your fate." "Don't run away, my son," cried Pilgrim. "If you want to fight, act like a fighter! Don't give me the excuse that it's getting late." With his rod, he rained blows indiscriminately on his opponent's head and face, but the swarthy fellow changed once more into a clear breeze and went back to his cave. Tightly bolting his stone doors, he refused to come out.

Pilgrim had no alternative except to go back to the Kuan-yin Hall. Dropping down from the clouds, he said, "Master." Tripitaka, who was waiting for him with bulging eyes, was delighted to see him; but when he did not see the cassock, he became frightened again. "How is it that you still have not brought back the cassock?" he asked. Pilgrim took out from his sleeve the invitation slip and handed it over to Tripitaka, saying, "Master, the monster and that old carcass used to be friends. He sent a little demon here with this invitation for him to go to a Festival of the Buddha Robe. I killed the little demon and changed into the form of the old monk to get inside the cave. I managed to trick him into giving me a cup of tea, but when I asked for the cassock, he refused to show it to me. As we were sitting there, my identity was leaked by someone on patrol in the mountain, and we began to fight. The battle lasted until this early evening and ended in a draw. When the monster saw that it was late, he slipped back into the cave and tightly bolted up his stone door. Old Monkey had no choice but to return here for the moment." "How's your skill as a fighter when compared with his?" asked Tripitaka. "Not much better," said Pilgrim. "We are quite evenly matched." Tripitaka then read the invitation slip and handed it to the abbot, saying, "Could it be that your master was also a monster-spirit?" Falling to his knees, the abbot said, "Old Father, my master is human. Because that Great Black King attained the way of humanity through self-cultivation, he frequently came to the monastery to discuss religious texts with my master. He imparted to my master a little of the magic of nourishing one's essence and feeding on breath; hence they address each other as friends." "This bunch of monks," said Pilgrim, "don't have the aura of monsters: each one has a round head pointing to the sky and a pair of feet set flat on the earth. They are a little taller and heavier than old Monkey, but they are no monsters. Look at what's written on the slip: your student-servant, the Bear. This creature must be a black bear who has become a spirit." Tripitaka said, "I have heard from the ancients that the bear and the ape are of the same kind. They are all beasts, in other words. How can this bear

become a spirit?" "Old Monkey is also a beast," said Pilgrim laughing,
"but I became the Great Sage, Equal to Heaven. Is he any different?
All the creatures of this world who possess the nine apertures can
become immortals through the cultivation of the Great Art." "You
just said that the two of you were evenly matched," said Tripitaka
again. "How can you defeat him and get back my cassock?" "Lay
off! Lay off!" said Pilgrim. "I know what to do." As they were discussing the matter, the monks brought in the evening meal for
master and disciple. Afterwards, Tripitaka asked for lamps to go to
the Zen hall in front to rest. The rest of the monks reclined against
the walls beneath some temporary awnings and slept, while the back
rooms were given to accommodate the senior and junior abbots. It
was now late. You see

The Silver Stream aglow;
The air perfectly pure;
The sky full of bright and twinkling stars;
The river marked by receding tide.
All sounds are hushed;
All hills emptied of birds.
The fisherman's fire dies by the brook;
The lamps grow faint on the pagoda.
Last night ācāryas sounded drums and bells.
Only weeping is heard throughout this night!

So they spent the night in the Zen hall, but Tripitaka was thinking
about the cassock. How could he possibly sleep well? As he tossed
and turned, he suddenly saw the windows growing bright. He arose
at once and called: "Wu-k'ung, it's morning. Go find the cassock
quickly." Pilgrim leaped up with a bound and saw that the monks
were bringing in washing water. "All of you," said Pilgrim, "take
care to minister to my master. Old Monkey is leaving." Getting up
from his bed, Tripitaka clutched at him, asking, "Where are you
going?" "Come to think of it," said Pilgrim, "this whole affair reveals
the irresponsibility of the Bodhisattva Kuan-yin. She has a Zen hall
here where she has enjoyed the incense and worship of all the local
people, and yet she can permit a monster-spirit to be her neighbor.
I'm leaving for South Sea to find her for a little conversation. I'm
going to ask her to come here and demand that the monster return
the cassock to us." "When will you be back?" said Tripitaka. "Probably right after breakfast," said Pilgrim. "At latest, I should be back

around noon, when everything should be taken care of. All of you
monks must take care to wait on my master. Old Monkey is leaving."

He said he was leaving, and the next instant he was already out
of sight. In a moment, he arrived at South Sea, where he stopped his
cloud to look around. He saw

A vast expanse of ocean,
Where water and sky seemed to merge.
Auspicious light shrouded the earth;
Hallowed air brightened the world.
Endless snow-capped waves surged up to Heaven;
Layers of misty billows washed out the sun.
Water flying everywhere;
Waves churning all around.
Water flying everywhere rolled like thunderclaps;
Waves churning all around boomed like cannonade.
Speak not merely of water;
Let's look more at the center.
The treasure-filled mountain of five dazzling colors:
Red, yellow, green, deep purple, and blue.
If this be Kuan-yin's scenic region true,
Look further at Potalaka of South Sea.
What a splendid place!
The tall mountain peak
Cut through airy space.
In its midst were thousands of rare flowers,
A hundred kinds of divine herbs.
The wind stirred the precious trees;
The sun shone on the golden lotus.
Glazed tiles covered the Kuan-yin Hall;
Tortoiseshell spread before the Tidal-Sound Cave.
In the shades of green willow the parrot spoke;
Within the bamboo grove the peacock sang.
On rocks with grains like fingerprints,
The guardians fierce and solemn.
Before the cornelian foreshore,
Mokṣa strong and heroic.

Pilgrim, who could hardly take his eyes off the marvelous scenery,
lowered his cloud and went straight to the bamboo grove. The
various deities were there to receive him, saying, "The Bodhisattva

told us some time ago about the conversion of the Great Sage, for whom she had nothing but praise. You are supposed to be accompanying the T'ang monk at this moment. How do you have the time to come here?" "Because I am accompanying the T'ang monk," said Pilgrim, "I had an incident on our journey which I must see the Bodhisattva about. Please announce my arrival." The deities went to the mouth of the cave to make the announcement, and the Bodhisattva asked him to enter. Obeying the summons, Pilgrim went before the bejeweled lotus platform and knelt down. "What are you doing here?" asked the Bodhisattva. "On his journey my master came across one of your Zen halls," said Pilgrim, "where you receive the services of fire and incense from the local people. But you also permitted a Black Bear Spirit to live nearby and to steal the cassock of my master. Several times I tried to get it back but without success. I have come specifically to ask you for it." The Bodhisattva said, "This monkey still speaks insolently! If the Bear Spirit stole your cassock, why did you come to ask me for it? It was all because you had the presumption, you wretched ape, to show off your treasure to sinister people. Moreover, you had your share of evildoing when you called for the wind to intensify the fire, which burned down one of my way stations down below. And yet you still want to be rowdy around here?" When Pilgrim heard the Bodhisattva speaking like that, he knew that she had knowledge of past and future events. Hurriedly he bowed with humility and said, "Bodhisattva, please pardon the offense of your disciple. It was as you said. But I'm upset by the monster's refusal to give us back our cassock, and my master is threatening to recite that spell of his at any moment. I can't bear the headache, and that's why I have come to cause you inconvenience. I beseech the Bodhisattva to have mercy on me and help me capture that monster, so that we may recover the garment and proceed toward the West." "That monster has great magical power," said the Bodhisattva, "really just as strong as yours. All right! For the sake of the T'ang monk, I'll go with you this time." When Pilgrim heard this, he bowed again in gratitude and asked the Bodhisattva to leave at once. They mounted the blessed clouds and soon arrived on the Black Wind Mountain. Dropping down from the clouds, they followed a path to look for the cave.

As they were walking, they saw a Taoist coming down the mountain slope, holding a glass tray on which there were two magic pills.

Pilgrim ran right into him, whipped out his rod, and brought it down squarely on his head, with one blow causing the brains to burst and blood to shoot out from the neck. Completely stunned, the Bodhisattva said, "Monkey, you are still so reckless! He didn't steal your cassock; he neither knew nor wronged you. Why did you kill him with one blow?" "Bodhisattva," said Pilgrim, "you may not recognize him, but he is a friend of the Black Bear Spirit. Yesterday he was having a conversation with a white-robed scholar on the grass meadow. Since they were invited to the cave of the Black Bear Spirit, who was going to give a Festival of the Buddha Robe to celebrate his birthday, this Taoist said that he would first go to celebrate his friend's birthday today and then attend the festival tomorrow. That's how I recognized him. He must have been on his way to celebrate the monster's birthday." "If that's how it is, all right," said the Bodhisattva. Pilgrim then went to pick up the Taoist and discovered that he was a gray wolf. The tray, which had fallen to one side, had an inscription on the bottom: "Made by Ling-hsü Tzu.[10]"

When Pilgrim saw this, he laughed and said, "What luck! What luck! Old Monkey will benefit; the Bodhisattva will save some energy. This monster may be said to have made a confession without torture, while the other monster may be destined to perish today." "What are you saying, Wu-k'ung?" said the Bodhisattva. "Bodhisattva," said Pilgrim, "I, Wu-k'ung, have a saying: plot should be met with plot. I don't know whether you will listen to me or not." "Speak up!" said the Bodhisattva. "Look, Bodhisattva!" said Pilgrim. "There are two magic pills on this little tray, and they are introductory gifts which we shall present to the monster. Beneath the tray is the four-word inscription "Made by Ling-hsü Tzu," and they shall serve as our contact with the monster. If you will listen to me, I'll give you a plan which will dispense with weapons and do away with combat. In a moment, the monster will meet pestilence; in the twinkling of an eye, the Buddha robe will reappear. If you do not follow my suggestion, you may go back to the West, and I, Wu-k'ung, will return to the east; the Buddha robe will be counted as lost, while Tripitaka T'ang will have journeyed in vain." "This monkey is pretty clever with his tongue!" said the Bodhisattva laughing. "Hardly!" said Pilgrim. "But it is a small plan!" "What's your plan?" said the Bodhisattva. "Since the tray has this inscription beneath it," said Pilgrim, "the Taoist himself must be this Ling-hsü Tzu. If you agree with me, Bodhisattva, you can change yourself into this Taoist. I'll take one of the pills and then change myself into another pill—a slightly bigger one, that is. Take this tray with the two magic pills and present them to the monster as his birthday gift. Let the monster swallow the bigger pill, and old Monkey will accomplish the rest. If he is unwilling to return the Buddha robe, old Monkey will make one—even if I have to weave it with his guts!"

The Bodhisattva could not think of a better plan and she had to nod her head to show her approval. "Well?" said Pilgrim, laughing. Immediately the Bodhisattva exercised her great mercy and boundless power. With her infinite capacity for transformation, her mind moved in perfect accord with her will, and her will with her body: in one blurry instant, she changed into the form of the immortal Ling-hsü Tzu.

Her crane's-down cloak swept by the wind,
With light, airy steps she walked.
Her face, aged like cypress and pine,
Was peerlessly fresh and fair.
Yesterday, today, forever:
An all transcendent Absolute!
To one Law all beings must turn,
But hers was no demonic self.

When Pilgrim saw the transformation, he cried, "Marvelous, Marvelous! Is the monster the Bodhisattva, or is the Bodhisattva the monster?" The Bodhisattva laughed and said, "Wu-k'ung, the Bodhisattva, and the monster—they all exist in a single thought, for originally they are nothing." Immediately enlightened, Pilgrim turned around and changed at once into a magic pill:

A rolling-pan pearl, it stabilizes all;[11]
Of formula unknown it's round and bright.
"Three time three,"[12] as if fused at Kou-lou Mount;[13]
"Six times six," as if formed with Shao Wêng's help.[14]
It blazes like glazed tile and yellow gold;
It shines like sunlight and the mani pearl.
Coated outside by mercury and lead,
Not easily measured such power it has.

The pill into which Pilgrim had changed was slightly larger than the

other one. Making a mental note of it, the Bodhisattva took the glass
tray and went straight to the entrance of the monster's cave. She
paused to look around and saw

Treacherous cliffs and ridges;
Clouds forming around the peak;
Jade-green pines and cypresses;
And wind rustling in the woods.
Treacherous cliffs and ridges:
Truly such a place was made for monsters and not for man!
But jade-green pines and cypresses
Might seem a fitting spot for hermits to seek the Way.
There was a stream in the mountain;
And there was water in the stream,
Its current murmured lightly as a lute
Worthy to cleanse your ears.
There were deer on the cliff;
There were cranes in the woods,
Where softly hummed the music of the spheres
To uplift your spirit.
So it was the luck of the bogus immortal that Bodhi came,
Who vowed unlimited mercy to vouchsafe.

After looking over the place, the Bodhisattva was secretly pleased and
said to herself, "If this cursed beast could occupy such a mountain, it
might be that he is destined to attain the Tao." Thus she was already
inclined to be merciful.

When she walked up to the cave's entrance, some of the little
demons standing guard there recognized her, saying, "Ling-hsü Immortal has arrived." Some went to announce her arrival, while
others greeted her. Just then, the monster came bowing out the door,
saying, "Ling-hsü, you honor my humble abode with your divine
presence!" "This humble Taoist," said the Bodhisattva, "respectfully
submits a magic pill as a birthday gift." After the two of them had
bowed to each other, they were seated. The incidents of the day
before were mentioned, but the Bodhisattva made no reply. Instead,
she took up the tray and said, "Great King, please accept the humble
regard of this little Taoist." She chose the large pill and pushed it over
to the monster, saying, "May the Great King live for a thousand
years!" The monster then pushed the other pill over to the Bodhisattva, saying, "I wish to share this with Ling-hsü Tzu." After this

ceremonial presentation, the monster was about to swallow it, but the pill rolled by itself right down his throat. It changed back into its original form and began to do physical exercises! The monster fell to the floor, while the Bodhisattva revealed her true form and recovered the Buddha Robe from the monster. Pilgrim then left the monster's body through his nose, but fearing that the monster might still be truculent, the Bodhisattva threw a fillet on his head. As he arose, the monster did indeed pick up his lance to thrust at Pilgrim. The Bodhisattva, however, rose into the air and began reciting her spell. The spell worked, and the monster felt excruciating pain on his head; throwing away the lance, he rolled wildly all over the ground. In midair, the Handsome Monkey King nearly collapsed with laughter; down below the Black Bear Monster almost rolled himself to death on the floor.

"Cursed beast." said the Bodhisattva, "will you now surrender?" "I surrender," said the monster without any hesitation, "please spare my life!" Fearing that too much effort would have been wasted, Pilgrim wanted to strike at once. Quickly stopping him, the Bodhisattva said, "Don't hurt him; I have some use for him." Pilgrim said, "Why not destroy a monster like him, for of what use can he be?" "There's no one guarding the rear of my Potalaka Mountain," said the Bodhisattva, "and I want to take him back there to be a Great Mountain-Guardian God." "Truly a salvific and merciful goddess," said Pilgrim laughing, "who will not hurt a single sentient being. If old Monkey knew a spell like that, he'd recite it a thousand times. That would finish off as many black bears as there are around here!"

So, we shall tell you about the monster, who regained consciousness after a long time; convinced by the unbearable pain, he had no choice but to fall on his knees and beg: "Spare my life, for I'm willing to submit to Truth!" Dropping down from the blessed luminosity, the Bodhisattva then touched his head and gave him the commandments, telling him to wait on her, holding the lance. So it was with the Black Bear:

Today his vaulting ambition is checked;
This time his boundless license has been curbed.

"You may return now, Wu-k'ung," instructed the Bodhisattva, "and serve the T'ang monk attentively. Don't start any more trouble with your carelessness." "I'm grateful that the Bodhisattva was willing to come this far to help," said Pilgrim, "and it is my duty as disciple to see you back." "You may be excused," said the Bodhisattva. Holding the cassock, Pilgrim then kowtowed to her and left, while the Bodhisattva led the bear and returned to the great ocean. We have a testimonial poem:

Auspicious light surrounds the golden form:
What maze of colors so worthy of praise!
With her great mercy she succors mankind,
This Revealed Gold Lotus scans the whole world.
She came for the cause of scripture seeking;
Then she withdrew, as ever chaste and pure.
The fiend converted, she left for the sea;
The Buddhist regained a brocade-cassock.

We do not know what happened afterwards, and you must listen to the explanation in the next chapter.

Eighteen

At the Kuan-yin Hall the T'ang monk escapes his ordeal;
At the Kao Village the Great Sage disposes of
  the monster.

Pilgrim took leave of the Bodhisattva; lowering the direction of his cloud, he hung the cassock on one of the fragrant cedars nearby. He took out his rod and fought his way into the Black Wind Cave. But where could he find even a single little demon inside? The fact of the matter is that when they saw the Bodhisattva revealed, causing the old monster to roll all over the ground, they all scattered. Pilgrim, however, was not to be stopped; he piled dried wood around the several doorways in the cave and started a fire in the front and in the back. The whole Black Wind Cave was reduced to a "Red Wind Cave"! Picking up the cassock, Pilgrim then mounted the auspicious luminosity and went north.

  We now tell you about Tripitaka, who was impatiently waiting for Pilgrim's return and wondering whether Bodhisattva had consented to come and help, or whether Pilgrim on some pretext had left him. He was filled with such foolish thoughts and wild speculations when he saw bright, rose-colored clouds approaching in the sky. Dropping down at the foot of the steps and kneeling, Pilgrim said, "Master, the cassock is here!" Tripitaka was most delighted, and not one of the monks could hide his pleasure. "Good! Good!" they cried. "Now we've found our lives again!" Taking the cassock, Tripitaka said, "Wu-k'ung, when you left in the morning, you promised to come back either after breakfast or sometime around noon. Why are you returning so late, when the sun is already setting?" Pilgrim then gave a thorough account of how he went to ask for the Bodhisattva's help, and how she in her transformation had subdued the monster. When Tripitaka heard the account, he prepared an incense table at once and worshiped, facing south. Then he said, "Disciple, since we have the Buddha robe, let us pack up and leave." "No need to rush like that," said Pilgrim. "It's getting late, hardly the time to travel. Wait until tomorrow morning before we leave." All the monks knelt down also and said, "Elder Sun is right. It is getting late, and, moreover, we have a vow to fulfill. Now that we are all saved and the treasure has been recovered, we must redeem our vow and ask the venerable elders to distribute the blessing.[1] Tomorrow we shall see you off to the West." "Yes, yes, that's very good!" said Pilgrim. Look at those monks! They all emptied their pockets and presented all the valuables they had managed to salvage from the fire. Everyone made some contribution. They prepared some vegetarian offerings, burned paper money to request perpetual peace, and recited several scrolls of scriptures for the prevention of calamities and deliverance from evil. The service lasted until late in the evening. The next morning they saddled the horse and took up the luggage, while the monks accompanied them for a great distance before turning back. As Pilgrim led the way forward, it was the happiest time of spring. You see

The horse making light tracks on grassy turfs;
Gold threads of willow swaying with fresh dew.
Peaches and apricots fill the forest gay.
Creepers grow with vigor along the way.
Warmed by the sun, ducks[2] rest on sandy banks;
By the brook the fragrant flowers tame the butterflies.
Thus autumn goes, winter fades, and spring is nigh half gone;
In which year will merit be made and the True Writ be found?

Master and disciple traveled for some six or seven days in the wilderness. One day, when it was getting late, they saw a village in the distance. "Wu-k'ung," said Tripitaka, "look! There's a village over there. How about asking for lodging for the night before we travel again tomorrow?" "Let's wait until I have determined whether it is a good or bad place before we decide," said Pilgrim. The master pulled in the reins as Pilgrim stared intently at the village. Truly there were

Dense rows of bamboo fences;
Thick clusters of thatched huts.
Sky-reaching wild trees faced the doorways;
The winding brooklet reflected the houses.
Willows by the path unfurled their lovely green;
Fragrant were the flowers blooming in the yard.
At this time of twilight fast fading,
The birds chattered everywhere in the woods.

As kitchen smoke arose,
Cattle returned on every lane and path.
You saw, too, well-fed pigs and chickens sleeping
     by the house's edge.
And the old, sotted neighbor coming with a song.

After surveying the area, Pilgrim said, "Master, you may proceed. It
appears to be a village of good families, where it will be appropriate
for us to seek shelter." The priest urged the white horse on, and they
arrived at the beginning of a lane heading into the village, where they
saw a young man wearing a cotton head-wrap and a blue jacket. He
had an umbrella in his hand and a bundle on his back; his trousers
were rolled up, and he had on his feet a pair of straw sandals with
three loops. He was striding along the street in a resolute manner
when Pilgrim grabbed him, saying, "Where are you going? I have a
question for you: what is this place?" Struggling to break free, the
man complained: "Isn't there anyone else here in the village? Why
must you pick me for your question?" "Patron," said Pilgrim genially,
"don't get upset. 'Helping others is in truth helping yourself.' What's
so bad about your telling me the name of this place? Perhaps I can
help you with your problems." Unable to break out of Pilgrim's grip,
the man was so infuriated that he jumped about wildly. "I'm licked,
licked!" he cried. "The grievances I have suffered at the hands of my
family elders are still not at an end and I have to run into this bald-
headed fellow and suffer such indignity from him!" "If you have the
ability to pry open my hand," said Pilgrim, "I'll let you go." The man
twisted left and right without any success: it was as if he had been
clamped tight with a pair of iron tongs. He became so enraged that
he threw away his bundle and his umbrella; with both hands, he
rained blows and scratches on Pilgrim. With one hand steadying his
luggage, Pilgrim held off the man with the other, and no matter how
hard the man tried, he could not scratch or even touch Pilgrim at all.
The more he fought, the firmer was Pilgrim's grip, so that the man
was utterly exasperated. "Wu-k'ung," said Tripitaka, "isn't someone
coming over there? You can ask someone else. Why hang onto him
like that? Let the man go." "Master, you don't realize," said Pilgrim
laughing. "If I ask someone else, all the fun will be gone. I have to
ask him if, as the saying goes, 'there's going to be any business!'"
Seeing that it was fruitless to struggle any more, the man said

finally, "This place is called the Mr. Kao Village in the territory of the Kingdom of Tibet. Most of the families here in the village are surnamed Kao, and that's why the village is so called. Now, please let me go." "You are hardly dressed for a stroll in the neighborhood," said Pilgrim, "so tell me the truth. Where are you going, and what are you doing anyway? Then I'll let you go."

The man had little alternative but to speak the truth. "I'm a member of the family of old Mr. Kao, and my name is Kao Ts'ai. Old Mr. Kao has a daughter, his youngest, in fact, who is twenty years old and not yet betrothed. Three years ago, however, a monster-spirit seized her and kept her as his wife. Having a monster as his son-in-law bothered old Mr. Kao terribly; he said, 'My daughter having a monster as her spouse can hardly be a lasting arrangement. First, my family's reputation is ruined, and second, I don't even have any in-laws with whom we can be friends.' All that time he wanted to have this marriage annulled, but the monster absolutely refused; he locked the daughter up instead in the rear building and would not permit her to see her family for nearly half a year. The old man, therefore, gave me several taels of silver and told me to find an exorcist to capture the monster. Since then, I have hardly rested my feet; I managed to turn up three or four persons, all worthless monks and impotent Taoists. None of them could subdue the monster. A short while ago I received a severe scolding for my incompetence, and with only half an ounce more of silver as a travel allowance, I was told to find a capable exorcist this time. I didn't expect to run into you, my unlucky star, and now my journey is delayed. That's what I meant by the grievances I had suffered in and out of the family, and that's why I was complaining at you just now. I didn't know you had this trick of holding people, which I can't overcome. Now I have told you the truth, please let me go."

"It's really your luck," said Pilgrim, "coupled with my vocation: they fit like the numbers four and six when you throw the dice! You needn't travel far, nor need you waste your money. We are not worthless monks or impotent Taoists, for we really do have some abilities; we are most experienced, in fact, in capturing monsters. As the saying goes, 'You have now not only taken care of the physician, but you have cured your eyes as well!' Please take the trouble of returning to the head of your family and tell him that we are holy monks sent by the Throne in the Land of the East to go worship

Buddha in the Western Heaven and acquire scriptures. We are most capable of seizing monsters and binding fiends." "Don't mislead me," said Kao Ts'ai, "for I've had it up to here! If you are deceiving me and really don't have the ability to take the monster, you will only cause me to suffer more grievances." Pilgrim said, "I guarantee that you won't be harmed in any way. Lead me to the door of your house." The man could not think of a better alternative; he picked up his bundle and umbrella and turned to lead master and disciple to the door of his house. "You two elders," he said, "please rest yourselves for a moment against the hitching posts here. I'll go in to report to my master." Only then did Pilgrim release him. Putting down the luggage and dismounting from the horse, master and disciple stood and waited outside the door.

Kao Ts'ai walked through the main gate and went straight to the main hall in the center, but it just happened that he ran right into old Mr. Kao. "You thick-skinned creature!" railed Mr. Kao. "Why aren't you out looking for an exorcist? What are you doing back here?" Putting down his bundle and umbrella, Kao Ts'ai said, "Let me humbly inform my lord. Your servant just reached the end of the street and ran into two monks: one riding a horse and the other hauling a load. They caught hold of me and refused to let go, asking where I was going. At first I absolutely refused to tell them, but they were most insistent and I had no means of freeing myself. It was only then that I gave them a detailed account of my lord's affairs. The one who was holding me was delighted, saying that he would arrest the monster for us." "Where did they come from?" said old Mr. Kao. "He claimed to be a holy monk, the brother of the emperor," said Kao Ts'ai, "who was sent from the Land of the East to go worship Buddha in the Western Heaven and acquire scriptures." "If they are monks who have come from such a great distance," said old Mr. Kao, "they may indeed have some abilities. Where are they now?" "Waiting outside the front door," said Kao Ts'ai.

Hurriedly that old Mr. Kao changed his clothes and came out with Kao Ts'ai to extend his welcome, crying, "Your Grace!" When Tripitaka heard this, he turned quickly, and his host was already standing in front of him. That old man had on his head a dark silk wrap; he wore a robe of Szechwan silk brocade in spring-onion white with a dark green sash, and a pair of boots made of rough steer hide. Smiling affably, he addressed them saying, "Honored Priests, please accept my bow!" Tripitaka returned his greeting, but Pilgrim stood there unmoved. When the old man saw how hideous he looked, he did not bow to him. "Why don't you say hello to me?" demanded Pilgrim. Somewhat alarmed, the old man said to Kao Ts'ai: "Young man! You have really done me in, haven't you? There is already an ugly monster in the house that we can't drive away. Now you have to fetch this thunder-spirit to cause me more troubles!" "Old Kao," said Pilgrim, "it's in vain that you have reached such old age, for you have hardly any discernment! If you want to judge people by appearances, you are utterly wrong! I, old Monkey, may be ugly, but I have some abilities. I'll capture the monster for your family, exorcise the fiend, apprehend that son-in-law of yours, and get your daughter back. Will that be good enough? Why all these mutterings about appearances!" When the old man heard this, he trembled with fear, but he managed to pull himself together sufficiently to say, "Please come in!" At this invitation, Pilgrim led the white horse and asked Kao Ts'ai to pick up their luggage so that Tripitaka could go in with them. With no regard for manners, he tethered the horse on one of the pillars and drew up a weather-beaten lacquered chair for his master to be seated. He pulled over another chair and sat down himself on one side. "This little priest," said old Mr. Kao, "really knows how to make himself at home!" "If you are willing to keep me here for half a year," said Pilgrim, "then I'll truly feel at home!"

After they were seated, old Mr. Kao asked: "Just now my little one said that you two honored priests came from the Land of the East?" "Yes," said Tripitaka. "Your poor monk was commissioned by the court to go to the Western Heaven to seek scriptures for Buddha. Since we have reached your village, we would like to ask for lodging for the night. We plan to leave early tomorrow morning." "So the two of you wanted lodging?" said old Mr. Kao. "Then why did you say you could catch monsters?" "Since we are asking for a place to stay," said Pilgrim, "we thought we might as well catch a few monsters, just for fun! May we ask how many monsters there are in your house?" "My God!" exclaimed old Mr. Kao. "How many monsters could we feed? There's only this one son-in-law, and we have suffered enough from him!" "Tell me everything about the monster," said Pilgrim, "how he came to this place, what sort of power he has, and so forth. Start from the beginning and don't leave out any details. Then I can catch him for you."

"From ancient times," said old Mr. Kao, "this village of ours has never had any troubles with ghosts, goblins, or fiends; in fact, my sole misfortune consists of not having a son. I had three daughters born to me: the eldest is named Fragrant Orchid; the second one, Jade Orchid; and the third, Green Orchid. The first two since their youth had been promised to people belonging to this same village, but I had hoped that the youngest would take a husband who would stay with our family and consent to have his children bear our name. Since I have no son, he would in fact become my heir and look after me in my old age. Little did I expect that about three years ago a fellow would turn up who was passably good-looking. He said that he came from the Fu-ling Mountain and that his surname was Chu (Hog). Since he had neither parents nor brothers, he was willing to be taken in as a son-in-law, and I accepted him, thinking that someone with no other family attachment was exactly the right sort of person. When he first came into our family, he was, I must confess, fairly industrious and well-behaved. He worked hard to loosen the earth and plow the fields without even using a buffalo; and when he harvested the grains, he did the reaping without sickle or staff. He came home late in the evening and started early again in the morning, and to tell you the truth, we were quite happy with him. The only trouble was that his appearance began to change." "In what way?" asked Pilgrim. "Well," said old Mr. Kao, "when he first came, he was a stout, swarthy fellow, but afterwards he turned into an idiot with huge ears and a long snout, with a great tuft of bristles behind his head. His body became horribly coarse and hulking. In short, his whole appearance was that of a hog! And what an enormous appetite! For a single meal, he has to have three to five bushels of rice; a little snack in the morning means over a hundred biscuits or rolls. It's a good thing he keeps a vegetarian diet; if he liked meat and wine, the property and estate of this old man would be consumed in half a year!" "Perhaps it's because he's a good worker," said Tripitaka, "that he has such a good appetite." "Even that appetite is a small problem!" said old Mr. Kao. "What is most disturbing is that he likes to come riding the wind and disappears again astride the fog; he kicks up stones and dirt so frequently that my household and my neighbors have not had a moment's peace. Then he locked up my little girl, Green Orchid, in the back building, and we haven't seen her for half a year and don't know whether she's dead or alive. We are certain now that he is a monster, and that's why we want to get an exorcist to drive him away." "There's nothing difficult about that," said Pilgrim. "Relax, old man! Tonight, I'll catch him for you, and I'll demand that he sign a document of annulment and return your daughter. How's that?" Immensely pleased, old Mr. Kao said, "My taking him in was a small thing, when you consider how he has ruined my good reputation and how many relatives of ours he had alienated! Just catch him for me. Why bother about a document? Please, just get rid of him for me." Pilgrim said, "It's simple! When night falls, you'll see the result!"

The old man was delighted; he asked at once for tables to be set and a vegetarian feast be prepared. When they had finished the meal, evening was setting in. The old man asked: "What sort of weapons and how many people do you need? We'd better prepare soon." "I have my own weapon," replied Pilgrim. The old man said, "The only thing the two of you have is that priestly staff, hardly something you can use to battle the monster," whereupon Pilgrim took an embroidery needle out of his ear, held it in his hands, and waving it once in the wind, changed it into a golden-hooped rod with the thickness of a rice bowl. "Look at this rod," he said to old Mr. Kao, "how does it compare with your weapons? Think it'll do for the monster?" "Since you have a weapon," said old Mr. Kao again, "do you need some followers?" "No need for any followers," said Pilgrim. "All I ask for is some decent elderly persons to keep my master company and talk with him, so that I may feel free to leave him for a while. I'll catch the monster for you and make him promise publicly to leave, so that you will be rid of him for good." The old man at once asked his houseboy to send for several intimate friends and relatives, who soon arrived. After they were introduced, Pilgrim said, "Master, you may feel quite safe sitting here. Old Monkey is off!"

Look at him! Lifting high his iron rod, he dragged old Mr. Kao along saying, "Lead me to the back building where the monster is staying so that I may have a look." The old man indeed took him to the door of the building in the rear. "Get a key quickly!" said Pilgrim. "Take a look yourself," said old Mr. Kao. "If I could use a key on this lock, I wouldn't need you." Pilgrim laughed and said, "Dear old man! Though you are quite old, you can't even recognize a joke! I was just teasing you a little, and you took my words literally." He went forward and touched the lock: it was solidly welded with liquid copper. Annoyed, Pilgrim smashed·open the door with one terrific blow of his rod and found it was pitch black inside. "Old Kao," said Pilgrim, "go give your daughter a call and see if she is there inside." Summoning up his courage, the old man cried, "Miss Three!" Recognizing her father's voice, the girl replied faintly, "Papa! I'm over here!" With his golden pupils ablaze, Pilgrim peered into the dark shadows. "How does she look?" you ask. You see that

Her cloudlike hair is unkempt and unbrushed;
Her jadelike face is grimy and unwashed.
Though her nature refined is unchanged,
Her lovely image is weary and wan.
Her cherry lips seem completely bloodless,
And her body is both crooked and bent.
Knitted in sorrow
The moth-brows[3] are pallid;
Weakened by weight loss,
The voice is feeble.

She came forward, and when she saw that it was old Mr. Kao, she clutched at him and began to wail. "Stop crying! Stop crying!" said Pilgrim. "Let me ask you: where is the monster?" "I don't know where he has gone," said the girl. "Nowadays he leaves in the morning and comes back only after nightfall. Surrounded by cloud and fog, he comes and goes without ever letting me know where he is. Since he has learned that father is trying to drive him away, he takes frequent precautions; that's why he comes only at night and leaves in the morning." "No need to talk anymore," Pilgrim said. "Old Man! Take your beloved daughter to the building in front, and then you can spend all the time you want with her. Old Monkey will be here waiting for him; if the monster doesn't show up, don't blame me. But if he comes at all, I'll pull out the weeds of your troubles by the roots!" With great joy, old Mr. Kao led his daughter to the front building. Exercising his magic might, Pilgrim shook his body and changed at once into the form of that girl, sitting all by herself to wait for the monster. In a little while, a gust of wind swept by, kicking up dust and stones. What a wind!

At first it was a breeze gentle and light.
Thereafter it became gusty and strong.

A light, gentle breeze that could fill the world!
A strong, gusty wind that nothing else could stop!
Flowers and willow snapped like shaken hemp;
Trees and plants were felled like uprooted crops.
It stirred up streams and seas, cowing ghosts and gods.
It fractured rocks and mountains, awing Heaven and Earth.
Flower-nibbling deer lost their homeward trail.
Fruit-picking monkeys all were gone astray.
The seven-tiered pagoda crashed on Buddha's head.
Flags on eight sides damaged the temple's top.
Gold beams and jade pillars were rooted up.
Like flocks of swallow flew the roofing tiles.
The boatman lifted his oars to make a vow,
Eager to have his livestock sacrificed.
The local spirit abandoned his shrine.
Dragon kings from four seas made humble bows.
At sea the ship of yakṣa ran aground,
While half of Great Wall's rampart was blown down.

When the violent gust of wind had gone by, there appeared in midair a monster who was ugly indeed. With his black face covered with short, stubby hair, his long snout and huge ears, he wore a cotton shirt that was neither quite green nor quite blue. A sort of spotted cotton handkerchief was tied round his head. Said Pilgrim, smiling to himself, "So, I have to do business with a thing like this!" Dear Pilgrim! He neither greeted the monster, nor did he speak to him; he lay on the bed instead and pretended to be sick, making moaning noises all the time. The monster could not tell the true from the false; walking into the room, he grabbed his "spouse" and at once demanded a kiss. "He really wants to sport with old Monkey!" said Pilgrim, smiling to himself. Using a holding trick, he caught the long snout of that monster and gave it a sudden, violent twist, sending him crashing to the floor with a loud thud. Picking himself up, the monster supported himself on the side of the bed and said, "Sister, how is it that you seem somewhat annoyed with me today? Because I'm late, perhaps?" "I'm not annoyed!" said Pilgrim. "If not," said that monster, "why did you give me such a fall?" "How can you be so boorish," said Pilgrim, "grabbing me like that and wanting to kiss me? I don't feel very well today; under normal conditions I would have been up waiting for you and would have opened the door myself. You may take off your clothes and go to sleep." The fiend did not suspect anything and took off his clothes. Pilgrim jumped up and sat on the chamber pot, while the fiend climbed into bed. Groping around, he could not feel anyone and called out: "Sister, where have you gone? Please take off your clothes and go to sleep." "You go to sleep first," said Pilgrim, "for I have to wait until I've dropped my load." The fiend indeed loosened his clothes and stayed in bed. Suddenly Pilgrim gave out a sigh, saying, 'I'm truly unlucky!'" "What's bothering you?" said the monster. "What do you mean, you're truly unlucky? It's true that I have consumed quite a bit of food and drink since I entered your family, but I certainly did not take them as free meals. Look at the things I did for your family: sweeping the grounds and draining the ditches, hauling bricks and carrying tiles, building walls and pounding mortar, plowing the fields and raking the earth, planting seedlings of rice and wheat—in short, I took care of your entire estate. Now what you have on your body happens to be brocade, and what you wear as ornaments happens to be gold. You enjoy the flowers and fruits of four seasons, and you have fresh vegetables for the table in all eight periods. Whatever makes you so dissatisfied that you have to sigh and lament, saying how unlucky you are?" "It isn't quite as you say," said Pilgrim. "Today my parents gave me a severe scolding over the partition wall, throwing bricks and tiles into this place." "What were they scolding you for?" asked the monster. Pilgrim said, "They said that since we have become husband and wife, you are in fact a son-in-law in their family but one who is completely without manners. A person as ugly as you is unpresentable: you can't meet your brothers-in-law, nor can you greet the other relatives. Since you come with the clouds and leave with the fog, we really don't know what family you belong to and what your true name is. In fact, you have ruined our family's reputation and defiled our heritage. That was what they rebuked me for, and that's why I'm upset." "Though I am somewhat homely," said the monster, "it's no great problem if they insist on my being more handsome. We discussed these matters before when I came here, and I entered your family fully with your father's consent. Why did they bring it up again today? My family is located in the Cloudy Paths Cave of Fu-ling Mountain; my surname

is based on my appearance. Hence I am called Chu (Hog), and my
official name is Kang-lieh (Stiff Bristles). If they ever ask you again,
tell them what I have told you."

"This monster is quite honest," said Pilgrim to himself, secretly
pleased. "Without torture, he has already made a plain confession;
with his name and location clearly known, he will certainly be
caught, regardless of what may happen." Pilgrim then said to him:
"My parents are trying to get an exorcist here to arrest you." "Go
to sleep! Go to sleep!" said the monster, laughing. "Don't mind them
at all! I know as many transformations as the number of stars in the
Heavenly Ladle,[4] and I own a nine-pronged muckrake. Why should
I fear any exorcist, monk, or Taoist priest? Even if your old man
were pious enough to be able to get the Monster-Routing Patriarch
to come down from the Ninefold Heaven, I could still claim to have
been an old acquaintance of his. And he wouldn't dare do anything to
me." "But they were saying that they hoped to invite someone by
the name of Sun," said Pilgrim, "the so-called Great Sage, Equal to
Heaven, who caused havoc in the Celestial Palace five hundred
years ago. They were going to ask him to come and catch you."
When the monster heard this name, he was rather alarmed. "If that's
true,' he said, "I'm leaving. We can't live as a couple anymore!"
"Why do you have to leave so suddenly?" asked Pilgrim. "You may
not know," said the monster, "that that pi-ma-wên who caused
such turmoil in Heaven has some real abilities. I fear that I may be
no match for him, and losing my reputation is hardly a desirable
prospect!"

When he had finished speaking, he slipped on his clothes, opened
the door, and walked right out. Pilgrim grabbed him, and with one
wipe of his own face he assumed his original form, shouting:
"Monster, where do you think you're going? Take a good look and
see who I am!" The monster turned around and saw the protruding
teeth, the gaping mouth, the fiery eyes, the golden pupils, the pointed
head, and the hairy face of Pilgrim—virtually a living thunder god!
He was so horrified that his hands became numb and his feet grew
weak. With a loud ripping sound, he tore open his shirt and broke
free of Pilgrim's clutch by changing into a violent wind. Pilgrim
rushed forward and struck mightily with the iron rod at the wind;
the monster at once transformed himself into myriad shafts of
flaming light and fled toward his own mountain. Mounting the

clouds, Pilgrim pursued him, crying, "Where are you running to? If you ascend to Heaven, I'll chase you to the Palace of the Polestar, and if you go down into the Earth, I'll follow you into the heart of Hell!" Good Heavens! We do not know where the chase took them to or what was the outcome of the fight, and you must listen to the explanation in the next chapter.

Nineteen

At Cloudy Paths Cave, Wu-k'ung apprehends Pa-chieh;
At Pagoda Mountain, Tripitaka receives the *Heart Sūtra*.

We were telling you about the flaming light of the monster, which
was fleeing, while the Great Sage riding the rosy clouds followed
right behind. As they were thus proceeding, they came upon a tall
mountain, where the monster gathered together the fiery shafts of
light and resumed his original form. Racing into a cave, he took out
a nine-pronged muckrake to fight. "Lawless monster!" shouted
Pilgrim. "What region are you from, fiend, and how do you know
old Monkey's names? What abilities do you have? Make a full confession quickly and your life may be spared!" "So you don't know
my powers!" said that monster. "Come up here and brace yourself!
I'll tell you!

My mind was dim since the time of my youth;
Always I loved my indolence and sloth.
I trained not my nature nor practiced Truth:[1]
I passed my days deluded and confused.
I met suddenly an immortal true.
Who sat and spoke to me of heat and cold.[2]
'Repent,' he said, 'and cease your worldly ways,
For taking life will bring you endless pain.
One day when you reach the end of your life,
For eight woes and three ways[3] you'll grieve too late!'
I listened and turned my will to mend my ways;
I heard, repented, and sought the wondrous gloss.
By fate my teacher he became at once,
Telling me the secrets of Heaven and Earth.
I was given the Great Pills of Nine Turns.[4]
My work[5] incessant went on night and day:
It reached the Mud-Pill Chambers[6] of my crown,
And the Jetting-Spring Points[7] beneath my feet.
Into the Floral Pool[8] kidney-water freely flowed,

My Cinnabar Field[9] was thus warmly fed.[10]
Baby[11] and virgin[12] mated as yin and yang:
Lead and mercury mixed as sun and moon.[13]
In concord Li-dragon and K'an-tiger used,[14]
The spirit turtle[15] sucked dry the gold crow's[16] blood.
Three flowers joined[17] on top, returning to the root;
Five energies as one[18] in perfect accord.
My work finished, I ascended on high,
Met by pairs of immortals from the sky.
Radiant pink clouds arose beneath my feet;
With light, healthy frame I faced the Golden Arch.
The Jade Emperor gave a banquet for gods:
They sat in rows according to their ranks.
Made a marshal of the River of Heaven,
Of the naval forces I took command.
Because Wang-mu[19] gave the Peaches Banquet,
When she met her guests at the Jasper Pool,
My mind became hazy for I was drunk;
A shameless rowdy, I reeled left and right.
Boldly I invaded the Lunar Palace,
Where I was by the charming lady met.
When I saw her lovely, soul-snatching face,
My carnal itch of old could not be stopped!
Without regard for manners or for rank,
I grabbed Miss Ch'ang-o,[20] asking her to bed.
Three or four times she rejected me;
Hiding here and there, she was sore annoyed.
I roared with passion boundless as the sky,
Almost toppling the arch of Heaven's gate.
The Inspector General[21] told the Jade Emperor;
I was destined that day to meet my fate.
The Lunar Palace completely enclosed
Left me no way to run or to escape.
Then I was caught by the various gods,
Still undaunted, for wine was in my heart.
Bound and taken to see the Jade Emperor,
I should by law have been executed.
It was Venus, the Gold Star, Mr. Li,
Who left the ranks and knelt to beg for me.

My punishment changed to two thousand blows,
My flesh was torn; my bones did almost crack.
Alive! I was banished from Heaven's gate
To make my home beneath the Fu-ling Mount.
My sins led me to an erroneous womb:
My common name is therefore Chu Kang-lieh!"
When Pilgrim heard this, he said, "So you are actually the Water
God of the Heavenly Reeds, who came to earth. Small wonder you
knew old Monkey's name." "Curses!" cried the monster. "You
Heaven-defying pi-ma-wên! When you caused such turmoil that
year in Heaven, you had no idea how many of us had to suffer
because of you. And here you are again to make life miserable for
others! Don't give me any lip! Have a taste of my rake!" Pilgrim, of
course, was unwilling to be tolerant; lifting high his rod, he struck
at the monster's head. The two of them thus began a battle in the
middle of the mountain, in the middle of the night. What a fight!

Pilgrim's gold pupils blazed like lightning;
The monster's round eyes flashed like silver blooms.
This one spat out colored fog;
That one spouted crimson mist.
The spouted crimson mist lit up the dark;
The colored fog spat out made bright the night.
The golden-hooped rod;
The nine-pronged muckrake.
Two heroes true most worthy of acclaim:
One was the Great Sage descended to earth;
One was a Marshal who from Heaven came.
That one, for indecorum, became a monster;
This one, to flee his ordeal, bowed to a monk.
The rake lunged like a dragon wielding his claws;
The rod came like a phoenix darting through flowers.
That one said: "Your breaking up a marriage is like patricide!"
This one said: "You should be arrested for raping a young girl!"
Such idle words!
Such wild clamor!
Back and forth the rod blocked the rake.
They fought till dawn was about to break,
When the monster's two arms felt sore and numb.
From the time of the second watch, the two of them fought until it

was growing light in the east. That monster could hold out no longer and fled in defeat. He changed once more into a violent gust of wind and went straight back to his cave, shutting the doors tightly and refusing to come out. Outside the cave, Pilgrim saw a large stone tablet, which had on it the inscription "Cloudy Paths Cave." By now, it was completely light. Realizing that the monster was not going to come out, Pilgrim thought to himself: "I fear that Master may be anxiously waiting for me. I may as well go back and see him before returning here to catch the monster." Mounting the clouds, he soon arrived at Old Kao village.

We shall now tell you about Tripitaka, who chatted about past and present with the other elders and did not sleep all night. He was just wondering why Pilgrim had not shown up, when suddenly the latter dropped down into the courtyard. Straightening out his clothes and putting away his rod, Pilgrim went up to the hall, crying, "Master! I've returned!" The various elders hurriedly bowed low, saying, "Thank you for all the trouble you have been to!" "Wu-k'ung, you were gone all night," said Tripitaka. "If you captured the monster, where is he now?" "Master," said Pilgrim, "that monster is no fiend of this world, nor is he a strange beast of the mountains. He is actually the incarnation of the Marshal of the Heavenly Reeds. Because he took the wrong path of rebirth, his appearance assumed the form of a wild hog; but actually his spiritual nature has not been extinguished. He said that he derived his surname from his appearance, and he went by the name of Chu Kang-lieh. When I attacked him with my rod in the back building, he tried to escape by changing into a violent gust of wind; I then struck at the wind, and he changed into shafts of flaming light and retreated to his mountain cave. There he took out a nine-pronged muckrake to do battle with old Monkey for a whole night. Just now when it grew light, he could fight no longer and fled into the cave, shutting the doors tightly and not coming out any more. I wanted to break down the door to finish him off, but I was afraid that you might be waiting here anxiously. That's why I came back first to give you some news."

When he had finished speaking, old Mr. Kao came forward and knelt down, saying, "Honored Priest, I have no alternative but to say this. Though you have chased him away, he might come back here after you leave. What should we do then? I may as well ask you to do us the favor of apprehending him, so that we shall not have any further worries. This old man, I assure you, will not be ungrateful or unkind; there will be a generous reward for you. I shall ask my relatives and friends to witness the drawing up of a document, whereby I shall divide my possessions and my property equally with you. All I want is to pluck up the trouble by the root, so that the pure virtue of our Kao family will not be tainted."

"Aren't you being rather demanding, old man?" said Pilgrim, laughing. "That monster did tell me that, although he has an enormous appetite and has consumed a good deal of food and drink from your family, he has also done a lot of good work for you. Much of what you were able to accumulate these last few years you owe to his strength, so that he really hasn't taken any free meals from you. Why ever do you want to have him driven away? According to him, he is a god who has come down to earth and who has helped your family earn a living. Moreover, he has not harmed your daughter in any way. Such a son-in-law, I should think, would be a good match for your daughter and your family. So, what's all this about ruining your family's reputation and damaging your standing in the community? Why not really accept him as he is?"

"Honored Priest," said old Mr. Kao, "though this matter may not offend public morals, it does leave us with a bad name. Like it or not, people will say, 'The Kao family has taken in a monster as a son-in-law!' How can one stand remarks of that kind?" "Wu-k'ung," said Tripitaka, "if you have worked for him all this while, you might as well see him through to a satisfactory conclusion." Pilgrim said, "I was testing him a little, just for fun. This time when I go, I'll apprehend the monster for certain and bring him back for you all to see. Don't worry, old Kao! Take good care of my master. I'm off!"

He said he was off, and the next instant he was completely out of sight. Bounding up that mountain, he arrived at the cave's entrance; a few strokes of the iron rod reduced the doors to dust. "You overstuffed coolie!" he shouted, "Come out quickly and fight with old Monkey!" Huffing and puffing, the monster was lying in the cave and trying to catch his breath. When he heard his doors being struck down and heard himself called "an overstuffed coolie," he could not control his wrath. Dragging his rake, he pulled himself together and ran out. "A pi-ma-wên like you," he yelled, "is an absolute pest! What have I done to you that you have to break my doors to pieces? Go and take a look at the law: a man who breaks someone's door and enters without permission may be guilty of trespassing, a crime punishable by death!" "Idiot!" said Pilgrim laughing. "I may have broken down the door, but my case is still a defensible one. But you, you took a girl from her family by force—without using the proper matchmakers and witnesses, without presenting the proper gifts of money and wine. If you ask me, *you* are the one guilty of a capital crime!" "Enough of this idle talk," said the monster, "and watch out for old Hog's rake!" Parrying the rake with his rod, Pilgrim said, "Isn't that rake of yours just something you use as a regular farm hand to plow the fields or plant vegetables for the Kao family? Why on Earth should I fear you?" "You have made a mistake!" said the monster. "Is this rake a thing of this world? Just listen to my recital:

This is fine steel colored like ice divine,
Polished so highly that it glows and shines.
Lao Tzu himself wielded the large hammer,
And Mars himself added charcoals piece by piece.
Five Kings of Five Quarters used all their powers;
Liu Ting and Liu Chia[22] spent all their resources.
They made nine prongs like dangling teeth of jade,
And brass rings were cast with dropping gold leaves.
Decked with five stars and six brightnesses,
To four and eight seasons its frame conformed.
Its whole length and its proportions throughout
Conformed to yin-yang, to the sun and moon.
Six-Diagram[23] Gods followed Heaven's rules;
Eight-Trigram Stars stood in ranks and files;
They named this the High Treasure Golden Rake,
A gift for Jade Emperor to guard his court.
Since I learned to be an immortal great,
Becoming someone with longevity,
I was made Marshal of the Heavenly Reeds,
And given this rake, a sign of royal grace.
When it's held high, there'll be bright flames and light;
When it's brought low, strong wind blows down white snow.
The warriors of Heaven all fear it;
The Ten Kings of Hell all shrink from it.

Are there such weapons among mankind?
In this wide world there's no such fine steel.
It changes its form after my own wish,
Rising and falling after my command.
I've kept it with me for several years,
A daily comrade I never parted from.
I've stayed with it right through the day's three meals,
Nor left it when I went to sleep at night.
I brought it along to the Peaches Feast,
And with it I attended Heaven's court.
Since I wrought evil relying on wine,
Since trusting my strength I displayed my fraud,
Heaven sent me down to this world of dust,
Where in my next life I would sin some more.
With wicked mind I ate men in my cave,
Pleased to be married at the Kao Village.
This rake can overturn sea dragons' and turtles' lairs.
And rake to pieces the mountain dens of tigers and wolves.
All other weapons there's no need to name,
Only my rake is the most fitting one
To win in battle, for it's no hard thing!
And making merit? It need not be said!
You may have a bronze head, an iron brain,
       and a body full of steel.
    I'll rake till your soul melts and your spirit leaks!"
When Pilgrim heard these words, he put away his iron rod and said,
"Don't brag too much, Idiot! Old Monkey will stretch out his head
right here, and you can give him a blow. See if his soul melts and
his spirit leaks!" The monster did indeed raise his rake high and
bring it down with all his might; with a loud bang, the rake made
sparks as it bounced back up. But the blow did not make so much as
a scratch on Pilgrim's head. The monster was so astounded that his
hands turned numb and his feet grew weak. He mumbled, "What a
head! What a head!" "You didn't know about this, did you?" said
Pilgrim. "When I caused such turmoil in Heaven by stealing the
magic pills, the immortal peaches, and the imperial wine, I was captured by the Little Sage Erh-lang and taken to the Polestar Palace.
The various celestial beings chopped me with an ax, pounded me

with a bludgeon, cut me with a scimitar, jabbed me with a sword, burned me with fire, and struck me with thunder—all this could not hurt me one whit. Then I was taken by Lao Tzu and placed in his eight-trigram brazier, in which I was refined by divine fire until I had fiery eyes and diamond pupils, a bronze head and iron arms. If you don't believe me, give me some more blows and see whether it hurts me at all." "Monkey," said the monster, "I remember that at the time you were causing trouble in Heaven, you lived in the Water-Curtain Cave of the Flower-Fruit Mountain, in the Ao-lai Country of the East Pūrvavideha Continent. Your name hasn't been heard of for a long time. How is it that you suddenly turn up at this place to oppress me? Could my father-in-law have gone all that way to ask you to come here?" "Your father-in-law did not go to fetch me," said Pilgrim. "It's old Monkey who turned from wrong to right, who left the Taoist to follow the Buddhist. I am now accompanying the royal brother of the Great T'ang Emperor in the Land of the East, whose name is Tripitaka, Master of the Law. He is on his way to the Western Heaven to seek scriptures from Buddha. We passed through the Kao Village and asked for lodging; old man Kao then brought up the subject of his daughter and asked me to rescue her and to apprehend you, you overstuffed coolie!"

Hearing this, the monster threw away his muckrake and said with great affability, "Where is the scripture pilgrim? Please take the trouble of introducing me to him." "Why do you want to see him?" asked Pilgrim. The monster said, "I was a convert of the Bodhisattva Kuan-shih-yin, who commanded me to keep a vegetarian diet here and to wait for the scripture pilgrim. I was to follow him to the Western Heaven to seek scriptures from the Buddha, so that I might atone for my sins with my merit and regain the fruits of Truth. I have been waiting for a number of years without receiving any further news. Since you have been made his disciple, why didn't you mention the search for scriptures in the first place? Why did you have to unleash your violence and attack me right at my own door?" "Don't try to soften me with deception," said Pilgrim, "thinking that you can escape that way. If you are truly sincere about accompanying the T'ang monk, you must face Heaven and swear that you are telling the truth. Then I'll take you to see my master." At once the monster knelt down and kowtowed as rapidly as if he were pounding

rice with his head. "Amitābha," he cried, "Namo Buddha! If I am
not speaking the truth in all sincerity, let me be punished as one who
has offended Heaven—let me be hewn to pieces!"

Hearing him swear such an oath, Pilgrim said, "All right! You
light a fire and burn up this place of yours; then I'll take you with
me." The monster accordingly dragged in bunches of rushweed and
thorns and lighted the fire; the Cloudy Paths Cave soon looked like a
derelict potter's kiln. "I have no other attachment," he said to Pilgrim.
"You can take me away." "Give me your muckrake and let me hold
it," said Pilgrim, and our monster at once handed it over. Yanking
out a piece of hair, Pilgrim blew onto it and cried "Change!" It
changed into a three-ply hemp rope with which he prepared to tie
up the monster's hands. Putting his arms behind his back, the
monster did nothing to stop himself from being bound. Then Pilgrim
took hold of his ear and dragged him along, crying, "Hurry! Hurry!"
"Gently, please!" pleaded the monster. "You are holding me so
roughly, and my ear is hurting!" "I can't be any gentler," said
Pilgrim, "for I can't worry about you now. As the saying goes, 'The
better the pig, the harder to hold!'[24] After you have seen my master
and proved your worth, I'll let you go." Rising up to a distance halfway between cloud and fog, they headed straight for the Kao Family
Village. We have a poem as a testimony:[25]

> Strong is metal's nature to vanquish wood:
> Mind Monkey has the Wood Dragon[26] subdued.
> With metal and wood both obedient as one,
> All their love and virtue will grow and show.
> One guest and one host[27] there's nothing between;
> Three mixes, three unions[28]—there's mystery great!
> Nature and feelings gladly fused as chên and yüan,[29]
> It's sure that they'll both be enlightened in the West.

In a moment they had arrived at the village. Grasping the rake and
pulling at the monster's ear, Pilgrim said, "Look at the one sitting in
a most dignified manner up there in the main hall: that's my master."
When old Mr. Kao and his relatives suddenly saw Pilgrim dragging
by the ear a monster who had his hands bound behind his back, they
all gladly left their seats to meet them in the courtyard. The old man
cried, "Honored Priest! There's that son-in-law of mine." Our
monster went forward and fell on his knees, kowtowing to Tripitaka
and saying, "Master, your disciple apologizes for not coming to meet

you. If I had known earlier that my master was staying in my father-in-law's house, I would have come at once to pay my respects, and none of these troubles would have befallen me." "Wu-k'ung," said Tripitaka, "how did you manage to get him here to see me?" Only then did Pilgrim release his hold. Using the handle of the rake to give the monster a whack, he shouted, "Idiot! Say something!" The monster gave a full account of how the Bodhisattva had converted him. Greatly pleased, Tripitaka said at once, "Mr. Kao, may I borrow your incense table?" Old Mr. Kao took it out immediately, and Tripitaka lighted the incense after purifying his hands. He bowed toward the south, saying, "I thank the Bodhisattva for her holy grace!" The other elders all joined in the worship by adding incense, after which Tripitaka resumed his seat in the main hall and asked Wu-k'ung to untie the monster. Pilgrim shook his body to retrieve his hair, and the rope fell off by itself. Once more the monster bowed to Tripitaka, declaring his intention to follow him to the West, and then bowed also to Pilgrim, addressing him as "elder brother" since he was the senior disciple.

"Since you have entered my fold," said Tripitaka, "and have decided to become my disciple, let me give you a religious name so that I may address you properly." "Master," said the monster, "the Bodhisattva already laid hands on my head and gave me the commandments and a religious name, which is Chu Wu-nêng." "Good! Good!" said Tripitaka, laughing. "Your elder brother is named Wu-k'ung and you are called Wu-nêng; your names are well in accord with the emphasis of our denomination." "Master," said Wu-nêng, "since I received the commandments from the Bodhisattva, I was completely cut off from the five forbidden viands and the three undesirable foods.[30] I maintained a strict vegetarian diet in my father-in-law's house, never touching any forbidden food. Now that I have met my master today, let me be released from my vegetarian vow." "No, no!" said Tripitaka. "Since you have not eaten the five forbidden viands and the three undesirable foods, let me give you another name. Let me call you Pa-chieh."[31] Delighted, Idiot said, "I shall obey my master." For this reason, he was also called Chu Pa-chieh.

When old Mr. Kao saw the happy ending of this whole affair, he was more delighted than ever. He ordered his houseboys immediately to prepare a feast to thank the T'ang monk. Pa-chieh went forward and tugged at him, saying, "Papa, please ask my humble wife to come out and greet the grand-dads and uncles. How about it?" "Worthy brother!" said Pilgrim laughing. "Since you have embraced Buddhism and become a monk, please don't ever mention 'your humble wife' again. There may be a married Taoist in this world, but there's no such monk, is there? Let's sit down, rather, and have a nice vegetarian meal. We'll have to start off soon for the West."

Old Mr. Kao set the tables in order and invited Tripitaka to take the honored seat in the middle; Pilgrim and Pa-chieh sat on both sides while the relatives took the remaining seats below. Mr. Kao opened a bottle of vegetarian wine and filled a glass; he sprinkled a little of the wine on the ground to thank Heaven and Earth before presenting the glass to Tripitaka. "To tell you the truth, aged sir," said Tripitaka, "this poor monk has been a vegetarian from birth. I have not touched any kind of forbidden food since childhood." "I know the reverend teacher is chaste and pure," said old Mr. Kao, "and I did not dare bring forth any forbidden foodstuff. This wine is made for those who maintain a vegetarian diet; there's no harm in your taking a glass." "I just don't dare use wine," said Tripitaka, "for the prohibition of strong drink is a monk's first commandment." Alarmed, Wu-nêng said, "Master, though I kept a vegetarian diet, I didn't cut out wine." "Though my capacity is not great," said Wu-k'ung, "and I'm not able to handle more than a crock or so, I haven't discontinued the use of wine either." "In that case," said Tripitaka, "you two brothers may take some of this pure wine. But you are not permitted to get drunk and cause trouble." So the two of them took the first round before taking their seats again to enjoy the feast. We cannot tell you in full what a richly laden table that was, and what varieties of delicacies were presented.

After master and disciples had been feted, old Mr. Kao took out a red lacquered tray bearing some two hundred taels of gold and silver in small pieces, which were to be presented to the three priests for travel expenses. There were, moreover, three outer garments made of fine silk. Tripitaka said, "We are mendicants who beg for food and drink from village to village. How could we accept gold, silver, and precious clothing?" Coming forward and stretching out his hand, Pilgrim took a handful of the money, saying, "Kao Ts'ai, yesterday you took the trouble to bring my master here, with the result that we made a disciple today. We have nothing to thank you with. Take this as remuneration for being a guide; perhaps you can use it to buy a few pairs of straw sandals. If there are any more monsters, turn them over to me and I'll truly be grateful to you." Kao Ts'ai took the money and kowtowed to thank Pilgrim for his reward. Old Mr. Kao then said, "If the masters do not want the silver and gold, please accept at least these three simple garments, which are but small tokens of our goodwill." "If those of us who have left the family," said Tripitaka again, "accept the bribe of a single strand of silk, we may fall into ten thousand kalpas from which we may never recover. It is quite sufficient that we take along the leftovers from the table as provisions on our way." Pa-chieh spoke up from the side: "Master, Elder Brother, you may not want these things. But I was a son-in-law in this household for several years, and the payment for my services should be worth more than three stones of rice! Father, my shirt was torn by Elder Brother last night; please give me a cassock of blue silk. My shoes are worn also, so please give me a good pair of new shoes." When old Mr. Kao heard that, he dared not refuse; a new pair of shoes and a cassock were purchased at once so that Pa-chieh could dispose of the old attire.

Swaggering around, our Pa-chieh spoke amiably to old Mr. Kao, saying, "Please convey my humble sentiments to my mother-in-law, my great-aunt, my second aunt and my uncle-in-law, and all my other relatives. Today I am going away as a monk, and please do not blame me if I cannot take leave of them in person. Father, do take care of my better half. If we fail in our quest for scriptures, I'll return to secular life and live with you again as your son-in-law." "Coolie!" shouted Pilgrim. "Stop babbling nonsense!" "It's no nonsense," said Pa-chieh. "Sometimes I fear that things may go wrong, and then I could end up unable either to be a monk or to take a wife, losing out on both counts." "Less of this idle conversation!" said Tripitaka. "We must hurry up and leave." They therefore packed their luggage, and Pa-chieh was told to carry the load with a pole. Tripitaka rode on the white horse, while Pilgrim led the way with the iron rod across his shoulders. The three of them took leave of old Mr. Kao and his relatives and headed toward the West. We have a poem as testimony:

The earth's mist-shrouded, the trees appear tall.
The Buddha-son of T'ang Court ever toils.

He eats in need rice begged from many homes;
He wears when cold a robe patched a thousandfold.
Hold fast at the breast the Horse of the Will!
The Mind-Monkey is sly—let him not wail!
Nature is one with feelings, causes in accord:[32]
The moon full with golden light is the hair shorn.[33]

The three of them proceeded toward the West, and for about a month
it was an uneventful journey. When they crossed the boundary of
Tibet, they looked up and saw a tall mountain. Tripitaka reined in his
horse and said, "Wu-k'ung, Wu-nêng, there's a tall mountain ahead.
We must approach it with care." "It's nothing!" said Pa-chieh. "This
mountain is called the Pagoda Mountain,[34] and a Crow's Nest Zen
Master lives there, practicing austerities. Old Hog has met him
before." "What's his business?" said Tripitaka. "He's fairly accomplished in the Way," said Pa-chieh, "and he once asked me to
practice austerities with him. But I didn't go, and that was the end of
the matter." As master and disciple conversed, they soon arrived at
the mountain. What a splendid mountain! You see

South of it, blue pines, jade-green junipers;
North of it, green willows, red peach trees.
A clamorous din:
The mountain fowls are conversing.
A fluttering dance:
Immortal cranes fly in unison.
A dense fragrance:
The flowers in a thousand colors.
A manifold green:
Divers plants in forms exotic.
In the stream there's water bubbling and green;
Before the cliff, petals of blessed cloud afloat.
Truly a place of rare beauty, a well-secluded spot;
Silence is all, not a man to be seen.

As the master sat on his horse, peering into the distance, he saw on
top of the fragrant juniper tree a nest made of dried wood and grass.
To the left, muskdeer carried flowers in their mouths; to the right,
mountain monkeys were presenting fruits. At the top of the tree, blue
and pink phoenixes sang together, soon to be joined by a congregation of black cranes and brightly colored pheasants. "Isn't that the

Crow's Nest Zen Master?" asked Pa-chieh, pointing. Tripitaka urged on his horse and rode up to the tree.

We now tell you about that Zen Master, who, seeing the three of them approach, left his nest and jumped down from the tree. Tripitaka dismounted and prostrated himself. Raising him up with his hand, the Zen Master said, "Holy Monk, please arise! Pardon me for not coming to meet you." "Old Zen Master," said Pa-chieh, "please receive my bow!" "Aren't you the Chu Kang-lieh of the Fu-ling Mountain?" asked the Zen Master, startled. "How did you have the good fortune to journey with the holy monk?" "A few years back," said Pa-chieh, "I was beholden to the Bodhisattva Kuan-yin for persuading me to follow him as a disciple." "Good! Good! Good!" said the Zen Master, greatly pleased. Then he pointed to Pilgrim and asked: "Who is this person?" "How is it that the old Zen recognizes him," said Pilgrim, laughing, "and not me?" "Because I haven't had the pleasure of meeting you," said the Zen Master. Tripitaka said, "He is my eldest disciple, Sun Wu-k'ung." Smiling amiably, the Zen Master said, "How impolite of me!"

Tripitaka bowed again and asked about the distance to the Great Thunderclap Temple of the Western Heaven. "It's very far away! Very far away!" said the Zen Master. "What's more, the road is a difficult one, filled with tigers and leopards." With great earnestness, Tripitaka asked again, "Just how far is it?" "Though it may be very far," answered the Zen Master, "you will arrive there one day. But all those māra hindrances along the way are hard to dispel. I have a *Heart Sūtra* here in this scroll; it has fifty-four sentences containing two hundred and seventy characters. When you meet these māra hindrances, recite the sūtra and you will not suffer any injury or harm." Tripitaka prostrated himself on the ground and begged to receive it, whereupon the Zen Master imparted the sūtra by reciting it orally. The sūtra said:

Heart Sūtra of the Great Perfection of Wisdom
When the Bodhisattva Kuan-tzu-tsai[35] was moving in the deep course of the Perfection of Wisdom, she saw that the five heaps[36] were but emptiness, and she transcended all sufferings. Śāriputra, form is no different from emptiness, emptiness no different from form; form is emptiness, and emptiness is form. Of sensations, perceptions, volition, and consciousness, the same is

also true. Śāriputra, it is thus that all dharmas are but empty
appearances, neither produced nor destroyed, neither defiled nor
pure, neither increasing nor decreasing. This is why in emptiness
there are no forms and no sensations, perceptions, volition, or
consciousness; no eye, ear, nose, tongue, body, or mind; no form,
sound, smell, taste, touch, or object of mind. There is no realm of
sight [and so forth], until we reach the realm of no mind-
consciousness; there is no ignorance, nor is there extinction of
ignorance [and so forth], until we reach the stage where there is
no old age and death, nor is there the extinction of old age and
death; there is no suffering, annihilation, or way; there is no
cognition or attainment. Because there is nothing to be attained,
the mind of the Bodhisattva, by virtue of reliance upon the Perfection of Wisdom, has no hindrances; no hindrances, and therefore, no terror or fear; he is far removed from error and delusion,
and finally reaches nirvāṇa. All the Buddhas of the three worlds[37]
rely on the Perfection of Wisdom, and that is why they attain the
ultimate and complete enlightenment. Know, therefore, that the
Perfection of Wisdom is a great divine spell, a spell of great illumination, a spell without superior, and a spell without equal. It can
do away with all sufferings—such is the unvarnished truth.
Therefore, when the Spell of the Perfection of Wisdom is to be
spoken, say this spell: "Gate! Gate! Pāragate! Pārasaṃgate!
Bodhisvāhā!"[38]

Now because that master of the law from the T'ang Court was spiritually prepared, he could remember the *Heart Sūtra* after hearing it
only once. Through him, it has come down to us this day. It is the
comprehensive classic for the cultivation of Truth, the very gateway
to becoming a Buddha.

After the transmission of the sūtra, the Zen Master trod on the
cloudy luminosity and was about to return to his crow's nest. Tripitaka, however, held him back and earnestly questioned him again
about the condition of the road to the West. The Zen Master laughed
and said:

The way is not too hard to walk;
Try listening to what I say.
A thousand hills and waters deep;
Places full of goblins and snags;

When you reach those sky-touching cliffs,
Fear not and put your mind at rest.
Crossing the Rub Ear Precipice,
You must walk with steps placed sideways.
Take care in the Black Pine Forest;
Fox-spirits will likely bar your way.
Griffins will fill the capitals;
Monsters all mountains populate;
Old tigers sit as magistrates;
Graying wolves act as registrars.
Lions, elephants—all called kings!
Leopards, tigers are coachmen all!
A wild pig totes a hauling pole;
You'll meet ahead a water sprite.
An old stone ape of many years
Nurses his anger over there!
Just ask that acquaintance of yours;
Well he knows the way to the West.

Hearing this, Pilgrim laughed with scorn and said, "Let's go. Don't ask him, ask me! That's enough!" Tripitaka did not perceive what he meant. The Zen Master, changing into a beam of golden light, went straight up to his crow's nest, while the priest bowed toward him to express his gratitude. Enraged, Pilgrim lifted his iron rod and thrust it upward violently, but garlands of blooming lotus flowers were seen together with a thousand-layered shield of blessed clouds. Though Pilgrim might have the strength to overturn rivers and seas, he could not catch hold of even one strand of the crow's nest. When Tripitaka saw this, he pulled Pilgrim back, saying, "Wu-k'ung, why are you jabbing at the nest of a bodhisattva like him?" "For leaving like that after abusing both my brother and me," said Pilgrim. "He was speaking of the way to the Western Heaven," said Tripitaka. "Since when did he abuse you?" "Didn't you get it?" asked Pilgrim. "He said, 'A wild pig totes a hauling pole,' and insulted Pa-chieh; 'An old stone ape of many years' was an insult to old Monkey. How else would you understand that?" "Elder Brother," said Pa-chieh, "don't be angry. This Zen Master does know the events of past and future. Let's see if his statement, 'You'll meet ahead a water sprite,' will be fulfilled or not. Let's spare him and leave." Pilgrim saw the

lotus flowers and auspicious fog near the nest, and he had little
alternative than to ask his master to mount so that they could
descend from the mountain and proceed toward the West. Lo, their
journey

Thus proves that in man's world pure luck is rare,

But evils and ogres are rife in the hills!

We really do not know what took place in the journey ahead, and
you must listen to the explanation in the next chapter.

Twenty

At Yellow Wind Ridge the T'ang monk meets adversity;
In mid-mountain, Pa-chieh strives to be first.

The dharma is born through the mind;
It will be destroyed, too, through the mind.
By whom it is destroyed or born,
You are asked to judge for yourself.
If it is through your own mind,
What do others need to tell you?
All that you need do is strive
To draw blood out of iron ore.
Let a silk cord puncture your nose
To tie a firm knot on the void;
And fasten that to the *wu-wei* tree,[1]
That you may not be vicious and wild.
Regard not the thief as your son,
And forget all dharma and mind.
Let not the other one fool me:
Strike him out first with one punch.
The manifest mind is no mind;
And Law that's manifest has stopped.
When both Bull[2] and Man disappear,
The jade-green sky is bright and clear.
The autumn moon is just as full:
You can't tell one from the other.

This enigmatic verse[3] was composed by Hsüan-tsang, master of the law, after he had thoroughly mastered the *Heart Sūtra*, which had, in fact, broken through the gate of his understanding. He recited it frequently, and the beam of spiritual light penetrated by itself to his innermost being.

We turn now to tell you about the three travelers, who dined on the wind and rested by the waters, who clothed themselves with the moon and cloaked themselves with the stars on their journey. Soon,

it was the scene of summer again, beneath a torrid sky. They saw
Flowers gone, and butterflies cared not to linger;
On tall trees the cicada chirp turned brazen.
Wild worms made their cocoons, fair pomegranates their fire,
As new lilies in the ponds appeared.

As they were traveling one day, it was growing late again when they
saw a hamlet beside the mountain road. "Wu-k'ung," said Tripitaka, "look at that sun setting behind the mountain, hiding its fiery
orb, and the moon rising on the eastern sea, revealing an icy wheel.
It's a good thing that a family lives by the road up there. Let us ask for
lodging for the night and proceed tomorrow." "You are right!" said
Pa-chieh. "Old Hog is rather hungry, too! Let's go and beg for some
food at the house. Then I can regain my strength to pole the luggage."
"This family-hugging devil!" said Pilgrim. "You only left the family
a few days ago, and you are already beginning to complain." "Elder
Brother," said Pa-Chieh, "I'm not like you—I can't imbibe the wind
and exhale the mist. Since I began following our master a few days
ago, I've been half hungry all the time. Did you know that?" Hearing
this, Tripitaka said, "Wu-nêng, if your heart still clings to the family,
you are not the kind of person who wants to leave it. You may as well
turn back!" Idiot was so taken aback that he fell on his knees and
said, "Master, please do not listen to the words of Elder Brother. He
loves to put blame on others: I haven't made any complaint, but he
said that I was complaining. I'm only an honest moron, who said that
I was hungry so that we could find some household to beg for food.
Immediately he called me a family-hugging devil! Master, I received
the commandments from the Bodhisattva and mercy from you, and
that was why I was determined to serve you and go to the Western
Heaven. I vow that I have no regrets. This is, in fact, what they call
the practice of strict austerities. What do you mean, I'm not willing
to leave the family?" "In that case," said Tripitaka, "you may get up."

Leaping up with a bound, Idiot was still muttering something as
he picked up the pole with the luggage. He had no choice but to follow
his companions with complete determination up to the door of the
house by the wayside. Tripitaka dismounted, Pilgrim took the reins,
and Pa-chieh put down the luggage, all standing still beneath the
shade of a large tree. Holding his nine-ringed priestly staff and pressing down his rain hat woven of straw and rattan, Tripitaka went to
the door first. He saw inside an old man reclining on a bamboo bed

and softly reciting the name of Buddha. Tripitaka dared not speak loudly; instead, he said very slowly and quietly, "Patron, salutations!" The old man jumped up and at once began to straighten out his attire. He walked out of the door to return the greeting, saying, "Honored Priest, pardon me for not coming to meet you. Where did you come from? What are you doing at my humble abode?" "This poor monk," said Tripitaka, "happens to be a priest from the Great T'ang in the Land of the East. In obedience to an imperial decree, I am journeying to the Great Thunderclap Temple to seek scriptures from the Buddha. It was getting late when I arrived in your esteemed region, and I would beg for shelter for one night in your fine mansion. I beseech you to grant me this favor." "You can't go there," said the old man, shaking his head and waving his hand, "it's exceedingly difficult to bring scriptures back from the Western Heaven. If you want to do that, you might as well go the Eastern Heaven!" Tripitaka fell silent, thinking to himself: "The Bodhisattva clearly told me to go to the West. Why does this old man now say that I should head for the East instead? Where in the East would there be any scriptures?" Terribly flustered and embarrassed, he could not make any reply for a long time.

We now tell you about Pilgrim, who had always been impulsive and mischievous. Unable to restrain himself, he went forward and said in a loud voice, "Old man! Though you are of such great age, you don't have much common sense. We monks have traveled a great distance to come and ask you for shelter, and here you are trying to intimidate us with discouraging words. If your house is too small and there's not enough space for us to sleep, we'll sit beneath the trees for the night and not disturb you." "Master!" said the old man, taking hold of Tipitaka, "you don't say anything. But that disciple of yours with a pointed chin, shriveled cheeks, a thunder-god mouth, and blood-red eyes—he looks like a demon with a bad case of consumption —how dare he offend an aged person like me!" "An old fellow like you," said Pilgrim with a laugh, "really has very little discernment! Those who are handsome may be good for their looks only! A person like me, old Monkey, may be small but tough, like the skin around a ball of ligaments!" "I suppose you must have some abilities," said the old man. "I won't boast," said Pilgrim, "but they are passable." "Where did you use to live?" asked the old man, "and why did you shave your hair to become a monk?" "The ancestral home of old

Monkey," said Pilgrim, "is at the Water-Curtain Cave in the Flower-
Fruit Mountain, in the Ao-lai Country of the East Pūrvavideha Continent. I learned to be a monster-spirit in my youth, assuming the
name of Wu-k'ung, and with my abilities I finally became the Great
Sage, Equal to Heaven. Because I did not receive any acceptable
appointment in Heaven, I caused great turmoil in the Celestial Palace,
and incurred great calamities for myself. I was, however, delivered
from my ordeals and have turned to Buddhism instead to seek the
fruits of Truth. As a guardian of my master, who is in the service of
the T'ang court, I am journeying to the Western Heaven to worship
Buddha. Why should I fear tall mountains, treacherous roads, wide
waters, and wild waves? I, old Monkey, can apprehend monsters,
subdue demons, tame tigers, capture dragons—in sum, I know a
little about all the matters which a person needs to know to go up to
Heaven or to descend into Earth. If by chance your household is
suffering from some such disturbances as flying bricks and dancing
tiles, or talking pots and doors opening by themselves, old Monkey
can quiet things down for you."

When that old man heard this lengthy speech, he roared with
laughter and said, "So you are really a garrulous monk who begs for
alms from place to place!" "Only your son is garrulous!" said Pilgrim.
"I'm not very talkative these days, because following my master on
his journey is quite tiring." "If you were not tired," said that old
man, "and if you were in the mood to chatter, you would probably
talk me to death! Since you have such abilities, I suppose you can go
to the West all right. How many of you are there? You may rest in
my thatched hut." "We thank the old patron for not sending us
away," said Tripitaka; "there are three of us altogether." "Where is
the third member of your party?" asked the old man. "Your eyes
must be somewhat dim, old man," said Pilgrim. "Isn't he over there
standing in the shade?" The old man did indeed have poor sight; he
raised his head and stared intently. The moment he saw Pa-chieh
with his strange face and mouth, he became so terrified that he
started to rush back into the house, tripping at every step. "Shut the
door! Shut the door!" he cried. "A monster is coming!" Pilgrim
caught hold of him, saying, "Don't be afraid, old man! He's no
monster; he's my younger brother." "Fine! Fine! Fine!" said the old
man, shaking all over. "One monk uglier than another!" Pa-chieh
approached him and said, "You are really mistaken, Aged Sir, if you

judge people by their looks. We may be ugly, but we are all useful."

As the old man was speaking with the three monks in front of his house, two young men appeared to the south of the village, leading an old woman and several young children. All of them had their clothes rolled up and were walking barefoot, for they were returning after a day's planting of young shoots of grain. When they saw the white horse, the luggage, and the goings-on in front of their house, they all ran forward asking, "What are you people doing here?" Turning his head, Pa-chieh flapped his ears a couple of times and stuck out his long snout once, so frightening the people that they fell down right and left, madly scattering in every direction. Tripitaka, alarmed, kept saying, "Don't be afraid! Don't be afraid! We are not bad people! We are monks in quest of scriptures." Coming out of his house, the old man helped the old woman up, saying, "Mama, get up! Calm yourself. This master came from the T'ang Court. His disciples may look hideous, but they are really good people with ugly faces. Take the boys and girls back into the house." Clutching at the old man, the old woman walked inside with the two young men and their children.

Sitting on the bamboo bed in their house, Tripitaka began to pro-test, saying, "Disciples! The two of you are not only ugly in appear-ance; you are also rude in your language. You have scared this family badly, and you are causing me to sin." "To tell you the truth, Master," said Pa-chieh, "since I started accompanying you, I have become a lot better behaved. At the time when I was living in Old Kao Village, all I needed to do was to pout and flap my ears once, and scores of people would be frightened to death!" "Stop talking rubbish, Idiot," said Pilgrim, "and fix your ugliness." "Look at the way Wu-k'ung talks," said Tripitaka. "Your appearance comes with your birth. How can you tell him to fix it?" "Take that rakelike snout," said Pilgrim, "put it in your bosom, and don't take it out. And stick your rush-leaf-fan ears to the back of your head, and don't shake them. That's fixing it." Pa-chieh did indeed hide his snout and stick his ears to the back of his head; with his hands folded in front of him to hide his head, he stood on one side of his master. Pilgrim took the luggage inside the main door, and tied the white horse to one of the posts in the courtyard.

The old man then brought a young man in to present three cups of tea placed on a wooden tray. After the tea, he ordered a vegetarian meal to be prepared. Then the young man took an old, unvarnished table full of holes and several stools with broken legs, and placed them in the courtyard for the three of them to sit where it was cool. Only then did Tripitaka ask, "Old patron, what is your noble surname?" "Your humble servant goes by the surname of Wang," said the old man. "And how many heirs do you have?" asked Tripitaka. "I have two sons and three grandchildren," said the old man. "Congratulations! Congratulations!" said Tripitaka. "And what is your age?" "I have foolishly lived till my sixty-first year," the old man said. "Good! Good! Good!" said Pilgrim. "You have just begun a new sexagenary cycle." "Old patron," said Tripitaka again, "you said when we first came that the scriptures in the Western Heaven were difficult to get. Why?" "The scriptures are not hard to get," said the old man, "but the journey there is filled with hazards and difficulties. Some thirty miles west of us there is a mountain called the Yellow Wind Ridge of Eight Hundred Miles. Monsters infest that mountain, and that's what I meant by difficulties. Since this little priest claims that he has many abilities, however, you may perhaps proceed after all." "No fear! No fear!" said Pilgrim. "With old Monkey and his younger brother around, we'll never be touched, no matter what kind of monster we meet."

While they spoke, one of the sons brought out some rice and placed it on the table, saying, "Please eat." Tripitaka immediately folded his hands to begin his grace, but Pa-chieh had already swallowed a whole bowl of rice. Before the priest could say the few sentences, Idiot had devoured three more bowlfuls. "Look at the glutton!" said Pilgrim. "It's like meeting a preta!" Old Wang was a sensitive person. When he saw how fast Pa-chieh was eating, he said, "This honored priest must be really hungry! Quick, bring more rice!" Idiot in truth had an enormous appetite. Look at him! Without lifting his head once, he finished over ten bowls, while Tripitaka and Pilgrim could hardly finish two.

Idiot refused to stop and wanted to eat still more. "In our haste we have not prepared any dainty viands," said old Wang, "and I dare not press you too much. Please take at least one more helping." Both Tripitaka and Pilgrim said, "We have had enough." "Old man," said Pa-chieh, "what are you mumbling about? Who's having a game of divination with you? Why mention all that about the fifth yao and the sixth yao?[4] If you have rice, just bring more of it, that's all!" So

Idiot in one meal finished up all the rice in that household, and then he said he was only half filled! The tables and dishes were cleared away, and after bedding had been placed on the bamboo bed and on some wooden boards, the travelers rested.

Next morning, Pilgrim went to saddle the horse, while Pa-chieh put their luggage in order. Old Wang asked his wife to prepare some refreshments and drinks to serve them, after which the three of them expressed their thanks and took leave of their host. The old man said, "If there is any mishap on your journey after you leave here, you must feel free to return to our house." "Old man," said Pilgrim, "don't speak such disconcerting words. Those of us who have left the family never retrace our steps!" They then urged on the horse, picked up the luggage, and proceeded toward the West. Alas! What this journey means for them is that

There's no safe way which leads to the Western Realm;
There'll be great disasters brought by demons vile.

Before the three of them had traveled for half a day, they did indeed come upon a tall mountain, exceedingly rugged. Tripitaka rode right up to the hanging cliff and looked around, sitting sideways on his saddle. Truly

Tall was the mountain;
Rugged, the peak;
Steep, the precipice;
Deep, the canyon;
Gurgling, the stream;
And fresh were the flowers.
This mountain, whether tall or not,
Its top reached the blue sky;
This stream, whether deep or not,
Its floor opened to Hell below.
Before the mountain,
White clouds rose in continuous rings
And boulders in shapes grotesque.
Countless the soul-rending cliffs ten thousand yards deep;
Behind them, winding, twisting, dragon-hiding caves,
Where water dripped from ledges drop by drop.
He also saw some deer with zigzag horns;
Dull and dumbly staring antelopes;
Winding and coiling red-scaled pythons;

Silly and foolish white-faced apes;
Tigers that climbed the hills to seek their dens at night;
Dragons that churned the waves to leave their lairs at dawn.
If one stepped before a cave's entrance,
The dead leaves crackled;
The fowls in the grass
Darted up with wings loudly beating;
The beasts in the forest
Walked with paws noisily scratching.
Suddenly wild creatures hurried by,
Making hearts beat with fear.
Thus it was that the Due-to-Fall Cave duly faced the Due-to-Fall
    Cave,
The Cave duly facing the Due-to-Fall Cave duly faced the mount.[5]
A blue mountain dyed like a thousand feet of jade,
Veiled by mists like countless piles of jade-green gauze.

The master rode forward very slowly, while the Great Sage Sun also
walked at a slower pace and Chu Wu-nêng proceeded leisurely with
the load. As all of them were looking at the mountain, a great whirlwind suddenly arose. Alarmed, Tripitaka said, "Wu-k'ung, the wind
is rising!" "Why fear the wind?" said Pilgrim. "This is the breath of
Heaven in the four seasons, nothing to be afraid of." "But this is a
terribly violent wind, unlike the kind which comes from Heaven,"
said Tripitaka. "How so?" said Pilgrim. Tripitaka said, "Look at this
wind!

Augustly it blows in a blusterous key,
An immense force leaving the jade-green sky.
It passes the ridge, just hear the trees roar.
It moves in the wood, just see the poles quake.
Willows by the banks are shaken to the roots;
Blown flowers in the garden soar with their leaves.
Fishing boats, nets retrieved, make their hawsers taut;
Vessels with sails down have their anchors cast.
Trekkers in mid-journey have lost their way;
Woodsmen in the hills cannot hold their loads.
From woods with fruits divine the apes disperse;
From clumps of rare flowers the small fawns flee.
Cypress before the cliffs fall one by one;

Bamboos downstream and pines die leaf by leaf.
Earth and dust are scattered while sand explodes;
Rivers and seas overturned, waves churn and roll."
Pa-chieh went forward and tugged at Pilgrim, saying, "Elder Brother,
the wind is too strong! Let's find shelter until it dies down." "You are
too soft, Brother," said Pilgrim, laughing, "when you want to hide
the moment the wind gets strong. What would happen to you if you
were to meet a monster-spirit face to face?" "Elder Brother," said
Pa-chieh, "you probably haven't heard of the proverb, 'Flee sensuality
like an enemy; flee the wind like an arrow!' We suffer no loss if we
take shelter just for a little while." "Stop talking," said Pilgrim, "and
let me seize the wind and smell it." "You are fibbing again, Elder
Brother," said Pa-chieh, with a laugh, "for how can the wind be
seized for you to smell? Even if you manage to catch hold of it, it
will slip past you at once." "Brother," said Pilgrim, "you didn't know
that I have the power to 'seize the wind.'" Dear Great Sage! He
allowed the head of the wind to move past but he caught hold of its
tail and sniffed at it. Finding it somewhat fetid, he said, "This is
indeed not a very good wind, for it smells like a tiger or else like a
monster; there's something definitely strange about it."

Hardly had he finished speaking when from over a hump of the
mountain a fierce striped tiger with a whiplike tail and powerful limbs
appeared. Tripitaka was so horrified that he could no longer sit on
the saddle; he fell head over heels from the white horse and lay beside
the road, half out of his wits. Throwing down the luggage, Pa-chieh
took up his muckrake and rushed past Pilgrim. "Cursed beast!" he
shouted. "Where are you going?" He lunged forward and struck at
the beast's head. That tiger stood straight up on his hind legs and,
raising his left paw, punctured his own breast with one jab. Then,
gripping the skin, he tore downward with a loud rending noise and
he became completely stripped of his own hide as he stood there by
the side of the road. Look how abominable he appears! Oh! That
hideous form:

All smeared with blood, the naked body;
Most sickly red, the warped legs and feet;
Like shooting flames, wild hair by the temples;
Bristlingly hard, two eyebrows pointing upward;
Hellishly white, four steel-like fangs;

With light aglow, a pair of gold eyes;
Imposing of mien, he mightily roared;
With power fierce, he cried aloud.

"Slow down! Slow down!" he shouted. "I am not any other person. I am the vanguard of the forces commanded by the Great King Yellow Wind. I have received the Great King's strict order to patrol this mountain and to catch a few mortals to be used as hors-d'œuvres for him. Where did you monks come from that you dare reach for your weapons to harm me?" "Cursed beast that you are!" cried Pa-chieh. "So you don't recognize me! We are no mortals who just happen to be passing by; we are the disciples of Tripitaka, the royal brother of the Great T'ang Emperor in the Land of the East, who by imperial decree is journeying to the Western Heaven to seek scriptures from the Buddha. You better stand aside quickly for us to pass, and don't alarm my master. Then I'll spare your life. But if you are impudent as before, there will be no clemency when this rake is lifted up!"

That monster-spirit would not permit any further discussion. He quickly drew near, assumed a fighting pose, and clawed at Pa-chieh's face. Dodging the blow, Pa-chieh struck at once with his rake. Since the monster had no weapons in his hands, he turned and fled, with Pa-chieh hard on his heels. Racing to the slope below, the monster took out from beneath a clump of rocks a pair of bronze scimitars, with which he turned to face his pursuer. So the two of them clashed right in front of the mountain slope, closing in again and again. Meanwhile, Pilgrim lifted up the T'ang monk and said, "Master, don't be afraid. Sit here and let old Monkey go help Pa-chieh strike down that monster so that we can leave." Only then did Tripitaka manage to sit up; trembling all over, he began to recite the *Heart Sūtra*, but we shall say no more of that.

Whipping out the iron rod, Pilgrim shouted, "Catch him!" Pa-chieh at once attacked with even greater ferocity, and the monster fled in defeat. "Don't spare him," yelled Pilgrim. "We must catch him!" Wielding rod and rake, the two of them gave chase down the mountain. In panic, the monster resorted to the trick of the gold cicada casting its shell: he rolled on the ground and changed back into the form of a tiger. Pilgrim and Pa-chieh would not let up. Closing in on the tiger, they intended to dispose of him once and for all. When the monster saw them approaching, he again stripped himself of his

own hide and threw the skin over a large piece of rock, while his true
form changed into a violent gust of wind heading back the way he
had come. Suddenly noticing the master of the law sitting by the road
and reciting the *Heart Sūtra*, he caught hold of him and hauled him
away by mounting the wind. O, pity that Tripitaka,

The River Float fated to suffer oft!

It's hard to make merit in Buddha's gate!

Having taken the T'ang monk back to the door of his cave, the
monster stopped the wind and said to the one standing guard at the
door, "Go report to the Great King and say that the Tiger Vanguard
has captured a monk. He awaits his order outside the door." The
Cave Master gave the order for him to enter. The Tiger Vanguard,
with the two bronze scimitars hanging from his waist, lifted up the
T'ang monk in his hands. He went forward and knelt down, saying,
"Great King! Though your humble officer is not talented, he thanks
you for granting him the honored command of doing patrol in the
mountain. I encountered a monk who is Tripitaka, master of the law
and brother to the Throne of the Great T'ang in the Land of the East.
While he was on his way to seek scriptures from Buddha, I captured
him to present to you here for your culinary pleasure." When the
Cave Master heard this, he was a little startled. "I have heard some
rumor," he said, "that the master of the law Tripitaka is a divine
monk who is going in search of scriptures by imperial decree of the
Great T'ang. He has under him a disciple whose name is Pilgrim Sun
and who possesses tremendous magical power and prodigious intelligence. How did you manage to catch him and bring him here?" "He
has, in fact, two disciples," said the Vanguard. "The one who
appeared first used a nine-pronged muckrake, and he had a long
snout and huge ears. Another one used a golden-hooped iron rod,
and he had fiery eyes and diamond pupils. As they were chasing me
to attack me, I used the trick of the gold cicada casting its shell and
succeeded not only in eluding them but also in catching this monk.
I now respectfully present him to the Great King as a meal." "Let's
not eat him yet," said the Cave Master. "Great King," said the Vanguard, "only a worthless horse turns away ready feed!" "You
haven't considered this," said the Cave Master. "There's nothing
wrong with eating him, but I'm afraid his two disciples may come to
our door and argue with us. Let's tie him instead to one of the posts
in the rear garden and wait for three or four days. If those two don't

show up to disturb us, then we can enjoy the double benefit of having his body cleaned and not having to bicker with our tongues. Then we can do what we want with him, whether we wish him boiled, steamed, fried, or sautéed; we can take our time to enjoy him." Highly pleased, the Vanguard said, "The Great King is full of wisdom and foresight, and what he says is most reasonable. Little ones, take the priest inside."

Seven or eight demons rushed up from the sides and took the T'ang monk away; like hawks catching sparrows, they bound him firmly with ropes. This is how that

Ill-fated River Float on Pilgrim broods;
The god-monk in pain calls Wu-nêng to mind.

"Disciples," he said, "I don't know in what mountain you are catching monsters, or in what region you are subduing goblins. But I have been captured by this demon from whom I have to suffer great injury. When shall we see each other again? Oh, what misery! If you two can come here quickly, you may be able to save my life. But if you tarry, I shall never survive!" As he lamented and sighed, his tears fell like rain.

We now tell you about Pilgrim and Pa-chieh, who, having chased the tiger down the slope of the mountain, saw him fall and collapse at the foot of the cliff. Lifting his rod, Pilgrim brought it down on the tiger with all his might, but the rod bounced back up and his hands were stung by the impact. Pa-chieh, too, gave a blow with his muck-rake, and its prongs also rebounded. They then discovered that it was nothing but a piece of tigerskin covering a large slab of stone. Greatly startled, Pilgrim said, "Oh, no! Oh, no! He's tricked us!" "What trick?" said Pa-chieh. Pilgrim said, "This is called the trick of the gold cicada casting its shell. He left his skin covering the stone here to fool us, but he himself has escaped. Let's go back at once to take a look at Master. Let's hope that he has not been hurt." They retreated hurriedly, but Tripitaka had long vanished. Bellowing like thunder, Pilgrim cried, "What shall we do? He has taken Master away." "Heavens! Heavens!" wailed Pa-chieh, leading the horse, as tears fell from his eyes, "where shall we go to look for him?" With head held high, Pilgrim said, "Don't cry! Don't cry! The moment you cry, you already feel defeated. They have to be somewhere in this mountain. Let's go and search for them."

The two of them indeed rushed up the mountain, passing the ridges and scaling the heights. After traveling for a long time, they suddenly beheld a cave dwelling emerging from beneath a cliff. Pausing to take a careful look around, they saw that it was indeed a formidable place. You see

A pointed peak fortresslike;
An old path ever winding;
Blue pines and fresh bamboos;
Green willows and verdant wu-trees;[6]
Strange rocks in twos below the cliff;
Rare fowls in pairs within the woods.
A stream flowing far away spills over a wall of stones;
The mountain brook reaches the sandy banks in small drops.
Wasteland clouds in clusters;
And grass as green as jade.
The sly vixen and hare scamper wildly about;
Horned deer and muskdeer lock to contest their strength.
Slanted across the cliff dangles an aged vine;
Half down the gorge an ancient cedar hangs.
August and grand, this place surpasses Mount Hua;[7]
The falling blooms and singing birds rival T'ien-t'ai's.

"Worthy Brother," said Pilgrim, "you may leave the luggage in the fold of the mountain, where it will be protected from the wind. Then you can graze the horse nearby and you need not come out. Let old Monkey go fight with him at his door. That monster has to be caught before our master can be rescued." "No need for instructions," said Pa-chieh. "Go quickly!" Pulling down his shirt and tightening his belt on the tiger-skin skirt, Pilgrim grasped his rod and rushed up to the cave, where he saw six words in large letters above the door: "Yellow Wind Cave, Yellow Wind Peak." He at once poised himself for battle, with legs apart and one foot slightly ahead of the other. Holding his rod high, he cried: "Monster! Send out my master at once, lest I overturn your den and level your dwelling!"

When the little demons heard this, every one of them was panic-stricken and ran inside to make the report: "Great King, disaster!" The Yellow Wind Monster, who was sitting there, asked, "What's the matter?" "Outside the cave door there's a monk with a thunder-god mouth and hairy face," said one of the little demons, "holding in his hands a huge, thick, iron rod and demanding the return of his master." Somewhat fearful, the Cave Master said to the Tiger Vanguard, "I asked you to patrol the mountain, and you should merely have caught a few mountain buffalo, wild boar, fat deer, or wild goats. Why did you have to bring back a T'ang monk? Now we have provoked his disciple to come here to create all sorts of disturbance. What shall we do?" "Don't be anxious, Great King," said the Vanguard, "and put your worries to rest. Though this junior officer is untalented, he is willing to lead fifty soldiers out there and bring in that so-called Pilgrim Sun as a condiment for your meal." "In addition to the various officers here," said the Cave Master, "we have some seven hundred regulars. You may pick as many of them as you want. Only if that Pilgrim is caught will we be able to enjoy a piece of that monk's flesh with any comfort. And if that happens, I'm willing to become your bond brother. But I fear that if you can't catch him, you may even get hurt. You mustn't blame me then!" "Relax! Relax! Let me go now!" said the Tiger Monster. He checked off the roll fifty of the toughest little demons, who began beating drums and waving banners. He himself took up the two bronze scimitars and leaped out of the cave, crying with a loud voice, "Where did you come from, you monkey-monk, that you dare make such a racket here?" "You skin-flaying beast!" shouted Pilgrim. "You were the one who used that shell-casting trick to take away my master. Why do you question me instead? You better send out my master immediately, or I'll not spare your life." "I took your master," said the Tiger Monster, "so that he could be served to my Great King as meat for his rice. If you know what's good for you, get away from here. If not, I'll catch you too, and you'll be eaten along with him. It will be like 'one free piece of merchandise with every purchase!'" When he heard this, Pilgrim was filled with anger. With grinding teeth and fiery eyes all ablaze, he lifted his iron rod and yelled, "What great ability do you have, that you dare talk like that? Don't move! Watch this rod!" Wielding his scimitars swiftly, the Vanguard turned to meet him. It was truly some battle as the two of them let loose their power. What a fight!

> That monster is truly a goose egg,
> But Wu-k'ung is a goose egg stone no less!
> When bronze swords fight Handsome Monkey King,
> It's as if eggs were attacking stones.

How can sparrows strive with the phoenix?
Dare pigeons oppose the eagles and hawks?
The monster belches wind to fill the mount with dust;
Wu-k'ung spits out fog and clouds hide the sun.
They fight for no more than four or five rounds.
The Vanguard grows weak, having no strength left.
He turns in defeat to flee for his life,
Hard pressed by Wu-k'ung, who seeks his death.

Not able to hold out any longer, the monster turned and fled. But since he had boasted in front of the Cave Master, he dared not go back to the cave; instead, he fled toward the mountain slope. Pilgrim, of course, would not let him go; holding his rod, he gave chase relentlessly, shouting and crying along the way. As they reached the fold of the mountain, which formed a wind break, he happened to look up, and there was Pa-chieh grazing the horse. Hearing all the shouts and clamor, Pa-chieh turned around and saw that it was Pilgrim chasing a defeated Tiger Monster. Abandoning the horse, Pa-chieh lifted his rake and approaching from one side brought it down hard on the monster's head. Pity that Vanguard!

He hoped to leap clear of the brown-rope net,
Not knowing he would meet the fisher's coop.

One blow from Pa-chieh's rake produced nine holes, from which fresh blood spurted out, and the brains of the monster's whole head ran dry! We have a poem as a testimony for Pa-chieh, which says:

He came back to True Teaching some years ago,
Keeping a chaste diet to reach the True Void.
To serve Tripitaka was his desire;
This, his first merit, as a new convert.

Idiot put his foot on the monster's spine and brought down the rake on him once more. When Pilgrim saw that, he was very pleased, saying, "That's right, Brother! He was audacious enough to lead scores of little demons against me, but he was defeated. Instead of fleeing back to the cave, he came here seeking death. It's a good thing you are here, or else he would have escaped again." "Is he the one who took our master with the wind?" said Pa-chieh. "Yes! Yes!" said Pilgrim. "Did you ask him the whereabouts of our master?" said Pa-chieh. "This monster brought Master to the cave," said Pilgrim, "to be served to some blackguard of a Great King as meat for his rice. I was enraged, fought with him, and chased him here for you to finish him off. Brother, this is your merit! You can remain here guarding the horse and luggage, and let me drag this dead monster back to the mouth of the cave to provoke battle again. We must capture the old monster before we can rescue Master." "You are right, Elder Brother," said Pa-chieh. "Go, go now! If you beat that old monster, chase him here and let old Hog intercept and kill him." Dear Pilgrim! Holding the iron rod in one hand and dragging the dead tiger with the other, he went back to the mouth of the cave. So it was that

The master of the law met monsters in his ordeal;

Nature and feeling in harmony wild demons subdued.

We do not know whether he managed this time to overcome the monster and rescue the T'ang monk, and you must listen to the explanation in the next chapter.

Twenty-one

The Vihārapālas[1] prepare lodging for the Great Sage;
Ling-chi of Sumeru crushes the Wind Demon.

We shall now tell about those fifty defeated little demons, who rushed into the cave carrying their broken drums and torn banners. "Great King," they cried, "the Tiger Vanguard was no match for the hairy-faced monk. That monk chased him down the eastern slope until the Vanguard disappeared." When the old monster heard this, he was terribly upset. As he bowed his head in silent deliberation, another little demon who stood guard at the door came to report: "Great King, the Tiger Vanguard was beaten to death by the hairy-faced monk and dragged up to our door to provoke battle." Hearing this, the old monster became even angrier. "This fellow does not know when to stop!" he said. "I have not eaten his master, but he has killed our Vanguard instead. How despicable! Bring me my armor. I have heard only rumors about this Pilgrim Sun, and I'm going out there to find out what sort of monk he really is. Even if he has nine heads and eight tails, I'm going to take him in here to pay for the life of my Tiger Vanguard!" The little demons quickly brought out the armor. After having been properly buckled and laced, the old monster took a steel trident and leaped out of the cave leading the rest of the demons. Standing in front of the door, the Great Sage watched the monster emerge with a truly aggressive appearance. Look how he is attired. You see

Gold helmet reflecting the sun;
Gold cuirass gleaming with light.
A pheasant-tail tassel flies from the helmet;
A light yellow silk robe topped by the cuirass,
Tied with a dragonlike sash of brilliant hues.
His breastplate emits eye-dazzling light.
His boots of suede
Are dyed by locust flowers.
His embroidered kilt

Is decked with willow leaves.
Holding a sharp trident in his hands,
He seems almost the Erh-lang Boy of old![2]

When he had come out, the old monster shouted, "Who is Pilgrim
Sun?" With one foot on the carcass of the Tiger Monster and the
compliant iron rod in his hands, Pilgrim replied: "Your Grandpa Sun
is here! Send my master out!" The old monster took a careful look
and saw the diminutive figure of Pilgrim—less than four feet, in fact
—and his sallow cheeks. He said with a laugh: "Too bad! Too bad! I
thought you were some kind of invincible hero. But you are only a
sickly ghost, with nothing more than your skeleton left!" "My son,"
said Pilgrim laughing, "how you lack perception! Your grandpa may
be somewhat small in size, but if you have the courage to hit me on
the head with the handle of your trident, I'll grow six feet at once."
"Harden your head," said the monster, "and have a taste of my
handle!" Our Great Sage was not in the least frightened. When the
monster struck him once, he stretched his waist and at once grew
more than six feet, attaining the height of ten feet altogether. The
monster was so alarmed that he tried to use his trident to hold him
down, shouting, "Pilgrim Sun, how dare you stand at my door, displaying this paltry magic of body protection! Stop using tricks! Come
up here and let's measure our real abilities!" "My dear son," said
Pilgrim with laughter, "the proverb says: 'Mercy should be shown
before the hand is raised!' Your grandpa is pretty heavy-handed, and
he fears that you won't be able to bear even one stroke of this rod!"
Refusing to listen to any such discussion, the monster turned his
trident around and stabbed at Pilgrim's chest. The Great Sage, of
course, was not at all perturbed, for as the saying goes: The expert
is never exercised. He raised his rod and, using the movement of the
"black dragon sweeping the ground" to parry the trident, struck at
the monster's head. The two of them thus began a fierce battle before
that Yellow Wind Cave:

The Monster King became enraged;
The Great Sage released his might.
The Monster King became enraged,
Wishing to seize Pilgrim to pay for his Vanguard.
The Great Sage released his might
To capture this spirit and to save the priest.
The trident arrived, blocked by the rod;

The rod went forth, met by the trident.
This one, a mountain-ruling captain of his hosts.
That one, the Handsome Monkey King who defends the Law.
At first they fought on the dusty earth;
Then each arose midway to the sky.
The fine steel trident;
Pointed, sharp, and brilliant.
The compliant rod:
Body black and yellow hoops.
Stabbed by them, your soul goes back to darkness!
Struck by them, you'll face King Yama!
You must rely on quick arms and keen sight.
You must have a tough frame and great strength.
The two fought without regard for life or death;
We know not who will be safe or who will be hurt.

The old monster and the Great Sage fought for thirty rounds, but neither could gain the upper hand. Pressing for a quick victory, Pilgrim decided to use the trick of "the body beyond the body." He tore from himself a handful of hairs which he chewed to pieces in his mouth. Spitting them out, he cried, "Change!" They changed at once into more than a hundred Pilgrims: all having the same appearance and all holding an iron rod, they surrounded the monster in mid-air. Somewhat alarmed, the monster also resorted to his special talent. He turned to face the ground to the southwest and opened his mouth three times to blow out some air. Suddenly a mighty yellow wind arose in the sky. Dear wind! It was indeed powerful.

Cold and whistling, it changed Heaven and Earth,
As yellow sand whirled without form or shape.
It stabbed through woods and mountains,
    toppling pines and plums;
It tossed up dirt and dust, cracking crags and cliffs.
Churning waves of Huang Ho[3] muddied all its floor;
Tide and current swelled up at River Hsiang.
The Polestar Palace in the blue sky shook;
The Hall of Darkness was almost blown down;
The Five Hundred Arhats all yelled and screamed;
The Eight Guards of Akṣobhya all cried and shrieked.
Mañjuśrī's green-haired lion ran away;
Viśvabhadra lost his white elephant.[4]

Snake and turtle of Chên-wu[5] left their fold;
Aflutter were the saddle-flaps of Tzŭ-t'ung's[6] mule.
Traveling merchants sent their cries to Heaven,
And boatmen bowed to make their many vows.
Their mistlike lives awash in rolling waves!
Their names, their fortunes, adrift in the tide!
Caves on genie mountains were black as pitch;
The isle of P'êng-lai[7] was gloomy and dark.
Lao Tzu could not tend his elixir brazier;
Age Star folded his fan of grapevine leaves.
As Wang-mu[8] traveled to the Peaches Feast,
The wind blew her skirt and pins awry.
Erh-lang lost his way to the Kuan Chou town;
Naṭa found it hard to pull out his sword.
Li Ching missed the pagoda in his hand;
Lu Pan[9] dropped his golden-headed drill.
While three stories of Thunderclap fell down,
The stone bridge at Chao Chou broke in twain.
The orb of the red sun had little light;
The stars of all Heaven grew obscure and faint.
Birds of south mountains flew to northern hills;
Water of east lakes spilled over to the west.
Fowls with mates broke up, they ceased their calls;
Mothers and sons parted, their cries turned mute.
Dragon Kings sought yakṣas all over the sea;
Thunder gods hunted lightnings everywhere.
Ten Kings of Yama tried to find their judge;
In Hell, Bull-Head ran after Horse-Face.
This wind blew down the Potalaka Mount
And whipped up one scroll of Kuan-yin's verse.
White lotus-blooms, cut down, flew beside the sea;
Twelve halls of the Bodhisattva were blown down.
From P'an-ku[10] till this time since wind was known,
There never was wind with such ferocity.
Hu-la-la!
The universe did almost split apart!
The whole world was one mighty trembling mass!

This violent wind called up by the monster blew away all those little
Pilgrims formed by the Great Sage's hairs and sent them reeling

through the air like so many spinning wheels. Unable even to wield their rods, how could they possibly hope to draw near to fight? Pilgrim was so alarmed that he shook his body and retrieved his hairs. He then lifted the iron rod and tried to attack the monster all by himself, only to be met by a mouthful of yellow wind right on his face. Those two fiery eyes with diamond pupils of his were so blasted that they shut tightly and could not be opened. No longer able to use his rod, he fled in defeat while the monster retrieved the wind, which we shall mention no further.

We tell you now about Chu Pa-chieh, who, when he saw the violent yellow windstorm arriving and the whole of Heaven and Earth growing dim, led the horse and took the luggage to the fold of the mountain. There he crouched on the ground and refused to open his eyes or raise his head, his mouth incessantly calling on the name of Buddha and making vows. As he was wondering how Pilgrim was faring in his battle and whether his master was dead or alive, the wind stopped and the sky brightened again. He looked up and peered toward the entrance of the cave, but he could neither see any movement of weapons nor hear the sound of gongs and drums. Idiot dared not approach the cave, since there was no one else to guard the horse and the luggage. Deeply distressed and not knowing what to do, he suddenly heard the Great Sage approaching from the west, making all sorts of noises as he came. Bowing to meet his companion, he said, "Elder Brother, what a mighty wind! Where did you come from?" With a wave of his hand, Pilgrim said, "Formidable! It's truly formidable! Since I, old Monkey, was born, I have never witnessed such a violent wind! That old monster fought me with a steel trident, and we battled for over thirty rounds. It was then that I used the magic of the body beyond the body and had him surrounded. He panicked and called up this wind, which was ferocious indeed. Its force was so overwhelming that I had to suspend my operation and flee instead. Whew! What a wind! Whew! What a wind! Old Monkey also knows how to call up the wind and how to summon the rain, but it's hardly as vicious as the wind of this monster-spirit!" "Elder Brother," said Pa-chieh, "how is the martial technique of that monster?" "It's presentable," said Pilgrim, "and he knows how to use the trident! He is, in fact, just about the equal of old Monkey. But that wind of his is vicious, and that makes it difficult to defeat him." "In that case," said Pa-chieh, "how are we going to rescue Master?"

Pilgrim said, "We'll have to wait to rescue Master. I wonder if there
is any eye doctor around here who can take a look at my eyes."
"What's the matter with your eyes?" asked Pa-chieh. Pilgrim said,
"That monster blew a mouthful of wind on my face, and my eyes
were so sorely blasted that they are now watering constantly."
"Elder Brother," said Pa-chieh, "we are in the middle of a mountain,
and it's getting late. Let's not talk about eye doctors; we don't even
have a place to stay." "It won't be difficult to find lodging," said
Pilgrim. "I doubt that the monster has the gall to harm our master.
Let's find our way back to the main road and see whether we can
stay with some family. After spending the night, we can return to
subdue the monster tomorrow when it's light." "You are right," said
Pa-chieh.

Leading the horse and carrying up the luggage, they left the fold
of the mountain and went up the road. Dusk was setting in, and as
they walked, they heard the sound of barking dogs toward the south
of the mountain slope. Stopping to look, they saw a small cottage
with flickering lamplights. Not bothering to look for a path, the two
of them walked through the grass and arrived at the door of that
household. They saw

Hazy clumps of purplish fungi;
Greyish piles of white stones;
Hazy clumps of purplish fungi with much green grass;
Greyish piles of white stones half coated with moss:
A few specks of fireflies, their faint light aglow;
A forest of wild woods both thick and dense;
The orchids so fragrant;
The bamboos newly planted;
A clear stream flowing through a winding course;
Old cedars leaning over a yawning cliff.
A secluded place where no travelers came:
Only wild flowers bloomed before the door.

Not presuming to enter without permission, they both called out:
"Open the door! Open the door!" An old man inside appeared with
several young farmers, all holding rakes, pitchforks, and brooms.
"Who are you? Who are you?" they asked. With a bow, Pilgrim said,
"We are disciples of a holy monk from the Great T'ang in the Land
of the East. We were on our way to seek scriptures from the Buddha
in the Western Heaven when we passed through this mountain, and

our master was captured by the Yellow Wind Great King. We have yet to rescue him. Since it is getting late, we have come to ask for lodging for one night at your house. We beg you to grant us this favor." Returning the bow, the old man said, "Pardon me for not coming to greet you. This is a place where clouds are more numerous than people, and when we heard you calling at the door just now, we were afraid that it might be someone like a wily fox, a tiger, or a bandit from the mountain. That's why my little ones might have offended you by their rather brusque manner. Please come in. Please come in."

The two brothers led the horse and hauled the luggage inside; after tying up the animal and putting down the load, they exchanged greetings again with the old man of the cottage before taking their seats. An old manservant then came forward to present tea, after which several bowls of sesame seed rice were brought out.[11] After they had finished the rice, the old man asked for bedding to be laid out for them to sleep. Pilgrim said, "We don't need to sleep just yet. May I ask the good man whether there is in your region someone who sells eye medicine?" "Which one of you elders has eye disease?" said the old man. Pilgrim said, "To tell you the truth, Venerable Sir, we who have left the family rarely become ill. In fact, I have never known any disease of the eye." "If you are not suffering from an eye disease," said the old man, "why do you want medicine?" "We were trying to rescue our master at the entrance of the Yellow Wind Cave today," said Pilgrim. "Unexpectedly that monster blew a mouthful of wind at me, causing my eyes to hurt and smart. At the moment, I'm weeping constantly, and that's why I want to find eye medicine." "My goodness! My goodness!" said the old man. "A young priest like you, why do you lie? The wind of that Great King Yellow Wind is most fearsome, not comparable with any spring-autumn wind, pine-and-bamboo wind, or the wind coming from the four quarters."

"I suppose," said Pa-chieh, "it must be brain-bursting wind, goat-ear wind, leprous wind, or migrainous wind!" "No, no!" said the old man. "His is called the Divine Wind of Samādhi." "What's it like?" asked Pilgrim. The old man said, "That wind

Can blow to dim Heaven and Earth,
And sadden both ghosts and gods.
So savage it breaks rocks and stones,
A man will die when he's blown!

If you had encountered that wind of his, you think you would still be alive? Only if you were an immortal could you remain unharmed." "Indeed!" said Pilgrim. "I may not be an immortal (for they belong to the younger generation, as far as I am concerned), but it will take some doing to finish me off! That wind, however, did cause my eyeballs to hurt and smart." "If you can say that," said the old man, "you must be a person with some background. Our humble region has no one who sells eye medicine. But I myself suffer from watery eyes when the wind blows in my face, and I met an extraordinary person once who gave me a prescription. It's called the three-flowers and nine-seeds ointment, and it's capable of curing all wind-induced eye troubles." When Pilgrim heard these words, he bowed his head and said humbly, "I'm willing to ask you for some and try it on myself." The old man consented and went into the inner chamber. He took out a little cornelian vase and pulled off the stopper; using a small jade pin to scoop out some ointment, he dabbed it onto Pilgrim's eyes, telling him to close his eyes and rest quietly, for he would be well by morning. After doing this, the old man took the vase and retired with his attendants. Pa-chieh untied the bags, took out the bedding, and asked Pilgrim to lie down. As Pilgrim groped about confusedly with his eyes closed, Pa-chieh laughed and said, "Sir, where's your seeing-eye cane?" "You overstuffed idiot!" said Pilgrim. "You want to take care of me as a blind man?" Giggling to himself, Idiot fell asleep, but Pilgrim sat on the mattress and did exercises to cultivate his magic power. Only after the third watch did he go to sleep.

Soon it was the fifth watch and dawn was about to break. Wiping his face, Pilgrim opened his eyes, saying, "It's really marvelous medicine! I can see a hundred times better than before!" He then turned his head to look around. Ah! There were neither buildings nor halls, only some old locust trees and tall willows. The brothers were actually lying on a green grass meadow. Just then, Pa-chieh began to stir, saying, "Elder Brother, why are you making all these noises?" "Open your eyes and take a look," said Pilgrim. Raising his head, Idiot discovered that the house had disappeared. He was so startled that he scrambled up at once, crying, "Where's my horse?" "Isn't it over there, tied to a tree?" said Pilgrim. "And the luggage?" asked Pa-chieh.

"Isn't it there by your head?" said Pilgrim. "This family is rather shifty!" said Pa-chieh. "If they have moved, why didn't they give us a call? If they had let old Hog know about it, they might have received some farewell gifts of tea and fruits. Well, I suppose they must be trying to hide from something and are afraid that the county sheriff may get wind of it; so they moved out in the the night. Good Heavens! We must have been dead to the world! How could we not have heard anything when they dismantled the whole house?" "Idiot, stop babbling!" said Pilgrim, chuckling. "Take a look on that tree and see what kind of paper slip that is." Pa-chieh went and took it down. It was a four-line poem which read:

This humble abode's no mortal abode:
A cottage devised by the Guardians of Law,
Who gave the wondrous balm to heal your sore.
Fret not and do your best to quell the fiend.

Pilgrim said, "A bunch of roguish deities! Since we changed to the dragon-horse, I had not taken a roll call of them. Now they are playing tricks on me instead!" "Elder Brother," said Pa-chieh, "stop putting on such airs! How would they ever let you check them off the roll?" "Brother," said Pilgrim, "you don't know about this. These Eighteen Protectors of Monasteries, the Six Gods of Darkness and Six Gods of Light, the Guardians of Five Points, and the Four Sentinels all have been ordered by the Bodhisattva to give secret protection to Master. The other day they reported their names to me, but since you have been with us, I have not made use of them. That's why I haven't made a roll call." "Elder Brother," said Pa-chieh, "if they were ordered to give secret protection to Master, they had reason not to reveal themselves. That's why they had to devise this cottage here, and you shouldn't blame them. After all, they did put ointment on your eyes for you yesterday, and they did take care of us for one meal. You can say that they have done their duty. Don't blame them. Let's go and rescue Master." "Brother, you are right," said Pilgrim. "This place is not far from the Yellow Wind Cave. You had better stay here and look after the horse and luggage in the woods. Let old Monkey go into the cave to make some inquiry after the condition of Master. Then we can do battle with the monster again." "Exactly," said Pa-chieh. "You should find out whether Master is dead or alive; if he's dead, each one of us can tend to our own business; if he's not,

we can do our best to discharge our responsibility." Pilgrim said,
"Stop talking nonsense! I'm off!"

With one leap he arrived at the entrance of the cave and found
the door still shut and the inhabitants sound asleep. Pilgrim neither
made any noise nor disturbed the monsters; making the magic sign
and reciting the spell, he shook his body and changed at once into
a spotted-leg mosquito. It was tiny and delicate. We have a testimonial poem:

A pesky small shape with sharp sting;
His tiny voice can hum like thunder!
Adept at piercing gauze nets and orchid rooms,
He likes the warmth of sultry climate.
He fears only incense and the swatting fan,
But dearly loves bright lights and lamps.
Airy, agile, all too clever and fast,
He flies into the cave of the fiend.

The little demon who was supposed to guard the door was lying
there asleep, snoring. Pilgrim gave him a bite on his face, causing the
little demon to roll over half awakened. "O my father!" he said.
"What a big mosquito! One bite and I already have a big lump." He
then opened his eyes and said, "Why, it's dawn!" Just then, the
second door inside opened with a creak, and Pilgrim immediately
flew in. The old monster was giving orders to all his subordinates to
be especially careful in guarding the various entrances while they
made ready their weapons. "If the wind yesterday did not kill that
Pilgrim Sun," he said, "he will certainly come back today. When he
comes, we'll finish him off."

Hearing this, Pilgrim flew past the main hall and arrived at the
rear of the cave, where he found another door tightly shut. Crawling
through a crack in the door, he discovered a large garden, in the
middle of which, bound by ropes to a pole, was the T'ang monk.
That master was shedding tears profusely, constantly wondering
where Wu-k'ung and Wu-nêng were to be found. Pilgrim stopped
his flight and alighted on his bald head, saying, "Master!" Recognizing his voice, the Elder said, "Wu-k'ung, I nearly died thinking of
you! Where are you calling from?" "Master," said Pilgrim, "I'm on
your head. Calm yourself and stop worrying. We must first capture
the monster before we can rescue you. "Disciple," said the T'ang

monk, "when will you be able to capture the monster?" "The Tiger Monster who took you," said Pilgrim, "has already been slain by Pa-chieh. But the wind of the old monster is a powerful weapon. I suspect we should be able to capture him today. Relax and stop crying. I'm leaving."

Having said that, he flew at once to the front, where the old monster was seated aloft, making a roll call of all the commanders of his troops. A little demon suddenly appeared, waving the command flag. He dashed up to the hall, crying, "Great King, this little one was on patrol in the mountain when he ran into a monk with a long snout and huge ears sitting in the woods not far from our entrance. If I hadn't run away quickly, he would have caught me. But I didn't see that hairy-faced monk who came here yesterday." "If Pilgrim Sun is absent," said the old monster, "it may mean that he's been killed by the wind. Or, he may have gone to try to find help." "Great King," said one of the demons, "it would be our good fortune if he had been killed. But suppose he's not dead? If he succeeds in bringing with him some divine warriors, what shall we do then?" The old monster said, "Who's afraid of any divine warrior? Only the Bodhisattva Ling-chi can overcome the power of my wind; no one else can do us any harm."

That Pilgrim resting on one of the beams above him was delighted by this one statement. He flew out of the cave at once and, changing back into his original form, arrived at the woods. "Brother!" he cried. Pa-chieh asked, "Elder Brother, where have you been? Just now a monster with a command flag came by, and I chased him away." "Thank you! Thank you!" said Pilgrim laughing. "Old Monkey changed into a mosquito to enter the cave to see how Master was doing. I found him tied to a post in the garden, weeping. After telling him not to cry, I flew around the roof to spy on them some more. That was when the fellow who held the command flag came in panting, saying that you had chased him. He also said that he had not seen me. The old monster made some wild speculations about my having been killed by the wind, or else having gone to find help. Then, without being prompted, he suddenly mentioned some-one else. It's marvelous, simply marvelous!" "Whom did he mention?" asked Pa-chieh. "He said that he wasn't afraid of any divine warrior," said Pilgrim, "for no one else could overpower his wind

save the Bodhisattva Ling-chi. The only trouble is that I don't know
where this Ling-chi lives." As they were thus conversing, they suddenly saw an aged man walking by the side of the main road. Look
at his appearance:

Robust, he used no cane to walk,
With flowing snowlike hair and beard.
Though wit and eyes were somewhat dim,
Thin bones and sinews were still tough.

With bent head and back he walked slowly,
With thick brows and a pink face, childlike.
You look at his features and he seems a man—
Though he's like the Long-Life Star no less!

Highly pleased when he caught sight of him, Pa-chieh said, "Elder
Brother, the proverb says: 'If you want to know the way, you must ask
the man on the road.' Why don't you approach him and ask?" The
Great Sage put away his iron rod and straightened out his clothes.
Approaching the old man, he said, "Aged Sir, receive my bow."
Somewhat reluctantly, the old man returned his greeting, saying,
"What region are you from, monk? What are you doing here in this
wilderness?" "We are holy monks on our way to seek scriptures,"
said Pilgrim. "Yesterday we lost our master here, and so I'm approaching you to ask where the Bodhisattva Ling-chi lives." "Ling-chi
lives south of here," said the old man, "about three thousand miles
away. There is a mountain called the Little Sumeru Mountain, which
has within it the plot of Truth, the monastery where the Bodhisattva
gives his discourses. I suppose you are trying to obtain scriptures
from him." "Not from him," said Pilgrim, "but I have something
which requires his attention. Will you please show me the way?"
Pointing with his hand toward the south, the old man said, "Follow
that winding path." The Great Sage Sun was tricked into turning his
head to look at the path, when the old man changed himself into a
gentle breeze and vanished. A small slip of paper was left beside the
road, on which was written this four-line verse:

Let the Great Sage, Equal to Heaven, be told:
The old man is in truth one Long-Life Li!
There is on Sumeru the Flying-Dragon Staff;
Ling-chi in years past received this Buddhist arm.

Pilgrim took up the slip and went back down the road. "Elder

Brother," said Pa-chieh, "our luck must have been rather bad lately. For two days we saw ghosts in broad daylight. Who is that old man who left after changing into a breeze?" Pilgrim gave Pa-chieh the slip of paper. "Who is this Long-Life Li?" asked Pa-chieh, when he had read the verse. "It's the name of the Planet Venus from the West," said Pilgrim. Pa-chieh hurriedly bowed toward the sky, crying, "Benefactor! Benefactor! Had it not been for the Gold Star, who personally begged the Jade Emperor to be merciful, I don't know what would have become of old Hog!" "Elder Brother," said Pilgrim, "you do have a sense of gratitude. But don't expose yourself. Take cover deep in the woods and carefully guard the luggage and the horse. Let old Monkey find the Sumeru Mountain and seek help from the Bodhisattva." "I know, I know!" said Pa-chieh. "Hurry up and go! Old Hog has mastered the law of the turtle: withdraw your head when there's no need to stick it out!"

The Great Sage Sun leaped into the air; mounting the cloud-somersault, he headed straight south. He was fast, all right! With a nod of his head, he covered three thousand miles; just a twist of his torso carried him over eight hundred! In a moment he saw a tall mountain with auspicious clouds hanging halfway up its slopes and holy mists gathered around it. In the fold of the mountain there was indeed a temple. He could hear the melodious sounds of the bells and sonorous stones[12] and could see the swirling smoke of incense. As he approached the door, the Great Sage saw a Taoist with a string of beads around his neck, who was reciting the name of Buddha. Pilgrim said, "Taoist, please accept my bow." The Taoist at once bowed in return, saying, "Where did the venerable father come from?" "Is this where the Bodhisattva Ling-chi expounds the scriptures?" asked Pilgrim. "Indeed it is," said the Taoist. "Do you wish to speak to someone?" "May I trouble you, sir, to make this announcement for me," said Pilgrim. "I am the disciple of the master of the Law, Tripitaka, who is the royal brother of the Great T'ang Emperor in the Land of the East; I am the Great Sage, Equal to Heaven, Sun Wu-k'ung, also named Pilgrim. I have a matter which requires me to have an audience with the Bodhisattva." The Taoist laughed and said, "The venerable father has given me a long announcement! I can't quite remember all those words." "Just say that Sun Wu-k'ung, the disciple of the T'ang monk, has arrived," said Pilgrim. The Taoist agreed and made that announcement in the

lecture hall, whereupon the Bodhisattva at once put on his cassock
and asked for more incense to be burned to welcome the visitor. Then
the Great Sage walked in the door and peered inside. He saw

A hall full of brocade and silk;
A house most solemn and grand.
Those pupils all recited the *Lotus Sūtra*;
An old group leader struck lightly the golden gong.
Set before the Buddha
Were all immortal fruits and flowers.
Spread out on the tables
Were vegetarian dainties and viands.
The bright, precious candles,
Their golden flames shot up like rainbows;
The fragrant true incense,
Its jadelike smoke flew up like colored mists.
So it was that after the lecture one would calmly meditate,
As white-cloud clusters circled the tips of pines.
The sword of wisdom quietly retired after Māra was slain;
Here was perfection of wisdom in this august assembly.

The Bodhisattva straightened out his attire to receive Pilgrim, who
entered the hall and took the seat of the guest. Tea was offered, but
Pilgrim said, "No need for you to bother about tea. My master faces
peril at the Yellow Wind Mountain, and I beseech the Bodhisattva to
exercise his great dharma power to defeat the monster and rescue
him." "I did receive the command of Tathāgata," said the Bodhisattva,
"to keep the Yellow Wind Monster here in submission. Tathāgata
also gave me a Wind-Stopping Pearl and a Flying-Dragon Precious
Staff. At the time when I captured him, I spared the monster his life
only on condition that he would retire in the mountain and abstain
from the sin of taking life. I did not know that he would want to harm
your esteemed teacher and transgress the Law. That is my fault."
The Bodhisattva would have liked to prepare some vegetarian food
to entertain Pilgrim, but Pilgrim insisted on leaving. So he took the
Flying-Dragon Staff and mounted the clouds with the Great Sage.

In a little while they reached the Yellow Wind Mountain. "Great
Sage," said the Bodhisattva, "this monster is rather afraid of me. I
will stand here at the edge of the clouds while you go down there to
provoke battle. Entice him to come out so that I may exercise my
power." Pilgrim followed his suggestion and lowered his cloud.

Without waiting for further announcement, he whipped out his iron rod and smashed the door of the cave, crying, "Monster, give me back my Master!" Those little demons standing guard at the door were so terrified that they ran to make the report. "This lawless ape," said the monster, "is truly ill-behaved! He would not defer to kindness, and now he has even broken my door! This time when I go out, I'm going to use that divine wind to blow him to death." He put on his armor as before, and took up the steel trident. Walking out of the door and seeing Pilgrim, he did not utter a word before aiming the trident at Pilgrim's chest. The Great Sage stepped aside to dodge this blow and then faced him with uplifted rod. Before they had fought for a few rounds, the monster turned his head toward the ground in the southwest and was about to open his mouth to summon the wind. From midair, the Bodhisattva threw down the Flying-Dragon Precious Staff as he recited some kind of spell. It was instantly transformed into a golden dragon with eight claws, two of which caught hold of that monster's head and threw him two or three times against the boulders beside the mountain cliff. The monster changed back into his original form and became a mink with yellow fur.

Pilgrim ran up and was about to strike with his rod, but he was stopped by the Bodhisattva, who said to him, "Great Sage, do not harm him. I have to take him back to see Tathāgata. Originally he was a rodent at the foot of the Spirit Mountain who had acquired the Way. Because he stole some of the pure oil in the crystal chalice, he fled for fear that the vajra attendants would seize him. Tathāgata thought that he was not guilty of death, and that is why I was asked to capture him in the first place and banish him to this region. But now he has offended the Great Sage and has attempted to harm the T'ang monk. Therefore I must take him to see Tathāgata so that his guilt may be clearly established. Only then will this merit be completed." When Pilgrim heard this, he thanked the Bodhisattva, who left for the West, and we shall say no more of that.

We now tell you about Chu Pa-chieh, who was thinking about Pilgrim in the woods when he heard someone calling down by the slope, "Brother Wu-nêng, bring the horse and the luggage here." Recognizing Pilgrim's voice, Idiot quickly ran out of the woods and said to Pilgrim, "Elder Brother, how did everything go?" "I invited the Bodhisattva Ling-chi to come here," said Pilgrim, "to use his

Flying-Dragon Staff to capture the monster. He was a mink with yellow fur who became a spirit and has now been taken by the Bodhisattva to Spirit Mountain to face Tathāgata. Let's go into the cave to rescue Master." Idiot was delighted. The two of them smashed their way into the cave and with their rake and rod slaughtered all the wily hares, the vixen, the musk deer, and the horned deer. Then they went to the garden in the back to rescue their master, who, after coming out, asked, "How did you two manage to catch the monster so that you could rescue me?" Pilgrim gave a thorough account of how he went to seek the Bodhisattva's help to subdue the monster, and the master thanked him profusely. Then the two brothers found some vegetarian food in the cave, which they prepared along with some tea and rice. After eating, they left and again found the road to the West. We do not know what took place hereafter, and you must listen to the explanation in the next chapter.

Twenty-two

Pa-chieh fights fiercely at the Flowing-Sand River;
By order Mokṣa brings Wu-ching to submission.

Now we tell you about the T'ang monk and his disciples, the three
travellers, who were delivered from their ordeal. In less than a day
they passed the Yellow Wind Mountain and proceeded toward the
West through a vast level plain. Time went by swiftly, and summer
yielded to the arrival of autumn. All they saw were some cicadas in
the cold, singing on dying willows, and the Great Fire rolling toward
the West. As they proceeded, they came upon a huge and turbulent
river, its waves surging and splashing. "Disciples," exclaimed Tripitaka, "look at that vast expanse of water in front of us. Why are there
no boats in sight? How can we get across?" Taking a close look,
Pa-chieh said, "It's very turbulent, too rough for any boat!" Pilgrim
leaped into the air and peered into the distance, shading his eyes with
his hand. Even he was rather frightened and said, "Master, it's very
difficult! Very difficult! If old Monkey wishes to cross this river, he
need only make one twist of his body and he will reach the other
shore. But for you, Master, it's impossible to get across." "I can't even
see the other shore from here," said Tripitaka. "Really, how wide is
it?" "It's just about eight hundred miles wide," said Pilgrim. "Elder
Brother," said Pa-chieh, "how could you determine its width just
like that?" "To tell you the truth, Worthy Brother," said Pilgrim,
"these eyes of mine can determine good or evil up to a thousand miles
away in daylight. Just now when I was up in the air, I could not tell
how long the river was, but I could make out its width to be at least
eight hundred miles." Sighing anxiously, the Elder pulled back his
horse and suddenly discovered on the shore a slab of stone. When
the three of them drew closer to have a look, they saw three words
written in seal-script, "Flowing-Sand River," below which there were
also four lines written in regular style. It read:

These Flowing-Sand metes, eight hundred wide;
These Weak Waters, three thousand deep.

A goose feather cannot stay afloat;
A rush petal will sink to the bottom.

As master and disciples were reading the inscription, the waves in the river suddenly rose like tall mountains, and with a loud splash from the midst of the waters a monster sprang out. Looking most savage and hideous, he had

A head full of wild and flamelike hair;
A pair of bright, round eyes which shone like lamps;
A bluish face which seemed neither black nor green;
An old dragon's voice like thunderclap or drum.
He wore a cape of light yellow goose down.
Two strands of white reeds tied around his waist.
Beneath his chin nine skulls were strung and hung;
His hands held an awesome priestly staff.

Like a cyclone, the fiend rushed up to the shore and went straight for the T'ang monk. Pilgrim was so taken aback that he grabbed his master and dashed for high ground to make the escape. Putting down the pole, Pa-chieh whipped out his rake and brought it down hard on the monster. The fiend used his staff to parry the blow, and so the two of them began to unleash their power on the bank of the Flowing-Sand River. This was some battle!

The nine-pronged rake;
The fiend-routing staff;
These two met in battle on the river shore.
This one was the Marshal of Heavenly Reeds;
That one was the Curtain-Raising Captain by the Throne.
In years past they met in Divine Mists Hall;
Today they fought and waged a test of might.
From this one the rake went out like a dragon stretching its claws;
From that one the staff blocked the way like a sharp-tusked
    elephant.
They stood with their limbs outstretched;
Each struck at the other's rib cage.
This one raked madly, heedless of head or face;
That one struck wildly without pause or rest.
This one was a man-eating spirit, long a lord of Flowing-Sand;
That one was a Way-seeking fighter upholding Law and Faith.

Closing in again and again, the two of them fought for twenty rounds, but neither emerged the victor.

The Great Sage meanwhile was standing there to protect the T'ang monk. As he held the horse and guarded the luggage, he became so aroused by the sight of Pa-chieh engaging that fiend that he ground his teeth and rubbed his hands vehemently. Finally he could not restrain himself; whipping out the rod, he said, "Master, sit here and don't be afraid. Let old Monkey go play with him a little." The master begged in vain for him to stay, and with a loud whoop he leaped forward. The monster, you see, was just having a grand time fighting with Pa-chieh, the two of them so tightly locked in combat that nothing seemed able to part them. Pilgrim, however, rushed up to the monster and delivered a terrific blow at his head with his iron rod. The monster was so shaken that he jumped aside; turning around he dove straight into the Flowing-Sand River and disappeared. Pa-chieh was so upset that he jumped about wildly, crying, "Elder Brother! Who asked you to come? The monster was gradually weakening and was finding it difficult to parry my rake. Another four or five rounds and I would have taken him captive. But when he saw how fierce you were, he fled in defeat. Now, what shall we do?" "Brother," said Pilgrim laughing, "to tell you the truth, since defeating the Yellow Wind Fiend a month ago, I have not played with my rod all this time after leaving the mountain. When I saw how delicious your fight with him was, I couldn't stand the itch beneath my feet! That's why I jumped up here to play a little with him. That monster doesn't know how to play, and I suppose that's the reason for his departure."

Holding hands and joking with each other, the two of them returned to the T'ang monk. "Did you catch the monster?" asked the T'ang monk. "He didn't last out the fight," said Pilgrim, "and he scrambled back into the water in defeat." "Disciple," said Tripitaka, "since this monster has probably lived here a long time, he ought to know the deep and the shallow parts of the river. After all, such a boundless body of weak water, and not a boat in sight—we need someone who is familiar with the region to lead us across." "Exactly!" said Pilgrim. "As the proverb says, 'He who's near cinnabar becomes red, and he who's near ink turns black.' The monster living here must have a good knowledge of the water. When we catch him, we should not slay him, but just make him take Master across the river before we dispose of him." "Elder Brother," said Pa-chieh, "no need for further delay. You go ahead and catch him, while old Hog guards

our master." "Worthy Brother," said Pilgrim with a laugh, "In this
case I've really nothing to brag about, for I'm just not comfortable
doing business in the water. If all I do is walk around down there, I
still have to make the magic sign and recite the water-repelling spell
before I can move around. Or else I have to change into a water
creature like a fish, shrimp, crab, or turtle before going in. If it were
a matter of matching wits in the high mountains or up in the clouds,
I know enough to deal with the strangest and most difficult situation.
But doing business in water somewhat cramps my style!" "When I
was Marshal of the Heavenly River in former years," said Pa-chieh,
"I commanded a naval force of eighty thousand men, and I acquired
some knowledge of that element. But I fear that that monster may
have some relatives down there in his den, and I won't be able to
withstand him if his seventh and eighth cousins all come out. What
will happen to me then if they grab me?" "If you go into the water
to fight him," said Pilgrim, "don't tarry. Make sure, in fact, that you
feign defeat and entice him out here. Then old Monkey will help
you." "Right you are," said Pa-chieh, "I'm off!" He took off his blue
silk shirt and his shoes; holding the rake with both hands, he
divided the waters to make a path for himself. Using the ability he
had developed in bygone years, he leaped through billows and waves
and headed for the bottom of the river.

We now tell you about that monster, who went back to his home
in defeat. He had barely caught his breath when he heard someone
pushing water, and as he rose to take a look, he saw Pa-chieh pushing
his way through with his rake. That monster lifted his staff and met
him face to face, crying, "Monk, watch where you are going or
you'll receive a blow from this!" Using the rake to block the blow,
Pa-chieh said, "What sort of a monster are you that you dare to bar
our way?" "So you don't recognize me," said the monster. "I'm no
demon or fiend, nor do I lack a name or surname." "If you are no
demon or fiend," said Pa-chieh, "why do you stay here and take
human lives? Tell me your name and surname, and I'll spare your
life." The monster said,

My spirit was strong since the time of birth.
I had made a tour of the whole wide world,
Where my fame as a hero became well known—
A gallant type emulated by all.
Through countless nations I went as I pleased;

Over lakes and seas I freely roamed.
To learn the Way I crossed the edge of Heaven;
To find a teacher I stumped this great earth.
For years my clothes and alms bowl went with me;
Not one day was I ever lax in spirit.
For scores of times I cruised cloudlike the earth,
And walked everywhere a hundred times.
Only then I met an immortal true,
Who showed me the Great Path of Golden Light.
I seized the baby and the fair girl first;[1]
Then released wood mother and the squire of gold.[2]
Kidney-water from Bright Hall[3] flowed to the Floral Pool;[4]
Liver-fire from the Tower[5] plunged to the heart.
Three thousand merits done, I saw Heaven's face,
And reverently bowed to the Hall of Light.
Then the Jade Emperor exalted me:
The Curtain-Raising Captain he made me.
An honored one in South Heaven Gate,
I was much esteemed at Divine Mists Hall.
I hung at my waist the Tiger-Headed Shield;
I held in my hands the Fiend-Routing Staff.
Just like the sunlight my gold helmet shone;
My body's armor flashed like radiant mists.
I was chief of the guardians of the Throne;
I was first among attendants of the court.
When Wang-mu[6] gave the Festival of Peach,
Serving her guests at Jasper Pool a feast,
I dropped and broke a crystal glass of jade,
And souls from all the hosts of Heaven fled.
Jade Emperor grew mightily enraged;
Hands clasped, he faced his counsel on the left.[7]
Stripped of my hat, my armor, and my rank,
I was bodily taken to the block.
Only the Great Immortal of Naked Feet[8]
Came from the ranks and begged to have me freed.
Pardoned from death and with my sentence stayed,
I was banished to the shores of Flowing-Sand.
Sated, I lie wearily in the stream.
Famished, I churn the waves to find my feed.

The woodsman sees me and his life is gone;
The fishers face me and they soon perish.
From first to last I've eaten many men;
I've sinned, repeatedly, taking human lives.
Since you dare to work violence at my door,
My stomach this day has its fondest hopes!
Don't say you're too coarse to be eaten now.
I'll catch you, and look!—that's my chopped meat sauce!

Growing terribly angry because of what he heard, Pa-chieh shouted:
"You brazen thing! You haven't the slightest perception! Old Hog is
tempting enough to make people's mouths water, and you dare say
that I'm coarse, that I'm to be chopped up for a chopped meat sauce!
Come to think of it, you would like to consider me a piece of tough
old bacon! Watch your manners and swallow this rake of your
ancestor!" When the monster saw the rake coming, he used the style
of "the phoenix nodding its head" to dodge the blow. The two of
them thus fought to the surface of the water, each one treading the
waters and waves. This conflict was somewhat different from the one
before. Look at

The Curtain-Raising Captain,
The Marshal of Heavenly Reeds:
Each showing most admirably his magic might.
This one waved above his head the fiend-routing staff;
That one moved the rake as swiftly as his hand.
The vaulting waves rocked hills and streams;
The surging tide the cosmos dimmed. ✒
Savage like Jupiter wielding banners and flags!
Fierce like Hell's envoy upsetting sacred tops!
This one guarded the T'ang monk devotedly;
That one, a water fiend, perpetrated his crimes.
The rake's one stroke would leave nine red marks;
The staff's one blow would dissolve man's soul.
They strove to win the fight;
They struggled to prevail.
All in all for the scripture pilgrim's sake,
They vented their fury without restraint.
They brawled till carps and perches lost their newborn scales,
And youthful shells of turtles, big and small, were hurt.
Red shrimps and purple crabs all lost their lives;

The sundry gods of water all bowed to Heaven!
You heard only the waves rolled and crashed like thunderclaps.
The world was astounded; sun and moon were dark!

The two of them fought for two hours, and neither prevailed. It was like

A brass pan meeting an iron broom,
A jade gong facing a golden bell.

We now tell you about the Great Sage, who was standing guard beside the T'ang monk. With bulging eyes he watched them fighting on the water, but he dared not move his hands. Finally, Pa-chieh made a half-hearted blow with his rake and, feigning defeat, turned to flee toward the eastern shore, the monster gave chase and was about to reach the river bank when our Pilgrim could no longer restrain himself. He abandoned his master, whipped out the iron rod, leaped to the river side and struck at the monster's head. Fearing to face him, the monster swiftly dove back into the river. "You pi-ma-wên!" shouted Pa-chieh. "You impulsive ape! Can't you be a bit more patient? You could have waited until I led him up to high ground and then blocked his path to the river. We would have caught him then. Now he has gone back in, and when do you think he'll come out again?" "Idiot," said Pilgrim laughing, "stop shouting! Let's go talk to Master first."

Pa-chieh went with Pilgrim back to high ground to Tripitaka. "Disciple," said Tripitaka, bowing, "you must be tired!" "I won't complain about my fatigue," said Pa-chieh. "Let's subdue the monster and take you across the river; only then shall we have realized a perfect plan." Tripitaka said, "How did the battle go with the monster just now?" "He was just about my equal," said Pa-chieh, "and we fought to a draw. But then I feigned defeat and he chased me up to the bank. When he saw Elder Brother lifting his rod, however, he fled. "So what are we going to do?" asked Tripitaka. "Master, relax!" said Pilgrim. "Let's not worry now, for it's getting late. You sit here on the cliff and let old Monkey go beg some vegetarian food. Take some rest after you eat, and we'll find a solution tomorrow." "You are right," said Pa-chieh. "Go, and come back quickly."

Pilgrim swiftly mounted the clouds and went north to beg a bowl of vegetarian food from some family to present to his master. When the master saw him return so soon, he said, "Wu-k'ung, let us go to that household which gave us the food and ask them how we may cross this river. Isn't this better than fighting the monster?" With a laugh, Pilgrim said, "That household is quite far from here, about six or seven thousand miles, no less! How could the people there know about the water? What's the use of asking them?" "You are fibbing again, Elder Brother!" said Pa-chieh. "Six or seven thousand miles how could you cover that distance so quickly?" "You have no idea," said Pilgrim, "about the capacity of my cloud-somersault, which with one leap can cover a hundred and eight thousand miles. For the six or seven thousand here, all I have to do is to nod my head and stretch my waist, and that's a round trip already! What's so hard about that?" "Elder Brother," said Pa-chieh, "if it's so easy, all you need to do is to carry Master on your back: nod your head, stretch your waist, and jump across. Why continue to fight this monster?" "Don't *you* know how to ride the clouds?" asked Pilgrim. "Can't you carry him across the river?" "The mortal nature and worldly bones of Master are as heavy as the T'ai Mountain," Pa-chieh said. "How could my cloud-soaring bear him up? It has to be your cloud-somersault." "My cloud-somersault is essentially like cloud-soaring," said Pilgrim, "the only difference being that I can cover greater distances more rapidly. If you can't carry him, what makes you think I can? There's an old proverb which says: 'Move the T'ai Mountain, and it's as light as the mustard seed, but carry a mortal and you won't leave the red dust behind!' Take this monster here: he can use spells and call upon the wind, pushing and pulling a little, but he can't carry a human into the air. And if it's this kind of magic, old Monkey knows every trick well, including becoming invisible and making distances shorter. But it is required of Master to go through all these strange territories before he finds deliverance from the sea of sorrows; hence even one step turns out to be difficult. You and I are only his protective companions, guarding his body and life, but we cannot exempt him from these woes, nor can we obtain the scriptures all by ourselves. Even if we had the ability to go and see Buddha first, he would not bestow the scriptures on you and me. Remember the adage: 'What's easily gotten, is soon forgotten.'" When Idiot heard these words, he accepted them amiably as instruction. Master and disciples ate some of the simply prepared vegetarian food before resting on the eastern shore of the Flowing-Sand River.

Next morning, Tripitaka said, "Wu-k'ung, what are we going to do today?" "Not much," said Pilgrim, "except that Pa-chieh must go into the water again." "Elder Brother," said Pa-chieh, "you only want to stay clean, but you have no hesitation making me go into the water." "Worthy Brother," said Pilgrim, "this time I'll try not to be impulsive. I'll let you trick him into coming up here, and then I'll block his retreat along the river bank. We must capture him." Dear Pa-chieh! He wiped his face and pulled himself together. Holding the rake in both hands, he walked to the edge of the river, opened up a path in the water, and went to the monster's home as before. The monster had just wakened from his sleep when he heard the sound of water. Turning quickly to look, he saw Pa-chieh approaching with the rake. He leaped out at once and barred the way, shouting, "Slow down! Watch out for my staff!" Pa-chieh lifted his rake to parry the blow, saying, "What sort of 'mourning staff' do you have there that you dare ask your ancestor to watch out for it?" "A fellow like you," said the monster, "wouldn't recognize this!

For years my staff has enjoyed great fame,
At first an evergreen[9] in the moon.
Wu Kang[10] cut down from it one huge limb;
Lu Pan[11] then made it, using all his skills.
Within the hub's one solid piece of gold;
Outside it's wrapped by countless pearly threads.
It's called the treasure staff good for crushing fiends,
Placed forever in Divine Mists to rout the ogres.
Since I was appointed a captain great,
The Jade Emperor gave it to me to use.
It lengthens or shortens after my desire;
It grows thick or thin with my command.
It went to guard the Throne at the Peaches Feast;
It served at court in Heaven's world above.
On duty it saw the many sages bowed,
And immortals, too, when the screen was raised.[12]
A divine weapon of transcendent power,
It's no mere human fighting piece.
Since I was banished from the gate of Heaven,
It roamed with me at will beyond the seas.
Perhaps it is not right for me to boast,
But swords and spears of man can't match this staff.
Look at that old, rusted muckrake of yours:
It's only fit for hoeing fields and herbs!"

"You unchastened brazen thing!" said Pa-chieh laughing. "Never mind whether it's fit for hoeing fields! One little touch and you won't even know how to begin putting bandages or ointment on nine bleeding holes! Even if you are not killed, you will grow old with chronic infection!" The monster raised his hands and again fought with Pa-chieh from the bottom of the river up to the surface of the water. This battle was even more different from the first one. Look at them

> Wielding the treasure staff,
> Striking with muckrake;
> They would not speak as if they were estranged.
> Since wood mother constrained the spatula,[13]
> The two engaged in a combat fierce.
> No win or loss;
> With determined minds
> They churned up waves and billows to fight a war.
> How could this one control his bitter rage?
> That one found unbearable his pain.
> Rake and staff went back and forth to show their might;
> The water rolled like poison in Flowing-Sand.
> They huffed and puffed!
> They worked and worked!
> All because Tripitaka must face the West.
> The muckrake so ferocious!
> The staff used with such ease!
> This one made a grab to pull him up the shore;
> That one sought to seize and drown him in the stream.
> They roared like thunder, stirring dragon and fish.
> Gods and ghosts cowered as the Heavens grew dim.

This time they fought back and forth for thirty rounds, and neither one proved to be the stronger. Again Pa-chieh pretended to be defeated and fled, dragging his rake. Kicking up the waves, the monster gave chase and they reached the edge of the river. "Wretch!" cried Pa-chieh. "Come up here! We can fight better on solid ground up here." "You are just trying to trick me into going up there," shouted the monster, "so that you can bring out your assistant. You come down here, and we can fight in the water." The monster, you see, had become wise; he refused to go up to the bank and remained near the edge of the water to argue with Pa-chieh. When Pilgrim

saw that the monster refused to leave the water, he was highly
irritated, and all he could think of was to catch him at once. "Master,"
he said, "you sit here. Let me give him a taste of the 'ravenous eagle
seizing his prey.'" He somersaulted into the air and then swooped
down onto the monster, who was still bickering with Pa-chieh. When
he heard the sound of the wind, he turned quickly and discovered
Pilgrim hurtling down from the clouds. Putting away his staff, he
dove into the water and disappeared. Pilgrim stood on the shore and
said to Pa-chieh: "Brother, that monster is catching on! He refuses
to come up now. What shall we do?" "It's hard, terribly hard!" said
Pa-chieh. "I just can't beat him—even when I summoned up the
strength of my milk-drinking days! We are evenly matched!" "Let's
go talk to Master," said Pilgrim.

The two of them went up again to high ground and told the T'ang
monk everything. "If it's so difficult," said the Elder, tears welling up
in his eyes, "how can we ever get across?" "Master, please don't
worry," said Pilgrim. "It is hard for us to cross with this monster
hiding deep in the river. So, don't fight with him any more, Pa-chieh;
just stay here and protect Master. I'm going to make a trip up to
South Sea." "Elder Brother," said Pa-chieh, "what do you want to
do at South Sea?" Pilgrim said, "This business of seeking scriptures
originated from the Bodhisattva Kuan-yin; the one who delivered us
from our ordeals was also the Bodhisattva Kuan-yin. Today our path
is blocked at this Flowing-Sand River and we can't proceed. Without
her, how can we ever solve our problem? Let me go ask her to help
us; it's much better than doing battle with this monster." "You have
a point there, Elder Brother," said Pa-chieh. "When you get there,
please convey my gratitude to her for her kindly instructions in the
past." "Wu-k'ung," said Tripitaka, "if you want to go see the
Bodhisattva, you needn't delay. Go, and hurry back."

Pilgrim catapulted into the air with his cloud-somersault and
headed for the South Sea. Ah! It did not even take him half an hour
before he saw the scenery of the Potalaka Mountain. In a moment, he
dropped down from his somersault and arrived at the edge of the
purple bamboo grove, where he was met by the Spirits of the
Twenty-Four Ways. They said to him, "Great Sage, what brings you
here?" "My master faces an ordeal," said Pilgrim, "which brings me
here specially to see the Bodhisattva." "Please sit down," said the
spirits, "and allow us to make the announcement." One of the spirits

who was on duty went to the entrance of the Tidal-Sound Cave, announcing, "Sun Wu-k'ung wishes to have an audience with you." The Bodhisattva was leaning on the rails by the Treasure Lotus Pool, looking at the flowers with the Pearl-Bearing Dragon Princess. When she heard the announcement, she went back to the cave, opened the door, and asked that he be shown in. With great solemnity, the Great Sage prostrated himself before her.

"Why are you not accompanying the T'ang monk?" asked the Bodhisattva. "For what reason did you want to see me again?" "Bodhisattva," said Pilgrim, looking up at her, "my master took another disciple at the Kao Village, to whom you had given the religious name of Wu-nêng. After crossing the Yellow Wind Ridge, we have now arrived at the Flowing-Sand River eight hundred miles wide, a body of weak water, which is difficult for Master to get across. There is, moreover, a monster in the river who is quite accomplished in the martial arts. We are grateful to Wu-nêng, who fought in the water with him three times but could not beat him. The monster is, in fact, blocking our path and we cannot get across. That is why I have come to see you, hoping you will take pity and grant us deliverance." "Monkey," said the Bodhisattva, "are you still acting so smug and self-sufficient that you refuse to disclose the fact that you are in the service of the T'ang monk?" "All we had intended to do," said Pilgrim, "was to catch the monster and make him take Master across the river. I am not too good at doing business in the water; so, Wu-nêng went down alone to his lair to look for him, and they had some conversation. I presume the matter of scripture seeking was not mentioned." "That monster in the Flowing-Sand River," said the Bodhisattva, "happens to be the incarnation of the Curtain-Raising Captain, who was also brought into the faith by my persuasion when I told him to accompany those on their way to acquire scriptures. Had you been willing to mention that you were a scripture pilgrim from the Land of the East, he would not have fought you; he would have yielded instead." Pilgrim said: "That monster is afraid to fight now; he refuses to come up to the shore and is hiding deep in the water. How can we bring him to submission? How can my master get across this body of weak water?"

The Bodhisattva immediately called for Hui-an. Taking a little red gourd from her sleeves, she handed it over to him, saying, "Take this gourd and go with Sun Wu-k'ung to the Flowing-Sand River. Call

'Wu-ching,' and he'll come out at once. You must first take him to submit to the T'ang monk. Next, string together those nine skulls of his and arrange them according to the position of the Nine Palaces. Put this gourd in the center, and you will have a dharma vessel ready to ferry the T'ang monk across the boundary formed by the Flowing-Sand River." Obeying the instructions of his master, Hui-an left the Tidal-Sound Cave with the Great Sage carrying the gourd. As they departed the purple bamboo grove in compliance with the holy command, we have a testimonial poem:

The Five Phases well balanced as Heaven's Truth,
He can recognize his former master.
The self's refined, the base's set for wondrous use;
Discerning good and evil he can see the cause.
Metal returns to nature—of the same kind are both.
Wood asks for mercy for they're all related.
The two-earths[14] completes the merit to reach the great void,
As water and fire are blended without a speck of dust.

In a little while the two of them lowered their clouds and arrived at the Flowing-Sand River. Recognizing the disciple Mokṣa, Chu Pa-chieh led his master to receive him. After bowing to Tripitaka, Mokṣa then greeted Pa-chieh, who said, "I was grateful to be instructed by Your Reverence so that I could meet the Bodhisattva. I have indeed obeyed the Law, and I am happy recently to have entered the gate of Buddhism. Since we have been constantly on the road, I have yet to thank you. Please forgive me." "Let's forget about these fancy conversations," said Pilgrim. "We must go and call that fellow." "Call whom?" said Tripitaka. Pilgrim said, "Old Monkey saw the Bodhisattva and gave her an account of what happened. The Bodhisattva told me that this monster in the Flowing-Sand River happened to be the incarnation of the Curtain-Raising Captain. Because he had sinned in Heaven, he was banished to this river and became a monster. But he was converted by the Bodhisattva, who had told him to accompany you to the Western Heaven. Since we did not mention the matter of seeking scriptures, he fought us bitterly. Now the Bodhisattva has sent Mokṣa with this gourd, which that fellow will turn into a dharma vessel to take you across the river." When Tripitaka heard these words, he bowed repeatedly to Mokṣa, saying, "I beseech Your Reverence to act quickly." Holding the gourd and treading half on cloud and half on fog, Mokṣa moved directly above the surface of the Flowing-Sand River. He cried with a loud voice, "Wu-ching! Wu-ching! The scripture pilgrim has been here for a long time. Why have you not submitted?"

We now tell you about that monster: fearful of the Monkey King, he had gone back to the bottom of the river and was resting in his den. When he heard someone call him by his religious name, he knew that it had to be the Bodhisattva Kuan-yin. And when he heard, moreover, that the scripture pilgrim had arrived, he no longer feared the ax or the halberd. Swiftly he leaped out of the waves and saw that it was the disciple Mokṣa. Look at him! All smiles, he went forward and bowed, saying, "Your Reverence, forgive me for not coming to meet you. Where is the Bodhisattva?" "My teacher did not come," said Mokṣa, "but she sent me to tell you to become the disciple of the T'ang monk without delay. You are to take the skulls around your neck and this gourd, and to fashion with them a dharma vessel according to the position of the Nine Palaces so that he may be taken across this body of weak water." "Where is the scripture pilgrim?" asked Wu-ching. Pointing with his finger, Mokṣa said, "Isn't he the one sitting on the eastern shore?" Wu-ching caught sight of Pa-chieh and said, "I don't know where that lawless creature came from! He fought with me for two whole days, never once saying a word about seeking scriptures." When he saw Pilgrim, he said again, "That customer is his assistant, and a formidable one too! I'm not going over there!" "That is Chu Pa-chieh," said Mokṣa, "and that other one is Pilgrim Sun, both disciples of the T'ang monk and both converted by the Bodhisattva. Why fear them? I'll escort you to the T'ang monk." Only then did Wu-ching put away his precious staff and straighten his yellow silk shirt. He jumped ashore and knelt before Tripitaka, saying, "Master, your disciple has eyes but no pupils, and he failed to recognize your noble features. I have greatly offended you, and I beg you to pardon me." "You bum!" said Pa-chieh. "Why did you not submit in the first place? Why did you only want to fight with me? What do you have to say for yourself?" "Brother," said Pilgrim laughing, "don't berate him. It's really our fault for not mentioning that we were seeking scriptures, and we didn't tell him our names." "Are you truly willing to embrace our faith?" said the Elder. "Your disciple was converted by the Bodhisattva," said Wu-ching. "Deriving my surname from the river, she gave me the religious name Sha Wu-ching. How could I be unwilling to take you as my master?" "In that case," said Tripitaka, "Wu-k'ung may bring over the sacred razor and shave off his hair." The Great Sage indeed took the razor and shaved Wu-ching's head, after which he came again to do homage to Tripitaka, Pilgrim, and Pa-chieh, thus becoming the youngest disciple of the T'ang monk. When Tripitaka saw that he comported himself very much like a monk, he gave him the nickname of Sha Monk. "Since you have embraced the faith," said Mokṣa, "there's no need for further delay. You must build the dharma vessel at once."

Wu-ching dared not delay; he took off the skulls around his neck and strung them up with a rope after the design of the Nine Palaces, placing the gourd in the middle. He then asked his master to leave the shore, and our Elder thus embarked on the dharma vessel. As he sat in the center, he found it to be as sturdy as a little boat. He was, moreover, supported by Pa-chieh on his left and Wu-ching on his right, while Pilgrim Sun, leading the dragon-horse, followed in the rear, treading half on cloud and half on fog. Above their heads Mokṣa also took up his post to give them added protection. In this way our master of the Law was safely ferried across the boundary of the Flowing-Sand River; with the wind calm and waves quiet he crossed the weak water. It was truly as fast as flying or riding an arrow; in a little while he reached the other shore, having been delivered from the mighty waves. He did not drag up mud or water, and happily both his hands and feet remained dry. In sum, he was pure and clean without engaging in any activity. When master and disciples reached solid ground again, Mokṣa descended from the auspicious clouds. As he took back his gourd, the nine skulls changed into nine curls of dark wind and vanished. Tripitaka bowed to thank Mokṣa and also gave thanks to the Bodhisattva. So it was that Mokṣa went straight back to the South Sea, while Tripitaka mounted his horse to go to the West. We do not know how long it took them to achieve the right fruit of scripture acquisition, and you must listen to the explanation in the next chapter.

Twenty-three

Tripitaka does not forget his origin;
The Four Sages test the priestly mind.

A long journey westward is his decree,
As frosted blooms fall in autumn's mild breeze.
Tie up the sly ape, don't loosen the ropes!
Hold back the mean horse, don't let him go fast!
Wood mother, metal squire—they mix so well.
Yellow hag[1] and red son[2] are all the same.
Bite open the iron ball—there's mystery true:
Perfection and wisdom will come to you.

The principal aim of this chapter is to make clear that the quest for scriptures is essentially the same as the need to attend to the fundamentals in one's life. We now tell you about master and disciples, the four of them, who, having awakened to the suchness of all things, broke the lock of dust asunder. Leaping clear from the flowing sand of the sea of nature, they were completely rid of any hindrance and proceeded westward on the main road. They passed through countless green hills and blue waters; they saw wild grass and untended flowers in endless arrays. Time was swift indeed and soon it was autumn again. You see

Maple leaves red all over the mountain
Golden blooms prevail over the night-wind.
The old cicada's song turns languid;
The sad cricket ever voices his plaint.
Cracked lotus leaves like green silk fans;
Oranges tangy like balls of gold.
Lovely, those rows of wild geese,
Spreading dots in the distant sky.

As they journeyed, it was getting late again. "Disciples," said Tripitaka, "it's getting late. Where shall we go to spend the night?" "Master," said Pilgrim, "what you said is not quite right. Those who have left home dine on the winds and rest beside the waters; they

444

sleep beneath the moon and lie on the frost; in short, any place can be their home. Why ask where we should spend the night?" "Elder Brother," said Chu Pa-chieh, "all you seem to care about is making progress on the journey, and you've no concern for the burdens of others. Since crossing the Flowing-Sand River, we have been doing nothing but scale mountains and peaks, and hauling this heavy load is becoming rather hard on me. Wouldn't it be much more reasonable to look for a house where we can ask for some tea and rice, and try to regain our strength?" "Idiot," said Pilgrim, "your words sound as if you begrudge this whole enterprise. If you think that you are still back in the Kao Village, where you can enjoy the comfort which comes to you without your exerting yourself, then you won't make it! If you have truly embraced the faith of Buddhism, you must be willing to endure pain and suffering; only then will you be a true disciple." "Elder Brother," said Pa-chieh, "how heavy do you think this load of luggage is?" Pilgrim said, "Brother, since you and Sha Monk joined us, I haven't had a chance to pole it. How would I know its weight?" "Ah! Elder Brother," said Pa-chieh, "just count the things here:

Four yellow rattan mats;
Long and short, eight ropes in all.
To guard against dampness and rain.
There are blankets—three, four layers!
The flat pole's too slippery, perhaps?
You add nails on nails at both ends!
Cast in iron and copper, the nine-ringed priestly staff.
Made of bamboo and rattan, the long, large cloak.

With all this luggage, you should pity old Hog, who has to walk all day carrying it! You only are the disciple of our master; I've been made into a long-term laborer!" "Idiot!" said Pilgrim with a laugh, "to whom are you complaining?" "To you, Elder Brother," said Pa-chieh. "If you're making complaints to me," said Pilgrim, "you've made a mistake! Old Monkey is solely concerned with Master's safety, while you and Sha Monk have the special responsibility of looking after the luggage and the horse. If you ever slack off, you'll get a good whipping in the shanks from this huge rod!" "Elder Brother," said Pa-chieh, "don't mention whipping, for that only means taking advantage of others by brute force. I realize that you have a proud and haughty nature, and you are not about to pole the luggage. But look how fat and strong the horse is that Master is riding: he's only carrying one old monk. Make him take a few pieces of luggage, for the sake of fraternal sentiment!" "So you think he's a horse!" said Pilgrim. "He's no earthly horse, for he is originally the son of Ao-jun, the Dragon King of the Western Ocean. Because he set fire to the palace and destroyed some of its pearls, his father charged him with disobedience and he was condemned by Heaven. He was fortunate to have the Bodhisattva Kuan-yin save his life, and he was placed in the Eagle Grief Stream to await Master's arrival. At the appropriate time, the Bodhisattva also appeared personally to take off his scales and horns and to remove the pearls around his neck. It was then that he changed into this horse to carry Master to worship Buddha in the Western Heaven. This is a matter of achieving merit for each one of us individually, and you shouldn't bother him." When Sha Monk heard these words, he said, "Elder Brother, is he really a dragon?" "Yes," said Pilgrim. Pa-chieh said, "Elder Brother, I have heard an ancient saying that a dragon can breathe out clouds and mists, kick up dust and dirt; he has the ability to leap over mountains and peaks, the divine power to stir up rivers and seas. How is it that he is walking so slowly at the moment?" "You want him to move swiftly?" said Pilgrim. "I'll make him do that. Look!" Dear Great Sage! He shook his golden-hooped rod once, and there were ten thousand shafts of colorful lights! When that horse saw the rod, he was so afraid that he might be struck by it that he moved his four legs like lightning and darted away. As his hands were weak, the master could not restrain the horse from this display of its mean nature. The horse ran all the way up a mountain cliff before slowing down to a trot. The master finally caught his breath, and that was when he discovered in the distance several stately buildings beneath some pine trees. He saw

Doors draped by hanging cedars;
Houses beside a green hill;
Pine trees fresh and straight.
And some poles of mottled bamboo.
By the fence wild chrysanthemums glow with the frost;
By the bridge, reflections of orchids redden the stream.
Walls of white plaster;
And fences brick-laid.
A great hall, how noble and august;
A tall house, so peaceful and clean.

No oxen or sheep are seen, nor hens or dogs.

After autumn's harvest the farm chores must be light.

As the master held on to the saddle and slowly surveyed the scenery, Wu-k'ung and his brothers arrived. "Master," said Wu-k'ung, "you didn't fall off the horse?" "You brazen ape!" scolded the elder. "You were the one who frightened the horse! It's a good thing I managed to stay on him!" Attempting to placate him with a smile, Pilgrim said, "Master, please don't scold me. It all began when Chu Pa-chieh said that the horse was moving too slowly; so I made him hurry a little." Because he tried to catch up with the horse, Idiot ran till he was all out of breath, mumbling to himself, "I'm done, done! Look at this belly of mine, and the slack torso! Already the pole is so heavy that I can hardly carry it. Now I'm given the additional bustle and toil of running after this horse!" "Disciples," said the elder, "look over there: there's a small village where we may perhaps ask for lodging." When Pilgrim heard these words, he looked up and saw that it was covered by auspicious clouds and hallowed mists. He knew then that this place had to be a creation of buddhas or immortals, but he dared not reveal the Heavenly secret. He only said: "Fine! Fine! Let's go ask for shelter."

Quickly dismounting, the elder discovered that the towered entrance gate was decorated with carved lotus designs and looped slits in the woodwork; its pillars were carved and its beams gilded. Sha Monk put down the luggage, while Pa-chieh led the horse, saying, "This must be a family of considerable wealth!" Pilgrim wanted to go in at once, but Tripitaka said, "No, you and I are priests, and we should behave with circumspection. Don't ever enter a house without permission. Let's wait until someone comes out, and then we may request lodging politely." Pa-chieh tied up the horse and sat down, leaning against the wall. Tripitaka sat on one of the stone drums while Pilgrim and Sha Monk seated themselves at the foot of the gate. They waited for a long time, but no one came out. Impatient by nature, Pilgrim leaped up after a while and ran inside the gate to have a look. There were, in fact, three large halls facing south, each with its curtains highly drawn up. Above the door screen hung a horizontal scroll painting with motifs of long life and rich blessings. And pasted on the gold lacquered pillars on either side was this new year couplet written on bright red paper:

Frail willows float like gossamer, the low bridge at dusk;

Snow dots the fragrant plums, a small yard in the spring.
In the center hall, there was a small black lacquered table, its luster half gone, bearing an old bronze urn in the shape of a beast. There were six straight-backed chairs in the main hall, while hanging screens were mounted on the walls east and west just below the roof.

As Pilgrim was glancing at all this furtively, the sound of footsteps suddenly came from behind the door to the rear, and out walked a middle-aged woman, who asked in a seductive voice, "Who are you, that you dare enter a widow's home without permission?" The Great Sage was so taken aback that he could only murmur his reply: "This humble monk came from the Great T'ang in the Land of the East, having received the royal decree to seek scriptures from Buddha in the West. There are four of us altogether. As we reached your noble region, it became late, and we therefore approached the sacred abode of the old Bodhisattva to seek shelter for the night." Smiling amiably, the woman said, "Elder, where are your other three companions? Please invite them to come in." "Master," shouted Pilgrim in a loud voice, "you are invited to come in." Only then did Tripitaka enter with Pa-chieh and Sha Monk, who was leading the horse and carrying the luggage as well. The woman walked out of the hall to greet them, where she was met by the furtive, wanton glances of Pa-chieh. How did she look, you ask.

She wore a gown of mandarin green and silk brocade,
Topped by a light pink vest,
To which was fastened a light yellow embroidered skirt;
Her high-heeled, patterned shoes glinted beneath.
A black lace covered her stylish coiffure,
Nicely matching the twin-colored braids like dragons coiled.
Her ivory palace-comb, gleaming red and halcyon-blue,
Supported two gold hair-pins set aslant.
Her half-grey tresses swept up like phoenix wings;
Her dangling earrings had rows of precious pearls.
Still lovely even without powder or rouge,
She had charm and beauty like one fair youth.

When the woman saw the three of them, she became even more amiable and invited them with great politeness into the main hall. After they had exchanged greetings one after the other, the pilgrims were told to be seated for tea to be served. From behind the screen

a young maid with two tufts of flowing locks appeared, holding a
golden tray with several white-jade cups. There were

Fragrant tea wafting warm air,
Strange fruits spreading fine aroma.

That lady rolled up her colorful sleeves and revealed long, delicate
fingers like the stalks of spring onions; holding high the jade cups, she
passed the tea to each one of them, bowing as she made the presentation. After the tea, she gave instructions for vegetarian food to be
prepared. "Old Bodhisattva," said Tripitaka bowing, "what is your
noble surname? And what is the name of your esteemed region?"
The woman said, "This belongs to the West Aparagodānīya Continent. My maiden surname is Chia (Unreal), and the surname of my
husband's family is Mo (Nonexisting). Unfortunately my in-laws died
prematurely, and my husband and I inherited our ancestral fortune,
which amounted to more than ten thousand taels of silver and over
fifteen thousand acres of prime land. It was fated, however, that we
should have no son, having given birth only to three daughters. The
year before last, it was my great misfortune to lose my husband also,
and I was left a widow. This year my mourning period is completed,
but we have no other relatives beside mother and daughters to inherit
our vast property and land. I would have liked to marry again, but
I find it difficult to give up such wealth. We are delighted, therefore,
that the four of you have arrived, for we four, mother and daughters,
would like very much to ask you to become our spouses. I do not
know what you will think of this proposal."

When Tripitaka heard these words, he turned deaf and dumb;
shutting his eyes to quiet his mind, he fell silent and gave no reply.
The woman said, "We own over three hundred mou[3] of paddies,
over four hundred and sixty acres of dried fields, and over four
hundred and sixty acres of orchards and forests. We have over a
thousand head of yellow water buffalo, herds of mules and horses,
countless pigs and sheep; in all four quarters, there are over seventy
barns and haystacks. In this household there is grain enough to feed
you for more than eight or nine years, silk that you could not wear
out in a decade, gold and silver that you might spend for a lifetime.
What could be more delightful than our silk sheets and curtains,
which can render spring eternal? Not to mention those who wear
golden hairpins standing in rows! If all of you, master and disciples,

are willing to change your minds and enter the family of your wives, you will be most comfortable, having all these riches to enjoy. Will that not be better than the toil of the journey to the West?" Like a dumb and stupid person, Tripitaka refused to utter a word.

The woman said, "I was born in the hour of the Cock, on the third day of the third month, in the year Ting-hai. As my deceased husband was three years my senior, I am now forty-five years old. My eldest daughter, named Chên-Chên, is twenty; my second daughter, Ai-ai, is eighteen; and my youngest daughter, Lien-lien, is sixteen; and none of them has been betrothed to anyone. Though I am rather homely, my daughters fortunately are rather good-looking. Moreover, each of them is well trained in needlework and the feminine arts. And because we had no son, my late husband brought them up as if they were boys, teaching them some of the Confucian classics when they were young as well as the art of writing verse and couplets. So, although they reside in a mountain home, they are not vulgar or uncouth persons; they would make suitable matches, I dare say, for all of you. If you Elders can put away your inhibitions and let your hair grow again, you can at once become masters of this household. Are not the silk and brocade that you will wear infinitely better than the porcelain almsbowl and black robes, the straw sandals and grass hats?"

Sitting aloft in the seat of honor, Tripitaka was like a child struck by lightning, a frog smitten by rain. With eyes bulging and rolling upward, he could barely keep himself from keeling over in his chair. But Pa-chieh, hearing of such wealth and such beauty, could hardly quell the unbearable itch in his heart! Sitting on his chair, he kept turning and twisting—as if a needle were pricking him in the ass. Finally he could restrain himself no longer. Walking forward, he tugged at his master, saying, "Master! How can you completely ignore what the lady has been saying to you? You must try to pay some attention." Jerking back his head, the priest gave such a hostile shout that Pa-chieh backed away hurriedly. "You cursed beast!" he bellowed. "We are people who have left home. How can we possibly allow ourselves anymore to be moved by riches and tempted by beauty?"

With a laugh the woman said, "Oh dear, dear! Tell me, what's so good about those who leave home?" "Lady Bodhisattva," said Tripitaka, "tell me what is so good about those of you who remain at home?" "Please take a seat, Elder," said the woman, "and let me tell you the benefits in the life of those of us who remain at home. If you ask what they are, this poem will make them abundantly clear.

When spring fashions appear I wear new silk;
Pleased to watch summer lilies I change to lace.
Autumn brings fragrant rice-wine newly brewed.
In winter's heated rooms my face glows with wine.
I may enjoy the fruits of all four climes
And every dainty of eight seasons, too.
The silk sheets and quilts of the bridal eve
Best the mendicant's life of Buddhist chants."

Tripitaka said, "Lady Bodhisattva, you who remain in the home can enjoy riches and glory; you have things to eat, clothes to wear, and children by your side. That is undeniably a good life, but you do not know that there are some benefits in the life of those of us who have left home. If you ask what they are, this poem will make them abundantly clear.

The will to leave home is no common thing:
You must tear down the old stronghold of love!
No cares without, tongue and mouth are at peace;
Your body within has good yin and yang.
When merit's done, you face the Golden Arch
And go back, mind enlightened, to your Home.
It beats the life of lust for meat at home:
You rot with age, one stinking bag of flesh!"

When the woman heard these words, she grew terribly angry, saying, "How dare you to be so insolent, you brazen monk! If I had had no regard for the fact that you have come from the Land of the East, I would have sent you away at once. Here I was trying to ask you, with all sincerity, to enter our family and share our wealth, and you insult me instead. Even though you have received the commandments and made the vow never to return to secular life, at least one of your followers could become a member of our family. Why are you being so legalistic?"

Seeing how angry she had become, Tripitaka was intimidated and said, "Wu-k'ung, why don't you stay here." Pilgrim said, "I've been completely ignorant in such matters since the time I was young. Let Pa-chieh stay." "Elder Brother," said Pa-chieh, "don't play tricks. Let's all have some further discussion." "If neither of you is willing," said Tripitaka, "I'll ask Wu-ching to stay." "Listen to the way Master is speaking!" said Sha Monk. "Since I was converted by the Bodhisattva and received the commandments from her, I've been waiting for you. It has been scarcely two months since you took me as your disciple and gave me your teachings, and I have yet to acquire even half an inch of merit. You think I would dare seek such riches! I will journey to the Western Heaven even if it means my death! I'll never engage in such perfidious activities!" When the woman saw them refusing to remain, she quickly walked behind the screen and slammed the door to the rear. Master and disciples were left outside, and no one came out again to present tea or rice. Exasperated, Pa-chieh began to find fault with the T'ang monk, saying, "Master, you really don't know how to handle these matters! In fact, you have ruined all our chances by the way you spoke! You could have been more flexible and given her a vague reply so that she would at least have given us a meal. We would at least have enjoyed a pleasant evening, and whether we would be willing to stay tomorrow or not would have been for us to decide. Now the door is shut and no one is going to come out. How are we going to last through the night in the midst of these empty ashes and cold stoves?"

"Second Brother," said Wu-ching, "why don't you stay here and become her son-in-law." Pa-chieh said, "Brother, don't play tricks on people. Let's discuss the matter further." "What's there to discuss?" said Pilgrim. "If you are willing, Master and that woman will become in-laws, and you will be the son-in-law who lives in the girl's home. With such riches and such treasures in this family, you will no doubt be given a huge dowry and a nice banquet to greet the kinsfolk, which all of us can also enjoy. Your return to secular life here will in fact benefit both parties concerned." "You can say that all right," said Pa-chieh, "but for me it's a matter of fleeing the secular life only to return to secular life, of leaving my wife only to take another wife." "So, Second Brother already has a wife?" said Sha Monk. "You didn't realize," Pilgrim said, "that originally he was the son-in-law of Mr. Kao of the Old Kao Village, in the Kingdom of Tibet. Since I defeated him, and since he had earlier received the commandments from the Bodhisattva, he had little choice but to follow the priestly vocation. That's the reason he abandoned his former wife to follow Master and to go worship Buddha in the Western Heaven. I suppose he has felt the separation keenly and has been brooding on it for some time. Just now, when marriage was mentioned, he must have been sorely tempted. Idiot, why don't you become the son-in-law of this household? Just make sure that you make a few extra bows to old Monkey, and you won't be reprimanded!" "Nonsense! Nonsense!" said Idiot. "Each one of us is tempted, but you only want old Hog to be embarrassed. The proverb says, 'A monk is the preta of sensuality;' and which one of us can truly say that he doesn't want this? But you have to put on a show, and your histronics have ruined a good thing. Now we can't even get a drop of tea or water, and no one is tending the lamps or fires. We may last through the night, but I doubt that the horse can; he has to carry someone tomorrow and walk again, you know. If he goes hungry for a night, he might be reduced to a skeleton. You people sit here, while Old Hog goes to graze the horse." Hastily, Idiot untied the reins and pulled the horse outside. "Sha Monk," said Pilgrim, "you stay here and keep Master company. I'll follow him and see where he is going to graze the horse." "Wu-k'ung," said Tripitaka, "you may go and see where he's going, but don't ridicule him." "I won't," said Pilgrim. The Great Sage walked out of the main hall, and with one shake of his body he changed into a red dragonfly. He flew out of the front gate and caught up with Pa-chieh.

Idiot pulled the horse out to where there was grass, but he did not graze him there. Shouting and whooping, he chased the horse instead to the rear door of the house, where he found the woman standing outside the door with three girls, enjoying the sight of some chrysanthemums. When mother and daughters saw Pa-chieh approaching, the three girls slipped inside the house at once, but the woman stood still beside the door and said, "Little Elder, where are you going?" Our Idiot threw away the reins and went up to greet her with a most friendly "Hello!" Then he said, "Mama, I came to graze the horse." "Your master is much too squeamish," said the woman. "If he took a wife in our family, he would be much better off, wouldn't he, than being a mendicant trudging to the West?" "Well, they all have received the command of the T'ang emperor," said Pa-chieh with a laugh, "and they haven't the courage to disobey the ruler's decree. That's why they are unwilling to do this thing. Just now they were all trying to play tricks on me in the front hall, and

I was somewhat embarrassed because I was afraid that Mama would find my long snout and large ears too offensive." "I don't, really," said the woman, "and since we have no master of the house, it's better to take one than none at all. But I do fear that my daughters may find you somewhat unattractive." "Mama," said Pa-chieh, "please instruct your noble daughters not to choose their men that way. Others may be more handsome, but they usually turn out to be quite useless. Though I may be ugly, I do live by certain principles." "And what are they?" said the woman. Pa-chieh said,

Though I may be somewhat ugly,
I can work quite diligently.
A thousand acres of land, you say?
No need for oxen to plow it.
I'll go over it once with my rake,
And the seeds will grow in season.
When there's no rain I can make rain.
When there's no wind I'll call for wind.
If the house is not tall enough,
I'll build you a few stories more.
If the grounds are not swept I'll give them a sweep.
If the gutter's not drained I'll draw it for you.
All things both great and small around the house
I am able to do most readily.

"If you can work around the house," said the woman, "you should discuss the matter again with your master. If there's no great inconvenience, we'll take you." "No need for further discussion," said Pa-chieh, "for he's no genuine parent of mine. Whether I want to do this or not is for me to decide." "All right, all right," said the woman. "Let me talk to my girls first." She slipped back inside immediately and slammed the rear door shut. Pa-chieh did not graze the horse there either, but led it back to the front. Little did he realize, however, that Great Sage Sun had heard everything. With wings outstretched, the Great Sage flew back to see the T'ang monk, changing back into his original form. "Master," he said, "Wu-nêng is leading the horse back here." "Of course he's leading the horse," said T'ang monk, "for if he doesn't, it may run away in a fit of mischief." Pilgrim started to laugh and gave a thorough account of what the woman and Pa-chieh had said, but Tripitaka did not know whether to believe him or not.

In a little while Idiot arrived and tied up the horse. "Have you grazed him?" asked the Elder. "There's not much good grass around here," said Pa-chieh, "so it's really no place to graze a horse." "It may not be a place to graze the horse," said Pilgrim, "but is it a place to lead a horse?"[4] When Idiot heard this question, he knew that his secret was known. He lowered his head and turned it to one side; with pouting lips and wrinkled brows, he remained silent for a long time. Just then, they heard the side door open with a creak, and out came a pair of red lanterns and a pair of portable incense burners. There were swirling clouds of fragrance and the sounds of tinkling girdle-jade, when the woman walked out leading her three daughters. Chên-chên, Ai-ai, and Lien-lien were told to bow to the scripture pilgrims, and as they did so, standing in a row at the main hall, they appeared to be most beautiful indeed. Look at them!

Each mothlike eyebrow painted halcyon-blue;
Each pretty face aglow with springlike hues.
What beguiling, empire-shaking beauty!
What ravishing, heart-jolting charm!
Their filigreed headgears enhance their grace;
Silk sashes afloat, they seem wholly divine.
Like ripe cherries their lips part, half-smiling,
As they walk slowly and spread their orchid-scent.
Their heads full of pearls and jade
Atop countless hairpins slightly trembling.
Their bodies full of delicate aroma,
Shrouded by exquisite robes of fine golden thread.
Why speak of the lovely ladies of Ch'u,
Or the good looks of Hsi-tzŭ?[5]
They look like the fairy ladies descending from the Ninefold Heaven,
Or the Princess Ch'ang-o leaving her Lunar Palace.

When he saw them, Tripitaka lowered his head and folded his hands in front of him, while the Great Sage became dumb and mute and Sha Monk turned away completely. But look at that Chu Pa-chieh! With eyes unblinking, a mind filled with lust, and passion fast rising, he murmured huskily: "What an honor it is to have the presence of you immortal ladies! Mama, please ask your dear sisters to leave." The three girls went behind the screen, leaving the pair of lanterns behind. The woman said, "Have your four Elders made up your mind which one of you shall be betrothed to my daughters?" "We have discussed the matter," said Wu-ching, "and we have decided that the one whose surname is Chu shall enter your family." "Brother," said Pa-chieh, "please don't play any tricks on me. Let's discuss the matter further." "What's there to discuss?" said Pilgrim. "You have already made all the arrangements with her at the back door, and even call har 'Mama.' What's there to discuss any more? Master can be the in-law for the groom while this woman here will give away the bride; old Monkey will be the witness, and Sha monk the go-between. There's no need even to consult the almanac, for today happens to be the most auspicious and lucky day. You come here and bow to Master, and then you can go inside and become her son-in-law." "Nothing doing! Nothing doing!" said Pa-chieh. "How can I engage in this kind of business?" "Idiot!" said Pilgrim. "Stop this fakery! You have addressed her as 'Mama' for countless times already! What do you mean by 'nothing doing'? Agree to this at once, so that we may have the pleasure of enjoying some wine at the wedding." He caught hold of Pa-chieh with one hand and pulled at the woman with the other, saying, "Mother-in-law, take your son-in-law inside." Somewhat hesitantly, Idiot started to shuffle inside, while the woman gave instructions to a houseboy, saying, "Take out some tables and chairs and wipe them clean. Prepare a vegetarian dinner to serve these three relatives of ours. I'm leading our new master inside." She further gave instructions for the cook to begin preparation for a wedding banquet to be held next morning. The houseboys then left to tell the cook. After the three pilgrims had eaten their meal, they retired to the guestrooms, and we shall say no more of them for the moment.

We now tell you about Pa-chieh, who followed his mother-in-law and walked inside. There were row upon row of doorways and chambers with tall thresholds, causing him constantly to stumble and fall. "Mama," said Idiot, "please walk more slowly. I'm not familiar with the way here, so you must guide me a little." The woman said, "These are all the storerooms, the treasuries, the rooms where the flour is ground. We have yet to reach the kitchen." "What a huge house!" said Pa-chieh. Stumbling along a winding course, he walked for a long time before finally reaching the inner chamber of the house. "Son-in-law," said the woman, "since your brother said that today is a most auspicious and lucky day, I have taken you in.

In all this hurry, we have not had the chance of consulting an astrologer, nor have we been prepared for the proper wedding ceremony of worshiping Heaven and Earth and of spreading grains and fruits on the bridal bed. Right now, why don't you kowtow eight times toward the sky?" "You are right, Mama," said Pa-chieh. "You take the upper seat also, and let me bow to you a few times. We'll consider that my worship of Heaven and Earth as well as my gesture of gratitude to you. Doing these two things at once will save me some trouble." "All right, all right," said his mother-in-law, laughing; "you are indeed a son-in-law who knows how to fulfill your household duties with the least effort. I'll sit down, and you can make your bows."

The candles on silver candlesticks were shining brightly throughout the hall as Idiot made his bows. Afterwards he said, "Mama, which one of the dear sisters do you plan to give me?" "That's my dilemma," said his mother-in-law. "I was going to give you my eldest daughter, but I was afraid of offending my second daughter; I was going to give you my second daughter, but I was afraid then of offending my third daughter; and if I were to give you my third daughter, I fear that my eldest daughter may be offended. That's why I cannot make up my mind." "Mama," said Pa-chieh, "if you want to prevent strife, why not give them all to me; in that way, you will spare yourself a lot of bickering that can destroy the harmony of the family." "Nonsense!" said his mother-in-law. "You mean you alone want to take all three of my daughters?" "Listen to what you're saying, Mama!" said Pa-chieh. "Who doesn't have three or four concubines nowadays? Even if you have a few more daughters, I'll gladly take them all. When I was young, I learned how to be long-lasting in the arts of love. You can be assured that I'll render satisfactory service to every one of them." "That's no good! That's no good!" said the woman. "I have a large handkerchief here, with which you can cover your head, blindfold yourself, and determine your fated marriage that way. I'm going to ask my daughters to walk past you, and the one you can catch with your hands will be betrothed to you." Idiot accepted her suggestion and covered his head with his handkerchief. We have a testimonial poem which says:

The fool knows not the true causes of things:
Beauty's sword can in secret the self destroy.

Proper rites have long been fixed by the Duke of Chou,
But a bridegroom today still covers his head!

After Idiot had tied himself up properly, he said, "Mama, ask the dear sisters to come out." "Chên-chên, Ai-ai, Lien-lien," cried his mother-in-law, "you all come out and determine your fated marriage, so that one of you may be given to this man." With the sounds of girdle-jade and the fragrance of orchids, it seemed that some fairy ladies had suddenly appeared. Idiot indeed stretched forth his hands to try to catch hold of one of the girls, but though he darted about madly this way and that, he could not lay hands on anyone on either side of him. It seemed to him, to be sure, that the girls were making all kinds of movement around him, but he could not grab a single one of them. He lunged toward the east and wrapped his arms around a pillar; he made a dive toward the west and slammed into a wooden partition. Growing faint from rushing about like that, he began to stumble and fall all over the place—tripping on the threshold in front of him, smashing into the brick wall behind him! Fumbling and tumbling around, he ended up sitting on the floor with a bruised head and a swollen mouth. "Mama," he cried, panting heavily, "you have a bunch of slippery daughters! I can't catch a single one of them! What am I to do? What am I to do?"

Taking off his blindfold, the woman said, "Son-in-law, it's not that my daughters are slippery; it's just that they are all very modest. Each defers to the other so that she may take you." "If they are unwilling to take me, Mama," said Pa-chieh, "why don't you take me instead." "Dear Son-in-law," said the woman, "you really have no regard for age or youth, when you even want your mother-in-law! My three daughters are really quite talented, for each one of them has woven a silk undershirt studded with pearls. Try them on, and the one whose shirt fits you will take you in." "Fine! Fine! Fine!" said Pa-chieh. "Bring out all three undershirts and let me try them on. If all fit me, they can all have me." The woman went inside and took out one undershirt, which she handed over to Pa-chieh. Taking off his blue silk shirt, Idiot took up the undergarment and draped it over his body at once. Before he had managed to tie the strings, however, he suddenly fell to the floor. The undershirt, you see, had changed into several pieces of rope which had him tightly bound. As he lay there in great pain, the women vanished.

We now tell you about Tripitaka, Pilgrim, and Sha Monk, who woke up when it began to grow light in the East. As they opened their eyes, they discovered that all the noble halls and buildings had vanished. There were neither carved beams nor gilded pillars, for the truth of the matter is that they had all been sleeping in a forest of pines and cedars. In a panic, the elder began to shout for Pilgrim, and Sha Monk also cried: "Elder Brother, we are finished! We have met some ghosts!" The Great Sage Sun, however, realized fully what had happened. Smiling gently, he said, "What are you talking about?" "Look where we've been sleeping!" cried the elder. "It's pleasant enough in this pine forest," said Pilgrim, "but I wonder where that Idiot is going through his ordeal." "Who is going through an ordeal?" asked the elder. Pilgrim answered with a laugh, "The women of that household happened to be some bodhisattvas from somewhere, who had waited for us to teach us a lesson. They must have left during the night, but unfortunately Chu Pa-chieh has to suffer." When Tripitaka heard this, he quickly folded his hands to make a bow. Then they saw a slip of paper hanging on an old cedar tree, fluttering in the wind. Sha Monk quickly took it down for his master to read. On it was written the following eight-line poem:

Though the old Dame of Li Shan[6] had no desire,
Kuan-yin invited her to leave the mount.
Mañjuśri and Viśvabhadra, too, were guests
Who took in the woods the form of maidens fair.
The holy monk's virtuous and truly chaste,
But Pa-chieh's profane, loving things mundane.
Henceforth he must repent with quiet heart,
For if he's slothful, the way will be hard.

As the elder, Pilgrim and Sha Monk recited this poem aloud, they heard a loud call from deep in the woods: "Master, the ropes are killing me! Save me, please! I'll never dare do this again!" "Wu-k'ung," said Tripitaka, "is it Wu-nêng who is calling us?" "Yes," said Sha Monk. "Brother," said Pilgrim, "don't bother about him. Let us leave now." "Though Idiot is stupid and mischievous," said Tripitaka, "he is at least fairly honest, and he has arms strong enough to carry the luggage. Let's have some regard for the Bodhisattva's earlier intention; let's rescue him so that he may continue to follow us. I doubt that he'll ever dare do this again." Sha Monk thereupon rolled up the bedding and put the luggage in order, after which Great Sage Sun untied the horse to lead the T'ang monk into the woods to see what had happened. Ah! So it is that

You must take care in the pursuit of truth

To purge desires, and you'll enter the Real.

We do not know what sort of good or evil was in store for Idiot, and you must listen to the explanation in the next chapter.

Twenty-four

At the Mountain of Longevity, the Great Immortal detains
  his old friend;
At the Temple of Five Villages, Pilgrim steals the
  ginseng[1] fruit.

We shall tell you about the three of them who, on entering the forest,
found Idiot tied to a tree. He was screaming continuously because of
the unbearable pain. Pilgrim approached him and said to him,
laughing, "Dear son-in-law! It's getting rather late, and you still
haven't got around to performing the proper ceremony of thanking
your parents or announcing your marriage to Master. You are still
having a grand old time playing games here! Hey! Where's your
mama? Where's your wife? What a dear son-in-law, all bound and
beaten!" When Idiot heard such ridicule, he was so mortified that he
clenched his teeth to try to endure the pain without making any
more noise. Sha Monk, however, could not bear to look at him; he
put down the luggage and went forward to untie the ropes. After he
was freed, Idiot could only drop to his knees and kowtow toward the
sky, for he was filled with shame. For him we have as a testimony
this tz'ŭ poem to the tune of *Hsi-chiang-yüeh*:

Eros is a sword injurious:
Live by it and you will be slain.
The lady so fair and lovely at sixteen
Is more vicious than a yakṣa!

You have but one principal sum;
You can't add profit to your purse.
Guard and keep well your precious capital,
Which you must not squander and waste.

Scooping up some dirt and scattering it like incense, Pa-chieh bowed
to the sky. "Did you recognize those bodhisattvas at all?" said
Pilgrim. "I was in a stupor, about to faint," said Pa-chieh. "How
could I recognize anyone?" Pilgrim then handed him the slip of paper.
When Pa-chieh saw the gāthā, he was more embarrassed than ever.
"Second Brother does have all the luck," said Sha Monk with a laugh,

"for you have attracted these four bodhisattvas here to become your wives!" "Brother," said Pa-chieh, "let's not ever mention that again! It's blasphemy! From now on, I'll never dare do such foolish things again. Even if it breaks my bones, I'll carry the pole and luggage to follow Master to the West." "You are finally speaking sensibly," said Tripitaka.

Pilgrim then led his master up the main road, and after journeying for a long time, they suddenly came upon a tall mountain. Pulling in the reins, Tripitaka said, "Disciples, let's be careful as we travel up this mountain before us, for there may be monsters seeking to harm us." "Ahead of your horse you have the three of us," said Pilgrim. "Why fear the monsters?" Reassured by these words, the elder proceeded. That mountain is truly a magnificent mountain:

A tall mountain most rugged,
Its shape both lofty and grand.
Its root joins the K'un-lun² ranges;
Its top reaches to the sky.
White cranes come oft to perch on junipers;
Black apes hang frequently on the vines.
As the sun lights up the forest,
Strands upon strands of red mist are circling;
As wind rises from dark gorges,
Ten thousand pieces of pink cloud soar and fly.
Mysterious birds sing wildly in green bamboos;
Pheasants do battle amidst untended flowers.
You see that Thousand-Year Peak,
That Five-Blessings³ Peak,
And the Hibiscus Peak—
They all glow and shimmer most awesomely;
That Ageless Rock,
That Tiger-Tooth Rock,
And that Three-Heaven Rock—
From which blessed air rises endlessly.
Below the cliff, delicate grass;
Atop the ridge, fragrant plum.
The thorns and briars are thick;
The orchids are pale and pure.
In the deep forest the phoenix musters a thousand fowls;
In an old cave the unicorn governs countless beasts.

Even the brook seems to care:
She twists and turns as if looking back.
The peaks are continuous:
Row upon row circling all around.
You see those green huai[4] trees,
Those spotted bamboos,
And those verdant pines—
Ever fresh in their dense luxuriance;
Those pears milk-white,
Those peaches red,
And those willows green—
Each rivaling the other in their Triple-Spring hues.
Dragons sing and tigers roar;
The cranes dance and the apes wail;
The musk deer from flowers walk out;
The phoenix cries facing the sun.
This is a mountain divine, land of true blessedness,
The same as P'êng-lai, the fairyland.
All you see are flowers blooming and dying—such, the view of the
    mount,
And clouds nearing or leaving the soaring peaks.

With great delight, Tripitaka said as he rode along, "Disciples, since
I began this journey to the West, I have passed through many regions,
all rather treacherous and difficult to traverse. None of the other
places has scenery like this mountain, which is extraordinarily beautiful. Perhaps we are not far from Thunderclap, and, if so, we should
prepare in a dignified and solemn manner to meet the World's
Honored One." "It's early, much too early!" said Pilgrim laughing.
"We are nowhere near!" "Elder Brother," said Sha Monk, "how far
is it to Thunderclap?" "A hundred and eight thousand miles," said
Pilgrim, "and we have not even covered one-tenth of the distance."
"Elder Brother," said Pa-chieh, "how many years do we have to
travel before we get there?" "If we were talking about you two, my
worthy brothers," said Pilgrim, "this journey would take some ten
days. If we were talking about me, I could probably make about fifty
round trips in a day and there would still be sunlight. But if we are
talking about Master, then don't even think about it!" "Wu-k'ung,"
said the T'ang monk, "tell us when we shall be able to reach our
destination." Pilgrim said, "You can walk from the time of your youth

till the time you grow old, and after that, till you become youthful again; and even after going through such a cycle a thousand times, you may still find it difficult to reach the place you want to go to. But when you perceive, by the resoluteness of your will, the Buddha-nature in all things, and when every one of your thoughts goes back to its very source in your memory, that will be the time you arrive at the Spirit Mountain." "Elder Brother," said Sha Monk, "even though this is not the region of Thunderclap, a place of such scenic splendor must be the residence of a good man." "That's true," said Pilgrim, "for this can hardly be a place for demons or goblins; rather, it must be the home of a holy monk or an immortal. We can walk leisurely and enjoy the scenery." We shall say no more about them for the time being.

We now tell you about this mountain, which had the name of the Mountain of Longevity. In the mountain there was a Taoist Temple called the Temple of Five villages; it was the abode of an immortal whose Taoist name was Chên-yüan-tzǔ,[5] and whose nickname was Lord, Equal to Earth. There was, moreover, a strange treasure grown in this temple, a spiritual root which was formed just after chaos had been parted and the nebula had been established prior to the division of Heaven and Earth. Throughout the four great continents of the world, it could be found in only the Temple of Five Villages in the West Aparagodānīya Continent. This treasure was called grass of the reverted cinnabar,[6] or the ginseng fruit. It took three thousand years for the plant to bloom, another three thousand years to bear fruit, and still another three thousand years before they ripened. All in all, it would be nearly ten thousand years before they could be eaten, and even after such a long time, there would be only thirty such fruits. The shape of the fruit was exactly that of a newborn infant not yet three days old, complete with the four limbs and the five senses. If a man had the good fortune of even smelling the fruit, he would live for three hundred and sixty years; if he ate one, he would reach his forty-seven thousandth year.

That day, the Great Chên-yüan Immortal happened to have received a card from the Celestial Honored Primordial, who invited him to the Mi-lo Palace in the Heaven of Exalted Purity to listen to the discourse on "The Taoist Fruit of the Chaotic Origin." That Great Immortal, you see, had already trained countless disciples to become immortals; even now he had with him some forty-eight disciples, all Taoists of the Complete Truth Sect who had acquired the Tao. When he went up to the region above to listen to the lecture that day, he took forty-six disciples along with him, leaving behind two of the youngest ones to look after the temple. One was called Clear Breeze, and the other was named Bright Moon. Clear Breeze was only one thousand two hundred and twenty years old, while Bright Moon had just passed his one thousand two hundredth birthday. Before his departure, Chên-yüan-tzŭ gave instructions to the two young lads saying, "I cannot refuse the invitation of the Celestial Honored One, and I'm leaving for the Mi-lo Palace to attend a lecture. You two must be watchful, for an old friend of mine will be passing by here any day. Don't fail to treat him kindly: you may, in fact, strike down from the tree two of the ginseng fruits for him to eat as a token of our past friendship." "Who is this friend of yours, Master?" asked one of the lads. "Tell us, so that we may take good care of him." "He is a holy monk serving the Great T'ang Emperor in the land of the East," said the Great Immortal, "and his religious name is Tripitaka. He is now on his way to the Western Heaven to acquire scriptures from Buddha." "According to Confucius," said one of the lads laughing, " 'One does not take counsel with those who follow a different way.'⁷ We belong to the Mysterious Fold of the Great Monad. Why should we associate with a Buddhist monk?" "You should know," said the Great Immortal, "that that monk happens to be the incarnate Gold Cicada, the second disciple of Tathāgata, the Aged Sage of the West. Five hundred years ago, I became acquainted with him during the Feast of the Ullambana Bowl, when he presented me tea with his own hands as the various sons of Buddha paid me their respect. That's why I consider him an old friend." When the two immortal lads heard these words, they accepted them as the instruction of their master. As the Great Immortal was about to leave, he cautioned them again, saying, "Those fruits of mine are all numbered. You may give him two, but no more." "When the garden was opened to the public," said Clear Breeze, "we shared and ate two of the fruits; there should be still twenty-eight of them on the tree. We wouldn't think of using any more than you have told us to." The Great Immortal said, "Though Tripitaka T'ang is an old friend, his disciples, I fear, may be somewhat rowdy. It's best not to let them know about

the fruits." After he had finished giving these instructions to the two
lads, the Great Immortal ascended to the region of Heaven with all
his disciples.

We tell you now about the T'ang monk and his three companions,
who were making a tour of the mountain. Looking up, they suddenly
discovered several tall buildings by a cluster of pines and bamboos.
"Wu-k'ung," said the T'ang monk, "what sort of place do you think
that is over there?" After taking a look at it, Pilgrim said, "It's either
a Taoist temple or a Buddhist monastery. Let's move along, and we'll
find out more about it when we get there." They soon arrived at the
gate, and they saw

A pine knoll cool and serene;
A bamboo path dark and secluded;
White cranes coming and leaving with clouds afloat;
And apes climbing up and down to hand out fruits.
Before the gate, the pond's wide and trees cast long shadows;
The rocks crack, breaking the moss's growth.
Palatial halls dark and tall as the purple Heaven;
And towers aloft from which bright red mists descend.
Truly a blessed region, a spiritual place
Like the cloudy cave of P'êng-lai:
Quiet, untouched by the affairs of man;
Tranquil, fit to nurse the mind of Tao.
Blue birds may bring at times a letter from Wang-mu;
A phoenix oft arrives with a Lao Tzu scroll.
There's no end to the sight of this noble Taoist scene:
It's the boundless home of immortals indeed!

As the T'ang monk dismounted, he saw on the left a huge stone tablet,
on which the following inscription was written in large letters:

The Blessed Land of the Mountain of Longevity.

The Cave Heaven of the Temple of Five Villages.

"Disciples," said the Elder, "it's indeed a Taoist temple." "Master,"
said Sha Monk, "with such splendid scenery, there must be a good
man living in this temple. Let us go in and take a look. When we return
to the East after completing our merits, this may be the place for
another visit because of its marvelous scenery." "Well spoken," said
Pilgrim, and they all went inside. On both sides of the second gate they
saw this New Year couplet:

Long-living and ever young, this immortal house.

Of the same age as Heaven, this Taoist home.

Pilgrim said with a laugh, "This Taoist is mouthing big words just to intimidate people! When I, old Monkey, caused disturbance in the Heavenly Palace five hundreds years ago, I did not encounter such words even on the door of Lao Tzu!" "Never mind him!" said Pa-chieh. "Let's go inside! Let's go inside! You never know, maybe this Taoist does possess some virtue."

When they passed through the second gate, they were met by two young lads who were hurrying out. Look how they appear:

Healthy in body and spirit and with visage fair,
They had on their heads some knotted tufts of hair.
Their Taoist gowns, falling free, seemed wrapped in mists;
Their feathered robes seemed more quaint for the wind-blown
    sleeves.
Tightly tied, their sashes had dragon-head knots,
And silken cords laced lightly their sandals of straw.
Such uncommon looks were of no worldly-born;
They were Clear Breeze and Bright Moon, two lads divine.

The two young lads came out to meet them, bowing and saying, "Old Master, forgive us for not coming to meet you. Please take a seat." Delighted, the elder followed the two lads to the main hall to look around. There were altogether five huge chambers facing south, separated by floor-length windows that had carved panes and were translucent at the top and solid at the bottom. Pushing open one of these, the two immortal lads invited the T'ang monk into the central chamber, with a panel hanging on the middle wall on which two large characters—"Heaven, Earth"—were embroidered in five colors. Beneath the panel was a cinnabar-red lacquered incense table, on which there was an urn of yellow gold. Conveniently placed beside the urn were several sticks of incense.

The T'ang monk went forward and with his left hand, he took up some incense to put into the urn. He then prostrated himself three times before the table, after which he turned around and said, "Immortal lads, your Temple of Five Villages is in truth a godly region of the West. But why is it that you do not worship the Three Pure Ones, the Kings of the Four Quarters, or the many Lords of High Heaven? Why is it that you merely put up these two words of Heaven and Earth to be the recipient of fire and incense?" Smiling, one of the lads said, "To tell you the truth, Master, putting these two words up is an act of flattery on the part of our teacher, for of these two words, the one on top,[8] may deserve our reverence, but the one below is hardly worthy of our fire and incense." "What do you mean by an act of flattery?" said Tripitaka. The lad said, "The Three Pure Ones are friends of our teacher; the Four Kings, his old acquaintances; the Nine Luminaries, his junior colleagues; and the God of the New Year, his unwanted guest!" When Pilgrim heard this remark, he laughed so hard that he could barely stand up. "Elder Brother," said Pa-chieh, "why are you laughing?" "Talk about the shenanigans of old Monkey!" said Pilgrim. "Just listen to the flimflam of this Taoist kid!" "Where is your honorable teacher?" said Tripitaka. "Our teacher," said the lad, "had been invited by the Celestial Honored Primordial to attend a lecture on 'The Taoist Fruit of the Chaotic Origin' at the Mi-lo Palace in the Heaven of Exalted Purity. He's not home."

No longer able to restrain himself after hearing these words, Pilgrim shouted: "You stinking young Taoist! You can't even recognize people! Whom are you trying to hoodwink? What kind of taradiddle is this? Who is that Heavenly Immortal in the Mi-lo Palace who wanted to invite this wild bull shank of yours? And what sort of lecture is he going to give?" When Tripitaka saw how aroused Pilgrim was, he feared that the lads might give some reply that would lead to real trouble. So he said, "Wu-k'ung, stop being quarrelsome. If we leave this place the moment after we arrive, it is hardly a friendly gesture. The proverb says, 'The egrets do not devour the egret's flesh.' If their teacher is not here, why bother them? You go to graze the horse outside the temple gate; let Sha Monk look after the luggage and Pa-chieh fetch some grain from our bags. Let's borrow their pans and stove to prepare a meal for ourselves. When we are done, we can pay them a few pennies for firewood and that will be the end of the matter. Attend to your business, each of you, and let me rest here for a while. After the meal, we'll leave." The three of them duly went about their business.

Clear Breeze, and Bright Moon, filled with admiration, said softly to each other: "What a monk! Truly the incarnation of a lovable sage of the West, whose true origin is not at all obscured! Well, our master did tell us to take care of the T'ang monk and to serve him some ginseng fruits as a token of past friendship. He also cautioned us about the rowdiness of his disciples, and he couldn't have been more correct. It's a good thing that those three, so fierce in their looks and so churlish in their manners, were sent away. For had they remained, they would certainly have to see the ginseng fruits." Then Clear Breeze said, "Brother, we are still not quite certain whether that monk is really an old acquaintance of Master. We had better ask him and not make a mistake." The two lads therefore went forward again and said, "May we ask the old master whether he is Tripitaka T'ang from the Great T'ang Empire, who is on his way to fetch scriptures from the Western Heaven?" Returning their bows, the elder said, "I am, indeed. How is it that the immortal youths know my vulgar name?" "Before our master's departure," said one of them," he gave us instructions that we should go some distance to meet you. We did not expect your arrival to be so soon, and thus we failed in the proper etiquette of greeting you. Please take a seat, Master, and allow us to serve you tea." "I hardly deserve that," said Tripitaka, but Bright Moon went quickly back to his room and brought back a cup of fragrant tea to present to the elder. After Tripitaka had drunk the tea, Clear Breeze said, "Brother, we must not disobey our master's command. Let's go and bring back the fruit."

The two lads took leave of Tripitaka and went back to their room, where one of them took out a gold mallet and the other a wooden tray for carrying elixir. They also spread out several silk handkerchiefs on the tray before going to the Ginseng Garden. Clear Breeze then climbed on the tree to strike at the fruits with the mallet, while Bright Moon waited below, holding the tray. In a moment, two of the fruits dropped down and fell onto the tray. The young lads returned to the main hall and presented the fruits to the T'ang monk, saying, "Master T'ang, our Temple of Five Villages is situated in the midst of wild and desolate country. There's not much that we can offer you except these two fruits, our local products. Please use them to relieve your thirst." When the elder saw the fruits, he trembled all over and backed away three feet, saying, "Goodness! Goodness! The harvest seems to be plentiful this year! But why is this temple so destitute that they have to practice cannibalism here? These are newborn infants not yet three days old! How could you serve them to me to relieve my thirst?" "This monk," said Clear Breeze quietly to himself, "has been so corrupted by the fields of mouths and tongues, by the sea of strife and envy, that all he possesses are but two fleshly eyes and a worldly mind. That's why he can't recognize the strange treasures of our divine abode!" Bright Moon then drew near and said, "Master, this thing is called ginseng fruit. It's perfectly all right for you to eat one." "Non-sense! Nonsense!" said Tripitaka. "Their parents went through who knows how much suffering before they brought them to birth! How could you serve them as fruits when they are less than three days old?" Clear Breeze said, "Honestly, they were formed on a tree." "Rubbish! Rubbish!" said the elder. "How can people grow on trees? Take them away! This is blasphemy!" When the young lads saw that he absolutely refused to eat them, they had no choice but to take the tray back to their own room. The fruit, you see, is peculiar: if it is kept too long, it will become stiff and inedible. So, when the two of them reached their room, they each took one of the fruits and began to eat them, sitting on the edge of their beds.

Alas, now this is what has to happen! That chamber of theirs, you see, was immediately adjacent to the kitchen, joined, in fact, by a common wall. Even the whispered words from one room could be heard in the other, and Pa-chieh was busily cooking rice in the kitchen. All that talk, moments before, about taking the golden mallet and the elixir tray had already caught his attention. Then, when he heard how the T'ang monk could not recognize ginseng fruits which were served him, and how they had to be eaten by the young lads in their own room, he could not stop his mouth watering, and said to himself, "How can I try one myself?" Since he himself was reluctant to do anything, he decided to wait for Pilgrim's arrival so that they could plan something together. Completely distracted by now from tending the fire in the stove, he kept sticking his head out of the door to watch for Pilgrim. In a little while, he saw Pilgrim arrive, leading the horse. Having tied the horse to a huai tree, Pilgrim started to walk toward the rear, when Idiot waved to him madly with his hands, crying, "Come this way! Come this way!" Pilgrim turned around and went to the door of the kitchen, saying, "Idiot, why are you yelling? Not enough rice, perhaps? Let the old monk have his fill first, and we can beg more rice from some big household along our way." "Come in," said Pa-chieh; "this has nothing to do with the amount of rice we have. There's a treasure in this Taoist temple. Did you know that?" "What kind of treasure?" said Pilgrim. "I can tell you," said Pa-chieh with a laugh, "but you have never seen it; I can put it before you, but you won't recognize it." "You must be joking, Idiot," said Pilgrim. "Five hundred years ago, when I, old Monkey, searched for the Way of Immortality, I went all the way to the corner of the ocean and the edge of the sky. What can there be that I have never seen?" "Elder Brother," said Pa-chieh, "have you ever seen the ginseng fruit?" Somewhat startled, Pilgrim said, "That I really have never seen! But I have heard that ginseng fruit is the grass of the reverted cinnabar. When a man eats it, his life will be prolonged. But where can one get hold of it?" "They have it here," said Pa-chieh. "The two lads brought two of these fruits for Master to eat, but that old monk could not recognize them for what they were. He said that they were infants not yet three days old and dared not eat them. The lads themselves were quite disobliging; if Master would not eat, they should have given them to us. Instead, they hid them from us. Just now in the room next door, each had a fruit to himself and finished it with great relish. I got so excited that I was drooling, wondering how I could have a taste of this fruit. I know you are quite tricky. How about going to their garden and stealing a few for us to have a taste of them?" "That's easy," said Pilgrim. "Old Monkey will go, and they will be at the reach of his hands!" He turned quickly and began to walk to the front. Pa-chieh caught hold of him and said, "Elder Brother, I heard them talking in the room, and they mentioned something about using a gold mallet to knock down the fruits. You must do it properly, and without being detected." "I know! I know!" said Pilgrim.

Our Great Sage used the magic of body concealment and stole into the Taoist chamber. The two Taoist lads, you see, were not in the room, for they had gone back to the main hall to speak to the T'ang monk after they had finished eating the fruits. Pilgrim looked everywhere for the gold mallet and discovered a stick of red gold hanging on the window pane: it was about two feet long and as thick as a finger. At the lower end there was a knob about the size of a clove of garlic, while the upper end had a hole through which a green woolen thread was fastened. He said to himself: "This must be the thing called the gold mallet." Taking it down, he left the Taoist chamber, went to the rear, and pushed through a double-leaf door to have a look. Ah, it was a garden! You see

Vermilion fences and carved railings;
Artificial hills ruggedly built.
Strange flowers rival the sun in brightness;
Bamboos match well the clear sky in blueness.

Beyond the flowing-cup pavilion,
One curvate band of willows like mists outspread;
Before the moon-gazing terrace,
Choice pines like spilled indigo.
Shining red,
Pomegranates with brocade-like sacs;
Fresh, tender green,
Grass by the ornamental stools;
Luxuriant blue,
Sand-orchids like jade;
Limpid and smooth,
The water in the brook.
The cassia glows with the wu-t'ung[9] by the golden well;[10]
The huai trees stand near the red fences and marble steps.
Some red and some white: peaches with a thousand leaves;
Some fragrant and some yellow: chrysanthemums of late fall.
The rush-flower supports
Complement the peony pavilion;
The hibiscus terrace
Connects with the shao-yao[11] plot.
There are countless princely bamboos which mock the frost,
And noble pines which defy the snow.
There are, moreover, crane hamlets and deer homes,
The square pool and the round pond.
The stream spills chips of jade;
The ground sprouts mounds of gold.
The winter wind cracks and whitens the plum blossoms;
A touch of spring breaks open the begonia's red.
Truly it may be called the best fairyland on Earth,
The finest floral site of the West.

Pilgrim could not take his eyes off this marvelous place. He came upon another door which he pushed open and found inside a vegetable garden,

Planted with the herbs of all four seasons:
Spinach, celery, mare's tail,[12] beet, ginger, and seaweed;
Bamboo shoot, melon, squash, and watercress;
Chive, garlic, coriander, leek, and scallion;
Hollow water-lotus, young celery, and bitter su;[13]
The gourd and the eggplant which must be trimmed;

Green turnip, white turnip, and taro deep in the earth;
Red spinach, green cabbage, and purple mustard plant.

Pilgrim smiled to himself and said, "So, he's a Taoist who grows his own food!" He walked past the vegetable garden and found another door, which he pushed open also. Ah! There was a huge tree right in the middle of the garden, with long, healthy branches and luxuriant green leaves that somewhat resembled those of the plantain. Soaring straight up, the tree was over a thousand feet tall, and its base must have measured sixty or seventy feet around. Leaning on the tree, Pilgrim looked up and found one ginseng fruit sticking out on one of the branches pointing southward. It certainly had the appearance of an infant with a tail-like peduncle. Look at it dangling from the end of the branch, with limbs moving wildly and head bobbing madly! It seemed to make sounds as it swung in the breeze. Filled with admiration and delight, Pilgrim said to himself, "What a marvelous thing! It's rarely seen! It's rarely seen!" With a swish, he vaulted up the tree.

The monkey, you see, was an expert in climbing trees and stealing fruits. He took the gold mallet and struck lightly at the fruit, which dropped at once from the branch. Pilgrim leaped down after it but the fruit was nowhere to be seen. Though he searched for it all over the grass, there was not a trace of it. "Strange! Strange!" said Pilgrim. "I suppose it could walk with its legs, but even so, it could hardly have jumped across the wall. I know! It must be the local spirit of this garden who will not allow me to steal the fruit; he must have taken it." Making the magic sign and reciting a spell which began with the letter *om*, he summoned the local spirit of the garden, who came bowing to Pilgrim and said, "Great Sage, what sort of instructions do you have for this humble deity?" "Don't you know," said Pilgrim, "that old Monkey happens to be the world's most famous thief? When I stole the immortal peaches, the imperial wine, and the efficacious pills that year, there was no one brave enough to share the spoils with me. How is it, therefore, when I steal just one of their fruits today, that you have the gall to snatch away the prime portion? Since these fruits are formed on a tree, I suppose even the fowls of the air may partake of them. What's wrong with my eating one of them? How dare you grab it the moment I knock it down?" "Great Sage," said the local spirit, "you have made a mistake in blaming me. This treasure is something which belongs to an Earth immortal, whereas I am only a demon immortal.[14] Would I dare take it? I don't even have the good fortune to smell it!" "If you didn't snatch it," said Pilgrim, "why did it disappear the moment it fell?" "You may know only about its power to prolong life, Great Sage," said the local spirit, "but you don't know its background." "What do you mean by background?" said Pilgrim. "This treasure," said the local spirit, "will bloom only once in three thousand years; it will bear fruit after another three thousand years; and the fruit won't ripen for yet another three thousand years. All in all, one must wait for almost ten thousand years before there are thirty of these fruits. A person lucky enough to smell it once will live for three hundred and sixty years; if he eats one, he will live for forty-seven thousand years. However, the fruit is resistant to the Five Phases." "What do you mean by resistant to the Five Phases?" said Pilgrim. The local spirit said, "This fruit will fall when it meets with gold; it will wither when it meets with wood; it will melt when it meets with water; it will dry up if it meets with fire; and it will be assimilated if it meets with earth. That is why one has to use an instrument of gold to knock it down, but when it falls, it has to be held by a tray cushioned with silk handkerchiefs. The moment it touches wood, it will wither and will not prolong life even if it's eaten. When it is eaten, it should be held in a porcelain container and should be dissolved with water. Again, fire will dry it up and it will be useless. Finally, what is meant by its assimilation into earth may be illustrated by what happened just now, for when you knocked it down, it at once crawled into the ground. This part of the garden will last for at least forty-seven thousand years. Even a steel pick will not be able to bore through it, for it is three or four times harder than raw iron. That is why a man will live long if he eats one of the fruits. If you don't believe me, Great Sage, strike at the ground and see for yourself." Whipping out his golden-hooped rod, Pilgrim gave the ground a terriffic blow. The rod rebounded at once, but there was not the slightest mark on the ground. "Indeed! Indeed!" said Pilgrim. "This rod of mine can turn a boulder into powder; it will leave its mark even on raw iron. How is it that there's not even a scratch on the ground? Well, in that case, I have made a mistake in blaming you. You may go back." The local spirit thus went back to his own shrine.

The Great Sage, however, had his own plan: after climbing up on the tree, he held the golden mallet in one hand and, with the other, pulled up the front of his silk shirt to make a little sack. Parting the leaves and branches, he knocked three of the fruits into the sack. He jumped down from the tree and ran straight to the kitchen. "Elder Brother," said Pa-chieh smiling, "do you have them?" "Aren't these the ones?" said Pilgrim. "I reached and took, that's all! But we shouldn't let Sha Monk pass up the chance of tasting this fruit. You call him." Pa-chieh waved his hands and cried, "Wu-ching, come!" Setting down the luggage, Sha Monk ran into the kitchen and said, "Elder Brother, why did you call me?" Opening the sack, Pilgrim said, "Brother, take a look. What are these?" When Sha Monk saw them, he said, "Ginseng fruits." "Fine!" said Pilgrim. "So, you recognize them! Where did you taste them before?" "I have never tasted the fruit before," said Sha Monk. "But when I was the Curtain-Raising Captain, I waited on the Throne to attend the Festival of Immortal Peaches, and I once saw many immortals from beyond the sea presenting this fruit to the Lady Queen Mother as a birthday gift. So I have seen it, but I have never tasted it. Elder Brother, will you let me try a little?" "No need to say anymore," said Pilgrim. "There's one for each of us brothers."

The three of them took the fruits and began to enjoy them. That Pa-chieh, of course, had a huge appetite and a huge mouth. When he had heard the conversation of the young lads earlier, he had already felt ravenous. The moment he saw the fruit, therefore, he grabbed it and, with one gulp, swallowed it whole. Then he rolled up his eyes and said in a roguish manner to Pilgrim and Sha Monk: "What are you two eating?" "Ginseng fruit," said Sha Monk. "How does it taste?" asked Pa-chieh. "Wu-ching," said Pilgrim, "don't listen to him. He ate it first. Why all these questions now?" "Elder Brother," said Pa-chieh, "I ate it somewhat too hurriedly, not as the two of you are doing, mincing and munching little by little to discover its taste. I swallowed it without even knowing whether it had a pit or not! Elder Brother, if you are helping someone, help him to the end. You have roused the worms in my stomach! Please fetch me another fruit so that I can take time to enjoy it." "Brother," said Pilgrim, "you really don't know when to stop! This thing here is not like rice or noodles, food to stuff yourself with. There are only thirty such fruits in ten thousand years! It's our great fortune to have eaten one already, and you should not regard this lightly. Stop now! It's enough." He stretched himself and threw the gold mallet into the adjacent room through a little hole on the window paper without saying anything more to Pa-chieh.

Idiot, however, kept muttering and mumbling to himself. When the two Taoist lads unexpectedly came back to the room to fetch some tea for the T'ang monk, they heard Pa-chieh complaining about "not enjoying my ginseng fruit," and saying that it would be much better if he could have a taste of another one. Hearing this, Clear Breeze grew suspicious and said: "Bright Moon, listen to that monk with the long snout; he said he wanted to eat another ginseng fruit. Before our master's departure, he told us to be wary of their mischief. Could it be that they have stolen our treasures?" Turning around, Bright Moon said, "Elder Brother, it looks bad, very bad! Why has the golden mallet fallen to the ground? Let's go into the garden to take a look." They ran hastily to the back and found the door to the flower garden open. "I closed this door myself," said Clear Breeze. "Why is it open?" They ran past the flower garden and saw that the door to the vegetable garden was also open. They dashed into the ginseng garden; running up to the tree, they started to count, staring upward. Back and forth they counted, but they could find only twenty-two of the fruits. "You know how to do accounting?" said Bright Moon. "I do," said Clear Breeze, "give me the figures!" "There were originally thirty fruits," said Bright Moon. "When Master opened the garden to the public, he divided two of them for all of us, so that twenty-eight fruits were left. Just now we knocked down two more for the T'ang monk, leaving twenty-six behind. Now we have only twenty-two left. Doesn't that mean that four are missing? No need for further explanation: they must have been stolen by that bunch of rogues. Let's go and chide the T'ang monk."

The two of them went out of the garden gate and came directly back to the main hall. Pointing their fingers at the T'ang monk, they berated him with all kinds of foul and abusive language, accusing him of being a larcenous bald-head and a thievish rat. They went on like this for a long time, until finally the T'ang monk could not endure it any longer. "Divine lads," he said, "why are you making all this fuss? Be quiet a moment. If you have something to say, say it slowly, but don't use such nonsensical language." "Are you deaf?" said Clear Breeze. "Am I speaking in a barbarian tongue which you can't understand? You stole and ate our ginseng fruits. Do you now forbid me to say so?" "What is a ginseng fruit like?" asked the T'ang monk. "Like an infant," said Bright Moon, "as you said when we brought two of them for you to eat just now." "Amitābha Buddha!" exclaimed the

T'ang monk. "I only had to take one look at that thing and I trembled all over! You think I would dare steal one and eat it? Even if I had a case of bulimia, I would not dare indulge in such thievery. Don't blame the wrong person." "You might not have eaten them," said Clear Breeze, "but your followers wanted to steal them and eat them." "Perhaps you are right," said Tripitaka, "but there's no need for you to shout. Let me ask them. If they have stolen them, I will ask them to repay you." "Repay!" said Bright Moon. "You couldn't buy these fruits even if you had the money!" "If they can't buy them with money," said Tripitaka, "they can at least offer you an apology, for as the proverb says, 'Righteousness is worth a thousand pieces of gold.' That should be sufficient. Moreover, we are still not sure whether it is my disciples who took your fruits." "What do you mean, not sure?" said Bright Moon. "They were arguing among themselves, saying something about the portions not being equally divided." "Disciples," cried Tripitaka, "come, all of you." When Sha Monk heard this, he said, "It's terrible! We've been discovered! Old master is calling us, and the Taoist lads are making all this racket. They must have found out!" "It is extremely embarrassing!" said Pilgrim. "This is just a matter of food and drink. But if we say so, that means we are stealing for our mouths! Let's not admit it." "Yes! Yes!" said Pa-chieh. "Let's deny it!" The three of them had no choice, however, but to leave the kitchen for the main hall. Alas, we do not know how they would be able to deny the charges, and you must listen to the explanation in the next chapter.

Twenty-five

The Chên-yüan Immortal gives chase to catch
  the scripture monk;
Pilgrim Sun causes great disturbance at the Temple of
  Five Villages.

We were telling you about the three brothers, who went to the main hall and said to their master, "The rice is about done. Why did you call us?" "Disciples," said Tripitaka, "I didn't want to ask you about the rice. They have something called the ginseng fruit in this temple, which looks like a newborn infant. Which one of you stole it and ate it?" "Honestly," said Pa-chieh, "I don't know anything about it, and I haven't seen it." "It's the one who is laughing! It's the one who is laughing!" said Clear Breeze. "I was born with a laughing face!" snapped Pilgrim. "Don't think because you have lost some kind of a fruit that you can prohibit me from laughing!" "Disciple, don't get angry," said Tripitaka. "Those of us who have left the family should not lie, nor should we enjoy stolen food. If you have in truth eaten it, you owe them an apology. Why deny it so vehemently?" When Pilgrim perceived how reasonable this advice of his master was, he said truthfully, "Master, it's not my fault. It was Pa-chieh who over-heard those two Taoist lads eating some sort of ginseng fruit. He wanted to try one to see how it tasted and told me to knock down three of the fruits; each of us brothers had one. It's true that we have eaten them. What's to be done about that?" "He stole four of the fruits," said Bright Moon, "and still this monk could claim that he's not a thief!" "Amitābha Buddha!" said Pa-chieh. "If you stole four of them, why did you only bring out three for us to divide among our-selves? Didn't you skim something off the top already?" So saying, Idiot began to make a fuss again.

When the immortal lads found out the truth, they became even more abusive in their language; the Great Sage became so enraged that he ground his steel-like teeth audibly and opened wide his fiery eyes. He gripped his golden-hooped rod again and again, struggling to restrain himself and saying to himself, "These malicious youths!

They certainly know how to give people a lashing with their tongues! All right, so I have to take such abuse from them. Let me offer them in return 'a plan for eliminating posterity,' and none of them will have any more fruit to eat!" Dear Pilgrim! He pulled off a strand of hair behind his head and blew on it with his magic breath, crying "Change!" It changed at once into a specious Pilgrim, standing by the T'ang monk, Wu-ching, and Wu-nêng to receive the scolding from the Taoist lads. His true spirit rose into the clouds, and with one leap he arrived at the ginseng garden. Whipping out his golden-hooped rod, he gave the tree a terrific blow, after which he used that mountain-moving divine strength of his to give it a mighty shove. Alas,

The leaves fell, the limbs cracked, and the roots became exposed;
Blasted was the Taoist's grass of reverted cinnabar.

After the Great Sage had pushed down the tree, he tried to look for the fruits on the branches but he could not find even half a fruit. The treasure, you see, would fall when it met with gold, and both ends of his rod were wrapped in gold. Moreover, iron is also one of the five metallic elements. The blow of the rod, therefore, shook loose all the fruits from the tree, and when they fell, they became assimilated to the earth once they touched ground, so that there was not a single fruit left on the tree. "Fine! Fine!" he said. "Now all of us can scram!" He put away his iron rod and went back to the front. With a shake of his body he retrieved his hair, but the rest of the people, like those of fleshly eyes and mortal stock, could not perceive what had taken place.

We now tell you about the two immortal lads, who ranted at the pilgrims for a long time. Clear Breeze said, "Bright Moon, these monks do take our reproach quite well. We have been upbraiding them as if they were chickens all this time, but not once have they even attempted to answer us. Could it be that they really did not steal the fruits? With the tree so tall and the leaves so dense, we could have made a mistake in our tallying, and we might have chided them unjustly. We should go and investigate further." "You are right," said Bright Moon, and the two of them accordingly went back to the garden. But what they saw was only a tree on the ground with broken boughs and fallen leaves, without so much as a single fruit on it. Clear Breeze was so aghast that his legs gave way and he fell to the ground; Bright Moon shook so violently that he could hardly stand up. Both of them were scared out of their wits! We have, as testimony, this poem:

Tripitaka went westward to the Longevity Mount;
Wu-k'ung cut down the grass of reverted cinnabar.
Boughs broken and leaves fallen, the divine root exposed:
Clear Breeze and Bright Moon were horrified!

The two of them lay on the ground, hardly able to speak coherently. They could only blurt out: "What shall we do? What shall we do? The magic root of our Temple of Five Villages is severed! The seed of this divine house of ours is cut off! When our master returns, what shall we tell him?" Then Bright Moon said, "Elder Brother, stop hollering! Let's pull ourselves together and not alarm those monks. There's no one else here; it has to be that fellow with a hairy face and a thundergod beak who used magic unseen to ruin our treasure. If we try to talk to him, he will probably deny it, and further argument may well lead to actual combat. In the event of a fight, how do you suppose the two of us could stand up to the four of them? It would be better if we deceived them now by saying that the fruits were not missing, and that since we made a mistake in our counting, we were offering them our own apology. Their rice is about cooked. When they eat, we shall even present them with a few side dishes. When each of them is holding a bowl, you stand on the left of the door and I'll stand on the right, and we'll slam the door shut together. We'll lock it and all the other doors of this temple too, so that they will not be able to escape. We can then wait for Master to return and let him do with them what he wills. Since the T'ang monk is an old acquaintance of Master, he might decide to forgive them, and that would be his act of kindness. Should he decide not to, however, we have at least managed to catch the thieves, for which we ourselves might be forgiven." When he heard these words, Clear Breeze said, "You are right! You are right!"

The two of them forced themselves to look cheerful as they walked back to the main hall from the rear garden. Bowing to the T'ang monk, they said, "Master, our coarse and vulgar language just now must have offended you. Please pardon us!" "What are you saying?" asked Tripitaka. "The fruits were not missing," said Clear Breeze, "but we couldn't see them clearly because of the dense foliage. We went back again to have a second look and we found the original number."

Hearing this, Pa-chieh chimed in at once: "You lads, you are young and impulsive, quick to condemn before you even know the truth of the matter. You throw out your castigations at random, and you have accused us unjustly. It's blasphemy!" Pilgrim, however, understood what was going on; though he did not say anything, he thought to himself: "It's a lie! It's a lie! The fruits were done with! Why do they say such things? Could it be that they have the magic of revivification?" Meanwhile, Tripitaka said to his disciples, "In that case, bring us some rice. We'll eat and leave."

Pa-chieh went at once to fetch the rice, while Sha Monk set the table and chairs. The two lads brought out seven or eight side dishes, including pickles, pickled eggplants, radishes in wine sauce, string beans in vinegar, salted lotus roots, and blanched mustard plants for master and disciples to eat with their rice. They also brought out a pot of fine tea and two mugs, and stood on either side of the table to wait on them. As soon as the four of them had taken up their bowls, however, the lads, one on each side, took hold of the door and slammed it tightly shut. They then bolted it with a double-shackle brass lock. "You lads made a mistake," said Pa-chieh with a laugh, "or else your custom here is rather strange. Why do you shut the door before you eat?" "Indeed!" said Bright Moon. "For good or ill, we will not open the door until after we have eaten." Then Clear Breeze lashed out at them, saying, "You bulimic and gluttonous bald thieves! You stole and ate our divine fruits, and you were thus already guilty of eating the produce of someone's garden without permission. Now you have even knocked over our divine tree and destroyed this immortal root of our Temple of Five Villages. And you still dare to speak to us defiantly? If you think you can reach the Western Heaven to behold the face of Buddha, you will have to ride the Wheel of Transmigration and do it in the next incarnation!" When Tripitaka heard these words, he threw down his rice bowl and sat there weighed down as if by a huge boulder on his heart. The lads then went to lock both the front gate and the second gate before returning to the main hall to revile them once more with the most abusive language. Calling them thieves again and again, the two lads assailed them until it was late, when they then left to eat. After the meal, the lads went back to their own room. The T'ang monk began to complain at Pilgrim, saying, "You mischievous ape! Every time it's you who causes trouble! If you stole and ate their fruits, you should have been more forbearing to their reproach. Why did you have to knock down even their tree? If you were brought into court, even if your old man were the judge, you would not be able to defend yourself when you behave like that!" "Don't scold me, Master," said Pilgrim. "If those lads have gone to sleep, let them sleep. We'll leave tonight." "Elder Brother," said Sha Monk, "all the doors have been locked securely. How can we leave?" Pilgrim said with a laugh, "Never mind! Never mind! Old Monkey will find a way!" "You have a way, all right!" said Pa-chieh. "All you need to do is to change into some sort of an insect, and you can fly out through a hole or a crack in the window. But what about those of us who don't know how to change into these tiny things? We have to stay and take the blame for you." "If he does something like that," said the T'ang monk, "and leaves us behind, I'll recite that *Old-Time Sūtra* and see whether he can take it!" When he heard this, Pa-chieh did not know whether to laugh or not. "Master," he said, "what are you saying? I have only heard the *Sūraṅgama Sūtra*, the *Lotus Sūtra*, the *Peacock Sūtra*, the *Kuan-yin Sūtra*, and the *Diamond Sūtra* in Buddhism, but I have never heard of anything called the *Old-Time Sūtra*." "You don't know about this, Brother," said Pilgrim. "This fillet that I wear on my head was given to Master by the Bodhissatva Kuan-yin. Master deceived me into wearing it, and it took root, as it were, on my head so that it could never be removed. There is, moreover, the Tight-Fillet Spell or the Tight-Fillet Sūtra. The moment he recites that, I'll have a terrible headache, for it's the magic trick designed to give me a hard time. Master, don't recite it. I won't betray you. No matter what happens, all of us will leave together."

As they spoke, it grew dark and the moon rose in the East. Pilgrim said, "When all is quiet and the crystal orb is bright, this is the time for us to steal away." "Elder Brother," said Pa-chieh, "stop this hocus-pocus. The doors are all locked. Where are we going to go?" "Watch my power!" said Pilgrim. He seized his golden-hooped rod and exercised the lock-opening magic; he pointed the rod at the door and all the locks fell down with a loud pop as the several doors immediately sprung open. "What talent!" said Pa-chieh, laughing. "Even if a little smith were to use a lock pick, he wouldn't be able to do this so nimbly." Pilgrim said, "This door is nothing! Even the South Heavenly Gate would immediately fly open if I pointed this at it!" They asked their master to go outside and mount the horse; Pa-chieh poled the luggage and Sha Monk led the way toward the West. "Walk slowly, all of you," said Pilgrim. "Let me go and see to it that the Taoist lads will sleep for a month." "Disciple," said Tripitaka, "don't harm them, or you will be guilty of murder as well as robbery." "I won't," said Pilgrim. Going inside again, he went to the door of the room where the lads were sleeping. He still had around his waist a few sleep-inducing insects, which he had won from the Devarāja Virūpāksa when they had played a game of guess-fingers at the East Heavenly Gate. Taking out two of these insects, he filliped them through a hole in the window. They headed straight for the faces of the lads who fell at once into a sleep so deep that it seemed nothing could arouse them. Then Pilgrim turned around and caught up with the T'ang monk, and all of them fled, following the main road to the West.

Throughout that whole night, the horse did not pause to rest, and they journeyed until it was almost dawn. "Monkey," said the T'ang monk, "you have just about killed me! Because of your mouth, I've had to spend a sleepless night." "Stop this complaining!" said Pilgrim. "It's dawn now, and you may as well take some rest in the forest here by the road. After you have regained a little strength, we'll move on." All that elder could do was to dismount and use a pine root as his couch. As soon as he put down the luggage, Sha Monk dozed off, while Pa-chieh fell asleep with a rock as his pillow. The Great Sage Sun, however, had other interests. Just look at him! Climbing the trees and leaping from branch to branch, he had a grand time playing. We shall leave them resting and make no further mention of them now.

We now tell you about the Great Immortal, who left the Tushita Palace with the lesser immortals after the lecture was over. Descending from the Green Jasper Heaven and dropping down from the auspicious clouds, they arrived before the Temple of Five Villages at the Mountain of Longevity, where they found the gates wide open and the grounds neat and clean. "Well," said the Great Immortal, "Clear Breeze and Bright Moon are not that useless after all! Ordinarily, they don't even bestir themselves when the sun is high, but today when we are away, they are willing to rise early to open the gates and sweep the grounds." All the lesser immortals were delighted, but when they reached the main hall, they discovered neither fire and incense nor any trace of a human person. Clear Breeze and Bright Moon were simply nowhere to be seen! "Because of our absence, the two of them must have stolen away with our things," said the rest of the immortals. "Nonsense!" said the Great Immortal. "How could those who seek the way of immortality dare to engage in such wickedness? They must have forgotten to close the gates last night and gone to sleep. They are probably not yet awake this morning." When they all reached the door of the Taoist lads, they found the door tightly shut and heard heavy snoring from within. They pounded on the door and attempted to rouse them, but the lads could not be wakened by all that clamor. Finally, the immortals managed to pry open the door and pull the lads off their beds; even then they did not wake up. "Dear immortal lads!" said the Great Immortal laughing. "Those who have attained immortality should not be so desirous of sleep, for their spirits are full. Why are they so fatigued? Could it be that someone has played a trick on them? Quickly, bring me some water?" One of the lads brought half a cup of water to the Great Immortal, who recited a spell before spitting a mouthful of water on the lads' faces. The Sleep Demon was thus exorcised.

Both lads woke up, and as they opened their eyes and wiped their faces, they suddenly saw all the familiar faces of their teacher, Lord, Equal to Earth, and the other immortals. Clear Breeze and Bright Moon were so startled that they knelt down at once and kowtowed, saying, "Master, your old friends, the monks who came from the East, were a bunch of vicious thieves!" "Don't be afraid!" said the Great Immortal smiling. "Take your time and tell me about them." "Master," said Clear Breeze, "Shortly after you left that day, a T'ang monk from the Land of the East did indeed arrive with three other monks and a horse. In obedience to your command, your disciples, having ascertained their origin, took two of the ginseng fruits and served them. That elder, however, had worldly eyes and a foolish mind, for he could not recognize the treasures of our immortal house. He insisted that they were newborn infants not yet three days old and absolutely refused to eat them. For this reason, each of us ate one of the fruits instead. We didn't expect, however, that one of his three disciples, a fellow whose surname was Sun and whose given name was Wu-k'ung Pilgrim, would steal and eat four of the fruits. When we discovered the theft, we tried to reason with him, speaking rather forthrightly to that monk. But he refused to listen to us and instead used the magic of the spirit leaving the body to—oh, this is painful!" When the two lads reached this point in their discourse, they could not hold back their tears. "Did that monk strike you?" asked the rest of the immortals. "He did not hit us," said Bright Moon, "but he struck down our ginseng tree." When the Great Immortal heard this, he was not angry. Instead, he said, "Don't cry! Don't cry! What you don't know is that the fellow with the name of Sun is also a minor immortal of the Great Monad; he has great magic power and has caused much disturbance in Heaven. If our treasure tree is struck down, all I want to know is whether you will be able to recognize these monks if you see them again." "Certainly," said Clear Breeze. "In that case," said the Great Immortal, "follow me. The rest of you disciples can prepare the instruments of punishment. When I return, they shall be whipped."

The various immortals took this instruction, while the Great Immortal mounted the auspicious luminosity with Clear Breeze and Bright Moon to give chase to Tripitaka. In a moment they had covered a thousand miles, but when the Great Immortal looked toward the West at the tip of the cloud, he could not see the T'ang monk anywhere. When he turned around and stared eastward instead, he found that he had overtaken the pilgrims by some nine hundred miles, for that elder, even with his horse galloping nonstop all night, had managed to travel only one hundred and twenty miles. Reversing the direction of his cloud, the Great Immortal made the trip back in an instant. "Master," said one of the lads, "that's the T'ang monk sitting beneath a tree by the road." "I see him," said the Great Immortal. "You two go back and prepare the ropes. Let me capture them by myself." Clear Breeze and Bright Moon went back to the temple at once.

Dropping down from the clouds, the Great Immortal changed himself into a mendicant Taoist with one shake of his body. "How was he dressed?" you ask.

He wore a priestly robe patched a hundred times
And a sash in the style of Mr. Lü.[1]
He waved a yak's-tail[2] in his hand,
And lightly tapped a fishlike drum.
Straw sandals with three loops on his feet;
A sinuous turban wrapped around his head.
With large sleeves aflutter in the wind,
He sang a song of the rising moon.

He came straight to the tree and said in a loud voice to the T'ang monk, "Elder, this poor Taoist raises his hands!" Hastily returning the salutation, the elder said, "Pardon me for not paying respects to you first." "Where did the elder come from," asked the Great Immortal, "and why is he sitting in meditation here beside the road?" Tripitaka said, "I am a scripture seeker sent by the Great T'ang of the Land of the East to the Western Heaven." Feigning surprise, the Great Immortal said, "When you came from the East, did you pass through my humble mountain abode?" "Which precious mountain is the abode of the venerable immortal?" asked the elder. The Great Immortal said, "The Temple of the Five Villages in the Mountain of Longevity is where I reside."

The moment he heard this, Pilgrim, having something very much on his mind, replied, "No! No! We came by another route up there." Pointing a finger firmly at him, the Great Immortal said with a laugh, "Brazen ape! Whom are you trying to fool? You struck down my ginseng fruit tree in my temple, and then you fled here in the night. You dare deny this? Why try to cover up? Don't run away! Go quickly and bring back another tree for me!" When Pilgrim heard this, he grew angry and whipped out his iron rod; without waiting for further discussion, he struck at the head of the Great Immortal. Stepping aside to dodge the blow, the Great Immortal trod on the auspicious luminosity and rose into the air, closely followed by Pilgrim, who also mounted the clouds. The Great Immortal changed back into his true form in midair, and this was how he appeared:

He wore a cap of purple gold,
And a carefree gown trimmed with crane's down.
He had on his feet a pair of shoes;
A silk sash was tied round his waist.
His body seemed that of a lad
His face, that of a lady fair,
But with flowing moustaches and beard.
Some crow feathers adorned his hair.
He faced Pilgrim but without a weapon,
Save a jade yak's-tail[3] which he twirled in his hand.

Above and below, Pilgrim struck wildly with his rod, only to be parried again and again by the Great Immortal wielding his jade yak's tail. After two or three rounds of fighting, the Great Immortal displayed his magic of the cosmos in the sleeve. Standing on the tip of a cloud and facing the wind, he gently flipped open the wide sleeve of his gown and sent it toward the earth in a sweeping motion. All four of the monks and the horse were at once scooped up into the sleeve. "This is dreadful!" said Pa-chieh. "We have been placed in a clothes bag!" "It isn't a clothes bag, Idiot!" said Pilgrim. "We've been scooped up into his sleeve." "In that case," said Pa-chieh, "it shouldn't be too difficult! Let me use my rake and make a hole in his gown. When we make our escape, we can claim that he was careless and didn't hold us securely, so that we fell out of his sleeve." Idiot started to dig into the garment madly with his rake, but all to no avail: although the material was soft to the touch, it was harder than steel when it came into contact with the rake.

Turning around the direction of his auspicious cloud, the Great Immortal went back to the Temple of Five Villages and sat down, ordering his disciples to fetch some ropes. As the little immortals went about their business, he fished out the pilgrims one by one like puppets from his sleeve: first he brought out the T'ang monk and had him bound to one of the large pillars in the main hall. Then he took out the three disciples and had them tied to three other pillars. Finally he took out the horse and had it tied up in the courtyard; it was given some hay while the luggage was thrown into one of the corridors. "Disciples," said the Great Immortal, "these monks are persons who have left home, and they should not be harmed by knives or spears, hatchets or battle-axes. Bring out my leather whip instead and give them a beating—as an act of vengeance for my ginseng fruit!" Some of the immortals went quickly to fetch the whip—not the sort made of cow hide, sheep hide, suede, or buffalo hide. It was, rather, a whip of seven thongs made of dragon hide. After soaking it in water for a while, one of the more robust little immortals took it up and asked: "Master, which one shall be flogged first?" The Great Immortal said, "Tripitaka T'ang is the unworthy senior member of his party. Beat him first."

When Pilgrim heard what he said, he thought to himself: "That old monk of mine cannot stand such flogging. If he's destroyed by the whip, wouldn't that be my sin?" Unable to remain silent any longer, he said, "Sir, you are mistaken! It was I who stole the fruits, and it was I who ate the fruits. Moreover, it was also I who pushed down the tree. Why don't you flog me first? Why do you have to whip him?" "This brazen ape," said the Great Immortal laughing, "does know how to speak courageously! All right, let's flog him first." "How many lashes?" asked the little immortal. "As many as the original number of the fruits," said the Great Immortal, "thirty lashes." Lifting high the whip, the little immortal was about to strike. Fearing that this weapon of an immortal's house might be a formidable one, Pilgrim opened his eyes wide to see where he was going to be struck and found that the little immortal was about to flog his legs. With a twist of his torso, Pilgrim said, "Change!" and his two legs became hard as steel, all ready to be flogged. With measured strokes, the little immortal gave him thirty lashes before putting down the whip. It was already almost noon, when the Great Immortal said again, "We should now give Tripitaka a flogging, since he did not know how to discipline his mischievous disciples and permitted them to indulge in unruly behaviour." As the immortal took up the whip again, Pilgrim said, "You are again mistaken, sir. When the fruits were stolen, my master was conversing in this hall with the two lads; he had no knowledge whatever of what we brothers had perpetrated. Though he might be guilty of not being strict enough in his discipline of us, those of us who are his disciples should receive the punishment for him. Flog me again." "This lawless ape!" said the Great Immortal. "Though he is sly and devious, he does possess some filial sentiments! In that case, let's flog him again." The little immortal again gave him thirty lashes. When Pilgrim lowered his head to take a look, he saw that his two legs had been beaten until they were shining like mirrors, though he had no sensation whatever, either of pain or of itching. By this time it was getting late, and the Great Immortal said, "Soak the whip in water. Wait until tomorrow, and then we shall punish them again." The little immortals retrieved the whip and placed it in water, after which everyone retired to his own chamber. When they had finished their evening meal, all went away to sleep, and we shall say no more of them now.

With tears flowing from his eyes, the elder began to complain bitterly to his three disciples, saying, "You all have caused this trouble, but I have to suffer with you in this place. What are you going to do about it?" "Stop this complaining," said Pilgrim. "They flogged me first, and you haven't even had a taste of it yet. Why do you have to grumble like that?" "Though I have not been flogged," said the T'ang monk, "this rope is causing me to ache all over." "Master," said Sha Monk, "there are others here who are your companions in bondage!" "Stop this racket, all of you!" said Pilgrim. "In a little while, we'll all be on our way again." "Elder Brother," said Pa-chieh, "you are fibbing again. We are tightly bound now in hemp ropes sprayed with water. They are not like the locks on those doors which you opened so easily with your magic!" "This is no exaggeration," said Pilgrim, "but I'm not afraid of a three-ply hemp rope sprayed with water. Even if it were a coir cord as thick as a small bowl, I would consider it as insubstantial as the autumn wind!" Hardly had he finished speaking when it became completely quiet everywhere. Dear Pilgrim! He contracted his body and at once freed himself from the ropes, saying "Let's go, Master!" "Elder Brother," said a startled Sha Monk, "save us, too!" "Speak softly! Speak softly!" said Pilgrim. He untied Tripitaka, Sha Monk, and Pa-chieh; they put on their clothes, saddled the horse, and picked up the luggage from the corridor. As they walked out of the temple gate, Pilgrim said to Pa-chieh: "Go to the edge of the cliff there and bring back four willow trees." "What do you want them for?" said Pa-chieh. "I have use for them. Bring them quickly." Idiot did possess some sort of brutish strength. He did as he was told, and with one shove of his snout he felled one of the willow trees. Knocking down three more, he gathered them up into a bundle and hauled them back. Pilgrim stripped the branches off the trunks, and the two of them carried the trunks inside, where they fastened them to the pillars with the ropes with which they had earlier been tied up themselves. Then the Great Sage recited a spell; biting the tip of his own tongue, he spat some blood on the trees and cried, "Change!" One of them changed into the elder, another changed into a figure like himself, and the two other trees changed into Sha Monk and Pa-chieh. They all seemed to look exactly alike; when questioned, they knew how to make replies; when their names were called, they knew how to answer. Only then did the two of them run back out and catch up with their master. As before, the horse did not pause to rest for that whole night as they fled the Temple of Five Villages. When morning arrived, however, the elder was nodding on the horse, hardly able to remain in the saddle. When Pilgrim saw him like that, he called out: "Master, you are terribly soft! How is it that a person who has left home like yourself has so little endurance? If I, old Monkey, went without sleep even for a thousand nights, I still would not feel fatigue. Well, you had better get off the horse, so that travelers won't see your condition and laugh at you. Let's find a temporary shelter beneath the mountain slope and rest awhile before we move on again."

We shall not tell you any more now about master and disciples resting by the way; we shall tell you instead of the Great Immortal, who rose at the crack of dawn and went out at once to the main hall after taking his morning meal. He said, "Bring out the whip. It's Tripitaka's turn today to be flogged." The little immortal wielded the whip and said to the T'ang monk, "I'm going to beat you." "Go ahead," said the willow tree, and he was given thirty lashes. Changing the direction of his whip, the little immortal said to Pa-chieh, "I'm going to flog you." "Go ahead," said the other willow tree, and the one which was changed into the form of Sha Monk gave the same reply when it was his turn. By the time they reached Pilgrim, the real Pilgrim, resting by the wayside, was suddenly sent into a violent shudder. "Something's wrong!" he said. "What do you mean?" asked Tripitaka. Pilgrim said, "I transformed four willow trees into the four of us, thinking that since they flogged me twice yesterday, they would not beat me again today. But they are giving my transformed body a beating, and that's why my true body is shivering. I had better stop the magic." Hastily Pilgrim recited a spell to suspend the magic.

Look at those frightened Taoist lads! The one who was doing the flogging threw away the whip and ran to report, saying, "Master, at first I was beating the Great T'ang monk, but now I am only striking at some willow roots!" When the Great Immortal heard these words, he laughed bitterly, saying, "Pilgrim Sun! Truly a marvelous Monkey King! It was rumored that when he caused great disturbance in Heaven, even the cosmic nets which the gods set up could not hold him. I suppose there must be some truth to that! So, you escaped! But why did you have to tie up these willow trees here to impersonate you and your companions? I'm not going to spare you! I'll pursue you!" Saying this, the Great Immortal at once rose into the clouds; he peered toward the West and saw the monks fleeing, poling the load of luggage and riding the horse. The Great Immortal dropped down from the clouds, crying, "Pilgrim Sun! Where are you running to? Give me back my ginseng tree!" Hearing this, Pa-chieh said, "We're finished! Our foe is here again!" "Master," said Pilgrim, "let's pack up that little word 'Kindness' for the moment. Allow us to indulge in a little violence and finish him off so that we can make our escape." When the T'ang monk heard these words, he trembled all over, hardly able to reply. Without even waiting for his answer, however, Sha Monk lifted his precious staff, Pa-chieh brought out his muckrake, and the Great Sage wielded his iron rod. They all rushed forward to surround the Great Immortal in midair and began to strike at him furiously. For this vicious battle, we have the following poem as testimony:

Wu-k'ung did not know the Chên-yüan Immortal,
The Lord, Equal to Earth, was wonderous and strange.
Though three weapons divine showed forth their might,
One yak's-tail flew up with natural ease
To parry the thrusts on the left and right,
To block the blows struck at the front and back.
Night passed, day came, still they could not escape!
How long would it take them to reach the West?

The three brothers all raised their divine weapons and attacked the immortal together, but the Great Immortal had only the fly brush with which to meet his adversaries. The battle, however, had not lasted for half an hour when the Great Immortal spread open his sleeve and with one scoop, recaptured the four monks, the horse, and their luggage. Reversing the direction of his cloud, he went back to his temple, where he was greeted by the other immortals. The Master Immortal took a seat in the main hall and again took out the pilgrims one by one from his sleeve. The T'ang monk was bound to a short huai tree in the courtyard, while Sha Monk and Pa-chieh were fastened to two other trees, one on each side. Pilgrim, however, was tightly bound but left on the ground. "I suppose," thought Pilgrim to himself, "they are going to interrogate me." After the immortals had finished tying up the captives, they were told to bring out ten large bales of cloth. "Pa-chieh," said Pilgrim with a laugh, "this gentleman must have the good intention of making us some clothes! He might as well be more economical and just cut us a few monks' bells!"[4] After the little immortals had brought out the homespun cloth, the Great Immortal said, "Wrap up Tripitaka T'ang, Chu Pa-chieh, and Sha Monk entirely in the cloth." The little immortals obeyed and wrapped the three of them completely. "Fine! Fine! Fine!" said Pilgrim, laughing. "We are prepared to be buried alive!" After they were wrapped, the Taoists brought out some lacquer which they had made themselves, and the Great Immortal gave the order that the wrappings of the pilgrims be completely coated with the varnish. Only their faces were left uncovered. "Sir," said Pa-chieh, "I'm all right on top, but leave me a hole down below so that I can unburden myself!"

The Great Immortal next gave the order that a huge frying pan be brought out. "Pa-chieh, we are lucky!" said Pilgrim laughing. "If they are hauling out a pan, they must want to cook some rice for us to eat." "That's all right with me," said Pa-chieh. "If they let us eat some rice, we'll be well-fed ghosts even if we die!" The various immortals duly brought out a huge pan, which they set up before the steps of the main hall. After giving the order that a big fire be built with plenty of dry firewood, the Great Immortal said, "Fill the pan with clear oil. When it boils, dump Pilgrim Sun into the pan and fry him! That'll be his payment for my ginseng tree!"

When Pilgrim heard this, he was secretly pleased, saying to himself, "This is exactly what I want! I haven't had a bath for sometime and my skin is so dry that it's getting itchy. For good or ill, I'll enjoy a little scorching and be most grateful for it." In a moment, the oil was about to boil. The Great Sage, however, was quite cautious; fearing that this might be some form of formidable divine magic which would be difficult for him to handle once he was in the pan, he looked around quickly. In the east he saw a little terrace with a sun dial on top, but to the west he discovered a stone lion. With a bound, Pilgrim rolled himself toward the west; biting the tip of his tongue, he spat a mouthful of blood on the stone lion, crying, "Change!" It changed into a figure just like himself, all tied up in a bundle. His true spirit rose into the clouds, from where he lowered his head to stare at the Taoists.

Just then, one of the little immortals gave this report: "Master, the oil is sizzling in the pan." "Pick up Pilgrim Sun and throw him in!" said the Great Immortal. Four of the divine lads went to carry him, but they could not lift him up; eight more joined them, but they had no success either. They added four more, and still they could not even budge him. "This monkey loves the earth so much that he can't be moved!" said one of the immortals. "Though he may be rather small, he's quite tough!" Finally, twenty little immortals managed to lift him up and hurl him into the pan; there was a loud splash, big drops of boiling oil flew out in every direction, and the faces of those little Taoists were covered with blisters. Then they heard the lad who was tending the fire crying, "The pan's leaking! The pan's leaking!" Hardly had he uttered these words when all the oil was gone. What they saw in the pan with its bottom punctured was a stone lion.

Enraged, the Great Immortal said, "That wretched ape! He's wicked indeed! And I've allowed him to show off right in front of my nose! So, he wanted to escape, but why did he have to ruin my pan? I suppose it's exceedingly difficult to catch the wretched ape, and even if one does catch him, trying to hold him is like trying to grasp sand or handle mercury, to catch a shadow or seize the wind! All right! All right! Let him go. Untie Tripitaka T'ang and bring out a new pan. We'll fry him instead in order to avenge my ginseng tree." The various little immortals accordingly went to untie the lacquer cloth, but Pilgrim, who heard this clearly in the air, thought to himself: "Master is utterly helpless! If he arrives in the pan, the first boiling bubble will kill him and the second will burn him up; by the time the oil sizzles three or four times, he'll be a messy monk! I had better go and save him!" Dear Great Sage! He lowered the direction of his cloud and went back to the main hall. With his hands at his waist, he said, "Don't untie the lacquer wrapping to fry my master. Let me go into the pan of boiling oil instead." "You wretched ape!" cried a somewhat started Great Immortal. "How could you have the nerve to make such a display and wreck my pan?" "If you have the misfortune of meeting me," said Pilgrim laughing, "your pan should be ruined! Why blame me? Just now, I was about to receive your kind hospitality in the form of oily soup, but I suddenly had the urge to relieve myself. If I opened up right in the pan, I was afraid that I might spoil your hot oil so that it could not be used for cooking. Now that I'm completely relieved, I feel quite good about going into the pan. Don't fry my master; fry me instead." When the Great Immortal heard these words, he laughed menacingly and ran out of the hall to catch hold of Pilgrim. We do not know what sort of things he has to say to him, or whether Pilgrim manages to escape again. You must listen to the explanation in the next chapter.

Notes

Introduction

1. See Liang Ch'i-ch'ao 梁啟超, "Chung-kuo Yin-tu chih chiao-t'ung 中國印度之交通," in *Fo-hsüeh yen-chiu shih-pa p'ien* 佛學研究十八篇 (1936; repr. Taipei, 1966); see also Ven Tungtsu 釋東初, *Chung-Yin Fo-chiao chiao-t'ung-shih* 中印佛教交通史 (Taipei, 1968), pp. 166–222.

2. See "T'ang shang-tu Chang-ching ssŭ Wu-k'ung chuan 唐上都章敬寺悟空傳," in *Sung Kao-sêng chuan* 宋高僧傳, *chüan* 3 (T. 50: 2061, no. 722); see also Sylvain Lévi and Édouard Chavannes, "L'itinéraire d' Ou-k'ong," *JA*, 9th ser. 6 (1895): 341–85.

3. Most modern scholars date his birth at 602, but Liang Ch'i-ch'ao seems to me to have conclusively demonstrated that 596 is the more probable year. See Appendix 3, "Chih-na nei-hsüeh-yüan ching-chiao-pên Hsüan-tsăng chuan shu-hou 支那內學院精校本玄奘傳書後," in *Fo-hsüeh yen-chiu*; cf. Lo Hsiang-lin 羅香林," "Chiu T'ang Shu Sêng Hsüan-tsang chuan chiang-shu 舊唐書僧玄奘傳講疏," in *Chi-nien Hsüan-tsang ta-shih ling-ku kuei-kuo fêng-an chuan-chi* 紀念玄奘大師靈骨歸國奉安專輯 (Taipei, 1957), pp. 66–67.

4. See the *Fa-shih chuan, chüan* 1. Other sources on Hsüan-tsang's life are to be found in the *Chiu T'ang Shu Hsüan-tsang chuan* 舊唐書玄奘傳, *Tao-hsüan hsü kao-sêng chuan Hsüan-tsang chuan* 道宣續高僧傳玄奘傳, *Chih-shêng k'ai-yüan shih-chiao-lu* 智昇開元釋教錄, *Ching-mai ku-chin i-ching t'u-chi* 靖邁古今譯經圖記, *Ming-hsiang Hsüan-tsang fa-shih hsing-chuang* 冥詳玄奘法師行狀, and *Liu K'o Ta-pien-chüeh fa-shih t'a-ming* 劉軻大遍覺法師塔銘. For English accounts of his life, see Arthur Waley, *The Real Tripitaka and Other Pieces* (London, 1952), pp. 11–130; René Grousset, *In the Footsteps of the Buddha*, trans. J. A. Underwood (New York, 1971).

5. Arthur F. Wright, "The Formation of Sui Ideology, 581–604," in *Chinse Thought and Institutions*, ed. John K. Fairbank (Chicago, 1957), p. 71.

6. See Huang Shêng-fu 黃聲孚, *T'ang-tai fo-chiao tui chêng-chih chih ying-hsiang* 唐代佛教對政治之影響 (Hong Kong, 1959); see also the important essays by Arthur F. Wright, "T'ang T'ai-tsung and Buddhism,"

and Stanley Weinstein, "Imperial Patronage in the Formation of T'ang Buddhism," in *Perspectives on the T'ang*, ed. Arthur F. Wright and Denis Twitchett (New Haven, 1973), pp. 239–64 and pp. 265–306.

7. *Fa-shih chuan, chüan* 1.

8. Kenneth Ch'en, *Buddhism in China: A Historical Survey* (Princeton, 1964), pp. 117–18. For a thorough discussion of the various interpretations of this sūtra prior to the time of Hsüan-tsang, see T'ang Yung-t'ung 湯用彤, *Han Wei Liang-Chin Nan-Pei Ch'ao fo-chiao shih* 漢魏兩晉南北朝佛教史 (2 vols., Shanghai, 1937), 1: 284–87; 2: 134–39, 189–218.

9. For the text and Hsuan-tsang's translation of the commentary by Vasubandhu, see *T.* 31: 97–450, nos. 1592, 1593, 1595, 1596, 1597, and 1598. For a modern commentary on this śāstra, see Yin-shun 印順, *Shê-ta-ch'êng lun chiang-chi* 攝大乘論講記 (1st published in 1946; reprinted in Taipei, 1972).

10. *Fa-shih chuan, chüan* 3. See also Jen Chi-t'ang 任繼唐, *Han T'ang fo-chiao ssŭ-hsiang lun-chi* 漢唐佛教思想論集 (Peking, 1963), pp. 61–62.

11. Most scholars follow the biography and set the date of Hsüan-tsang's departure in 629. I have, however, found Liang Ch'i-ch'ao's argument for an earlier date to be much more convincing, and his conclusion is further supported by Lo Hsiang-lin's additional research. See Lo (n. 3 above), pp. 66–67.

12. *Fa-shih chuan, chüan* 6.

13. *Chiu T'ang Shu, chüan* 191.

14. Glen Dudbridge, *The Hsi-yu Chi: A Study of Antecedents to the Sixteenth-Century Chinese Novel* (Cambridge, Eng., 1970). Hereafter cited as *Antecedents*.

15. *Fa-shih chuan, chüan* 1.

16. *TPKC, chüan* 92.10:606.

17. *Ou-yang Wên-chung kung wên-chi* 歐陽文忠公文集, *chüan* 125, 4b–5a.

18. The *ch'ü-ching chi* was examined in 1916 by Lo Chên-yü 羅振玉, who published a photographic facsimile of it in his *Chi-shih-an ts'ung-shu* 吉石盦叢書 with his own postface 跋. The *shih-hua* was examined by both Wang Kuo-wei 王國維 and Lo in 1911, who also published it in 1916 with postfaces by himself (dated 1916) and by Wang (dated 1915). Modern editions of the *shih-hua* include the 1925 edition by the Commercial Press of Shanghai, and a 1954 edition by the Chung-kuo ku-tien wên-hsüeh ch'u-pan-shê of Shanghai. All future references are to the 1954 edition.

19. On the importance of the Deep Sand God (*shen-sha shên*), see Hu Shih (1923), pp. 364–65; for the earlier sources of this deity, see Dudbridge, *Antecedents*, pp. 18–21.

20. In the *tsa-chü* version of the story, kuei-tzu-mu became the mother of the Red Boy 紅孩兒, and both of them were subdued by Kuan-yin. Dudbridge, in *Antecedents*, p. 18, n. 2, has noted that the name Kuei-tzu-mu appears only incidentally in the hundred-chapter narrative, but it is nonetheless significant that its appearance occurs in the very episode of the Red Boy. Cf. *HYC*, chap. 42, p. 485.

21. *Hou-ts'un hsien-shêng ta-ch'üan chi* 後村先生大全集, *chüan* 43, 18b. The reference to *Hou hsing-chê* in *chüan* 24, 2a, only mentions an ugly face of the ape novice without any overt relation to the theme of the quest for scriptures. See Dudbridge, *Antecedents*, pp. 45–47, for a discussion of these two poetic passages.

22. G. Ecke and P. Demiéville, *The Twin Pagodas of Zayton*, Harvard-Yenching Institute Monograph Series, 11 (Cambridge, Mass., 1935), p. 35.

23. Ōta Tatsuo 太田辰夫 and Torii Hisayasu 鳥居久靖, in "Kaisetsu 解説," in *Saiyuki*, Chūgoku koten bungaku taikei, 31–2 (Tokyo 1971), 432, have challenged Ecke and Demiéville's interpretation of the carving by pointing out that the figure at the upper righthand corner should be thought of simply as a figure of Buddha (not Hsüan-tsang), which Monkey will become by virtue of bringing back the scriptures. It may be added that Sun Wu-k'ung of the hundred-chapter narrative did use a sword or scimitar 刀 (*JW*, chaps. 2 and 3) before he acquired his famous rod. None of the scholars consulted here sees fit to discuss the significance of what seems to be a headband worn by the carved figure.

24. The story, which appears in the third volume of the fragment from the *Ch'ing-p'ing-shan t'ang hua-pên* 清平山堂話本, also exists in slightly revised form in *chüan* 20 of the anthology *Ku-chin hsiao-shuo* 古今小說. For the possible date of this story, see Patrick Hanan, *The Chinese Short Story*, Harvard-Yenching Institute Monograph Series, 21 (Cambridge, Mass., 1973), pp. 116, 137–38.

25. So dated by Dudbridge, *Antecedents*, p. 133.

26. Ibid., p. 128.

27. Dudbridge's arguments (pp. 126–27) against any connection between the white ape legend and Sun Wu-k'ung of the full-length *Hsi-yu chi* do not seem to me to be wholly convincing. He has already conceded that the Sun Hsing-chê of the twenty-four-act *tsa-chü* is explicitly represented as an abductor of women, but insists that this may not be part of the "authentic" tradition because of (1) "the liberties taken with the materials in the cause of dramatic expediency," and (2), the Kōzanji version, "earliest and, in its own way, most genuine of the sources, [which] shows no trace of any such characterization in its monkey-hero." To these arguments, it may be pointed out (1) that there is no reason why the Kōzanji version, just because it is the earliest text, should contain every significant element

of a *developing* tradition; (2) that the name Ta-shêng (though without the qualifying Ch'i-t'ien) is already found in the Kōzanji account (sec. 17); and (3) that the Sun Wu-k'ung of the *JW*, though less ribald in speech and manner than his dramatic counterpart, is no stranger to sexual play when it is called for (cf. *HYC*, chap. 60, p. 694; chap. 81, pp. 927–28).

28. See Hu Shih (1923), pp. 368–70; Lu Hsün 魯迅, *Chung-kuo hsiao-shuo ti li-shih ti pien-ch'ien* 中國小說的歷史的變遷 (Lectures given originally in 1924; repr. Hong Kong, 1957), p. 19; Huang Chih-kang 黃芝崗, *Chung-kuo ti shui-shên* 中國的水神 (Shanghai, 1934), p. 178; Wolfram Eberhard, *Die chinesische Novelle des 17.–19. Jahrhunderts*, suppl. 9 to *Artibus Asiae* (Ascona, Switzerland, 1948), p. 127; Wu Hsiao-ling 吳曉鈴, "*Hsi-yu chi* yü *Lo-mo-yen shu*," *Wen-hsüeh yen-chiu* 文學研究 2 (1958): 169; and Ishida Eiichirō 石田英一郎, "The *Kappa* Legend," *Folklore Studies* (Peking) 9 (1950): 125–26.

29. Dudbridge, *Antecedents*, p. 148.

30. See Hu Shih (1923), pp. 370–72. After Hu's essay, the Indian prototype of the monkey hero was advocated again by Ch'ên Yin-k'o 陳寅恪, "*Hsi-yu chi* Hsüan-tsang ti-tzŭ ku-shih ti yen-pien 西游記玄奘弟子故事的演變," *LSYYCK* 2 (1930): 157–60; by Chêng Chên-to 鄭振鐸, "*Hsi-yu chi* ti yen-hua 西游記的演化," first published 1933, repr. in *Chung-kuo wên-hsüeh yen-chiu* 中國文學研究 (3 vols., Peking, 1957), 1: 291–92; and most recently by Huang Mêng-wên 黃孟文, *Sung-tai pai-hua hsiao-shuo yen-chiu* 宋代白話小說研究 (Singapore, 1971), pp. 177–78.

31. Wu Hsiao-ling, pp. 168–69. Whether the author of the *HYC* has read in the Buddhist canon or not is a question which cannot be settled without careful examination of the narrative itself. For a recent discussion of Tibetan versions of the *Rāmāyāna*, see J. W. de Jong, "An Old Tibetan Version of the *Rāmāyāna*," *T'oung Pao* 58 (1972): 190–202.

32. Dudbridge, *Antecedents*, p. 162.

33. Surviving remnants of the *Yung-lo ta-tien* have been published in facsimile by Chung-hua shu-chü (Peking, 1960). For the Chinese text of the particular section under discussion, see also Chêng Chên-to, 1: 270–72.

34. Dudbridge, *Antecedents*, p. 63; see also pp. 179–88 for the Chinese text and translation.

35. See ibid., pp. 73–74 for a detailed listing.

36. Ibid.

37. Originally in *Shibun* 斯文 9,1–10,3. I use here the text included in the *Yüan-ch'ü-hsüan wai-pien* 元曲選外編, ed. Sui Shu-sên 隋樹森 (3 vols., Peking, 1959), 2: 633–94.

38. See Sun K'ai-ti 孫楷第, "Wu Ch'ang-ling yü tsa-chü *Hsi-yu chi* 吳昌齡與雜劇西游記," first published 1939, repr. in *Ts'ang-chou chi*

滄州集 2 vols. (Peking, 1965, 2: 366–98; Yen Tun-i 嚴敦易, "*Hsi-yu chi* ho ku-tien hsi-ch'ü ti kuan-hsi 西游記和古典戲曲的關係," first published 1954, repr. in *LWC*, pp. 142–52; and Dudbridge, *Antecedents*, pp. 76–80.

39. Glen Dudbridge, "*Hsi-yu chi* tsu-pên k'ao ti tsai shang-ch'üeh 西游記祖本考的再商榷," *Hsin-ya hsüeh-pao* 新亞學報 6 (1964): 497–518; "The Hundred-chapter *Hsi-yu chi* and its Early Versions," *Asia Major*, n.s. 14 (1969): 141–91, hereafter cited as "Early Versions."

40. Dudbridge, "Early Versions," p. 151.

41. Ibid., p. 184.

42. See *HYC*, pp. 1–7.

43. See my "Narrative Structure and the Problem of Chapter Nine in the *Hsi-yu chi*," *JAS* 34 (1975): 295–311.

44. See *Wu Ch'êng-ên shih-wên chi* 吳承恩詩文集, ed. Liu Hsiu-yeh 劉修業 (Peking, 1958); and Liu Ts'un-yan 柳存仁, "Wu Ch'êng-ên: His Life and Career," *T'oung Pao* 53 (1967): 1–97.

45. *T'ien-ch'i Huai-an Fu-chih*, chüan 19, 3b.

46. Quoted in Hu Shih (1923), p. 378.

47. Tanaka Iwao 田中嚴, "*Saiyuki* no sakusha 西游記の作者," *Shibun* 斯文, n.s. 8 (1953): 37.

48. See ibid., 33–34 for some samples of Li's annotations.

49. Liu Ts'un-yan, "Life and Career," pp. 17–20.

50. See Kuo Shao-yü 郭紹虞, *Chung-kuo wên-hsüeh p'i-p'ing shih* 中國文學批評史 (2 vols., Shanghai, 1947), 2: 242–46. See also Wu Tsê 吳澤, *Ju-chiao p'an-t'u Li Cho-wu* 儒教叛徒李卓吾 (Shanghai, 1949), pp. 59–228; Jung Chao-tsu 容肇祖, *Li Cho-wu p'ing-chuan* 李卓吾評傳 (Shanghai, 1936), pp. 69–106; and C. K. Hsiao, "An Iconoclast of the Sixteenth Century," *Tien Hsia Monthly* 6 (1938): 317–41. The most recent study of Li's view of history is Chao Ling-yang 趙令揚, "Li Chih chih shih-hsüeh 李贄之史學," *Journal of Oriental Studies* 東方文化 11 (1973): 122–42.

51. Hu Shih's translation in the Preface to *Monkey: Folk Novel of China by Wu Ch'eng-en*, trans. Arthur Waley (London, 1943), p. 1; for the Chinese text, see the *shih-wên chi*, p. 62.

52. Liu Ts'un-yan, "Life and Career," 68–70.

53. *Huai-an Fu-chih*, chüan 16, 13a.

54. See, for example, the poems written to the tune of 如夢令 (p. 171), to the tune of 浣溪沙 (pp. 172–73), to the tune of 菩薩蠻 (pp. 173–74), the fourth poem written to the tune of 西江月 (p. 175), the second poem written to the tune of 滿江紅 (p. 178), the poem written to the tune of 送我入門來 (p. 182), and the poem written to the tune of 滿庭芳 (p. 184), in the *Shih-wên chi*.

55. Ch'in Kuan 秦觀, *Huai-hai chü-shih ch'ang-tuan-chü* 淮海居士長
短句 (Peking, 1957), p. 11.

56. Jên Pan-t'ang 任半塘, *T'ang hsi-lung* 唐戲弄 2 vols. (Peking, 1958),
2: 876–888.

57. Maurice Winternitz, *A History of Indian Literature*, trans. S. Ketkar
and H. Kohn, 2 (Calcutta, 1933): 91.

58. Winternitz, in ibid., p. 115, cites the *Saddharma-puṇḍarīka sūtra* to
point out that "Buddha teaches by means of sūtras, gāthās, legends and
jātakas."

59. See the *"Miao-fa-lien-hua-ching* chiang-wên 妙法蓮華經講文,"
and the *"Wei-mo-chieh-ching* chiang-wên 維摩詰經講文," in *Tun-huang
pien-wên chi* 敦煌變文集, ed. Wang Chung-min 王重民 et al. 2 vols.
(Peking, 1957), 2: 501–645.

60. Hu Shih, *Pai-hua wen-hsüeh shih* 白話文學史 (Shanghai, 1928;
repr. Taipei, 1957), pp. 204–10.

61. See James I. Crump, "The Conventions and Craft of Yüan Drama,"
JAOS 91 (1971): 14–24; "The Elements of Yüan Opera," *JAS* 17 (1958):
425–26; Cyril Birch, "Some Formal Characteristics of the *hua-pen* Story,"
BSOAS 17 (1955): 348, 357; Jaroslav Prušek, "The Creative Methods of
Chinese Mediaeval Story-Tellers," in *Chinese History and Literature* (Dor-
drecht, Holland, 1970), pp. 367–68; Patrick Hanan, "The Early Chinese
Short Story: A Critical Theory in Outline," *HJAS* 27 (1969): 174; idem,
"Sources of the *Chin P'ing Mei*," *Asia Major*, n.s. 10 (1963): 28; idem,
"The *Yün-men Chuan*: From Chantefable to Short Story," *BSOAS* 36 (1973):
302–3.

62. There are thirty-two poems in the *Hsi-yu chi* which may also be
found, with minor modifications, in the *Fêng-shên yen-i* 封神演義, a work
whose date and authorship are by no means firmly established, though it
is generally regarded as approximately of the same period as the hundred-
chapter *Hsi-yu chi*. The following table will make clear the location of these
poems in the two narratives.

Poem	Hsi-yu chi	Fêng-shên yen-i (All references are to the 1960 edition, published in Hong Kong by Chung-hua shu-chü)
1.	Chap. 1, p. 2	Chap. 43, p. 401
2.	Chap. 1, p. 8	Chap. 38, pp. 348–49
3.	Chap. 1, p. 9	Chap. 37, p. 335
4.	Chap. 1, p. 10	Chap. 61, p. 585
5.	Chap. 4, p. 37	Chap. 12, p. 116
6.	Chap. 5, p. 51	Chap. 45, p. 419

7.	Chap. 7, p. 70	Chap. 78, p. 765
8.	Chap. 7, p. 76	Chap. 78, p. 764
9.	Chap. 16, p. 185	Chap. 64, p. 621
10.	Chap. 17, p. 191	Chap. 49, p. 465
11.	Chap. 18, p. 204	Chap. 52, p. 494
12.	Chap. 28, p. 318	Chap. 55, p. 520
13.	Chap. 28, p. 315	Chap. 66, p. 641
14.	Chap. 36, p. 411	Chap. 55, p. 518
15.	Chap. 37, p. 421	Chap. 54, p. 514
16.	Chap. 41, p. 472	Chap. 71, p. 694
17.	Chap. 41, p. 476	Chap. 64, p. 623
18.	Chap. 42, p. 486	Chap. 83, p. 819
19.	Chap. 47, p. 542	Chap. 88, p. 880
20.	Chap. 48, p. 555	Chap. 88, p. 879
21.	Chap. 48, p. 555	Chap. 89, p. 889
22.	Chap. 50, p. 575	Chap. 45, p. 426
23.	Chap. 56, p. 643	Chap. 59, p. 567
24.	Chap. 65, p. 742	Chap. 63, p. 613
25.	Chap. 66, p. 751	Chap. 58, p. 559
26.	Chap. 70, p. 796	Chap. 63, p. 606
27.	Chap. 84, p. 953	Chap. 62, p. 595
28.	Chap. 85, p. 966	Chap. 61, pp. 583–84
29.	Chap. 86, p. 976	Chap. 62, p. 601
30.	Chap. 96, p. 1080	Chap. 85, p. 841
31.	Chap. 98, p. 1103	Chap. 71, p. 687
32.	Chap. 98, p. 1106	Chap. 65, pp. 628–29

Liu Ts'un-yan in *Buddhist and Taoist Influences on Chinese Novels. Vol. I: The Authorship of the "Fêng Shên Yen I"* (Wiesbaden, 1962), pp. 204–42, and Wei Chü-hsien 衛聚賢 in *"Fêng-shên pang" ku-shih t'an-yüan* 封神榜故事探源 (private edition; Hong Kong, 1960), II, 207–9, have both claimed that the *Fêng-shên yen-i* might have been the source for the *Hsi-yu chi*. However, Nicholas Koss, graduate student at Indiana University, has completed an M.A. thesis in which he made exhaustive comparisons of the poems in the two works. His preliminary conclusions, on the basis of variations in diction, syntax, meter, rhyme, and the probable changes induced by different contexts, seem to point to the fact that it is the author of the *Fêng-shên yen-i* who has deliberately borrowed from the *Hsi-yu chi*.

63. C. T. Hsia, *The Classic Chinese Novel: A Critical Introduction* (New York, 1968), p. 120. Hereafter cited as *Introduction*.

64. Cf. Eugene Eoyang, "The Solitary Boat: Images of Self in Chinese Nature Poetry," *JAS* 32 (1973): 593–622.

65. C. H. Wang is certainly right, therefore, in saying that the poetry of the *Hsi-yu chi* lacks "weight and solidity" in "Towards Defining A Chinese Heroism," *JAOS* 95 (1975): 26. But that is precisely the reason why these poems must not be read as poetic entities by themselves; it is their complete integration into the narrative as a whole that gives them their "epic" force. Divorced from their contexts, the lengthy similes of Homer or Vergil are no more impressive than the balladic lines of "Chevy Chase."

66. William Whallon, "Old Testament Poetry and Homeric Epic," *Comparative Literature* 18 (1966): 113–31; see also his *Formula, Character and Context: Studies in Homeric, Old English and Old Testament Poetry* (Cambridge and Washington, D.C., 1969), pp. 68–70.

67. See also Arai Ken 荒井健 "Saiyuki no naka no Saiyuki 西游記の友かの西游記," *Tōhō Gappō* 東方學報 36 (1964): 591–96, for some suggestive comments on this point.

68. Průšek, pp. 386 and 393.

69. Erich Auerbach, *Dante: Poet of the Secular World,* trans. Ralph Manheim (Chicago, 1961), p. 95.

70. C. M. Bowra, *Heroic Poetry* (London, 1952), p. 31.

71. *Ssŭ-pu ku-tien hsiao-shuo p'ing-lun* (Peking, 1973), p. 67.

72. *Hsin-k'ê ch'u-hsiang kuan-pan ta-tzu Hsi-yu chi* 新刻出像官板大字西游記, *chüan* 1, 2b–3a.

73. See the commentary at the end of the first chapter of the *Hsi-yu chên-ch'üan.*

74. The text of the *Hsin-shuo Hsi-yu chi* here is that published by Shu-yeh-kung 書業公; the manuscript is located at the library of the University of Tokyo.

75. Hu Shih (1923), pp. 383, 390.

76. Waley, p. 5.

77. Lu Hsün, *Chung-kuo hsiao-shuo-shih lüeh* 中國小說史略 (1923; repr. Hong Kong, 1967), p. 173.

78. Tanaka Kenji 田中謙二 and Arai Ken 荒井健, "Saiyuki no Bungaku 西游記の文學," in *Chūgoku no Hachi-Dai Shōsetsu* 中國の八大小說 (Tokyo, 1965), p. 193.

79. Hsia, *Introduction,* p. 138.

80. Chin Meishin, "Saiyuki to Shikai 西游記と志怪," *Chūgoku Bungaku Kenkyū* 中國文學研究 4 (1966): 56–58. See also C. T. Hsia and T. A. Hsia, "New Perspectives on Two Ming Novels: *Hsi-yu chi* and *Hsi-yu pu,*" in *"Wen-lin": Studies in the Chinese Humanities,* ed. Chow Tse-tsung (Madison, 1968), pp. 229–45; and Karl S. Y. Kao, "An Archetypal Approach to *Hsi-yu chi,*" *Tamkang Review* 5 (1974): 63–98.

81. Andrew H. Plaks, "Allegory in *Hung-lou mêng* and *Hsi-yu chi*" (unpublished paper presented at the Princeton Conference on Chinese Narrative, 20–22 January, 1974).

82. Dudbridge, *Antecedents*, p. 176.

83. *Shih-wên chi*, p. 95.

84. Liu Ts'un-yan, "Life and Career," pp. 82–83.

85. Cf. Dudbridge, *Antecedents*, pp. 167–76.

86. Fu Ch'in-chia, *Chung-kuo Tao-chiao shih* (Shanghai, 1937), p. 137.

87. C. T. Hsia, *Introduction*, p. 130.

88. See the pertinent titles under the sections on "Fang-fa lei方法類" and "Chung-shu lei 眾術類" in the *Combined Indices to the Authors and Titles of Books in Two Collections of Taoist Literature*, compiled by Weng Tu-chien, Harvard-Yenching Institute Sinological Index Series, no. 25 (1935), p. xi.

89. See Jen Pan-t'ang, 1: 393–412.

90. See, for example, the *Lung-hu yüan-chih* 龍虎原旨 and the *Lung-hu huan-tan chüeh* 龍虎還丹訣 in *TT*, 84: 741; *Chin-tan chih-chih* 金丹直指 in *TT* 83: 739, 6b.

91. Okuno Shintarō, "Mizu to honō no denshō; *Saiyuki* seiritsu no ichi sakumen 水と炎の傳承;西游記成立の一側面," *Nihon Chūgoku Gakkai Hō*日本中國學會報 18 (1966): 227.

92. C. T. Hsia, *Introduction*, p. 126.

93. Cf. Fung Yu-lan, *Chung-kuo chê-hsüeh shih* 中國哲學史 (2d ed., 1933; repr. Hong Kong, 1959), pp. 552–64; Joseph Needham, *Science and Civilisation in China* (Cambridge, England, 1954–), 2: 332.

94. See Liu Ts'un-yan, "Taoist Self-cultivation in Ming Thought," in *Self and Society in Ming Thought*, ed. W. Theodore de Bary and the Conference on Ming Thought (New York, 1970), pp. 301–3; Manfred Porkert, *The Theoretical Foundations of Chinese Medicine: Systems of Correspondence*, M.I.T. East Asian Science Series, 3 (Cambridge, Mass.: 1974), pp. 9–43.

95. *TT* 84: 742.

96. A small, spoonlike instrument used as a dry measure for small amounts of powdered medicine, it is also frequently a metonym for Sha Wu-ching in the narrative (cf. *JW*, chap. 22).

97. Cf. Wolfram Eberhard, "Beiträge zur kosmologischen Spekulation Chinas in der Han-Zeit," *Baessler Archiv* 16 (1933): 1–100; Needham, pp. 253 ff.; Porkert, pp. 43–54.

98. *TT* 84: 743.

99. C. S. Lewis, *The Allegory of Love* (New York, 1958), p. 68; Henri de Lubac, however, seems to think that the allegorical presentation of internal realities is a distinctive Christian accomplishment. "*Altum intus*! Ainsi s'achève l'allégorie chrétienne," he declares in his *Exégèse médiévale*, pt. 1 Paris, 1959), p. 513.

100. See Arthur F. Wright, "Fu I and the Rejection of Buddhism," *Journal of the History of Ideas* 12 (1951): 33–47.

101. *Fa-shih-chuan, chüan* 1, 14a.

102. Dudbridge, *Antecedents*, pp. 18–21.

103. Hu Shih (1923), 358.

104. Dudbridge, *Antecedents*, p. 44.

105. See the essays collected in the *LWC* and Sa Mêng-wu 薩孟武, *Hsi-yu chi yü Chung-kuo ku-tai chêng-chih* 西游記與中國古代政治 (Taipei, 1969).

106. Arthur Wright, *Buddhism in Chinese History* (Stanford, 1959), p. 98.

107. See Marie-Thérèse de Mallmann, *Introduction a l'étude d'Avalokiteçvara* (Paris, 1948), pp. 86–115.

108. Okuno, 225–26.

109. Some of the more common Buddhist sources for this metaphor are Kumārajīva's translation of the *Vimalakīrti sūtra*, the *Mahāprajñapāramitā śāstra* (*Ta-chih-tu lun* 大智度論), Sanghabara's translation of the *Mañjuśripariprcchā* (*Wên-shu-shih-li wên ching* 文殊師利問經), and the *An-lo chi* 安樂集 by Tao-ch'o. For sources in the *Tao Tsang*, see, for example, the *Shang-ch'ing t'ai-hsüan chi* 上清太玄集, chüan 5, 27, in *TT* 83:730; *chüan* 9, 5 in 731; *Hsüan-tsung chih-chih wan-fa t'ung-kuei* 玄宗直指萬法同歸, chüan 2, 11 in 734; *Ming-ho yü-yin*, chüan 6, 5 in *TT* 84:745.

110. Dudbridge, *Antecedents*, p. 176.

111. The incident occurs during the episode of the Cart-Slow Kingdom, where Sun Wu-k'ung engages in a magic contest with his Taoist adversaries. When at one point the Tiger Strength Immortal proposes a duel in meditation to see who can sit perfectly still for the longest period, Monkey is immediately defeated (cf. *HYC*, chap. 46, pp. 528–29; Waley, pp. 234–35).

112. Hsia, *Introduction*, p. 126.

113. D. T. Suzuki, *Outlines of Mahayana Buddhism* (New York, 1963), p. 173.

114. Plaks, pp. 48–49.

115. Arai Ken, "*Saiyuki* no naka no *Saiyuki*," pp. 601–7.

Chapter One

1. In Chinese legend, P'an Ku was said to be the first human, born from the union of the yin and yang forces. See the *Wu-yün li-nien chi* 五運歷年記 and the *Shu-i chi* 述異記. He also assisted in the formation of the universe.

2. This is probably a reference to a shorter (or abridged) version of the Tripitaka story, compiled by Chu-Ting-ch'ên of Canton and published in the late sixteenth century (probably during the reign of Wan-li) by a Fukien bookseller, Liu Ch'iu-mao. The exact title of this work, according to the title page of the Library of Congress edition, is *Hsin-ch'ieh ch'üan-hsiang T'ang San-tsang Hsi-yu shih-ni* (=o) *chuan*. See Introduction (pp. 13–14) for a brief discussion of its relation to *JW*.

3. Shao Yung, a Sung scholar and an expert in the *I Ching*.

4. The Three Kings and the Five Emperors refer to the legendary sage rulers at the dawn of Chinese civilization. There has been no agreement on who the Three Kings or the Five Emperors were, and ancient Chinese texts present several varied combinations. See the entries under *san-huang* and *wu-ti* in the *Chung-wên ta tz'ŭ-tien* or the *Tz'u Hai*.

5. The Ten Islets and the Three Islands were famous abodes of immortals.

6. The twenty-four solar terms are seasonal divisions of a year established in the Han period. They are: *li-ch'un* (spring begins), *yü-shui* (rain water), *ching-chih* (excited insects), *ch'un-fên* (vernal equinox), *ch'ing-ming* (clear and bright), *ku-yü* (grain rains), *li hsia* (summer begins), *hsiao-man* (grain fills), *mang-chung* (grain in ear), *hsia-chih* (summer solstice), *hsiao-shu* (slight heat), *ta-shu* (great heat), *li ch'iu* (autumn begins), *ch'u-shu* (limit of heat), *pai-lu* (white dew), *ch'iu-fên* (autumnal equinox), *han-lu* (cold dew), *shuang-chiang* (hoar frost descends), *li-tung* (winter begins), *hsiao-hsüeh* (slight snow), *ta-hsüeh* (great snow), *tung-chih* (winter solstice), *hsiao-han* (slight cold), and *ta-han* (great cold).

7. A quotation from a poem of the T'ang period.

8. "Blessed Land" and "Cave Heaven" (*tung-t'ien fu-ti*) are frequently used by Taoists as euphemisms for their residences.

9. Confucius, *Analects*, II, 22.

10. Yellow-sperm (*Polygonatum gigantum* var. *thunbergii*): a small plant whose roots are often used for medicinal purposes by the Chinese.

11. According to ancient Chinese custom, the five divisions of living creatures are: the winged creatures, the hairy creatures, the armored creatures, the scaly creatures, and the naked creatures (i.e., humans).

12. The dragon's pulse is one of the magnetic currents recognized by geomancers.

13. The rotted ax handle (*lan-k'o*) alludes to a mountain by such a name (Lan-k'o Shan) in the province of Chê-chiang, south of Chü-chou. According to the *Shu-i chi* 述異記 a certain Wang Chih (王質) of the Tsin (晉) period went to this mountain to gather wood. He saw two youths playing chess who gave him a fruit to eat shaped like the pit of a date, after which he felt no hunger at all. When at last the game was finished, one of the youths pointed to his ax and said, "Your handle has rotted!" When Wang returned to his home, a century had elapsed. There is also a chess classic in Chinese named *Lan-k'o Ching*; see *JW*, chap. 10.

14. A Taoist classic, generally regarded as one of the five major canonical texts of Taoism.

15. A probable allusion to the three samādhis, in the meditation on three subjects, which are (1) *k'ung*, or emptiness, purging the mind of all

ideas and illusions; (2) *wu-hsiang*, or no appearance, purging the mind of all phenomena and external forms; and (3) *wu-yüan*, or no desire, purging the mind of all desires. The Double Three is the advanced type of meditation, in which the term of each is doubled (e.g., *k'ung-k'ung*, etc.).

16. A pun on the words "surname" and "temper," both of which are pronounced *hsing*.

Chapter Two

1. In Buddhism, *māra* has the meaning of the Destroyer, the Evil One, and the Hinderer.

2. The three vehicles (*triyāna*) are the conveyances which carry living beings across mortality to the shores of *Nirvāṇa*. They are generally divided into the categories of great, medium, and small. Here it is used as a metonym for Buddhism.

3. The tail of the yak or deer was adopted by the great conversationalists of antiquity as a ceremonious instrument. Used sometimes as a fly-brush or duster, it became inseparably associated with the Taoist or Buddhist recluse and served as a symbol of his purity and detachment.

4. I.e., Confucianism, Taoism, and Buddhism.

5. I have not been able to determine the meaning of the metaphor "treading the arrow," though it probably refers to some practice (possibly sexual) in alchemy.

6. Red lead is the name for a virgin's menstrual discharge, while autumn stone refers to the urine of a virgin boy. These are considered indispensable elements for the alchemical process.

7. Tzŭ means 11:00 p.m. to 1:00 a.m.

8. In alchemy, the gold elixir is the medicine of immortality; it is supposedly refined in the body and hence it is sometimes called internal elixir (*nei-tan*).

9. On this teaching, see Henri Maspero, "Les procédés de 'nourrir le principe vital' dans la religion taoïste ancienne," *Journal asiatique* 228 (1937): 177–252, 353–430.

10. A symbol of perfection as well as a symbol for brazier in alchemy, the moon may also refer to the heart in the writings on internal alchemy.

11. Snake and the tortoise are frequently used as Taoist symbols of polar opposites, such as the forces of yin and yang.

12. According to the literature of internal alchemy, there are five forces in the human body which correspond to the Five Phases: *ching* (essence, water), *shên* (spirit, fire), *hun* (soul, wood), *p'o* (vigor, metal, or gold), *i* (will, earth). If the forces are allowed to follow their natural course, then the fluids become blood, and the blood becomes vital discharges (sperm or

vaginal fluids) which may flow out of the body. The teaching of reversing the five forces is aimed at retaining them within the body.

13. Wu means 11:00 a.m. to 1:00 p.m.

14. The nine apertures are: the eyes, the nostrils, the ears, the mouth, and the urinal and anal passages.

15. Oxen made of cast iron were placed in streams or fields; farmers used them as a charm to prevent floods.

16. The eight epochs are: the first days of spring, summer, autumn, and winter, the two equinoxes, and the solstices.

17. The Three Regions: the Buddhist division of the world into the three realms of desire, form, and pure spirit. Hence the term frequently means the world or the universe.

18. The Five Phases are: metal, wood, water, fire, and earth. For the precise meaning of the term *Wu-hsing* (Five Evolutive Phases), see Manfred Porkert, *The Theoretical Foundations of Chinese Medicine: Systems of Correspondence* (Cambridge, 1974), pp. 43–54.

19. An inconsistency in the text.

CHAPTER THREE

1. The ten species include the five kinds of beings (ecclesiastical, earthly, human, divine, and demonic) and the five divisions of living creatures (see chap. 1, n. 9). The Hell of Ninefold Darkness (*chiu-yu*) is a Taoist hell.

2. The Heavenly River: i.e., the Milky Way.

3. The Great Yü is the reputed founder of the Hsia dynasty (2205 B.C.) and the mythic conqueror of the Flood in China.

4. I.e., the wheel of karma. For the translation of these ten kings, I am following Arthur Waley. See his discussion in *A Catalogue of Paintings Recovered from Tun-Huang by Sir Aurel Stein* (London, 1931), pp. xxvi–xxx.

5. Waley's translation is so apt that I have adopted it here.

6. Subduing dragons and taming tigers are metaphors for the alchemical process.

CHAPTER FOUR

1. The verse here is alluding to the Indra heaven with its thirty-three summits (*trayastrimśās*) and to the six heavens of desire (*devalokas*). The first of these heavens is situated halfway up Mount Sumeru, where Indra is said to rule over his thirty-two devas. For descriptions of the Heavens, see the *Ta-chih-tu lun* (the śastra ascribed to Nāgārjuna on the greater *Prajñā-pāramitā sūtra,* translated by Kumārajīva), and the *Chü-shê lun* (the *Abhidharma-kośa śāstra*), translated into Chinese by Paramārtha and the historical Hsüan-tsang.

2. In Chinese mythology, this is the Star of Long Life.

3. Special judges in the Underworld, traditionally robed in red, blue, and green.

4. The brilliant scarlet color reserved only for royalty.

5. The jade rabbit and the golden crow are Taoist metaphors for the sun and the moon.

6. In Chinese folklore, the monkey is said to be able to ward off sickness from horses. This title is a pun on the words *pi* (to avoid, to keep off), *ma* (horse), and *wên* (pestilence, plague).

7. In this poem, which is exceedingly difficult to translate, the author has made use of numerous lists of horses associated with the emperors, Chou Mu-wang (ca. 1001–942 B.C.), Shih Huang-ti (221–209 B.C.), and Han Wên-ti (179–57 B.C.). To construct the poem, some names are used merely for their tonal effects (e.g., *ch'i-chi* and *yao-niao*), while others have ostensible meanings as well. In my translation I have tried to approximate the effect of the original. Those interested in famous and legendary horses in Chinese lore should consult the relevant sections on horses in the *T'a-p'ing yü-lan* 太平御覽, *chüan* 9.

8. The modern Khokand, where the best horses are said to be raised.

9. This is Chang Tao-ling, the first pope or patriarch of popular Taoism.

10. This is the Chinese counterpart of Vaiśravaṇa or Dhanada, one of the twenty great heavenly devarājas (*t'ien-wang*).

11. The term, "spreading flower" (*hsüan-hua*), may also be translated "spreading virtue," since flower (*hua*) and virtue (*tê-hua*) have the same pronunciation but different tonal inflection.

12. The Three Platforms (*san-t'ai*) are the offices of Taoist Star Spirits, which are said to correspond to the Three Officials (*san-kung*) in imperial government. See the *Tsin Shu, T'ien-wên-chih* 晉書天文志.

13. Star Spirits of Five Poles (*wu-tou hsing-chün*) are Taoist deities.

Chapter Five

1. The Three Pure Ones are the highest gods of the pantheon in popular Taoism. They are: the Jade-Pure Honorable Divine of the Origin (Yü-ch'ing yüan-shih t'ien-tsun) the Exalted-Pure Honorable Divine of Spiritual Treasures (Shang-ch'ing ling-pao t'ien-tsun) and the Primal-Pure Honorable Divine of Moral Virtue (T'ai-ch'ing tao-tê t'ien-tsun, also named T'ai-ch'ing t'ai-shang lao-chün). The last one is Lao Tzu.

2. These may be the Four Heavenly Emperors in Chinese folklore. They are divided according to locations and colors: green (east), white (west), red (south), and black (north). The Yellow Emperor of the Center is often added to the group to make up the Five Emperors, and thus they may be another form of the Four (Five, if the Center is included) Deva Kings.

3. The Nine Luminaries are: Āditya (the sun), Sōma (the moon), Aṅgāraka (Mars, also in Chinese, the Planet of Fire), Budha (Mercury, the Planet of Water), Bṛhaspati (Jupiter, the Planet of Wood), Sukra (Venus, the Planet of Gold), Śanaiścara (Saturn, the Planet of Earth), Rāhu (the spirit that causes eclipses), and Ketu, a comet.

4. The Generals of the Five Quarters are the five powerful Bodhisattvas who are guardians of the four quarters and the center.

5. These constellations are the twenty-eight nakṣatras, divided into four mansions (east-spring, south-summer, west-autumn, and north-winter), each of which has seven members.

6. The Four Devarājas are the external protectors of Indra, each living on a side of Mount Meru. They defend the world against the attack of evil spirits or asuras, whence the name the Four Devarājas, Guardians of the World. They are: Dhṛtarāṣṭra, Upholder of the Kingdom; Virūḍhaka, King of Growth; Virūpākṣa, the Broad-eyed Deva King; and Vaiśravaṇa, the God of Great Learning. Kuvera, the God of Wealth, is also a member of this group.

7. The Twelve Horary Branches are: Tzŭ (Rat, 11 p.m.–1 a.m.), Ch'ou (Ox, 1–3 a.m.), Yin (Tiger, 3–5 a.m.), Mao (Hare, 5–7 a.m.), Ch'ên (Dragon, 7–9 a.m.), Ssŭ (Serpent, 9–11 a.m.), Wu (Horse, 11 a.m.–1 p.m.), Wei (Sheep, 1–3 p.m.), Shên (Monkey, 3–5 p.m.), Yu (Cock, 5–7 p.m.), Hsü (Dog, 7–9 p.m.), Hai (Boar, 9–11 p.m.).

8. These deities of the Taoist pantheon represent the essences (*ching*) of the Five Phases.

9. The Queen Mother, sometimes called the Lady Queen Mother (Wang-mu niang-niang) or the Queen Mother of the West (Hsi wang-mu), is the highest goddess of popular Taoism. She lives in the Palace of the Jasper Pool located on Mount K'un-lun in Tibet.

10. A Sung document by Wang Ming-ch'ing has told the story that the crown prince, Ch'ao-ling, who later became the Emperor Jên tsung, was fond of taking off shoes and socks as a boy. He was thus nicknamed the Immortal of Naked Feet, which was explained also as another name for Lao Tzu.

11. Dragon livers, phoenix marrow, bear paws, lips of apes: these were four of the eight dainties (see the wine makers' complaint later in this chapter), the rest being rabbit embryo, carp tail, broiled osprey, and koumiss.

12. According to the fourth chapter (*Chin Tan*, "On golden elixir") of the *Pao p'u tzu nei-p'ien* attributed to the alchemist Ko Hung (283–343), the classification of the efficacy of the elixir is as follows: "The elixir of one turn, if taken, will enable a man to become an immortal (*tê hsien*) in three years; that of two turns, if taken, will enable a man to become an immortal

in two years; . . ." And so on, until one reaches the elixir of nine turns, which, if taken, "will enable a man to become an Immortal in three days." The "turn" apparently refers to the process of cyclical chemical or physical manipulations of the elixir ingredients; hence the greater the number of turns, the more powerful the elixir. See Nathan Sivin, *Chinese Alchemy: Preliminary Studies* (Cambridge, Mass., 1968), pp. 36–52; Needham, 5/2, 62–71.

13. Fearless Guards: fierce custodians of the Law.

14. The Guardians of the year, the month, the day, and the hour.

15. The Five Great Mountains are: T'ai (east), Hua (west), Hêng (south), Hêng (north), Sung (central); and the four rivers are: the Yangtze, the Yellow River, the Huai, and the Chi.

16. Five Plagues: possibly a reference to the five epidemics in Vaiśālī during Buddha's lifetime: eye-bleeding, nose-bleeding, pus from the ears, lockjaw, and foul taste of all food.

17. All the names in the following five lines of verse are the members of the Twenty-Eight Constellations.

18. In Buddhism, the ten evil things (*daśākuśala*) are: killing, stealing, lying, double-tongue, deceitful language, filthy language, covetousness, anger, and perverted thoughts.

Chapter Six

1. The Potalaka Mountain, located southeast of Malakūta, is the home of Avalokiteśvara. In the Chinese tradition of popular Buddhism, the equivalent place is the P'u-t'o Mountain, east of the port city of Ningpo in the Chê-chiang Province, where it is the center of the cult of Kuan-yin.

2. In Chinese folk religions, the Immortal Master Erh-lang has been variously identified with Chao Yü 趙昱 of the Sui dynasty, with Li Ping 李冰 of Szechuan, and with a certain Yang Chien 楊戩 the powerful magician and warrior in the *Investiture of the Gods*, another folk novel of approximately the same period as that of the *Hsi-yu Chi*. For further discussion, see Huang Chih-kang 黃芝崗 *Chung-kuo ti shui-shên* 中國的水神 (The Water Gods of China) (Shanghai, 1934), pp. 7–84; Dudbridge, *Antecedents*, pp. 146–54; Li Ssŭ-ch'un 李思純, "Kuan-k'ou-shih shên k'ao 灌口氏神考," and Liu Tê-hsing 劉德馨," Tu Kuan-k'ou-shih shên k'ao ti shang-ch'üeh 讀灌口氏神考的商榷," in *Chiang-ts'un shih-lun* 江村十論 (Shanghai, 1957), pp. 63–74, 75–78.

3. The eight emblems could refer to the eight marks of good fortune on the sole of Buddha's foot—wheel, conch shell, umbrella, canopy, lotus flower, jar, pair of fishes, and mystic signs—which, in turn, were symbols of the organs in Buddha's body. On the other hand, the emblems (lit., treasures) may refer to the magic weapons of the Eight Immortals of Taoism: sword, fan, flower basket, lotus flower, flute, gourd, castanet, and

a stringed musical instrument.

4. The City of Ch'ih may refer to the mountain in Chê-chiang Province called the City of Red Rampart (Ch'ih-ch'êng), another name for T'ien-t'ai Mountain. Or, it can refer to the Prefecture of Kuan-chou in Szechuan Province. The second is the more likely, since the Erh-lang cult was supposed to have originated from this province.

5. In popular accounts, Erh-lang is said to have an extra eye of magic power and vision in the middle of his forehead.

CHAPTER SEVEN

1. This is the first of several instances in the chapter (e.g., the poem on p. 168) and in the book (e.g., the titles of chapters 14, 30, 35, 36, and 41) where reference is made to the phrase "Monkey of the Mind and Horse of the Will." For the history and significance of this term in Buddhist writings, see Dudbridge, *Antecedents*, pp. 168–69; Introduction, pp. 59–61.

2. Lord of the East: possibly a reference to the Sun God.

3. Samādhi fire: the fire that is said to consume the body of Buddha when he enters Nirvāṇa. But in the Buddhism of popular fiction, this fire is possessed by many fighters or warriors who have attained immortality, and it is often used as a weapon. Cf. chapters 24 and 48 of the *Fêng-shên Yen-I* (The Investiture of the Gods).

4. The time is calculated according to the sacred number 7.

5. Mercury is one of the crucial elements in alchemy.

6. The "three refuges," or Triśaraṇa, refer to three kinds of surrender: to surrender to the Buddha as master, to the Law (*Dharma*) as medicine, and to the community of monks (*Saṅgha*) as friends. The "five commandments" (*pañca veramaṇī*) are prohibitions against killing, stealing, adultery, lying, and intoxicating beverages.

7. Tathāgata: one of the highest titles of Buddha. It may be defined as: He who comes as do all other Buddhas; or, He who took the absolute way of cause and effect, and attained to perfect wisdom.

8. The twin Sāl trees in the grove in which Śākyamuni entered Nirvāṇa.

9. The maṇi pearl, said to give sight to the blind, is known for its luster.

10. I.e., he is reduced to an animal.

11. According to the *Sui Shu*, the Six Women Officials were established in the Han dynasty. They were in charge of palace upkeep, palatial protocol, Court attire, food and medicine, banquets, and the various artisans of the court.

12. Pinning of corsages: supposedly a custom of the Sung dynasty. After offering sacrifices at the ancestral temple of the imperial family, the emperor and the subjects would pin flowers on their clothes or on their caps.

13. Wu-ling is the prefecture (*chün* 郡) in which is located the town of Ch'ang-tê, in Hunan Province. Its fame rests on the "Peach-Blossom

Spring," poems written by T'ao Ch'ien (365–427) and later by Wang Wei (655–759). The spring is near the town.

14. "Sun and moon . . . vase": a metaphoric expression for the alchemical process.

15. Ten Islets: legendary home of the immortals.

16. The three wains are the three vehicles (*triyāna*), drawn by a goat, a deer, and an ox to convey the living across the cycles of births and deaths (*saṃsāra*) to the shores of Nirvāṇa.

17. "Nine-grade" refers to the nine classes or grades of rewards in the Pure Land.

18. The Mādhyamika or San-lun School advocates the doctrine of formlessness or nothingness (*animitta, nirābhāsa*).

19. "Form is emptiness and the very emptiness is form" is the famous statement of the *Heart Sūtra* (the *Prajñāpāramitāhrdaya*). See JW, chap. 19, and also *Buddhist Texts through the Ages*, trans. and ed. Edward Conze, et al. (New York, 1964), p. 152.

20. Buddha's transformed body is said to be sixteen feet, the same height as his earthly body.

21. Pears and dates are the traditional fruits of *hsien*-Taoism.

22. *Om . . . hūm*: said to be a prayer to Padmapāṇi, this is a Lamaistic charm. Each syllable is supposed to have its own mystic power of salvation.

23. Good stock (善根, *kuśala-mula*): the Buddhist idea of the good seeds sown by a virtuous life which will bring future rewards.

CHAPTER EIGHT

1. Ch'ang-an: the capital of the T'ang dynasty (A.D. 618–906); renamed Hsī-an in modern times, it is located in Shen-hsi Province.

2. "Polishing . . . foodstuff": metaphors for useless labor.

3. The mustard seed, or *sarṣapa*, is considered in Buddhist lore to be the smallest grain, whereas the Sumeru is the central mountain range of the Buddhist cosmos. Hence these are references to the paradox that the smallest may contain the greatest.

4. Another name for the Golden Dhūta is Mahākāśyapa. He was one of Śākyamuni's principal disciples who was also chief of the ascetics before the enlightenment. He was said to have first compiled the canon of the first patriarch. One tradition also has it that the esoteric tradition of *ch'an* (Zen) Buddhism was imparted to Kāśyapa by Śākyamuni himself, who revealed the secret by plucking a flower to show to his disciples without, however, a word of explanation. Kāśyapa alone nodded his head and smiled gently in comprehension, and thereafter, he was said to have passed on the mystery of this meditative method to other patriarchs. Twenty-eight generations later, Bodhidharma brought the teachings to China.

5. The ten stages (*daśabhūmi*) belong to the fifty-two stages of the development of a bodhisattva into a Buddha. What these stages are varies according to the different schools of Buddhism.

6. The four creatures or four forms of birth (*catur-yoni*) are: those born of the womb or stomach (*jarāyuja, viviparous*), as are mammals; those born of eggs (*aṇḍaja, oviparous*), as are birds; those born of moisture (*saṁsvedaja*), as are worms and fishes; and those which evolve from different forms (*aupapāduka*, metamorphic), as are certain insects.

7. A reference to the six ways of reincarnation: that of hell (*nāraka-gati*), that of hungry ghosts (*preta-gati*), that of malevolent spirits (*asura-gati*), that of animals (*tiryagyoni-gati*), that of man (*manuṣya-gati*), and that of heavenly beings (*deva-gati*).

8. Ts'ao-ch'i: a stream in Kuang-tung Province. In the T'ang Period, the Sixth Patriarch of Zen Hui-nêng taught here.

9. Chiu-ling: literally, the Vulture Peak (*Gṛdhrakūṭa*). This is supposedly the place frequented by Śākyamuni, and where the *Lotus sūtra* was preached. The full name of the mountain is Spiritual Vulture Mountain.

10. The Three Treasures (*triratna*) refer to the three precious ones: the Buddha, the Dharma, and the Saṅgha.

11. *Prajñā*: wisdom and understanding.

12. *Sārī* or *satrīra* is usually associated with the relics of Buddha.

13. The *bhūtatathatā* is the permanent reality underlying all phenomena.

14. T'ien-chu: India.

15. Formlessness School: the Mādyamika School.

16. Jetavana is a park near Śrāvastī, said to be the favorite resort of Śākyamuni.

17. The Feast of All Souls, celebrated in China by both Taoists and Buddhists. For a description of this and other "masses" for the dead, see K. L. Reichelt, *Truth and Tradition in Chinese Buddhism: A Study of Chinese Mahayana Buddhism* (Shanghai, 1927), pp. 77–126.

18. Lokajyeṣṭha: "The most venerable one of the world," an epithet for Buddha.

19. The five skandhas (*pañcaskandha*) refer to the five substances or components of an intelligent being like the human being. They are form (*rūpa*), reception (*vedanā*, i.e., sensation and feeling), thought (*sañyñā*, i.e., discernment), action (*saṁskāra*), and cognition (*vijñāna*).

20. According to Confucianism, the four virtues are filial piety, brotherly submission, loyalty, and honesty (*hsiao, ti, chung*, and *hsin*). But according to the *Mahāyāna-Nirvāṇa Sūtra*, the four virtues are: permanence, joy, the reality of the self (*wo* 我), and purity.

21. Candana: a kind of sandalwood from Southern India.

22. The Weak Water (Jo Shui 弱水) is a river located in Northwestern

China (now Kansu Province), and the entire region had the name of Liu-sha (Flowing sand). See Albert Herrmann, *An Historical Atlas of China,* new ed. (Chicago, 1966), maps 4 and 5.

23. Wu-i refers to Wu-i-shan-li, or Arachosia. See Herrmann, map 16, A4.

24. It was Buddha's custom to lay his hand on top of his disciple's head while teaching him.

25. *Sha* means sand, and *Wu-ching* means "he who awakes to purity."

26. A pun on his religious name, as the Gate of Sand refers to the sand of Ganges; hence Buddhism.

27. Heavenly Reeds (*T'ien-p'êng* 天蓬) is one of the Four Sages (*ssŭ-shêng* 四聖) in the Taoist pantheon, who serve as aides to the Jade Emperor.

28. Goddess of the Moon: literally Ch'ang O, wife of the legendary famous archer, Hou I, who was said to have obtained drugs of immortality from the Lady Queen of the West (Hsi Wang-mu). Ch'ang O stole them and fled to the moon. Cf. the end of the Lecture on Viewing the Dark (*Lan-ming*), book 6 of the *Huai-nan Tzu* 淮南子.

29. *Luan* means egg.

30. "Standing backward in the door," a colloquial phrase of the Huai-an region, refers to a man living in the woman's house after marriage.

31. *Chu* means pig, and *Wu-nêng* means "he who awakes to power."

32. The five forbidden viands, according to various teachings of Buddhism, may refer to spices (leeks, garlic, onion, green onion, and scallion) or to kinds of meat (the flesh of horse, dog, bullock, goose, and pigeon). The three undesirable foods, prohibited by popular Taoism, are wild goose, dog, and black fish.

33. In popular Chinese fiction, the wandering monk with scabby sores or leprosy is frequently a holy man in disguise.

CHAPTER NINE

1. The eight waters are the eight rivers and their tributaries in Shensi Province: Wei, Ching, Pa, Liao, Chü, Hao, Li, and Ch'an.

2. T'ai-tsung was the second emperor of the T'ang dynasty. He reigned from 627 to 649.

3. The cyclical name of a year is derived from combining the Ten Celestial Stems with the Twelve Branches or Horary Characters.

4. Wei Chêng (魏徵) was a great statesman of the early T'ang period, highly respected by Emperor T'ai-tsung. He had the reputation of being a fearless remonstrant to the throne. He also was one of the editors of the *Chou Shu,* the *Sui Shu,* and *Pei-ch'i Shu,* dynastic histories of the Chou, Sui, and Northern Ch'i periods. See Howard J. Wechsler, *Mirror to the Son of Heaven: Wei Cheng at the Court of T'ang T'ai-tsung* (New Haven, Conn., 1974).

5. The three sessions of examination probably refer to those tests taken by the candidate for the *ming-ching* (men who understood the classics) degree. According to Ho Ping-ti, *The Ladder of Success in Imperial China: Aspects of Social Mobility, 1368–1911* (New York, 1962), p. 13, "the first required the completion by the candidate from memory of ten test passages (*t'ieh*) from each of the following classics, namely, either the record of ritual *Li-chi* or the history of feudal states *Tso-chuan*, the treatise on filial piety *Hsiao-ching*, the Confucian analects *Lun-yü*, and the work on semantics *Erh-ya*. The candidate was given several words as a clue and could pass this first test by completing five or more of the ten passages for each of the four classics. The second test consisted of oral interpretation of ten passages selected from classics, of which correct answers to six or more were required. The third test required a fairly lucid expositon in essay form of three assigned problems dealing with current affairs or aspects of administration, which was called *ts'ê*." Cf. also E. A. Kracke, Jr., "Religion, Family, and Individual in the Chinese Examination System," in *Chinese Thought and Institutions*, ed. John K. Fairbank (Chicago, 1957), pp. 251–68; and Robert des Rotours, *Le traité des examens* (a translation of chaps. 44 and 45 of the *Hsin T'ang Shu* [Paris, 1932]).

6. Imperial documents were written on yellow paper.

7. *Wên-chiao* literally means "warm and coy." *Man-t'ang-chiao* means a roomful of coyness.

8. When a mendicant monk begs for alms, he frequently sits in front of a home with a bowl on his head.

9. Since the time of Sung, the most urgent military matters or documents of official pardon were sent on tablets with gold letters. See the *Sung Shih*, *Yü-fu-chih* (宋史．輿服志．).

10. *Cintāmaṇi*, the magic pearl which is capable of responding to every wish and is produced by the Dragon King of the ocean.

11. In the *Hsü Po-wu-chih* (續博物志．), it is recorded that there are nine grades of pearls from Vietnam, the second largest kind being named rolling pearls (*tsou-chu*). But the name "rolling-pan" may refer to an essay of Su Tung-p'o which reads: "There are four rolls of Lêng-chia (the *Laṅkāvatāra sūtra*) which can stabilize the heart, . . . as pearls roll on the pan." See *Tung-p'o Ch'i-chi* 東坡七集, 49, 8 (SPPY edition).

12. *Chiao-hisao*, raw silk spun and sold by mermaids, according to Chinese legend. A bale (here, *tuan*) is eighteen feet in length.

CHAPTER TEN

1. The following section is adapted from the encyclopedic chronicle *Yung-lo ta-tien*, compiled in 1403–8 under commission of the Ming

emperor Ch'êng-tsu. For the Chinese text, see the facsimile version published by Chung-hua shu-chü, Peking, 1960; for a translation of this particular episode, see Dudbridge, *Antecedents*, pp. 177–79. On the poetic dialogues between the fisherman and the woodcutter, C. T. Hsia in his *Introduction*, p. 347, note 13, has noted its parallel to a similar episode in the *Fêng-shên yen-i* (chap. 23), and written that "the Chinese have traditionally associated fishermen and woodcutters with an idyllic life of contemplation detached from worldly cares. The phrase *yü ch'iao* occurs frequently in T'ang poetry. The Northern Sung philosopher Shao Yung wrote, a short dialogue between a fisherman and a woodcutter entitled *Yü-ch'iao wên-ta.*" Illustrations in the older editions (e.g., the 1592 Shih-tê-t'ang's version) bear the explicit title *Yü-ch'iao wên-ta.*

2. The *tz'ŭ* poetry as a genre developed toward the end of the T'ang period (907). Originally appearing as popular songs and ballads from the teahouses and brothels, the poems were further influenced by musical modes from central and northern Asia. Their tonal patterns and rhyme schemes resemble the regulated verse (*lü shih*) of the T'ang period, but their distinctive feature is the irregularity of rhythm, although each poem (in conformity to a tune identified by a specific name such as *Tieh-lien-hua*) is written in a set metrical form.

3. "Chicken heads": seeds of *Euryale-ferox*, so named because of their shape.

4. *Ch'un* leaves: *Cedrela sinensio* or *Cedrela odorata*.

5. *Lien* sprouts: *Melia japonica*.

6. This poem is an explicit adaptation of another *tz'ŭ* poem, *Man-t'ing-fang*, by the Sung poet Ch'in Kuan (1049–1100), which has been included in many anthologies. Introduction, pp. 20–21.

7. Encircling chess: the game of *Go*.

8. This is a quotation from the last two lines of the first of two poems on "Small plum blossoms in a mountain garden (*Shan-yüan hsiao-mei*)" by the early Sung poet, Lin Pu (967–1028), better known as Lin Ho-ching.

9. The linking-verse is a long poem which is composed by two or more persons, each offering alternate lines.

10. This first line would be spoken presumably by Chang Shao, the fisherman, to be followed in the next line by the woodcutter, and so on.

11. Lung-mên: a place in the Shanhsi Province famous for the carp making their annual ascent up the rapids of the Yellow River.

12. One of the twenty-four solar terms, Frost Descends is approximately 23 October in the calendar.

13. The ninth day of the ninth lunar month is a famous festival. For the legends associated with it, see A. R. Davis, "The Double Ninth Festival in Chinese Poetry: A Study of Variations Upon a Theme," in *Wen-lin: Studies*

in the Chinese Humanities, ed. Chow Tse-tsung (Madison, Milwaukee, and London, 1968), pp. 45–64.

14. The three chief ministers of state have traditionally been understood to be the T'ai-shih (the Grand Tutor), the T'ai-fu (the Grand Preceptor) and the T'ai-pao (the Grand Guardian or Protector) of the Chou dynasty. For a recent critical reconstruction of the various governmental officers and agencies, see Herrlee G. Creel, *The Origins of Statecraft in China,* Vol. 1 (Chicago and London, 1970), pp. 101–32.

15. I.e., the call from the emperor.

16. This line of verse is a paraphrase of the Confucian statement: the benevolent takes pleasure in the hills, the wise in the waters. See *Analects,* 6.

17. "I'll never . . . woe on earth": a quotation of the famous statement by Chu-ko Liang to Chou Yü before the battle of Red Cliff with the forces of Ts'ao Ts'ao. See the *San-kuo chih yen-i,* chap. 49.

18. K'ung and Mêng: Confucius and Mencius.

19. Chou and Wên: the duke of Chou and King Wên, the latter of whom was considered to be the founder of the Chou dynasty (1111–256 B.C.) by orthodox Chinese history. In *Analects,* IX, 5, Confucius names King Wên as the source of his tradition, for he was reputed to be a man of great virtue, learning, refinement, and compassion for his subjects. See further discussion in Creel, *Origins,* pp. 62–68.

20. I.e., the wrap is quite flat, since the word "one" in Chinese is written as a single horizontal stroke. This is the traditional attire of a student or scholar.

21. Dragon, Tiger: references to the astronomical signs under which these people were born.

22. Treasure duck: an incense burner shaped like a duck.

23. I.e., A portrait of Kuei-ku Tzu, legendary *hsien* Taoist of antiquity, who had over a hundred disciples.

24. Tuan-ch'i: a stream in Kuang-tung Province, famous for its stones which can be made into ink slabs.

25. Kuo P'u: a famous *Fu* poet of the Tsin Period (265–419 A.D.), who was well known also as a master occultist. There is an error in the Chinese text here, as the personal name P'u 璞 is given as 樸.

26. Waley's translation of these four lines can hardly be improved on.

27. The hours of Dragon, Serpent, Horse, Sheep: 7–9 a.m., 9–11 a.m., 11 a.m.–1 p.m., and 1–3 p.m. respectively.

28. Hour of the Monkey: 3–5 p.m.

29. Silver stream: the Milky Way.

30. Time float: a clepsydra or water clock. In this device, water drips from a large jar, and the receding liquid is measured by a bamboo index. By the time the water falls to a certain marking, it will be the first watch.

31. A reference to the *Chuang Tzu*, chapter 2, where the narrator dreams that he is transformed into a butterfly.

32. Hour of the Rat: 11 p.m.–1 a.m.

33. Royal flags are decorated with the feathers of kingfishers or halcyons.

34. Yao and Shun: the legendary sage emperors of China's antiquity. Shun was said to have served Yao with complete loyalty and obedience before he succeeded him as emperor.

35. Mountain-river (*shan-ho*) is usually a metaphor for the world or empire; I have kept the literal translation here to preserve the metrical parallel with the preceding line.

36. The three signs: the sun, the moon, and the stars.

37. Literally, the colors are in accordance with the yin and the yang.

38. The Chess Immortal is literally, in the Chinese, the immortal with the rotted ax-handle. See chap. 1, no. 13.

39. Ching-tê: frequently the name of Yü-ch'ih Kung in popular Chinese fiction.

40. This last line of the poem is undoubtedly a satirical comment on the fact that the two famous early T'ang warriors, Ch'in Shu-pao and Yü-ch'ih Ching-tê, became in popular culture the guardian spirits of the home. Their portraits are often pasted on either side of the main entrance to a house.

41. Shên Shu 神荼 and Yü Lü 鬱壘 are also guardian deities of the home, their portraits similarly pasted on either side of the main entrance. See Derk Bodde, *Festivals in Classical China* (Princeton and Hong Kong, 1975), pp. 127–38.

42. In a famous episode in the *San-kuo chih yen-i* (chap. 85), the dying emperor, Liu Pei, entrusts the affairs of state to his prime minister, Chu-ko Liang. To the faithful and able subject who has served him for nearly two decades, the emperor says, "If my heir can be helped, then help him. But if he turns out to be worthless, then take the throne at Chengtu yourself."

CHAPTER ELEVEN

1. "Even termites disband . . .": a reference to the T'ang short story *Nan-k'o Chi* 南柯記 or the *Nan-k'o t'ai-shou chuan*, by Li Kung-tso. A certain man who had a huge locust tree (*sophora japonica*) in his garden dreamed of journeying to a distant country, where he married the princess and stayed for two decades before returning. When he awoke, he discovered a huge ant hill beneath the tree in the garden, and close examination revealed that its structure was a miniature replica of the places he had visited in his dream. The sight brought to the man the realization of the brevity and vanity of

human life, and he became thereafter a Taoist. The story in Chinese literature has been regarded as one of the classic treatments of *sic gloria mundi
transit.*

2. The sound of the cuckoo is said to imitate the Chinese phrase *pu-ju
kuei*, which may be translated, "Why not go back?"

3. A stiff, loose belt was worn by ministers as part of their official regalia.

4. To eliminate rivalry, T'ai-tsung defeated and killed his brothers before
becoming emperor himself. See *T'ang Shu*, I, 1, 17. Shih-min is the given
name of the emperor.

5. *Ting*: a huge, three-legged sacrificial vessel of bronze already in use
in the Shang dynasty.

6. Eastern melon is actually winter melon, or white gourd, the name
here being a pun since east and winter (*tung*) are homonyms. Western and
southern melons are water melons and pumpkins respectively.

7. The mountains in Szechuan Province are known for their rugged-
ness.

8. Mount Lu is a famous resort in Kiangsi.

9. Hungry ghosts: the *pretas*, the hungry spirits of the three lower
destinies. They are in different kinds of suffering, and they vary in numbers
from nine to thirty-six.

10. The lowest and deepest of the eight hot hells in Buddhism. For a
convenient discussion, see Daigan and Alicia Matsunaga, *The Buddhist
Concept of Hell* (New York, 1972).

11. The name *Nai-ho* (奈 河 = 奈 何), "Without alternative or remedy,"
may have been a popular corruption of the River *Nei-ho* (漆 河) in Shan-
tung Province, where according to the *Ch'ing i-t'ung chih*, 清 一 統 志 there
is another bridge, the Gold-Silver Bridge 金 銀 橋, southwest of the bridge
proper. Popular legends locate the river's origin in Hell; the blood of damned
souls and demons is supposed to flow in the Nei-ho. The height and the
narrowness of the bridge are such that anyone trying to walk across it
inevitably falls into the river; hence its name.

12. The mass, which offered food for both water and land spirits, was
instituted supposedly by Wu Ti of the Liang dynasty, who became an ardent
believer in Buddhism during the last years of his reign.

13. Sage Kings: literally, in Chinese, Yao and Shun.

CHAPTER TWELVE

1. *Hsiang-kuo* simply means "prime minister." The author of the *Hsi-yu
Chi* apparently invented this episode, constantly punning on the phrase.
The temple, supposedly, was first built in the K'ai-fêng district of Honan

during the period of the Warring States (403–222 B.C.). Destroyed repeatedly, it was finally rebuilt by the T'ang Emperor, Jui-tsung (A.D. 684).

2. Historically, Fu I was one of the most ardent critics of Buddhism. See Arthur F. Wright, "Fu I and the Rejection of Buddhism," *Journal of the History of Ideas* 12 (1951): 33–47.

3. Ming Ti (A.D. 58–76) was an emperor of the Later or Eastern Han Dynasty.

4. Wu Ti of the Northern Chou dynasty ruled A.D. 561–78. The Three Religions are Confucianism, Taoism, and Buddhism.

5. The Fifth Patriarch of the Ch'an Sect was Hung-jen (A.D. 601–74). It is said that when his mother was carrying him, their whole house was illuminated by divine light night and day for over a month. At his birth, he was enveloped in a strange fragrance. See the *Sung Kao-sêng Chuan* 宋高僧傳, 2, and the *Ching-tê ch'uan-têng Lu* 景德傳燈錄, 3.

6. In the T'ang Dynasty, this tower was established as a sort of national Valhalla, where portraits of meritorious officials were displayed.

7. A hat with the picture of the Vairocana Buddha on its brim.

8. A spiritual master, or preceptor, used frequently in Chinese writings as a synonym for Buddhist priest.

9. Temple of Transformation: *Anpapādaka*, meaning direct metamorphosis or birth by transformation.

10. The Three Modes: the former, the present, and the after life.

11. Lokajyeṣṭha: the most honorable one of the world.

12. Ch'an monks: the meditational or intuitive sect, whose founder is said to be Bodhidharma.

13. The seven ancient Buddhas, or Sapta Buddha: Vipaśyin, Śikhui, Viśvabhū, Krakucchanda, Kanakamuni, Kāśyapa, and Śākyamuni.

14. Ice Silkworms: i.e., silkworms white as ice.

15. The luminescent pearl: a pearl which glows at night.

16. Vajradhātu: the golden or diamond element in the universe, signifying the indestructible and active wisdom of Vairocana.

17. Literally, when held, the staff scorns to see green bones grow thin; i.e., it has the magic of prolonging life.

18. The Chinese name for Mahāmaudgalyāyana, one of the chief disciples of Śākyamuni, who was famous for his journey to Hell to save his mother from the *pretas*.

19. Yü Shan: Jade Mountain, another abode of Hsi-wang-mu.

20. Geya: a metrical piece, one of the twelve classes of sūtras in Hīnayāna Buddhism.

21. Kṣitigarbha, guardian of the Earth, was one of the eight Dhyāni-Bodhisattvas who, with Yama, ruled the Underworld.

22. Ṣaḍ-varṣa: the sexennial assembly of Buddha's disciples.

23. Jetavana: see chap. 8, no. 16.

24. Caturdiśaḥ: name of a famous monastery.

25. *Sūtra* . . ., *Chronicle* . . ., *Scroll* . . . : these documents seem to be fictitious inventions of the author.

26. Dharmakāya: the true, spiritual form or "body," the embodiment of essential Buddhahood.

27. The full name of Kuan-yin, which means "the one who heeds the voices of the world."

28. "Namo": I yield to, or submit to.

29. *Sung*: a kind of eulogistic ode.

30. Mahāyāna: the Great Vehicle.

CHAPTER THIRTEEN

1. Vulture Peak: see chap. 8, n. 9.

2. For *māra*, see chap. 2, no. 1.

3. The Wheel of the Law is *dharmacakra*, the truth of Buddha able to vanquish all evil and all resistance. It rolls on from man to man and from age to age.

4. Bamboo sticks were struck by the watchman as he announced the time.

5. "Sixteen feet tall": see chap. 7, n. 20.

6. Huang Kung, a man of the Han period and a native of Tung Hai (in Kiangsu Province), was reputedly a tamer of tigers. See the *Hsi-ching tsa-chi* 西 京 雜 記, chap. 3.

7. From antiquity, the dream of a bear had been interpreted by Chinese as a sign of the imminent birth of a male child. See the "Hsiao-ya" chapter in the *Shih Ching* (The Book of Odes).

8. The lion king, or *shih-man*, was supposedly a pastry decoration made of flour and shaped like a barbarian king with a lion head. This ornament also appeared on belt buckles; hence the name.

9. Bhikṣu: a mendicant monk.

CHAPTER FOURTEEN

1. The six robbers, or *cauras*, refer to the six senses of the body which impede enlightenment; hence they appear in the form of bandits in this chapter.

2. Pariṇāmanā: to turn toward; the term also refers to the bestowal of merit by one being on another.

3. Wang Mang (45 B.C.–A.D. 23) was a prime minister during the Early Han period who usurped the throne of the emperor, P'ing-ti. He was also a reformer.

4. Dhūta: literally the word means shaken, shaken off, or cleansed. It points to the practice of asceticism as an antidote to worldly attachments.

Hence it is also used in colloquial Chinese as a name for any mendicant.

5. Literally, in Chinese, *Hsing-chê* 行者, one who practices austerities or asceticism, or one who journeys.

6. Sugar in Chinese is also *t'ang*.

7. Horse-face fold: a colloquialism in the southern dialects which refers to the making of a folded lining. The term is still in use in Cantonese.

8. The tenth month of the lunar year is often referred to as Little Spring.

9. Chang Liang, Hsiao Ho, and Han Hsin were the three master tacticians who helped Liu Pang found the Han dynasty.

10. "Made his plans . . . away": a quotation from *chüan* 8 (高祖本紀) of the *Shih Chi* (史記). It was a compliment to Chang Liang by Liu Pang himself, and the saying has been used in subsequent generations as a hyperbolic description of the achievements of any military strategist.

11. Red Pine Seed: a legendary immortal of antiquity, who was supposed to be a rain deity in the time of Shên-nung 神農. See Liu Hsiang 劉向, *Lieh-hsien chuan* 列仙傳.

CHAPTER FIFTEEN

1. According to certain teachings of Taoism, the Three Worms are spirits which reside in the brain, the forehead, and the stomach of the human body. See the *Yu-yang tsa-tsu* 酉陽雜俎 (SPTK edition), *chüan* 2, 2.

2. "Came home": literally, returned to the Real.

3. "Thusness": i.e., *chên-ju* or *bhūtatathatā*.

4. The three beasts: the cow, the sheep, and the pig.

5. The six domestic creatures: the cow, the sheep, the pig, the dog, the chicken, and the horse.

CHAPTER SIXTEEN

1. Jetavana: see chap. 8, n. 16.

2. Ṣaḍ-varṣa: the sexennial assembly of Buddha's disciples.

3. Grapevine: literally, dragon whiskers (*Juncus effusus*), a kind of rush used for weaving mats.

4. "Hoisted . . . petard": literally, "I shall lead the sheep astray conveniently and meet plot with plot."

5. Sui-jên: the legendary Chinese Prometheus, who was said to have invented fire by rubbing sticks of wood together.

6. Red Cliff Campaign: the famous episode in the *Romance of the Three Kingdoms*, where Ts'ao Ts'ao is defeated by the combined tactics of Chu-ko Liang and Chou Yü, who attack with burning boats.

7. O-P'ang: a palace built in the capital, Hsien-yang, in Shensi by Shih Huang-ti (221–209 B.C.) of the Ch'in dynasty. It was razed by the warrior Hsiang Yü, and the fire was said to have lasted for three months. The

incident was memorialized in the *O-P'ang Kung Fu* by Tu Mu of the T'ang dynasty.

8. Ch'ang-an: literally, Peking, an inconsistency probably caused by the requirement of rhyme of this *Lü-shih* poem.

CHAPTER SEVENTEEN

1. The *ting* (tripod) and the oven may refer to the utensils of external alchemy, or they may refer to the internal cavity of the human body. White snow and yellow sprout are names for mercury and lead.

2. Mount P'êng-lai: one of three famous mythical mountains in the east, the abode of immortals.

3. Mount Ling-t'ai: the Mountain of Heart and Mind (see chap. 1).

4. Literally, sun and moon copulated as male and female (*li, k'an*) in my body. According to the lore of internal alchemy, the sun and the moon may represent the heart and the kidneys respectively, which in turn are correlated with the male and female symbols (離 and 坎) in the eight trigram lore. When the energies (*ch'i* 氣) of the heart and the kidneys are in proper balance, the internal elixir (*tan*) is formed and immortality is achieved.

5. In this context, "without leaks" probably refers to the retention of the *ch'i*, the essences or energies of the body, also mentioned in the oral formula given to Wu-k'ung by his teacher in chapter 2. But *wu-lou* 無漏 in Buddhism can also mean perfection in the sense of beyond the stream of passion (*anāsrava*) and of transmigratory suffering. It is thus a kind of purity which functions as a cause for attaining nirvāṇa.

6. Hsien-shêng: the Immortal Master of Illustrious Sagacity, the God Êrh-lang (see chap. 6).

7. Wu-hsing Mountain: the Mountain of the Five Phases.

8. The Buddha is said to have had luminous eyebrows the color of white jade.

9. The references to the tiger and the dragon in these two lines may well be the descriptive names of certain poses or postures in Chinese martial art.

10. Ling-hsü Tzu: the Master of the Transcendent Void.

11. For rolling-pan pearl, see chapter 9, note 11.

12. The numbers, "three times three" and "six times six" in all likelihood refer to the lines of the *Ch'ien* and the *K'un* (☰, ☷) Hexagrams of the *I Ching*. They are not only regarded as the parental *kua* of all the sixty-four hexagrams, but they are also the definitive symbols of male and female, hence of the yin and the yang. See *The I Ching or Book of Changes*, The Richard Wilhelm Translation rendered into English by Cary F. Baynes, 3d ed., with a Preface by Hellmut Wilhelm (1967), Bollingen Series 19 (Princeton, 1971), pp. 3–20.

13. The Kou-lou or Chü-lou Mountain (幻漏 = 句漏) is located at the north of Kwangsi Province. It is so named because it has many caves which are joined to one another. Legend has it that the famed alchemist Ko Hung (283–343), did some of his work here.

14. Shao Wêng 少翁 was supposed to be some kind of magician from the Ch'i State. See the *Shih Chi, chüan* 12 and 28.

CHAPTER EIGHTEEN

1. After rites involving sacrificial offerings, the sacrificial meat and fruits are then distributed among the celebrants. Hence the name "blessing."

2. Literally, mandarin ducks.

3. Moth-brows, i.e. mothlike eyebrows, is a common phrase describing the delicately painted and curved eyebrows of a beautiful woman.

4. I.e., thirty-six (see chapter 2). The Heavenly Ladle is the name for the thirty-six stars of the Big Dipper revolving around the North Star.

CHAPTER NINETEEN

1. Truth: literally, the arts of the realized immortal (*chên-jen*).

2. Heat and cold (*han, wên* 寒溫) may be references to alchemical interpretations of the "Heat and Cold" chapter (chap. 41) of the *Lun hêng* by Wang Ch'ung (A.D. 27–ca. 100). However, the phrase as it is used in classical Chinese is also synonymous with *han-hsüan* (to talk about the weather, i.e., to exchange conventional greetings).

3. The eight woes (*pa-nan*) or ordeals are the situations wherein it is difficult to see Buddha or hear his law; hence they are also called the eight conditions of no leisure (*pa wu-hsia*). These conditions include: the state of hells; the state of hungry ghosts (*pretas*); the state of animals; the state of Uttarakuru (the Northern Continent, where no affliction exists); the state of the Heaven of Long Life; the state of being deaf, blind, and dumb; the state of the worldly-wise; and the state of those who exist in the intermediate period between a Buddha ·and his successor.

The three ways, according to Buddhism, consist of (1) the way of fire, where one is burned in the hells; (2) the way of blood, which is the realm of animal existence where one preys on another; and (3) the way of the sword, where hungry ghosts are tortured by the sword.

4. See chapter 5, n. 12.

5. What follows in the next eight lines are allusions to the various processes of internal alchemy.

6. The Mud-Pill Chamber (*Ni-wan kung* 泥丸宮) refers to the spot at the very top of one's head.

7. Not only in acupuncture lore, but even in alchemy, the human body is divided into a system of interconnecting points or holes (*hsüeh* 穴). The

Jetting-Spring Points (*Yung-ch'üan* 湧泉) are points at the center of the soles.

8. The Floral Pool (*hua-ch'ih* 華池) refers to the spot beneath the tongue in the mouth, where saliva supposedly originates. The idea here seems to be that the energy refined in the kidney system, which corresponds to the phase Water (*shui* 水) of the Five Phases (*wu-hsing*), flows throughout the body. See Porkert, pp. 140–46, 162–63.

9. Cinnabar Field (*tan-t'ien* 丹田) refers to the lower part of the abdomen, three inches below the navel.

10. Literally, nourished or replenished (*pu* 補).

11. In external alchemy, baby, or young lad (*ying-ërh* 嬰兒), probably refers to lead, but in terms of internal alchemy it can also take on the meaning of the essence or energy (*ch'i* 氣) of the kidney.

12. Literally, the beautiful girl (*ch'a-nü* 奼女), which means mercury, or the *ch'i* of the heart. The idea here is the blending of the essences or energies of the kidney and heart. For a convenient discussion of these and related ideas, see Needham, 2: 329–35.

13. Sun and moon are other names for the heart and the kidney.

14. K'an-tiger: see chapter 17, n. 4.

15. Spirit turtle: another name in alchemical lore for the dark liquid in the kidneys.

16. Gold crow: the sun; hence, the heart. The line refers to the union of yin and yang through the absorption of yang energy by yin.

17. Literally, three flowers in conglomeration at the top (*san-hua chü-ting* 三花聚頂). It refers to the process whereby the body's three internal elements of essence (*ching* 精), vital potential or matter-energy (*ch'i* 氣), and spirit (*shên* 神) are brought together at the top of the head. The elixir so distilled would be regarded as the "fruit" 結子 of the union of the three flowers.

18. Literally, "Five energies facing the one (*wu-ch'i ch'ao-yüan* 五氣朝元)," referring to the *ch'i* of the five viscera (the heart, the liver, the spleen, the lungs, and the kidneys) in harmonious balance. See, for example, the *Chin-tan ssŭ-pai-tzŭ* 金丹四百字, in *Tao Tsang*, 84/741, *chüan* 2.

19. Wang-mu: the Lady Queen Mother of the West.

20. Miss Ch'ang-o: the famed immortal lady who resides in the moon.

21. Inspector General: the same figure as Wang Ling-kuan of chapter 7, he is regarded as the prime guardian of the faith in Taoist temples.

22. Liu Ting and Liu Chia: the Six Gods of Darkness and Six Gods of Light.

23. In the development of the *I Ching* tradition, the diagrams and hexagrams (*kua*) were sometimes hypostatized as celestial beings.

24. "The better . . . hold": Waley's translation.

25. This poem is the first of many passages in which the relations of the pilgrims one to another are depicted by means of the Five Phases (*wu-hsing*) theories.

26. Throughout the novel, the pig is identified with wood (he is called Wood Mother, or *mu-mu* 木母, many times); hence "Wood Dragon" here.

27. In alchemy, lead is sometimes regarded as the host (*chu* 主) and mercury as the guest (*k'ê* or *pin* 賓), and vice versa. It is said in the *Hsien-hsüeh tz'u-tien* 仙學辭典 (Taipei, 1962), p. 76, that when gold attacks (*fa* 伐) wood, lead will be acting as host and mercury as guest.

28. *San-chiao san-ho* (三交三合). According to the *yin-yang* theorists, this union refers to the *ch'i* of the *yin*, the *yang*, and Heaven (*t'ien* 天); nothing can be created if one is lacking. Later, the idea is expanded to the correlation of the Five Phases with the cycles of the year, the month, and the day, which is also thus called *san-ho*.

29. *Chên-yüan* 貞元 has been the name of at least two reigning periods: of the emperor Tê-tsung in T'ang (785–805), and of the Southern Sung Chin-hai Ling-Wang (1153–56). But *chên* 貞 (perseverance, continuance, single-mindedness) is also last of the four attributes of the *ch'ien* 乾 hexagram with which the *I Ching* begins, and *yüan* 元 (beginning, greatness, sublimity) is the first of its four attributes. Thus this combination may point again to the union of opposites, the first and the last, and such a combination is then further correlated with psychological realities. See, for example, the *Chou-i ts'an-t'ung ch'i* 周易參同契, *chüan* 2, chap. 5.

30. Undesirable foods: see chap. 8, n. 32.

31. Pa-chieh: i.e., eight commandments. These are the first eight of the ten commandments in Buddhism forbidding killing, stealing, sexual immorality, lying, the use of cosmetics and other personal comforts (e.g., a fine bed), strong drink, the use of dancing and music, and eating out of regulation hours. The last two deal with specific forbidden foods and the rule for fasting.

32. Literally, the various causes are fused (諸緣合), a probable reference to the harmonious working of the cycle of twelve *nidānas*.

33. The shorn hair refers to the story of the immortal, Huang Wêng 黃翁. According to the *Han-wu tung-ming-chi* 漢武洞冥記 *chüan* 1, Tungfang Shuo met during one of his travels an Immortal, Huang Wêng. He told him, "I fasted and fed on my breath for some nine thousand years. The pupils of my eyes have all turned blue-green, and I can discern objects even in the dark or when they are hidden. Once in three thousand years, my bones were changed and the marrow was drained; and once in two thousand years, my bones were stripped and my hair was shorn. Since my birth, my marrow has been drained three times, and my hair shorn five

times." Thus the meaning of the line seems to be that when the process of internal alchemy is completed, immortality is achieved.

34. *Fou-t'u*, the Chinese name for this mountain, can mean both Buddha and pagoda.

35. Kuan-tzu-tsai: i.e., Kuan-yin, the Onlooking Lord.

36. *Pañcaskandha*: the five aggregates or constitutive elements of the human being. They are (1) *rūpa*, physical phenomena related to the five senses; (2) *vedanā*, sensation or reception of stimuli from events and things; (3) *sañjñā*, discernment or perception; (4) *sainskāra*, decision or volition; and (5) *vijñāna*, cognition and consciousness.

37. Three worlds: the past, the present, and the future.

38. "Gate! . . . Bodhisvāhā": "Gone, gone, gone beyond, completely gone beyond! O what an awakening! All hail!"

CHAPTER TWENTY

1. *Wu-wei* tree: the tree of passivity, nonactivity, spontaneity, and non-causality.

2. The Buddha is sometimes referred to as the king of bulls, possibly because his name, Gautama, is thought to be a derivative of *gaus*, ox or bull.

3. Enigmatic verse: i.e., a *gāthā*, a short metrical hymn or chant, usually composed for moral or religious instruction.

4. A pun on the words *yao*, meaning the lines in a hexagram of the *I Ching*, and *yao*, meaning dainty viands.

5. The puns in these lines are virtually untranslatable.

6. *Wu*-trees: *Sterculia platanifolia*.

7. Mount Hua and T'ien-t'ai Mountain are famous mountains located in Shensi and Anhwei provinces respectively. For a good description of these mountains and their significance in the history of Chinese religions, see Mary Augusta Mullikin and Anna M. Hotchkis, *The Nine Sacred Mountains of China* (Hong Kong, 1973).

CHAPTER TWENTY-ONE

1. Vihārapālas: guardian spirits of a monastery.

2. Erh-lang, who uses a weapon with three points and two blades, sometimes uses a trident also.

3. Huang Ho: the Yellow River.

4. Mañjuśri and Viśvabhadra or Samantabhadra are frequently depicted as two disciples who appear on the left and right of Tathāgata; the former rides a green lion and the latter a white elephant. For a discussion of these two disciples as idealizations of Śāriputra and Maudgalyāyana, see Yin-shun 印順, "Wên-shu yü P'u-hsien 文殊與普賢," in *Fo-chiao shih-ti k'ao-lun* 佛教史地考論 (Taipei, 1973), pp. 233–44.

5. Sometimes called the Warrior of the North, Chên-wu 真武 was traditionally identified as the Exalted Emperor of the Primal Heaven 玄天上帝, who gained his fame as the one who subdued the great turtle and snake under his feet. The best-known account of this story is the *Pei-yu chi* 北游記 by Yü Hsiang-tou 余象斗 of the Ming period.

6. Tzŭ-t'ung 梓橦: name of a Taoist god, who rides a mule.

7. P'êng-lai: one of the three famous mountains, and a home of the immortals.

8. Wang-mu: the Queen Mother of the West.

9. Reputedly a craftsman of marvelous skills in the Spring and Autumn period, Lu Pan was subsequently venerated by carpenters and builders as their patron deity.

10. P'an-ku: chap. 1, n. 1.

11. Sesame seed rice: an allusion to the story of Liu Ch'ên 劉晨 and Juan Chao 阮肇, who went to gather herbs on T'ien-t'ai Mountain and met immortals there. They were fed peaches and rice with sesame seeds.

12. Sonorous stones: the *ch'ing*, a small gong-like stone with the inside hollowed out, to be struck in religious services.

CHAPTER TWENTY-TWO

1. For baby and fair girl, see chap. 19, nn. 11 and 12.

2. In the lore of alchemy, mercury is often called wood mother (*mu-mu*), while lead is called the squire of gold, or squire of metal (*chin-kung* or *chin-wêng*). The name may derive from the fact that the word *ch'ien* 金公, another word for lead in Chinese, is made up of 2 characters: *chin* 金, meaning gold or metal, and *kung* 公, meaning duke, lord, or an aged man. I owe this suggestion to Professor Nathan Sivin.

3. Bright Hall (*ming-t'ang*) refers to the space, one inch inside the skull, between the eyebrows.

4. See chap. 19, n. 8.

5. The Tower (*ch'ung-lou*) refers to the windpipe or the trachea. Since the Chinese alchemists thought that it had twelve sections, it was frequently called the Twelve-Tiered Tower (*shih-êrh ch'ung-lou* 十二重樓).

6. Wang-mu: the Queen Mother of the West.

7. "On the left": a sign of imperial anger.

8. Great Immortal of Naked Feet: this deity also appeared in chapter 5.

9. Evergreen: literally, *so-lo* (*Cunninghamia anceolata*).

10. Wu Kang was supposedly an immortal of the Han period, who took up residence in the moon. There he tried frequently to cut down a cassia tree, which would grow again the moment it fell. See the *Yu-yang tsa-tsu*.

11. Lu Pan: see chapter 21, n. 9.

12. When the emperor holds court, the screen or curtain separating his throne and his subjects would be raised.

13. *Tao-kuei* 刀 圭, the spatula or knifelike instrument which the alchemists use to separate or measure their herbs and chemicals. In the narrative, it is used as a metaphor for Sha Wu-ching.

14. A word play on the word *kuei* 圭 (gem-token or spatula), which is composed of two *t'u* 土, meaning mud or earth.

CHAPTER TWENTY-THREE

1. In internal alchemy, the secretion of the spleen, called *huang-p'o* (黃 婆 yellow hag), is considered vital to the nourishment of the other viscera. In the narrative, the term is frequently used to designate Sha Monk (see, for example, the titular couplet of chapter 53).

2. "Red son" or "red boy" is synonymous with infant or baby, for that is the color of the newborn. In internal alchemy, however, the formation of the baby can refer to the state of achieved immortality within the human body, and it is in this sense that the term is occasionally used in the narrative to identify Tripitaka (see the titular couplets of chapters 37 and 79).

3. *Mou*: a Chinese acre, measuring $733\frac{1}{2}$ square yards.

4. "To lead a horse" in Chinese slang means to be a marriage go-between.

5. Hsi-tzŭ: the legendary beauty and concubine of King Fu-ch'a of *Wu*.

6. Li Shan Lao-mu, or the Old Woman of Li Mountain, seems to have been originally a river demon (see Dudbridge, *Antecedents*, pp. 144–46); in this episode, however, she is apparently elevated to the status of a goddess.

CHAPTER TWENTY-FOUR

1. Ginseng: *Panax schinseng*, a plant highly treasured in traditional Chinese medicine both as an aphrodisiac and as a long-life herb.

2. K'un-lun: the largest mountain range in China, beginning in Tibet and extending eastward to form three ranges in North, Central, and South China. Regarded commonly as the most important sacred mountain of folk Taoism, it is the legendary home of the Lady Queen Mother of the West and the Celestial Honored Primordial (*Yüan-shih t'ien-chün*).

3. The five blessings are: long life, wealth, health, love of virtue, and a natural death.

4. *Huai*: *Sophora japonica*.

5. Chên-yüan-tzŭ: literally, "one who has fortified his origin."

6. For the possible origin of the phrase "reverted cinnabar" (*huan-tan*), see the *Pao-p'u tzu* (SPTK edition), 4.3a and 7b. See also *Alchemy, Medicine,*

and Religion in the China of A.D. 320: The "Nei P'ien" of Ko Hung, trans. James R. Ware (Cambridge, Mass., 1966), pp. 70 and 77.

7. "One does not . . . way": see *Analects, XV*.

8. "The one on top": i.e., *t'ien*, or Heaven.

9. *Wu-t'ung: Sterculia platanifolia*.

10. The railings on top of a well in the households of wealthy families are frequently painted gold; hence the frequent references to a "golden well" in classical Chinese verse.

11. *Shao-yao: Paeonia albifora*.

12. Mare's tail: *Hippuris*, a plant used primarily to feed goldfish.

13. *Su: Dipsacus asper*.

14. For the classification of immortals, see Needham, V/2 (1974), pp. 11–12, 92–113.

CHAPTER TWENTY-FIVE

1. Probably Lü Tung-pin, one of the famous Eight Taoist Immortals.

2. Yak's-tail: see chap. 2, n. 3.

3. Jade yak's tail: a yak's tail with a jade handle.

4. The monk's robe is sometimes called a bell because it is shaped like one—tight and narrow on top, loose and wide at the bottom.